Also by Ella M. Kaye

<u>Dancers & Lighthouses</u>
Pier Lights
Shadowed Lights
Pieces of Light

<u>Artists & Cottages</u>
Shadows of Greens & Memories
Shadows of Blues & Echoes
Shadows of Rust & Reels

<u>Anthology</u>
Music of the Heart from Fire Star Press (2017)
includes the EMK novella *A Melody in the Dark*

All books are stand-alone titles, related as series by similar locations
and art forms. They can be read separately or in any order.

Elucidate Publishing
United States of America

The Texture of Glass

Ella M. Kaye

One

Stepping carefully over the lake-smoothed mostly flat stones along Beach 1, Isabel tuned into a teenager complaining loudly to a nearby adult about the rocks hurting her feet. Put your shoes on, the adult said. I don't want them wet, was the reply. Then why did you bring those? They're my favorites. Why would you wear your favorite shoes to scuff through sand? They're comfortable. Then put them on or don't whine about your feet...

Isabel couldn't help a grin. It wasn't all that long ago that she'd been a teenager and would have done the same. If she'd come out to Presque Isle as a teenager. Which she hadn't. Her parents had no interest and no time: There are three rivers in Pittsburgh, said her mother, that should be enough water. But there's not a beach, Isabel replied. You don't swim. That's not the point of the beach. Then the rivers will do...

It wasn't the same. Even as an adult, she couldn't buy that one. You didn't find sea glass along a city's river bank. You couldn't look out over the water and only see water. It was nice, but it wasn't as peaceful, as tranquil. It wasn't quiet. So as soon as she moved out, up to Meadville, she'd started making almost weekly treks to Lake Erie, almost always on Presque Isle.

It only took one time walking along the stones that looked too smooth to hurt your feet to realize they hurt your feet. They'd not only *hurt* her used-to-shoes city feet; they'd bruised her feet.

They did until you got used to it. Which she was by now. Ever since she'd been in her own place, Isabel only wore shoes when absolutely necessary. In decent weather, she often pulled off her sandals and walked barefoot along the sidewalk to go up to the corner store for a couple of things. And she'd been coming to the beach looking for sea glass long enough now that her feet were hardened. Now and then she still grimaced when she stepped on one of the sharper rocks, and it took a little time each spring to get used to it again, but generally she could walk across them without pain.

She considered telling those who apparently didn't come often that some of the other beaches were much easier on bare feet, but she didn't make a habit of talking to strangers. Isabel generally tried to avoid that as much as she tried to avoid shoes. Possibly more.

Making her way farther from their continued bickering, she headed toward the little half submerged dock. She suspected it used to be a boat launch since it sloped down into the water where it eventually disappeared, but she had never seen it used for that. The metal tube things coming up along each side from within the concrete were rusted and at least one of them had lost the cap and looked dangerous to step on, so she always stayed away from the edges when she wandered down to where the water got deeper. Beside it, though, collected at the top edge, she often found a good bit of sea glass.

Crouching there, where the water ebbed over her feet but wouldn't get her capris wet past her knees, she sifted pebbles through her fingers. At times, she gathered some of the little rocks instead, since so many were beautiful and interesting. Mostly, she left them in favor of glass.

As usual, there were quite a few small opaque white pieces, but they were too common and too small to bother with. The five tiny pieces of green and one even tinier piece of dark blue, she stuck in her pocket. There were a few browns, but she didn't take brown glass since they reminded her of beer bottles. It could be they were oil bottles or something else, but that's not what she thought of, so she left them.

After a good bit of searching with not much luck and her knees and ankles starting to ache, she moved away, up into the sand.

Was that pink glass? Turning back to where she thought she'd seen a flash of color, Isabel crouched and dug through the damp sand. It wasn't glass. It was plastic. A small pink troll with a silly grin plastered forever on its face and damp sand caked in its fake pink hair. She wondered if the little girl who lost it cried over its loss or quickly forgot it in favor of other things.

What should she do with it? Rebury it and let some other kid have the fun of finding it? Maybe. But maybe the child would come back for it. She could leave it lie, but it seemed wrong to toss it down as though it was garbage, when she wouldn't even do that with garbage, so after going back to the water to rinse the sand out of its hair, she decided to make the little thing a castle to help her be found.

How long had it been since she'd made a sand castle? Her grandparents took her to Maine once, and while her grandma attended whatever business she had there, she and her grandpa went to the beach. He'd helped her build a huge sand castle, nice enough to attract other kids, including a little boy with light brown hair who kept smiling shyly at her while they played together. She'd kept asking Gramps if he'd take her back to that Maine beach until he built a big sandbox behind his Pittsburgh town house. They'd spent many hours designing perfect castles. She'd even started drawing them to plan out the next design to try, which gave her a nice escape while hiding in her room to avoid her father. She didn't draw the boy, but she imagined him playing there with her. Until she got too old for that kid stuff and lost interest in sand castles.

And her mom was right. She didn't swim. She didn't trust the water. Gramps put her in swim lessons to help her learn, but she wouldn't do it. Wading was nice. Anything above the knees was too deep. Still, the water called to her. She came to Presque Isle to walk along one of the beaches or trails while listening to the roaring or creeping waves sweeping against the shore. It was her newest escape. It helped her head and soul unwind.

And often, it inspired a song, or at least a line or two of a song.

Today, it was not relaxing. It was not bringing words or music from anywhere within. She hadn't found one decent piece of glass. Today, two years to the day the jerk walked out on her, she got nothing but a troll. So be it.

Tucking the thing into her pocket so it wouldn't get lost again, she dropped her sandals and moved toward the water. She had no bucket to haul wet sand or water farther up onto shore, so she chose a spot at the edge of where it was wet enough to work with but out of reach of the soft rolling waves.

It was slow going, but she had all day. No one was waiting on her. She'd run her errands the day before. Isabel always took care of her errands on Saturday to get them out of the way. Work was tomorrow. Today was her own. If she wanted to stay and build a sand castle, she could take as long as she needed.

Except that it was atypically warm for May, and without western Pennsylvania's typical partial cloud cover buffering some of the glaring midday sun, her shoulders warmed fast. By the time she had a decent castle made, her legs felt the work of crouching, standing, bending, and her shoulders were getting a pink tinge that she would definitely feel later. But the wide, rather messy but stable castle was complete with a turret to stand Little Pink Troll on top of so it could look out in wait for its ... owner. At least it was only a piece of plastic. Replaceable. Unlike...

Telling herself not to go there, Isabel took the thing from her pocket and gently nudged it into the sand of the turret, leaned up against the wall for support, looking out. And then she changed her mind and turned it away. Little Troll would be annoyed about being left behind, wouldn't it? As though not important enough to be kept safe in its owner's care? It should have its back turned.

With a deep sigh, she took a few steps backward, pulled her phone from her bag, and snapped a photo of the troll in her castle with Lake Erie in the background. Maybe she'd post it to a local lost and found page. Chances were good, though, that it would be taken by a different child by then, or the waves would come in and claim it.

Because she hated to see it with its back turned, she fixed it to look forward, as though it hoped her original mom, original owner, would find her and take her home. Or maybe she would hope not to be found and was watching to run if a stranger came near, even a stranger that maybe looked like her, because she'd be too angry about being left.

"Stop it. It's just a toy." Grabbing her sandals, she ambled back up the beach to the softer sand and down farther away from the lifeguarded area, when there was a lifeguard there, and there wasn't always. She preferred off-season when there wasn't.

Watching for any glimmer in the sand that might turn out to be something worth keeping, Isabel didn't hold much hope of that. It was late May, just past Memorial Day. Tourist season had already set, and pre-season glass-hunting season had already hit, so the water-smoothed glass was pretty well scavanged, either by a curious child or a collector. It was harder to find these days, since sea glass had lately became the *in* thing. Still, it was always possible.

The clear tall straight glass vase she'd been dropping them in was two-thirds full. After finding the first one, found her first time on the Isle, two years ago, it became an obsession. She loved the mystery of where they had come from, of how long they'd been at the bottom of the lake or swirled along strong currents, of what they had been before. There was also the simple beauty of each piece.

Her roommate laughed when she started throwing it into the vase, the vase that had held the first bouquet her first real boyfriend had given her way back when. "It's just broken glass, Izzy. Why are you collecting bits of garbage?"

Glass wasn't garbage, though. Glass was made of sand, and like sand, sea glass came in a lot of shades, and different textures. It could be shiny or satin or matte. It could be crushed and melted to make new glass. She'd read they sometimes used it in asphalt, which made roads shine in the sun, which she thought was pretty cool. It could be also be crushed to become sand again. Glass and sand went together like ... guitar and voice. Both were wonderful alone when done right, but together they were a versatile and beautiful combination. Trying to explain to Libs was pointless. She barely even got music references, since she was barely into any music.

Lisbon Garcia, named after the Portuguese capital city, was the only friend Isabel had left from her school days. They looked about as different as they could, with her own strongly Irish heritage and Libs' Portuguese heritage, but Libs had asked about Isabel's Spanish-spelled name one day when she didn't look Spanish, and somehow, that led to a so-far life-long connection.

Isabel overlooked the lack of music appreciation, and the laughter. It was friendly laughter, no harm meant. She loved how easily her friend laughed. And she understood the point. She did. She didn't even know why she was obsessed with the search. It called to her, so she did it even without understanding why.

A shine caught her eye and she bent to pick it up out of the sand. Glass, but not smooth. Dark green. A piece of broken bottle. Beer bottle, probably. Maybe the color faded over time. Maybe the water changed the color. Maybe this piece would be worth collecting some day after it had time to be smoothed and faded. When it didn't look like a beer bottle.

Bracing herself in the sand that shifted under her bare feet, she threw the piece as far as she could out into the water, which wasn't very far since she'd never had any arm strength. Then she wondered if she should have. What if it hit a fish? Not likely, she guessed. The smack of the small piece against the surface of the water would slow it down, and it would drift slowly into the depth. Any self-respecting fish would be able to move away from it.

Continuing down the shoreline, Isabel watched for glass, but also for sharp rocks to avoid since she was leaving the sandier part of the beach. Most of the rocks weren't sharp. Most had been in or along the water too long to still be sharp. The lake smoothed everything, even broken hearts after a while, if you gave it enough time.

With enough time, it would. Once she filled her vase, she would tell herself it had been enough time. She would stop expecting the phone call that hadn't come in two years, the one she knew wouldn't come but still could. Two-thirds. She had only a third of the vase left, and then she'd let him go.

~~

James eyed the blonde girl staring from the passenger side of an old green Plymouth held together by gray Bondo badly applied over rust. It was stuck at a red light, and she took full advantage of the time to leer while he walked along the sidewalk toward and past her, cautious of edges of pavement raised by tree roots or holes eroded by salt.

Yeah, so he took his shirt off after his run. It was damned hot and his shirt was soaked enough to tug at him. Had she never seen a guy walking down the sidewalk without a shirt? Yeah, so he was in decent shape. He was workout fixated, his buddies said. When you didn't have a girl and didn't want to pick one up temporarily, what else did you do with your energy? Play that war game and jump up and down yelling at the big screen because your fake guy didn't do what you wanted him to do? Yeah, no thanks. Not that he had an issue with games. He'd been known to play a mean game of Centipede and Asteroids on the old Atari that had been his uncle's prize possession in his younger days. He got it. It was good entertainment, sometimes a good brain workout. But too much sitting time about killed him. It was a great thing to do in your early teens when you were naturally lazy due to all the hormonal crap, but that was about half a lifetime ago by now.

He would be thirty next month. And despite his deformity, he could work circles around any early twenty, even the fit ones. He supposed he should be flattered by the girl's stare.

Yeah, so he was flattered. He also didn't want to think about it.

A pretty girl. Right enough age. Full wavy neat hair and nice features. She grinned as the driver, a guy about his age but not so much in shape, let off the brake with the change of light from red to green. The girl was his type, definitely, looks-wise, anyway. Not that his type had turned out well for him yet. Which only meant he hadn't found the right his type.

Maybe it was time for another beach jaunt. Beach girls were different than small city girls. Very small city girls.

Greenville, Pennsylvania was barely a city, technically a borough of only some six thousand people, and in recent years it had fallen into disrepair about as bad as he had himself. It was the kind of town where people stopped at Sheetz for $10 worth of gas and a single pack of cheap cigarettes to get them through till payday. But more recently, it was coming back into its own. As he was. They both had a ways to go, but a start toward a goal was at least a start.

His roommates wanted him to go to Sam's later. James shuddered at the thought. He hadn't been there in seven months. The place was a dive, and not even a nicer dive, but a true dive, known for cheap beer and often for ... well, cheap women who went for the cheap beer and the guys who were there drinking plenty of it.

Himself included.

That was before he started his workout routine. These days after work, he grabbed some jerky and downed a quarter bottle of Gatorade while shoving into his shorts and running shoes, then he walked down Shenango Street, up Race, across the river to Riverside Park. At the ball field entrance, he stretched some and then ran the length of the narrow road that circled the park, detouring to the amphitheatre where he bypassed the shorter steps along each side and used the middle area where the stones were deeper. He did at least one jaunt up and down, often two or three times, before continuing on around the park.

Sunday was his play day. He had a standing time slot at Carried Away Outfitters for a ten mile kayak rental. Some day, he would buy his own kayak. The problem was finding a place to keep it. His parents said he could store it at their place, just outside Mercer in the middle of the trees where they had a big three car garage, a big shed, and a big rolling lawn, but that was a trip out there and a trip back and James too often got stuck talking forever. It screwed up his routine and took too much time.

Right now, his routine mattered too much. In time, he hoped it wouldn't.

Sam's could be okay by now. Seven months. Could be it was time for a self-test, with Bruce at his side in case seven months hadn't been long enough. Next weekend. That would give him time to prepare.

~~

When some girl looked at her funny, Isabel realized she was humming louder than she thought. She often hummed songs in progress when she didn't have her guitar handy. This one was about getting over him, the long-term unsordid three year affair of the heart rather than the body. Most of what she wrote was about him, sadly. She'd long ago stopped playing her songs for her mother because she was tired of hearing, "Another one, Isabel? Let it go, already. He wasn't worth it then, as I told you at the time, and he's not worth it now, either."

Easy for her mom to say. At eighteen, Jocelyn Dillon met the man she believed was intended for her, became Josie Dillon Sanderson at nineteen, and had Isabel at twenty. Everything perfectly in order, like everything in her mother's life. Nothing got to her. Nothing distracted her from her goals.

Completely unlike Isabel who was distracted by everything and was always meandering through shifting sand. She'd have to wonder if they were even related except for their nearly twin-like looks. Along with the same square facial structure, too-narrow eyes, and too-long nose, their hair was the same shade of mousy ashy light brown. Except her mom had red tints; in sunlight the red was nearly like fire burning along the edges of her head. Isabel was lacking even that much vibrancy. She was dull, inside, outside. Dull. The word Mickey had used when he left. "You're just too ... too dull, Izzy. I kept waiting for you to pop out of that gray shell, and I know it's in you, but you won't let it out. If you'd let me in more, I could help you, you know, but since you won't and I'm tired of trying, I have to give up. Sorry."

Sorry. The jerk actually said Sorry like, Yeah, no big deal. Three years of dating after being school friends for years and your only real boyfriend, the only one who knows your whole story and still swore to be there for you. Let you think it was going to be forever. But hey, see ya 'round.

She knew exactly what he meant by wouldn't *let him in*. He meant it physically, even if he was trying to make it sound like more than that. She couldn't do it. The risk was too high. He hadn't committed enough. What choice did she have but to stay inside herself when she had to try so hard not to repeat her mistakes? Especially the biggest one.

He hadn't actually wanted her enough. It wasn't like they'd done nothing. She wasn't that much of a prude, and he knew it. But she wanted someone who wanted her, not just sex, but *her*. She needed the *want*, not the *need*. She wanted and needed the whole thing together…

She wanted and needed… The phrase struck her and Isabel repeated it within the melody she'd been humming. *Wanted and needed and no one could tell her/ she loved him and… she loved and adored him and no one could tell her/ he wouldn't stay long/ he wouldn't be 'round/ when she wanted and needed his strength and his … needed his need of her…*

His need of her. Wanted his need of her. He *had* needed her.

Until he didn't.

Pausing her trek through the damp sand, she stared out at the restless waves, the constantly moving and mixing and churning water that drew her to Lake Erie so often. She didn't come for the glass, not really. She came for the lake. The crying seagulls.

She wanted his need of her. But not that one, the real boyfriend. Her thoughts had gone back further. Back to the one who had thrown her so far off balance.

Isabel frowned at the thought. He had needed her. He had. Deeply. Like no one else in the world. Is that all it was? Not love, but the feeling of being so desperately needed? She'd spent much of her childhood alone while her father worked more than full time and her mother took care of the house in between her realtor work and playing with the thought of becoming an interior decorator. Someday she'd do more with it, so she said. The day had yet to come when she actually took a step toward that dream, though. Her mother was far more full of talk than action. She dressed the part of go-getter but lacked the gumption to actually get up and go for what she wanted. The realty thing was something she just fell into through an acquaintance and accepted it because it was offered.

Isabel was her only child because Jocelyn Dillon Sanderson wanted no more than one. She spent what little social energy she had showing houses to people who *wanted everything for nothing* because they had nothing due to dreaming more than doing, without seeing the irony in her own statement, or who *had everything and still wanted more*. Her mother clearly believed those were the only two kinds of people in the world.

The truth was: her mother didn't like people much. Isabel's grandpa once said it had to have come from her biological father, since it wasn't from him or from her grandma, both big believers there was good in everyone. Isabel was somewhere between the two. She was optimistically cautious with new people, but fairly avoidant overall. Meaning she was basically a loner and yet craved companionship and adventure, all while being afraid of that adventure.

Wanted and needed… She wanted… what? Someone who understood her, who wouldn't make her wary. Someone stable who listened. Someone who didn't particularly *need* her, but wanted her anyway.

Repeating the new lines along with the melody in her head that had been waiting for words for some time, she found herself singing aloud while she walked the shoreline despite people stopping to stare. She didn't care if they did. Maybe it would help more than open mic nights to sing out and about where people didn't expect it.

Except that she didn't have her guitar. Singing without her guitar was like that old dream of going to school naked and somehow managing to get through the day. She could do it. She'd always been able to hold a tune well. Gramps had always encouraged her to sing, said he loved her sweet, true voice and the way she stayed on key without music. She hadn't realized everyone couldn't do it until he mentioned it.

It was her grandfather who bought Isabel a guitar, to give her something to do other than sneaking out to "find trouble." He picked up on her love and understanding of music and the need to keep her hands busy and decided she could do both together.

If she was honest with herself, Isabel wasn't sure whether the love for music was hers or his and she was only going along with it because he pushed her that direction.

The thought threw her out of writing mode and out of beach mood. Between that and her warm shoulders, she turned back and made her way to the rocky narrow path through the shrubs that led to the parking and picnic area. As she did every Sunday, she allowed herself the splurge of stopping at Sara's just outside the isle for a cheesy hamburger and a turtle sundae. She ate the sundae first, in her car with the windows open for air, then opened napkins over her lap and unwrapped her burger to eat on the way home.

Maybe it was time to find out whether this whole music thing was what she wanted or what she'd only fallen into out of lack of knowing what else she wanted.

Two

"Come on, man. We'll check out the no-talent hacks and heckle them off the stage."

Barely preventing the full mug of ice water from sloshing all over his jeans, James shoved his most annoying roommate in return for the purposeful hard knock into his shoulder. "Seriously, when are you going to grow up?"

"Never. What for?" Davis took a gulp of beer loud enough it echoed out into the room. "You deserve a night out. And it'd be less pathetic to drink water out of a huge-ass beer mug if you'd stir some scotch or something in with it."

"It's not pathetic to use my favorite mug." Although a touch of scotch mixed in with his water didn't sound like a bad idea, especially since he was considering going to Sam's with them, even if he shouldn't.

"It's a beer mug. So put beer in it. One here and there won't hurt."

Bruce jumped in between. "Ignore that, but you do need a night off, J. You do nothing these days but work and run. It's great that it's doing well for you so far, but you have to get back into living too, if it's going to keep working."

"I'm living just fine. Want to go kayaking with me tomorrow?"

"No. I want to be a vegetable tomorrow since it's my one day off."

"Be a vegetable tonight and go out tomorrow instead. The fresh air will do you good after sitting in that little office all day."

"I don't stay in the office all day. I walk back and forth to the courthouse all day. And I get plenty of fresh air in here since you keep opening the windows."

"Need the air."

"Great, but it's hot as hell and you're letting the cool out." Bruce went over to shut them again.

"Real air is healthier than fresh air."

"Yeah, yeah, whatever." Davis pushed against him again. "The health kick is getting annoying. Come hang with us, have a beer or two, and help me heckle the idiots more pathetic than you who think they can sing but can't hold a fucking tune in a steel jar. You oughtta get back up there and show them how it's supposed to be done. I'll buy you the first round to get you started."

Bruce shoved Davis away. "Knock it the fuck off already."

"Oh, yes, sir, Mr. Big Shot Lawyer. Whatever. You know he's no fun anymore. Won't even go to a damn bar to hang out."

"If you'd shut up, maybe he would."

"You laugh at the idiots who can't sing, too. Don't get all high and mighty with me."

"Not so they can hear me. I at least hide it."

James cut in before they went at it. Again. "You know what? Some of them can't sing. I get it. But it matters to them, and they have the guts to follow their passion, which is more than a lot of people will do. Leave them be and I'll go with you."

"Don't push alcohol at him, either."

Davis bitched back at Bruce until Gavin stepped in to separate them. Always the mediator, and the quiet one of the four, Gavin slapped a hand on his shoulder. "It'll be cool to have you there again. The hell with the drinks. Let's find some girls. I mean, if it's time to start living again instead of just surviving, you've got to start with a girl, right?"

"From Sam's? Not likely."

Davis snickered. "Used to work for you just fine. You've become a real pretentious ass, you know. Liked you better as a drunk."

Bruce shoved him again.

Gavin ignored them both. "I didn't say you had to keep one, or get serious or anything. Start slow. Ask a girl to dance, enjoy the company, then give her a good night and say see ya 'round and keep looking. Have to start again somewhere. How long has it been?"

"Too fucking long." He took a long swallow of his ice water. Way too long.

"There you go. Put something sexy on and let's see what we find."

With a roll of his eyes, James gulped a good bit more water and went to change from sweats and a loose tee to jeans and one of his nicest Henleys. A good-fitting one that showed his physique, now that his physique was worth showing again. His thoughts gravitated to the girl in the car. Maybe it was time to at least do a dance and a dinner here and there. If he avoided restaurants that served alcohol. Which left most of his favorite places out.

Including Sam's. And it wasn't pretention. It was the smell of alcohol on a girl's breath. It's why he'd given up dating. Even when he ordered cola, she was likely to get wine or some mixed thing and he could smell it, even taste it when it went that far. Didn't work. It was damned unlikely he'd find a girl at Sam's who wasn't drinking. Still, he could go listen to the music.

~~

"*What* are you *doing?*"

Isabel shrugged at her roommate through the white-framed bathroom cabinet mirror as she chopped off another chunk of hair. "Got tired of it."

"But ... but, there are *salons* for that." Lisbon gaped from the bathroom doorway, her own hairdo so perfect it could have been laughing at Isabel. But Libs had gorgeous, dark, curly, shiny hair that looked amazing no matter what she did with it. Even fresh out of bed, Libs was gorgeous.

"I don't want a salon do." Isabel lifted her chin as though she knew exactly what she was doing. "That's not me. Just want something different, you know?"

"You're nuts. I can't watch this."

"Don't. Hey, I have another open mic tonight, new place this time. Coming? I could use the support."

"Can't." She called from the hall as she walked away. "Big date. Real dinner, not Eat 'N Park."

"Hey, I like Eat 'N Park. Their melts are amazing." Isabel knew her roommate would say nothing more. Libs also did only the salad bar when they went for lunch. An amazing salad bar, but Isabel could never resist the sandwich of the day along with it. So her figure wasn't amazing like her roommate's, either. She didn't care. She liked food. She loved a good sandwich, as melty and drippy as possible. She also loved chocolate and caramel, particularly over ice cream.

It sounded good about now. Maybe she'd run through Dairy Queen after her show as a reward and pick up a Peanut Buster Parfait, because chocolate and caramel with vanilla ice cream was bested only by peanuts being added to the mix.

With another whack of hair chopped off, she grabbed the hand mirror and turned to see the damage. She nearly regretted what she'd done. It was kind of cool, maybe. At least it was different. Still to her shoulders in front and long on the sides and top, but chopped up above her neck in a kind of V shape. It definitely didn't look salon. It looked ... messy and punky and ... well, different. Now, though, she had to wonder if she had anything to wear that would be cool enough to go with her hair. "Hey, Libs." She stuck her head out the bathroom door. "Can I borrow something that'll go with my new do?"

"I have nothing to go with that mess, but I'll drive you to a salon."

"Funny. Thanks." Grabbing the broom to clean the long strands of hair off the scuffed white and cream speckled vinyl floor that was curling up along a couple of wall edges, Isabel went to her own closet and shuffled through. Nothing cool. Maybe it wasn't her songs that were lacking. Maybe it was her style. Or lack of. With no time to shop before she had to head to Greenville, she pulled some stuff out, mixing and matching pretty pastel scarves with a black tank top and her oldest jeans with their seams threatening to give way. It would have to work. It didn't matter that much. It was about her songs, if anyone bothered to pay attention to them.

Isabel wished Libs would come. She hated going to new venues on her own, especially since she'd finally screwed up the nerve to go to Sam's. Her grandma said if she played there and did well, she'd be on her way, since it was Western Pennsylvania's answer to Playing in Peoria. Isabel wasn't sure it was true, at least not these days, but she couldn't deny her grandmother's wisdom, either, since *the* Meladee Dillon had long ago become part of the elite crowd of highly successful songwriters. She was also the wisest person Isabel knew. Her grandma didn't talk much, but when she did, people listened. She often threw the credit to her husband, insisting she would be nowhere if not for her dear Niall. He constantly refuted it, with a sparkle in his eyes, and constantly said her name would be far bigger if she'd performed her own songs rather than selling them. But her grandma didn't want to be on stage. She only wanted to write songs.

Isabel felt the same way, but for more reason: her singing just wasn't that good, not star material by a long shot. It was her songs that mattered. She'd been at it for years, to no avail. So it was time to take the plunge and try Sam's.

~~

Kicked back on his regular chair at their regular table, James made himself answer anyone who came to greet him. A couple of girls he knew asked how he was doing. Hard to keep a secret in Greenville. He imagined everyone he used to hang with knew why he hadn't been there in weeks. No one could keep their mouth shut. When he started to get edgy, Bruce started shoving them away. To distract himself from the questions and the okay-enough guy at the mic doing his best with some recent cover songs, he studied Sam's with sober eyes. Definitely a new experience.

The place was dark, notoriously dark, purposely to hide the fact that it was a hole in the wall. The talk was it had been that way since the 70s and had a few necessary repairs since then, but otherwise it hadn't changed, including the tall weeds covering the stone block base beneath the grayed and peeling white-washed barn siding. The stained glass window by now was so old or so dirty you could hardly tell it wasn't just shades of dirt-gray. Only when the sun hit it just right did any of its colors show. No image, only colors, not even in a set pattern. Looked like someone had extra pieces and shoved them together however they fit. Some said it was painted glass with black lines to make it look like it could possibly be stained glass. With the ceiling so high and the window up by the ceiling, it was hard to tell. It was rumored to be an old church, but James wasn't sure that was true, based on the design that didn't look like any old church he'd ever seen. From what he heard, the original owners were somewhat eccentric. The design said that could be true. Why else would you build a bar with high ceilings that would make the place harder to heat and cool? It was wasted space for a bar. Good acoustics, though. Not that quality acoustics were necessary for the low quality bands willing to play there.

The new owners had nearly taken the window out to replace it with a larger, more energy efficient window that would actually let light in, but too many old-timers complained, said it was part of the place. Some of them were still going to Sam's as they had back in the 70s, which they called its heyday, only because one of the biggest bands in rock back then somewhat got its start there, they said. James had his doubts the story was true; they probably had never been near the place. But a story was a story and you couldn't tell old-timers anything.

They glorified the shanty of a bar. When the stage area had been on the other side of the room, they said, the light from that window would glow in on the performers before the sun went down like they were some kind of rock and roll angels. Yeah, James definitely didn't buy that one. Rock and Roll Angels was an oxymoron to beat all the others, as far as he could see, especially any of them that might have played at Sam's way back when. These days, there was no stage, only a place kept cleared of tables that was mainly used for some guy with a guitar playing for tips, as well as for open mic nights.

Open mics were easier to take when he was lit, too. He hadn't missed hearing the warblers who should have been told long ago to sing only in their showers. Now and then one came through that wasn't bad, but mainly he'd gone to Sam's to take the edge off his night after whatever his current job was in between wandering. Pretty much every night. Although when Denton was still around, they'd made it a quest to hit up every bar in the area that had any kind of music.

He missed his buddy. And he hoped he was doing well.

Either way, the place was far more dark and musty than he remembered, or he noticed it more since his senses had cleared. Barely in the door, he'd got a sharp whiff of alcohol and nearly turned right back around. But not touching alcohol himself was only half the battle. He had to be able to do this, to hang with his buddies, to be able to see others drinking, to smell it, and not give in. It was the next test.

Maybe he wasn't ready. The urge to go straight to the bar and grab a drink was too strong.

Still, there was something comforting about the old place with the scratched up wooden bar top, water-stained wooden tables, and the wood plank floor that was so well-used the planks curved in from wear. James would love to think that Raucous had been there and walked on the same floor, sat at the same tables. In the middle of the western Pennsylvania boonies, though, he didn't figure it was likely.

Sipping tea, unsweetened, which Davis also harassed him about, and studying people in the bar, as well as the bar itself, with different eyes than last time he'd been there, James thought it might be cool to buy the place and remodel, turn it into more of a social hangout than the seedy run-down cheap entertainment it was now. And draw better acts, screened and paid acts rather than open mic, or even screened open mic acts mixed in with others who did have talent and needed a place to start. Music wasn't in his plans anymore, though. Hard enough to sit and watch others do it.

~~

"You're up next."

Isabel jumped at the deep, hoarse voice behind her. She was warmed up and tuned up and ready, technically, but her heart pounded. Odd. She'd pretty well conquered her fear of performing, mainly by telling herself to expect little response, that many wouldn't even pay attention. Often that was true. Something about tonight was throwing her. The place, maybe, and her grandma's emphasis about how important it was. Still, she'd played in front of A&R guys before and she wasn't this nervous. What was it?

She considered walking back through the little hallway that connected the bar to a small house now serving as performer warm up space and employee break area and running out through the old squeeky screen door and jumping into her car and going for chocolate of any kind. "Stop it. You can do this. It's just an open mic. Just an open mic."

When the guy with the voice raised his eyebrows and asked if she was going out there, she took a deep breath and nodded. Then she had to remind herself not to bite her lip and mess up her lip color if she hadn't already. She used only a bit of light mauve in an expensive brand that stayed on well and didn't smear and wasn't sticky or pasty to hide the whiteness of her lips. She wasn't big on make up in general. Mostly, she didn't need it due to the time she spent outside. But her lips...

"Now or never, lady."

Her feet nearly took her right back down the hall and out of the building, but her head took over and forced them to walk toward the stage area where the current performer was just finishing, to only slight applause. Polite, anyway. At least that was a good sign.

~~

After three not-so-good acts, a couple of which were local favorites he'd heard before and hadn't like then, either, James was ready to go somewhere without singers who couldn't hold a proper tune and guitarists who screwed up their chords and laughed about it. Davis and Gavin had been keeping their remarks low enough for only their table to hear, but after a few beers with whiskey chasers, they were getting loud, despite Bruce and James trying to hush them. Two girls had come over to ask him to dance and he refused politely by saying it was too early in the night, his usual reply until he got at least half lit and then always agreed. His buddies hassled him about refusing, but for now, he was trying hard just to hold it together. A couple more girls threw looks at him and giggled with their friends. Only a matter of time before they got up the nerve to approach, he figured. Between the childishness at his table and his urge to order beer, with the urge growing stronger the longer he was there, and girls hitting on him, which he both wanted and didn't want, he had to get out.

"I'm out of here." He stood and shoved his chair in. Good thing he'd driven his truck. Bruce might have a beer once he left, but he'd stay sober enough to get the other two back safe.

Waving off their objections, he headed toward the exit, got stopped by another girl who asked if she could buy him a drink, brushed her off, and was nearly out the door when the newest bait from the stage began to sing. Even with the noise in the room, including his roommates still at it, her soft voice came through. A nice voice. Not a song he recognized yet. Unable to resist, he turned to watch. The girl hesitated when Davis yelled his typical "Freebird!" request at her, but she continued.

And she was good. A bit more vocal training wouldn't hurt. She occasionally took breaths at the wrong times. Still, her tone was nice and he noted not a trace of arrogance. She wasn't singing to hear her own voice, as some did. She felt the song. Possibly her own.

Ambling back toward the open mic area, he studied her stage presence along with the music. She was dressed boyish, in a black tank top too big for her and old jeans, topped by ultra feminine blue and purple scarves that matched the prettiness of her voice. Her hair was short and kind of jagged, as much as he could see of it. Some brown color he couldn't tell in the bar's bad lighting, even with the spotlights over the performing area that weren't much better. She wasn't a looker at all, and it didn't look as though she was trying to be. But the song was real, heartfelt, with beautiful soft strong words that came from deep within. Her voice was deep, lower alto but not contralto, and clear, with enough vibrato to create a rich tone but not enough to overshadow the voice and words. Her range was good. She shifted into falsetto seamlessly, without getting thin or tinny. Unique. It was a unique voice. And pretty, although the girl did not put off a "pretty" vibe. It was more like a "stay the hell away" vibe. Except for her voice. And the lyrics.

Her acoustic guitar, an older Martin, not too expensive, was tuned well and she played it well. Technically good, but without the heart that was in her voice. Due to nerves, maybe.

He crept closer, swerving tables and chairs shoved out in his path. Before he realized it, he was standing right in front of her and his buddies were heckling him instead, but he blocked them out to keep his focus on the singer. She was still somewhat faltering, nervous, with glances over at the stupid comments, and at him, also, questioning why he was so close, he guessed.

Davis yelled "get off the stage" in his drunken garble and the girl stopped singing, stopped playing. She gazed at the floor as though trying to decide whether to actually get off the stage. Chuckles flooded in from around the room, along with some kinder people trying to hush the rest.

"He's an idiot. Keep going." James caught and held her eyes. Light brown eyes. He was close enough to see them well. "Keep going."

After a slight hesitation, she played a couple of measures and then started the song where she'd stopped.

People behind him told him to sit down, but he paid no attention. He was too drawn in. Not only to the music, but to her, to her eyes, her softness, her strength to put up with the idiots who likely couldn't hold a tune if their life depended on it, to include his roommates, and to keep singing, not even a cover, but her own music. He knew it was hers.

He turned long enough to tell Davis to shut the hell up, and returned his focus to the girl.

He recognized the next song. Infiniti's *When You Tell Me*. One of his favorites. Coincidence. It was a big song, not so surprising that she'd sing it. Back in the early two thousands, it was a big song. Fifteen-some years ago. Still, it was popular. Lots of bands covered it in local shows, or they used to. He had to wonder if the Raucous connection was intentional due to being at Sam's. She did it well. It meant something to her.

It was definitely more than the music pulling him. It was something inside her. How everyone in the crowd wasn't standing there awestruck, he couldn't figure. The girl was mesmerizing. Her voice needed some sharpening, some fine-tuning, but it was a pretty voice, luring. Unique. This one could do something in music.

~~

Isabel barely made it through her alotted time, and she cut it a couple of minutes short. She couldn't wait to get out of there. It wasn't even the heckling. She'd been heckled before. All performers were when they started out. But not like that. And that guy who stared gave her the creeps standing there so close, just staring. She'd wanted to tell him to back out of her face, but after he yelled at the group of cretins to stop heckling, which could have been risky if they had been prone to violence, she couldn't quite do it. Still, he could have pulled up a chair. It's not like there weren't any available.

Never again. She wasn't going back. So much for making it at Sam's. She'd gone because she needed to expand her reach, and her grandma had a special fondness for the bar and for Greenville because her musical idol she supposedly met way back in early 70-something had met his friend there who pulled him into what became one of the biggest rock bands of her time. Isabel's mom shrugged when she asked if it was true. It was before her time, she said, at least that she could remember.

And her mom didn't care much for the whole music scene, which Isabel found odd considering both of her parents were into it. Grams was a big name songwriter by the time Isabel was born, and Gramps was a local roadie for quite a few years. He'd met tons of big name bands during his time working at the Pittsburgh Civic Arena, which no longer existed. Papa Niall was depressed for months when they tore the place down. So far, he absolutely refused to set foot in Consol Energy Center, or whatever they called it now. "When you make it big and play there, my sweet girl, I will go to that new monstrosity, but not before." Isabel told him again she wasn't a performer. Again, her grandpa argued.

He was glad to know she was trying her luck at Sam's, and on June 4th, the birthday of her Grandma's long-time crush, no less, he laughed. A good omen, he'd said. So much for that.

In her car, she locked the door and dropped her head onto her steering wheel. Maybe it was time to stop. Maybe her skin was getting too thin after pushing so hard for the past few years and getting nowhere and cutting her hair so it looked stupid out of desperation. *Nothing will go with that mess.* Libs was right. Kind of like Isabel herself, really. Nothing, and no one, maybe, went with the mess that was her life. Her only direction for the past ... well, forever, was music, and it was going absolutely nowhere.

He's an idiot. Keep going.

The guy's words echoed through her head. Maybe he was creepy, but he was also listening. Intently. Creepily. But still, he'd been listening.

Maybe he was someone. Maybe he'd been an A&R guy and ... and she'd rushed out of there so fast after her set, he wouldn't have had a chance to talk to her if he'd wanted to. Did she even tell them her name when she was done, as she normally did? Before her set and after, she said her name. Name recognition mattered. Isabel was sure she'd forgotten, since she was so shaken.

"Just go home. Go home." With a deep breath, she picked her head up, started the engine of the hand-me-down black Aveo her grandpa gifted her with when the old thing she'd picked up upon moving away from home needed more repair than it was worth, and headed back to her little apartment in Meadville. She almost headed south to Pittsburgh instead, to her grandparents' place. She was tired, though, and the half hour home would be bad enough. It was more than twice as long the other direction, and Pittsburgh traffic was heavier, especially on a Saturday night. Isabel was far too tired to deal with that.

And she was too frustrated.

The jeering words telling her to get off the stage rang through her head mercilessly as she pulled out, made her way to Main Street, and across town to find I-79. She just wanted to be home. Maybe after work Monday, she would find a salon to fix the mess of her hair. Or she wouldn't. She was a mess. What did it matter if she looked like it?

Of course, the office where she worked might not like it. It wasn't at all a professional look. She hadn't thought about that while chopping away. Could be they would tell her to go fix it. She worked with people coming in the door. A receptionist. The first person they saw. She knew better than to do that to herself.

Trying not to let the thought throw her even more, she noticed a little bakery across the road from the Sheetz. Exactly what she needed, something sweet and fully indulgent. Sadly, the lights were out. Closed. She'd missed it. Still, she needed indulgence, so she pulled into the gas station and went in to find a sweet and fattening snack to serve as a temporary mood lifter while she drove home.

~~

"Hey, wait up!" James spotted her getting back in her car at Sheetz and yelled through his open window as he illegally pulled around someone to get into the parking lot. She closed her door as the guy blared his horn and gave him the finger. Whatever. He wanted to get her name. Stupidly, he hadn't listened when she said it before her set and she hadn't said it at the end. She'd packed up fast and bolted. Not that he could blame her.

The manager at Sam's said he wasn't sure of her name. Lizzy, he thought, but it didn't make any difference to him. He'd only written in *chick hard to understand* when she called to reserve a spot. Since the bar didn't have to pay open mic performers, he didn't need her name.

She pulled her Aveo out of the parking lot and he tried to follow, but his truck didn't fit through the small space left between the car at the pump and the one parked where it shouldn't be, so he had to back up and go around. He headed down Main for some time, but he didn't see any sign of her car that he could tell for sure. It looked too much like every other car in the dark.

Maybe she'd come back to Sam's. Not that he expected she would after Davis and Gavin acted like stupid rude drunks. Gavin wasn't a stupid drunk, exactly, but he followed Davis too close and Davis was every bit of one. Not that James had a lot of room to talk. Nothing worse than a reformed drunk, Davis told him more than once. He figured being an unreformed drunk was worse, actually, but it did no good to argue.

Giving up on the search for the night, he headed back to the apartment. But he didn't want to go home. He wanted... No, he would not acknowledge what he wanted. Seven months. He was not going to ruin seven months because of one girl and two stupid roommates.

He also would not go back to Sam's for a while. The urge was still too strong. How would he look for the little songbird without going to bars?

Social media.

The thought hit him that she would be advertising her shows. Of course, without her name it would be hard to look her up. He could check out the local music scene sites and every local bar and winery he could find online that hosted live music and watch for her face. That could work. Shouldn't be too hard.

Veering around to the park, James headed to the gravel parking area behind the amphitheatre, locked his doors, and used his phone as a flashlight to walk through the weeds to slip through the narrow opening. Sitting on the highest step, he leaned back against the stone wall and began searching the places he knew off the top of his head.

Three

"Put that thing down and come out with us."

"*Don't* hit anything. Might have found a lead." Jumping up from the couch to reclaim the phone Bruce grabbed from his hand, James checked the screen. "Damn. You *lost* the page. It might have been *her.*"

"Three weeks, bud. Give it up. You didn't even talk to the girl."

"I did." He tapped on recent screens trying to go back to where he was. No dice. It wouldn't reload.

"Yeah, you told her to keep going. So what? You like her voice. There are a hundred out there just as good. Besides, she's kinda young for you. Come on out with us and find someone your own age."

James rolled his eyes and replanted himself on the couch to try to get back to the page he'd found. "It's not about that. It's about her music. I don't want to hook up with anyone yet. I'm not ready."

Lowering beside him, Bruce set a hand on the back of his shoulder. "Eight months, J, and you're doing great. I think you could risk a date here and there. It would be better than turning the obsession onto a girl you don't know, and before you argue, it is just an obsession, something to focus on as a distraction. You know it is. Time to move on."

"Not eight months yet. Seven months and three weeks."

"Close enough. I know Sam's wasn't a good idea, but you can do Hicks. We'll grab wings, sit out on the patio, and listen to the music. Local acoustic, your specialty. And Felix said he'd try to drop by. It's been forever since he's seen you, so he said."

Maybe it was an obsession. Maybe a distraction. But it worked. As often as he'd wanted a drink, he managed to think of her instead and spend that time searching rather than drinking. Whatever worked, his counselor said, as long as it was safe. Nothing unsafe about researching a local singer.

Hicks in Mercer had been updated recently, to include a sidewalk patio area. His parents liked it. And it had been some time since he'd seen his little brother. Burt stopped in fairly often, to say hi, so he said. To check on him, is what he meant. He always suggested James could at least come by for Sunday dinner now and then. He joked back that if he was going to get leftovers by way of Brother Express faking camaraderie as pretense for being sure he was still being good, there was no point in actually going. Being home was hard since they were wary of him, of how he was doing, of whether he'd given in and was trying to hide it. Again.

"So? Coming or what?"

Local acoustic. Maybe the girl had gravitated toward nicer places, and her own set up rather than open mics at rundown bars. Hicks was a better location for her music. Much more appropriate. Along with that, local musicians tended to know each other. He could ask whoever was playing if they knew her, try to get some kind of lead. He closed out the screen and stood. "When are we leaving?"

~~

Isabel sat in her car and let it idle while she tried to decide whether or not to go inside. She hadn't tried an open mic for the past three weeks, and if she let herself wait any longer, she wouldn't start again. Tuning into the oldies rock station and the deejay's deep sensual voice, she closed her eyes and pictured one of her songs playing on the radio.

That wouldn't happen if she didn't keep going. Submitting them through proper channels hadn't worked at all. Too much competition. She had no idea if anyone had even looked at them. She constantly reminded herself of her grandma's words: *Not getting accepted doesn't mean your songs aren't good. It only means it wasn't in one person's interest range.*

Great, but how did you get past that? *Get out there and play*, her grandpa said, *and don't stop.*

"Okay, Grandpa. Okay." She reached up to turn off the ignition, but the beginning chords through the radio grabbed her. One of her favorites. *Magic Power.* Isabel sang along with Triumph in her best rock voice, which wasn't so great, but it was a good warm up, anyway. Energized and impassioned by the end notes, she turned off the car, got out, grabbed her guitar case from the back, and held her head and shoulders up while she walked into the little bar in Meadville she'd done okay at several times already.

Sometimes she had to go back to comfort zone areas to get rebooted. Then, she could head out farther again. But maybe not back to Sam's.

~~

During the acoustic band's break, a husband and wife duo he enjoyed well enough, James went up to the bassist since he seemed the most engaged with the audience. Describing Isabel, he waited for some spark of recognition that didn't come. The guy shrugged. He didn't know anyone with her description. No one in their circle. Just in case, he cornered the other three, the couple and their rhythm guitarist, and asked them, also. Nothing. No idea. He'd already asked the bartender about the girl and she didn't have a clue, either. Someone hanging by the singer, a friend, James assumed, suggested the girl might have been a stop through, not local. Not likely true. If she was trying to make a name by traveling to new areas, she would have been far more obvious about what that name was. And she didn't seem confident enough to travel outside her home base. She had to be nearby.

With thanks, he headed back to his roommates who had staked claim at a patio table on the sidewalk within one of two small fenced-off areas. Bruce was talking with a girl, so he veered away ... to the bar. For a cola. Or a beer. Just one. He could do one by now, he figured.

Like hell he could. He knew better. The bartender waited for his order. James hesitated. The bar stools were full of laughing people, some of which were enjoying the specials hand-written on the mirror behind the bar, although he knew most ordered their personal specialties, their known favorites. He wouldn't mind asking for his own go-to, a Scotch and soda, light on the soda, with a touch of lemon juice.

"Want me to come back? Our specials are…"

"Yeah, I see them. I'll do a, um…" Maybe a whiskey shot to go with a cola instead of a beer. Or gin, since it wouldn't smell.

"He'll take a Pepsi, and make that two." Bruce set a hand on his shoulder and gave him a look to say he knew damned well what he'd been about to do. "That's it for us, but I think my buddies over there could use a new beer. Add it to my tab." When she nodded and left, he leaned closer to James. "You okay?"

"So you keep me from getting one and send more over to Davis, never mind he's had more than enough?"

"He's not even making an attempt. Nothing I do's gonna change that. You, on the other hand, are not blowing it now."

James considered decking him, more so when the bartender set two glasses of what he knew was only Pepsi in front of them.

The girl who'd been flirting with his buddy over at the table came to find him, introduced herself with a noxious amount of alcohol on her breath, leaning forward enough her slinky tank top allowed even more view of her cleavage, and asked if she should bring her friend over.

"Of course, bring her over." Bruce gave her that half grin girls seemed to like, for some reason. Tall and slender, with dark brown round eyes and matching dark brown hair long enough to hit his shoulders, along with confidence nearly oozing from his pores, Bruce was too much a girl magnet. The last thing James wanted while still so unsteady with his resolve was some chick hitting him up while she stood around the bar drinking and laughing. If he kissed her with the alcohol on her breath...

"I gotta go. Give me a buzz when you're ready."

Bruce grabbed his arm. "Go where?"

He shrugged. "I'll walk around town, sit and star gaze or something. Can't be here."

"Bullshit. I know where you'll end up if you leave by yourself, down at the Legion where I can't stop you. You're staying with me. We'll have our Pepsis and then go on home if you're ready. You're not blowing it."

Seething frustration built up fast. He wanted to strike out. He wanted a damned drink. Just one. Or two.

"Come on." Bruce yanked his arm and steered him over to a table of girls that included the one who'd been hitting on him. "Hey. This is my buddy James and he could use someone to talk to, maybe slow dance with. Any takers? He's single. Has a job. Not bad looking, right? And yes, he's straight."

James rolled his eyes and tried to shove Bruce away.

"I will." A girl beside Bruce's current interest stood and came to him. "I'm Jackie. Also single and straight. No job. I'm a student. But I will have. I'm studying to be an IT tech." Her eyes sparkled, blue eyes, pretty color, but narrow, rather squinty. Her too-blonde hair was an obvious dye job, bobbed short but with enough length to swing when she twisted her head, making her look far too perky.

"Perfect." Bruce nudged him. "My friend, here, is a near genius with electronic stuff, computers, anything. You'll have plenty to talk about."

When the girl smiled, he gave in. Why not? If he couldn't drink, he could at least ... flirt, socialize, whatever. There was still a chance his little brother would make it there, although he hadn't yet and hadn't checked in. Typical Felix. James had learned long ago not to count on him.

~~

"Hey baby, how 'bout singing to me private-like? Then I'll make you sing." The guy laughed like he was hysterical.

Isabel did her best to ignore him. Why hadn't the bouncer taken care of this guy yet? He was a regular. She'd seen him plenty often, but he'd never bothered her before. While she continued her song, she shifted her gaze around to try to find assistance. Libs had offered to come, but she was sick, and this was a comfort zone, so Isabel told her it was fine, to stay home and rest. She'd never thought about security in the bar. It was a small place. Friendly. It could be they knew the guy was only bluster and nothing to worry about.

Ignoring him didn't help. His buddies were laughing and egging him on. One more song. She had time for one more song. Instead of doing one of her own, she closed her eyes for a second to remember the chords she used to play and then did her best with Triumph's song that spoke of being wild and free, the way she felt when she sang…

"Come get wild with me, baby. I'm free, too." The jerk yelled it out. A couple of people told him to quiet down. He only yelled back.

Between the drunk idiot and the lack of interest and attention, Isabel threw up her hands. She cut the song short, packed up her guitar, and veered around people in her path. Using the guitar case as a blockade, she made it to and out the door into the cool, humid night air. With a long deep breath, she gazed up at the few stars visible through the clouds. Always so many clouds. She longed for a clear night so she could see the sky speckled with millions of lights. Those nights were too rare.

"Hey, nice job. Good to hear that song again." A middle-aged guy walked past and gave her a pleasant grin as he accompanied a woman at his side, obviously his wife, to their car.

That song. He liked her cover song. She thanked him, but inside she screamed, "What about *my* songs?" At least she got a *nice job* out of it and some decent tips. Better than a lot of nights.

With a sigh, she picked up her guitar case from where she'd propped it on the ground and decided to be happy enough with the compliment and the tips. Tomorrow was beach day. Sunday. Her down time.

As she opened the back door of her car, a hand clutched her arm. "Hey baby, where're ya running to so fast? How about that private song I requested?" He yanked her up against his large smelly body.

She tried to push away, but his grasp was too tight. "Let go of me."

He laughed. Her heart sank. Laughter wasn't good. The swaying that said he had way more than his limit wasn't good. The parking lot was mostly empty and dark other than a couple of too-dim lights under the bar's eaves. She felt the guitar case pulled from her grasp, felt him pushing her into the car, his hot gut-wrenching stench of breath on her neck, his hand under her shirt.

Fighting, scratching whatever skin she could reach, she tried to get her knee in a position to immobilize him only for a minute, enough to climb out from underneath, but he was heavy and large and determined. He laughed while she yelled at him to get off, got her jeans unzipped, his hand inside. Her heart pounded. She pushed at his head…

"Get *off* her." A female voice. Not one she knew. More voices. Male. The heaviness was pulled away enough she could breathe easier. Someone asked if she was okay. A girl, helping her sit up, helping to cover her up again. Apologies from someone. He was too drunk, didn't mean it, wouldn't do it otherwise. The guy's friends? Acquaintances? She didn't care who they were. She asked where her guitar was and someone handed it to her while they asked again if she was okay and kept apologizing and Isabel grabbed it and put it on the back seat and shut the door and opened the driver door and told them to back up as she found her keys and shut them all out.

She nearly rammed another car veering out of the gravel parking area, drove just down the road, pulled into a parking lot, well lit, to catch her breath, and decided she was done. No more shows. No more assholes. No more jeers or propositions or… No more.

With anger and resolve keeping her emotions in check, she went home, refused to answer Libs when her friend asked how it went, if she was okay, if she'd caught the stomach bug, and locked herself in the bathroom for a long, hot shower.

Tomorrow was beach day. She would go look for sea glass and…

Sobs took over, and by the time she could make herself get out from under the hot water, she only had the energy to tell Libs she was done with music before dropping onto her bed.

Four

The end of June already. It had been nearly a month since James had seen the singer girl at Sam's, and since then, he'd spent most every night after work checking every bar in the area that did open mic nights, dragging Bruce or Gavin or Burt with him in case the urge to get a beer got too strong. No one knew her by the name Sam's manager gave him, Lizzy something, or by description, not even other singers. Of course, he figured he could have her name wrong since she ran out of there like a scared rabbit instead of repeating it to her audience, as she should have. Major rule of shows: say your name at least in the beginning and the end. In between didn't hurt, either. He couldn't quite blame her for running out of there, although she'd have to develop thicker skin if she wanted to go anywhere, but he hoped she hadn't given up.

How did he find her when social media didn't work and neither did bar hopping?

Putting his head back in his job long enough to be sure he measured the right amount of chlorine to add to the water tank, James figured he might as well give up his quest. He'd spent too much time and money at bars, and along with making it harder to stay dry, the food he ordered to have an excuse to be there was wracking his system. It was also eating into his beach tour fund. He desperately needed another beach-hopping trip soon. His buddies harassed him about wanting to spend his off time at the water after doing his forty a week at the water treatment plant, but one had nothing to do with the other. The smell of natural lake or ocean water was a salve to the smell of chemicals, both those added to the waste water to clean it and those he used to clean the tanks and equipment.

He didn't care much about the smell of the chemicals; he was too used to it. But there was something about the beach that made him breathe heavy and slow. And the girls at the beach, of course. More on the east coast than along lake Erie. As the Beach Boys said, east coast girls were different. That one he'd met at Snapper Jack's on Folly Beach, South Carolina, the girl on crutches he'd tried hard to get to beach-hop with him, she still crawled back into his thoughts from time to time although it had been a few years. Four years, wasn't it? Maybe five. Crutches or no, that girl was sensuous. He loved the way she moved.

The little songbird had nothing on that, looks-wise. She was cute, but she wasn't what James would call sensuous. It wasn't *her*... well, it was her, but not her looks that pulled him in. It was the music. The lyrics.

Okay, more than that. It was something inside her.

An odd feeling. It was always looks and the eyes that had pulled him before, and the way they moved. But Lizzie, or whatever her name actually was, would likely pull at him for some time, as well. He'd even started watching for her while out about. Like an idiot. Definitely time to go up to Presque Isle, to swim and sun bathe and run one of the paths, to see if would take his mind off the girl.

Of course there was Jackie. He'd seen her a couple of times since spending the night with her after their set up rescue dance. James couldn't quite make himself not see her, but he hadn't slept with her again. It was too much encouragement. She was interesting as a conversationalist as long as they kept it on information technology and related subjects. But she didn't like the beach. She swam, in pools only because they were clean, so she believed, despite evidence to the contrary, which he decided not to mention. But she hated the feel of "slimy" moss on her feet and between her toes, hated the fish smell, and the sound of seagulls. Definitely, she would not beach hop with him.

Maybe the little songbird would be the same. Didn't matter. He only wanted to hear her sing, to hear more of her songs.

A glance at his watch said he had nearly an hour until the figurative whistle blew. Maybe he'd wander farther away, or toward smaller places. Maybe Sandy Lake or Hadley. He could see her as a rural girl, which would help explain her nerves. It was possible he could run into her just cruising the sidewalks or diners. How did you look for someone when you had no idea where to look?

~~

Just outside the door of the one story office building in a little strip mall area, Isabel glanced around the large parking lot. It was daylight, a steamy day, in a work area, not dark and outside a bar. It was fine. Two weeks after the drunk jerk attacked her and she was still fighting the fear of going out alone. She hadn't even gone to the lake. Going to work was hard enough, and it was only down a few blocks from her place. The parking lot was a large open space with scattered cars and several people going to or from or wandering the sidewalks. No one paid attention to her. Still, she was wary.

But it was time to get past it. She missed the beach. And she needed the relaxation that came with the sounds and smells of the lake, the feel of her feet in the sand.

Watching everything while making her way quickly from the doorstep, across the grayed asphalt that threw heat up at her sandaled feet, she held her key in her hand, pointed out ready to unlock the door. At least she wasn't in the middle of the parking deck somewhere. She often wished she was because of the rain through much of the year and snow and salt making a mess of her shoes the rest of it. For now, she was glad it was an open area. And bright. Bright enough that even with her sunglasses, she held a hand over her forehead to block the rays.

By the time she reached her car, clicked it open at the last second, and closed and locked it behind her, her heart was pounding and her underarms were drenched, partly from heat, more from fear. It was ridiculous. One scare outside a bar at night could not keep her from everyday activities. She had to work. And she needed the lake.

Maybe she would have her hair fixed on Saturday, since her manager badgered her about it not being "presentable" no matter how she tried to fix it up with barrettes and hair bands, and then brave Presque Isle on Sunday. She supposed it was time to move along, fix herself up, and prepare for the world of offices and professionalism.

Five

Two weeks and a few days without touching her guitar and Isabel still heard music in her head. But mainly, she heard words: *Wanted and needed and no one could tell her/ she loved him and ... no one could sell her/ he wouldn't stay long/ he wouldn't be 'round/ when she wanted and needed his...*

It buzzed through her brain too often, but it wouldn't gel. She had to get it on paper.

Not that she had paper on her. Generally, she did. Generally, when Isabel went to the beach, she carried a notebook in the small laptop bag she used as a purse and traveling office. It was made of a heavy sand-colored material with smaller pockets in front that worked for her keys, sunglasses, and guitar picks. She'd chosen it specifically so if she set it on the beach, the sand sticking to it wouldn't show. But she'd quit music, and so she hadn't brought her notebook. There was damp sand, though.

Finding a small stick, she wrote the words into the sand next to the water: *He wouldn't stay long/ he wouldn't be 'round/ when she...*

When she what? Told him she was ready to give in, to give him what he wanted in order to stay? Would he have stayed? Or would he have stayed only long enough to get what he wanted and...

She shuddered. "Forget him, Isabel. He doesn't matter." Erasing the last two words, she paused. Wouldn't be around... and what? Closing her eyes to concentrate, she hummed the music, studying the rhythm, the mood she'd already created and wanted to emphasize.

"Hey. It's you."

She jumped at the voice and saw a shadow move over her words.

"Sorry. Didn't mean to startle you. New song?"

Wiping her lyrics away, she stood and backed up. A tall, sturdy male. In khaki shorts and tennis shoes and nothing else.

"You don't recognize me. I shouldn't have expected you would. I saw you sing. A bit more than a month ago. At Sam's."

Sam's. She held a hand over her forehead to block the sun and found his face. The guy who had stood right in front of her while she sang. The creepy guy. Cute. Well built. But creepy.

"You're from Erie?" He took a couple of steps closer. "Guess that's why I've had trouble finding you. At clubs. I've been hoping I might catch up with you again."

A quick check to see how close others might be satisfied her well enough. No one was terribly close, but enough they'd hear her if needed.

The guy crept forward, his head in a slight tilt. The sun behind his head made the edges of his blond hair glow. "I just wanted to ask where you'll be singing next so I can drop by without my idiot buddies. The hecklers. And I'm sorry they did that. You didn't deserve it."

To let him know he was close enough, she stepped backward. He was pretty cute, really, and built nicely, with sturdy shoulders, but not overdone. Tall, but not overly tall. His hair was trimmed neat and short in the back, his bangs slightly longer and swept back, with a nice wave to it. The green eyes were a darker green, close to brown but not brown. His gaze was friendly, pretty much. He didn't look threatening, exactly, but his sharp face had an edginess, as did his eyes. She forced herself to answer, to try not to look afraid of him. "No one deserves that."

"Yeah, well, that may be true, but someone should tell people they can't sing when they can't. Nicely, of course. You, though..."

"A lot of them are songwriters trying to get their songs out there, not themselves. They aren't trying to show off their voices. They just want their songs heard and you do what you have to do. They don't deserve that." She backed away farther. A few more steps and she'd turn to walk faster. First, she wanted a head start.

"Wait. I'm not..." He stuck his hands out in a shrug. "I just want to talk a minute. I'll stay put right here. Promise." He studied her in return, too hard, reading her fear. "So, where are you singing next? I enjoyed your songs, and your voice. The whole thing. I can try to help gather some people who won't be idiots, get you a bigger crowd, a better crowd, those who actually want to listen to an emerging songwriter."

Her heart raced. "Why?"

"Like I said, I enjoyed your music. I have a habit of supporting music I enjoy."

"Are you in the business? A&R?" Isabel used the short version of Artists and Repertoire, meaning those who scout out new talent, purposely to see if he understood.

He laughed. "No, nowhere close. I'm a technician at a local wastewater treatment facility. I clean tanks, check equipment, and add chemicals to used water to make it safe for consumption. In Greenville, where I live, which is why I was at Sam's. That's it. Not exciting, but a job. At least that's what I do currently." He stuck his thumbs into the pockets of his shorts. Possibly, they were swim trunks, and probably they were. Probably he was about to go swimming since he wasn't wearing a shirt, or carrying one. His feet were bare other than tennis shoes, the *in* kind of shoe people paid way too much for with as basic and boring as they were. And he was built really nice. His abs were muscular and flat. He boasted a nice tan. The small amount of hair on his chest that trailed down to his stomach showed he was actually a blond.

She had to try to slow her heart rate between the way he'd come up on her so fast and … well, because he was the kind of guy she'd stop and stare at in any other situation. She tried to focus on what he said while trying not to look at him. "Currently?"

"Yeah, I work a while to save up money to travel and then take off for a while, then come back and get something else, or sometimes the same thing if it's available. Depending."

She nodded without saying it must be nice to work only part of a year, and took a couple more steps backward. "Well, thank you. For the compliment. I have to go."

"Wait. Where will you be next?"

"Nowhere."

"You didn't quit? Because of those idiots? I'd hoped you hadn't, and you shouldn't. You're good … Lizzie? Do I have your name right? I wasn't sure."

Isabel wondered whether to correct him and decided against it. She was either right that she hadn't said her name at the end of her set or he didn't bother to hear it right or remember it right. Either way, it didn't matter now. And she wasn't telling this guy anything. She took another step back.

"Um, okay. You can sing on a stage to strangers, but you can't stand here and talk to me a minute?"

"You are a stranger."

"Okay, but... Wow, what's up with this? I'm only trying to talk. Not hitting on you or anything. No offense, but you're not my type."

Jerk. She was right. He was creepy. "I couldn't care one ounce less if I am or not." Isabel swiveled and walked away from him. Too much nerve. She didn't like too much nerve in a man. And she didn't have to talk just because he felt like it.

"Fine, Lizzy from Erie. Just quit. Let the idiots chase you off. If you do that all your life, you're never going to get anywhere with anything. Your loss, I guess."

She swiveled back. "Have you tried it? Have you tried getting up in front of people purposely letting them judge you, not just your voice or just your songs, but *you*, as they think you are, just to have them act like you're a waste of time? Have you done that not once or twice but over and over and over until you believe they're right? Yeah, maybe they're right. Maybe I can't keep doing that to myself when it gets me nowhere at all. Ever. Who in the hell are you to judge me for it?"

~~

James stared for some time, silent. Waste of time? He focused on her light brown eyes, her square jaw, the light brown hair dangling down her face and her shoulder with the back cut up roughly around the base of her neck. A hack job, it looked like. Style, maybe. He didn't know anything about girls' fashion or hair or anything of the sort and didn't care one way or another. Maybe it was on purpose. But then, maybe it wasn't. Wary. Most of what he saw from her was wariness, but with an obvious fire within.

He shrugged as though he couldn't care less if she cared nothing about him or his opinion, even if it wasn't true. "I know more about that than you can imagine. But whatever. I only meant to be encouraging..."

"It wasn't encouraging. It was insulting."

"Okay, I'm sorry." He watched her body language. She seemed to be not sure whether to turn away or stay, so she remained frozen, watching his every move. James decided to change tactics. "Hungry?"

"What?"

"Being out here always makes me hungry. Not sure what it is. Want to go get something to eat with me so I don't have to go alone?"

"No." She looked at him like he was crazy.

"I'm not asking you to get into my truck, okay? I can meet you. Maybe at the hot dog stand just off the island. Haven't been there yet, but I've thought about it a lot. Is it good?"

"Sara's?"

"I guess so. The little place covered in bright red."

"Sara's. Why do you assume I know whether it's good?"

"You're from here, right?"

"Why do you think that?" She brushed a strand of longer hair behind her ear when the light breeze pushed it into her face. Her ears were pierced, but she wore no earrings, allowing the tiny holes that scarred her lobes to show as though she didn't care. Maybe she always took them out for the beach.

"You just kinda seem to fit." Her loose navy T-shirt over loose blue jean capris made her look comfortable with where she was, like it was an everyday kind of thing to be out there. Plus, she had a nice, gradual healthy tan that hinted at a lot of natural outdoor time instead of the forced tan look that changed the natural skin tone to something odd. "You grew up on the lake, I assume."

"You assume one hell of a lot. Are you aware of that?"

"Maybe. But I have a hell of a lot of experience to back it up."

"Right. Well, I have to go." She moved away, but not as fast as she'd started to walk earlier.

James caught up, grimacing when sand seeped inside his sneakers and rubbed his feet. She was carrying her shoes, basic brown sandals, probably the much smarter thing to do. "Hey."

She jumped away when he touched her shoulder.

"Ooookay, got it. You don't like physical contact. Won't have to tell me again, or show me, whatever the case may be. And it's my treat. Just a hot dog or burger. No big deal. Okay?"

"Are you some kind of nut job?"

He laughed. "Probably so, but a safe one."

"Right. They all say that. I really have to go so I can get to work."

"Work? It's Saturday, nearly four o'clock."

"Yeah. And?"

"You have a show? No, you just said you quit music. So what do you do? Or did you just tell me you quit so I won't show up at one of your gigs and stand in front of you? I won't do that again. Promise. I think I promise. At least I'll try not to stand so close next time."

She started walking backward. "Sara's is wonderful, so you should try it. I have to go. Don't follow me or I will yell."

James watched her hurry through the sand, past the peeling-white picket fence loosely held together with wire, back up toward the parking area. He considered following, but he was afraid she might actually yell for help and that was the last thing he needed.

With a sigh, he continued his trek down the shoreline. If she'd given up, it didn't much matter if he lost contact.

~~

Isabel locked her car door as soon as it was closed and watched for signs of him. Figured creepy guy would find her at the lake, on the one day she was free to go. How? She usually came on Sundays, not Saturdays, so if he'd been following or anything, it should have thrown him off track. He asked if she was from Erie. Obviously he wasn't following enough to know better, or he did and he wanted to sound like he didn't. It was hard to tell. A shudder shook her whole body.

She didn't want to leave yet. She'd only been there a couple of hours and the plan had been to spend the afternoon into evening. She could drive around and go to another beach on Presque Isle, or drive west along Lake Erie and maybe stop at Lake City. He hadn't followed her. He wouldn't know. With the thought in mind, she started the engine and pulled out, keeping an eye out for any sign of him. How did he happen to choose the same beach area she had? Which vehicle was his? Truck. He mentioned his truck like it was some kind of status symbol. The guy was full of himself. Arrogant. And creepy. She could not let herself believe he wanted to help. She would not believe him.

With the intention of pulling into another beach area, Isabel found herself driving all the way off Presque Isle. She did not veer right toward Lake City or left toward the shoreline up along Erie. With a glance at Sara's, where she would stop if not afraid he would be there, Isabel wound around the small roads through the edge of Erie and back to I-79 toward Meadville.

~~

James ambled along the non-swimming part of the beach for some time, considering her reaction, her wariness. Why had he said she wasn't his type? It was petty, because he felt rebuffed. She wasn't the type to play that kind of game with. After looking for her so long, he blew it.

Maybe he could find her at Sara's. She could have stopped. Find her why, though? She'd quit singing. But he didn't want her to quit. He wanted to convince her to continue.

Unwilling to bother her again too soon even if she had stopped, he made his way back to the beach area, left his shoes with his shirt, stuck his wallet and keys in the locking cooler that held his water and some jerky, tied the key to the string of his trunks and zipped it into his pocket, then treaded out into the water. He swam the perimeter of the roped off area which marked the boundary between safe and unsafe with a fast breast stroke that made his chest heave, and then made the return path with a slower front crawl. In his younger years, he would have dived down below the water and come out on the other side of the roped area, just to be out where no one else was, beyond the safe border.

No more. He'd done enough of that for a lifetime, or for a few more years at least. Hard to say how he'd feel about it after memories had faded some, after his current struggle stopped being a struggle. At the moment, that was enough of a danger zone. He didn't need to add to it.

Rubbing his hair with the towel and leaving the rest to drip dry, he carried his things to a rocky place, sat on the towel, and tented his hands behind him, his knees in front, drying off. Enjoying the sun and the heat, the humid heat rather than the dry heat. He hated dry heat. The joke about ridiculous temperatures at least being dry made him roll his eyes. A couple of times, he'd jumped someone for saying something so stupid. Dry heat was excruciating. At times PA's humidity was stupid-humid, but mostly it was plenty bearable. Better than the dry heat that made your skin feel like sandpaper.

She'd been writing in the sand. What had it said? He closed his eyes and tried to remember. Wouldn't be there. Wouldn't... stay long. He wouldn't stay... or be around. The girl had been hurt. Left? Was that what the wariness was about? She'd had her trust in someone get crushed? Nothing new. Who didn't? It happened. He'd been dumped by someone he was sure would wait for him while he was away and she hadn't bothered to tell him until he was back home Shit happened. You just moved on.

With a shake of his head, he got up again, grabbed his belongings, and climbed over the rocks, farther from people, away from the swimming area, out where it was quiet.

Wouldn't stay long. He wanted to hear the rest. That much could lead anywhere. Hell, he could sit down and write a song around those words and it would be a hundred percent different than hers.

She had been hurt, though, maybe far more than the norm.

The thought made James shiver and he put his shirt and shoes back on to head toward his truck. It was a good ways down the path, since he'd parked and walked as usual. Some days, he'd park in the first available space, swim a bit, walk the path to the next beach, swim a bit, and continue. Then he'd turn and walk back.

At least it's what he'd been doing this summer now that he was sober and in shape enough. Before then...

No, he wouldn't think about before. He had to focus on ahead, not behind.

Six

No matter how much Isabel had pleaded with Lisbon not to make it sound like a double date, it felt exactly like that. Except that Isabel wanted no part of it.

She'd agreed to go to Greenville's fireworks when Libs begged. The all-important boyfriend, Charlie something, had a friend in the band that was entertaining until dark descended, and Charlie's cousin insisted on going along since the friend was a mutual friend, and he didn't want to be a third wheel. But it was a not a date. Isabel told Libs it was *not* a blind date. Absolutely not. She just wanted to see the fireworks.

Still, Cousin Dale spent far too much time brushing up against her arm, talked mainly to her when he bothered to say anything, and had tried to grasp her fingers while they ambled along the road between the short row of face-to-face food vendors deciding what to get. Isabel veered away in guise of wanting a corn dog. It did nothing to deter him. He even paid for the thing while she was telling him she could get it.

She should have driven instead of riding in Charlie's car with Libs and Charlie's cousin. Now she was stuck.

Dale was a nice enough guy, and she actually liked him far better than she liked braggart, know-it-all Charlie, but his lips were soft and big, too prominent amid the rest of his face, which wasn't a bad face, even if it spoke of an always indoors type that rarely got any sun or exercise. Not that she had much room to talk. Her body advertised the fact, with an extra twenty-five pounds, that exercise was not her thing, either. She did, though, have a healthy tan from all of her beach time. She did not look like she sat inside glued to the TV all day.

An unfair assumption that he was, and she knew it as she thought it, but she couldn't unthink it.

At least the band was pretty good. She wouldn't follow them around, but she didn't mind listening, until Dale put his hand on her back. A cringe ran from where he touched her and rushed through her body.

The guy from Sam's came to mind. Did he give her his name? She didn't remember. She did, however, vividly remember what he said: *Got it. You don't like physical contact.* Idiot. Just because she didn't want strangers touching her didn't mean she didn't like physical contact. There was a line. He'd crossed it. And so had this guy.

Leaning around him to tell Libs she'd be right back, Isabel headed over to the port-a-potties she did not actually intend to use. While she walked, she thought about hiding out from Dale. It would be easy enough to blend into the fast-growing crowd in the creeping dark. Blankets and folding chairs were filling in the grassy area. Kids sported light-up necklaces and wands that lit up and blew bubbles. Vendors and rides were shutting down in preparation for the main event. If she didn't come right back, Libs would call her and Isabel would say she'd meet them when they were ready to leave. Simple.

Except she didn't want to wander alone after dark. Even if she had to put off Dale's advances, it would be better than being alone after dark. The thought still made her too nervous.

Trying to brush off the heaviness in her soul, she started back toward the pavilion, and stopped. Creepy guy from Sam's. Her stomach tightened. He said he lived in Greenville, so she'd been keeping an eye out for him. He was at the pavilion listening to the band. Music. He'd also said he supported music he liked. Was he one of their fans?

When he turned, she ducked around behind a group of older teens, hoping he wouldn't see her. A girl was with him. Slim and curvy. In a tight cream-colored tank top and brown shorts. Wavy blonde hair in a very neat little cutesy bob. Hanging all over him. Of course.

You're not my type. As if Isabel hadn't known that already. Jerk. He didn't have to say it. And really, assuming she thought he was interested in her was fully obnoxious.

Instead of returning to Libs and the men, she veered away, back to the area full of blankets, and sat in the grass close to a family with three half-grown kids. No one would bother her there. And it was dark enough creepy guy wouldn't notice, if he bothered to notice anything beyond that girl, which she highly doubted.

He hadn't said he had a girlfriend. Really, that would have been a more polite line than *you're not my type.* Somewhat more polite. But it still inferred she could be interested in him, which was not only obnoxious, but terribly conceited. To be fair, he may have noticed her admiring his body, but admiring did not equal interested. It did not.

~~

"These guys are really good."

James made himself not roll his eyes at Jackie. They were okay. Their guitarist was good. All of the songs he'd heard so far were covers, nothing original. The lead, though, tended to be pitchy, which he tried to cover with a growl kind of thing that didn't come off well. He heard a couple of girls talk about how "sexy" they were. He figured that might be the big appeal for Jackie, also.

While she focused on the band, he glanced around the area, watching people. Watching for her, the little songbird from Sam's. Long shot she'd be there, he supposed, but it was one of the few places that had fireworks on the Fourth rather than the weekend before, so there was a chance, if that mattered to her, if she liked fireworks at all. Could be she didn't. Could be she was at work if she worked evenings. What would she be doing? Retail probably. Maybe he'd start looking around the local Wal-marts in the evenings, or grocery stores... Hell, could be anything since most everyone was open late these days.

He wanted to keep moving, either way. "Want to walk around more before fireworks start?"

Jackie took his arm, but kept her focus to the band. "You don't want to listen? Thought you were into music."

"I am, but..." He shrugged.

"You don't like them?" Her voice was loud enough to turn a few heads, her gaze, which was finally on him, throwing fake shock.

"Not enough to stand around here another thirty minutes."

"Wow. I don't get it, but okay, then. How about you walk around and meet me back here in twenty? They only play for another twenty minutes."

Because watching these guys mattered more than being with him? He'd brought her to not be there alone. He wanted to honor his country's independence day and the sacrifices that were made for that independence. Fireworks were rough to take these days. He loved them, always had, but the memories were still too fresh, including concern for his battle buddy still over there. He supposed he could wander alone until time to find somewhere to sit, though. "You're good by yourself?"

"Yep. Go ahead. But don't use too much of that energy, okay?" She tapped his hip with a wink.

~~

Isabel did answer when Libs called to see where she was. She did not agree to meet up with them again until time for fireworks, but she also didn't want to sit until then. Making arrangements to meet at the ticket tent at 9:45, which would give them fifteen minutes to settle before the show, she took a deep breath and wandered toward the small path that ran between food vendors. It was still hot, still humid. She was sweaty and annoyed. Part of her annoyance was being sweaty, which she hated. She needed water.

And she had to be able to walk around by herself. It was a must. No matter how much she did not want to be by herself after dark. She'd done much harder things and she could do this, also. Especially when it was only dusk, not dark, the place was well lit, and people were everywhere.

Pulling the hand-size pepper spray from her bag, she stuck it in her front pocket for easier access. At least she'd thought to bring it. She nearly forgot her phone, but she no longer went anywhere without her pepper spray.

The smells flooding her senses – nacho cheese, popcorn, sausage – were tempting, but she didn't want to carry it around and she'd already eaten, so she settled for a small slushee instead of water, crossed her arms in front of her while she stood in line, looked at the girl taking her order only as long as she had to, and made a bee-line back to where she'd been sitting. The food area was too crowded. It was too obvious she was alone. It was easier to sit by herself than to walk around by herself.

Finding the spot she'd settled in earlier, Isabel changed her mind. A young couple with a baby was now next to the family. A cringe in her gut said she couldn't do quite that much, so she headed away, closer to a group of young twenties. At least listening to their inane, and very loud, conversation would give her something to think about while she waited, and maybe it would give her a song idea, if she was lucky. If she wanted a song idea.

~~

James sipped on a bottle of water while he wandered the outskirts of the crowd. At one point, he thought maybe he caught a glimpse of a girl that could have been her, but a couple of kids nearly ran him over and he moved out of their way and then she was gone.

Stupid search, anyway. Too much a long shot.

He got bored with being on his own before the twenty minutes were up, so he headed back to Jackie. Better to listen to okay music and watch his date half drool over the guys in the band than to wander on his own on a ridiculous quest, especially since the little songbird wanted nothing to do with him.

He jumped at the buzz of his phone and pulled it from his pocket. Burt. With a grimace, James remembered he was supposed to have called his brother about his Fourth plans. He thought about ignoring it, but he couldn't quite do it. "Hey."

"Hey? C'mon James. You were supposed to call me. I've left three messages. Where are you?" His oldest brother sounded half annoyed and half worried.

"Riverside."

"Okay, so Bruce said you'd be here, but I haven't caught sight of you yet. Whereabouts?"

"Caught sight?" He looked around for the familiar face.

"We're here, bud. All of us. Set up on about twenty blankets waiting on fireworks with the kids all lit up like mini Christmas trees. Not hard to find. Where are you?"

"Wandering around the food." He wasn't going to admit he was back behind the vendors away from people while watching them.

Burt laughed. "Of course you are." He relayed it to someone else, his family, James figured. "I'll meet you at the popcorn stand. Kids are begging. Be right there."

Clicking it off, he rubbed his chin, trying to decide whether to be grateful for the rescue or annoyed by the interruption. Making his way back to the popcorn stand, he wished there was a beer stand, also. The whole crew was there. It was good. He still hadn't gone to visit, or for Sunday dinner, although his mom called to invite him every Sunday morning on her way to church, trying to entice him by letting him know what was on the menu. And less obviously, calling early enough to see how he sounded.

Grabbing four huge bags of popcorn, three for his nieces and nephews to share and one for himself and Jackie, he tucked three of them under his arm, holding the fourth with the two fingers of his left hand that still worked. The woman taking the money looked at him funny when he mishandled the damned change and again when he grasped the bag. With his jaw gritted to ignore it, he turned and nearly ran into his brother.

"Hungry?" Burt grinned.

"Only one's mine. Here. Take a couple."

"You didn't have to do that." Grabbing all three from under his arm, holding them all by the tops in one hand, Burt set the other hand on his shoulder. "You wanted to be alone for this?"

"I'm not here alone."

"No? Dating again, finally?"

"More or less. She's over listening to the crappy band playing. That mattered more than walking around with me."

"Considering the mood you're in, not sure I blame her. And they're only crappy if you're an arrogant classically trained musician who went rogue and turned uppity about it."

"Whatever." He headed that direction.

"They sound okay to me."

"Of course they do."

His brother shook his head and stopped to get water. "Want one or two?"

"Rather have a beer."

Burt raised his eyebrows. "This'll have to do. Sharing one with your girl, or..?"

"Fuck, no. But I'll get it."

Insisting, since James bought the popcorn, Burt tucked three of them in his arm and handed the other two over. "So." He continued the path toward the music. "Is this girl decent enough to bring over to sit with us?"

James gave him a not amused look, although to be honest, he wasn't so sure, considering she'd been all over him since he picked her up. "Why are you here? Thought you were doing Grove City this year."

"Changed our plans when Bruce said you'd be here. Think we were going to let our heroic vet brother celebrate the Fourth without us?"

He felt his eyes roll. "Don't call me that."

"What? Our brother? You are, you know. You can ditch us most of the time, but we're still your family, like it or not."

"Don't be a jackass. You know what I meant."

Grabbing his arm to get him to stop, Burt stepped in front of him. "You are, and you deserve the accolades, think so or not. Can't stop us being proud of you, either."

"Fully undeserved."

"Like hell it is. I've seen your record."

With another roll of the eyes, he pulled from his brother's grasp and moved around him to find Jackie. He had to call her name twice before she pulled attention from the music, and some guy she was talking to, offered the water, and introduced Burt. She was at least friendly. And she agreed to go sit with his family, as soon as the band was done.

~~

Isabel tried to sit on the other side of Libs and Charlie, but Dale moved over beside her, too close. Under cover of the dark night and everyone being focused up at the sky where the sparkling remnants of exploded fireworks looked at times like they might fall down right on top of her head, Dale nudged in with an arm around her back, then around her shoulders, his fingers playing with her hair which he'd called unique and "kinda cool" which she knew was a put-down. She tried to politely back away, but he only moved in closer, and spoke into her ear.

"I'd love to see you again." It was a loud whisper too close to her ear and she pulled away. Still, he didn't get it. She ignored him and he didn't get it. Or he did and wasn't backing down even if she did show every sign of having no interest. When she shuddered, he asked if she was cold and tried to warm her with his arms.

She shrugged out of the too tight embrace. "Stop, okay?"

"Too many people around?" The glint in his eyes said he had more in mind than she wanted him to have in mind.

"I just want to watch the fireworks."

"Got it." He winked.

He absolutely did not get it. He was absolutely too dense to get it. She wanted to go home. He was even ruining the fireworks for her, and that was hard to do considering how much she loved them.

~~

James had to stop Jackie from her too-blatant flirting, making it far too obvious she wanted to go home with him. Although not her home. She lived with her parents while still in school, so she wanted to go back to his place before he took her home. Since it was dark, he wouldn't have minded much if his family wasn't right there. Twice he'd had to move her hand to a more family-appropriate place to be touched. Still, Denny saw it and smirked at him. The kids were all safely in front of the adults, lining the front edge of the blankets, their little faces tilted up at the sky, with oohs and ahs and some jumping and laughter. Between his three brothers, there were eight kids, twelve years to three months. His little brother had started before him. Felix's baby was a beautiful little girl and obviously not easily scared since she was sleeping through the noise in her dad's arm. Her three-year-old cousin was cuddled tight into her mom's lap, peeking now and then, but not fond of the noise.

Watching them, James jumped at a series of those single explosion white light things meant more for noise than beauty. He hated them. Too realistic.

Jackie laughed and slid her hand to his inner thigh. "Did you really jump at fireworks?"

"We're still in public, you know." He moved her hand back up to the top of his leg.

"It's dark and everyone's watching the sky. Why did you jump?"

Ignoring her amusement, James stopped her when she tried to return it to where it had been. "Don't do that out here."

"What? Laugh at you or touch you?"

"Either. Can we just watch? It'll be over soon."

"I didn't mean to insult you. It's cute."

Getting up before he said something he'd regret, he walked toward the port-a-potties in case she was watching, and then veered behind the crowd to watch uninterrupted. *Cute.* Damn, he wanted a beer.

"You okay?"

He jumped at the voice behind his shoulder. Burt. "Fuck."

"Sorry. She's um…"

"Temporary."

"Good. No offense. This is still hard." He glanced up at the sky.

"At times. But I'm good. You can go back to your family."

"You're my family, too, J. How about coming for dinner Sunday? Been a while."

"Maybe."

"Maybe don't bring that girl."

"Definitely not."

"But maybe think about finding one you can bring."

His thoughts went straight to the singer girl. Shouldn't have. But they did.

"Still thinking you need a beer?"

A deep breath paused his reply. "More than I'm gonna admit."

"Don't."

"Yeah, I won't."

"Promise me, James."

"Promise. I hate it, but I promise."

"Good. Let's go sit over there." He nodded to an open space.

"You should go back to your wife and kids."

"They're fine. And they need you to be. We all do. Come on."

Of course Charlie had to walk Libs all the way inside, which meant his cousin tagged along. Inside their apartment. Where Libs took her boyfriend to her room to "say goodnight" in private.

Being polite as taught, Isabel asked if Dale wanted water or tea. With a *no thanks*, he took her hands, pulled her up against him, and kissed her. A soft, slobbery kind of kiss. Unsure whether she was more grossed out or angry, she shoved him away. "You can wait on the porch for your cousin. Good night."

"What the hell? Wait outside? Come on, you've been hitting on me all night."

"No, I haven't. You were. I kept moving away..."

"Teasing." He approached again.

"No. I do not tease. I am not interested. Please, wait outside or in the car."

"He has the keys and it's locked. Isabel, really..."

"Fine. Wait here if you want." Turning, she hurried into her room, closed the door, and locked it. She had to pee, but it would wait. Who knew where he might be lurking? On the couch, she supposed, so really, she could run to the bathroom real quick and back again. Her heart pounded at the thought. She was not risking it. So she waited, far too long, until she heard Libs talking in the hallway, heard Dale say her friend was nuts and tell his cousin not to set him up like that again, and finally heard the front door close.

Unlocking her door, after cursing at the stubborn lock that didn't want to unlock, she almost shoved Libs out of her way and slammed the bathroom door behind her.

"Izzy?" Libs called through the door. "What happened?"

"Nothing. I'm going to bed." *Nothing.* She couldn't talk about it anymore than she could ever tell her friend about what happened after her last gig. Too humiliating. Maybe she'd call off work in the morning and give herself the day to unwind.

~~

"Guess I should get you home." James rolled to the edge of the bed, but he was stopped from getting up by soft fingers reaching around to his chest.

"I told my parents I was staying with a friend, so I can stay." Jackie kissed his shoulder. "If you want. Or if you don't mind."

Hell. He should have taken her straight home or straight to the friend's house, not to his place. Now he was stuck, considering he'd given in to her advances and she was naked in his bed after what turned out to be a fast and rather unfulfilling romp. It got the job done, but it felt only like getting the job done.

What could he say? Wasn't much choice without being callous. "You

can stay, but I have to be at work by eight, so it'll be an early drop-off."
He took her hand to keep it from wandering any lower. "Your choice."

"Or you can go in late; call and say you overslept." Cuddling up
against him, she continued the kisses, up to his neck.

"That's not going to happen. I don't go to work late."

"Okay, then. Go on to work and I can lock up behind me and walk
from here. It's not far."

Leave her in the apartment alone? Wasn't going to happen. He'd
been taken that way once. He was not about to let himself, or his
roommates, get taken again. "Sorry. Can't do that. You'll have to leave
when I do. So, tonight or early morning?"

She sat up and stared at him. "Fine. I'll go now, and don't bother to
take me. I'll walk."

"Not at this time of night." While she pulled into her clothes, James
did the same. No matter how much she insisted she could walk, by
herself, he insisted on either driving her or walking with her. Wasn't like
she could keep him from following along if she insisted on walking.
Luckily, she let him drive. And she apparently didn't hold a grudge long,
since, when he walked her up to her friend's door, she gave him a deep
kiss and whispered in his ear that she couldn't wait to see him again.

He supposed he would.

Bruce was there by the time he got back. Asked about his night,
James thanked him, with possibly more than a touch of sarcasm but also
some truth, for sending his family to meet up with him, said it was fine,
and went to his room. Opening his laptop, he planned to do some IT
work for a regular client, but soon found himself searching videos for
anything with the lyrics he remembered from her show. Lizzy from Erie,
or whatever her name actually was from wherever she was actually from.
Her reaction had told him he had her name wrong, but since he had
nothing else to call her, he was going with that until corrected.

Two hours later, his eyes burned and his head was fuzzy. After two
a.m. and he had work in a few hours. And he'd found nothing.

Why did he care? He didn't. Shouldn't.

Still. The thought of finding one of her videos and therefore more of
her work, some possible contact info, excited him more than his romp
with ... with ... Jackie. Her name was Jackie.

And he didn't care much. Maybe he wouldn't see her again.

How did he find... Sara's. The little songbird said Sara's was *wonderful*.
Maybe he could find her there.

Seven

"I need this by four o'clock. Possible?"

Isabel pulled back from the sheets of handwritten paper shoved in her face and took them from her office manager. "If the phone doesn't keep ringing non-stop as it has all day." It was after three. As always, the handwriting was nearly illegible.

"I have complete confidence you can do it. I'll have to practice my typing sometime when I have nothing better to do." The woman gave her a fake-sweet smile and pranced away in her tight off-white skirt that showed every movement of her ass while she pranced. "Oh." She swiveled, brushing her hair back behind her ear as though she was a teenage girl trying to impress a boy. "And that hairdo? Nice try, honey, but it's still not working. You'll have to have it cut short and try again."

Not working? She'd pulled it together and put it in a bun with one of those cute bun wrap things, suggested by Libs who *was* all things *in fashion*. Libs said it was perfect, cute and kicky but still professional. Why did the girl with the bright blue streak down her head not get fussed at? At least Isabel's hair was her natural color.

She considered saying as much, and she considered saying it wasn't her job to do the typing, since it was absolutely not in her job description, but again, she kept quiet and just did it. By four. With the phone ringing constantly, talking and typing at the same time. She was a good typist, usually 75 words per minute without mistake, if uninterrupted. But while trying to sort out what it said, it was not fast. Her stomach was in knots while trying to get it done, being pleasant to idiots on the phone, and watching the clock. And then she'd have to go out to the parking lot alone. Again. The big, open parking lot in not one of the better parts of Meadville, which seemed to be declining as fast as ... well, as she was. And she was in a skirt since it was required, in low heels, since heels were required and they were as low as she could get away with. There was no point in it. Her feet were under her desk, her desk that went down to the floor in front. Really, tennis shoes would have worked. And pants.

It wasn't worth this. She wanted more than this.

At five till four, the notes typed and printed and ready to go, Isabel pulled up a new document and typed her resignation, giving them two weeks, as required. She handed it to her manager along with the notes.

"You can't…" The woman scanned it, her mouth hanging open.

"See you tomorrow." With a huge weight lifting off her shoulders and a pit starting in her gut, she grabbed her office-approved purse, since they wouldn't allow her laptop bag, and slipped out the front door, grabbing the pepper spray she also wasn't supposed to have, watching every movement from anywhere around while she hurried to her car and locked the door.

Two weeks. She had to find another job within two weeks.

The woman couldn't let her have the last six days? Not that she wanted them, but she wanted the pay. She didn't have one lead on another job yet and since she'd quit, she wouldn't get unemployment. She wanted those six days of pay. Even if her manager had turned into a full-out witch since she'd resigned and stacked on as much work as possible. Flirting with the UPS guy? She had not. Not close. So we was kind of cute, and so he invited her to a bonfire with some friends. She hadn't accepted, and she hadn't hit on him. The witch told her to go ahead and leave.

Her hands shook while she packed the few items on her desk that were hers into her purse. She even did it in front of the guy, to make things worse. It was humiliating. But he tried to make it better by walking her to her car and giving her his phone number in case she wanted to accept the invitation. After opening her door and holding it for her, he took her hand and kissed her fingers.

The odd thing was it didn't bother her. It also didn't attract her. He was nice, sweet, polite, but she didn't feel more than that. She'd have to at least call and let him know she wasn't interested in the bonfire, since he'd been so nice, but then he'd have her phone number, so maybe she wouldn't.

She'd deal with that later. She had to pee and she was starving, so she headed down the road to Arby's for a roast beef smothered in cheese and Arby's Sauce, plus a large curly fry and a mint chocolate shake, grabbing a second shake for Libs, just because. Might as well spend the money while she had it.

While waiting for her order, she pulled her hair out of the stupid bun and her feet out of the stupid shoes. Maybe she'd go to Presque Isle tomorrow since she was free. Maybe she'd go every day in between job hunting until she found a job. Why not?

He'd asked her out. After getting over the embarrassment of being called down in front of him and accused of wanting his *package* and being told to leave, it hadn't really sunk in that he'd asked her out.

Focusing on that and the upside of not having to go to that office again, Isabel was nearly deliriously happy by the time she got back to her apartment. She'd eaten the food on the way but waited on the shake. Libs wouldn't be home yet, so she'd put them both in the freezer and they could celebrate her freedom, short-lived freedom since she'd have to find something soon.

Unlocking the door, she heard noise inside and hesitated. Lisbon's shoes were just inside the door, dropped... dropped, not carefully placed as normal. Her blouse, the pretty lacy green one, was on the floor, beside Charlie's shoes. They were in her room, thankfully, but it sounded like the door was open.

Cursing to herself, she set the shakes on the coffee table, changed her heals for her sandals, stripped off the stupid hose and stuffed them in her office purse, grabbed her laptop bag with her notebook in it, and left again, taking her shake with her.

Not sure where she wanted to go, she considered walking Ernst Trail, but it felt like far too much effort, and she didn't want to go alone. She wanted the beach. But she didn't want to do that alone, either. Stupid thought. She always went to Presque Isle alone. If she could go to her room to get a few things, she'd head down to her grandparents' and stay for the weekend. Not without at least one change of clothes, though, and her toothbrush and...

The Greenville park. It was small, and there was the little river running through it. She could sit and enjoy the rare sunny day and work on lyrics. Except she'd quit music. Or not. She'd quit shows, not music. She'd send her songs out again rather than playing them herself. Maybe she'd look for jobs there instead. Somewhere smaller. Less city. It would be more of a drive, but less anxiety-provoking. Why not?

~~

"Gilbert. You have a minute?"

James closed his locker and turned to his manager. Damn, he hoped his fumble of the chemicals due to his stupid hand hadn't been noticed and reported, or the fact that he'd been so distracted by words running through his head about the little songbird from Sam's that he'd messed up a few times in the past couple of weeks. Minor mistakes. Not a big deal. Still... "Sure." Following to the office, he tried to turn off his natural defensiveness. Could be he wasn't getting fired, or warned. Could be it was something else. If they were about to can him, he wasn't about to let it show that it mattered.

"The boss has been notified of your work." His manager stood propped against the desk.

"Just a fumble today. Doesn't happen often."

"Fumble?"

"Who reported it? It was one mess up, due to the stupid hand. It was easily fixed. I took care of it..."

"James." He grinned and stood, walked around the desk, and sat back partly on it. "I have no idea what you mean, but we all have mishaps. Relax." Walking back around the desk, he pulled something from his top drawer and handed it across. "Bonus."

"For what?"

"For accepting the shift supervisor position. If you want it." He leaned back in his chair. "Your work ethic hasn't gone unnoticed, and the fact that you jump in to help your coworkers is appreciated. As is your military service, which, I'll have to admit, helped you get hired despite your job jumping past. If you accept, we'll want you to stick around for the next couple of years. Can you give us that?"

Two years? Probably he could. It would be more money. Still, the fact he got it only due to his service grated on him, or he was using it as an excuse to not want to be locked in. "Can I think about it?"

The man acted like he expected a fully different answer. "Of course. Take the weekend and let us know by Tuesday, Wednesday latest. After that, we'll have to move to the next in line."

"Understood." The next in line, technically, would be the incompetent jerk he ended up helping more often than should be needed. James didn't want to be under him. He also wasn't sure he wanted to be locked in, but it would help his record. "I'll let you know by Monday." Standing, he offered his hand and gave the check back.

"No, that's yours either way. You've earned it."

Rubbing his chin as he made the trek out to his truck, he considered the offer. No reason he shouldn't. He could still use his earned two weeks of vacation to hit a southern beach during the winter and get out of the cold. A couple of weeks wasn't much, but it would be paid. Of course, two years would mean all this summer and most of the next summer, and he was already getting jittery about wanting to travel. A long trip. Month or so. Not a couple of weeks that would include getting there and back.

~~

Isabel woke to the smell of strong coffee and stumbled out to the kitchen in her robe. At the sight of Charlie in his pajama pants, a look she hated on men, and without the T-shirt that went with it, so his pasty white no-muscle upper body glared at her, she briefly said hi to him and otherwise tried to avoid seeing him. She greeted her roommate instead. "Did you find your shake?"

Libs sighed. "It melted all over the table. Thank you."

"It was in a cup."

"Okay, slight exaggeration. Still had to throw it out. You know I don't touch melty ice cream. It's gross. Why were you home so early?"

"She told me to leave for inappropriate behavior."

"What? You?" Libs' eyes widened even more. "Did you finally slug the witch in the jaw?"

"I wish. No, the UPS guy invited me to a cookout and she heard."

"So? Wait. UPS guy? Is he like fifty?"

"Um, he's about my age, and pretty cute, very polite..."

"You have a date? You're telling me you actually have a date?"

Offended by her friend's surprise, Isabel changed tracts. "Why aren't you getting ready for work?"

"Oh. Well. I'm ... taking a couple of weeks vacation."

Giving herself time to try to remember whether she knew Libs was taking vacation, Isabel shoved a mug of water into the microwave and shuffled through the drawer to find the tea she wanted. She remembered nothing about vacation. "All of a sudden?"

Libs went to Charlie and wrapped her arms around him from behind. "We're heading to Vegas today and getting married, so I'll be moving out. But I'll fulfill my part of the lease until it's up."

Eloping and moving out? She hadn't been dating him long. And Isabel had always hoped to be her maid of honor. A Vegas wedding? She'd wanted a big wedding, always talked about it...

"You could say congratulations." Charlie was eyeing her, a dare.

Congratulating her friend with a quick hug, Isabel went to her room, grabbed clothes, and headed to the shower. No job and now no roommate. Why should she bother to stay in Meadville? There was nothing there for her now. Except for her apartment, and giving up one more thing all at once was just too much. So was paying the full rent by herself. The lease was up in a couple of months. She couldn't do it alone.

She needed time to think, and maybe some good advice. Time to visit her grandparents.

"You can't hide here forever, baby girl."

Isabel sighed. Of course Papa Niall was right. He was always right. She took the hand he set on her shoulder and focused on the softness of the back of the thin hand compared to the rough hardness of the palm and long fingers. Working hands. Even now, although technically retired, her grandpa was a hard worker. He often helped neighbors with maintenance of their houses or their yard equipment. Refusing pay, he was constantly bringing home fresh-baked pies or garden vegetables. He grew his own cucumbers and squash and lettuce but could never get the hang of tomatoes and was happiest when a neighbor had extra to share.

"Bella?" His soft, understanding voice brought her back to the issue at hand. She'd been there two weeks already, since the day after Libs left. She hated being at the apartment alone at night. One night had been enough. She hadn't slept. But she was going to have to figure something out. "I know, Grandpa, but I don't really know where to go from here."

"Are you still writing?" He sipped overly sweet coffee with his free hand. No matter how much Grandma Meladee fussed at him about his caffeine and sugar habit, he wouldn't let it go. He figured all of the fresh fruits and vegetables he grabbed from the local markets to supplement his own made up for it.

She sipped the vanilla milkshake he made for her, using real vanilla beans and cream from a local dairy. He'd made it for her every time he knew she was down about something she didn't want to talk about. "No. I keep trying to start, but the words won't come."

"Force them. Write gibberish if you have to. Just write something. That's what your grandmother does when she's stuck. You should see some of the gibberish scribbled on scraps I've kept during the years. They amuse me all over again when I pull them out."

"Thanks for the warning. If I write gibberish, I'm burning it so no one ends up laughing at me for however many years."

"Oh, baby girl." He cupped the side of her head. "You need to learn to laugh more, at yourself, especially. You take things too seriously. We're here and then we're gone and the next line takes over and then they're gone and the next line takes over etcetera, etcetera. Why obsess so much about the right now? Just shrug your shoulders, take a deep breath, and leap to the next whatever's going to happen."

"I wish I could do that like you do. I've always wished I could."

"If you truly wished you could, you would."

"It's not that easy."

"Nothing is easy. You're tough. You're smart. You're resourceful. You don't need easy. You only need to pick up your feet and keep walking."

Keep walking. It had been a month since she'd been to Presque Isle, because of that creepy guy. He'd told her not to quit singing because of the cretins and then she quit walking on the beach at her favorite place in the world because he'd been there. Once. A coincidence.

Except it was too creepy to be coincidence.

Still, since she'd given up her two favorite things in the world, she felt stuck, blocked, ready to explode at the tiniest thing. She'd even fought with her mother, which she generally didn't bother to do since it never came out well. She should have been smart enough to find another job before quitting the one she had. When her mother said as much when she'd dropped by to check on her parents and found Isabel there, she should have just said, "I know, but I didn't because I can't even think right now because I don't know who I am anymore," but she didn't because she could never stand up to her mother, and she could never admit weakness in front of her.

Her mother did not understand weakness you had to hide any more than she understood Isabel still mourning her ex. She couldn't. Jocelyn Dillon-Sanderson – who went by Josie as a kid because she hated the name Jocelyn and yet now only went by Jocelyn so she would be taken seriously – so often talked about a boy who "broke her heart" before Isabel's father, but only for two days, and that was enough grieving time. If she hadn't let go and moved along, she wouldn't have given Isabel's father the time of day when they met and then Isabel wouldn't be there. *Think about what you might be missing, Isabel May. It's not worth it.*

What she might be missing? Like the way her mother these days only put up with her father because they were married and for no other reason? Why would she want that? Just because her mother was strong enough to live that way didn't mean she wanted to, or could. She wanted no part of that kind of life.

Isabel had even dropped the second part of her hyphenated last name that used to match her father's, so instead of Isabel May Dillon-Sanderson, she was now simply Isabel Dillon, no middle name, although her mother still always called her Isabel May, possibly to protest her dropping the part of her name that came from one of her mom's favorite decorators, Dorothy May Parish. She dropped Sanderson because it represented her father, and she chose to be a Dillon instead, like her grandparents. She'd dropped her middle name out of spite, really.

It was one of the first things she'd done when she turned eighteen. She'd already been living with her grandparents for a couple of years, and then Libs found the little place in Meadville and asked her to move in with her. It was a cheap place, and barely affordable for the two girls starting out in their jobs, but workable. And away from her parents. Away from a past she was still trying to outrun.

It wasn't a pretty past, but it made for good songs, even if no one but those who dropped in on open mic nights in the area would ever hear them. And now no one would hear them.

The last show was strike three. Just like her love life. At only 25, Isabel already had three big heart-breakers, even though she'd only officially dated one of them. The first was young love, Gramps called it, and she hardly said two words to him, but she'd adored that boy. In eighth grade. Lead clarinet, with such a sweet smile. But he laughed when she asked him to the vice-versa dance and she was crushed. "You give your heart too easily," her mother said. Her grandmother tended to agree, even if she was a fellow songwriter, Isabel's greatest muse. Her grandpa, though, he understood her. He wasn't even her biological grandfather, but they were so much more alike than she and her mother.

Jocelyn/Josie was a baby when her mother, Melodee Lerner, moved to Pittsburgh to escape Josie's sperm donor, as she called him, and four when she met Niall Dillon at a park. Josie had hit young, hard-working Niall in the nose with a Frisbee while he was relaxing between jobs. Melodee apologized over and over, handing him tissues to stop the bleeding. He'd willingly, from that moment, taken them both into his heart and his life. Isabel's mother loved her adoptive father as much as she loved anyone. Isabel loved her grandfather more than anyone else in the world, if she was honest with herself. But Papa Niall understood her and supported her and told her to take whatever time she needed and not to let anyone tell her she was wrong, while her mother only lectured and her grandmother tried not to be in the middle.

He went to the pantry disguised as a door-sized memory board, cork on top for tacking to-do notes, with an iron sheet painted dark red on the bottom to highlight the magnets he'd collected over the years from places he'd traveled. The kitchen was white, silver, and dark red, a modern feel mixed with antique servers and glass vases, and still somehow homey rather than cold. Her grandmother's doing. She was such an odd combination. Pulling out a big package of a beer nut mix, he dumped some in a wooden bowl between them. "So where have you applied for work?"

"Nowhere." She picked out a few pieces of flavored dried corn.

"In the two weeks you've been hiding out here, you have not even one job application out there?"

"Can't find anything I want to do."

His round, friendly face wrinkled in a frown. "Now, Bella, you are not going to become a house bum letting others support you because you don't want to pick yourself up. You know we love having you here, but it's not in your best interest to sit and mope. So go get the paper and let's see what's out there."

"Paper?"

He scratched his head through a half-and-half mixture of reddish-blond and gray curly hair. "That thing with the news in it? You realize it has job offerings, as well as news and other entertainment."

"No one uses the paper for that anymore, Gramps. They do it online. Most places won't even take a mailed-in application."

With a grimace, he drained his cup. "Fine, then. Get on that electronic gadget and start looking them up. *Now*, punkin pie. While I see that you're doing it."

Isabel had to laugh at the electronic gadget phrase. Papa Niall was probably the master of electronic gadgets for his age. He could run any of them and fix most. Still, he talked as though he thought they were some kind of evil that would rot the brains of obsessed users. He had no worry about that with her; Isabel hardly used her laptop for more than checking mail and watching music videos. Libs said she should type her songs into documents to save on disc, but so far, her pretty journals and hand scratches with pencil worked fine. She got enough typing at work.

With an exaggerated sigh that got a teasing scornful look, she pushed away from her chair and went to get her laptop to prop on the table beside the bowl of beer nuts.

"Good girl. I'll make your special dinner as a reward."

Eight

The first two weeks were always hardest at a new job, and this was temporary: a medical scheduler that took only organization skills and a high school diploma, temp to start, with possible full time hire. At least it was something. Her grandpa was happy to know she was working. He also said she should have found something closer to what she wanted, and she better keep looking for that. The problem was, she didn't quite know what she wanted.

Except to walk along Presque Isle unbothered to search for any possibly remaining sea glass that hadn't been picked over. Fat chance, she knew, by mid August. Still, it was a gorgeous hot day, Saturday after a very long stressful first week of a new job, and she wanted the sun on her shoulders and the breeze in her hair. She could do her errands the next day when rain was expected.

Just for the hell of it, she took her music notebook.

The drive from Meadville to Erie passed quickly with her stereo blasting Anna Nalick. She studied the lyrics, as always, considering what made her like them so much. Sometimes she sang with them and sometimes she only listened. As a last-second thought, she turned into Sara's, not for a hot dog. Isabel did not eat hot dogs. For a turtle sundae. If creepy guy had asked about the ice cream, she could have answered him, not that she would have volunteered that much information.

Since she didn't want it to melt while driving, she wandered over to an empty table in front of Sally's, an old silver diner with windows lining the front and bright red stripes accenting the silver, and sat at a bright red metal table behind the bright red barrier. She could feel the warmth of the metal on her legs while she savored the caramel, chocolate, and pecans mixed with vanilla ice cream. As always, she watched cars pulling in and out, particularly the license plates. They were mainly from Pennsylvania and Ohio, but she also spotted Illinois, Michigan, and Indiana. Nothing unusual about that. There was one from Massachusetts, which was less common but still not too uncommon. Maryland. Ontario, of course. There were always a lot of plates from Ontario.

Isabel did have to wonder if Canadians didn't have closer beachfront views to explore or if they'd done that and needed new beaches. She wasn't sure why it mattered. One beach was like another, wasn't it? Sand.

Water. Seagulls. Seashells. Lifeguards. Stone breakers. Tall grasses waving. Of course, she didn't really know other than photos since she hadn't been far outside Pennsylvania other than the one trip to Maine when she was so young she only remembered the beach and rocks. Huge rocks. Maybe someday she would go back and refresh her memory.

If her songs ever caught on so she could afford it.

With a sigh, she spooned the last of the sundae into her mouth and got up, thinking about adding a fish sandwich. Although, taking fish to eat at the beach seemed a little too wrong, so maybe something else.

"Is this you?"

She turned to the woman holding a black and white printed wanted poster and nearly asked if she was crazy, but it did look like her, from the back. Her hack job haircut that had somewhat grown out by now. On the beach. It *was* her. What the hell?

She took it to look closer. A photocopied homemade poster described her, using the name Lizzy, said she was a songwriter and she'd lost something he wanted to return. There was a name and a phone number. James at 724... James. Creepy guy. The one who called her Lizzy and accused her of not liking physical contact. "Really? What kind of a jerk does this?"

"Sounds like he wants to return something you lost." The woman gave her a grin.

"I didn't..." She felt her eyes roll. "Thanks. I'll call him." Oh, she would definitely call him. After that, she might call the cops, too. They could find this James guy by his number and warn him to back off.

~~

James climbed up over the rocks along the non-beach part of the island and lowered onto one of the smooth, mostly flat rocks to watch the waves and the boats and the seagulls. Every Saturday for the past month he'd been there. For nothing. Not quite nothing. He enjoyed the scenery. It was why he'd been there in the first place. But he'd put that poster up three weeks ago, and nothing.

Of course she could be on a different beach since they went all the way around, with different parking areas. Or she could be on the walking trail. He had tried once to run on the main trail, but there were far too many people, bicycles, and unscooped dog shit to work around. Not worth it. A couple of years ago, he'd taken Gull Point Trail now and then, just to walk the mile and a half through tall saw grass, avoiding the quicksand around the ponds, to sit out by the secluded beach front with his cooler that included Pepsi bottles he'd drained part way and topped up with gin, plus an emptied water bottle filled with straight gin.

Bruce went out with him once or twice, but he railed on James for getting carried away and passing out on the beach that got cold at night and having to stay all night because he didn't want to leave his drunk ass there alone, so he started going alone to cut out the bitching.

Due to the memories, he wouldn't go alone now that he was sober even if he could. Lake Erie had reached in and claimed Gull Point, creating a large water barrier and turning it from a hiking trail into a small island. Just as well. Sitting on the less isolated rocks was safer. One thing he'd learned was to avoid too much isolation, to stay around people.

He jumped when his phone buzzed in his pocket. James rarely had the thing on in his pocket. It generally sat next to him where he could see any incoming message or notification. He usually had it on silent and vibrate because he couldn't stand the tinny fake sound of ringtones.

Not recognizing the number, he nearly ignored it since he didn't particularly want to be hit up by a solicitor, although often he had fun with them, chatting about the weather or whatever until they hung up. Maybe he would do that again, just because he was on his own and annoyed that he was again on his own. He answered as though he knew the number. "Hey, man, what's up?"

"What the hell are you doing? Was that supposed to be funny?"

Not a telemarketer. An irate female. "You've gotta have the wrong number, lady."

"Is this James?"

"Yeah?"

"Fine, James, what in the hell do you want from me?"

"Well, hard to tell since I have no clue who you are."

"No shit, you don't. What was that poster about? You posted a picture of my ass walking away from your ass? Really? What's wrong with you? Do I need to file a leave me alone thing with the cops?"

The poster. "Lizzie."

"That's not my name, but yes, that's what you called me. What is this about?"

"Hey. I figured by now it wasn't going to work. Apparently you don't go to Sara's as often as you made it sound like you did."

"I didn't say I went a lot, only that it was good. Why in the hell did you do that to me?"

Frustrated by her tone, he stood to wander. He couldn't sit when frustrated. "What's your problem, whatever your name actually is? I'm only trying to hear you sing again..."

"Yeah well, I'm not. Okay? And I told you that. So you can stop."

"Wait. Why aren't you?" Silence came over the phone. At least he had her number now, so he could call back. But he figured she wouldn't answer. "Hello? Still there?"

"You saw why." Her voice came at him softer, sad instead of angry. "A person can only take so much of that, you know."

His eyes rolled. A person could actually take a hell of a lot if they decided to, or had to. But he didn't want her to hang up, so he tried hard to see it her way. "I'm sorry. Really. But my offer to get you a gig somewhere more classy where they don't act like idiots was sincere. I wasn't trying to make a stupid joke or harass you or anything. I meant it. So, would you consider giving this thing one more shot?"

A long pause made him start to wonder if she hung up. But she came back on the line, softer. "What are you? Honestly."

What was he? "I told you."

"Yeah, water treatment guy. But why does that make you think you can help me and why do you care?"

"The job is just a paycheck. I love music. I've always loved music. If I could do it myself, I would, but I can't, so I live vicariously through those who can and I honestly love to listen to a good voice in a small venue where you're up close and really get the soul of the music, not just speakers and electronics and such. Okay? That's all there is to it." At least all he was willing to say at this point. Her silence encouraged him. "I know a nice place you should try if you haven't, and I can get people there, decent people, not those idiots who heckled you. Will you think about it?"

More silence.

"How about you at least tell me your first name? No big risk in a first name, right?"

"Isabel. I go by Izzy on stage."

"So I was close."

"Yeah. You were close. Actually, you were too close. To the stage. It gave me the creeps."

"Sorry again. My buddies say I don't understand personal space. Guess they're right. It's nice to meet you, Isabel. I'm James, as you know. James Gilbert. I'm from Greenville, born and raised. You can look me up. I'm on Facebook as JamesAG, no periods or spaces, and most of my stuff is friends only, but you can look me up if you want. We might even have mutual friends. You never know."

"And you're assuming I'm on there."

He stopped walking. "Oh. Yeah, I did assume. Isn't everyone?"

"I'm there. Kind of. Not much, and not under my real name. I barely know how to use it."

"Well, you might want to learn well enough to advertise your shows, you know. It's a good spot for that."

"I don't have shows. I do open mics."

"Yeah, okay. You can advertise that, as well." He started ambling again, down toward the water.

"Why? So more people will come and tell me to get off the stage because they don't like my looks even before I sing a note? Why?"

A glimmer in the sand caught his eye and he crouched to check on it. "You've been at this a while."

"Four years, with nothing to show for it. I didn't quit because of that one night of cretins being cretins..."

He laughed. "Now, that's a good word. Cretins. I'll have to use that." Only a piece of glass, partly worn down. He carried it down to the edge of the lake.

"Okay. Anyway..."

"Yeah, so, four years of that?"

"Right. Okay, not always. Sometimes they're nicer, but they're never real interested. So am I more pathetic now or less?"

Pathetic? "Isabel, you're not. At all. Like I said, you should be up there. Too many people just don't get it, but the right people will." Throwing the piece as hard as he could, he waited until he saw the splash in the distance. Not a bad throw. "Will you try it once more?"

"I don't know. I'm pretty burned out and I'm probably moving very soon and I'll be busy..."

"Moving where?" Silence came back at him. "Look, I don't even know your last name, so it's not like I can look you up."

"Back to Pittsburgh where I was born and raised. I only haven't yet because my job's in Meadville, but I don't like it much, so as soon as I find something in Pitt, I'm packing up."

Pittsburgh. Not all that far. Hour and a half or not quite, depending what part. If she did shows north of Pittsburgh, it would be an easy enough drive. "Okay, so it's not like you're moving across the country or anything. How far are you willing to drive for a show?"

"Depends how worth it it might be."

"Right." He could start scouting out places in the Butler and Cranberry areas. Maybe New Castle. Some of those he knew of should still be open, along with newer openings.

"So, where is this place they won't heckle because they're too classy?" She was a definite firecracker, full of attitude. Enough he considered bowing out.

But maybe he deserved it. Picking up a fairly flat rock, he rolled it between his fingers. "Beans on Broad. Grove City. Have you been there?"

"I've been to the outlets."

He chuckled. "Yeah, hasn't everyone? I mean Old Town."

"No. Not since I can remember. Beans?"

"A coffee shop."

"Really?"

"They do open mics. I've started following people I've heard there. It's a cool place. Small. More upscale than Sam's. No cretins." If he wasn't mistaken, she chuckled. Barely.

"How hard is it to get in?"

"Not sure. Haven't been there lately. Want me to check into it for you, see what dates are available?"

More silence preceded the soft question. "Where are you now?"

He grinned. She would only ask if she was willing to meet with him. James had to try to make himself not sound as excited about that thought as he was. "North Pier Lighthouse."

"On Presque Isle?"

"Yep. Should I ask where you are?"

"At Sara's. Just drowned myself in a turtle sundae and may need to eat something along with it."

"Serious this time?"

"Yeah. Sorry about that. Kind of sick of cretins and you never know who they are. I'm still not sure about you, but if you want to meet me here, I have nowhere I have to be today."

"Absolutely. Hang tight and I'll be there in a few."

~~

Isabel thought about leaving, driving away fast. Why had she told him where she was? Why was he so close to where she was, again? Coincidence? Too many. One might be. Two...

She headed to her car, unlocked it, got in, and started the engine. But she didn't pull out. He loved music. He followed local singers after hearing them. He gave her his full name and town. If he was telling the truth, he could be a good contact, but Isabel was not at all good at deciphering who was and wasn't being truthful. Her grandpa would tell her to give it a careful chance. *Stay watchful, punkin pie, but don't shut out opportunity.* She could hear him say it.

"Okay, Grandpa. Let's see what happens, right?" Turning off the engine, she took a deep breath and got out of the car. Then she wondered whether she should have eaten real quick before he came or if she should wait because maybe he would get food while he was there. Did she want to eat with him? Maybe not. But she hated to stuff her food down, and it wouldn't take long for him to get there and...

"Aye aye aye, Isabel, be a little bit decisive for a change, would you?" She rolled her eyes at herself and saw an older man look over with a grin. Her face heated and she walked over to the menu and then walked back again. She didn't want to stand there in line and wait and ... and...

With another sigh, she went back to her car and stood against it, watching other vehicles pull in and out and drive past. She hadn't asked what he drove. A truck, she remembered, but there were a lot of trucks in the area. Between snow and rural areas, every other guy had a truck, and some girls, too. But she supposed he would see her.

She should have just gone home. She shouldn't have told him where she was. It would take a good ten minutes or so to get from where he was back off the island, maybe more depended where he'd parked and how fast he walked. She had time to leave still. But he had her number. As angry as she'd been, she hadn't thought about that. It could be changed if needed...

"Isabel?"

She started at the voice and looked over at the man approaching. Creepy guy. Maybe not quite as creepy as she thought. Actually, he looked nice enough. Neat. Together. He wore cargo shorts, tan, with a plain tee over top, navy and fitted but not tight, meaning he wasn't trying to show off his stature. The shirt wasn't tucked in, meaning he wasn't uptight. Not wrinkled, meaning not a slob. His arms dangled at his sides. Not holding a phone like he was ready with an excuse to have to go or to entertain himself if she was boring. No thumb tucked into his pocket like he was trying to look cool or smug. His thick dark blond hair was trimmed nicely around his neck but not too short to hide the wave in it. No facial hair. Not trying to look older. Just casual. And friendly.

She forced herself to meet him rather than waiting until he came all the way to her car. "Hi. I was just trying to decide..." She tucked a thumb into her pocket and then pulled it out so she wouldn't look like she wanted to look cool or smug...

"You thought about leaving before I got here."

"Yeah."

He grinned. "Glad you didn't. Did you eat?"

"No. Other than the ice cream. Should have done it the other way around, but you know..."

"I like a girl who can have dessert first if she wants."

Isabel felt herself pull back. She should have left.

"Hey, no double meaning or anything. I only mean good for you. But I'm in need of something substantial and this is smelling pretty good. Do you have a favorite here?"

"No. Anything but hot dogs. Fish usually, but..."

"Yeah, that sounds good. Want to walk over with me, or find a table, or should I bring it back here?"

"Um. No, I'll get mine. I just didn't know if I should wait or..."

"It's on me for harassing you. Find somewhere to sit. I got it."

Isabel did not want him to buy her lunch and she seriously wished she'd either left or bought her own before he came, but she was too unsure of herself, of whether or not she wanted to talk with him, of whether or not to let him arrange a coffee shop open mic, of ... anything to argue, and so she found a place close to the road away from the biggest part of the crowd.

When he joined her, she thanked him out loud for the sandwich and silently for sitting across from her instead of beside her.

"I hope tea is okay. Grabbed sugar in case you want it." Setting three packets on the table, he didn't hesitate to plunge in to his fish.

"Yes, thank you."

"You said that already." It came out mumbled between his food and she stared. "Sorry." He covered his mouth while he spoke this time and swallowed. "Bad habit. The cretins I hang with don't care."

"Or the girls you date?" She felt herself get warm again when she realized she'd said that out loud.

He swallowed and laughed. "Yeah, generally, but I'm more careful then. So. The coffee shop. Are you willing?"

"Maybe." She dumped in one of the packets and stirred it with the straw while keeping her eyes from him. Generally, she'd used two for a large tea, but she wasn't sure if he'd want some of it.

Reading her hesitation, possibly, he talked about the coffee place and its name, Beans on Broad, because it's on Broad Street, the main road through Old Town, Grove City, where he used to hang out a lot while dating one of his exes, about a folk/soft rock/country pop band called Mandolin Whiskey that he first saw there and followed a bit until they broke up, sadly, and about other bands and singers he still followed, including a husband and wife acoustic duo, 50 Miles to Empty, and a folk/Americana group, Treebeard Brown, that had a big following. He used names and flaunted enough music knowledge to let her know he did actually love it and know something about it. He didn't add any sugar to his tea, which she found annoying. He assumed she'd want three packets for herself? Did she look like she would? Sadly, she did look like she would. Maybe she'd do something about that. Sometime. When she had the mental energy.

When silence filtered between them, with Isabel far less willing to talk about herself than he was, he asked why she was moving to Pittsburgh.

"My family's there. I can stay with my grandparents until I find a place reasonable enough to afford on my own. My long-term roommate just eloped with her not-so-long-term boyfriend, so there goes half the rent. I can't do it on my own with the job I have."

"So get another roommate."

"Right, but how do you know what you're getting?"

"How'd you meet the last one?"

"We went to school together. I'd known her for years."

He eyed her as he took another bite and waited to swallow it. "You're not real crazy about people."

She shrugged. "I haven't been treated all that well by people."

"Why?"

Isabel looked away, over at cars going past.

"Okay, I mean we all have trouble with people. Some of them are just trouble. Or cretins. I'll give you that. But most aren't. So...?"

"No? Maybe they aren't when you look like you, but we don't all look like Mr. America or whatever and it's not the same experience when you don't."

"Mr. America?" He laughed. "First time I've been called that. And yeah, I'm sure that's true, but you're a cute girl, and I don't mean that offensive or anything, but I still don't get it."

Cute? "First time I've been called that."

"No, it isn't." He stared like he was waiting for the joke. "Serious? Hm. You are, though."

"I'm not. If I were, those cretins wouldn't have told me to get off the stage before I even sang. Pretty girls can sing off key, songs that make no sense whatsoever, and they just shake their pretty hair and bat their eyes and people stand up and cheer them on. Even other girls do. When they do it for not pretty girls, they're just trying to make us feel good. None of it is about the actual songs. That's why I stopped. It's not worth it."

"Ah. Well. It could just be the wrong crowd, too. People aren't the same everywhere, no matter what they say."

"Maybe."

"Have you traveled much?" He took another large bite.

"No." To give him time while he chewed, she took another small bite and took longer than really needed to chew it. Still, he waited as though she was supposed to explain. "Not because I don't want to. I haven't really had anyone to travel with and I won't go alone and I'm picky about ... well..."

"Who you let that close."

"Yeah."

"Not that I can blame you, but I tend to be opposite. Anyone I can find who's willing, I'll invite along just for the company and go see some place I haven't. East coast especially. My favorite. If you like it here, you'd love walking around Folly Beach or Tybee Island..."

"Where's that?"

"Folly is in South Carolina, near Charleston. I met a girl there once I tried to convince to go beach hopping with me, a dancer, no less, with a messed up foot, but it was a no go. Of course I wasn't at my best at the time, so I can't blame her." He swallowed a couple of gulps of his soda. "Tybee is in Georgia near Savannah. Gorgeous place. I stayed there longer than I probably should have because of..."

"Another girl?"

"Bingo." He shrugged. "I like meeting people." James shoved more fish in his mouth and wiped tartar sauce off his lip.

"And you just pick up people to take with you?"

"Sometimes. I have a buddy who used to go, but he's tied down with his career, and most I used to hang with have a wife and kids, so I make do and I'm okay with going alone, if need be. It's cool to get to know new people, and traveling with them is a good way to get to know them fast. Now and then I've regretted it. Even ditched one of them halfway through the trip."

"Really? You just left her somewhere?"

"Him, not her, and he was fully capable of getting back on his own. Just couldn't handle his constant negative talk about everything. Nothing, no matter how nice, was ever nice enough. Ruins a trip. I'm a deal-with-what-comes type. About anything can be decent if you want to see it that way." He bit into the sandwich again and barely swallowed before he continued. "Of course, since he was my manager at the time, it wasn't a smart move. I got fired not long after that. No big loss. Jobs are just travel money."

"And ... rent? Food?"

"Yeah, that too, of course. But I split a place and don't do much other than go listen to local music and I save the luxury eating for my travels, so it works."

"Guess that depends what you're making."

"Well, yeah, it would. Jobs in Pitt should pay pretty well, right? So if you stay with your grandparents, you'd be able to save up some travel cash."

The guy was crazy if he thought she was just going to take off and go wander somewhere with him. "I'll only stay with them long enough to get on my feet. I'm not living off them. I don't believe in that, and they'd kick me out if I tried."

"Your grandparents would? Are your parents not close by?"

"A few blocks from my grandparents, but ... let's just say I'd rather not get that desperate."

"Interesting. And probably explains a lot. So if you have no plans today, why don't we run out to the coffee shop and check it out?"

"You talk like it's just down the street."

"It is." He crumpled up his wrapper.

"You said Grove City. That's ... like..."

"About an hour. Just down the road. If you want, we can drop your car at your place and you can ride with me. If it's okay. Call and tell someone where you're at if you want. Give them my name, number, truck model, whatever, if you feel better. Promise I'm not a cretin of any kind. And I'll drop you back home again. I won't leave you out there."

"From Greenville to Erie to Meadville to Grove City back to Meadville and then back to Greenville? All today?"

He shrugged. "I like to drive. A good way to listen to my music uninterrupted, which is one of the biggest issues of having three roommates. Of course I'll keep it down while you're in the truck. I don't blast it around others."

Get in his vehicle with him and go out to a place she didn't know? She could follow him out, but it was a lot of driving, after already coming up to Erie. Leave her number with who, exactly? Her grandparents? What were they going to do from down in Pittsburgh, and how did she know he gave her his real name?

"Okay, you're nervous about me. Understood. Hold on." Jumping up, he went to the counter and came back with another of those flyers, plus a girl who worked there. "Look." He held the flyer where the girl could see the picture. "As you can see, I found her. She doesn't know me, but she's a heck of a singer/songwriter and I want to help her out. Being as smart as she is, she's hesitant to go with me to a place I think she'll do well. So." He pulled out his driver's license to show Isabel first, so she could see the same information he gave her, and then to the girl. Borrowing her pen, he wrote something on the flyer. "Name, address, and driver's license number. Same, right?" He let the girl compare the two. "So, if anyone's looking for Isabel..." He looked at her.

Why not? Take a careful chance, her grandpa would say. "Dillon."

"Isabel Dillon." With a light grin and nod, he wrote her name on the flyer, also, and drew an arrow to the photo. "They can contact me." He shrugged at her. "Good enough?"

"You're nuts."

"No. I'm pretty stable, really, overall. I just don't want you to quit music and I want to help you so you don't want to quit music."

The girl looked between them and smiled. "I think he's probably okay. And I'll hold onto this if it makes you feel better."

"Fine. But write down what you're driving, too. If you kidnap me for no obvious reason, I want to make it easy on anyone who might actually look for me." She was kidding, of course.

He stared a second, then laughed and reclaimed the paper, talking as he wrote. "Metallic blue Ford 150 2-door, 2012, with a hard cover. License plate number included. Taking I-79 to Grove City with a stop in Meadville, then back to Meadville. Good enough?"

She was an idiot. Isabel knew better, even with his safety flyer, than to get into a stranger's vehicle, but she knew she wasn't going to refuse.

Nine

"Why not, right? What's one more rejection on top of three hundred?" Isabel figured she might as well be honest.

"No rejection this time. I'll guarantee it." He thanked the girl who
took the paper back with her, giving him a somewhat flirtatious grin that
said she might use his number. "Go ahead and finish first."

"I eat slow. Sorry."

"No, no problem. I eat fast, always have. With three brothers, you
do that before they get it all." He grinned. A charming friendly warm grin
that made her want to trust him. But then, her ex had done the same. It
was what pulled her in.

And then he took up with a prettier, less boring girl and he was gone.
No warning. No fights. He just said sorry and left.

Which didn't matter this time, with James. It was only business.
About the music. Her music. Which he believed in. And he thought she
was cute, a term she hated, really, except it was too much a compliment
in her current state of mind to really hate that he'd called her that. She'd
been called far worse.

Before he asked more about her, she tried to keep him talking. "You
have three brothers? Wow."

"Yeah, our poor mother. She wanted a girl, but after my youngest
brother came out a boy, she gave up. Nice thing is she gets along well
with all of my sisters-in-law, so she now has four boys and three girls,
plus eight grandkids, four from the oldest, three from the second, and
one from the youngest, and she says she should have thought about that
before."

"I bet your holidays are loud."

"Very loud. I love it. Not all of us do."

"I can imagine."

"Yeah? So what are your holidays like?"

Giving herself time to decide how or whether to answer by chewing
slowly, Isabel didn't figure there was any harm in it. "Quiet. We go to my
grandparents and have dinner and that's about it."

"We? How many are there?"

"My grandparents, my parents, and me. Every other year, my aunt
and uncle and their two kids come, one year on Easter and the next on

Christmas. The other years, they go to the other side of the family out of state. Sometimes in the years they don't come, my grandpa will bring in someone who doesn't have anywhere else to go for dinner, so there could be a stranger or two, also, which is nice, I guess, but not so easy for me. Hard to relax that way."

"Homeless, you mean?"

"No, people he knows through work or his daily excursions or so on. He's extremely social, but too careful to bring a stranger in to scope the house. He probably would, actually, but Grandma wouldn't have it."

"That is nice, though."

"Yeah." Isabel crumpled her wrapper and stood. "Thanks again for lunch. How about I buy you a coffee when we get there?"

"Sounds good. I'll follow you to your place to drop off your car. Want to give me an address in case we get separated?"

"Nope. Don't lose me." She headed to her car. He had her number since she'd called him. It wasn't like he couldn't find her again.

Isabel wasn't about to call anyone and admit she was going to get into a car with a virtual stranger, but she did want some precaution other than the flyer, since that girl could be a friend of his and a set up, so she called her own number and left the info on her answering machine. Just in case. So they'd have a lead to start looking if necessary.

Of course she was being ridiculous. But you never knew.

He stayed plenty close on the interstate, closer than was necessary or comfortable, kept up easily as she wound her way through the streets of Meadville, pulled into the driveway behind her, and left his truck running. A newer truck but a small one, only two seats. Dark blue with some shimmer to it. He had told the girl it was metallic blue and two door. Isabel walked to his window. Leather seats. Of course he had leather seats in a truck with shimmery blue paint. So he did have some showiness about him, apparently. "I'll be back in a second, okay?"

"Sure. No rush."

"I'd ask you in, but…"

"No, it's fine. I'll be here." He turned off the engine.

Using the bathroom quickly, Isabel brushed her hair out and brushed her teeth, then added a long vest over her loose knit top and capris, just to dress it up a bit. Debating far too long whether to take her guitar, she finally decided to leave it. If this guy wasn't as trustworthy as she thought maybe he was, she at least wanted her guitar safe at home. And they were only going to check the place out, to talk to whoever was there about joining an open mic. Not a big deal. She'd never had to audition for one.

Checking to be sure her pepper spray was in her bag, Isabel grabbed a deep breath and her keys and locked the apartment.

Leaned back against his truck, James grinned and pushed away to walk her to the other side. He opened her door, offered a hand up, and closed it carefully behind her. The gesture threw her. How long had it been... Actually, only her grandpa had done that for her in the rare times they went out together in a car rather than walking. Even her long term friend turned boyfriend hadn't bothered.

"So what music do you listen to?" He started talking before he closed his own door.

"Pretty much whatever is fine. No screaming. Or nasty lyrics. Anything else..."

"I don't have any of that. I have Atlanta Rhythm Section on shuffle at the moment. Does that work?"

"Really? Sure." She had to wonder if he had it ready to play only because she'd done a couple of 70s songs during her open mic at Sam's. As a tribute, kind of, to Sam's background, and just as part of her repertoire because she liked it. Most of her older stuff was late 90s and early 2000s. It's what she modeled her own work after.

He turned on the engine and the big display in the center of the dash came up to the end of one of the band's lesser known songs, on high. Turning it down, he yanked his seat belt around and hooked it, then pulled out gently and headed down Arch Street. She appreciated that he wore his seat belt and didn't fly out into the street.

As *So Into You* started, one of her favorites, he turned onto Liberty, then to Linden, and to Conneaut Lake Road where he could veer onto I-79. Without asking directions. "You know your way around Meadville."

He checked to be sure he had plenty of room before pulling onto the interstate. "Yeah, around most of the area. But some of it is just knowing which direction I want to head and zigzagging till I get there."

"You're a homing pigeon."

He glanced at her. "What?"

"You just know where you are. Like Grandpa. He can find his way out of anywhere. Me, I need specific directions and main roads."

"Ah, yeah, Mom's that way, too. All of us boys are like dad. We just sense what direction we're heading."

"That would be nice."

"When you have a map, it's not so necessary, and especially if you have GPS. No one needs to have to find their way out of a paper bag anymore. A shame, I think, you know, to not have to figure stuff out on your own. So. You know the words to this?"

Isabel tuned into *Imaginary Lover* while trying to beat back the thought that James reminded her a little too much of her grandpa. "Some. Most people know this, I'd think."

"Not that I've found. Most of my crowd won't even bother with the words for current songs, much less the more classic stuff."

"Not much to be worth learning in current stuff." Isabel muttered under her breath, but when he chuckled, she figured he heard her. "Sorry, that was rude, wasn't it?"

"Not to me. You like older music."

"Yeah. I grew up with that. It's like comfort food: rich and lyrical and meaningful. Not like... Well, I guess a lot of people would argue that current stuff is, too." She shrugged. "I'm just not a big fan."

"Of anyone current?"

"Well, yes, there are some I like."

"Who?"

"Anna Nalick, though she's not real current. Melissa Etheridge. Pink, the non-political songs, Sarah McLaughlin. Sara Evans does one of my favorite songs. Sheryl Crow. Jennifer Nettles. Stevie Nicks. Infiniti is one of my top favorites. I have everything they've done and always hope for more soon. Dani's voice is incredible..."

"So, you only like female singers?"

"Oh. No, but I do tend to listen to them more, studying their techniques, I guess. Don't judge me, but I fell in love with Taylor John Williams during *The Voice* a few years ago. When he puts anything out, I'll be the first in line to grab it. I just hope they don't take what he has and ruin it, as they have with some."

"No judging. He was good. Wonder what happened with him."

"He put out an EP, and I have that, but that's been a while."

"A good start, hopefully. Everyone has to start somewhere and run in their own path." James veered out and around a car creeping along the interstate with a shake of his head as he checked his rearview. "They should have taken 19 instead if they're out for a Sunday drive."

Isabel considered teasing about the interstate being their chosen path, but she thought it sounded corny, so she let it go.

"You realize no one you mentioned is actually current. Okay, some are still out there working, but I meant new, as in the past couple of years."

"Um." She had to think about that a moment. "I'm not sure. I mainly listen to stuff I own instead of the radio these days. Who do you consider current?"

"Ariana Grande, Billie Eilish, Halsey, Demi Lovato. Sticking with females."

"I've heard the names, but I don't really know their music. They're pop rock?"

"Well, I wouldn't call it that, but that's what's current. Billie Eilish is big among the more pop sound."

"I've heard her. You might be stretching the genre definition."

He laughed. "That's where it is now. As a songwriter, you should know that."

"But there has to still be a market for what I would call pop rock, right? I mean, like those I mentioned?"

"Could be, but you'll likely have to go indie and put it out yourself."

"I wouldn't have a clue how to do that."

Rubbing his chin, he gave her a soft shrug. "We can deal with that later. First, we need you to get going with shows again."

We? She considered asking what he meant by we, but for now, she let it go.

Playing with the console, he switched the music over to shuffle everything and it started with Foreigner's *Waiting For A Girl Like You.*

"You have a lot of old music."

"Yeah, my buddies call me old man because I picked up a lot of Dad's attitudes and I like what I call real music, meaning you can actually hear the words and instruments and such. They all like the new stuff. Me, I could sing every word of this one, and most of its contemporaries."

"Me, too."

He glanced over. "Nice. I'm impressed. It's okay if you want to sing along. Don't worry, I won't."

"I don't care if you do."

He laughed. "Yeah, you'd care. Trust me on that. Of course, don't feel like you need to just because I'm anxious to hear your voice again."

"Thank you, I think. And I'm nervous enough already, so I probably won't. No offense."

"None taken." He switched the music again, to Chris Cornell's *The Promise.* "You know this one? Song or artist?"

"I don't recognize him. Should I?"

"No particular reason you should. Just wondered. Sad that we lost him already. He was doing good things beyond music. Look him up when you get a chance." His expression switched from thoughtful to curious. "So... Isabel Dillon?"

"Yeah?"

"No relation to Meladee Dillon, is there? Or do you know?"

Isabel's gut tightened. She never imagined he'd connect the name. It was always the singer's names people knew, never the songwriter's, unless they were both and high on the charts.

"Pittsburgh. You're from Pittsburgh? Isn't that where she's settled?"

"Why do you know that?"

"I'm into music, especially local music. Just like I know Trent Reznor isn't from Cleveland, as he's claimed, or as someone claimed for him. My mom knows his dad." He looked over at her. Too long while driving, she thought, although he stayed perfectly within his own lane. "So you obviously know who she is. Are you related?"

Isabel had to consider whether she should answer. But if he was going to help her, they couldn't start on the wrong foot, any more than they already had. "I'm her granddaughter. But I don't tell people that."

His jaw dropped, but he kept his eyes on the road. "Um, okay. That's pretty cool."

"You'd think."

"It's not?"

The music switched to a Seventies song. She supposed that's why he knew Meladee Dillon. Her grandma was still putting out songs. By now, they were largely picked up by country/rock singers rather than pop stars, for obvious reasons, but the late Seventies was when she hit big. "It hasn't gotten me anywhere. Not that I'm trying to use her name. But I figured the name might catch attention in the industry so they'd at least listen."

"Too many change their names to try to do that. No one automatically expects a relationship unless the person with the name pushes their relative out there, often when they aren't worth being pushed, to be honest. Too many have broken through only due to family in the business. You don't want to do it that way."

"No, and I keep it quiet. I want to do it with my own talent, if it's good enough to get anywhere."

"Good for you."

"You know a lot about the industry."

He started to answer, then stopped and shrugged before actually answering. "I'm pretty much music obsessed, so I've studied it. Should I admit I have three iPods because I have too much I want to carry around to put it all on one? Might have to buy another one soon."

"Wow. Really? I thought I was bad. I just rotate them from different playlists."

"Too much trouble. I'm lazy."

Isabel expected that wasn't true, especially with as fit as he was. At least he was a good driver, not a speed demon, not an I Have To Be First In A Line Where There Is No First competitive driving nut. Like her ex. The only thing she'd disliked about him. Well, other than that he'd walked out on her.

She was starting to wonder if she even cared anymore.

The thought of it shocked her enough, Isabel lost all track of what James was saying. Maybe she didn't care anymore. Her beach glass vase wasn't full yet, though. She cared. She just... She was tired of thinking about it. She didn't not care. She was numb. Was that the same? Couldn't be, could it?

"Hello?"

She looked back over at him from where she'd been staring out at the roadside. "Um. Sorry. I was..."

"You okay? You're not worried about me, right?"

"Yeah. I mean, I am, but ... I don't know. I'm just kind of lost these days." Why had she told him that? Why was she even in his truck?

"Shutting off a part of you that you really need can do that. I know, Isabel. I've been there. You need to start singing again, or writing, whichever you most need, and everything else will come back."

"How have you been there?"

His chest rose and fell hard. "Well, how about we do that conversation another time?"

"Sorry. I guess I..."

"No need to be sorry. I just know you're really unsure of me and so maybe we need to only talk about music and such for now. Right?"

"Yeah." She turned her attention back out the window. In other words, keep her problems to herself. Nothing new. She could do that.

~~

Needy. The girl was needy. Scared, but needy. Could be why she didn't have a boyfriend, not that he should assume she didn't, but he expected she would have mentioned one by now, if for no other reason, to let him know what he'd be up against if he tried to hit on her. He was almost surprised she hadn't made one up if she didn't have one, as a wall of sorts. But she seemed too genuine. Too up-and-up. Maybe too naive for her own good.

Too nice, he guessed. Maybe why she distrusted people so much. It would be hard to be so up-and-up in a world where most weren't. You'd expect them to be mostly the same, he supposed. Like the way he didn't expect them to be since he wasn't so much himself. Protection first. Say what you need and go from there. Truth was flexible for the most part. His truth wasn't the same as hers. Maybe she hadn't caught onto that yet.

She was young, after all. Younger by several years, he expected, nine or ten years maybe, but he didn't want to ask because then she'd think he had a particular reason to ask, and she didn't trust him. No reason to make her trust him less. Although he figured she could hardly trust him much less. She did get into his truck, though.

Her stop at home could have been for protective reasons. She could be carrying in that purse. Anyone that wary and mistrusting was pretty likely to be protected. Not that he cared. But he wouldn't push her too far, either.

Turning off the interstate onto Route 208, James noticed her getting jittery, so he switched the media player to the radio and put it on a country/pop mix station, partly to see how she reacted to which songs. It was as close to her style as he could think of for current music.

~~

Isabel looked out over the outlets, and at Primanti Brothers, as James headed left toward Grove City. She'd never tried Primanti, although she knew they were one of Pittsburgh's biggest thing and there was one up in Erie, as well. She didn't remember there was one by the outlets, though. New, maybe. It had been some time since she'd been out this way. It was supposed to be amazing...

"So are you a Pittsburgh Primanti fan?"

She looked over at him. Had he read her thoughts?

"Isn't that what you were staring at? Or just hungry again?"

"No. I'm not."

"You're not which?"

"Hungry, and I don't know. I haven't tried it."

"Serious? I didn't figure there was a Pittsburgher who hadn't."

"It's always crowded and I don't like to wait in line for food when I'm hungry. Makes me grouchy."

"Ah. Guess I might want to remember that. This one doesn't usually have a line, depending what time you go."

"Are you down this way a lot?"

"Used to be, when I was dating the Grove City girl. Not too much recently. She didn't like the place, so now and then I went before or after I dropped her off."

"By yourself?"

"Sure. I sit at the bar and there's always someone to talk to. Even met another girl there about the time the other called it quits, so it all worked out."

"You're still with that one, the one you met?" She shouldn't have asked. Isabel couldn't think for the life of her why she had.

He tried, not well, to hide a smirk. "No. That was a while back." But he thought he knew why she asked. The guy probably thought she was interested. Probably most girls were, because of his looks. He had beautiful hair for a guy. It was a nice medium blond, naturally highlighted, by the sun, she expected. She wondered if it got darker during the winter and if his nice tan faded. He had the figure of a baseball player, tall, fit, muscular but thin muscular, not stocky. More normal sized, but tall. She was 5'7" and he still made her look short without towering over her. His features were sturdy, not gorgeous, a bit odd here and there although she couldn't place why. Still, she supposed he was well used to girls hitting on him.

When he glanced over at her gaze, she turned away and noticed a little brick building on the left side of the road nearly enveloped by trees and weeds. An old schoolhouse, she guessed, but one room, since it wasn't big enough for more than that, and abandoned, sadly. She could almost see herself turning it into a little music store with guitar lessons.

Guitar lessons. Maybe she could do that, except she wasn't certified as a teacher. Did you have to be? Maybe you didn't have to be. She could check. But did she want to teach strangers?

Isabel considered the idea as she put her attention on the song. Keith Urban. She recognized his voice but not the song. She didn't often listen to country, only bits and pieces of it. She also didn't listen to much pop from the past decade. Not her style. Too out there and in your face and kind of all the same. She supposed most people thought that about music they didn't like. Her own songs might sound "all the same" to people, also. Maybe that's what was wrong with it? But how did she change that?

Maybe she should turn to giving lessons instead. At least that was sure money; well, it was sure if she had students. She could start inexpensive to draw interest and work up.

At a main intersection, James turned left in front of a college and headed down a two-lane one-way road that reminded her of Pittsburgh's many one-way roads. It threw Isabel to find it in such a quaint part of a town rather than in the city. Cars lined both sides, all faced the same way, and they pulled out from the left. She hated one way roads in Pittsburgh, but for some reason, she hated it more here.

Or her nerves were far too taut.

He pulled into a space on the right in front of an ice cream shop on the other side of the street, as though trying to torture her. She'd already had a sundae. She did not need more. But the store window was horribly inviting.

"Things have changed some since I was here last. I would have sworn that was Daffin's." He noticed where she was looking.

"Daffin's. I've heard of that. The chocolate shop?"

"Right. You haven't been there?"

"I haven't been here before, as I said."

"This is, or was, a branch. The main store with the big candyland display is in Sharon."

"Oh. No, I haven't been to Sharon, either, at least not in a lot of years. I think we might have gone to see Santa there once years ago when I was young. I remember the long line in the cold waiting to get in, and lots of decorations."

"At Kraynak's."

"I guess."

"You don't get around much, do you?"

Isabel shrugged. She supposed not, other than her open mics, and they were usually the same few places. She focused on day to day, and other than the outlets in between Pittsburgh and Erie, she found what she needed in the Meadville Wal-Mart. She wasn't a big shopper. She hated to go out by herself. She also hated to go anywhere with anyone she wasn't very comfortable with. Being out here with James was harder than she wanted to let him know.

"Okay, well, Beans on Broad is right up there." He pointed up the street and scanned the area. "Looks like the music shop is gone, too, sadly. I used to stop in there a lot. Still, there are some nice shops here. Do you want to walk around a bit first to settle your nerves?"

"Do I look nervous?"

He chuckled. "Yeah, Isabel. You look way beyond nervous. Relax. They're very sweet people. And it's not big enough to be too awfully crowded."

"Then why come all the way out here to sing?"

"Different audience, and open mic nights do pretty well. They draw music lovers. Like me. It could really be worth your time."

She shrugged and he got out, dodging cars flying or crawling past so close to his door. When she got out on the other side, he looked over. "I would have gotten that for you."

"Why? We're not on a date, you know. It's business."

"Well, yes, but…"

"No need. Really."

"Okay."

She made her way over to him and they used a break in traffic to cross the little road. Nearly pulling back when he grasped her hand, Isabel realized he was being protective, and she wasn't sure whether to object or to be flattered.

He released it once they were on the sidewalk and she missed the warmth, or the comfort. Why a strange man's hand should feel comforting, she didn't understand. She didn't understand any part of this, at all, especially why she was even there. The coffee shop looked like a nice little place, but she hesitated at the door.

"Let's just start with coffee. Okay? Not a big deal to go in and get coffee, right?"

"Right." She didn't balk about him holding the door for her, and she returned the grin and greeting from a young woman behind the counter.

"Well, James, it's been a while. How have you been?" The girl gave him a warm smile.

"I've been good, thanks, Ashley. I brought a new customer. She might need a minute to check your features. You know what I want."

"Okay, but some day you'll have to try something different. We have Milky Ways on special. Milk and white chocolate blended with caramel. What do you think?"

"Too much extravagance for me. But you can add a shot of caramel to my Americano."

The girl grinned and put her attention on Isabel. "Take your time. I'll get his going. If you have questions, ask. We can mix different flavors if you'd like, also."

"Thank you. I'll have a chai tea, please."

"Too many choices for the coffee?" The look on his face said he figured he had her pegged already.

"I don't drink coffee. I love the smell, but I can't handle the taste."

"That only means you haven't learned to like it yet." With a wink, James asked her to pick a table and she chose the one next to the window, but she jumped back up when he started to pay for it. "No, my turn. You agreed."

Luckily, he didn't argue. She would have backed down if he'd argued since she was so far out of her element and she wouldn't embarrass him at one of his usual haunts. A coffee shop being one of his usual haunts was a comforting thought. Although he'd looked plenty familiar with Sam's, also.

As she waited, and to help calm her nerves by not just sitting, she wandered to the little rack that held a few books and knick knacks.

"Local authors and artists." James took her side. "The owner's great about helping to support local arts."

Isabel picked up a book that featured a lake and two people, young people, standing with their backs turned looking at the water. The girl's hair was long, curly, thick. Gorgeous. The boy wore a jacket that might have been his father's since it was big on his thin frame. The way they stood there side by side, but obviously separate, intrigued her. She flipped to the first page, read two paragraphs, and took it to the counter. It was about music. Between that, the cover, the intriguing title, and the water, she couldn't resist.

Settling with her tea, in the chair closest to the window, she scanned the part of the street she could see. Quaint. Energetic. Well kept. She loved the small brick store fronts and inviting entrance signs and windows allowing plenty of preview to the store contents. And the little business district was small enough to easily walk up and down to each shop without getting tired. Old Town was as charming as James himself. As polished and appealing as James. She wasn't at all surprised he spent time here.

"What do you think?"

Isabel looked back at his voice. "It's good. I could do this again."

"Well, I'm glad, but I meant the place. Oh, come look." He stood and led her to the back area, past tall steep stairs roped off, to an almost separate hallway-like room with a brick wall that made it look like an outdoor patio at night. A big couch and chair with a long, low table made a nice socializing area. Behind it were tables for four, with tall two person tables along the opposite wall. James pointed out a small empty space on the other side of the dividing wall from the coffee counter. "This is the music area. Nothing big. Minimal equipment needed. Very intimate. You could do this."

Too intimate. Too close to the audience. They would actually be listening, she expected, which was good. It was also more frightening than playing in noisy bars where she was largely background noise. James was right, of course, the potential here was what she needed for her songs, but... did she really want this? "I don't know."

While he was trying to convince her she could, the girl behind the counter came over and joined the conversation, said she needed a CD or MP3 to hear her sound before signing her up. Isabel had neither and said so and she didn't have anything uploaded to any social sites, so he said she could sing for her right there, Accapella...

And she walked away from him. By the time he caught up, she was out the door and down the sidewalk.

"You left your book on the table."

Accepting, she kept walking.

"Okay. So you're nervous. I get it. But there won't be hecklers."

"The tables there are too close, too in my face."

"Which means you'll have their attention." He grasped her hand to stop her. "Okay, look, I know it's hard to put yourself out there, especially when your songs are so personal. It would be different if you did all covers, and you could, but it won't help get your songs heard, if that's what you want. Doing them for random open mics was a good start, but getting in there and singing them up close and personal is the next step. You can do it."

"How do you know? Have you done it? Because well-meaning advice is great and all, but unless you've been there, had your heart torn out and then tried to sing about it to the world, or even for a few cretins, your advice is pointless. So spare me the lecture if you haven't been there."

~~

James considered giving it up, letting her just walk if she wanted. What did it matter to him? Getting her back out there wouldn't help his own ex career at all. She was willing to throw it away for nothing but nerves, because of some heckling. If she didn't have the grit for it, why should he waste his time?

She pulled her fingers out of his and walked down the sidewalk, looking into windows, pausing at an antique shop before moving along, past Sweet Jeanie's, down to the end of the sidewalk in front of Nonni's Italian restaurant. Then she stopped. "Can we just go?"

"Fine." He headed toward the street, waited for a couple of cars, and crossed over, figuring she could cross on her own. If she wasn't going to do it, she could have said so before he drove her all the way out there.

By the time he got halfway across the road, he felt like an ass to be so rude, so he waited for her, moved to the side cars would come from, and let her lead. On the other sidewalk, she slowed, looking up at the theater and in through the window of B'Gifted. He told her they could go in and look around if she wanted, but she shook her head and kept walking, past his truck, past Beans on Broad on the other side of the street, and paused to stare up at the mural on the side of the building at the parking area where the farm market was held on Thursday nights.

With a sigh at the mix of frustration and determination on her face, he took her side and drained the rest of his coffee. Fine. If it would help convince her to keep going, she could know. It made no difference if she knew. "Yes, actually."

"Yes, what?"

"I used to play."

She threw a questioning gaze.

"Before this." He held up his left hand and bent his pointer finger and his thumb. "The other three are useless except for looks. They tell me I'm lucky to have good use of the two most important digits. Lucky to them, I suppose. Makes it impossible to play guitar, though."

When she looked from his hand to the sidewalk, as though wondering what to say about it, he cut the idea off. "Come sit with me." With a nod at the white gazebo next to the sidewalk, close to the bright, bold wall-size mural featuring music, he headed that way, dropping his cup in the trash. Letting her sit first, he sat across from her. "Isabel, yes, I know how hard it is. I know it eats into your soul when stupid asses throw stupid comments about songs you pour your soul into when they're not really even listening or just because it's not their style. It's tough. The music business is tough, but I figure you should know that. Didn't your grandma ever tell you it was?"

"She only says I can if I will. And yes, I understand it's tough, but you ... you have looks going for you, and you're male, so there is that."

He felt his back stiffen. "Please. Don't give me that *it's easier for men* crap. No, it's not."

"Really? If girls get drunk and throw themselves at you, I bet you can get away from them easily enough, if you want to, and based on most of the men I've seen, they're happy enough to have drunk girls throw themselves on them. Doesn't mean I like it when guys do it, or that it's easy for me to get away from them since there aren't many who aren't bigger and stronger than I am."

His gut tightened. "Something happen recently?"

She sipped her tea and watched cars go past. She did not want to answer, which answered him to some extent.

"Okay, I'll give you that. I can't say I've worried much about girls throwing themselves at me." At her look, he rephrased. "I didn't really say that the way I meant it. I mean it never worried me." Also wrong. "Damn. I'm going to stop because…" Because he couldn't say it without sounding conceited, which, really, he wasn't, or without pushing her to tell him more about what happened. It was too soon, and her clenched jaw said it wouldn't work. "Okay, I get that. I know too many men can be real assholes. Otherwise…"

"Otherwise, as I said before, your looks pull people in. Mine push them away. It matters more if girls look right because they're more expected to be pretty and charming and whatever. Men just have to be good and act like they know they are. Don't tell me it's not true. It is true. You know how many homely, and even ugly, guys are out there living like music gods because of their talent, which isn't always even great? I can name tons of them. How many girls can you see doing the same? They're either very talented and nice looking, or they're not very talented but they are sexy. And heaven help if they gain too much weight or lose too much weight. They get slammed, even if their talent is incredible. The standards aren't the same."

"Fine. Maybe you're right on that count." He leaned forward and rested his elbows on his knees to get a bit closer. "But you know what? It's more your attitude than your looks. You turn people off because you come off as distant and drawn into yourself. Nothing at all wrong with your looks, except you seem to be trying to tell people to stay the hell away from you and that's never going to work in your favor. You want to get somewhere, you've got to lose the chip on your shoulder. Self-focus is great while writing, not great while performing."

"Yeah well, I don't want to be a singer. I only want…"

"It's obvious. That's why you're getting heckled so bad. You want your songs heard, right? Then *want* to be a singer for a while. You have a nice voice, Isabel. You could be a stand-out if you'd let yourself."

Silent for some time while she sipped at her tea, her shoulders rose and fell softly. "I bet you were good at stage presence."

"I was good at it, even better on guitar. My voice doesn't have the quality yours does, but it didn't matter, because I acted like it did. You're definitely right on that one. I acted as though they should pay attention and enjoy my music, and so they did, overall, not always. It's all about attitude."

"But you have that or you don't."

"You can learn it. I can help teach you, but you have to be willing."

A deep breath overtook her and she looked anywhere but at him. She watched cars, people walking, birds searching the sidewalks for dropped food bits, studied the buildings, the mural... "There's a lot of art here."

"It's a very artsy area. That's why I think you'd do well starting here. Can we go back in and try to set up a date?"

"They want a CD. I don't have anything recorded anywhere. When I was still trying to get a record company deal, or interest, I sent song sheets. I figured it would do better than my voice since it's not good enough and I know it's not..."

"Bad call. They would have just tossed the sheets. You've got to send CDs. Still a long shot. Anyway, you need to get them recorded. But for now, just sing for her. Between that and my recommendation, it should work."

"You've played here."

"Used to play here a lot. I've also followed a lot of others who do and have."

"I don't have equipment other than my amp. I do open mics because they provide the mic and speakers. I can't afford to buy them right now, not decent ones."

"I can bring what you need. Already have it. It's just sitting doing nothing. Might as well get some use from it."

She brushed a strand of hair behind her ear. "Um, why did you..?"

"Keep it if I can't use it? I didn't. My buddy hid it at my parents' place for safekeeping."

"Safekeeping?"

"Yeah, I'll explain that one later." He stood and offered his good hand. "Come on. Give this a shot. I'll help you prepare for it."

He forced himself to walk slow, not pushing her. When they entered the coffee shop, Isabel looked at the group of people sipping drinks at a table, but she gave in when James convinced Ashley to let her sing right there. He promised to send a music file over if still needed. He suggested the one he'd heard her sing at Sam's that pulled him in. Open Doors. He found it a bit ironic that a song about open anything would have pulled him in when she was so very closed. But the song told him she didn't particularly want to be so closed. It was fear. She needed to get past that.

With a deep breath and closing her eyes for a moment first, she got a slow, shaky start, but then focused on him and grew in confidence. It was beautiful. As haunting as it had been that night he'd first seen her. It had haunted him since. And it was so much better without the crowd, even without the guitar. Just her and her voice.

She only sang about two thirds of it and stopped.

Ashley set a hand over her chest. "Okay. So let's schedule you a night. Do you have enough songs to fill a couple of hours? A mix of your own and covers would work."

James nearly jumped on Isabel when she looked at him, hesitated, and agreed.

~~

Isabel wasn't sure how he talked her into doing her own two hour show with only three and a half weeks to get ready, but she also agreed to go to Primanti's, and then wondered why she agreed. She would have to watch that. The guy was far too persuasive.

The restaurant was basically an upscale sports bar, with a large bar and large televisions broadcasting games or other guy stuff, plus huge chalkboards on a wall with the menu scrawled over it. At least he didn't ask her to sit at the bar. They found a booth against a window, since he'd already picked up on the fact she liked to stay by the window or by the street, as much on the outskirts of the crowd as possible. The place was doing well, with plenty of customers, and their waitress was super friendly. She was glad he ordered soda rather than alcohol, agreeing to the brand they had rather than the one he asked for, with a bit of a grimace that made Isabel have to try not to laugh and the waitress apologize, somewhat flirtatiously.

She almost never agreed to go anywhere that served alcohol with anyone if she wasn't driving herself. Actually, she rarely went anywhere that served alcohol other than her shows, which couldn't be helped. But if coffee shops would work, she would gladly go that direction instead. At least there shouldn't be drunk cretins at coffee shops.

James laughed when she pulled the French fries off her ham, turkey, and cole slaw sandwich, and then pulled off half the cole slaw. It was too big with everything on it, and she preferred the separate tastes. He also looked at her funny when she asked for a side order of French dressing and then dipped her fries in it. But he tried it when she offered. He admitted it wasn't half bad. He left his own fries on the sandwich that dripped its juices down his fingers.

Something about the way he licked his fingers off before wiping them on a napkin both amused her and ... well, he was charming her a little too much for not being his type, or for him not being her type. He wasn't. At all. Not even close. He had to have been one of the popular sports kids who wouldn't have even spoken to her. But they weren't still in high school, thank goodness. They were both very much adults who had been around enough blocks to have some of their edges worn off.

Thinking about his fingers made her want to ask what happened to his hand, but after telling her earlier to leave their conversation at music and such, she couldn't ask. Instead, she stayed in safe territory. "So, what cover songs would you recommend for the coffee shop? Since you know the style they're looking for."

"Which ones do you already do?"

"Not a lot lately since I've been trying to get my own out there and I don't have a lot of time in open mic slots. I have a bunch I used to do."

"Right, you want your own out there, but you've gotta pull them in with stuff they know in order to hold their interest."

"Then they'll compare me to the original and I can't stand up to that."

"Don't. You shouldn't stand up to the originals. You should make them your own."

"But if they hate my version…"

"Then they aren't the right audience for you, Isabel. You can't worry about those people. Your job is to grab the ones who will appreciate you, and your versions. Forget the rest. We all have different tastes. It's not a reflection on you, only on their personal taste. You have to remember that. It's crucial. Don't try to please everyone or you'll be done before you start." He took another large bite and gave her time to think about that while he finished it. "So, what songs do you play that I'll know?"

"Um. I do *Breathe* by Anna Nalick, *Come To My Window* and a couple of others by Melissa Etheridge. *Try* by Pink is a current favorite. That's kind of recent, right?"

He grinned with a slight tilt of the head. "I'll give you that as recent.

What else?"

"*Barely Breathing* by Duncan Sheik. A few Infinity songs. *Let You In* is a favorite. Also *Not Because Of Him*. Um." What else did she like to do? "*Unlove You* by Jennifer Nettles usually goes over well, and I'm working on *I Can Do Hard Things*. *Perfect* by Ed Sheeran. Stuff like that."

"Sounds good. Anything else more current?" He picked up fries that fell out of his sandwich and dipped them in her French dressing to stuff in his mouth.

"I've been working on *Someone You Loved* by Lewis Capaldi, but I haven't performed it yet."

"Yeah, I see you doing that well. Okay, so we're going to have to get together soon and compare music. Maybe look for current chart toppers that'll work for your voice. And maybe more … upbeat? Do you do upbeat?"

"Not really." At his raised eyebrows, she sighed. "I shouldn't have agreed to this."

"You'll be fine. We'll get you updated a bit before then and you'll knock 'em dead."

"Have to love your optimism, even if it's hard to believe."

"Guess we'll have to work on that, too."

A huge pit formed in her gut. She wasn't ready for her own show. She was singing too much for herself, not enough for the audience. It took too long to learn new songs. Upbeat wasn't her style.

"Isabel, you'll be fine. Trust me."

"You will be there?"

"Of course." He winked and downed part of his soda, using his left hand, balancing the glass with the palm. She tried not to notice, but she could tell he knew she did.

"You're wondering what happened to the hand."

"Thought I shouldn't ask. You know, no deep talk. Right?"

"It's not all that deep." He took another bite and luckily chewed and swallowed before he continued. "My parents own a farm, and I grew up working on it like all of my brothers did. A couple of years ago or so, I was being stupid and not paying attention well enough and caught the hand in the bailer. Two of the fingers had to be fully reattached; the other was only half severed. My poor mom nearly fainted when I ambled into the house carrying them in my palm, half in shock. She's hardy and all, but that was a bit much even for her. She thought fast, though, stuck them in a plastic bag and stuck that in a bag of ice, wrapped my hand up to slow the bleeding and took me to the ER. She drove like she was flying a jet, which she never does. Denny, the second oldest, still harasses me about making her so sick she couldn't eat for the next two days.

"I'm lucky I still have them, so they say. Guess it looks better to have them, but looks don't help much, not as much as you think." He shrugged. "Didn't gross you out, did I? Should I have waited till you were done eating?"

"No. It doesn't matter. I'm not that touchy." She bit into her sandwich as though proving it.

"Good to know." His face took on a fully serious tone for a moment. Then he shrugged. "I gave up music entirely for a long time, wouldn't even go listen to it. And I did stupid things to compensate. Screwed up my work record and... Well, with help from my family and my buddy Bruce, I finally decided I had to get over it and quit screwing up my life more than I already had. That's why this matters to me, Isabel. You can't give up on this when you're so good and still able. I'd trade you most anything..." He looked away with a deep breath and took a long swallow of soda.

"I'm sorry."

"No reason. You didn't do it."

"I mean about being so whiny. I'm not. Really, I'm not. It's just been ... a rough month with ... well, too much going on. I won't always be. I'll pull out of it."

He smiled and reached across for her hand. "We all have those times. Don't worry about it. Trust me, I was plenty whiny for the longest time. Surprising I still have friends left. So I'll give you time. And if you want to talk..."

"You said it was too soon."

Releasing her hand, he nodded and grabbed a fry. "Yeah, so I can be an ass at times. Something you'll have to overlook. Too many defensive instincts that kick in at bad times."

"Defensive?"

"That surprises you?"

"Yes."

"I'm deeper than I come off." He grinned. "Yeah, I know how I come off. I've been told. But I'm not actually that shallow. You know, other than being a guy, and I can't help that much."

Yeah, way too charming. She couldn't even help going along with it. "Well, for a guy, you seem not too bad."

He laughed. "I'll take it."

He didn't seem too bad at all, Isabel didn't think. His easy laughter and easy-going relaxed casualness reminded her of Lisbon. And still, something about him reminded her of her grandpa.

She turned down dessert when he offered since she had the sundae earlier, and he insisted on getting the check, although she offered since the trip out there was for her. They were parked back behind the restaurant, in the outlet stores parking area, and she saw a couple of new stores, or at least stores she didn't remember, as they wound through the little side path under the trees and crossed into the parking area. When he opened the passenger door, he set a hand on her back and closed the door behind her. But he didn't start it when he got in behind the wheel.

"So I have to ask." James kept his gaze out the window, watching cars and people go by. "You were evasive earlier, about fending off attacks. Something happened at Sam's, other than the heckling."

"No." She felt her body tense and tried to calm it with a deep breath. "Not at Sam's. After Sam's, it took me three weeks to force myself back out to another open mic, in a place I've been several times. My room-mate, ex roommate, was sick and I went alone, as I usually do." Talking about it stirred the memory too far and brought back the fear.

"Isabel." He shifted to face her better. "What happened?"

Her jaw was clenched tight enough it hurt her teeth, so she forced it to relax and kept her eyes on people getting out of their cars to head to the restaurant's back door just to have to go on around. It was an exit door, not an entrance door...

He took her hand and she looked back at him. Her heart pounded. She swallowed. She hadn't even told Libs, couldn't do it. But he was concerned, probably thinking it was worse than it was. His look said he definitely expected it was worse than it was.

"Okay." She soothed herself with a deep, slow breath. "I haven't really had trouble before. I'm not the type to get that kind of attention, so I didn't expect it."

"Not the type to get attention?"

"No. And I know I'm not. It's fine. I don't care. Except for my music. That's what matters." She shoved hair back behind her ear and wished she'd done something with the mess.

His head tilted. "I think you're far too hard on yourself."

"I'm realistic. I'm too awfully realistic, so I've been told. But at least I can see what is."

"Maybe. As far as out there." He nodded toward the window, the people walking around. "But I don't think you see yourself very well."

She shrugged. How would he know?

"So? Someone gave you more attention than you wanted? Worse than I did by getting up in your face at Sam's?"

"Far worse than you did." She picked at her green nail polish that was flaking off. She wished she'd done something with them, also.

"What happened?" His voice was soft and low. Patient. Concerned.

"Not exactly what you're probably thinking, but close enough." Giving up on the nail polish that would have to have remover, she looked out at the road, the slight hill just past the two lane one-way road, wondering where it went. "This drunk guy, old enough to be my father, which makes it twice as disturbing, had been throwing passes during my set and I ignored it. I've dealt with that. Just part of the territory. Typical drunk guy. Turns them into assholes, and maybe they do it just so they can be the assholes they want to be. Anyway, it happens, and I didn't think much of it other than how annoying he was."

"You shouldn't have to deal with that. Where was management?"

"He's a regular. I've seen him there before and he's commented before, but nothing major. A friend of management, maybe. Who knows?"

"Okay. So..?"

"So he followed me outside. Alone. By the time I knew he was behind me, I had the back door open, putting my guitar in, and he..." She shook her head and turned toward the side window so he couldn't see the moisture in her eyes.

"Did you have him arrested?" Anger streamed from his voice.

"It didn't... A couple of people stopped him. They knew him, I think. Probably more worried about him than me. He had me down in the back seat and ... and his hands were on me and I couldn't get him off. If they hadn't..." Her head shook again and a deep breath flooded her body, making her eyes water more. "I had to drive just down the road and stop and pull myself together enough to be able to get home without shaking. And that was it. I was done."

"I'm sorry." Silence fell between them while she couldn't answer, while she pulled herself together with her fingertips brushing away the couple of tears she couldn't stop, turned to the window to try to hide it from him as well as possible.

"Okay, so there are things I don't have to, didn't have to, deal with. I get it. And I was an ass to talk to you that way on the beach without understanding. I am sorry."

She nodded. It was the best she could do.

"You might want to consider carrying. I can teach you. I'm trained. But other than that, I'm glad to go with you so you won't have to quit and you won't have to worry about the jackasses. I'm pretty good at defense, more than I look like I'd be. And if you didn't report him, you should do that. No matter who he is."

"Wouldn't help anything. Especially since I waited this long. And there are plenty more where he came from."

"Which is why you need self protection if you're going to be out and about alone at night, especially outside bars."

"I carry pepper spray. I just... I was unprepared, so..."

"Well, that's something, but I can also teach you about what to watch and so on. If you want. I've done that for a couple of female friends. Anyway..." He set his hand along her face, his left hand, to pull her gently back. "I'm glad whoever stopped him was there and it didn't go farther. But you know, if he's a regular, we could still take care of it."

Her head shook. Her heart raced. "Don't go play vigilante and get hurt or in trouble because of me."

"No playing vigilante. Just a friendly warning."

"James..."

"We'll talk more later. I should get you home." He rubbed his thumb along her face and then turned back to start the engine.

~~

He shouldn't have touched her face. A mistake. She pulled back, not too fast, and looked out the window most of the way back to her place. He kept trying to find something to talk about, to lighten the mood, hoping he hadn't scared her off. She had really soft skin. James kept telling himself to stop thinking about it, but really, she had soft skin, more than any other girl he could remember. She definitely underesti- mated herself because she was getting to him, and she wasn't even his type. Could be it was only her emotions that got to him. He felt for her. No girl should have to deal with that.

Maybe he could at least get the name of the place out of her. Later. After she'd calmed. Then he'd take Bruce, or Denny, his scrappiest brother, and hang out there now and then, just to watch. If she would tell him where she'd been. There was a good chance she wouldn't.

Since he couldn't think of anything to say, he flipped through radio stations and stopped at a hip hop/pop fusion song. Finally, she looked over at him. He bopped along with it as much as he dared while driving and brought out a light smile from her wary face. "Bruno Mars fan?"

She shook her head.

"No? I thought all the girls were by now."

"He dances well. I like a couple of his songs."

"Yeah, so I've heard. About his dancing. Last girlfriend was obsessed with the guy." He rolled his eyes big, with an exaggerated twist of his mouth.

She chuckled, a beautiful sound. "Hard to compete with that?"

"Hey, I'm a good dancer. Really. Okay, maybe not Bruno Mars good, but white guy from Greenville good, anyway."

She laughed. An actual laugh.

"You don't believe me?"

"I believe you. And thank you."

"For?"

"I know what you're doing. I hate getting emotional. Hate it with a passion. I don't, usually. Didn't even tell my roommate about it, any of it, so I wouldn't break down in front of her. So ... thank you. For everything."

He glanced at her and turned off onto the street that would take him to her place. Waiting to answer until he didn't have to worry about watching for traffic and such, James pulled into an empty space on the street behind her car and left the truck running. "Let me get your door, okay? Just because I was taught to open a door for a lady. Makes me feel better."

With a light grin and a nod, she waited while he got out and walked around and opened her door, then accepted a hand down from the truck. She still, somehow, smelled like the lake. And he was maybe standing too close if he could tell she did. But he didn't back up. "Thank you, Isabel, for trusting me enough to come with me today. I know it was hard for you. And I'll wait here until you're in to be sure you're in. But we're going to get together to talk about music for your show, right?"

"If you're sure you want to bother."

Bother. Definitely underestimating herself. "No bother. I look forward to it." Taking her fingers gently, he gave them a light squeeze and released them. "Can I have your number now?"

"You should have it since I called you."

"Oh. Right." He pulled his phone from his pocket and scanned through. "This one?" Getting her nod, he programmed her name in it, showing her that he put it in as Lizzy to be funny. It worked. She grinned with a light shake of the head. "Okay, then. I'll give you a call. You want my number so you'll know it's me?"

"I have your number from the flyer. I'll know it's you."

"Yeah, guess I better take the rest of them down."

"The rest?"

"I have them in a few places. Sorry."

"Don't be. It was kind of sweet, now that I know you're not a crazy stalker or something."

"Glad you feel that way." Dusk was settling in and he told himself to leave. Now. Just go. But he was having a hard time doing it.

"Good night, James. Thank you again." She raised to her toes and set a hand on his arm to give him a kiss. On the cheek. And then she fled to her apartment building and didn't look back.

Ten

Pulling flattened boxes out from beside the apartment's small washer/dryer combo, Isabel grabbed the bag of junk mail flyers she usually took to recycle and started packing up things she wouldn't need until she had her own place again. Luckily, she hadn't accumulated much other than furniture, and although she and Libs bought it together, her friend told her to keep it all. Her new husband already had a place set up, and it would compensate for her sudden departure.

It didn't, really. But at least she didn't lose half of that, too.

With a frown at her phone when it rang, she went to find it. James. Eleven o'clock Sunday morning. "Hey, did I call at a bad time? You're not in church or anything?"

"No. I wouldn't have answered if I was."

"Good. Tried to wait long enough just in case. Are you free today?"

"Um..."

"I have song ideas, and some news I'd rather tell you in person. Can we meet up somewhere?"

She found herself shaking her head. Too much too fast. She'd just seen him yesterday. "I'm..."

"You have plans. Sorry. Guess I shouldn't assume you didn't. Not that I assumed you didn't, but..."

"Are you always this wound up in the morning?"

"Not always. Not for a long time, actually. So, when would be good? Can you do an after work thing? I can meet you up there by six or so."

"Um, maybe. We can't just talk about songs over the phone?"

"Easier in person." A male voice in the background told him to calm down two hairs. "Okay, I guess I threw all of that at you kind of fast. How about if you can find time this week after work, let me know. I'm good with any night." Another voice, but she didn't catch what it said. "I can skip that for one week. No big deal." He said it somewhat away from the phone and then came back. "Sound okay?"

"I'm ... not actually busy today. I was just going to work on some songs to run them by you..."

"Yeah? Cool, so is there somewhere you want to meet or can I pick you up? What time works?"

"You're exhausting me, James. I am not a morning person, especially on Sunday." Isabel thought she might as well just tell him.

He laughed. "Sorry. I'll hush and you talk now."

Against her better judgment, she agreed to meet him in Conneaut Lake, at Ice House Park. Although it was closer to her than to him, he agreed with no hesitation and said he'd bring lunch.

~~

James paced back and forth on the sidewalk along the street of the little grassy area Conneaut Lake called a park. In reality, it was no more than a semi-circle around a little harbor with metal benches and information plaques scattered around. He was fifteen minutes early, but with his roommates heckling him about being too overdressed to go kayaking and not wanting to explain what he was actually doing, it was easier to go ahead and leave.

Two chef salads in the cooler hung over his shoulder would suffice for lunch, along with crackers, a small cheese plate, and two thermoses of ice water. After eating out twice the day before, he figured they'd both feel better if they cleansed their systems.

He walked the sidewalk circle a couple of times, checking out the different boats docked and swaying in the breeze, thinking about which he'd most like to have at some point in the future, and then wandered down the sidewalk back to the parking area. He didn't see her car, so he turned back again. About the time he considered going to stand in front of the boats instead of walking in circles, a little black Chevy approached.

Following her to the parking area, he caught up as she was pulling her guitar case out of the trunk.

She was dressed a bit nicer than the day before, but still casual in loose gray capris and a long white tank that hung down to her thighs and flared out at the bottom, plus a loose short-sleeved knit shirt that partially hung off her shoulder and flared out around her waist. She looked like she was doing all she can to cover her shape. "I'm not late, am I?"

"No, I'm early." He reached for her guitar. "Can I take that?"

"I'm used to carrying it, but thanks."

He didn't argue. This time. He understood wanting to keep hold of your guitar, no matter how good peoples' intentions when they offered to help. A guitar was a personal item, like his wallet.

They ambled over to the circle and she chose one of the red benches closest to the water. "It's so beautiful today." Sitting, she brushed hair behind her ear and propped the case against the bench on her other side.

"I always enjoy seeing this when I go past, but I've never stopped."

"No? I jog here now and then, down the sidewalk, not in circles, of course." He set the cooler in front of the bench.

"Of course you jog." She gave him a half disdainful smile.

"You don't?"

"Someone would have to be chasing me. I detest running."

James knew that feeling was pretty prevalent, although he didn't understand it. To avoid the conversation, he pulled out a small towel to spread on the bench between them, and then the salads and water. "Hope this works."

"Looks wonderful. I could have brought something."

"Next time. So, since I'm impatient today, I got you an open mic spot at Sweet Jeanie's for next Saturday. Not this coming, but next. Gives you prep time if you need it..."

"Wait. Where?"

"The ice cream parlor in Olde Town, the one you saw yesterday." He handed her a fork and napkin. "I did some research last night when I got home and found they do it occasionally, so I sent a message, figuring they might respond by tomorrow, and they already answered. They have space if you want it. Before you say anything, I have a couple of other singers coming, so it won't be just you. Only a twenty minute set, kind of a warm up for the Beans show. And you can say no if you want, of course, but it would be good local publicity before the other. So..."

"An ice cream shop open mic? I can do that."

"Cool. I'll tell them yes, then. Tomorrow. I'm not going to bother her on a Sunday. So after we eat, we'll talk about songs for both."

"Or we can do that in between eating? I brought the list of stuff I do already." She pulled out a piece of notebook paper and handed it to him. It still had some of the paper shredded by tearing it out of a spiral notebook dangling, and he badly wanted to pull them off, but he figured that would look judgmental, so he resisted the thought and scanned her list while they started on their salads.

"These are all covers."

"Yes. Mine are on a different list. I figured the names of songs you haven't heard wouldn't mean much to you."

"Okay, so..." He shoved a slice of cucumber into his mouth and pulled a pen from the cooler's side pocket. "Can I write on this?"

"Sure. I copied it for you."

"Most would use their printer."

"I don't have them typed, only like this."

His head shook before he could stop it. "We need to bring you into the twenty-first century, Isabel. No offense."

"I type a lot for work, but it feels better to do my songs by hand. More personal, I guess."

"Well, I guess I get that, but a back up is always good to have. So, about this list, can I make some suggestions?"

"Of course. That's why we met up, right?"

"That we could have done over the phone. I want to hear more of your own stuff. In person."

James hadn't planned to stay so long. He'd have to call his mother and apologize for not making it for dessert. He'd gotten out of dinner by saying, honestly, that he had plans, so she asked him to at least drop by for homemade raspberry pie, which he loved. Every year, she picked the raspberries she protected from the birds with nets and tended herself rather than leaving it to any of the men in the house, and made pie out of the first batch. It wasn't something he missed very often.

But Isabel had gathered a small audience sitting there beside the boats on the gorgeous mid-August day playing her own songs and some of the covers he didn't know or that she'd changed to fit her own style, and she kept going, kept working with him, taking suggestions well, honestly listening to his thoughts, and he couldn't possibly stop her. Some of the small audience asked her name and if she had CDs. He gave them the dates he had lined up so far. Since she didn't have a public page of any kind yet, he gave them his personal Facebook page and said he'd announce her shows there publicly until she was set up with her own.

By the time she'd had enough, his stomach was growling. That was the trouble with salad. It didn't hold well. Afraid she would balk at eating with him again, he tried anyway, suggesting Silver Shores so they could walk up there together rather than worrying about having separate vehicles, and still look out over the sun and clouds reflecting in the water. One of his most favorite sights in the world. Maybe his most favorite, above everything.

"One condition. It's my turn to buy."

Although, the sight of Isabel beside the water under clear skies playing guitar, occasionally brushing hair behind her ear while she met his eyes, watching for his reaction, was getting up there pretty fast. And she'd agreed to dinner. "But it was my idea."

"Take it or leave it. I owe you for everything you're doing."

"No, you don't, but I'll accept this time." Especially when she smiled that little teasing victory smile.

~~

Isabel studied the bobbing boats tied to the docks out by the imitation lighthouse at the restaurant, its black and white swirled stripes a nice attention-getter. They were still talking about music off and on, but also about water, the lake, traveling, and whatever else came to his mind. He was a talker. She couldn't possibly keep up. But he didn't seem to care.

His phone rang a couple of times. One he answered and apologized for not making it, whatever *it* was, but assured whoever was worried that all was fine. The other he silenced without answering, and then he silenced his phone with an apology.

After they ate, which neither of them rushed, they ambled back toward their cars, except he detoured to the water, asking if she was in a hurry to get home. She wasn't, really, other than needing to do some laundry and stop at the store since she hadn't the day before, and needing to start packing since she'd already told her grandparents she was planning to come that way soon.

Still, she told him she was in no hurry.

The heat of the day had drifted into a nice late afternoon respite, including a breeze off the lake. A glacier-made lake where they used to harvest ice. She knew because James mentioned it. Ice House Park, a small bit of maintained grass lined with benches, was named after what used to be the area's main way to refrigerate food during the summer.

He was rambling, giving her the feeling he didn't want to leave, didn't want to end the day with her. He had buddies, though, roommates he lived with and hung out with. It wasn't like he had to go home to an empty apartment, like she did.

"Well, I should let you get back, I guess." He shoved a thumb into his shorts pocket and took it out again. "Give me a call if you have questions. About the show, or songs, or whatever. Okay?"

She nodded.

"Okay, then." He headed back toward their vehicles, silent all of a sudden, and waited beside her car while she unlocked her doors and set her guitar in the back. "Thanks for meeting me. I look forward to your show."

"Me, too."

"Yeah? Honestly?"

"Yes. I've missed it. Well, not the hecklers, you know, but..."

"Promise. No hecklers. I'll throw them out myself if needed. But it won't be needed. Fully different audience."

"Okay. I'll see you then."

"Have a good night, Isabel. Drive safe."

"You, too." Somewhat grudgingly, she got into her car.

"Hey, text me when you get in so I know you are."

"Why? It's not late."

"I know. Just ... because. Please."

"Okay. See you."

He nodded and stepped back, waiting until she pulled out before he went to his truck.

Two weeks. She would see him again in two weeks. In the meantime, she needed to work on her songs. And maybe do something with her hair, and her nails. Maybe find a new outfit more appropriate for a coffee shop show than the stuff she wore to bars. If he was going out of his way to help her, she should at least do her part as well as possible.

Eleven

He couldn't sit inside. James had already gone out for a run, through the humid and heavy August air that made running harder, came back to shower, made breakfast for himself and his roommates, cleaned the kitchen area back up again, including the wall behind the counter, and vacuumed the thin, old carpet he wanted to replace with hardwood. Still, he couldn't sit. So he grabbed his laptop bag and headed to the door, assured Bruce he was fine and just going to the park to work, accepted the offer of an IT job from one of his buddy's coworkers, although it was still slower going while adjusting to having to type with only two fingers on the left hand, and decided to drive rather than walk in case it started to rain. In which case, he'd move to the coffee shop.

Half jogging down the apartment stairs, he breathed deeply when he stepped out into the warm summer air. As heavy as it was, James still preferred it to the cool, conditioned air in the apartment. It didn't look much like rain, so he changed his mind and walked. His laptop case was waterproof. He'd learned that the hard way. If needed, he'd throw his phone in there, also.

Reaching the amphitheatre, he sat on one of the steps, halfway up, in about the middle of the thing, and pictured her doing a show right there, standing on the cement block at the bottom of the steps. Built a lot of years ago by the USO to entertain troops stationed at Fort Reynolds next door to Greenville, it hadn't been used in his lifetime, that he knew of. By now, it was just an abandoned amphitheatre with cracks made by persistent weeds facing a large concrete square, and nothing more. He'd have to get speakers and mic her and her guitar, plus a canopy to protect her from the sun or drizzle, if he could get permission for her to play there. Could be they wouldn't allow it. Maybe he'd check into doing some of the local craft shows to get her name out there and work up.

First, she needed a social media presence, and business cards. He'd order some cards... Of course, he had to know what she wanted to go by and what to use as contact info other than a web page, which he'd design today and fill in later, once he got photos and such. The cards would have to wait. In the meantime, he could use his own, for his IT work. Or not. That would look too much like he was promoting himself, and that wasn't what he wanted.

For now, he could put her name and social media sites on a few self-print cards, as soon as he had her other sites set up well enough. Or he could give her a call to tell her what he planned...

Too soon. He needed to let her do at least the open mic first and maybe the Beans show before he inundated her with all of that. He could call, anyway, just to ... see if she'd meet up and, well, maybe show him what she'd been working on for the past week. Except she worked all week and only had evenings and this weekend to prepare, so he figured he should leave her be to work.

~~

Isabel should have been working on her songs and the new covers he suggested. Instead, she was packing to move to Pittsburgh. Her Saturday errands were done, groceries bought and put away, laundry washed and put away, floors vacuumed and mopped. It was quiet without Lisbon there bouncing around getting in her way. Good work time. Still, she was packing instead.

Maybe she'd take her guitar out to the beach tomorrow and work there. If the weather held. Possibly, she should have switched her schedule and gone out there today while it was decent, since it would likely rain by the next day. She could still go if it was only rain and not a storm, but she couldn't take her guitar.

Either way, she should be working on her songs. And she wasn't. She didn't even know why she wasn't. Fear, maybe. Accepting the open mic and the show were one thing; actually doing them was another.

She jumped at the ringtone on her phone signaling a text. Grinning at his name, Isabel flipped it open.

Hope I'm not bothering you while you're working. Actually I hope I am. Hows it going?

Should she admit the truth? Since it was a text, she didn't have to answer right away, which she appreciated. Maybe she'd start working on the songs and then text him after she was working so she could say...

No. It would be unfair when he was helping her of his own accord. At least as far as she could tell, it was only for her, without a hidden agenda. Hard to tell. She could be wrong, and she'd watch close to see if she could find what other purpose he might have. Still...

With a sigh, she hit reply: Um.. no. You interrupted me telling myself I should be working on songs.

His reply was fast, much faster than hers: Other things in the way?

Other things. Well, like her fear or her lack of confidence or... How did she say that?

Another text came before she could figure out how to answer: Can I call?

Call? So she'd have to answer coherently quickly? It would be easier, she supposed, overall. Sure. Even expecting it, she jumped at the ring.

"Hey, Isabel. So, what's up?"

"I'm ... just doing some stuff around the house."

"Uh huh. I know how that goes. You're procrastinating. Why? You're not backing out, right?"

"No."

"That was a very unconvincing no. Do you want to meet up? I can come that way."

"No. I mean, you don't need to. And no, I'm not backing out." How could she when he sounded like it mattered so much?

"Then what's up?"

Her head shook. She had no idea how to answer.

"Okay. I get it. It's hard to go back once you've decided you're done. I've done that, too. Got way too convinced my stuff was crap and just stopped. But you know what? I regret losing that time now. Not that it matters at this point, not for me, but it will matter to you. So work. Okay? I'm holding you to the two shows you've agreed to do and we'll go from there. No excuses. Just do this."

"James..." What? What was there to say?

"It's going to be fine. Promise."

"And you'll be there."

"Absolutely."

"Okay."

"Good. I'll let you go, but call if you need. My phone's always on. I don't always answer if I don't feel like it, but I'll always answer your calls. Okay? You know, unless I'm in the shower or whatever, but I'll call right back. Whatever you need. Even not music related."

She felt moisture well in her eyes and fought it back. He was too sweet. He couldn't be as sweet as he seemed so far. There had to be something in his background...

"And you know, if you want to get together tomorrow, I'm free. To help conquer your nerves. Or for song feedback."

"Thanks, but no, I need to just work. I'll do that. Promise."

A chuckle came through the line. "Good enough. See you next weekend, then. Have a good rest of the night. Working. Bye, Isabel."

She managed a simple goodbye and wandered the quiet little apartment that was more Lisbon's style than her own. She'd said she would work, promised she would, so she went to grab her guitar and notebook from her room and crossed a leg up on the couch.

New lyrics came to her. Not about the ex, as usual. About James.

When had she last thought about her ex? She wasn't even sure. Too much of her time was spent thinking about James. "Work, Isabel. Stop thinking about him and work."

Except she liked the words that were coming out onto her notebook. He wouldn't have to know it had anything to do with him.

You saw through me when I was at a low point/
not my lowest but then again maybe so
Ready to give up, to walk away/ start with something easier to say
You said you know, you understand/ even offered to hold my hand

Across that street I walked with head held high/
and my gut telling me to turn back around
Ready to give up, to walk away/ to say leaving it behind would be okay
You said I'd regret it, I needed the sand/ to hold firm like it's dry land

Then again I found my sea legs/ I found my seagull wings
entwined with melodies and words and chords/
and I could fly, could hold myself high
on my own, but then again…

He would absolutely know it was about him. What else could it be? Still, she liked it so far, so she tucked it in the "to finish" file with several others she'd abandoned because she couldn't find endings.

A dull piece of coal. *I know it's inside you, Isabel, but you won't let it out.* Since his words wouldn't go away, she figured she might as well use them. Other girls had to feel the same. They could relate. Maybe she could provide some light for them. Or at least some empathy.

Sometimes you just needed someone to really understand.

As James did. Or seemed to. Maybe someday, she could sing this one to him.

Twelve

Isabel wasn't sure if she was more nervous about the open mic or about seeing James again.

The thought of moving back to Pittsburgh now gave her mixed emotions. It would be nice to stay with her grandparents while she resettled and restarted. But it would be a two hour plus drive to Lake Erie rather than just under an hour. Once she got outside Pittsburgh, it was an easy drive, but still a long one.

She was also moving farther away from James, but they didn't really need to meet in person other than for shows. They could do it through an online chat. Her grandparents had wifi that would work with her laptop. Really, it would be safer if they didn't meet in person too often. He was too infectious. Too fun to be around. Too addicting.

She had, at least, worked on her songs last weekend after he called to say she should. She also let herself go out to Presque Isle on Sunday to unwind before going home to work again. She needed the beach time to clear her head, to rest, to find inspiration. To get distance.

Not that he allowed too much distance. James called her often through the week around dinner time when they were both home, and Isabel often packed while talking to him but didn't tell him as much. And she wasn't moving because of James, at least, not only because of him. If she was going to go forward with this music thing, she needed to be in a bigger place with more people, more venues. Whether she did would depend on the open mic at the ice cream parlor, but more on the coffee shop gig, her own show. On what reaction she got. On how it felt to her.

If it didn't feel right, she would go back to her old method of sending her songs out in hopes that they would reach the one right person who would give them a chance. It was a slow and frustrating process, but it was far less scary. She would, as he said, have to get them on CD, though. Maybe he could recommend a singer who could do them better.

Her nerves nearly made her turn around before she got to the door of Sweet Jeanie's, but since she promised, she gritted her teeth and went in. The wood floors and casual style, along with kid stuff in the display windows, felt homey and comfortable. Especially when James came over to greet her with a sweet smile and walked her back to the three people he'd been talking with. The other singers. They welcomed her warmly, and they obviously knew him well. She had to wonder if he'd been one of the group before, while he could still play. Likely, he was. Maybe he'd been a group leader of sorts. The girl at the coffee shop asked if he'd run an open mic for them. Isabel could easily see him doing it.

And she was glad he'd asked them to go on before her, to give her time to settle in.

~~

James had to force himself not to hold a Cheshire cat grin on his face the whole time she sang. No need to freak the girl out. Alternately, he had to try to keep his emotions in check so he wouldn't weep like a child over the beauty of her performance. She was the whole thing. Even if she was only singing to showcase her songs, it would be wrong to have anyone else sing them. Not wrong, exactly, but not right enough. The combination was perfection.

She was just beautiful.

When not singing, she was kind of cute, as he'd told her. Not stand out. Not stop on the street to look twice pretty. Her figure was more boyish, straighter and stockier than what usually attracted him, but when she sang, none of that mattered. She was beautiful when she sang. Her inside came outside and the effect was stunning.

As he promised, there was not one heckler. The small audience at Sweet Jeanie's was enjoying it nearly as much as he was, by the looks on their faces and the way they were truly paying attention to the words. Patrons who obviously only meant to grab ice cream and leave lingered a while to listen instead.

She looked at him before starting her last song and gave him a sweet soft quick smile. It melted his heart right through his chest. He didn't recognize it. A new one? Unlike most of her songs, it was hopeful, upbeat, soft, sweet.

Along with handing out her new website address which linked to an in-progress Spotify page, he took photos of her performing. A couple of them would work until they got something more professional.

Ending with the song he'd asked her to do for the owner, a soft version of Infiniti's *If You Say So*, she thanked the audience, packed her guitar in its case, and came to him. He gave her a quick hug. "You were fantastic. Can't wait for your longer show. How about dessert?"

"I think my stomach would object right now, but thank you."

"Hamburger? Their burgers are wonderful."

"Maybe that, but I can…"

"I got it." He kissed the side of her head. Her hair smelled of coconut and something else he couldn't place. For a moment, it reminded him of the mojitos one of his exes used to drink and made him wonder what Isabel preferred. So far, sweet tea and Coke. Which made it easier to eat with her, to go out with her. Meaning, to shows and…

Shoving the thought aside, he requested a cheeseburger with everything and one with a few condiments on the side since a small crowd was talking with her and he didn't want to interrupt. While he waited for the burgers, he stood back and watched her handle it. She did well, looked very professional. Regardless of how people-wary she was, it didn't show. She was together and appreciative and gave them more reason to remember her name. Definitely the whole package. This girl could go places. He wanted to help her do it.

While they ate, the owner came over and thanked them for drawing a nice crowd and offered to let them come back any time. When they finished, she helped him pack up his equipment. Getting it loaded into his truck, he walked her down the sidewalk to where she'd parked and held her door. "You were wonderful, Isabel. This was a better venue for your music. More upscale, which is what you'll need."

She gave him a hug. A full, long, meaningful hug. "Thank you for pushing me to do it. I needed this."

She actually felt really good in his arms, and the thought was surprising. "You're welcome. Since you're out this way and it's still early, how about working a bit on your show?"

"Where?"

"Follow me back into Mercer. I know just the place. Yeah?"

Her nod was like a burst of sun through the dark.

Inside the gazebo at Brandy Springs Park, they worked on songs some, and they talked some. A couple of teen girls stopped at a distance to listen and James beckoned them over. After talking a bit, and accepting a card with her name written on it, the girls moved along down by the pond that only had a touch of water left in it.

She shivered when the sun fell into dusk and waved a bug away. He generally ignored the little pests, but she shooed away anything that came close, and with the sun setting, they were starting to swarm.

"Guess we should call it a night." At their vehicles, her car sitting behind his truck in the little semi-circle drive in front of the lower pavilion, he hesitated. "How about dessert now that your stomach's had time to settle? Or do you need to get going?"

"It sounds good, actually. I shouldn't, since I've splurged enough recently, but..."

"You earned it. Follow me."

~~

Isabel sat next to him instead of across from him at one of the picnic tables outside the little Dairy Queen in Mercer. The table was up on the grassy hill on the inside of the parking area away from the street so they could see the lights of passing cars but didn't get much of their noise, except for those trying to make noise and the few bikes that were still out this late.

He teased about her again ordering turtle pecan ice cream and she admitted she generally stuck to the familiar stuff she knew she liked.

"Makes dating hard, doesn't it?"

"Yes." She expected from his raised eyebrows he hadn't expected her to be so frank. "It takes so long to know who they really are, and by then, you're used to them, or, well, shattered by them. I haven't bothered lately."

His head tilted in between spooning out his Peanut Butter Crunch Blizzard. "How long is lately? Can I ask?"

"Two years."

"Wow. You're not that old, right? You would have barely started dating that long ago, wouldn't you have?"

"How old do you think I am?"

He shrugged. "Twenty, maybe twenty-one."

"Okay. In ten years, that might be flattering." She looked over at a car full of teenagers jumping out harassing each other with laughs and shoves while making their way inside. Isabel hoped they would stay inside or leave.

"Um, okay. So..?" He took a big enough bite it would have frozen her mouth.

"I'm twenty-five."

"Serious?" He covered his mouth with a napkin and waited until he swallowed the ice cream. "Sorry. You don't look it."

"It's the baby face. Runs in the family. I don't like it any more than Mom liked it. Or Grandma." She looked away. He knew her grandma's name. Isabel did not want to talk about her, not professionally.

"Nothing bad about it. But why two years, Isabel?"

"I got shattered." She shivered, not sure if it was from the cool night, the ice cream, or talking about him. "I'm still not even sure why. We'd been together for more than twice that long. High school sweethearts and all. We hung out in the same group for years. We were friends first. It's not like it was something I rushed into."

"Did he cheat on you?"

"Yeah, apparently, he had been for some time, like, months at least, but I didn't know he had until one day he said ... well, that I was too dull and he'd met someone who wasn't, and that was that."

"He called you dull? I mean, he actually said that?"

"Yeah, and I guess that's fair. I am to anyone else. I'm always in my own head too much, like Mom always said. But it's comfortable there, you know. I kind of thought after all that time, I wasn't dull to him, that he would see me deeper than that, than most people did. Either he didn't, or I am that dull."

"You're not dull."

She pulled ice cream from her spoon with a shrug, and studied a little path into a clearing within the trees, their branches high enough from the pine covered ground to make a perfect place for kids to play and explore, and tempting for any who noticed it. "You don't have to be nice. I can handle truth."

"Isabel." He shifted to face her more directly. "No one who writes the way you do is close to dull. That guy was an idiot, probably just not smart enough to understand you."

"Thank you. I'll take that." She gave him a grin and watched two of the teenagers step back outside to light cigarettes. Luckily, they stayed by the building. "I'm guessing you date often, from what you've said. Not hard to believe since you're so upbeat and all."

"Well, at times I am. And I date somewhat often. Nothing serious. I'm not really a serious tied-down type, but I like to be out and about around people. So anyway, are you looking forward to your own show now that tonight went so well?"

"Yeah."

"Yeah? Nice. I'm glad to hear it. Guess I should tell you what I've done, then."

She listened, her visual attention on the peeling paint of the old picnic table and the lighter wood that showed where it had been most recently peeled, while he talked about the website he was designing and that he wanted to add one of the photos he'd taken at the ice cream shop. If she okayed it, he would set up a Youtube account so they could link to her videos from her page, along with a couple of social media accounts where people who loved indie music hung out. He'd recorded some bits from the open mic but would do better at the full show. Once they got some of her songs recorded professionally, he would set up a CD Baby account to sell them and a Spotify account to find new fans.

Isabel was flattered to no end, but something about it still seemed fishy. "So, really. Why are you doing all of this? No one goes to this much effort without wanting something. And don't tell me it's only because you like music. So do I. Most people do, right? But this is a lot of effort for someone you hardly know. I don't get it."

"Well." He shoved more ice cream in his mouth and scratched his head. "I was kind of thinking you could use a manager. I want to volunteer. I'm not asking for pay, just to be part of it, to see what I can do to help get you out there. If it works well, I might be able to use it to get my foot into a music job of some kind. A&R work, maybe. Artist and repertoire, the guys who do the scouting for labels…"

"I know what A&R is. I mentioned it already. Remember?"

"Oh. Yeah, you did. Sorry. So anyway, although I do actually want to help you just for your sake, there is an ulterior motive of sorts, but it's nothing shady."

Isabel felt her spirit suddenly sink, and she wasn't sure why. Free promotion from someone who seemed to know what he was doing was a good thing. Manager. Scouting. Not personal interest, only business. Like he'd said from the beginning.

And it didn't matter. She wasn't looking to date and … and… It had crossed her mind, though. He'd thought she was twenty…

"Why do you suddenly look not happy? Like I said, I'm not asking for part of what you make. I know that won't be much, at least for some time. If you hit big, we can renegotiate. You can always say no. I just want to help you do this."

"Because you can't do it yourself? Or is there another reason? I mean, it's a long shot that it would actually help you, and I am smart enough to know that much."

His chest rose and fell and he focused on the large Harley pulling in with its two passengers, a middle-aged couple both wearing helmets, which many didn't since they didn't to, legally. "Because … well…" He was trying to avoid the question. But then he looked up, into her eyes. "You captivated me that night at Sam's and I can't stop thinking about the way I felt while listening to you, to your words, how much they affected me. If I feel that way, so will others, and … music … it's a life saver. It is. I want your stuff out there to help others, and I want to help make that happen. Lots of people need to hear what you have to say. Honestly."

If she'd been two ounces bolder, Isabel would have leaned in to kiss him right on the mouth. She wasn't. Thankfully. He wanted to be her manager. It was only about the music. "Okay."

"Yeah? All of it?"

"Yeah. And thank you. That... Telling me that..." She bit her lip and shook her head. "I can't tell you how much that means. So okay, let's do this. When you have time, I have stuff I've never played for anyone because I'm not sure about them, so maybe you could listen and..."

"Absolutely. Tomorrow?"

She couldn't help but laugh. "You do like to be out and about, don't you?"

"Have to keep myself busy."

For a moment, Isabel saw a deep, dark side within him. Hiding from something, or from himself. *Music is a life saver.* Yes, but what did he need to be saved from, other than the accident with his hand? Something was stirring down inside that charming, friendly exterior. Maybe it was a good thing he only wanted to be her manager. "Tomorrow's fine."

As soon as she got home, had the door locked behind her, and had scanned the apartment with pepper spray in hand, she texted James to let him know she was in. His reply was quick, as though he was waiting to hear from her: Good. Night, Isabel. Rest well.

She doubted she'd sleep much, at least not for a while. She was revved up from the show, but more from their conversation. People needed to hear what she had to say? She'd told herself as much, but it was a far different thing to have him say so. He'd been avoidant, until he wasn't, until he got direct. Complimentary. Sweet. But then…

Pulling out her folder of unfinished song lyrics, she grabbed the newest and a pencil. And added to it.

> *You saw through me when I was at a low point*
> *not my lowest but then again maybe so*
> *Ready to give up, to walk away/ start with something easier to say*
> *You said you know, you understand/ even offered to hold my hand*
>
> *Across that street I walked with head held high*

and my gut telling me to turn back around
Ready to give up, to walk away/ to say leaving it behind would be okay
You said I'd regret it, I needed the sand/ to hold firm like it's dry land

Leading me home where my name should be in lights
as a light to others struggling to glow

Then again I found my sea legs/ I found my seagull wings
entwined with melodies and words and chords
and I could fly, could hold myself high
on my own, but then again…

Is the light within me or am I only/   reflecting it off what I see in you?
Can it stay if you don't?/ Is it only a tease, a dream,
a dull piece of coal disguised/ in a sheen of smoothed broken glass?

It wasn't quite right. Repetition was fine when it made enough sense, but… maybe…

And then I found my sea legs/ I found my seagull wings
entwined with melodies and words and chords/ and I could fly, could hold myself high
on my own, but then again…

Still repetitive, but she liked it better. Was it on her own if he was helping her, lifting her up, pushing her back into the game? Would she keep going without his help? Would she have restarted if he hadn't pushed her?

Maybe. But not nearly so soon.

Isabel hoped it was a good idea to allow him to push, and to help.

Thirteen

As much as she hated having her picture taken, Isabel decided to cooperate and at least try to get a good one. Instead of letting him pick her up, she met him in Greenville, in the park beside the little river branch, after an emergency shopping and beauty parlor trip with Libs to fix her hair and find something appropriate to wear.

She found two outfits, a gray lightweight scarf with stripes of white lace and shimmers of silver over a light gray button-front shirt that she could put over her nice dark gray capris for the pictures, and a light gray and deep red sleeveless long sweater to go over the dark gray one piece plain, flowing maxi dress. Her friend complained that she needed more color in her wardrobe, but Isabel liked everything to go together. She liked what she knew.

Her hair was harder to deal with. She didn't want it shorter, but it did need to look more professional, so with Libs' input, the stylist cut it into a layered short but full bob leaving the front longer. It allowed her to leave it down natural or pull it back into a barrette for more elegance. At least for whatever amount of elegance she could fake.

Libs insisted she had to meet James and mentioned a double date, scoffing when Isabel said they weren't dating, so she'd have to come to a show to meet him. She couldn't imagine when that would happen since her new husband had gone to one of Isabel's shows and refused from then on, and Libs now did nothing without him tagging along. He'd even gone shopping with them and hung out at the little restaurant attached to the mall while he waited, which meant Libs was distracted and on a time limit. So she stopped at two outfits. Just as well, since her funds were limited and about to be limited even further with rent coming due soon and no roommate to split the cost.

As she veered off Greenville's Main Street headed toward Riverside Park, her heart pounded. She figured it was not good that she was nervous about meeting up with James and showing off her new look. It beat harder the farther she walked down the steps of the amphitheater from the gravel parking area above. He was there already, sitting at the edge of the concrete square at the bottom of the semi-circle of stone steps, notebook and pen in hand.

She was glad she wore her flat sandals since the steps weren't terribly smooth or even. The last thing she needed was to trip down the things and skin herself up. It was a cool place, though. It would be nice to watch a performance there, or to give one. When he looked up and gave her a smile, she paused. He was too freaking cute. And her manager. James was her manager. And she was not his type.

She repeated that to herself when he grabbed the notebook and jogged up the steps to meet her halfway. Tilting his head, he walked around behind her, stepping up onto the next seat, and smoothly back down to her other side. "Nice. I like it."

"Yeah? Thought I should have it fixed. Libs helped me choose a style since I'm really bad with fashion."

He grinned. "It looks great. It looks like you." He glanced down, as though appraising her for a modeling job. "All of it. You look great, Isabel. Perfect for a profile photo. Want to start there?"

Giving him a shrug since her heart was too fluttery to talk easily, she read his T-shirt, a well-fitted black T-shirt with big MR in the middle of a circle, and Born 2 Rise around the ring.

"You like them?" He'd caught her checking him, it, out.

"MR?"

"Madison Rising."

"Oh. Um, I don't know their work. I've heard of them."

"Wow, Iz, you've gotta get better acquainted with newer music. Here." He flipped screens around on his phone and music started playing. Loud, harsh ... the Star-Spangled Banner, but in rock form. She found herself nodding.

"Nice, huh?"

"Yeah. I love the lead's voice on this."

"It's the passion he puts into it. You can do that. Different, of course, since your style is different, but it'll be equally impressive once you let yourself go some and throw yourself all the way in."

"And you assume I can do that."

"Yep. I assume you can. Okay, so, pull your guitar out and we'll try some photos with it and then without it."

He had her sitting on the gritty stone steps right where they were and took way too many photos from different angles. Finally she said one of them would have to work and he sat next to her and flipped through, back and forth, until they agreed on a close up to use for her profile photo on social media sites, and another to use as a cover image for her website, focused more on the guitar. He'd actually made her look pretty good. Isabel was surprised how much she liked it. The girl in the photo looked very professional, artsy, just confident enough, with just enough of a smile to look friendly and not goofy. She'd been smiling at him while he teased about her pretending to enjoy the photo session or to like people. He made her relax enough she could focus on him and not the camera.

He moved without pause from photos to music. Kicking her left shoe off, she crossed her left leg underneath and let the right rest on the step below, turned toward him somewhat but not too directly.

She had to use her notes to play, since so far she was doing songs she'd written long ago, and she hadn't worked on them. Now and then he got up and moved around to take more photos or short video clips. And he was honest. He didn't like all of her songs. He liked parts of some that he thought needed work. Others he loved just as they were. It made her trust his opinion. If he'd loved them all, she wouldn't have believed anything he said, altogether. All songwriters wrote duds. They did. You couldn't write good without writing bad.

She wrote notes beside each one in a green pen to signify they were his comments. Her first thoughts were in red, with later thoughts in blue and then black. She always used the same color code.

James asked her to do the one that had caught his attention that night at Sam's. He wanted the whole thing on video. While she sang, he often caught her eyes and grinned or nodded. She was afraid it might show that she kept looking at him while singing, but he didn't complain about it. He thanked her, and Isabel stood. She wanted to walk off her nerves.

He insisted on carrying her guitar. As her manager, he said, it was part of the job, and she wasn't at all sure that was true, but she gave in and he slung it over his back like it belonged there. A guitar did belong on his back, in his hands. He should have been carrying his own around instead of hers. It had to be awful to want it so much, to practice enough to get really good at it, as she was sure he had been, and then have it taken away just like that.

"Can I ask you something?" She stepped down onto the grass at the bottom of the stone steps and walked over to the concrete square.

"Sure." He followed, but when she stepped up on it to wander the edge, he walked around the outside instead, just below her.

"How did you..? I mean, what pushed you to start supporting music when you couldn't do it yourself anymore? What you're doing for me, who did it for you?"

"Heck of a question." He looked down at the grass but kept up with her. "My family, of course, helped me deal with it, personally, mentally. As for the music, well... You know, I think it's not time for that yet. Later, okay?"

"Sure." She tried to make it sound like it didn't matter that he wouldn't answer her, but it did. She'd told him about her ex, about how she hadn't dated in two years and why. She only wanted to know who it was who reached him, who pulled him back from the pits of what had to be a huge dark hole. It would be for her. She'd only quit for a couple of months, not even that. But to do it for... Well, he hadn't said how long he'd been away from music. Or if he had, she didn't remember. She couldn't admit it if she didn't remember. She'd have to wait to ask.

Jumping down from the block when she got back to where she'd started, Isabel let him lead. The park was mainly deserted, which was nice but sad, and they walked down to the edge of the little river, then alongside its bank.

"Do you canoe or kayak at all?"

She felt her eyebrows raise. "Really? Do I look like I do?"

He chuckled. "You really need to get out more, Isabel. There's a place upriver that rents them. I'm out there usually every Sunday, although sometimes I go up to Lake Erie instead. Interested in going with me some day? Kayaking, that is."

"Um, you should know I have absolutely no arm strength, so that's probably not such a good idea."

"Kayaks don't take much strength if you're not doing rapids or anything. You could do it."

"Yeah, I don't think I want to be out there in that thing by myself when I've never paddled anything. Well, years ago, Gramps took me on one of those two people boats they have in parks, just for fun, but he steered and did most of the paddling. It was leg paddling, not arms. Anyway..."

He grinned. "Well, then a canoe instead of kayaks, so I can help you out and keep it steered in the right direction."

"Help? You'd have to just do it. You think I'm kidding."

"That bad?"

"Yeah, that bad."

"Maybe we should work on that a bit first, then." He lowered to the ground, propped the guitar over his back enough it would stay, and went into pushup position. "Come on."

"You're kidding, right?"

"Nope. You'll be glad you did."

"Uh huh."

He grinned and did a bunch of pushups. Showing off. The boy was showing off his plentiful arm muscles.

"At least let me take the guitar out of your way."

"Then it would be in your way. Come on. Let's go. I'm speaking as your manager. You have to be fit enough to go on tours and such eventually. Canoe first. Tours later." He did more, more slowly, and then looked up at her from plank position, waiting.

"Not in my good clothes. I just bought them."

"Roll them up."

"Not here."

"No one's around."

When she still refused, he stood and dusted off his hands. "Okay, then. Start on your own first so you're more comfortable. I want to go canoeing in a couple of weeks, as a change from the kayak, and I don't want to go alone, since canoes are meant for two, or four."

"Take one of your buddies."

"They're far too damn lazy."

"Hm, so am I."

"Not anymore, you're not. Think of it as vocal training."

Isabel wasn't sure whether to laugh or to punch him, and she was starting to think that could be a common theme with them. Not that she wouldn't be glad to have a few arm muscles, or that she hadn't thought about working on them, and canoeing did sound like it could be fun, but he couldn't just assume she would because he said so.

He tilted his head.

"What?"

"Well, I'm trying to decide whether you're about to walk away from me or tell me off. Is that what you're trying to decide?"

"Honestly, it was more like whether or not I should punch you."

He laughed. "Okay, that's fair, but the idea might be appealing to some extent, I'm guessing, right?"

"Which idea?"

"Canoeing."

"Oh. Maybe." The idea of punching him didn't sound too bad, either, but she didn't say as much.

He watched ducks waddle off and fly away. "Tell you what. Let's give it a try next weekend. We can make it a short trip and work up to longer excursions if you enjoy it."

"I'll think about it."

"Good enough." He walked again, moving farther down along the river. "Have you had time to check your Facebook page?"

"Yeah. Thanks. It looks good."

"I can make you admin if you want so you can make changes and such. You'll have to give me your user name or find me and send me a friend request."

"Oh, I'm not terribly computer literate outside office programs. I'd hate to screw it up so you have to start over."

"Not likely. Look." He pulled out his phone and sat down in the grass, one knee up, the other leg straight in front of him. "Have a seat." He patted the grass next to him.

"It's damp. Don't look at me like that. I'm not a prima donna or anything. If I was in jeans, I wouldn't care, but…"

"Right. You just bought those. Fine." Jumping back up, he led her over to a picnic table. They spent a good half hour or so going over basics of working social media. She could see the interest in the thing, at least for voyeurs, and for those selling stuff to voyeurs, but it felt far too open, too intrusive.

If he wanted to do it, she wouldn't complain, though. Maybe it kept him from doing other stupid things, more stupid things. Could be, she supposed. The same way her grandpa gave her a guitar to try to keep her from doing stupid things.

He sent her a friend request, helped her connect her personal page to her business page, and then showed her tips on how to use it. She stopped him to look at something he'd posted.

"You know you can see those from your page now. Anything I post, you can see, since we're friends."

"Oh. What if there's something you don't want me to see?"

"Then I won't post it. Simple."

"But if you want others to see it and not me?"

"Why would I?"

She shrugged.

"I don't put anything too personal on here, Iz. Privacy online is a misnomer. There's no such thing, no matter how you set it, so remember that. Anything can be found by someone who knows how."

"Okay."

"But you can make lists for some people to see things others can't. Here. I'll add you to my close friends like this ... and now you can see what others may not. I just create a post, mark it as close friends only, and it stays hidden from casual friends."

"And you can take me off there again if you want."

"Could, but I don't plan to. So. Got it?"

"Yeah, I guess it's not that big a deal."

"Didn't figure it would be for you." Closing the app, he stuck the phone in his back pocket, and stood, offering her a hand up. "Hungry? There's a great Italian place up the road. Do you like Italian?"

"I do, but..." Dinner? Again? And Italian? That was a little bit... too much on the romantic side. And people usually had wine with Italian, which she didn't want to do and didn't particularly want him to do...

Still holding her hand, he dipped his head closer. "Will you have dinner with me, Isabel?"

A date? It sounded like he was asking as a date, or at least in a date manner. "Are you sure? You're not tired of me yet or have something else you need to do?"

"Not at all, and laundry, but it'll wait." He grinned.

~~

James wasn't a big fan of the greens and reds combination that was so often used in Italian restaurant decorating, but the staff was friendly and the food was always good. They talked, taking their time, and he considered stalling her even after they were done with conversation, but he didn't want to push. She was pleasant company, not too talkative, not too quiet. She actually listened well enough to respond to what he said, not only to whatever thoughts it triggered of her own, but she had plenty of her own thoughts and wasn't easily swayed by his. He appreciated that. She was very pleasant company, easy to be around.

And she ordered iced tea. Not wine. Of course she had to drive home, so there was that. Still, he didn't remember when he'd last been out with a girl who hadn't ordered an actual drink with dinner. At least one. The invitation had partly been a test. For himself. To see how well he could handle it to have his date, dinner date not real date, sit across from him nursing wine or whatever. He was just as glad he hadn't had to find out yet, glad she was good with drinking tea instead. Still, he had to wonder why.

He was also still wrapping his head around the fact that she was five years older than he expected. Or maybe he was trying to see her too young. For safety purposes. Twenty-five, though, made things less complicated. More, but less. Both. She wasn't close to off-limits at twenty-five.

At her car, he gave her a casual hug, told her to drive safe, and asked her to text him when she got home so he knew she was in. She raised her eyebrows, but she agreed.

Back at his apartment, the ridiculously loud action movie starring The Rock slammed his brain after the quiet, relaxed outing, so he grabbed the laundry and his laptop and headed to the laundromat. He could start editing her videos while he waited for his clothes to clean.

Fourteen

James hadn't called in a couple of days, which was fine, except Isabel had new songs written and wanted to let him know. She had his number on a special ringtone so she could ignore every call but his while she was working. Writing. She was even writing during lunch breaks since her curiosity about him triggered a creative spark. They weren't really about him, though, only about the effect of him. She hoped they could get together over the weekend, but it was Thursday and ... canoeing. She'd nearly forgotten. She said she'd let him know.

Trying not to be too intrusive, since she thought he might be trying to unwind after work, or getting dinner or something, she sent a quick text: No pushups done. Sorry. Still on for canoeing if I can't paddle my own weight?

She barely set the phone down when it buzzed: Management slapping your hands, but sure. And I bet you can paddle your own. Canoe weight is a different story. When?

He called instead of debating date and time by text. The forecast looked better for Saturday, so they agreed on mid morning and she insisted on meeting him there. "I have new songs, by the way. That's why it took so long to answer about the canoe thing. I get obsessed while writing and kind of forget everything else."

"Yeah? Bring your guitar so I can hear them when we're done playing in the water. I look forward to it, Isabel."

"Me, too, and you can call me Izzy if you'd rather."

~~

Call me Izzy.

James considered that for far longer than he should have. Izzy. She said she used it for her stage name. She wanted him to call her by her stage name? Except everything he set up online used her full name: Isabel Dillon. She hadn't said anything. He liked it much better than Izzy, which didn't suit her.

Closing the door to his room behind him, shutting out the noise of the television and his roommates, along with Bruce's look and question about whether it was Jackie he'd arranged to meet, which James didn't answer, he picked up a notebook and plopped on his bed. *Call me Izzy.* Something about it wouldn't leave his thoughts, so he started to write, free-write nonsense, which is always how his songs began. He just grabbed a thought and wrote whatever came to mind and then went back to pick out phrases he liked to pull together into some kind of sense. The music came later, inspired by the words. Of course, adding music now would be an issue since he had to play while writing music.

The words came together fast. It turned into one about a girl, from her perspective, trying to be what she thought she wasn't but turned out she was that exactly. He liked it. Except it had no music.

Staring at his favorite guitar tucked back into the corner of his room, locked inside its case without seeing daylight for ... how long now? Two years? Two and a half? No, he'd pulled it out now and then, but only long enough to tune the thing, get frustrated, and shove it back inside.

James allowed himself a rare heavy, long sigh. Rubbing his chin, he went to open it, admired the beauty of the curly maple grain with only a natural finish and matte varnish rather than gloss. He'd had it made. His one big splurge. And now it sat nearly untouched.

At least he could tune it again. It took some time since it had been awhile, but the instrument felt good in his hands. With that thought and plenty of longing to return to his craft, what he was better at than anything else in the world, or used to be, he gripped the thin neck and reconfigured a C chord using his thumb and forefinger. It was awkward as hell, but some guitarists did use their thumb for chords, so he knew it was doable.

Or he could get a left-handed guitar as Bruce suggested more than once. The hell with that. He'd never get back to where he had been by playing left-handed. And he didn't want to start over.

Dropping his fingers down over the strings hard, he clenched his eyes and his jaw and considered throwing the instrument against the wall. If he couldn't play it, no one else could, either. Not his custom-made baby.

"Hey."

Startled by the voice, he jumped about five feet and stared at his roommate. "What the hell? Ever hear of knocking?"

Bruce came in and closed the door. "Sorry. Heard the guitar."

"Yeah." With a roll of his eyes, he got up to lock the thing back in its case before he did anything stupid. "Want to go have a drink?"

"No. And neither do you."

"Like hell I don't. I've got this great song, lyrics for what could be a great song. Came out just like that. A good omen. And I can't write even two fucking measures for it without playing. I've never been able to hear a tune until it comes out." He tried to push past Bruce, out the door.

His buddy held him back with a hand on his chest. "Not letting you do it. Come on out and watch a movie with us."

"Not interested."

"Then ... we can go for a quick jog."

"You hate to jog."

"Yeah, I do. But I will. What do you say?"

"Fuck." He shoved his good hand through his hair.

"Agreed. But other than that..."

Other than that. With another sigh, his thoughts went to Isabel and he calmed. She had new songs. He was anxious to hear them, more than he maybe should be.

"Is Jackie free tonight?"

James wasn't going to get around that conversation. "Wouldn't know."

"Didn't you just talk to her?"

"No. It was Isabel. Don't make a big deal of it."

"Okay then." Bruce rubbed the whisker shadow on his chin. He never shaved on weekends. "When did you last call home, or go home? Talk to your brother, any of them?"

Call home. Only twenty minutes from his parents' place and he hadn't been or called in maybe a month now other than to say he couldn't be there.

"Want me to ride out with you?" Bruce looked far too worried, which was nice, he guessed, but also annoying.

"I'm not going out there tonight."

"Okay, so how's the new IT job coming?"

"It's not yet. Guess I should do that. Fine. Got it. I'll work on something I can still do."

"Yeah?"

He gave Bruce a quick grin. "Yeah. Thanks."

With too much nervous energy and too many thoughts of eluding his buddy and heading down to the new brew house he'd seen talk of online, James dropped to the floor and did pushups and thought of Isabel standing there watching him and refusing to do even one. He hadn't expected she would; he only wanted to get her reaction.

And he'd been showing off. Flat out fucking showing off.

She hadn't seemed to mind.

He looked forward to Saturday way too fucking much.

Fifteen

She wasn't sure when she'd last laughed so much. And her arms didn't get tired quite as soon as she'd expected, but of course James was doing the brunt of the rowing, after he'd taught her the basic technique. Isabel dropped a paddle a couple of times when the water seemed to grab it right out of her hands, but he chuckled and caught it, once nearly falling overboard to reach it, and then said he should have let himself because the cool water would feel good. The idea of him going overboard scared her, though, since she didn't know how she'd manage to get the canoe back to him or to the shore so he could catch up without his help to steer the thing, so she kept a better grip, and then her hands got sore.

Still, it was a lot more fun than she'd expected. Along with the water itself and the scenery of tree-lined Shenango River, and his company, the exercise had actually felt good, to her surprise. Maybe it would be the impetus she needed to keep going, to at least work at toning her muscles.

She helped him pull the canoe up to the Carried Away docking point, or at least tried to look like she was helping, and accepted her bag of belongings tied in plastic to keep them dry. He had small zip bags for their phones and keys, plus a waterproof canvas bag he'd had made for his excursions big enough to hold a couple of jackets along with the plastic bags. Isabel had teased him about being a prepared Girl Scout and he quietly admitted to being an Eagle Scout but that it was more his dad's life training lessons that prepared him for whatever life threw at him. He'd obviously spent quite a lot of time with his dad. She had to wonder what her own father could have maybe taught her if not for…

"What do you think?" James set a hand on her back, thankfully interrupting her thoughts, as they headed toward the parking area. "Worth doing again sometime?"

"Definitely, once I get over being sore, because I'm guessing I will be for a day or two."

"Did we go too far?"

For a moment, she didn't realize he was talking about the distance in the canoe. His hand was warm and tender against her thin shirt. She hoped the sweat running down her spine into her capris wouldn't be obvious. "Not at all. I'll have to at least consider a few pushups here and there so we can make it longer next time. If you want."

"I can be out there all day if it's up to me, so whatever you're up to, I'm willing." His hair, mussed by the wind, flickered highlights from the sun. "You enjoyed it."

"I did. Thank you."

"No need. It was nice to not go by myself. Much more fun this way." With a wink, he lowered his hand. "So, songs or lunch first?"

"Lunch. I'm starving after that exertion. And I brought it, so we don't have to go out. Hope you like chicken salad because that's my specialty. If not, I threw lunch meat in the cooler, too. Your choice."

"You're amazing, and I happen to love chicken salad, or about any kind of sandwich salad."

"Yeah? Or are you playing nice?"

He leaned in and kissed her head. "I won't be anything but honest with you, Isabel, so you don't have to wonder. Okay? We're pals, right? Pals don't do that to each other."

She wasn't sure whether it was the kiss to her head or his ability to just be straight with her, or that he called her a pal, which was far more flattering than if he'd called her a friend, but she thought she might mind if he kept treating her like a little sister, since her thoughts were going a very different direction.

He spread the old blanket she always carried in her car over the grass and she pulled paper plates and a couple of plastic bottles of water out of a bag, then food from the cooler she'd had to buy since she didn't have one. Again, they didn't rush. They talked, about canoeing and water and how they were both attracted to the shore. She agreed she'd love to see the actual ocean again someday, relaying the trip years ago with her grandparents, although she was happy with the lake, and she'd spent plenty of time wandering Pittsburgh's River Walk and crossing bridges just to cross them.

Eventually, they got to her songs, and she was amused and impressed that he took notes on paper while she sang. He asked her to repeat certain phrases and questioned a couple of key changes. He knew music every bit as well as she did, and that impressed her, as well. Playing guitar didn't always mean the player really knew music. Often, they just imitated what they heard and then sometimes learned how to take that and change it and create their own, without really knowing the fundamentals. James knew the fundamentals, and while she appreciated that, it also made her more sad for him, since it showed he was serious about it.

She had to believe there was a way he could play again. Maybe if he could switch it around… That could work. If the accident had taken his right fingers rather than his left, he could still play. It would make other things harder, she supposed, since he was right-handed, but it wouldn't have screwed up his music. Had he considered that maybe he still could?

Pondering whether to ask while she finished playing as much as she had done of one of her new ones that needed work, she set her Martin down and grabbed a bottle of water. "Can I ask you something?"

"Iz, stop asking if you can ask. Yes, you can. What?"

"Well, I just wondered if you'd thought about trying to play left handed. I can't imagine it would be easy, but it would be doable, wouldn't it? At least worth a try?"

He echoed her swallow of water before answering, looking like he wished she had not asked, after saying she could. "Should be doable, and would be for some, I guess, but some people can learn to write with their non-dominant hand, too. Not me. Tried it once by restringing one of my guitars to make it left-hand compatible. I got so damned frustrated trying to start all over again doing everything backward after my brain was so well trained to do it the other way that I smashed a perfectly good guitar against the wall. Destroyed the guitar and the wall. One was fixable. Still mad at myself for doing that. I could have at least sold it. My smart ass brother, Denny, the middle one, pulled it from the garbage and turned it into a shelf. Says he'll give it to me if I ever want it, like I'd want that reminder. Anyway, no, it doesn't work for me, so that's that." Finishing off his second sandwich, he studied his notes.

He'd smashed it? She wouldn't have guessed he had that kind of temper. But she supposed anyone could have if they were too awfully frustrated.

"About that line where you say 'And it isn't what it was, not what I saw at the time,' what about changing the second time to 'And I'm not what I was, not what I saw at the time'. It would go along with the way looking back to see things differently with distance changed you, changed your perspective." He spoke the line in rhythm, almost but not quite singing it. Isabel couldn't imagine his singing was as bad as he said since his almost singing voice was so nice, but she let that go for now. Later, she would ask him to let her hear it. Far later when she was more comfortable with him. More personally comfortable. She was casually comfortable with him, more than with maybe anyone else, even more than with the ex she'd known for years, since they were kids.

Odd. But nice.

And he understood her songs, which meant he understood her, at least decently. *Not what I was.* It would have more impact, she supposed, but maybe later in the song? She needed to hear it to know if it was right.

Shuffling through heavy, wet sand,/ my eyes on the edges, hoping to spy a glimpse of color, a shimmer of light…

She stopped. Hoping to spy a shimmer of light.

"What?"

Her heart jumped slightly as she stared at him. A shimmer of light.

"Iz?"

"Um, nothing. I think you're right. Hold on." Grabbing her notebook, she pulled a leg up to both create a table and to block him from seeing while she wrote. A shimmer of light within the brown sand… *Browns and tans and shards, all most ever see, the … sea-smoothed edges of what I'm meant to be…* It was about changing with a different perspective, but it was about more than that. It was… about who she really was that most didn't see…

Trading the notebook for her guitar, she started again.

Shuffling through heavy, wet sand,/ my eyes on the edges, hoping to spy
a glimpse of color, a shimmer of light/ browns and tans and shards prevail but
like a snail, I slog forward
I'm looking back on those days, those early days with you,
through a distance, in a slow-clearing haze
like a mirror old and etched, its gray background
peeking though, erasing what's true, now
And it isn't what it was/ not what I saw at the time

She played a longer version of the music she'd written for in between the verses, because she needed time to think. It had become more personal, if that was possible. Definitely, it was changing from what she'd planned. And he knew she was stalling.

I'm looking at my todays, the way they were shaped by you,
through the blues and the grays, there's no way…through
like a maze with no map, it was only a trap/ I believed what wasn't true
And … and I'm not what I was/ not what I saw at the time

She stopped, since it was all she had. There were thoughts for the chorus, but they weren't written, so she wouldn't try to play them.

"I think I like it that way." He was studying her too close. "I mean, I know you were only pausing to think with the *And…and I'm not what I was*, but I like it. It adds emphasis."

Made it sound more personal, he meant. More gritty. It let listeners more inside. "Maybe." She wrote a note to consider it, but she was done playing it for now.

~~

James sipped his water and wished he could offer to share a bottle of wine with her. "Tell me more about the song."

She hesitated, suddenly wary. "Tell you what?"

"It's about the ex that called you dull."

"No. Well, it is about an ex, but not the main ex, more of a... Well, I'm not sure I'm ready to admit that much." She strummed through a couple of measures from another song. A distraction.

Something made him push when he knew he should let it go. "One night stand?" At her look, he threw his hands up. "I'm joking."

Still, she held his gaze. "Barely more than that. Not something I'm proud of. Although I did expect it to be more than that."

He found himself nodding but unsure what to say, since he figured his joke was far from the truth. He couldn't see her as a one-night-stand girl, or even close.

"He said the right words, he spoke the right tune, until she was so gone she knew what she would do, when he asked... and then... he was gone with the breeze like a nightingale's lie, and she was so struck down, she couldn't even cry... 'cause she knew... she wanted his need of her, wanted his truths to be lies full of blossoms and honeys and sighs, she wanted what came of him, all that he left her, and then it was gone like the breath of a cold night, in white wisps of blue..."

He recognized some of the words: the one she'd been writing on the beach, in the sand. Her guitar took over and she watched her fingers, hiding within herself while letting so much out through her music.

"She wanted and needed him and no one could tell her... and no one could sell her the truth... that he wouldn't stay long, he wouldn't be 'round, when her need said he'd stay and his lips said he may... and she knew she was wrong, yet she felt he belonged..."

Her head shook and she stopped playing. "Not quite right. I'll work on it." She set her guitar back in its case and closed it.

"Are we done for the day?"

"Yes. I'm tired. Your fault."

He couldn't help a grin. She was too cute. "But it was worth it. Yes?"

"It was."

Unwilling to leave, to let her go home, James got up and stretched and then lay on his back in the cool grass, shifting to get away from a rock under his hip. She stayed on the bench, pulling a leg up in front of her and wrapping an arm around.

"So. You're sounding pretty ready for your show next weekend. Yeah?" He focused up at the cumulus cloud spotted light blue sky behind the swaying tree tops.

"Guess so."

He looked over at her. "Say yes. Whether or not you feel it, say yes like you mean it. Let's try this again: You're ready for your show, right?"

"Yes?"

"Not good enough. No virtual question mark at the end. Just yes."

"But I'm not sure I am, and..."

"Get sure. You are. You'll be great. I'm your manager and I say you'll be great. Right? Artists are too subjective. It's why they need managers..."

"Well, that and because artists are artists and usually not so good at both."

"Never mind that. Go with where I'm going. Either way, you're subjective about your music. I'm not. You're ready, Iz. Tell me you're ready and mean it."

"You're still going to be there?"

"Of course."

"If something happens and you can't be..."

"Then you'll do it, anyway, because you said you would, but it won't. I'll be there."

"I don't want to do it if you're not." She was focused on a group of ducks beside the river making a bunch of racket.

Her soft words were far more flattering than he wanted them to be. Sitting up, he swiveled to face her and tented his knees in front of him. "Isabel, I'll be there. I wouldn't miss it for anything. Okay?"

She held his eyes a moment. "Okay, then. I'm ready."

It sounded sure enough. And he was far too enamored... flattered. He was flattered by her faith in him. "Well." He stood and wiped grass off the back of his shorts. "I need a shower and you have stuff to do, I'm sure. I should let you get going." He offered a hand to help her up and nearly kept it, but instead, he took her guitar.

"You don't need to..."

"Like you said, you'll probably be sore by tomorrow, anyway. Least I can do for coming with me today." Glad she didn't argue, he walked her to her car, waited while she put the guitar in the back seat, keeping enough distance not to make her nervous, and held her door. "A hot shower tonight will likely help your muscles."

"I'll do that. Thanks."

"Epsom salt helps, too, if needed."

"Okay."

"Drive safe, Iz. See you Friday."

She gave him a nod and tossed a wave out her window as she drove away. Maybe he'd jog around the park before he went home.

~~

James turned his phone over and over in his hand. She should have been home at least half an hour ago. He hadn't asked her to let him know, but she'd realize he'd want her to let him know. Wouldn't she? A quick text to check wouldn't be too intrusive, would it?

Whether or not it was, he did it, anyway, so he wouldn't have to keep wondering. And then he paced around in front of his building while waiting for her to answer. He needed a shower. He'd jogged long enough to drench his shirt and for sweat to run down into his shorts. But if he texted her in front of Bruce, his buddy would make an issue of it, and he wasn't in the mood to explain.

After five minutes of pacing, he stopped to stretch instead.

Ten minutes. Where was she? He should have checked in earlier, or asked her to... He jumped at the buzz.

Yes half hour ago. Was in the shower

Relief flooded his system as he answered: Good. Heading there now, too. Sweat dripping in my shorts. After he sent it, he wondered why he did.

Um okay nice to know. Ac isnt working?

Not outside. I was jogging.

A pause. Really? After canoeing?

Impressed or rolling your eyes?

Both. Thanks for checking in.

Did that mean she was done talking? Probably. He couldn't help asking, though. Muscles sore? He headed inside and up the stairs while waiting for the response. If she wanted to keep talking, well, texting, Bruce could just deal with it.

No answer. Could be she was saying she was done.

The noise of the apartment was a shock wave after the mostly quiet of nature and music. He answered briefly when his buddy asked how it went and veered straight to his room, announcing he was hitting the shower in two minutes in case anyone needed in there first. By the time he grabbed clean shorts and his towel that he hung in his room so it wouldn't get shared by the cretins, there was still no response, so he started the water and pulled out of his clothes.

About to step in, the text came: Sorry was getting dressed. Not yet.

Good. Wait. You were chatting with me naked? He knew darn well he should not have sent that one. Especially since it took her a bit to respond.

No in a towel. Is that a ? mngmnt shd ask

He chuckled, glad he hadn't thrown her. Of course not. It was a pals question. Teasing. But I'm naked and not in a towel. Back in a few. He most definitely crossed the line with that one.

~~

Isabel had to wonder why he was giving her so much personal detail. A test? Or was he that open in general? Could be, she supposed. And he could have just said bye or later or busy or something. Shaking her head, she grabbed a bag of chips and a new jar of sour cream and onion dip and plopped onto the couch to browse channels.

When her phone buzzed and she saw his name, she laughed.

Okay, dressed and unsweaty. What are you up to?

Are you bored

Nailed it. Am I bothering you?

No

Good. Can I call instead?

Sure. She turned the television volume down to take the call.

"So, I had a thought. How far are you willing to travel for shows? Because there's this place in New Castle that could be a good match..."

"New Castle's fine."

"Yeah? Great. I'll check there, then. There's also a place in Cranberry. I know that's a bit of a drive from Meadville, but you could come this way and I'd drive the rest, so it wouldn't be bad. Does it have to be Saturday, or what time do you get off work? Because it's often easier to get in on a week night while you're starting out. Weekends are often full..."

"James?"

"Yeah?"

"Are you seriously not at all tired after canoeing and jogging?"

"No. It energizes me. Oh, you're tired and I'm talking your ear off. Sorry."

"It's fine. I need some of your energy."

"Well, Iz, if you keep hanging out with me, that may happen since much of what I do is active. I have to keep busy..."

"Why?"

Silence took over.

"I mean, you're bored easily, right?" It wasn't exactly what she meant, but there was still something about him she was trying to figure out that he obviously didn't want to talk about. "Don't you have a girlfriend?"

Still, he was quiet. For a moment. "Um, probably not anymore. I totally forgot to call her … three days ago. And it was nothing, really. What made you ask? I don't remember mentioning one."

She couldn't admit she saw him with a girl and hid so he wouldn't see her, could she?

"Why do you think I have a girlfriend?"

She pretty much had to now. "Okay, so … I saw you … on the Fourth of July, at the park. Pretty girl. She looked pretty into you. Not my business, but, I guess I wonder why…"

"Why I'd call you instead when I'm bored? Simple. You're more interesting to talk to."

"Um, thank you. I'm flattered." Now she wanted to ask why he'd date someone not interesting to talk to…

"You could have said hello, at the park, if you saw me."

"Well, at that point, you were still some creepy guy who stood too close at my open mic."

He chuckled. "Break point."

"What?"

"Tennis term. Means you win. You don't do sports at all, do you?"

"I like to watch swimming."

"Watch it? Do you swim?"

"No. I don't swim or want to swim. I like to watch it and I like to walk along the edge of the water."

"So, you're obsessed with it but afraid of it? And yet you enjoyed canoeing."

"I'm not afraid. I just don't want to be that far in the water. I don't even do baths, only showers. But yeah, canoeing was kind of great."

He was silent a moment. "That's … interesting, Isabel. Odd, but interesting. And it could be a song, you know."

"Anything could be a song." Unable to resist the chips at her side, she put one in her mouth and tried to chew it quietly.

"Okay, I give. What about baseball? Ever go to a Pirates game?"

"No. I know nothing about it, really. When I was little, Grandpa put me in softball, but apparently all I did was pick clovers and build little sand castles, depending whether I was infield or outfield."

He laughed, and Isabel decided it was worth telling him just to hear that laugh. "Would you go?"

To a baseball game? "Is this work related in some way I'm missing?"

"Oh, I don't know. Everything can be work related when you're a songwriter, can't it? You know, *Put Me In Coach* and all."

"Okay, your point."

"Point break."

"Whatever. And the title of that song is *Centerfield*."

"Glad you know it. Would you? Go to a game, that is."

"With you, I would, if you wanted." Maybe she shouldn't have admitted that, but she was in deep already, had already said far more to him than she should have.

"Might have to do that, and I'll let you go now. Have a nice relaxing Sunday. You've earned it."

"You, too. Good night." Part of her hated to let him go, and she still didn't know why he'd texted beyond *are you home okay* or why he called after that. He hadn't really said anything. Go to a baseball game? And not even a local game, but the Pirates?

Her grandpa went at times. He'd invited her often. She never found any interest in sitting out on plastic seats surrounded by people she didn't know to watch a game she didn't understand. Throw the ball. Try to hit it. Run. Repeat. Whatever. For three hours or more. She didn't get it.

Still, she told James she would. Because he asked. Because it would be something different. Because ... doing pretty much anything with him sounded okay.

Sixteen

You have a girlfriend, don't you?

Pacing around town, James ran last night's conversation with Isabel through his head. Yes, it should be the girl he was kind of seeing he should call when he just needed to hear someone's voice other than his roommates or his family. He expected Jackie might not speak to him again, though, since it had now been four days since she called and a couple of weeks or so since he'd seen her.

Taking side streets, he stayed away from traffic as much as possible. Many were heading to church, he supposed, like his parents would be about now. He wanted the beach. It was a beautiful morning, the end of August, and summer was passing by fast. Maybe Jackie would go with him. At least it would be a reason to call.

She took her time answering and sounded hurried.

"Hey, sorry I'm late replying..."

"Who is this?"

"James. The guy you've been seeing? Or one of them at least."

"Oh. Now?"

"Why not now?" He stepped over a pothole in the side street and moved into the grass where it was smoother, and while considering why she hadn't jumped him for the *one of them* comment.

"It's Sunday morning."

"Okay?"

"I'm on my way to church."

"Ah. Sorry. I just wondered if you wanted to run to Presque Isle later. Say, elevenish? We can stop at..."

"For what?"

For what? What else did you do on Presque Isle? "To enjoy the beach? We can swim or just..."

"I hate sand and you know I only swim in pools. I have to go."

"Wait. We can..."

"Call me later." She hung up.

She hated sand? He didn't like it in his shoes, but... Okay, she was mad. Fine. Still... Still, he felt no need to see her, and he wouldn't bother calling back. He should go out to his parents' for Sunday dinner since it had been a while and they kept asking. Instead, he found himself calling

Isabel. She picked up right away and he quickly repeated the offer, knowing she might tell him to back off…

"Sounds good. Did you want to meet there?"

"Yeah?" James stopped walking. "No. I can pick you up. No sense in us both driving."

"Okay. Or come here and I'll drive the rest. What time?"

He gave himself enough time to walk back to his place and drive up to hers and suggested it, knowing it could be too early…

"Okay."

Okay? Okay. Just like that. Okay. He had to like a girl who could be spontaneous and almost last minute, even if she didn't like sports or exercise. She did great with canoeing, though, so maybe she only needed better introduction to the right kind of exercise. To build her energy, and strengthen her lungs, her cardio…

And just because she was nice to spend time with.

~ ~

Isabel went out to meet him as soon as he pulled in. Maybe it looked too anxious, but otherwise, he might want to come in, which would be fine, except she had boxes, partially packed, scattered around the living room. She wasn't ready to discuss that with him yet.

He smiled and got out to open and hold her door, told her she looked nice, which made her glad she'd dressed better than usual when she went to the beach but still beach-casual, with a barrette holding back one side of her hair so it wasn't just down and messy-looking. Messy was the planned style and it was okay down, but she thought doing something more with it looked like … she had thought to do something with it.

They mainly talked about songs that came on the radio until he switched over to a CD, one she hadn't heard. He let her know it was a local musician from just over the border in Ohio. J.D. Eicher got some national fame when he did a song for a Nicholas Sparks movie, but he had a large local following even before that. James suggested she listen to the way he put his lyrics and melodies together, being that it had a uniqueness to it, as hers did, and they fit into the same genre.

When he pulled into Sara's, he asked what she thought.

"It's nice. All the same, kind of, but not the same. Which is something I've been thinking about with mine, how to make each song different enough to not get boring, but still mine."

"The big artist conundrum. We all have that thought. I don't think you need to worry, though. You have plenty going on inside your head to create variety. There's a depth to you that comes out in your songs. As long as you have that, you're good. Although, repetition is good, too. People buy the same artists over and over because it's comfort food. So, you do what you need to do and people will follow because it's you."

"You sound sure of that."

"I am sure of that. And speaking of comfort food, lunch is waiting." With a grin, he got out and came around to hold the door she'd opened.

"Does he play around here or only in Ohio?"

"Ohio is around here, Iz. It's like half an hour."

"Okay, but…"

"He does jump over the moat to come this way at times."

"You're making fun of me? Really?"

"Might be. Sorry. No offense intended." He leaned over to kiss her head. "He's been to Foxburg Winery and to Buhl Park recently. I'll check the schedule if you want to go to one. And really, we could jump over the moat, too, and manage to find Ohio. You know, if we can get a couple of passports and read a map."

"You can stop now."

His grin was far too charming. Pals. He'd joked with her about being naked as a *pals* comment. Was kissing her head part of that? Was he so friendly with all of his pals?

She had the fish again while he ate three hot dogs and large fries, and then he drove out onto the island and pulled in next to Perry Monument. "This okay?"

"Of course."

"You know…" He held her door again and leaned against the truck when he closed it. "Maybe you shouldn't be too entirely easy to get along with. You can say so if you'd rather go somewhere else on the isle."

"I could. But I haven't been out here for some time. It's good. Anywhere out here is good."

"Careful, Iz. I might end up asking you to go beach hop with me if you keep being so easy to get along with."

Her first thought was that she couldn't, she had to work. Her next was that he was crazy if he thought she'd just take off with some guy she still barely knew, although she knew him better already than that other one, the one the song was about, since James talked so often and so freely. And then the scariest thought came, that maybe she would, whether or not she should.

"What are you thinking so hard about? Whether you'd accept?" His head tilted. Too entirely charming.

"Yes. I mean yes, that's what I was thinking."

He grinned. "Don't worry. Way too soon. And we have work to do here first." James led the way toward the monument and they walked silently for some time, enjoying the lake air, the view from the edge of the circular grass- and tree-filled area, and finally sat on the raised step circling the Battle of Erie war hero commemorative obelisk.

"I've been thinking about your song." He propped his elbows on his spread legs, his gaze out at the water.

"Which one?"

"Wanted his need of her. Wanted the one thing he left her."

Her gut lurched and she wished she hadn't played it for him. "It's not done. They're just thoughts so far."

"Right. I got that. But..." He shifted, his head again slightly tilted, his gaze directly on her. "Tell me about him. It's not about the guy you were with from back in high school."

"No." Her heart pounded and she wandered over to the water.

He followed. "No, you don't want to talk about him, or no, it's not the same guy?"

"Not the same guy. And ... I don't know. Probably not." She walked and he stayed quietly by her side.

Until she sat on the grass under a tree for the shade from the sun's intense August heat. James crouched beside her rather than sitting. Afraid of grass stains on his tan khaki shorts? She was in denim capris with a tank top in dark blue and a sleeveless loose white shirt, long to mostly cover her backside. It was unbuttoned until her waist, to try to help hide the extra flab on her stomach.

"Okay, so what do you usually do here on the isle when you're not being harassed by a creepy guy who gets too much in your face?"

She grinned. "Sometimes I sit and write. Mostly I walk."

"Just walk?"

"Well, and ... I search for sea glass."

"Sea glass? You mean the broken glass the lake throws back out now and then?"

"Yes. Lake Erie is supposed to be full of sea glass and maybe it is in different areas. I've had some luck west and east of here. But there are too many tourists on the isle who find it early in the season. So..."

"You walk around looking for glass."

"Not just any glass. I don't bother with the clear or white glass. Or brown. If you're really lucky, you can find a cobalt blue that's amazing, but usually it's greens and pale blues and corals."

"What do you do with it?"

"Collect it."

"For?"

She shrugged. "It's beautiful." And when her glass vase was full, she would move on, but he didn't need to know that.

"Okay, so you love everything to do with the water, except swimming. Why? If you're not afraid, why wouldn't you want to be in it?"

"I do. I like to wade in it. Only to my knees."

"Um..?"

"I don't know why. I always hated baths, too, from the beginning. Mom hated bathing me because I screamed every time. Once she started doing showers instead, I was good with that. I'm still that way."

"There has to be some reason."

"I guess. I don't know."

"But you're not afraid of it?"

"No. I took swim lessons because Gramps insisted I know how. Hated it, but I did it. I wasn't afraid; I just didn't like it."

With a nod, he looked out over the lake silently for some time, then pointed out at the horizon. "Look." A large boat headed their direction. "It's the cruise boat. Come on." Taking her hand, James helped her to her feet and kept hold of it while he led her down the little sidewalk leading to the boat dock area. "Let's go for a tour."

"Really?"

"Always wanted to do it, but haven't had anyone willing to go with me." Checking in at the little cabin where they sold tickets, he was nearly giddy tto find two available. "Is this okay? You want to go?"

"It's fine, but I can..."

"My idea. I got it."

~~

In hindsight, James wondered if he should have taken her out on the Lady Kate. She loved it, and he was glad she loved it, but her beauty came through with her excitement and relaxation. It was a business arrangement. He kept telling himself he had to keep it that way, that she had too much unresolved stuff to deal with, and he ... he hadn't even been dry for a year yet. He still had too many lapses where he wanted a drink so strongly, he could almost spit nails when Bruce stopped him.

It wasn't fair to her. He had to take it slow, give himself time.

Even now, while they walked along the beach in a non swimming area where it was quiet, with the sun starting to descend, he could see he had to be careful. She was guarded. And yet, she was needy, and beautiful. The red cast from the sky highlighted her hair and brought out a nice red-brown shade that didn't normally show. She was a true beach girl, well, more a *real* beach girl, more real than all of the showy girls in their bikinis he generally paid attention to more than he should. She belonged there along the water, enjoying the beach for its own sake, for its earthiness...

"Look." She crouched and dug in the sand to pull out a good sized hunk of translucent pastel glass. Light green. "Sea glass."

He accepted it and turned it over in his hand. Part of a Heineken bottle, his guess, but rounded so it was all smooth, and lightened with time. "Okay, I have to admit this is kind of pretty when you look past what it used to be. I'd pick it up if I noticed it." If he found sharp glass, he always picked it up to find somewhere safe to trash it. But rounded like this, it was a different effect. "Guess I just had to stop and notice."

She caught his eyes, with an expression that made his heart beat a little too fast. To keep himself from saying it would look nice in a necklace, that it would go well with her eyes, that she was beautiful in the dusk, beside the water, he focused on the glass, on the feel of it in his hand. "Can I have this?"

"Sure. But be careful. It's becomes an addiction to try to find more once you start keeping it."

He had far worse addictions, but he didn't say so. "I'll take my chances."

With a nod, and those eyes peering in as though wondering if there was hidden meaning behind his words, she lowered onto the sand to watch the sun set, her legs wrapped into a yoga position. James lowered beside her, maybe too close, with an arm propped part behind her.

She didn't complain or move away. She sat quietly, and when the sunset was at its brightest, she started singing. *"Browns and tans and shards, all most ever see, the sea-smoothed edges of what I'm meant to be..."*

"Keep going." He spoke barely loud enough for her to hear him, right next to her ear, afraid to break the spell of music and sunset.

"It's from *Not What I Saw*, the one I was playing yesterday."

"I remember. Go ahead."

"That's all I have. For the chorus, I think. I have trouble writing without working out the music at the same time."

"I'm opposite. Have to write the lyrics out all the way first."

"Yeah, I think that's more normal. That's how Grandma works, too. She also writes the whole thing in her head before she puts anything on paper. Sometimes, she'll have three or four songs in her head before writing them down."

"Serious?"

"Serious." She grinned as she threw his word back at him. A beautiful grin. Alluring. Too alluring. Leaning in, he let his lips meet hers. Barely. Softly. She didn't move into him, but she also didn't move away. A nice kiss. Sweet. Chaste. But nice. And he shouldn't have. "I... I'm sorry. I shouldn't have done that."

She caught his eyes but turned her face back to the fading light.

He was infinitely relieved she didn't make anything of it, for good or for bad. She didn't storm off. She didn't press the issue. She accepted the kiss and accepted his apology. Maybe he shouldn't have apologized, but he was her manager. She was still trying to decide whether to trust him.

When she started singing again, his body gave in to a deep breath and he lay back and closed his eyes. She stopped only for a moment and started again, off and on, changing and rearranging words. A line she sang got to him and he stopped her. "That should be the title."

"What?"

"The Texture of Glass. It's a good line. Pulls people to think. And it fits. Having life smooth you from what you used to be, but still having what you used to be within you somewhere. Right?"

"*Underneath the polish and shine, the texture of glass, is ... is sharp enough to cut and rough enough ... to survive.* Not sure I like that, but yeah, I like the phrase."

"Or... underneath the polish, the texture of glass, still sharp enough to slice and rough enough ... to shine. Right? Because you have to be rough inside to really shine, don't you? It's only those who've been through a lot of fires, or at least one big one, to have it within them to reach others. I mean, to care about reaching others because they know they need to be reached."

"I love that. *Underneath the polish, the texture of glass, still sharp enough to slice and rough enough to shine.*" She nodded. "Much better." She pulled out her notebook and made notes.

His little songbird. She was his artist. His fuel and inspiration. His courage. So often when he thought about finding a drink, he focused on her instead, on her songs, on the way she had given up but kept going with his push, on... on her. Damn, he wished he could play for her, with her. They could be a good duo, he could complement what she was doing well, if he was still able, if he hadn't screwed himself over by being so stupid.

"You okay?"

He opened his eyes to find her turned toward him, searching his face, and he realized his eyes were moist. "Yeah." Getting up, he brushed sand off his shorts and offered a hand to help her up. "It's getting late. Ready to go?"

"Sure. You're driving today. It's your call."

His call? Had he kept her too long? Stopping her by taking her hand, he moved in front of her. "Isabel, you know you can say so if you want to leave. Any time."

"I know. I didn't. I mean, I wasn't in a hurry, but we both have to work tomorrow, so..."

"It's not that late."

"No, I mean... Yes, I'm ready to go if you are."

Maybe he wasn't. But he had to, anyway.

~~

Isabel lay awake far too long thinking about that nothing kiss. It was appreciation for her music, nothing more. She knew it was... Well, maybe it was nothing more. She'd acted like it was nothing. She had to. It surprised her. Overwhelmed her. It flooded her system too much to be able to react appropriately, and she didn't know what appropriate would be. She didn't even know for sure how she felt about it. Her manager. Her impetus to keep moving, to start again, to get back to herself, to her inner being. She needed him to keep being her manager.

She enjoyed her attraction to him because it was no more than that. It was only fun, song-inspiring. She loved the little flutters that stirred at times but didn't turn into more. Isabel didn't want more than that. After it became more than that, it changed. It became hard, complicated, mind numbing...

Her work had suffered while she'd been so hooked to her ex. He took too much time, energy, her inner being... He took too much of what she was away and made her bend to what he wanted. She did not want that again. It was better that he left.

Better.

Rolling over onto her back, she stared up at the ceiling she could barely see through the dark. It was better that he left. It was. She didn't even care anymore. Well, yes. She cared. Maybe. And maybe...

Who needed him? Why had she thought she did?

A surge of relief spread throughout her body and Isabel got up out of bed to pad through her too-empty apartment. Time to make up her mind: get a smaller place nearby or move back to Pittsburgh? Or to Greenville. But that was smaller than she liked, and why did she even..? She knew why. And she knew why she'd suddenly given up caring about him after two years, two long years of such useless grief and missing him, for no good reason.

That kiss was nice, as brief as it was, even as much as he regretted it, and he did. She knew he did. She'd known immediately that he regretted it. Even if he hadn't apologized, she would have known.

Yeah, that wasn't confusing at all.

One song from the CD he played on the way home to get her thoughts kept running through her head. *Not Everybody Runs*. No, she imagined that was true, even if she hadn't found one yet who wouldn't. She hadn't looked, really, either. She'd closed that part of herself off, for protection.

Why had he wanted her thoughts about the album? He'd said that song was his favorite. The same artist also did an acoustic version of *Let It Be* that he loved more than the original, even. Not recorded, he didn't think. Why had he focused on that song? Telling her he could be one who wouldn't run, or that he knew she wasn't sure everybody wouldn't? Or was he looking for someone who wouldn't?

He did not want to open up that much to her yet. It was too obvious. Unless he did and she was missing the signs.

Isabel opened the fridge door and stood there looking for something that would make sense of everything. A ridiculous thought. Not all the chocolate in the world could do that. Although maybe it could make her stop thinking about it and get some sleep so she could work relatively well in the morning. Or...

Closing the door, she went to her laptop, searched the iTunes store, and downloaded the J.D. Eicher album he'd played. Were there other messages in it she had missed? Very possible. Just because, she also bought the rest of his work.

~~

James did his best to act interested in the movie he and his roommates, a couple of their buddies, and a couple of girlfriends, or temp girls, were all watching, loudly, at his place, but it wasn't happening. His thoughts were too distracting. He shouldn't have kissed her, or he should have done it better, at least not brushed it off. Something. Not at all sure what he should have done, he at least knew he hadn't done it right.

They could go on like it didn't happen and she would let him. He knew she would let him.

She was cool. Level-headed. Down to earth. And so very much not his type. He had to keep professional distance. If not, if they started anything else and it fell apart, she'd fire him as her manager, and that, he didn't want more than he didn't want most anything else.

When the noise got too much, he got up, grabbed his keys, and went out the door.

"Hey, where are you headed?" Bruce grabbed his arm.

"Need air."

"Windows are open."

"Still stuffy, and loud."

Bruce stopped him when he tried to pull away. "What's up with you lately, J? You seemed to be coming out of it, doing better. But..."

He shook his head, not wanting to explain yet about Isabel and the way he was starting to feel that he wasn't ready for.

"Come back in. I'll kick everyone out if you need."

"No, it's all good. Just don't want the noise. I'll be back."

"Not happening, bud. I know this look and you've put me through enough. Hold on till I get my shoes. I'm going with you."

He heard the comments from in the hallway, but Bruce told them to eff off in his normal casual way and came back with his shoes on and his keys in hand.

"I only plan to walk."

"Yeah, well, if they all pass out or whatever, I don't want to knock for twenty minutes to get back in." Following down the hall and down the stairs, he waited to talk until they were out in the dark away from anyone who would hear. "Was their drinking getting to you? We can tell Gavin and Davis it's time to find their own place so we keep it out of the apartment."

"No, it's good. Wasn't that." He knew he was walking faster than Bruce liked to walk, but so far he didn't complain.

"Okay. So..."

"Look, it's just ... this girl. Okay? Can we leave it at that? Just trying to figure things out and can't do that with people all over the place."

"You always want people all over the place. Can't stand quiet. Why is this girl changing that?"

"She's not. I am."

"Jackie?"

"No. I think we broke it off."

"You think?"

James shrugged. "It was too cutesy, anyway. James and Jackie. Doesn't work for me."

"You broke it off because of her name?"

"No. Just didn't call back because I didn't feel like it and she gave me a bunch of attitude I don't need. Doesn't matter. Has nothing to do with her."

"Okay, so..." Bruce grabbed his arm and stopped walking. "Your songwriter. It's your songwriter, isn't it?"

Pulling from his friend's grip, he walked farther along the sidewalk, turned off, and went down the hill to the edge of the river. Street lights sparkled in the water's reflection. Now and then a fish or frog broke the surface and created spreading circles.

"Tell me about her." Bruce sat in the grass and tossed a pebble in, creating larger circles.

"She's ... guarded, like ridiculously guarded. But also, she's ... calm, patient, very smart but doesn't see it, seriously earthy and stable..."

"Doesn't sound like anyone you've ever been interested in."

"No."

"Could be a good thing."

"Can't be."

"Why not?" Bruce waited through the silence broken only by a few passing cars and crickets and a dog barking somewhere in the distance. "Does she know?"

Know. That he was an alcoholic. Recovering alcoholic, but barely recovering. "No. Can't tell her."

"Well, then you can't start anything with her. You've gotta be able to trust a girl enough to talk to her about it before you get close to serious. If she's guarded, she's been hurt already..."

"Obviously."

"She's said as much?"

"Not a lot. It's in her music, mostly."

"Well." He stood again. "If you haven't... You haven't slept with her, right?"

"Not even close."

"Good. Give yourself more time, J. Jackie or someone like Jackie who's just looking to go out will work better for you right now."

"Except..." His head shook and he crouched to be closer to the water.

"Except?"

"I think I'm past that kind of thing. Not what I want anymore."

"Good. But still, if you can't tell her, you can't get serious with her."

"Yeah, I got it. Not that she's interested, anyway. I'm helping her out and she appreciates it, but it doesn't mean... And she's seriously not my type. Except she loves water, the beach, didn't exactly agree to beach hop with me in time but didn't say she wouldn't, either. And her music is..."

"Maybe she is your type."

"She's not, but I'm not sure I care that she's not."

"Okay, so, I'm going to have to meet her." Bruce slapped his arm. "Come on. Let's go grab a cola and wait out the noise in the apartment. Tomorrow, call and tell her your best buddy wants to meet her."

"I'm not doing that." He did start back up to the street and let Bruce take him into Steph's Corner where they found a small out-of-the way table and ordered two colas and some wings and watched the game that was on. Cleveland. Lots of Indians fans in the area. You could almost always find one of their games on in a local bar. Whenever he could, he asked to change it to the Pirates. On days he wanted to be a jerk, he said loudly that they were in Pennsylvania, for fuck's sake, not Ohio, so the PA game should be on. But then there were always those who jumped in to throw comments about the team being nothing but a farm team and start in on bitching about the manager and owner and certain players. He wasn't up to it tonight.

By the time they got back to the apartment, the crowd had dispersed and James thanked his friend and went to shower quick before bed.

But he was too bothered to sleep, so he grabbed his phone to send her a text: Hope this doesn't wake you. Just want to be sure we're still cool. Answer when you want, or if you want. Or ignore it. Night. Or morning. Maybe a stupid thing to send, but it was out there. He set the phone down and went to piss and came back to find a new message:

Of course. Night James.

He grinned and got under the covers. She was definitely cool. He'd have to keep it that way.

~~

Isabel considered his text as much as she'd considered the kiss. He sounded vulnerable, very much opposite of the thoughts she had of him. But definitely they were still cool. She was glad, if it worried him, that he would just ask. She did not want him to worry about her. She did not want him to think she was a silly little ninny who would fall apart with a kiss and run, with as nothing as it was, or even if it hadn't been nothing. She was not close to that clingy.

Putting the chocolate ice cream back in the freezer, she grabbed her notebook and her guitar. Reading through what she had, Isabel realized why he would think it was about the long-term ex. …*those early days with you.* It made it sound like a long-term thing. Maybe… those early days *of* you. That gave it a whole different meaning. Early dating days. Young and stupid days. Yes, it needed to be *of* rather than *with*.

And the next stanza… not shaped *by* you. That's where the *with* needed to be. Her life hadn't been shaped by him. He didn't have that much power. Too much, because of the outcome, but not that much. Her early days had been shaped *with* him, with her choices that included him but could have been anyone, really. They were her choices. Her actions. And her parents' actions, but that was partly up to her, as well. She could have left, run off somewhere they wouldn't be able to interfere. Like her grandma had. On her own. She could have. How different would things have turned out?

And I'm not what I was rather than *And it isn't what it was?* As James suggested. *I'm not what I was, not what I saw at the time.*

He was telling her she read herself wrong. She wasn't what she thought. Wasn't… what?

He'd had trouble believing she'd had a short fling. He thought highly of her, more than she did of herself. He'd been telling her that ever since they met. *Rough enough to shine.* An incredible compliment, the way she saw it.

Seventeen

So Im kind of seriously freaking out about the show by now. Suggestions Mr Manager?

James laughed at her text and shook his head. He had to think about her question before he answered. In the meantime, he went to the fridge and not finding what he wanted, and didn't want, both, he poured a large glass of tea and picked up his phone. Starting to tell her to relax, she had nothing to worry about, he knew that sounded like a dismissal of her feelings and deleted it. He paced while trying to decide what to say, what might help calm her without sounding demeaning. Humor. He decided to be funny while taking her nerves seriously: Try counting your vase of sea glass. If sheep work for sleep, pretty glass should work for nerves.

Very funny try again

Deep breaths?

Serious?

LOL okay. I have to admit I have no good tips about nerves.

U never got nervous?

He set the phone down and paced more, swallowing too much tea too fast, and tried to figure out what to say. Hard to be nervous after a few neat scotches while tuning. Or half a dozen beers. Yeah, he knew about nerves, but he wouldn't suggest she drown them the way he had.

He heard the buzz of a new text and hesitated before he looked.

You can say you didnt you know

Starting to answer in a way that would avoid the question and still make an attempt at helping her, he cursed, thought about going out to grab beer, just one, sighed, and called. The hell with the texting thing.

"Hey." Her voice sounded wary. "Did I ask something wrong?"

"No. And hey back. Just thought it would be easier to talk in person, well, in voice, anyway. What exactly are you freaking out about? Not your first rodeo."

"No, but it's ... well, it is, really. I've never had my own show. No one has ever come to listen to me, specifically, and not just whoever shows up, although I guess they'll just be going because they like checking out new acts, right? Not really for me, since they don't know me or my name and maybe no one will actually come since they don't know me or my name. And I'll just be singing to you and people who don't care for two hours. Or the house will be packed and they'll hate my songs or my voice or me or they'll not bother to listen because I'm not much to look at and that matters in entertainment. You know it does, so I don't know whether to hope for an audience or hope for no audience..."

"Whoa. Stop there." James perched on the edge of the couch. "First, some will come because they know your name, since you're up to nearly 60 likes on your page due to my management work, which is more publicist work right now, but anyway, several already said they'd be there. Now, some will follow through and others won't. Still, you will have *your* audience, plus whoever likes to just drop in to check the music or to support the coffee shop. Okay?"

"Yeah, I'm not sure that makes me feel better."

"Well, number two, your songs are good. They would have to be cretins with no music sense at all or no emotional sense whatsoever and it's rare they'd be there if that was true. This isn't Sam's, Isabel. You'll have a decent crowd of decent people, not cretins. I'm not even telling my buddies about it, so there's no chance they'll show up. Except one and he's actually not a cretin like the other two."

"You seriously hang out with cretins?"

"Well, a few of them are. Mostly they only are when they're drinking, which they were the other night. Not an excuse, but anyway, they aren't the coffee shop crowd..."

"And you are. Isn't that odd, to hang out with those so different than you?"

He gritted his teeth and took a long deep breath before he could answer. "Not all that different. Anyway, number three: Isabel, you are worth looking at. You are. You're more worth looking at than, well, to be very frank, those girls I usually would look at and probably chase. You're more worth it because ... because there's so much more inside you and that comes out when you sing. It comes out in your songs and it's beautiful." He made himself stop there. "So relax. You'll be great. Okay?"

Silence came from the other end of the line. "Isabel?"

"Yeah. Thanks. I'll make myself try to believe you."

"Good. Work on that. You have four days to convince yourself you should believe me. And you should, of course, since I'm your manager. If you can't trust your manager, who can you trust?" A faulty line of reasoning and he knew it as soon as he said it. Still...

"Right. Okay. I'm not backing out, in case you're worried. I won't do that to you after all you've done."

She wouldn't do it to him? "Don't do it to *you*. It's not about me. You deserve this."

"Wait. Sixty people? Last I saw it was like twenty something, barely over twenty."

"Yeah. I've added a few more, and by added, I mean pulled them in. Have you checked the hits on your videos?"

"No."

"Maybe you should. Or if it'll make you more nervous, wait a few days. Whichever would help more. Okay? Are you less freaked out now?"

"I think I'm more freaked out now, but I won't cancel on you."

"Good enough. You'll be fine." Standing again, and pacing, because he couldn't sit knowing that was nothing advice and she deserved better, he decided it would be better to talk about it in person. "How about dinner tomorrow? Cracker Barrel? I could use a good chicken fried chicken."

"Oh, that's not fair."

He stopped pacing. "Not fair?"

"I'm trying to be good, healthier, even doing sit ups and pushups and such, and you want to blow it with chicken fried chicken?"

Being good? He hoped it wasn't because of his stupid comments. "They have salads, but you know..."

"Who in their right mind goes to Cracker Barrel for salad?"

Had he screwed up again? He couldn't remember the last time he'd been so fucking nervous around a girl. Possibly, he never had been. "Okay, so ... no dinner tomorrow or you want to pick something else?"

~~

Dinner? He wanted to have dinner in the middle of the week? She wandered her living room, doing circles around the growing pile of moving boxes mostly full. "It's a work night, you know."

"Yeah, but you're still going to eat, right?"

"Don't be a smartass."

"Sorry, my M.O., in case you don't know that already."

Dinner. Just because. As far as she knew, the only Cracker Barrel around was in Meadville, so he'd have to come her way. Of course that meant she'd have to let him into her apartment, since by now it would be fully rude not to let him in. She supposed it would be the easiest way to tell him she was moving. Somewhere. "Cracker Barrel sounds good, actually. I'll count it as my metabolism boost day, since I have been really good for several days, with one ice cream night exception, but I only had a bit, so that was still pretty good for me."

"A bit of ice cream is absolutely necessary at times. I'll pick you up about six?"

"Okay." Why? Was he worried about that kiss the other day? She told him it was fine. They'd texted every night after work about songs and such. It was fine. There had to be a reason he wanted to drive up to Meadville. "Really, James, I won't cancel. You don't have to come up here for my sake."

"Who says I'm doing it for you? See you tomorrow, Iz. Night. Sleep well, please. Fatigue will make it worse."

Not for her? He'd sounded a bit worried, or otherwise off somehow. What was going on with him? Was it too soon to ask? Maybe. But maybe he really wanted her to ask.

Eighteen

He was too early. James considered driving around a while in order to show up at a more decent time rather than thirty minutes early, but he could wait if she wasn't ready. And he didn't feel like driving around. Too anxious. Too full of thoughts wondering if he was a true idiot asking her to dinner for no good reason. She knew he didn't have a good reason. She'd tried to ask why he was asking. He'd said too much. Not for her. It wasn't, really. It was... Hell, he didn't even know why he asked.

Hesitating in front of the white-painted building with cheap red brick balconies, he realized he didn't even know which apartment was hers, other than that she used the ground door on the right rather than on the left. He didn't even know if the ground doors were locked.

Giving it a try, he found it open and stepped in. Small mailboxes lined the wall beside one of the apartment doors. Dillon. Apt 2. Okay, easy enough. Apartment two... The one beside the mailboxes. Ground floor. He would have felt better if she was in an upstairs apartment.

With a deep breath, he tapped on the heavy door with peeling dark green paint to match the dark green and cream-speckled entrance carpet that badly needed cleaning. Silence came from the other side until he heard the click of a deadbolt opening.

"Hey." James stood just outside her door doing his best to look like he had no intention of going inside. "I know, I'm early. Sorry. Ready?"

Isabel looked down at a bleach-stained too-big bright pink T-shirt topping purplish-red sweat pants. "Are you kidding?"

"Well, I figured you could be going grunge, right? Take your time. I'll wait outside." He took a couple of steps backward.

"You can come in. Just don't mind the mess."

"Mess? You mean you're not a neat freak?"

She halted opening the door farther. "You're being funny, right? Do I give the impression I am?"

"I'm not, and you do, kind of."

"Hm, okay." She backed up and let him pass beside her. "Have a seat. I'll just be a couple of minutes."

He was taken aback by the sparseness of her place. There were no photos and no wall hangings on the white walls. The couch was a dark rose color almost brown. A couple of nearly flattened pillows had two different designs in different colors. The curtains were green and brown. Stripes. Plain. The thin carpet was beige and somewhat thread-bare.

Her small square black coffee table held a notebook of some kind, a few picks and a tuner, an empty glass, and a wide candle on a black, flat candle holder that looked like a previously used wall tile. The orange candle, well burned, was circled by a few used matches scattered atop the holder.

He didn't sit when she went to get ready. He was too nervous to sit. Instead, he wandered, not that there was much wandering space. It was a very tiny two bedroom with a tiny kitchen area. The messy stack of papers on the end of the counter island that somewhat blocked the kitchen from the living room took about a third of the otherwise open space. Spice containers sat around the stove, some flipped open. Dishes sat in the strainer.

James had to laugh to himself. She was right. He had to quit assuming. Too often, he was wrong.

Moving over to the front window, he shook his head about the view, or lack of. The overgrown evergreen shrub in front of the building blocked most of what he should have been able to see, not there was much to see other than the street and the buildings across the way. More apartments, he thought, although he hadn't looked closely.

Maybe it would be better if he sat while he waited so it didn't look like he was scoping her place. Except that he was and there was no point in acting like he wasn't. The notebook on the coffee table turned out to be an open planner, and being nosier than he should, he scanned it. Her show date was written big enough to fill the box for Saturday. In red. An appointment of some kind was written in black for next week. Doctor, maybe? But most of his attention was pulled by the green ink. Song notes. Not notes, but ... what she'd worked on each day. Most days were filled up to the current day. He was mentioned in her notes. What they'd done on what day...

Too nosy. He walked away from the planner, toward the black bookcase where not only books were stuffed in, but papers and knick-knacks, all jumbled together.

"Change your mind?"

He turned to find her in a dark gray skirt that stopped above her knees and a loose knit shirt, blue, different shades of blue in an abstract design. "About?"

"My neatness ability."

"Artists are seldom tidy; isn't that what Picasso or someone said?"

"Someone did, probably as an excuse to be lazy. I also told you I was that."

"Yeah, you did. Guess I didn't believe you."

"Good thing this is just business, huh? Because my guess is you *are* a neat freak. And I'm ready as I'm going to be."

Just business? Maybe not quite. There was no business need for them to go to dinner, or to the beach, or canoeing. Or for her to wear a cute skirt that accented her cuteness. He wouldn't say as much. "Well, I guess your assumptions are a bit better than mine. I am. But I'm not an extremist about it. You look nice, Iz."

"I'm glad, and thank you. So do you." She scanned his clothes, just jeans and a polo. Nothing fancy. Still, it made his heart lurch, only a touch, enough to tell himself to knock it off.

She talked much of the way to the restaurant, about her job a bit, a new one because she'd been stupid enough to quit the last one, a long term thing, before she had anything else lined up and had to take what she could to pay the bills, that she would have to find something less boring since she kept thinking about her lyrics in between typing up medical notes and making mistakes she had to fix that slowed her production, but mainly she talked about the show. He expected it was nerves. In general, she'd become more relaxed around him every time they got together, but she was definitely more ramped up tonight. He enjoyed this side of her.

James almost expected her to get a salad since he'd teased her about it, or since she'd teased him – he wasn't real sure which way it was – but she ordered chicken fried chicken with mashed potatoes and sausage gravy with green beans, banana bread rather than rolls, and he dittoed her order, to her raised eyebrows.

"Okay, so you did exactly what I was going to do." He raised his glass of tea in a salute. "Glad you skipped the salad so I don't feel like a pig next to you."

"Except you can afford the calories better than I can."

"Well, you know, the staying active thing helps."

"Being a guy helps, too."

He laughed. "There is that. So far. Won't always work."

"So are you like..." She seemed to not want to ask whatever was on her mind.

"Am I what?"

"Well, ADHD or something? No offense. I have, or used to have, a good friend who was and she never stopped moving. Never. Or talking. And she ate like crazy, but she was super skinny."

"Nah, I'm not. I'm just social. And I have to stay busy or I get bored, and getting bored is a very bad thing for me."

"Why?"

He nearly told her, and it would have been a good opportunity, but he couldn't yet. Bruce telling him he had to keep distance until he told her rang through his head, but he wasn't ready. Maybe he could start leaning into it, though. "Well, I guess I don't want to be accused of being a cretin. Seems to me that if you stay busy enough, productively, you don't have as much chance to do what you shouldn't. Right?"

"Have you been talking to my mom?"

"What?"

"Nothing. Sorry. It just... I heard that a lot when I was young, before Grandpa bought me a guitar to help keep me busy, and it did, so I guess you're right."

James found himself smiling and had to ask. "Don't try to tell me you were a troublemaker. I really see you as the typical good girl always doing what you should be doing and nothing else."

Her eyebrows raised. "You are really, seriously bad at reading people, aren't you?"

"Not generally."

"No? Because almost every assumption you've made about me has been wrong."

"Honestly?"

"I'm very honest. And yes, I got in trouble a lot as a kid. Mostly for sneaking out, but also for not doing my homework or doing it and forgetting to take it in, for hanging with the wrong crowd, as my mother kept saying, which is what I did when I snuck out."

"You were bored at home?"

"I was alone at home. Most of the time, they didn't even know I'd been out after school, and sometimes during school, since they weren't home until after six. Always. The routine never changed, so it was easy to work around."

"How'd they find out?"

"Someone who knew them and saw me out and about called Mom to ask if she knew who I was with."

"The old parents stick together chain. Got plenty of that myself. So, it was a boy you were with? Because that's usually when my parents got a call, if I was hanging out with the 'wrong' girl."

"You did that a lot?"

He gave her a light shrug. "Not a lot, I'd say. Depends on your definition. And generally, we were only hanging out, nothing more. You know how overprotective parents and their friends are, though." He thanked their server for the tea refill and noted her smirk at his comment before she walked away. "Can I say I'm glad to know you snuck out of the house?"

"Why?" She smoothed hair back behind one ear.

"Makes you more human. Less... Well..."

"You think I'm being judgmental about your dating history."

"I didn't say that. I only mean..."

"You wouldn't be the first to think I'm judgmental just because I live pretty clean and plain now, but you'd be wrong about that, too. In case you're wondering. I've done plenty I shouldn't have. I'm still paying for some of it. So, yeah, I imagine you've had a lot of girlfriends and such, and I'm sure you could have been a cretin at times, too, but it's not an accusation. We all have our things, right?"

"Yeah." Clean? Did she mean that the way he hoped she didn't? He studied her face, but she turned it away to look around the room.

When their food came, he changed the subject, although he was still curious about her family life and whoever she was with that someone thought they had to report. The guy in the songs, he supposed.

She'd only eaten half her meal by the time he'd cleaned his plate and he told her not to hurry. But she was done. Full, she said. So he asked their server for a box.

Isabel shook her head. "I don't eat leftovers."

"At all?"

"No. Can't. The idea of it... I can't."

"Interesting." When asked, he said he still wanted the box. "I don't waste food. With four boys in the family, we were taught better. If you don't mind, I'll take it."

"I ate off it."

"I'm not worried." From her expression, James figured he might have grossed her out. Still, chicken fried chicken wasn't something you just tossed out. "Once you nuke it, any germs you might have are going to disappear, right?"

"I don't nuke food. Can't do that, either. I know, I'm odd. It just seems wrong."

"You don't do a microwave at all?"

"No. I use a small pan to heat water for tea and a toaster oven for toast or other small things."

"Okay, then. So your music knowledge isn't the only thing that goes back a few decades." Glad she grinned at the teasing, he argued when she insisted on paying, but he decided to give in rather than offend her. Back in the truck, he wasn't sure what to do next. Take her home, he figured. But just going to dinner and back to her place didn't work. "Feel like finding some music to check out? Maybe we can start moving you into this decade."

"Find it where?" She hooked her seat belt and brushed hair behind her ear again.

"You don't know the best places around here?"

"I know where to find music on weekends, but they mainly only do weekends. I'm usually home on weeknights."

He pulled his phone out to do a search. "Here we go. Interested? If not, so say. I can just take you home."

"No, it sounds like it might be okay."

"Okay? Not fun?"

"We'll see."

~~

Isabel wondered why she hadn't done this more often. She should have been out more, checking out other acts, getting inspired by what they were doing, watching what the audience liked and what they didn't, when they were listening closely or when they only halfway heard it through their chatter.

Of course she wouldn't go by herself, and her roommate, ex roommate, only listened to hard stuff that hurt Isabel's brain. Her ex... They only did what he liked. Heaven forbid she ask him to do anything she wanted to do that didn't interest him. Really, why had she stayed with him so long? Why hadn't she been the one to leave? What an idiot to put up with it for so long and then to mourn his loss for way, way too long.

"Did you hear me at all?"

She looked over at James and nearly hit her nose against his, he was so close to her. "Sorry?"

"Sorry, question mark? Are you not sure you're sorry for ignoring me for ten minutes?"

"Not ten minutes, and I meant sorry as in I didn't hear you."

"I knew what you meant. I'm just not sure why people say that. If they're sorry, why don't they just say sorry instead of sorry question mark?"

"I have no idea." A nice light masculine scent wafted between them. "What did I not hear you say?"

"When did you stop listening?"

"Are you purposely being a smartass?"

He laughed and leaned even closer. "Yes. I do that. One of my things. And I just asked what you were thinking about since you suddenly became so serious."

What was she thinking about? It was hard to remember when he was so close, smelling so nice, his eyes sparkling with humor. "Um, I don't even remember now."

"Serious?"

"Yeah." The ex. "Oh, I do, I guess. Wish I didn't."

"Not good? You want to leave?"

"No. Well, yes and no. I was... Well, I just realized I've been a huge idiot for two years. More than two. A lot of years, actually."

He straightened somewhat. "Don't call yourself names. It's bad for the psyche. And why?"

"Because... Truth is truth. I don't make a habit of it, but we are all idiots at times, right? No harm in acknowledging that. I just realized I should have left the jerk long before he left me and I can't even imagine now why I didn't. I was an idiot. I'm not in general, at least I don't think I am in general, but I was, and I wasted so much time mourning something... It wasn't worth all of that. It was idiotic and..."

He raised his hand to her face, his palm cradling her cheek, fingers on either side of her ear. "I'm glad you realized it. He was the idiot, Isabel, not you. You got some good songs out of the deal, right? You have that. You have the lesson. Move on and don't let it get to you. At least you learned. Some never do. A shame. I've seen too many girls sell themselves out and never figure out the guys they're going through hell for aren't worth it. I hate seeing it."

"Like I did."

"Short term. Don't sweat it. Two years isn't a big deal in the long run. Some never realize what they've done, or are doing to themselves. You're a ton of steps ahead of that."

"How do you know he didn't deserve that much wasted energy?"

"Easy."

The heat from his palm felt like a deep blush, but better. "Why?"

"He walked away from you when you were loyal to him, when you're smart, funny, honest, deep, and ... beautiful inside and out. Definitely makes him an idiot, Iz."

Manager. Just business, Isabel. Stop that thought in its tracks. Slow that heart rate right back down. As she stared at him, listening to the soft smooth voice of another local singer, a singer and guitarist duet doing only covers, a couple, she thought, as she felt the warmth of his hand against her face and the heat of his gaze all the way through her body, James gave her a wink, took his hand down, and added distance, shifting his chair close enough his shoulder touched hers when one or both of them moved just right.

She watched the duo quietly for some time, trying to focus on the sound, the relationship, the way they looked at each other that said they were close in some way, more than just a duo. His body being so close to hers, though, and the coolness on her face where the warmth of his palm had rested so gently, was horribly distracting. *Some never realize what they've done.* She wondered if he had personal experience, if it was why he didn't get close to anyone. It could explain his distance.

Although he didn't seem to want too much distance tonight.

"Thank you." She spoke close to his ear and again nearly bumped into his nose.

"For?" He held her eyes.

"Well." She started to say for thinking the ex wasn't worth her time, but it was for so much more than that. He made her feel ... so much she had never felt, more worthy than she had ever thought she was. Not that she thought she wasn't, but, he was right, she'd...

"For what?"

"For being here." It was the best she could say.

He grinned and gripped her fingers without looking to see where they were. "You, too."

~~

Closing the door behind him after he walked her in and kissed the side of her head, she sensed a horrible silence. An aloneness she'd gotten used to, somewhat, since Libs left, but now... She had to stop. He'd made it clear he didn't get too involved. She wasn't his type. He'd said more than once he wasn't her type. A hint. It was only gratitude, what she felt for him. Immense gratitude, but only that.

At least he'd replaced her nerves about the show with bigger thoughts, bigger concerns. She had to find a way to work with him, to hang out with him, without falling for him and messing things up. He'd think she was jumping from the ex to him just because she finally got over the ex and he was right there and ... and that's all it was.

Except it wasn't and she wasn't anywhere near idiot enough to convince herself it was. She cared for him. Deeply. She hadn't wanted him to leave, and she'd wanted to offer her lips rather than the side of her head, although that was terribly sexy, as well. Comforting. Friendly. Caring. It was a caring gesture, but like a sister. He treated her like a little sister, or like an artist he was managing who needed moral support.

Maybe she could just unpack those boxes she'd moved to what used to be Lisbon's room so he wouldn't see them and ask if he wanted the room. He got sick of so many roommates. He'd said as much. It would make things easier. They could still keep it business only, couldn't they? But of course, he worked in Greenville, so it would be a heck of a drive every day. She could move his way instead. Probably, neither would be a good idea. Considering.

With a sigh, she went in to shower on her way to bed. She had to work in the morning, to go on like her world hadn't just shifted all angles of topsy-turvy.

~~

For the first time in a very long time, James had managed to go to a bar and order a soda, straight, and not have an intense craving to add whiskey. He'd even smelled beer breath on some guy who talked to him too close and all he thought of was that it stunk.

Isabel drank tea all night. Sweetened, advertising her sugar addiction, which he thought was kind of cute, although unhealthy. He'd offered a drink, and she ordered tea. Maybe she didn't drink at all. Maybe she objected to it. He partly hoped that was the case and he wouldn't have to worry about the taste of alcohol on her tongue that would make him want his own.

Not her tongue. Her breath.

He stopped just inside his apartment and shook off the thought. On her breath, he meant. As often as they talked close, he meant... Hell. He meant exactly what he thought. He wanted to taste her lips, her tongue.

Holy hell. He was her manager. She was wary. She deserved better than... But he was getting better. He would keep working at getting better. Until then, it had to stay only...

Or it didn't. Maybe it didn't.

Nineteen

Not freaking out yet, right?

Isabel frowned at his text while she shuffled through her cabinets trying to find something she could eat that wouldn't annoy her stomach. Yes, she was freaked out. She shouldn't have agreed to do her own show. With a fast, deep breath, she made herself answer. Yes but will be there

I know you will. I'm picking you up and getting you there.

No youre not

You think not?

Too much driving

Nah it's fine. I like to drive. Four o'clock?

Shows not till six

I'm bringing a late equivalent of brunch. Up to a celebration dinner after the show?

Isabel tried hard to tell him no, to both, that she would get there on her own and feed herself and ... and that it would be far safer to go home by herself since, if it went well, she'd be hyped up and too likely to show him she was, and if it didn't, she'd be too depressed for him to be around her, especially all the way from Grove City to Meadville. And then he'd think he had to stay until she wasn't, which would be a mistake and… Just no. She had to go by herself.

She started to text three times, saying it differently each time, and kept deleting it. When it rang, she jumped and greeted him cautiously.

"You're trying to tell me no, right?"

"If you always know what I'm thinking, why do I bother to talk at all?"

He chuckled. "Waste of time. I mean to try to tell me no. I'm your manager. It's my job."

"To manage, which you're doing incredibly well. Wow, the numbers on the page are incredible. All friends of yours?" She paced out of the kitchenette and around the moving boxes that she'd been working on instead of her music like she should have been.

"Serious? You think I have that many friends?"

"I think you could very well have."

"I'll take that as a compliment, but no, there are a lot of names I don't recognize. They're watching your videos and following only for that reason. Should get a decent crowd tonight. Don't get nervous about a possible crowd."

"I'm fine with crowds, if they're polite enough."

"Then you'll be fine."

"How can you be so sure?"

A pause came from the other end. "Because if they're not polite, as I said, I'll turn into your bouncer, too. Don't worry."

Good thing he wasn't right there in front of her. Isabel wanted to hug him.

Of course she gave in to let him pick her up, after trying to say she'd at least drive to his place so he wouldn't have to go north and then south and then all the way back up north to Meadville and south again to get home. It was bound to be another late night. At least not a work night this time. He could hang out as late as he wanted. She'd be fine with that.

~~

Beans was jumping already by the time they arrived. The manager greeted them, asked what they wanted to drink, and waved him off when he tried to pay for it.

After getting her set up and staying with her while she tuned, James kissed her head, handed her her guitar, and told her she'd be great. Then he took a chair at the reserved tall table closest to her and leaned back to watch her shine. Every table was full and several people stood around the back of the room. When she introduced herself, he could tell her soft sweetness was charming them the way it did him. They applauded lightly, with smiles, and they quieted when she strummed the first chord, starting with the song from Sam's that had pulled him in.

She looked nervous, but her voice came through beautifully, soft and sweet, and still with enough strength for those in the back to hear well plus enough emotion to make the words ring true. Before the end of the first song, some of the patrons who were lingering around the coffee counter came back to see who was singing, and stayed, moving around behind the tables as well as they could without blocking anyone's view. With his suggestion, she opted to do a tip jar rather than a cover charge, since she was unknown and they wanted people to take a chance. Tips started to come in early, and she gave each person a smile between lyrics whenever someone added to it.

Before she was half through her show, most had given up sitting and the place was standing room only, with management pulling a couple of tables out of the way to make room for a bigger audience. She grinned at him when she saw the tables moved.

At the familiar faces coming in, he got up to greet Bruce and his new girlfriend. "Glad you got here."

"Figured it was time I checked the girl out for you since you've been so obsessed. You should have saved us seats. Wow, look at this."

"Would've been hard to do. Nice, huh?"

"Yeah, and... you're right. She's good."

"Think so now? Give it more time." He saw Isabel notice and gave her a grin.

Never one to miss anything whatsoever, Bruce glanced between them, listened a bit longer, then leaned in, his gaze still on Isabel. You're sure she's twenty-five? She doesn't look it."

"She is. As you get to know her, you'll see that. Shows more in her maturity than in her face."

Brushing off the disbelief, he offered his chair to the girlfriend. For the rest of the show, his attention was split between Isabel and Bruce, watching his reaction, the occasional nods, and getting comments about what songs he especially liked, quietly, where only James could hear him. For being a lawyer, Bruce was pretty music knowledgeable. A long-standing harassment. His buddy had actually learned a fair bit of music theory from James, and in return, Bruce had shared a good bit of legal knowledge. They used to talk about Bruce becoming his legal manager when he hit it big. Maybe he'd do the same for Isabel.

Now and then in between watching, Bruce mentioned his girlfriend's name. Purposely, he expected. Bruce knew he almost always greeted people by their names, so when he didn't, he didn't know it. The fact that Bruce cared that he remember Abby's name told him this one meant something.

The applause at the end of the show was good and when people asked Isabel how to find future shows, she looked over at him and said they should talk to her manager, thanking him publicly for setting up the show and for keeping her going when she had doubts. His chest must have swelled to twice its size at the way she looked at him, because Bruce muttered "business only, my ass" into his ear.

He took her guitar to leave her free to talk with those who wanted to say hello. As soon as the crowd cleared enough, Bruce helped to pack the gear and carry it out to his truck while she talked with Abby and a few fans who lingered. Returning, he threw her guitar case over his own shoulder. He had to brush away the thought that it felt good to carry a guitar.

Just before they left, the owner complimented her and offered to have her back any time. Again, she gave James a smile. Out in the semi-dark of the sidewalk after those telling her good show and so on had left them alone so it was down to just the four of them, he set a hand on her back. Maybe he shouldn't have, since it looked possessive, but in spite of himself, he felt very possessive at this moment. The girl was radiant in the glow of the window and street lights and the successful show.

"Thank you. Again." Her eyes sparkled into his. If she thought he was being possessive, she didn't apparently mind.

"You were great. I enjoyed every minute. Are you hungry?"

"Starving, now that the adrenaline has been pumping all night."

"I always was, too."

"You play?" Abby was holding Bruce's arm, looking as though she had no intention of letting him get away.

James saw the glance from Bruce, wondering if he should interfere. Might as well address it straight on if the girl was going to be hanging around. "I did. Before this." He held up his left hand and moved the fingers that still worked. "Farm equipment mishap."

"Oh, that sucks. It at least could have been your other hand, right?"

"You know something about playing guitar?"

"Well, I tried it. For about two months." Holding up her own hands, Abby shrugged. "Short, fat fingers don't do well with guitar chords. Or piano. I tried that, too. No big deal for me. It was only a hobby, or intended hobby. I hope it wasn't anything serious for you."

"It was, but there are worse things." Suggesting Timber Creek beside the outlets, he invited Bruce and Abby. Always the gentleman, Bruce asked Isabel if she wanted the intrusion and she graciously accepted. James was glad she did. They needed to get to know each other.

On the way, she tried to give him half the tips since he wasn't getting anything out of it, so she said. "Nope. That wasn't the deal."

"But I used your equipment, and your time matters. You should have something to show for the work you put in. Setting it up and…"

"I enjoyed the show. Told you I wanted to hear you play again."

"Okay. Thank you for that, but I mean money-wise…"

"Well, you know, if money was that big an issue, I wouldn't have turned down the promotion I was just offered, so no need to worry. Okay? Told you I'm not taking anything from you while you're getting started. That was our agreement."

"Yes, but… You turned down a promotion?" She said it like he'd just turned over an airplane or something.

"They wanted to lock me in for another two years with it, and I'm not willing to be that tied down. I'm also not in desperate need for money. So yeah, I turned it down." He pulled into the parking lot and watched to see where Bruce was parking. "I don't intend to stay that much longer. When I get to the right place, I'll gladly grab any promotion I can get. Let me get your door."

Setting a hand on her back again when the hostess offered to lead them to a table, he couldn't help a grin when Isabel stopped abruptly in front of the cutout in the floor replaced by thick glass allowing a view of the brewing center below. She studied the big silver vats brewing their house specialties, but she would absolutely not walk over the glass. "Afraid of heights?"

"No."

"It's safe to walk on."

"No thank you." Taking it into her own hands, she swerved to the right and went all the way around it to where the hostess and their friends were waiting.

He held her chair. "So, it's like water? You don't mind being in it, but not too far, and you're not afraid of heights but won't walk over the glass?"

"It's … a trust issue. I guess I don't trust it to hold me up."

Hold her up? "With water, you hold yourself up."

"Yeah, and I can do that, but water is unpredictable. It can swirl without warning and suck you under. Right?"

"Well, in certain places…"

She shrugged. "I don't trust it. Like glass on a floor. Glass is for windows."

"Okay, then." As she sat and he helped push her in, he looked over at several young people, likely college students, at a nearby table drinking heartily and laughing aloud.

"Sure you're okay with this?" Bruce was at his side. "There's a family restaurant down the road that's…"

"I'm good."

"Yeah?"

"Yeah." He hoped Isabel hadn't heard, but the question in her gaze said she had. No surprise. Bruce, even in low voice, wasn't particularly quiet. She didn't ask, though. Again, she ordered iced tea and he did the same. Abby ordered wine and Bruce glanced over to see if he should ask her to change her order, but James gave him a quick light shake of the head. His friend ordered a Dr. Pepper. Idiot. It made Abby ask if she shouldn't be drinking, since no one else was.

"No reason you shouldn't. Get what you want." He felt Isabel's gaze and saw Abby's unasked question. At least Bruce hadn't forewarned his girlfriend. There was that. To change the subject, he focused on Isabel. "So, you know that glass is thick, tempered glass. Safe as the floor. Everyone's walking over it."

"People walk over grates in the road, too. I don't. It just looks too unstable."

Unstable. Like he was. He was about as unstable as she could have found. And she'd only done open mics that already had built-in audiences, never her own show, before tonight. Was it innate or something she'd learned? He guessed it was the latter.

Deciding to think more about that later, he skimmed the menu. "You like fried pickles?"

"I love them. I don't need them, though." She set a hand on her stomach.

That again. The *being good* thing. He had to think it was due to his stupid comments. "This is a celebration for a very successful first show of your own. No calorie counting."

"Yeah? Well, that chocolate dessert is looking really tempting." She nodded toward the card in the middle of the table. "I might skip the meal and do that instead."

"Do both. Just save room and ... I know you don't do leftovers, but I do." He gave her a wink. Of course Bruce raised his eyebrows.

~~

Isabel wanted to ask, but she wouldn't now. *I'm good.* After they both looked over at the kids getting lit. It echoed through her head while the other chattered around her and mixed with *I'm not staying long.* Was he moving, too? Farther than she was? He loved the ocean. He wasn't stuck to his job. He didn't talk about his family hardly. Maybe he was getting ready to pull up roots and go live close to the ocean.

She felt him watching her off and on and allowed him to pull her into the conversation when he tried. But she was focused on trying to figure out what he was "good" about. Loud people in restaurants? She hated that, too, especially in nicer places where people went to relax and enjoy, not get inundated with extra noise. But he was social, so she doubted that was it. It had to be the drinking. Again, at a place that brewed its own beer, he ordered tea. His buddy ordered cola. While watching James. Was that his dark secret? The thought made her shiver.

"Cold?" He'd noticed.

"Oh. No. Just... unwinding, I guess. I'm fine." Actually, she was plenty warm, even with the air conditioning set high enough she often would think it was too cold. Nerves. It was the alcohol. Had to be. Maybe he was only avoiding it for fitness? Not likely. His roommate wouldn't be so worried about it if it was that. He had to be...

She couldn't even say it in her mind. Not her James. Cheating wouldn't be as bad as that, she didn't think. She'd always said as much. Although, the thought of James being with another girl, cheating on her, hurt her stomach every bit as much as...

It wouldn't be cheating. They weren't together.

But she wanted them to be together. She did.

It had to be the alcohol. He'd never ordered an actual drink. Not even a beer at the bar when they went to listen to music. And he changed jobs a lot. The beach hopping could be an excuse. It had to be. Everything added up too much for it to be anything else.

They were all talking about music, about her songs, and she made herself pay attention enough to answer, to participate.

And then she couldn't. They were too far from the door, in a back corner, and he... He was an alcoholic. She knew. He'd tried to hint now and then. She'd tried so hard not to believe it, to hope it was almost anything but that. Why? Why, when she was finally getting ready to move on, to trust, to recover, did it have to be..?

Hardly able to breathe, Isabel used the excuse of going to the ladies' room and she did that but it wasn't good enough so she stepped outside into the dark, the fresh air. Wandering down the sidewalk, she pondered why there was a large log in the planting section between road and parking area and considered how big of a truck it took to get it there. The name. *Timber Creek.* Of course it made sense...

"Isabel?"

She jumped at the voice and turned to James. Holding her position while he came to her, she crossed her arms in front of her stomach. "Sorry. I needed air."

"You okay?"

"Yes, just... Adrenaline wore off, I guess. I'm a little jittery now. I just need a minute. You don't have to stay out here. Go back to your friends."

"Only Bruce is my friend. I barely know his current girl."

"Okay. I'll be back in a minute…"

"I'm not leaving you out here alone. What's up?" He moved closer when she didn't answer. "You heard what he said, about whether I was going to be okay here."

She looked over at a car passing in the dark, too fast for the small road. Trying to hold it together, to not break down in front of him. Really, she wanted to walk away, to refuse to deal with it. Not this, too, on top of everything…

"Okay, so." His voice lowered. He hooked his thumbs into his pockets, making him look far too vulnerable. It made her want to cry. For him, mainly. For what he was dealing with and covering so well. For knowing he had to try to cover it. For… For herself. Even if it was selfish, she wanted to cry for herself.

"I've been trying to figure out how to tell you, in case you haven't figured it out." He moved a touch closer, his head dipped toward hers. Gently. Like he was asking for permission to keep talking. Or asking if she'd figured it out. She couldn't. Couldn't say it. Couldn't talk.

"Before I do, I want you to know you don't have to worry about it. Okay?"

Like hell, she didn't. Gritting her teeth, trying to grit her gut, as well, Isabel met his gaze. "Tell me."

With a deep breath, he nodded lightly. "I'm an alcoholic."

Involuntarily, she stepped back. Away from him. Like she'd done when they met. Her gut hurt. No amount of gritting could stop it. She wanted to cry. She hadn't cried in a lot of years. How many now? No, she had recently, after that man attacked her. The drunk jerk. But not otherwise. Not even when the one guy she'd counted on walked out. She'd learned not to long ago. Because it pissed her father off, made everything worse. So she didn't. Still, she didn't. But this…

James moved in and touched her face, prompting her to meet his eyes. "Isabel, it's under control. I'm recovering. I haven't touched it in months. You don't have to worry about it."

"Your roommate is worried."

"He's a mother hen." Lowering his hand, he shrugged. "Okay. Full truth. I've been an alcoholic for years, and I mean, a lot of years, but I always kept it under control enough no one knew. I didn't even know, to be honest. Until I … went off the deep end for a while. Bruce helped to pull me back, sometimes physically." His chest rose and fell. Hard. "I am recovering. For nearly nine months now. I can't touch it or that recovery part is gone, but I'm good. Okay? Even when I wasn't good, even at my worst, I wasn't violent. I would never hurt you, if you're worried about that. Never did hurt anyone else. Only myself."

Her head spun. *A lot of years.* She wanted to sit. "Yourself?"

He held up his left hand. "Wouldn't have happened if I hadn't been ... way too out of it. Just ... had trouble adjusting, when I um..."

Her eyes watered, but she had to know. "Tell me. Please."

"How about after dinner? Okay? Give this time to process and we'll talk afterward." He offered a hand, looking as though he thought she might walk away right then.

Accepting it, she realized he'd offered his left hand. A test? Fine. She squeezed his palm lightly and saw his head tilt to look at her but she kept her focus ahead. Just get through dinner and let it process. That's all. Later, they could deal with the rest. *She* could deal with it. Or not. At least she had a choice this time.

Silently, they went back across the driveway to the sidewalk. But she stopped there. Her gut churned and she focused on crickets off in the trees in between the swoosh of tires on pavement.

"What are you thinking?" He stood on the drive beside the high sidewalk, still grasping her hand with his two good fingers. Finger and thumb. Whatever he thought about how useless the hand was now, it wasn't. He had a lot of strength in the one finger and thumb, enough he'd be able to hold her tight if he decided to. The hold was gentle, comforting, not threatening. Still, it came to mind that he could be threatening if he decided to be. "Isabel?"

She had to turn to see him, better able to see his eyes with the extra height from standing up on the curb. "Honestly?"

"Of course. We're pals. Pals are honest with each other."

Pals. Her heart pounded and she swallowed hard. "It scares the hell out of me."

He looked surprised for a moment. "Okay. Understood. But like I said, I've never hurt anyone because I was drunk. I wouldn't hurt anyone, drunk or not, other than to protect those I love, even those I don't know, if they need it. I won't hurt you. Okay? It's not something I do."

"There's more than one way to hurt someone, James. It doesn't have to be physical." She could barely breathe. He didn't understand...

"Granted. But, if I screw up as your manager, you can walk away and find someone else. We have no contract. No binder. And you don't have to see me, or take my calls, if I do screw up and you decide you're done. So there's no real risk here, right?"

No risk? Moisture filled her eyes and she walked away, away from him, away from the main building, away from people heading in or out, along the edge of the curb, toward the trees. No real risk? Who was he kidding?

"Food'll be ready soon, Iz. Can we go in? We'll talk more later." He was walking along beside her, still down on the pavement.

Go in and eat. Sure. Why not? As though her world wasn't crashing around her again. With a nod, she brushed the light moisture from under her eyes and turned to head to the door.

"Isabel." Before they got far, he took her hand again, stopping her. "You're not okay with this. I can take you home if you'd rather." His voice was soft, concerned.

Her heart hurt and she took a hugely deep breath and held it until her lungs burned. The way she'd learned to control tears way back when. Then she exhaled slowly and turned to him. He was still down on the road, lessening their height difference, making it easy to see the question in his beautiful, concerned, wary eyes.

And she couldn't stop herself, because it was a big deal, it *was* a big risk on her part. To show him it was, she met his lips.

Expecting him to pull away as fast as when he'd kissed her, she froze when he didn't pull away, when he pressed in gently, accepting. Tingles ran through her tense body and made her shiver. He did pull softly away at that, leaving her wanting far more and trying to catch her breath. "Should I apologize now?" It was barely more than a whisper, since she was barely able to speak.

"Fuck no, and I shouldn't have, either. I'm sorry for that." He returned to her, strengthening the kiss, his arms slipping around her back, pulling her in against him. Strong arms, so warm and soft around her already warm body. Heated from deep within, from the way she felt about him coming out every pore. Her arms went up around his shoulders of their own accord, closing her body against his as though drawn by a force she couldn't resist. Her senses exploded in warmth, excitement … passion. He was bringing far too much out of her, and when he released her, she rested her head on his shoulder, letting herself calm down and yet still revel in the feel of him, in the feel of longing for him. It was a nice kiss. So … so everything.

"Okay. So. Maybe a little bit of a risk." His voice was soft.

She gripped him tighter, clenching her eyes.

He kissed the side of her head. "I guess you'll have to decide whether it'll be worth it." A thumb, his left thumb, caressed her spine. "Isabel, look at me."

Biting her lip, she raised her head.

Holding her eyes, he stroked fingers alongside her face, back behind her ear. "Would you rather get the food to go so we can talk alone? Bruce will understand."

"No."

"You're not afraid of me now?"

"No." Releasing him, she took his hand. His left hand. "But I very badly need that dessert and it's going to be best warm." Glad he laughed, she accepted when he replaced his hand with his arm.

~~

James could hardly eat thinking about the kiss, about her reaction. Scared the hell out of her. Not that he blamed her. It scared him enough, the thought he wouldn't be able to hang onto the recovery part, that something would trigger him and he'd have to start all over. Her leaving him could do it. Already, he knew it could. Still, he was willing to take the chance. He only hoped she would be, and that she'd be strong enough to deal with his struggle. That, he wasn't at all sure about.

She got along decently with Bruce, although she was a bit wary, likely because of the way Bruce was studying her so intently. James tried to nudge him to tell him to knock it the hell off, but it didn't work. She hesitated about ordering the chocolate brownie sundae, so he ordered it, and he nearly laughed at her expression when she so obviously enjoyed it. There was something so beautiful about a girl who could enjoy the good things in life with such gusto.

And that kiss. That kiss was fucking amazing. Maybe because his senses weren't constantly dulled anymore or something, but that kiss was beyond any other he remembered.

Bruce grabbed both checks declaring it was his celebratory gift. James didn't figure he was talking about the show, but he didn't say as much. His friend read him too well. He even walked his date to his car and came over to the truck as James closed the door behind Isabel. "So okay, no more bullshit about only business, if you don't mind. I can see better than that."

"Yeah, well, it's evolved a bit tonight."

"Uh huh. Just tonight?" When James refused an answer, his friend shrugged. "This one could be a keeper. I like her. But be careful and don't push her too fast. The girl's unsure of you still, and…"

"Yep, I know that already. Both. But thanks. For dinner, too, although you didn't have to do that."

"Good to see you doing so well. Hell of a relief on my part, you know. Just hang on to the *I'm good* thing, alright?"

"I'm damned sure going to try. Don't want to scare her more than she already is."

"You told her."

"Yeah. After she figured it out and walked off."

"What'd she say?"

"She said it scares the hell out of her."

"Well, I can't blame her on that one. And it's good she was honest about it. Just don't make her have to worry, okay? Show her you're worth it, because you are."

James gave him a hug, told his friend he'd be home late, and made sure he got in his own car okay. Then he rubbed his face, felt the slight stubble starting to grow back already, and got in behind the wheel.

He studied her a moment, as she silently watched him, and raised a hand to the side of her soft, round face. "Thank you. For not bailing on dinner. I would have understood, but I'm glad you didn't."

"So tell me now. How under control is it? Honestly? How did you know… I mean, sometimes it's just … habit, not really a full addiction, from what I've heard…"

"It's not just habit. And I still have urges. I still have to fight against it. When things go wrong, the first thing I want to do is grab a drink. But it has been nine months since I've given in. I am recovering, not recovered. They don't technically count it as recovered until it's been a year, so yeah, you might want to remember that, too."

"You're getting help."

"Had to commit myself to a center for a couple of months to get it out of my system and deal with the withdrawal stuff. Now it's just AA meetings. Not so often anymore. I have someone who checks up on me."

"You think you're going to beat it? Long term?"

"I sure as hell hope so. I've never given up easily. Guess I'll have that in my favor."

She was silent a moment while watching passing headlights. "How did you know? I mean..."

"That it wasn't just a habit?" At her nod, he grabbed a deep breath. She had to know the whole story if she was going to be able to trust him. "I told myself for years that it was habit, just a want, not a need. Then several years ago, I joined the Army. It was kind of a dare from a buddy who was signing up. My best friend, since we were kids. I don't remember a time before we were friends, and a lot of it was based on pushing each other. He wanted me to sign up with him, and I laughed it off at first, but he kept at me and… well, it is kind of a family thing and it felt right one day, so I went with him and signed my name. We got stationed together, by request, and both ended up in the same unit in Afghanistan.

"The drinking didn't start because of that, as people have assumed. It was there already, but like I said, it was controlled so it just looked like I was hanging out with the guys and going a bit too far now and then. I passed all my PT tests and everything, so no warnings were set off. They didn't see that I started wandering farther away than I was supposed to so I could drink by myself, or that I was hiding it in water bottles, or that I often passed out rather than falling asleep. I'd already become top notch at hiding it before I joined."

With another deep breath and a shake of the head, he forced himself to continue. "But out there, with everything I saw, it got so I couldn't sleep without the heavy whiskey at the end of the day, and then I started doing it during breakfast as well as sneaking it during the work day, with plenty of breath mints to cover it, and it just multiplied to the point I couldn't function without it. So when my enlistment was up, I came home instead of reupping. Denton, my buddy, gave me a whole wrath of shit about not staying, about abandoning him, but he hadn't even figured out what I was doing, and I knew it had to stop before my body shut down. I figured I'd be fine once I was home.

"Turns out being out in the field on Dad's farm by myself for hours at a time, even though it's a long way from all of that, wasn't a good idea. I should have just said I couldn't, should have told someone, but I've never in my life admitted to being unable to handle anything myself. So I started taking gin out to work with me, in water bottles, and…" He raised his hand.

"Losing the fingers threw me in deeper for a long time, since I lost music, and I didn't care how much it showed. Bruce figured it out when I started getting the shakes because I was on meds for the pain and couldn't do both, so I stopped the meds and went out for booze and he jumped me for it and I ... went off about needing it. I could see he knew right then.

"My family tried to help, tried to never leave me alone. It was hell on them for a long time, because I kept brushing them off and finding ways to get it. Finally, Dad drove me to rehab and told me to go sign myself in. He hated doing it, but it was life or death by that point. I'll always regret what I put them through, and I think of that whenever I'm tempted. I'm doing good by now, Iz. I am. I never want to put my family through that again, never want to see that look in Dad's eyes again. Not something I'll forget."

She was silent, swallowing hard, watching car lights cut through the dark. When she shuddered, he took her hand, gently, watching her. And then she leaned over the center con, slid her other hand around his head, and pulled him in for a soft, quick kiss. "Don't give in to it again, James. You deserve better."

"Glad you think so, and I'll do my damnedest. Promise."

"Call me if you need to talk. Any time. Wake me up if you need to. If…"

"Thank you." He kissed her nose. "For not jumping out of the truck and running the other direction."

"Thank you for telling me."

Brushing her lips, gently, teasing, he felt his body heave a relaxed sigh. "Guess I should get you home. It's getting late."

"I don't care."

"No?"

"No." It was a soft whisper next to his ear and she trailed her lips from his ear to his lips. After a bit of teasing, she allowed him to slip his tongue inside her mouth. She tasted of rich chocolate and sweet tea and lusciousness. He wanted it to last far longer than he expected she'd allow.

~~

Isabel shifted, moving closer; her hand lowered to his neck, slid down to his chest. The feelings she'd hidden for so long, fought off as though they didn't matter, burst through, and she clung to him as though she was the one who needed to be rescued. She didn't. She was fine. She'd gotten out...

He broke the kiss and caught her eyes in the dim light of the parking lot. "Okay, let's ... slow this down a bit."

Slow down? She was being too aggressive. "I'm sorry. I just..."

"No, Iz. Don't be." He stroked the side of her face, back behind her ear. Watching her. Studying, really.

"I'm not needy, James. Okay? I'm not."

"I think maybe you are, but it's fine. Don't apologize. And don't worry. I won't take advantage of that like some would, maybe ... as some have?"

She couldn't honestly refute that. But it wasn't... "Okay, I get it. Maybe I was, but I'm not. That's not what this is about. I just... I don't want to lose you." She heard her own whisper as it came out and wished she hadn't said it. It sounded desperate, and she wasn't. She absolutely was not. She meant she couldn't lose him to his addiction. She meant he had too much going for him to give in to it, to lose who he was. She meant she needed his friendship, his guidance. She meant so much more than she could make herself say.

"Iz." He ran his fingers down her shoulder, her arm, to her hand, gripping it lightly, his focus on their hands entwined. "You want to know who it was who most helped me deal with not having my music? You asked once who inspired me, pushed me to where I should be, to do what I should do as much as I still can, as I've tried to do for you."

"Bruce?"

With a light grin, he kissed her forehead. "For starters, yes. He was the one who realized I had a problem I couldn't control and he helped pull me from it, told my family so they could get me the help I needed, and he's been right there doing his best to keep me straight. But it was only somewhat working. And then the night I saw you sing..." His head shook and his chest rose and fell hard. "I was about to leave by myself and find somewhere to go where Bruce wouldn't stop me. I was nearly out the door when I was drawn back by your voice. Not your voice by itself, but ... by you."

She shivered and he raised her hand to kiss her palm. The feel of it, the security of it, flooded her body with warmth. Her palm. Not the back of her hand. He'd kissed her palm. It was so very intimate, so much it made her eyes water.

"It was you, Isabel. Even during those two months it took to try to find you when it was driving me crazy that I couldn't find you, whenever I had the urge I couldn't shake, I'd grab Bruce and we'd go workout or walk around town and I'd think of your face, your voice, your words, and force myself to leave the alcohol alone. And I got back into music, back to listening, studying. Back to the urge to do something with it rather than let it sit and smolder and drive me crazy. It was you."

Her gut wrenched and she pulled back with a shake of the head. "You shouldn't have told me that." Her eyes watered. "I'm here, okay, but I don't want that kind of responsibility. What if..."

"It's not your responsibility, Isabel. It's mine. No matter what."

She couldn't respond, could hardly breathe. Too much too soon. A war vet. Years of drinking. Rehab. Too much. "Take me home, please."

"Look, don't take that too seriously, okay? I only meant you were an inspiration, nothing more. It's not your responsibility."

"James. Please. I can't. I'm not needy, but I'm not all that stable yet, either, and I can't... Please. Take me home."

~~

He nodded although he figured she didn't see it. She was turned to look out the window. James bitched at himself as he pulled out of the parking lot. Too soon. He'd known better, but it just came out.

They were silent all the way back to Meadville, with the radio breaking the tension, not well enough. He kept running words through his head to try to explain, to not scare her, or to un-scare her if possible. It was too much for one night. He should have waited. Patience wasn't close to one of his strong points, though.

When he pulled in front of her building, he expected she might jump out and run, but she didn't move, so he took a chance and turned off the truck. "Isabel?"

She brushed fingers under her eyes and turned to him. "I'm sorry."

Sorry? A lump formed in his throat. "Don't do this. Don't give up on this. We can take it slow..."

"I mean ... James..." A tear ran down her cheek.

"Don't, Iz. It's okay. I'm good. I'm not looking for a savior. It's my job to do it myself. Just ... be my pal." He wanted more than that, but he'd take what he could get until she could trust him. "If you can't do this, whatever we just started tonight, I get it. Serious. Just ... let's at least keep this music thing going, okay? Can you still do that? Because I don't want you to give up on it. You have real talent and you can't give up..."

She swiveled in the seat, struggling against the seat belt and then unhooking it, and moved closer, as much as possible with the center con between them. Her fingers smoothed back through his hair, pulling him in, and she pressed her lips hard against his.

He could feel her tears on his cheeks and the desperation in her kiss. He'd known better. He'd known she wasn't ready to deal with his shit. A stupid mistake. He had to keep it more casual. When she released his lips, he held her as close as he could. "Don't cry. It's okay. I'm good, Iz. I promise I won't be a burden on you..."

"You don't understand." She pulled back to brush moisture from her face. "I'm..."

"It's okay."

"No, it's not okay. You..." Her head shook and she took his hand. "I'll be here. Screw my little freak out, my fear of it. It doesn't matter. Just remember to call if you need. I don't care if it's three a.m. I don't care if you call three times a night in the middle of the night. Just call me. Okay? I want you to be okay, James. I very much want you to be okay. And it has nothing at all to do with my music."

Something about her words, her tears, triggered a notion in his brain. She knew too much. It scared her for a reason. It wouldn't do this to most people. Most people didn't really get it. They'd say a casual hey, sorry bud but it's cool and all or something similar and then move along to something else. She knew too much about it to be affected this deeply.

Rubbing his chin, he pulled a fast food napkin from his center con where he always kept the ones he didn't use, generally pulling them out to check the oil and such, and offered it to her. He wasn't used to girls crying. He didn't date girls who tended to cry, not more than once.

But she got it. He nearly didn't want to ask why, but it was major important. He had to know if they were going to move forward. "You have experience with this. Someone drinking."

She nodded, swallowed hard, trying hard not to cry. She was at least trying not to. There was that.

"Who?" At her silence, he claimed her hand. "Your turn. Tell me."

"My father. It was one of the reasons I got out as soon as I could, and I don't like to be there. He only does it at home. No one knows outside the family. So yes, I understand about how you can hide it so people don't know."

"Did he hurt you? Your mother?"

"Not on purpose. He ... knocked into me or knocked me over a few times when he was so out of it, he didn't know what he was doing, but never purposely. It was more... Like I said, pain isn't always physical."

Fuck. No wonder she was scared. He rubbed his chin again. He should back off, let her be. At least until he was more sure of himself. The girl didn't need his shit on top of everything she'd dealt with already. How much? He had to know. Smoothing his thumb over her jaw, he urged her eyes back to his. "Isabel, I want to understand. I want to know what you've already been through."

Her head nodded slightly, her jaw tensed. Then she grabbed a fast breath. "He ... used to yell at Mom that it was her fault, that she drove him crazy. I grew up hearing it. He would call her names, in front of me, and she would just stand there and take it. I finally realized she didn't care what he thought and didn't let it get to her. When he figured that out, too, he started doing it to me instead, blaming, name calling. Criticizing. He criticized me for everything: the way I dressed, what I said, what I did or didn't do. He jumped on every little thing, any little noise he didn't like, which was never the same thing twice. He would rant and throw things. Never his own things. Mom's, or sometimes mine if I forgot and left anything outside my room. Mom kept saying to act like it didn't matter, to not let it get to me, but I've never had her strength, and it did. It did matter."

"Of course it did. He's your father."

She sniffed and grabbed another fast breath. "He only did it when he got drunk. Not otherwise. He was a decent man when he was sober, but he just wouldn't stop. He said it kept him sane. I could never figure that one out since it actually turned him into a crazy person. But I ... don't react well to criticism. That night at Sam's... I am touchy. I'm not as strong as Mom. It gets to me, even if I tell myself it shouldn't."

"Understandable. And I'm truly sorry you had to deal with that. Also for what I've said when I didn't get it." She was going to have a hell of a time making it in the music business if she couldn't brush off criticism. Maybe he could help her learn to ignore it, help her realize how worthy she was so she could ignore it. If he could stay clean. "Iz, I want you to promise me that if I am ever stupid enough to do the same, if I get overly critical or make you feel uncomfortable in any way, you'll walk away and stop taking my calls."

"James..."

"I mean it. I never want to hurt you. If I treat you that way, I don't deserve you. Not that I do, anyway..."

"I don't want to lose you. And I mean ... I don't intend to lose you. Okay? I mean I want to help you stay on track, and I'll do what I can. So call me. Lean on me when you need. That's kind of what pals are for, right? Don't let my little freak out scare you. I can deal with it. I can. And I want to be here for you the way you have been for me."

His own eyes moistened at the intensity in her face, her voice. Maybe it wasn't too soon. Maybe he was underestimating her. Maybe she was far stronger than she thought, even stronger than her mother. Likely, she was far stronger than her mother. He'd have to try to help her see that. "Okay, then. I have something for you. Let me turn the lights on so you can see it."

"Or come in."

Into her apartment? Alone. "You don't have to invite me in. It's okay if you want me to just walk you to your door."

"Come in, James. It's fine." She got out of the truck and was at the apartment door by the time he closed and locked his doors.

He wasn't at all sure he should step foot inside after such a huge night, after so much emotional stuff. And her kisses that turned him on far too far. But he couldn't quite refuse and he brushed lightly against her body while she unlocked her apartment door, gratified that she didn't pull back.

Isabel switched the light on and he looked over at stacks of boxes piled on top of each other. Moving boxes. His gut twisted.

She dropped her keys and bag on a little entrance table and noticed where his focus was. "Oh. I kind of forgot..."

"You're leaving?"

"Moving back to Pittsburgh. I told you I was."

"Yes, but..."

"You'll have to let me drive up to meet you after I move since it's farther."

He caught her hand. "Why?"

"I told you. It's too expensive by myself and I can't just bring some girl in I don't really know. I can't do it. Besides, there are more opportunities there, for singing gigs. If I'm going to do this..."

"You just started a new job."

"Which I hate. I'm giving them notice on Monday. In two weeks, my grandparents are coming to help me move."

Pittsburgh. It was too far. An hour and a half each way, depending what part. Even if he did like to drive, it was too far for too many visits.

"We can meet in New Castle, kind of halfway in between, not bad for either of us." Obviously, she was better at reading him than he was at reading her.

He wandered over to the boxes as though he could make them disappear. If she moved, he'd lose her. It was too far. He'd never be able to hold her interest well enough for that. Now that she'd done her own show, had such a great reaction, a good start..."

She rubbed a hand up his back, slowly.

No, he couldn't lose her now. "Don't move. Or..." He thought fast, desperate to change her mind. "Move to Erie since you like it so much."

"It's the beach I like, not the city, and it's nearly as far from you."

"Half as far if you figure in Pittsburgh traffic, and you could stay a bit south. Edinburo's a nice little place with a lake. I've thought of that myself..."

"I don't have family to stay with in Erie or Edinboro."

"Then..." He almost said he'd move in with her, into her second room, but it was too pushy and too much after everything and far too soon. For several reasons.

"I'll make it work. And the phone still works no matter where I am." She slid soft fingers up his arm to his shoulder. "I have to do this. For myself. I feel stuck in Meadville, like I'm drowning."

That one, he understood. He used to feel that way about Greenville when his family was living there, before they moved to Mercer and surrounding towns. Before he'd been away and had a chance to miss it. Forcing a deep breath, he nodded. "Then you should." He kissed her forehead. "Will your grandparents be okay with me visiting?"

"They'll have to be." She slid an arm around his neck. "Is it really odd that I feel this comfortable with you already?"

"I guess comfortable is something, anyway." He grinned, teasing.

"Maybe more than comfortable, too, but I like comfortable. That's a really hard thing for me to find."

"I know, Iz. I'm glad you are." With any luck, he wouldn't screw that up. "So." Still holding the little box, he opened it and took the necklace out to hand to her.

She studied the pendant made of sea glass with music notes dangling underneath like a chime. "This is the piece I found the other day, after the boat tour."

"Yes. Hoped you'd remember."

"How..."

"Gavin, one of my roommates, is a whiz with jewelry. Works at a shop, kind of a funky little custom shop. I told him what I wanted and he made it for me. It's a congratulations gift, for making yourself pick up and keep going when it was so hard for you, and for a successful first show."

Her eyes watered. "This is magnificent. It's gorgeous." She put it around her neck and clasped it behind her head. "Thank you."

He kissed her gently and held her until he felt his body react too much. Pulling back, he kissed her forehead where it was safer. "You're welcome, but it's late, so I'm going to get out of here." Before he lost too much control, he went to the door.

She came to him and wrapped her arms around his shoulders. "Stay a bit. I have iced tea, but I can make hot tea if you want that."

"No beer in the house?"

"No..." She pulled back. "No."

"I'm teasing, Iz. Thank you, but it's nearly one a.m."

"You work tomorrow?"

"No, but..."

"Neither do I. Will you get too tired to drive?"

"Possibly." Although that wasn't the big problem.

"I have an extra room." She kissed him. Too long. Too deep.

He pulled her in close to his body and they made their way to her couch and somehow she ended up lying nearly on top of him cuddled into his chest and it was the most beautiful feeling in the world. She was needy. The girl was most definitely needy, and the idea of it was also too much of a turn on. That's what he'd been looking for: someone who very much needed him. Her song... *she wanted her need of him...* Right. Well. Sometimes it worked both ways and maybe it should. Maybe that was a good thing.

They lay there for some time until she grew heavier as though she was falling asleep, so he coaxed her up to sitting and kissed her head. "I'm not sure how safe it'll be to stay. I should go."

"I won't go into your room. Promise."

"I wasn't worried about that."

"Me, either." She stroked his face. "I trust you. Stay. I'll make breakfast. I'm really good at breakfast."

"You're really good at a lot of things."

Isabel held his eyes a good long while. "Thank you. Not something I've heard much in my life, other than from my grandpa, and people say he's a little nuts."

"I think they're probably wrong."

She grinned and gave him a light kiss.

Twenty

"You're right." James got up to gather the breakfast dishes and kissed Isabel on the head. Her hair was still damp and smelled of an herbal shampoo. "You're good at breakfast. Thank you."

"You're very welcome." She took the dishes from his hands. "I'll get this."

"You cooked. Least I can do is help you clean up." He couldn't keep himself from rubbing his arm against hers while they worked together or touching her fingers when she handed him dishes to put back in the cabinet. She caught his eyes now and then in return.

They'd stayed up far too late, until nearly three a.m., just talking, snuggling some, and now and then a bit more than that. But he fully respected her boundaries that were easy enough to see and gave her a soft kiss at her bedroom door. She'd offered to move stuff out of the way and off the bed in the spare room, but it was too much trouble, so he accepted a pillow and blanket and crashed on the couch.

By the time she'd come out, he'd been lying there awake for nearly an hour, thinking. Some of his thoughts were about venue possibilities, and about recording some of her work to send out farther. Mostly, they kept returning to the big one: was she strong enough to deal with it if he relapsed, or would she walk? Not that he intended to relapse. He did not intend to relapse. But there were no guarantees. Ever. About anything. Life happened and you had to learn to roll with it.

She offered more hot tea since she didn't have coffee or a coffee maker, but he wasn't a fan of hot tea. He was barely okay with iced tea. He needed coffee, and he'd already teased her about it. Pouring more hot water into her mug to add with the tea bag she'd already used, she came up in front of him where he leaned back against the counter. "Do you have plans today?"

He smoothed fingers along her hair. "I don't know. Do we?"

The light brown eyes glistened. "Do I get to have you all day?"

He grinned, unable to help himself.

"Ooookay. Not what I meant."

With a chuckle, he pulled her in and kissed her nose. She had an awfully cute short nose. "I can be yours all day if you want. Something you have in mind to do?"

"Nothing in particular."

"What would you do if I wasn't here?"

"Pack."

He felt a deep sigh run all the way through his body and she looked up at him.

"It's only Pittsburgh. Not that far. Not across the country or any-thing."

"With your family, so I can't exactly stay in your second room, or on your couch. Not that I planned to make that a routine thing. I'm not assuming. I only meant..."

"I'll only be with them temporarily until I can get my own place."

"Right." Which he figured would be a few months minimum, but maybe she'd come stay at his place now and then. "Anyway, I'll help if you want."

"Or we could find something much more fun to do and I'll pack after work at night when you're back home."

"Yeah? Sounds good. What do you do around here if you want to be out and about?"

~~

She saw his surprise when she suggested walking the nature trail that was just across town, but he was all for it, after stopping at Wal-Mart for a T-shirt so he wouldn't have to hike in the button shirt he'd worn the night before with his jeans and tennis shoes. He'd taken everything off except his jeans to sleep and she'd come out to find him with the blanket only covering the middle of his torso, leaving his chest bare.

He was definitely well built and very much in shape, and when he changed shirts in the parking lot, she could see he was tanned all the way to just above the top of his jeans where there was a lighter streak of skin. His swim trunks sat a touch higher than his jeans, she expected.

Not only did he look far more fit than she was, he had to slow down for her more than once while they walked Ernst Trail. Technically, it was a bike trail, but Isabel didn't have a bike, had never ridden a bike, and she liked the slow pace of walking, which was far slower than he was used to, apparently. "Sorry. I should have warned you I don't walk fast. Is it annoying?"

"Not at all." He slipped his arm around her back. "We're not in a hurry. It's just habit." With a quick kiss, he took her hand instead.

By the time they reached the covered bridge, Isabel could feel the burn in her legs. She needed to walk more. Once she moved, she'd start walking along the river path again. She missed doing that. She missed a lot about living in Pitt. He would like it, too, if he gave it a chance. And he didn't want to stay in his job forever. Maybe he could come her way. Maybe she could start him thinking about it. "Do you like German food?"

"Hungry already?"

"No. I used to walk all the time, before I moved up here and got lazy. My favorite place to walk in Pittsburgh is along the river. They've built it up recently, and there's a gorgeous walking trail, so I hear. I haven't been on it yet. But there's an incredible German restaurant at the Waterworks..."

"Hofbrauhaus?"

"Yes." The thought of it made her yearn for a schnitzel with polka playing in the background and the river breeze blowing on her face while she watched tugboats and tour boats. "You've been there."

He was silent while they made their way underneath the covered bridge and he hesitated in its dappled light. "Yeah, I've been there."

"You don't like it?"

"Couldn't say about the food." His gaze was on the rafters, on a bird building a nest, flitting back and forth.

"You went to a restaurant and didn't eat?"

"They have good beer. Stronger than American beer. Takes less to feel the effects. Got kicked out of there once, and rightly so. Damn was I sick the next day, even with the ridiculously high tolerance I'd built up. No idea how I got home, to be honest."

Her eyes tried to water at the thought of what kind of danger he could have been in. "Oh. I didn't even..."

"Do you drink at all, Isabel?"

"No."

"Never?"

"I've tried it. Barely. Not otherwise."

"Because of your father?"

"Well, partly. I can't say I enjoyed it, and the smell makes me sick if it gets too strong. Could be from smelling it and then seeing what it does. Mental, maybe. I'm not sure. I just don't."

"But you can handle being with people who do?"

"If they don't get stupid." Her face warmed. "Sorry."

He smoothed a strand of hair back from her face. "No problem. It is stupid to get stupid with it. I'll never disagree. But I wouldn't mind trying the food there if they'll let me back in. Always smells good."

"They should if you're not..."

"Yeah, I imagine. It has been a while, more than a year."

"And you'll be okay with being there?"

"I can't avoid everything from the past. Avoidance doesn't let you heal and move forward." His hand cupped the back of her head and he held her eyes. A message.

She knew avoidance wasn't healing, but then sometimes avoidance was the best you could do until you healed enough first. "So, after I move, you can come walk with me along the river and we can get a nice schnitzel afterward. Yeah?"

"Sounds like a plan." He leaned toward her, offering or asking.

She met his lips and he drew her body in against his. Maybe she didn't want to move farther from him. She loved the all weekend hanging out thing. She loved the occasional week night get-togethers. He wouldn't do that if she was an hour and a half away. He definitely wouldn't be able to stay over at her grandparents' house. It would be some time before she could afford her own place in the city, which would be even harder than the tiny place she had now.

Maybe she could find a roommate and stay, or... Or she could move closer to him. "So, um." She slid her hands back down his shoulders to his chest. "What kind of apartment availabilities are there in Greenville? Any idea?"

He tilted his head. "Serious?"

"Maybe."

He was quiet for some time until his chest rose hard and fell. "Iz, don't change your plans for me. I don't want you to do that. We'll work around it."

"Will we? How long before it becomes more hassle to you than it's worth? Because..."

"It won't."

"No? Are you sure?"

"Yeah. Besides, you'll still be just as easy to harass by text." With a wink, he took her hand and continued down the trail.

~~

James kicked himself for blowing his chance to keep her closer, but he couldn't do it. He couldn't push her to be who she was and to keep going on her path and then turn around and become a road block. However much he wished she would stay close.

Or he could move.

He could. If he changed jobs again. He could do that, since he'd turned that promotion down, and since he wasn't in love with his work. But he didn't mind it, either, and he was trying to build up time since he had so much job jumping in his work history already that it was hard to get someone to trust him to stay long enough to be worth hiring him.

Still, he could. If he found something there first, or close to there. Cranberry or Butler would work. Denny had a ritzy place in Wexford, so he'd still have someone nearby if needed. He couldn't afford Wexford, himself, and Bruce wouldn't move that far from his job in Greenville, where he was known by everyone. And liked by everyone, the asshole. Good thing, really. Turned out well for James more than once since so many local authorities knew him as Bruce's buddy. Still, it was annoying at times. And yet he wasn't ready to move that far away from his biggest support. Denny was his least-close brother. Often, they only tolerated each other. Not a great option for a fall back.

Truth was, it was too soon to make that big of an adjustment. This thing with Isabel was bound to throw him enough for a while.

She'd made more chicken salad and packed another picnic lunch for their trail walk and they sat on a bench overlooking French Creek while they ate. When she was done, she pulled out a small notepad and started writing something. She was on his right and the notepad was on her right, so he couldn't read what she wrote and he didn't want to disturb her thoughts, so he looked out over the water and thought about putting a boat out there with a fishing pole with Isabel and her guitar working while he fished.

How long had it been since he'd bothered to get a fishing license? Far too long if he couldn't remember.

Leaning forward, elbows on his knees, he thought about his young days that felt so far away by now. Being the second youngest of four boys, rowdy small town farm boys, he'd learned fast and well how to put up a good resistance to heckling and minor pummeling. It hadn't taken long to give as good as he got, all in fun and fair brotherly play. He'd worked hard days on the farm, rested little during harvest season and still kept running full steam, to include football and basketball, and a couple of seasons of baseball until he decided it wasn't for him.

And his music. Through it all, as tired as he was, he always ended his days playing, even if only one song.

He'd taken the thing with him to Afghanistan, soothing himself and his buddies by playing tunes from home while they sang along. They didn't care at all that he couldn't sing half as well as he could play, not even a quarter as well. It was home comfort. He'd come home without a scratch on his guitar or on himself, physically.

When Isabel said her father hadn't hurt her physically, but did mentally, he understood. Some would brush that off as not so important since it didn't show on the outside, but he knew better. What he saw, he couldn't just erase. Nothing he'd done to himself physically, except for the hand, could come close to touching the mental scars. His mom had warned him, had cried when he said he was going to Afghanistan, although she wasn't a crier, either. Hardly ever had he seen her cry. The day that prompted his father to push him into rehab was another time. No amount of apology would erase the disappointment in her eyes. Damn, that had hurt even if he was still part drunk. He still didn't remember shooting at the baler with his dad's shotgun, but even drunk, his aim had been good. Got the wires and the working mechanisms. Denny said he could have at least shot up the side of the thing, instead, so it'd still work. Felix complimented him on not hitting the brand new tractor attached to it. Burt said he was just glad nothing ricocheted and came back at him. His father had said nothing until the next morning, just locked his guns up. But his mom...

A fish jumped and left circular ripples in its wake. Catfish, possibly. Bottom feeders. They'd eat anything and they were ugly creatures. Made good eating, though. Someday he'd go to a good clean lake or stream, camp out, fish, and eat them fresh from the water after cooking them over open flame. Out west. Montana, maybe. And someday, he'd have a little house beside a beautiful body of water, not necessarily big, but beautiful. And sparse, neat. Without a lot of frillery.

She'd asked if he was a clean freak. He couldn't tell her yet that he hadn't been before, that it was all the stuff he saw, the garbage just dumped here and there, dead animal carcasses left to rot along roads after they starved or got hit, trash thrown in ditches and left uncovered, locals shitting in holes or pots and wiping it with their hand, which was why they offered only their left hand to shake, the cleaner hand. He never shook anyone's hand anymore without thinking of it, and he washed his own just as soon as possible when he couldn't get out of accepting someone's handshake. Too many men he'd seen in the States didn't even wash their hands after they pissed. Fucking disgusting. He assumed some women didn't, either, although he had to hope the number was far lower. He hated handshakes, no matter how social he was. But to actually wipe with your hand…

His solace through all of it other than his guitar had been to keep every bit of his gear cleaner than demanded, and himself as well as possible. When a shower wasn't an option, he used a water bottle or two or three to clean the sand and sweat from his body. Twice a day when he could. Wasn't always possible, but when it was…

A sudden pressure on his shoulder made him jump up, off the bench. Regaining his bearings as he realized it was Isabel, his heart slowed somewhat back to normal. "Sorry."

"No, it's my fault. I didn't mean to startle you. Are you okay?"

"Yeah. Ready to walk more?"

"How about looking at this first?" She held out the notepad.

He wanted to walk, to help his nerves ease, but he couldn't resist her. He also didn't sit. Taking it, he wandered while he read, not just once, but three times. She'd finished *Not What I Saw*, a title he wasn't sure fit.

Now I'm looking at my tomorrows, the days far beyond you/ and the clouds are shifting hues, adding brightness to the blues…

It was okay, but not… "What about the clouds are shifting shades instead of hues, so it's not quite so many rhymes?"

"You don't like the rhymes?"

"I do, but not three together."

"Let me see." She took the notebook, wrote something, and handed it back. "Agreed. It's nice alliteration." She'd crossed out *hues* and written *shades* above it.

"Also, and I may be pushing my job description, here, but I think you could change the title."

"To?"

"The Texture of Glass. The song is about you, not what you saw, which puts more emphasis on him. And it's not really about him, is it? It's about you."

She nodded, thinking. "Both."

He lowered next to her, needing the closer connections. "Not really, Iz. It's… and I mean the song, not the relationship, since that's way out of my place to say, but the song is about his effect on you, which still makes it about you. And I love that line. The texture of glass, since it's kind of an oxymoron, or at least it feels that way. Like water. It has texture, but it doesn't. Does that make sense?"

"Sure. Like something so natural you just take it for granted too much to think about the actual properties of it. Glass suggests sharp or see-through but that's only..."

"Outward appearance. And there's more. Like your sea glass. It says more to you than a broken bottle."

"It says ... beautiful things can come from common things, and broken things can still be beautiful and worth..."

"Worth hanging onto."

"Yeah."

James sifted fingers through her hair, his useless fingers and the one good one. "You're definitely worth hanging onto, Isabel. I only hope that I can and that I can deserve to." Before she could answer, he handed the notebook back. "Is there music in your head to go with this? I know there is. I can nearly hear it in the lyrics."

"What do you hear? Sing it for me."

"As I told you, I can't sing, not well enough to do this justice, but I hear it."

"I want to know what you hear, James. Yes, I do have music with it, but I don't want to show you until I hear what you hear."

"And how do you expect me to do that?"

"Write it if you won't sing it."

"I only write with my guitar and ... well, that's not going to happen."

"You'll figure it out." She pushed the notebook into the bag she always carried. "In the meantime, I'll work it onto paper and we can compare notes later. I'll email you the lyrics." Standing, she moved in front of him, between his legs, and wrapped her arms around his neck. "Now I'm ready to walk again."

"Yeah, well." He pulled her down onto his leg. "In a minute. Or two, or three."

~~

Isabel overheard him telling Bruce over the phone that he was fine, everything was good, and he could stop being a mother hen. He looked up at her from the couch when she returned with chips and sour cream and onion dip, told his friend he'd be in late, and hung up, dropping his phone on the table. "He's seriously worse than my family."

"It's nice."

"I guess. Did the salad not last well enough?"

"It didn't, and it is nice. Libs hasn't checked in on me even once since she moved out. Okay, once. We did get together once. Still."

"Your family?"

"Gramps has called a couple of times."

"So, does he know about your show? Your videos?"

"No. Haven't gotten that far." With a shrug, she opened the bag and pulled out a tortilla chip. "Not about you, either. Guess I'm not ready for that whole conversation."

"Don't think he'd approve of me?"

"Oh. I hadn't thought about that, actually. Probably he would, other than, well..."

"The recovering thing."

"Yeah. With my father... He'd worry. He's the one who helped me get away from it, argued with Mom, insisted, really."

He slid a hand through her hair. "Tell me about it."

"No. You don't..."

"I do." Setting the chips and dip on the table, he moved in close. "You need to talk about it, and I need to know better where you're coming from."

"I told you..."

"Barely. Talk to me, Iz."

She gave in to his look, the way he touched her face, the kiss to her head. So she let him know that she couldn't ever have a friend over out of fear he'd embarrass her and scare the friend, that her mother told her she should be more cooperative and not bother him so much, so he wouldn't get annoyed so often, that she begged her mother to leave him so they could both be away from it and her mother was horrified by the request, said it was her job to help him as much as she could and Isabel's job to help her, not make things harder, that she was often awake far too late into the night because he was ranting and thumping around and blasting the television with loud action-filled screaming girls movies. She told him a couple of her teachers constantly asked if everything was okay at home and she always lied and said it was because it was humiliating enough to be asked and her mother would have thrown her out, she suspected, if she'd told the truth, which might not have been a bad thing.

"She wouldn't actually have thrown you out."

"She threatened to. I always thought it was only a threat, but I'm not sure. She did much worse than that, so she might have."

"She did what?"

Isabel shook her head. She couldn't talk about that yet.

"Okay. Enough for tonight. Want to find a movie to watch while we eat this whole bag of chips?" He retrieved them from the table.

"You plan to stay that late?"

"If you're not ready to kick me out."

"I'm not. And we can. But I only want a few."

"Well, we'll see how it goes." He handed her the dip.

"You're not exactly helping my diet, you know."

His chest rose and fell and he tilted his head to look at her directly. "I think maybe you're doing that because of me, and you shouldn't. You're perfect as you are, and I don't want my workout comments earlier to be taken wrong. I only meant…"

"I know I'm too out of shape. I know it would be better for my vocals to have better airflow. I'm not offended."

"Good. That's all I meant, about the vocals." He ran fingers along her face. "You are beautiful, you know."

"I'm not, but thank you."

Instead of arguing, which he looked about to do, he kissed her. Moving the chips and dip back to the table, he returned to her lips, gathered her into his arms, and leaned her backward, against the pillow he'd used the night before.

She clung to him, reveling in his warmth and strength and masculine outdoorsy scent and longing. Badly wanting to ask him to take her to her room and stay all night, Isabel resisted the thought. Too soon. Too much risk. Way too much risk. She couldn't count on him staying. If they went that far, she would want him to stay; she'd want forever.

He'd promised her nothing, other than to call if he needed to talk. Not nearly good enough. "Mm, James."

"I know." He kissed her neck and she nearly changed her mind.

"You know what?"

"Movie. We need to find a movie."

"Right."

"Hm." He teased her mouth, then caught her eyes. "Right." It was a question, whether or not he said it that way.

"I can't do this yet. Not that far."

"I know." His thumb stroked her eyebrow. "Not asking you to."

"It feels like you are." Her body sure as heck felt like he was, and it was nearly begging her to give in to him.

His chest rose and fell and he sat up, helping her up beside him. "Too soon for that." He kissed her head. "So, what kind of movie should I look for?"

Twenty-one

"Shit." James woke to his phone alarm scaring the hell out of him, in an unfamiliar place. Not unfamiliar. Isabel's place. Her guest room where he'd stayed so he could sleep in his shorts instead of in his jeans again. He had to pull himself up, go home to shower, and get to work.

Sitting at the edge of the bed, he rubbed his hands over his face and wished he could call off. There wouldn't be much point in it, though, since she had to work, also. She was putting her two week notice in. He had her this close only for two more weeks and then her grandparents would be there with a rented truck to pick up her things to store in their garage until she had a place for them and she'd be gone. To Pittsburgh. An hour and a half away.

More than two hours from Lake Erie, by the posted speed limit.

The rivers were nice enough, but they weren't the lake. There was no beach in the city, only river banks and cement walks along a thin shoreline, with one of the riverboats going by at times along with the little motor boats and such that buzzed around on nice days, especially on game days for the Pirates when they'd congregate around the water at PNC park waiting for a rare ball to fly out of the park into the Allegheny. Didn't happen much, especially with the new roster.

If he moved to Pitt or Cranberry, it would be easier to get to games. There would be that, he supposed. Especially if he found a place with city transportation and he could hop a bus rather than driving and dealing with the traffic. That wouldn't be a bad thing. Maybe they could share a place, one with two rooms. Might be a hell of a lot more than she was ready for, though. Even with two rooms and using both. He wasn't sure how long that would last. He'd had a hard time not pushing to stay with her the night before.

She hadn't dated in two years. James had to wonder if she hadn't done anything else that usually went along with dating in two years, either. A good chance, he supposed.

Scratching the scruffiness on his chin, he sighed, got up, and pulled into his jeans. When he went in to buy a shirt the morning before, she'd picked up a small coffeepot and small thing of coffee. For entertaining, she said. She'd set the coffee on a timer so it would be ready by the time he said he'd need to get up. She even set out a travel mug to let him borrow.

The girl had thought of nearly everything.

Everything except how hard it would be to walk out the door knowing she was asleep in her room.

While he poured the coffee into the mug, James considered going in to tell her good morning and enjoy the sight of her sleeping body waking to his touch and looking up at him with sleepy eyes. He supposed he wouldn't. Too much privacy invasion for so early in their relationship.

"Morning." Her voice startled him and she apologized while her hands slid around his sides to his stomach, her head resting between his shoulder blades. Such a sensual feeling. He didn't remember the last time he'd been hugged from behind.

"Morning, Iz." He set his arms over hers. "Did I wake you? I tried not to."

"No, I set my alarm. Would you have slipped out without saying you were leaving?"

"I was just debating which I should do. Wasn't sure I should go into your room."

"You could have, but I figured you wouldn't."

"Yeah? So if we have a repeat performance in the future, I'll just come in to say bye so you don't have to get up." He turned in her arms and stroked the hair alongside her face. "I do have to get going. Hope you'll go back to sleep."

"I probably won't, but it doesn't matter." She released him slowly, her fingers lingering on his skin.

James couldn't help but chuckle at what she was wearing. A large red T-shirt with the red M&M character smirking on the front hung to her thighs over pajama pants covered in the M&M figures. "You look ... um, edible. Is that safe to say?"

"I'm not much into fashion. I am into M&Ms. Too often. Sorry, coach, I'm not likely to give that up."

He slid his fingers into her hair and cupped her cheek with his palm. "Your chocolate habit is kind of cute. I'll look the other way on that one. So are these pajamas." He bent to meet her lips, quickly. And moved away. "Guess I should grab my stuff and get on the road." On the way out her door, he claimed her hand and planted a soft kiss on her palm.

~~

Two minutes into his lunch break, he grinned at the Jack and the Bones song that signaled her text. He hadn't admitted he did some searching after Isabel mentioned her *The Voice* contestant obsession and found the duo featuring Taylor John Williams and *American Idol* contestant Amelia Hammer Harris. Their *Hole In My Head* worked well for her ringtone, maybe too well. He'd had to do some finagling to get the thing on his phone, but he got it there.

Sitting away from his coworkers with the chicken salad she'd sent along so he wouldn't have to find something for lunch, he opened the message.

Home and unmplyd. Decided they didnt need me 2 more weeks. Want to meet in Grnvlle wn ur off?

"Shit." A coworker walking past asked if everything was okay. "Yeah. Thanks." Except it meant she might move earlier. He would, in the same position. She was nearly packed and would likely spend the rest of the day doing more of it. With a sigh, he called her.

"Hey, you didn't have to call. You should be eating."

She sounded up enough. He hoped that was a good thing. "I am. Loving this chicken salad. Thanks again."

"No need. I'm glad you are."

"You okay with getting canned today?"

"I wasn't canned. I quit."

"Okay, but I mean..."

"Yep, I'm fine. So? Are you tired of me or can we walk or something tonight? I can be there pretty much any time."

"I'm not at all tired of you. Actually, I'm wondering if this is going to change your moving date." Silence filtered through. "Iz?"

"Yeah, probably. I need the rest of the week to pack and clean the place thoroughly, but..."

His gut churned. A few more days instead of two weeks. Not good enough. "Your rent is paid through the month, right? So give me the two weeks you'd planned. Can you do that?" He stood and paced.

"Sure. Not that it'll make much difference, but okay. I won't have to try to change the rental truck reservation that way, so... Where should we meet tonight and what time?"

Relief spread through his system. He wanted those two weeks. He very much needed that time to get used to the idea, to figure out how to make it work easier than he was afraid it would be. "How about just coming to my place?"

"With your dozen roommates there?"

"Three doesn't equal a dozen, Iz."

"Maybe."

"Well, that could be fair, but I'll convince Gavin and Davis to go crash someone else's place for the evening, so just Bruce and his girlfriend tonight. That okay?"

"Sure. How do I find it?"

~~

James kicked back on the couch and enjoyed listening to Isabel give Bruce a run for his money. The girl had a sharp wit he hadn't seen much of yet, and it amused him like crazy. He was fairly sure she'd even be able to handle his brothers. One of these days, he'd give that a try, after they had more time together, after things were more certain.

But his roommate, his most important roommate, approved. It showed all over Bruce's face, along with the way he laughed when she came back at him for outrageous comments. James had started to tell his buddy to back off and behave, but she handled it fine.

Abby laughed along with them, or shook her head. She was more earthy than most girls Bruce dated, fairly quiet, but friendly when spoken to. James was fine with her and Isabel chatted with her well.

When Davis came home, too early, and obviously lit, he took a look at Isabel and tilted his head. "Aren't you that singer?"

"Isabel Dillon, Davis McGraw, one of the two cretins who owes you an apology for hassling you at Sam's."

Davis shrugged. "They expect that. Isn't that right? It's part of the entertainment." Going to grab a beer from the fridge, he came back, stood too close, and popped it open. "So you're the one keeping him too busy to hang with us."

Getting up, Bruce moved to Isabel's other side and asked if anyone needed a refill.

"Here." Davis pushed his beer at James. "Your girl want one, too?"

Bruce pushed him back. "Knock it off or I'll knock you out myself."

"He can handle himself. No need to defend him like you're his bitch."

James stepped in to grab Bruce before he did knock him out. "Let's go find somewhere else to be while he sleeps this off."

"Sleep, hell. I'll knock it out of him. More effective." Bruce shoved their roommate's shoulder when he pressed in, pushing the beer again.

"You didn't do that to me."

"You weren't this obnoxious."

"Yeah, I was. And you know it." Separating them enough to be sure they didn't jump into another fist fight, James offered Isabel a hand. "Interested in finding music?"

"Of course." She kept an eye on the guy now laughing to himself in between making comments about James not being any fun anymore.

Warning Davis not to make a mess he didn't want to clean up, he grabbed his keys and steered everyone else out the door. "Sorry about that. Didn't expect him back so soon."

Isabel took his arm. "Why does he do that to you?"

"He's an ass." Bruce interrupted. "We gotta get him out of here. Seriously, J, it's not worth it."

"Where's he going to go?"

"Who gives a rat's ass? He's been baiting you the whole time, making it impossible..."

"Obviously it wasn't impossible. I'm good, bud. Really." He slipped his arm around Isabel and explained that Davis was between jobs, looking, but had a hard time keeping them since he never showed up on time, and he hoped to reel him in the way Bruce had for him.

"He's not an alcoholic, though, J. He's just a self-centered ass. Huge difference. He'll go two weeks without thinking about it and then get pissed just for the excuse to be an ass. You can't fix that."

James shrugged. "Maybe. But I can't kick a man out with nowhere else to go."

"I sure as hell could."

~~

Isabel tended to agree with Bruce, and she'd wanted to punch Davis every bit as much as Bruce wanted to punch him. However, she understood James's view, as well. If not for her family, she would be fairly desperate by now, also, or stuck bringing a stranger in to help with expenses, which would also be desperation. So she understood, but still, when someone was helping you and you stabbed them in the back, not once but consistently, you were asking to get thrown out. And probably, you should be, just for the lesson of it.

Since it was a weeknight, finding local live music nearby didn't happen and Abby didn't want to go far on a work night. She was a guidance counselor at the local middle school and tended to avoid places in town that might not look good to parents, although obviously they were there themselves if they saw her, so they ended up at Fresh Grounds for coffee and chai tea.

It was a nice atmosphere. Open. Friendly. With a pretty brick wall and a fireplace. Bookshelf cubes decorated each side. Accent walls were painted the colors of cinnamon and lemon. After ordering, they settled around a low table with easy chairs on one side and a couch on the other and James set a half dozen brownies in the middle.

Isabel gave him a teasing scornful look. "You realize I don't need this kind of encouragement, right?"

"You call it encouragement. I call it bribery. Whatever works."

Bruce rolled his eyes at his friend. "Oh for pete's sake, it's just Pittsburgh. What happens when her songs get big and she has to go out to L.A. for a few weeks at a time, or move there?"

He ran his fingers along the back of her neck. "Well, then I guess I get to see the beaches on the west coast. About time I did. I keep saying I will, since I have the east coast pretty well covered by now."

"You'd go with me?" She knew she shouldn't put him on the spot, shouldn't ask, shouldn't hope to presume, but she did hope he might go with her if she ever got that far, which at this point was ridiculously laughable to even consider.

"I should hope so. I am your manager, after all."

"Is that why?" Bruce laughed.

James set an arm around her with his fingers brushing her shoulder. "Whatever works."

"Well, in that case, maybe I actually could. I've been wondering if I'd have the nerve to go if needed. I'm not sure I do."

"Of course you could." He kissed her head. "But I would absolutely want to go with you."

Her body tensed and a shiver ran from underneath his warm arm all the way down her spine. As much as she hated public affection of most any kind, she didn't shy away from a light kiss. It felt like a test, or a show of possession. A statement.

"So how do you feel about moving to the west coast?" Bruce's voice pulled her a bit farther from James. He sounded half amused and half serious. He was asking Abby.

She gave him a shrug. "I'm up to moving. Pretty much anywhere."

"Yeah? Figured you wouldn't want to leave your job."

"Well, that's the good thing about my career. I can do it anywhere, since there are schools everywhere. I would have gone already if I had an opportunity."

"How about to Pittsburgh?" Isabel felt James's stare, but she was kidding, maybe. Maybe she wasn't. "I'm going to need a roommate in a couple of months or so..."

"Wow, I'd love to."

The men couldn't figure out whether to stare at each other or at their dates and Isabel nearly laughed at their heads turning. She grinned at Abby. "They're both trying to figure out whether or not we're serious."

"Oh. You weren't? Sorry..."

"Maybe I was. I will need a roommate when I'm ready to get a place, and I have trouble finding anyone I can deal with so closely."

She nodded and sipped her cappuccino. "I know what you mean. So many freaky girls out there, or vain or silly or so full of themselves I don't know how they walk a straight line while checking their mirrors and taking selfies right and left." Abby rolled her eyes in nearly exact imitation of Bruce. "Or don't-touch-anything-I-own neat freak types where you can't even relax in your own place. Oh, are you a neat freak?"

James chuckled and Isabel glanced over at him. "I think he just answered you. Clean, yes, freaky about it, no. If dishes and clothes stay washed and food isn't left on the table, I'm good."

"Right, the important stuff. No smelly mess. I have a horrible nesting habit, as my mom calls it. My area is always piled up with stuff I'm doing. No food remnants, just papers and thread and colored pencils... I'm kind of into the coloring craze and I have a ton of different kinds of pencils, gel pens, markers. Do you do it at all?"

"No." Isabel took a swallow of her tea and considered what she might be getting into. "But from what I hear, it's relaxing."

"It is. I use it at school for kids too restless to listen calmly. I give them coloring sheets and different drawing tools and let their teachers know they are to use them during lectures and such because it really helps to keep their brains activated and attentive rather than wandering around thinking about other things more interesting, and let's face it, most of us were not interested in most school lectures. But it's helped quite a few of them. I'm getting good results..." She suddenly quieted. "Sorry, I get carried away with the subject."

"No, that is interesting." Isabel wouldn't mind having one of those pages at the moment to keep her hands busy. "Actually, I might have done better in school if I had a counselor like you."

"Didn't you?" Bruce tilted his head curiously. "I mean, do well in school? I have trouble believing you wouldn't."

"Why?"

"You seem, well, attentive, studious. I figured you were one of the, excuse the expression, nerdy kids who got all As."

She turned to James. "That's really how I come off?"

"You already know that's what I thought. But Bruce is kind of calling the kettle black, since he was definitely a school nerd."

"Don't tell her that. I have Abby convinced I was a bad boy and had all the girls chasing me."

James chuckled. "Half right. Don't let him fool you. He was a straight A homework always done early nerd boy, who also loved a good party and had girls all over him."

"Now that, I believe." Abby grinned at her date. "Not had. Still has. Even when we're out together, they flirt with him. Good thing I'm not a jealous type."

"Yeah, yeah." Bruce grabbed a second brownie and turned focus back to her. "You weren't the typical good girl straight A student?"

"Not close. I drove my mother nuts with my grades. Not that I couldn't do the work. I could. It was easy enough, but I can't tell you how often I was in detention for not doing my schoolwork, for not listening in class, for doodling all over anything I could find."

"You were bored." Abby studied her as though Isabel was a child she was guiding.

"Part bored. Part disinterested. Much of what I doodled were lyrics, some mine but mostly from songs I liked, plus music scales and notes and such. Much of it, though, was ... rebellion, really."

"Against?" Bruce again, studying her worse than Abby was.

"Well, my home situation for one. Mainly, I wanted to go into music and nothing else mattered, but Mom kept saying I was too smart for that. There's a whole big history I won't go into, but anyway, I figured if I did bad at school stuff, she'd have to agree with me. It was a stupid idea, and by now I know it was. I just cheated myself, but kids are stupid overall, really. Most of them."

Abby grinned. "Well, most kids think of themselves as bigger and more mature than they are, and that can come off as..."

"Stupid."

"Sometimes, but don't quote me on that."

Conversation turned to Abby and her work at the school and it turned out she was one of those nerdy straight A kids who tutored others because she understood them and understood how to reach them, and Isabel thought Abby might be the first nerdy kid she actually really liked. Not exactly true. She liked them fine. She just didn't have enough common ground with them to really get where they were coming from.

When Abby excused herself to go to the restroom and Bruce stepped to the counter for a coffee refill, James leaned in. "You know, she might be willing to move into an apartment here in town with you. If you were seriously considering it. Seems like someone you could probably get along with, right?"

"Maybe. It's really short notice, though."

"You could go on to your grandparents' place and think about it from there, come up on weekends and get to know her better." His eyes held hers, looking very much like he wished they were alone.

"But I have to find another job, so..."

"Or let me set up more shows for you and spend the time working solely on your music for a while, if your grandparents won't be in a rush for you to leave. I'm not pushing. I just..."

"Yes, you are." At his look, the debate of how to answer in his face, she grasped his fingers. "But it's okay. I'm glad it matters."

"It matters." His thumb caressed her hand.

Her gut tightened and she wished every bit as much as he looked like he did that they were alone. "So, how about coming to my place tomorrow night? Bring them if you want. I'll make dinner."

"I don't know; alone time sounds good, too."

She badly wanted to kiss him. "They can drive separately and leave earlier. And you can..."

"Stay?"

"Yeah, if you want." She saw the question in his eyes. "In the other room. Just so there's no confusion."

He threw a big fake sigh at her and grinned with a squeeze to her fingers. "That'll be hard to do when you have a roommate again."

"I have a couch."

"And if Abby moves in with you and she invites Bruce to stay over at times? You're going to be okay with that?"

Isabel saw Abby start to head over, notice them talking quiet and close, and join Bruce at the counter instead. Was she okay with that? How together they were was none of her business, but in her apartment it would be her business, or at least her comfort or discomfort factor. "Well, as long as they're decent about it and all, it doesn't matter. Libs did it often enough. Guess I wouldn't wear my M&Ms around the place when he's there, though."

A charming smile warmed his face and his eyes. "You can save those for me."

They stayed at the coffee shop until it was getting ready to close. In the apartment, Davis was passed out on the couch, snoring loudly. Bruce went over and shoved him to wake him up and he and James helped him move to his room, out of their way.

She couldn't quite refuse when they talked about putting a movie on, although it was late already. Isabel did not want to leave him yet. It was too nice, too comfortable, too easy, including how well she liked his best friend and the best friend's girlfriend. It was all too easy.

Somehow, the thought made her nervous.

Still, she leaned back against him, resting her head on his shoulder while they half watched an older movie she'd seen years ago in a theater with Libs and talked through half of it. When they got to the scene that had embarrassed her in the theater, a fairly graphic sex scene, Bruce stood and took Abby back to his room with a quick good night.

James shook his head. "He doesn't need much encouragement."

"Well, this is pretty much porn. It'd be better without it."

"Meaning it makes you uncomfortable? I'll fast forward."

"No, it's about done, anyway. I just think it didn't need to be in the movie, and it throws it off."

"It does kind of make you think of other things than the somewhat weak plot. But there is that." He grinned, teasing.

"But that's what I mean. I saw this years ago, and the biggest thing I remembered about it was just this scene." At his smirk, she almost wanted to slug him. "I mean, it takes over until the rest of it doesn't matter when, really, it's a nice story without it."

"It's a story accent. It adds to it."

"It doesn't, though. In some movies, yes. When it feels more like a natural progression and it's not so much in your face. But this is just... It detracts from the story. It changes the whole feel."

"Maybe that was their point? It's kind of reality, if you think about it. Sex is kind of a central focus of a relationship, right? If you do or if you don't, it sets the whole tone..."

"But it shouldn't."

"Well, maybe it shouldn't at first. There are other things that should come first. They don't always. But you know, if they're both happy with that kind of thing, just do it to do it and enjoy each other's company without making a big deal out of it, why not? Right? As long as it's mutual and you're safe and smart about it..."

"You know, I should actually go. It's ... late, and..." She hesitated at the soft brush of his fingertips along her face.

"I'm only saying not everyone wants the same thing."

"Oh, trust me. That much, I know."

His fingers slid back through her hair while he studied her. "He wouldn't stay long, he wouldn't be 'round...'"

Isabel pulled back when he repeated the words from her own song, the one still in progress.

"Who did this to you?"

"Did what?"

"You know what I mean. You're afraid of getting too close. I don't think it's only me. I think it's in general."

"I don't want to talk about it."

"Of course you do, or you wouldn't put it into lyrics for people to hear."

"They're just..."

"Truth. They're your truth. Your experience."

Her heart raced and she stood to get farther away from him. It was too soon. She didn't know him well enough yet. Was he one of those who only wanted the physical relationship without a lot of fuss? Possible. Too possible. And if he was going to pull away because she didn't want that, she might as well know. "It's late, James. I have a long drive..."

He stood beside her and took her hand. "Stay tonight. You can take my room. I don't want you driving all the way back up to Meadville when you're tired already and I've just upset you."

"No, you didn't. I'm just..."

"Or I can drive you home, but then your car would be here..."

"And you have to work in the morning."

"Right. So..."

She kissed him the way she'd been wanting to do for hours. Maybe it was the wrong move after their conversation, since he didn't seem to need much encouragement, either. He moved them back to the couch and leaned her backward while he kissed her, adjusting pillows to support her head. His body lowered over hers, slowly, gently, one leg against the couch and the other between hers, and he slid a hand up along her side, to her breast.

She pulled air deeply into her lungs and debated whether she wanted him to stop or wanted him to take her to his room and...

And she couldn't. Far too soon. Too much she didn't know about him yet. Too much he didn't know... "James." She gently pushed him away.

His gaze questioned her.

"I can't. I'm sorry, but..."

"I'm not trying to take you to bed." He smoothed fingers through her hair alongside her face. "I know you're not ready for that." He kissed her nose and then teased her lips until her eyes closed. His fingers smoothed along her neck, down her shoulder. He kissed her, gently at first and then deeper.

Her body arched up into him, despite her head telling her they had to stop. Maybe he didn't intend to, but it would happen. It would. Because she had too little control, because it had been so, so long, and she wanted to say yes. But she couldn't. "No. Please, get up."

He sat up and shoved a hand through his hair.

Sitting, she wrapped her arms around the leg she pulled in front of her body. And again... He'd tell her to get out, then, to just go. She waited for it with her gut aching. But he was silent. So she asked. "Should I go?"

He turned to her, still with a question in his eyes, but a different question.

"I wasn't trying to..." She shrugged, watching him. "I'm sorry if it looked like I was trying to start something and then... I wasn't. I just..."

"Iz, no." With a quick move of his whole body, he captured her in his arms and held her head against his shoulder. "I'm sorry. I didn't mean to scare you."

"You didn't."

He met her eyes.

"You didn't scare me. I just... Don't tell me to go, okay? I need more time since this is really new, but I don't want to lose this because..."

"Hell, Iz, I'm not breaking up with you because you're not ready for sex two days after our first kiss. What do you think I am?"

She stared. Her heart pounded.

"That's happened before?" His head raised; a sign of understanding crossed his face. "The last boyfriend? The one who called you boring?"

"It's why he left. Because I wouldn't."

"Then he was an asshole."

"No. He was... We dated for a long time. Three years, actually. So I understood why he got annoyed whenever I said no. I do. It is a long time. But..."

"But, you didn't want him."

"I, um..." Her head shook. "I couldn't."

"Couldn't? Medical reason?" His voice softened and he moved closer, claiming her hands. "You can tell me."

"No. Personal reasons."

"Okay. So... You're not interested in that any more than you are in drinking? Because..."

"No. I just... Well, they can both lead to places you don't want to go. One can be as harmful as the other. I just can't... I'm not ready for the risk. I am interested. Trust me. I'm far more interested than I want to be at this point."

He nodded, his gaze at the floor.

"So... should I go? I will."

"No way in hell." He met her eyes. "I'm sorry for making you uncomfortable. It's the last thing I wanted to do. And, as far as risk, I will protect us if you decide you want to go that far at some point. I'm not one of those assholes who refuse to use protection. Just so you know. I'll also never push you to do anything you don't want to do. Promise." Gently, slowly, he reached over to caress the side of her face. "Stay tonight. Okay? I won't come into the room. I'll stay on the couch."

She nodded as relief flooded in. She'd never been able to just talk about it. Matter of fact. Simple. Like it was everyday conversation. Maybe for some, it was. Not when you'd been raised where the topic was absolutely taboo, it wasn't. If her mom had just talked to her...

"Good. We're okay, then?"

"Of course."

His chest rose and fell and he leaned back against the couch, inviting her back into his arm, where she stayed until the movie ended. By then, her body was heavy and her eyes fought to stay open. He grabbed sweats to sleep in and a long shirt to let her borrow for bed, then escorted her to his room and told her to lock the door since Davis was in the apartment. Just outside his room, he gave her a soft, sweet kiss.

His bed was incredibly luxurious, softer than hers, enough she sank into it as though it was hugging her, and it smelled like him, which was absolutely heavenly.

Twenty-two

Isabel woke with the sun streaming in through wide open blinds, smiled at the smell of him surrounding her, and cuddled into his blankets. They were nice quality, very soft sheets, over an incredible mattress, and they had a fresh laundry smell mixed with his smell that told her they were recently washed but that he'd slept in them for a couple of days and the effect was pure luxury. He'd offered to change them, but she didn't want to put him to that much trouble. She was glad she hadn't. Unlike her ex who always smelled of BO, even just out of the shower, James always smelled nice. Even out walking, when sweat tinged his shirt over his chest, he didn't smell bad.

Since she didn't have to work, she considered staying right there all morning, then going for a walk to get lunch, and coming back to putter with songs. Her guitar was in the corner where he set it for her, in front of his own. She loved the color and texture combination: his was a black hard case, hers a gray soft case that made it lighter to carry.

She was tempted to open his case and look at his guitar, but it was too personal and too invasive. It was up to him to share or not. And after last night when she'd somewhat come on to him and turned him away, he wasn't likely to be that amenable.

Still, he'd given her a sweet goodnight kiss.

Puttering around his place all day would be nice, homey, except... His roommate. Isabel wondered if Davis was there still sleeping off a hangover or if he'd be out and about. What time was it? Reaching for her phone to check, she found a digital alarm clock showing 9:15. Nine fifteen? James would have been gone for nearly two hours. She should have left the door unlocked so he could come in to say he was leaving, but she was too concerned about Davis, and apparently so was he, since he told her to lock it. She should have told him to wake her so she could leave when he did if the cretin was in the apartment.

Sitting up, she saw something sticking under the door and got up to retrieve it. A note, on a scratch pad with his company's logo:

Morning, Iz. Had to get to work. Breakfast is on the counter. We're all out for the day, including the cretin (took his key so he can't get back in until we are), so kick back and write or relax or whatever. I'll call during lunch. Call before then if you need. I'll break rules a bit and have my phone on for you. Stick around till I'm off if you can and we'll do dinner. Love, J.

Love. He'd taken care of Davis. She had his place to herself.

Going back to the bed, she let herself fall over onto it and enjoy its comfort, his smell, and the *love* on his note, and in his note.

He had pretty handwriting. Isabel read it again, just because, and admired the neatness, the artistry, of his half cursive, half print writing. She would truly love to see him play guitar.

Considering how hard it would be to play left handed rather than right, she got up and went to use the restroom. Another note on the counter beside a still-packaged toothbrush and travel-sized toothpaste had her name and a heart on it. Did he have last minute overnight company often enough to keep a supply on-hand? Or maybe he kept extra for when he needed a new one.

Either way, she was glad to have it.

Still in his shirt and her underwear, she went to see what he'd left or set out for breakfast. There were two packages of bagels, whole wheat and blueberry, with a tub of cream cheese and a rectangular plastic butter holder, complete with plate and knife. There was also a box of a variety of doughnuts from Sheetz with this morning's date on the label, a banana, an apple, and another note.

Take your pick. There's also lunchmeat and cheese in the fridge, in the drawer. Help yourself. The key is to the apartment so you can get back in if you go out.

He didn't have a toothbrush supply. He'd gone out already, first thing in the morning, to get it for her.

"Okay, Mr. Gilbert, you're just going too far now. This isn't fair." Maybe it wasn't too soon. Maybe she should just grab him and say yes to whatever and do her best to make him think he should want forever.

Debating which thing she wanted, she jumped when her phone rang. Not a ring. A text. A James text: Sleep okay?

There were about a thousand things she wanted to say, the first of which crossed her mind was I miss you, but that would sound stupid since she'd just seen him last night, also that she was sorry she hadn't just talked to him, but she wasn't ready yet to just talk to him, and she was sorry she had such a high wall that would be hard to break through, although he was doing a really good job of it already. She wanted to tell him to take the day off and come be with her, but of course she wouldn't. She wanted to say they could kick out the cretin and let her move in there, but he didn't want to kick the cretin out because of his soft heart...

His soft heart. He did have.

She loved his soft heart mixed with his strong countenance. It had to take incredible strength to come through what he had and still be so soft to others.

What would her grandpa say? With a start, Isabel realized she wanted her grandpa to meet him. Before she made any big decisions, she had to introduce them, listen to them talk, see their reactions.

That's what she needed to do.

Realizing she hadn't answered James yet, she decided to keep it light: Shouldnt you be working?

It only took him a second to answer: Sh don't tell the boss. Did I wake you?

No. Trying to make the right choice instead of the one Im leaning toward.

A pause: Are we talking about breakfast?

His question took her back enough she had to think about how to respond. Yes but maybe both

Another pause. Compromise. Have a doughnut and an apple

She figured he might be talking about more than breakfast. Fine. He could take it the way he wanted. Might do that. Thanks for breakfast. Slept great btw

I'm glad. Staying today?

Isabel hadn't quite decided whether she'd stay for the day or go on home, but his question made up her mind. Might go to the park to work since I see sun but will be back

Good. Beautiful day. I'll make dinner. Have to go. LU.

LU? Her heart skipped a beat as she stared at his message. Love You? Did he actually just tell her he loved her over a text? Or maybe he didn't mean it that seriously. People often said stuff through texts they wouldn't usually say. His *have to go* said she shouldn't answer even if she knew how. Maybe his boss was coming around. Or a coworker that would rat him out for being on his phone. Something. It was a good excuse not to answer.

Taking his advice and grabbing a doughnut, the chocolate cake doughnut with chocolate frosting, and an apple, she found a selection of tea bags and a clean mug on the counter beside the stove, plus a clean small pot on the stove for heating water, she assumed, since she said she didn't ever use a microwave. And he'd remembered, had thought about it. "Oh James, please just stop."

She shook her head and put water on the stove. Leaning against the counter savoring her doughnut while she waited, Isabel noted how neat his nearly empty countertops were, with no dried droplet streaks on the wall behind the stove, no bits of stuff around the back edge of the toaster, not even that finger oil buildup around the cabinet door handles that she hated but had a hard time trying to get rid of without stripping the varnish, also.

The whole apartment was orderly. James was definitely a neatnik.

Could be someone else, of course, but she didn't see Bruce as that type, since he'd left his glass on the table when he went off to bed, and the cretin... No way. Maybe the other one. But likely, it was James.

His Army training? She didn't know much about that other than movies where everything had to stay perfect. Or they had someone come in and clean. With four men in the apartment, that could be. And if it mattered enough they paid someone to do it...

She would drive him nuts.

Probably, she would drive him nuts in all kinds of ways.

Foregoing the apple, Isabel put the cream cheese in the fridge, which was also orderly with nothing growing in containers in the back, poured the lightly steaming water into the mug and plopped a bag into it, then propped herself on the couch with her guitar.

Nothing came. She was too obsessed with thinking about James and his neat habit and his roommate he wouldn't kick out and his sweet notes and the way he was taking care of her when he had his own stuff he was going through.

Maybe she was a distraction from having to deal with his own issues. Was that a good thing or would it backfire? She knew plenty about alcoholics but nothing about recovering alcoholics. Setting her guitar aside, she grabbed her phone and started searching.

~~

James walked in to an amazing smell and even better sight. Isabel was on the couch with her guitar, and she smiled when she saw him. He'd been worrying half the day about that text he'd sent. He shouldn't have done it. The LU was inappropriate considering he hadn't said it in person. It wasn't even like him to put that in a text. He never had.

Putting his shoes under the long, low oak entrance table, one he'd made back in woodshop class, he tried to keep things casual. "Hey, Iz. How was your day?"

"Nice, actually." She came to him and set a light kiss on his lips. "Hi.

How was yours?"

"Same old. Better knowing you'd be here." He pulled back when she tried to hug him. "Let me change first."

"You don't look dirty."

"I use chemicals at work. Don't want it on you." He kissed her forehead. "Something in here smells amazing."

"Meatloaf and fried red potatoes. Least I could do."

"Damn, you're beautiful. Be right back." In his room, he took a deep breath of relief. She wasn't acting different. A good thing. After pushing too far the night before and then the text, she could easily make some kind of an issue out of it.

Pulling out of his shirt, he grabbed clean jeans and went through a two minute shower to rid himself of whatever might be in his hair and on his skin. Her toothbrush was on the counter in front of the holder only he and Bruce bothered to use, so he put it in beside his. On his way from the bathroom back to his room, he paused. She was singing.

Carrying his towel, he stepped out where he could hear better.

Then again I found my sea legs, found my seagull wings entwined with melodies and words and chords, and I could fly, could hold myself high, on my own, but then again…

Is the light within me or am I only reflecting it off what I see in you? Can it stay if you don't? Is it only a tease, a dream, a dull piece of coal disguised in a sheen of smoothed broken glass?

He moved closer and when she looked up and saw him, she stopped. "That's beautiful, Iz. You've been working on it today?"

"Yes. And thank you. It's still in progress." Her gaze flickered down his chest. "So are you. Beautiful, I mean."

His stomach tightened. The girl was openly admiring him. "Well, the other is probably far more true."

"I might have to argue that."

"Hm. On that note, let me, um…" He raised his towel as though it explained that he figured he should finish dressing, went back to his room, and gave himself a couple of minutes to unwind his thoughts. Too soon. She said it was too soon. She couldn't. Not didn't want to. Couldn't. Her words had also floated around his head all day: *They can both lead to places you don't want to go. One can be as harmful as the other.*

Something major had happened, other than the assault attempt after her bar gig, other than the long-term guy leaving because she wouldn't sleep with him. There was something bigger. He needed to know.

By the time he went back out to her, Bruce had come in and was trying to convince her to keep playing the new song.

"When it's done." She grinned at James. "Only my manager gets to hear them unfinished."

"Uh huh. So is it a manager's job to go out first thing in the morning to get breakfast and a toothbrush for his overnight ... um, artist?"

"Nope." James took her side and raised her hand for a kiss. "That was purely unprofessional, as in, not management duty. Now that I'm clean..."

She set the guitar aside and gave him a nice hug, with her arms around his shoulders and a kiss to his neck.

~~

Gavin raved about the meatloaf even more than James did, after asking how she liked the necklace she was wearing, the sea glass necklace she only took off to shower and always put right back on, and bragging about his own handiwork. Bruce called to invite Abby for dinner since Isabel made three pounds of it to be sure there was plenty, but she had a meeting. Davis never showed up, luckily, as far as Isabel was concerned.

James tried to call him. Gavin tried to call him. He didn't answer. It worried James to no end. Bruce shrugged and said if he was still out by the next night, they'd file a missing person report.

"It'll be too damned late by then."

Bruce shrugged again. "Gonna happen sooner or later."

"Does your girlfriend know you have this much of a hardass side to you?"

"Yep." He took a long swallow of tea. "She also knows it's why I put up with your shit for so long." He glanced at Isabel. "Sorry, but facts are facts, and that's what I deal in. Be glad you didn't meet him a year sooner."

"Okay, enough, thank you." James rubbed her back. "For the record, it's not always easy being buddies with a public defender, either."

Bruce laughed. "Especially since you used to be on the wrong side of the law so often?"

"Not often."

"Often enough."

Isabel had a hard time seeing Bruce as a lawyer, although he was definitely charming enough to convince people of whatever he needed to convince them of. Maybe he dealt in facts, but there was no way he didn't use that charm to his advantage. He really could have been a magazine model with his dark shiny hair and tall, slender build, along with a kind of Johnny Depp face structure. She wasn't sure if he was trying to test her or warn her, but it was making James edgy, so she leaned up against him and set a hand on his chest. "I probably shouldn't stay much later."

"Or, you can stay."

"Wearing the same clothes two days in a row was bad enough."

He glanced down at her. "Only the same jeans, but we can run to Wal-Mart real quick."

She was wearing one of his T-shirts, not the one she slept in, but one she found in his drawer that was smaller, the Madison Rising shirt he was wearing at the park the day they went canoeing. "I never wear new clothes before I wash them. That's gross."

Bruce laughed at the thought and James mentioned he'd done it the other day before they went hiking, but she couldn't. Too many hands were on them while they were in the store, or on the way to the store. And the stuff they put on them to make them look nice also made them stiff or rough. She couldn't do it. Not even socks.

"Besides, I do have to pack."

James groaned. Loudly.

"Funny. Doesn't change anything."

"I know. Fine. If you won't stay, I won't hold you here until it's later than it is."

"Let me change so I can leave your shirt."

"Keep it. It looks good on you and it's on the small side for me."

She heard Bruce say something with some kind of surprise in his voice, but she was too focused on James to hear what it was. "Maybe I'll wear it to my next show."

He leaned close and stroked her hair. "Do that. With a pretty scarf."

"You think I won't?"

"No, I think you might. Oh. Next show. This Friday night?"

"Okay. Where?"

"Mercer. J. Hicks. They have an opening due to someone cancelling. A warning, though: my parents might drop in if you agree since they like the place and it's close to them."

"You've told your parents about me?"

"Of course." He pulled his head back slightly. "You still haven't told your grandparents. Anything?"

"No."

"Why not, Iz?"

She shrugged. Too much to explain at this point.

"Okay. Well, let me walk you out." His mood changed suddenly and she saw Bruce say something to him while she gathered her things.

Silent while they walked down to her car, she hesitated after unlocking her door. "Oh." Glad she remembered, she took his apartment key off her ring and handed it to him.

He turned it over in his fingers a couple of times while he stared at it in the soft buzz of the dark city that was barely a city, if it qualified as that. She wasn't sure.

Isabel had to try to explain before she left. "I haven't told them because they'll ask questions I'm not ready to answer."

"Hey, it's fine. Your business." He kissed the side of her face, a quick kiss. "Drive safe and let me know when you get there."

"I will. I hope Davis is okay. Let me know if he comes home. When, I mean."

"You were right the first time, and thanks. I know he's an ass, but I also know he could be more. Still hoping he will. The potential's there."

"I understand. Really."

"Iz." He met her eyes. "I'm a good listener. You know, if you need one. Despite anything else. Okay?"

Her eyes watered and she nodded. "Yeah. Thank you. I'm just ... not ready yet."

"Meaning you don't trust me enough yet."

She started to argue, but it was pointless to argue. He was right.

He nodded.

"Don't take that wrong. I've just learned the hard way not to be so trusting."

"I get it, Isabel. I can see it." He pulled her in for a hug. "Last thing I'd ever want to do is hurt you more than you already have been." With a kiss to her head, he released her. "We're pals first, right?"

"Right."

"So. Next weekend in Mercer, and I have a couple others I'm working on. Maybe Saturday night, also. Is two a weekend going to be..."

She kissed him and slid her arms over his shoulders, then whispered next to his ear. "This matters, too. It does."

He pulled her tight against his body, cradling her in his arms. "God, I love you so much. I just want to help however I can. Not only the music, but you, Iz. This is about *you*, you know. I've met lots of local musicians I could probably help, but I never bothered to reach out to them. It's *you*. You need to know that."

Nearly melting right there on the pavement, she clung tight, her tears barely held back, listening to the strong heart beat in his chest.

His hands slid up her arms, to her head, gently moving it to where he could see her eyes. And he kissed her nose, her eyes, her forehead, and her lips, taking her in, his warm palms on her neck, his thumb and fingers on each side of her ears.

She wanted to stay. She wanted to open up to him, tell him everything. But she had to let him meet her grandpa first. She could not trust herself enough. Maybe she'd invite her grandparents to the Mercer show. Except if his parents would be there, that was enough.

"Can I come up tomorrow after work?" It was a whisper beside her ear that made her spine tingle all the way to her toes.

"If you want."

He planted a kiss in front of her ear. "I'll help you pack."

"Or help me unwind after I spend the day packing." She let her hand slide down his chest to his stomach.

"Whichever. Or both."

"Should I pick up a toothbrush?"

He grinned. "I'll bring one." With a light kiss, he backed up. "Go before it gets too late, and before I try to change your mind."

She nodded and tried to tell him she loved him, but she couldn't. She couldn't say anything.

He loved her. Not even just "I love you," but "I love you so much." Why did he? What was it about her that made someone like him..? Did he, really? Or was she a coping strategy? From what she'd found during her research, relapses could occur at any stage, not only the beginning, but even years later, that his exercise obsession was likely a distraction, a coping mechanism. He hadn't been doing so much of it since he'd been helping her. Bruce had mentioned that. Was he only turning that toward their relationship? If so, how careful did she have to be?

He'd said it was his responsibility, not hers, but that wasn't true. Everything she read said he needed a good support system, one that wouldn't stress him out, one he could count on. Bruce was there. Bruce was stable and knew better what he was doing.

Still, she wanted to help him as much as he said he wanted to help her. How did she do that when she was so afraid of messing up, and of getting closer?

Artistic expression. One thing that stood out from her research was that artistic expression could help. He needed to get back to his own music. He could learn to play left-handed. Okay, so he'd tried it once and said it didn't work, but maybe it hadn't been the right time to try yet. He could do it. She was sure he could. At least she was pretty sure he could. Maybe she'd try it herself first and see how hard it was. It would take a left-handed guitar, though, since she didn't want to restring her own. Maybe she could find one second-hand and not too expensive.

Twenty-three

Isabel spent most of the week at his place, with a mid week exception to grab more clothes and do more packing. She'd been back in Greenville by the time he got home. The other days, she spent the mornings in his room working on songs, ready to close and lock the door in case his wandering roommate happened to come back, and went to the park or Fresh Grounds the rest of the day, depending on the weather, using that time to search for jobs and apartments. After dinner, they walked around town for privacy and exercise, unless it was raining and then they'd take the night off and watch a movie with Bruce and Abby. Gavin apparently had a girl he was seeing and wasn't there much.

By now, Isabel was nervous about the Mercer show, mainly because his parents hadn't answered yet as to whether they'd be there. She hoped they wouldn't, although she knew he hoped they would. He wanted to show her off, her talent, he said. The thought was terrifying, enough that she'd called Lisbon and asked if she was free to come to the show, just in case it was meet the parents night.

Maybe she would, depending on what Charlie wanted to do. Everything now depended on what Charlie wanted to do. Which likely meant an absolute no.

Isabel paced in front of his apartment since her nerves made her return sooner than she knew he'd be there. He'd said he would have a key made for her, but with Davis showing up sometime the day before with a shrug at their questions about being out and not needing to check in, she did not want to go into his place without James, or at least Bruce.

Another thought crossed her mind. Would Davis come to the show because his roommates were both going? It didn't matter. James would interfere if the jerk harassed her again. Or Bruce would, since he seemed to be always looking for an excuse to deck his unwanted roommate.

"Hey, Isabel."

She startled at the voice, and Bruce smiled. "Deep in thought?"

"Yeah. Hi. I'm back early."

"So I see. Come on in." He waited until she took his side. "Want me to take that?" He nodded at her guitar. She always took it, along with her laptop case, when she went out in the afternoon because if she didn't trust herself in there with Davis, she didn't trust her guitar in there with him, either. With her refusal, he led the way upstairs. "So, according to my inside source, with inside being J's brother Felix, the youngest, he and his parents will likely be there tonight. You okay with that?"

Her stomach twisted. "Um..."

He laughed and unlocked the apartment door, holding it for her. "Understood. Doing the parents thing is rough, or can be, but they're cool, so don't get all worried about it. Want some tea?"

"Please. And it's too late not to worry."

Heading to the kitchen, he came back with two glasses, a normal size he handed to her and a huge plastic thing he always used. "They're good people. Honestly. No need to worry."

"I wouldn't expect otherwise. It's not what worries me."

"You think they won't approve."

She shrugged and partly hid behind her glass for a couple of seconds.

"Well, you know what? I approve." He touched her arm. "I've known J forever, with forever being as far back as I can remember, and I think you're really good for him. If I can see that, so will they. So relax. And by the way, if he's ever a jerk to you, let me know. I love the guy like I'd love my own brother if I had one, but, he is still more moody than he should be at times. It's one of the effects of recovery, not normal for him. Normally, he's as stable as they come. I have to hope he gets back to that. It's early still. Just remember he's still in maintenance stage and there will be some sways with that."

"I know."

"You did your homework."

"Of course. I always did when it was something I cared about."

He threw her a grin. "Good to have you on the team. And I mean it. Tell me if he goes out of bounds. I'll talk to him. There's nothing disloyal about it. He would want you to. Trust me. I'm going to find something far more comfortable than this." He tugged on his suit jacket. "Make yourself at home. Oh. Let me see your phone."

"Why?"

"Please." He held out a hand until she gave in. "Wow, how old is this?"

"Four years, but it still works."

"Amazing." He played on it a minute and showed her his name as a contact. "In case you need it. Never be afraid to call me."

~~

James stood back and talked with his parents in between listening to

Isabel captivate the audience. Hicks was always crowded on Friday nights and it was a small place, with a bar on one side, a separating wall between that and a few tables on the other wall, plus a small bit of space in the back with a few more tables and a few square feet left open for performers. Even back out of the way somewhat, they were still close. His buddies and brother had moved out to the fenced-off patio section where they could hear but be out of the way.

She wore the Madison Rising T-shirt he gave her, along with a pretty, lightweight purple and blue scarf wrapped around her neck and hanging down her back out of her way. Instead of jeans, she wore a dark purple skirt that fell to her ankles and black boots that matched the shirt. The girl was way too adorable.

"You said these are her own songs?"

He gave his mom a nod. "Most are. This one is."

"She doesn't seem to be a very happy person."

"She's nervous, especially since you came."

"I mean from her songs, James."

"Oh. Yeah, most of them are a few years old and even the new ones tend to be reminiscing in a way. You missed the newest, but there are a couple more coming up that are lighter."

"Still." She eyed him, too intently. "Is this what you need right now? And I mean nothing against her. I only worry…"

"I'm fine, Mom. Honestly. And yes, she's wary. She has ghosts. But she also has a beautiful soul and a kind heart. And this…" He looked back at his little songbird and she caught his eye and gave him a quick grin. His breath caught at the grin. "This doesn't even touch the depth she has. She's still holding back so far."

"Wasting your breath, Nora." His dad leaned toward them both with a smile in his eyes. "The boy's a goner. I know that look. About time, I'd say. This one looks a hell of a lot more real human than most of your girls, if I can say so."

"You can, as though you have to ask, and she is. She's very much real, very down to earth."

"Bring her to dinner Sunday." His mom was still very much uncon-vinced. "It's nice to hear her sing, but it would be good to talk with her if you're as much goner as your father thinks you are."

Dinner with the family. The thought made him cringe. "Might be too soon. I'll see what she thinks."

"If she won't, at least come yourself." An order guised as an invitation. His dad told his mom to leave him be, he'd come when he wanted and they couldn't make rules for him any longer, but his mom's look said she expected him to be there.

~~

Isabel managed to speak to Nora and Ted Gilbert without too much tremble in her voice. Thankfully, they didn't stay long. After flirting far worse than his son ever had, Ted called bedtime and told her to come on out for Sunday dinner, that maybe James would come sometime in the next decade if she brought him.

His younger brother, Felix, gave her a firm hug, said it was nice to have met her and he hoped his father hadn't scared her off.

"She doesn't scare easily. Not even Gavin and Davis have done it yet." Bruce gave her a smile and pulled Felix with him to load some of her gear, James's gear, into his truck.

Finally alone for a moment in the back of the still noisy bar, James handed her a fresh iced tea. "You were as incredible as always."

"What did your parents think?"

"They enjoyed your music, even if it's not their norm."

"That's not what I meant."

"Doesn't matter."

"You mean they don't like me."

"No. I mean it doesn't matter. Dad likes you plenty well, or he wouldn't have been so obnoxious. Sorry for that. Mom is always a lot more reserved in her opinions. And it doesn't matter if they do or not. I like you. Quite a lot, actually." He ran fingers along her cheek.

"I like you a lot, too."

With a light grin and a soft kiss, he told her to sit and relax while he helped to pack the rest of the gear. The bar owner came over to talk and to offer to have her back again, stayed with her talking music until James returned, and handed him an envelope.

After a quick goodbye to Felix and Bruce, he helped her into the truck, got in next to her, and handed her the envelope. Her night's pay.

"Are you sure you won't take part of this? You've earned it."

"Nope. It's yours. Dessert to celebrate?"

"If we do that every time, I'm going to have to start jogging, which I hate, you know."

"Nah, singing is good cardio, and we can always add canoeing when you want. But you really don't need to worry so much. Just save dessert for after your shows so it doesn't mess up your voice." With a wink, he drove down 62 a ways and pulled up to a little white building in what looked like a rest stop, but with a big sign out front advertising ice cream. "Ever had a Jones shake?"

"Um. No. I don't think so." Even with it being late, several cars were there and a couple of people were waiting in line.

"Time you did." After holding her door, he led her to the menu board and told her to take her time.

Isabel was overwhelmed and amused by the ridiculous amount of shake flavors, including combinations she never would have considered putting together. Chocolate bacon. M&M popcorn. Cinnamon. "Um, okay, so what should I try?"

"Anything. My favorite is Mango Habanero, but you have to like spicy. Do you?"

"I do, but in ice cream?"

"Try mine if you want, but get what looks good."

"Pecan pie? That sounds pretty amazing."

"That's what you want?"

"I think?"

"Let's start there and see how it goes." At the counter, the girl behind it smiled and addressed him by name. He ordered a large for them both, despite her argument, and added an order of ranch bacon fries.

"You're seriously trying to force me to go jogging with you. I know what you're doing, Mr. Gilbert."

"Hell, don't call me that. It makes me sound ancient."

"Well." Isabel wrapped a hand around his arm. "You are kind of ancient. Bruce says you'll be 31 next month."

"Great; remind me to thank him." After paying, he moved them away from the counter to allow the next customer to order. "So 31 is ancient?"

"No, I just thought maybe she should know she's too young for you, since she was very much flirting."

"Nah, I know her. Rather, I know her older brother. We've hung out a bit. Wait." He took her farther away from the people drifting around waiting for their orders. "You have a jealous streak. You were worried about her because she smiled at me? Serious?"

"I do have. And I wasn't worried. I just think it's tacky to flirt with a guy who's obviously with someone else."

A chuckle highlighted the sparkle in his eyes, those pretty green eyes with long lashes that she loved. Running fingers through her hair, he set a light kiss on her forehead and held her loosely against him. "Don't worry, Iz. I have plenty of faults, but I don't cheat. Won't happen. Okay?" Without letting her answer, he met her lips briefly. Obviously he wasn't trying to look like they weren't actually together. When they got their shakes, he led her to a picnic table at the back edge of the parking area and sat next to her. Close.

"So." He tasted his ice cream and nodded as though in approval. "I might be able to get you in at Margarita King tomorrow night. They have an event scheduled, but they're not sure it won't get cancelled. It's just down the road from the courthouse, beside the highway." He pointed south. "Could be we'll get some people who planned to go to that and will be glad to have something else going on instead. What do you think?"

"Guess I should have brought something else to perform in. I only brought jeans and casual tops, other than what I'm wearing. I mean, if it's still okay to stay tonight through tomorrow. I can go home and..."

"You're always welcome to stay."

"Your roommates may start asking me for rent, though."

"They wouldn't dare. Not as often as they have girls over. Oh. Forgot to have you try this. Is it too late since I've been drinking it?"

"No. Apparently I'm not afraid of your germs."

With another sparkle in his eyes, he offered it. It was a lot hotter than she expected. Different. Not bad. But hot. "Um. Wow."

"Good wow or bad wow?"

"Not something I want more of. Mine's incredible, though."

"Glad to hear it. Good thing I got a large?"

"I don't know. It's a lot."

"Leave what you don't want. No big deal. Or take it home and we'll stick it in the freezer."

"I don't do..."

"Leftovers. I know. But I do. And I'm apparently not afraid of your germs, either." Leaning in slowly, he met her lips. She tasted the heat of the habanero and the sweetness of the mango all together with his warmth and gentleness.

Silence fell between them while they enjoyed the shakes and watched passing cars in the dark from the tall poles casting light around them, tall enough the bugs attracted to the light flitted about well above their heads. She knew what he was thinking, especially after the comment about his roommates having girls stay over. He was right. It was always there if they did or if they didn't. The thought was always there, in the way, always. It was a big reason she hadn't dated in the past two years.

"So tell me something about yourself you haven't yet." He shoved smothered fries into his mouth.

"Like what?"

A shrugged hand spoke for him.

Something about her. What did she admit? Something simple, like... "I hate ranch dressing."

A laugh through his food made him nearly lose it, until he swallowed. "Really? Why?"

"I have no idea. The first time I remember trying it, it made me gag. Literally. Mom thought I was choking."

"Okay. So, that's why you're picking the fries off the edges. I guess I better wash it down with the shake so you don't taste it later?"

"I wouldn't mind if you did."

"Damn, you're cute. Do you realize that?"

"I'm not cute."

"You are. And I mean it in a good way."

"I always wanted siblings, sisters especially."

"Now we're getting somewhere."

"Are we?"

He brushed hair behind her ear. "What else?"

"I think it's your turn."

"Okay. So..." He shoved more fries in his mouth and thought a moment. "I'm often jealous of my brothers. And that's not something I admit."

"Why are you?"

"This is going to sound whiny, and I don't mean it that way, but their paths have been pretty smooth overall. They were all popular..."

"And you weren't?"

"I was Burt and Denny's little brother. Not a bad thing since they were popular, big time school athletes. Or Felix's big brother, and that kid, well, you met him. Charming as hell, talks to everyone, always very attention-getting naturally. So I was... Well, I'm the only one not married with kids, which surprises no one. Mom says I'm particular and should be. My brothers say I'm overbearingly picky and too much of a smartass. They're probably more right."

"I don't find you overbearing."

"Give me time." He grinned.

"And your smartass tendency is kind of cute."

"So far, maybe. Give me time."

She shrugged. Picky and smartassy weren't big deals, not after other things she'd dealt with. "Felix is a dad?"

"Yeah. He has an adorable baby girl who is the spitting image of him, which his wife loves but complains about endlessly. She would have come tonight, but baby girl is sick. Nothing major, but she wouldn't leave her. I had some misgivings about Alicia, his wife, at first, but she's a really good mom and Felix is out-of-the-world happy with her."

Baby girl. Wonderful. Isabel didn't want to play anymore. "Can we take these with us?"

"You want to go?" The question sounded like she shouldn't.

"I think they're closing."

"We're outside."

"But it's loitering, right? To stay after they close?"

"Okay, Iz. You win." He stood and offered his hand. "However." Standing in front of her, he leaned his head down to nearly touch her nose. "It's still your turn next."

Continuing the game all the way from Mercer to the time he pulled into his building's parking area in Greenville, she revealed more likes and dislikes and he countered everything she said with something similar. It was a sign, maybe, that he didn't intend to go deeper until she did, or a way to try to wear her down to get to her big thing he kept hinting about. But her wall wasn't nearly so thin he could punch a hole in it that easily.

He grabbed a speaker from the back and she put her guitar over her shoulder and took the amp and the mic, despite his protest he'd come back for them. The amp was plenty small enough she could carry it. She set it just inside the door and held it while he went to get the second speaker, then waited while he took the stuff down to their locked storage area. Then he took her guitar without asking.

But he didn't go upstairs. "Feel like walking?"

"Now? It's nearly midnight."

"Right, and it'll be quiet."

~~

Could be it was a mistake to take her up to the park so late at night. She was nervous despite his reassurances. Bruce called to check on them. Her friend, Lisbon, texted an apology for not getting to the show, which Isabel didn't bother to answer. He found that odd.

"Mad at her?"

She looked at him, finally. "Who?"

"Your friend. Because she didn't come."

"No, I'm used to her not coming, especially now that she's married. She doesn't have time for me anymore. And that sounded really whiny, didn't it?"

"Can't blame you for that one. Sucks when a good friend turns away, regardless of the reason. Come here." Taking her hand, he led her over to the bleachers at the baseball field and sat on the top row.

Her arm pressed against his when she joined him. "I haven't done this in a lot of years."

He slid his around her back and inched closer. "What? Make out on the bleachers?"

"We're not exactly..."

Meeting her lips, he loved the way her arms went around him, her body pressing closer. A definite sign she was turned on by him, if he hadn't already seen it. "Hm, okay. Try again. You haven't done what in a lot of years?"

"Sat on bleachers. They're cold, and this is a thin skirt."

Setting the guitar beside him, he took her hands and pulled her over to sit on his leg. When he kissed her again, she leaned in even closer against his body, one hand sliding around his stomach to his back, the other streaming through his hair, holding him in, her tongue so deep in his mouth he could taste the pecans.

Forcing himself not to push too far too fast, he caressed her neck with his fingertips, then with his lips, nipping her lightly but not enough to leave a mark. Her fingers slid just underneath the back of his shirt and his whole body tightened. It was so fully different than with any other girl, so much more.... just more. "Isabel..."

"Hm."

"I love you."

She squeezed him tigher. "I love you, too, James. I think I've loved you ever since I found that poster and nearly threw it in your face."

"Could've fooled me. Thought I'd really messed up, with as angry as you were."

"You got my attention. That's not easy to do."

"Why?"

Her chest rose and fell and she pulled her fingers from under his shirt to touch his cheek, and his lips. "Okay, another thing about me." Her eyes turned up to the dark sky and several moments passed, filled only by a soft woosh of leaves and the song of crickets. Her hand settled on his chest, her face lowered. "I've only been with one man. A boy, really. I was too young. I gave in too easily. I promised myself I would never do that again, never be with someone I couldn't depend on..."

Depend on. "To stay. He wouldn't be 'round..."

"Right. And Mickey, the long-term life-long friend turned more than that, he knew the whole story, knew why I... And still, he left me because I wouldn't, because I couldn't trust him enough. He made it too hard to trust him and then he left because I wouldn't. I was stupid to stay with him so long, and more stupid to mourn his loss for so long."

"Not stupid. In love, yes?"

"No. Not really. Love, maybe. Not really *in* love, not close to what I feel with you." She shrugged. "He pulled me up when I was in a really bad place, and I was appreciative and I didn't think I'd ever want that kind of relationship again, anyway, at least not for a long time to come, but he kept trying to make it more. He stayed out of pity, I suppose, for as long as he did."

"Or maybe he loved you too much to keep getting pushed away? I mean, three years is a long time to be in a platonic love relationship."

She stared, and then stood and grabbed her guitar and made her way down the bleachers.

"Iz. I didn't mean..." He grabbed her hand to stop her. "Hey..."

"If he loved me, he wouldn't have been screwing around on me, even if I wouldn't. So, what, James? If you try and I push you away, you're going to go find someone who won't? Behind my back? Or you'll tell me to get lost? Which one? I mean, we haven't even known each other that long yet..."

"I'm not him."

"No, but really, what in the hell's the difference? I've yet to know of one guy who's not so set on *getting some* that it matters more than *anything else*." Shrugging away from his hand, she walked. Fast.

He stood watching her for a while as she started to fade into the darkness. More than anything else? No, it was *part* of *anything else*. They weren't kids. She wasn't that damned young anymore. When he couldn't see her, he ran to catch up, which took longer than he expected. She could move fast when she wanted.

"Isabel." He tried to grasp her hand, but she yanked it away. "I'm not the one you're mad at, here."

Swiveling around to face him, her expression said otherwise. "If you're going to break it off because I can't get myself into that again, just say so."

"Already told you I wasn't."

"Yeah? And so that thing about it being *my* fault he left because he couldn't stand to be turned away was, what? A hint, right?"

"No."

"Then what was it?" Her voice shook. "I suppose it was okay for the one person in the world I could count on through that time to go out and screw other girls because I wouldn't screw him, right? Never mind I had his promise ring and we *lived* together. Separate rooms, okay, but still, *he* broke the promise *he* made, voluntarily, and it was *my* fault, right?"

James badly wanted to take her in his arms, but he knew she'd bolt if he tried. "He convinced you it was your fault before he left."

"For a hell of a long time, until I woke up, until I admitted to Grandpa what happened and... I spent a full year thinking the jerk was right, there was something wrong with me and he had every right to turn to someone else no matter how much I counted on him, and I spent the next year trying to convince myself I wasn't stupid, and now... I don't know what to think, because you ... you're the last thing I need to deal with, and yet I..." Her chest rose and fell hard and she started walking again, back toward the apartment.

The last thing she needed to deal with? Because of his recovery, her father who... criticized. Her father criticized her. Often. And then that jerk played on it.

Catching up again, he stayed silent while walking beside her, keeping an eye on their surroundings, trying to think what in the hell he could say to her that would make any difference. When they got back to the building, she went straight to her car and unlocked the door.

Moving between her and the car to prevent her from getting in after putting her guitar in the back, James was silent. Waiting. She stood with her arms crossed in front of her stomach. His truck was beside her car and she moved back until she bumped into it, then sank to the pavement, sitting with her back against the metal, or fiberglass, rather.

He closed her car door and did the same, his back against her car, facing her. "We aren't all the same, you know." When she didn't answer, he sighed. "Okay, I know this is still pretty new and you don't trust me yet, but I have never in my life cheated on a girlfriend. It's not in me. I believe in loyalty, maybe to a fault, as Bruce claims. Could be true. I won't apologize for it. So even if I do think three years is a hell of a long time to be celibate out of loyalty, I get that you were still pretty young, like, twenty, right? when it started? and if you can't stay loyal, you need to end it first, not sneak around. I get that. I agree. He should have ended it first. There is no good excuse for that." He smacked a mosquito that started to bite his arm. "How are you not getting bit?"

"Lemongrass oil. I'm allergic and react badly, so I always wear it when I might be outside more than a minute or two."

"Is that what that scent is? It's nice. Okay, you're only allergic to mosquitoes or all bugs?"

"It's the only one I know of, but I've never been stung by a bee. I'm trying not to find out. I carry Benadryl in my bag, just in case."

"A good thing to know. I can't do shellfish. I puff up like Hitch. You know the movie? It's not attractive."

Finally, a slight grin.

"Okay. So. Back on topic, I already told you I wasn't walking away because you turn me down for sex. Okay? I won't. At least not at any time in the near future. I can't guarantee three years, though, with getting ancient and all. I mean, I have my limits, but they aren't nearly that short. You'll have to try harder if you're sick of me."

"I'm not. I'm afraid you will be soon." She wiped fingers under her eyes. "Even if we do... It won't keep you from leaving. I know that just as well."

"The first guy walked out on you, too. The one you were with."

"Yeah."

"Another girl?"

"No."

"So what happened?"

Her head shook. "It's too soon to talk about it."

"Is it? I don't think it is. About anything. Because I'm in love with you, Iz. So yeah, I think some of this stuff might matter. There's a bit of risk on my end, too."

She stared, silent, watching his face in the dim light of the street lamps that filtered down between their vehicles along with the damned mosquitoes.

James sat quietly and watched her for some time, avoiding him but not running. Too soon. Maybe. Or she was only afraid of something she wouldn't say. Love was a risk. It was always a risk. Hell, living was a risk. Everything was. You just jumped in and dealt with the fallout. Most of life was fallout. Maybe she hadn't learned that yet.

"Want to hear a story about my grandma?"

Her grandma? The Meladee Dillon? Should he say yes and sound like he wanted inside info? He didn't. But he did want to know why a story about her grandma mattered now. "Okay."

Isabel took a deep breath and pulled her legs up to wrap her arms around them. "I'm not sure how much you already know about her..."

"Nothing. Except some of the songs she's written and that she's from Pittsburgh."

"She actually isn't from Pittsburgh. She grew up over in eastern PA, in the sooty coal city where Lizzie Bordan was from."

"Yeah? That would be..."

"Freaky."

"A little."

"She always thought it was. She hated it there, enough she took refuge in the first non-sooty guy who took an interest in her. Not a good move, so she said. She wasn't close to in love with him, but she ended up pregnant anyway and he tried to use it to trap her into a marriage she didn't want. My grandmother doesn't trap easily. She's ... well, not emotion-ruled by a long shot. Pretty inside herself. The only way you really know what she's feeling is in her songs.

"Mom always said I was a lot like her, and it wasn't a compliment since she always talked about her mother being too cold to people in general and yet too easily attached to good-looking men. I think maybe she shouldn't have kept saying so, because it goes to a kid's head, what their parents think they are. And I love my grandma. I'm far closer to her than to Mom, so being like her didn't seem bad to me, even if it was meant as a warning." She reached over and slapped a mosquito between her palms, then rubbed it off onto the road.

"Anyway, Grandma refused to marry him because she was leaving town as soon as she could. When she said as much, he went east to find a different job, high paying, prominent, and kept writing to her about how she'd love it there, and how many opportunities there were for their child.

"She bided her time, working, saving money as she could around buying groceries for herself and her crazy mother, and she had Mom on her own, but then she couldn't work because she couldn't leave her child alone with her mother and she had no one else."

"Crazy mother?"

"She was... I never met her and I think she died a lot of years ago, but from what I know, she never had a grasp on reality, always saw things that weren't there..."

"Schizophrenic?"

"Maybe."

"Something must have been in the air over there."

"Coal dust. Fumes. Smog. Otherwise, I don't know, and maybe none of it had anything to do with anything. Anyway, one night when Mom was a few months old and they were nearly starving because her mother traded her food stamps for... well..."

"Alcohol."

She nodded, not meeting his eyes. "Grandma got desperate enough to sit out on the porch dressed in her best things after the baby was asleep and tucked upstairs in the tiny two story falling apart building. She sat out there waiting for someone to come along to ... well, help buy some food for the next week."

"Soliciting."

"One way to say it."

"That's sad. I never knew that."

"Because it didn't happen."

"She changed her mind?"

Isabel finally met his eyes. "You know the story about Sam's Shack, right? And why it got so famous?"

"Of course. The two Raucous guitarists met there and history was made. So they say. I never believed it."

"She says it's true. That's why she moved this direction. She figured it would be a good place to start over."

True? It was true? Bypassing that at the moment, he made himself stay on track. "She used to live in Greenville?"

"No, she wanted something bigger where she could disappear, so she went to Pittsburgh, on her own with her daughter, and that's where she met Grandpa, who was born and raised there. He didn't care that she had a five-year-old..."

"Whoa. You missed a couple of years there. What happened to change her mind that night?"

"It's... You have to promise not to repeat this. It's private."

"Of course, Iz. I won't betray your trust."

Her chest rose fast and fell slowly. "The Raucous guitarist. She met him that night, but it was before they were well known, one of their first tours beyond their own area..."

"You mean she went to a show and saw him?"

"No. He was out walking along the sidewalk while she was sitting there doing what she didn't want to do, and she tried to invite him in. She said he was cute as heck, even more in person than in pictures, and she wouldn't have even minded if he'd agreed, even for nothing, but he didn't. He said he had a girlfriend, handed her two twenties, which was a big deal back then, and told her to go on inside out of the rain, there were better ways. He wouldn't leave from his spot on the rainy cold sidewalk until she went in, and then he turned and went back the way he came."

"No way. Serious?"

"So she says. Of course there's no proof or anything other than an old twenty dollar bill framed on her bedroom wall along with a dried carnation she said he gave her when he ran across her again the next morning after she bought groceries with the other twenty. She says it's a reminder that there are always people willing to help, and there's always another way." She squashed another mosquito. "It also reminds her of her desperate days, so she never gets too full of herself."

"That's..." James was sitting straight up by now. "Pretty incredible."

"You mean you don't believe it."

"Do you?"

"I don't know. I'd like to, and I'd like not to. But probably it is. She's, like I said, not emotion-driven or prone to fantasy for star chasing or anything. She's met quite a few big names by now, but it doesn't matter to her half as much as that night, she says. She still has a thing for him. Grandpa thinks it's cute. He took her to see them more than once and offered to get her backstage to say hello to him, but she wouldn't do it. By that time, it had been several years and he was married. She said it was better left alone.

"Still, it's cool to think about the impact he had on her, more than just the music. That's when she picked up and left, applied for government help until she could find work around her baby. By the time she met Grandpa, she was paying her way with her songs, barely making it, but making it on her own."

"That's ... really pretty incredible. And I don't mean unbelievable. I only mean really cool. She's even more inspiring now that I know where she started."

"Don't repeat it. I've never told anyone that story. Neither has she. She told me back when I was ... at a desperate point myself. Probably the only time we had a deep heart-to-heart."

"Desperate how, Iz?"

Her head shook. "I... Can we um... I can't do this right now." She shoved herself up to standing, paced away a few steps, and came back to crouch beside him. "You're not the only one with your skeletons. I just can't yet. I have to..."

"Okay." He reached up to stroke her hair. "I get it. Whenever you're ready, I'll still be here if you let me. I'm not going anywhere. If you believe nothing else, believe that." He wrapped his arms around her and pulled her in for a long kiss.

"Mm, you don't feel like you're thinking of leaving."

"Because I'm not." He kissed her nose. "You don't seem too much like your grandma, either, since, well..."

"I don't come off as cold? Most people think I do."

"You come off as careful, particular. Nothing wrong with that."

"No? How long will you think so?"

"I'll always think so. I mean, I'll always understand you have your reasons like anyone."

"Not exactly what I was asking."

"Iz, look at me." He encouraged her to reposition until she was between his legs, leaning against one of them, her knees tented under her long skirt with her feet underneath his other leg. He cradled her face in his hands. "I love your company. I love talking with you. You are the furthest thing from boring I have ever found. I love being with you. I love you, Iz, and I'll wait. But I'm not giving up until you talk to me. I'll wait on that, too, since it's late and you're tired and..."

"Emotional. You can say it."

"See? Not like your grandma too awful much."

"I love you, too, James." She set her forehead against his.

"You're not just being rhetorical, right? Or a smartass?"

"No. Not this time."

"Good. Stay tonight. It's too late to drive home."

~~

The Raucous guitarist. Had her grandma actually met him?

James lay on his couch, his arms folded under his head, and stared at the ceiling, the white popcorn texture he hated. It was a stupid style choice from forever ago. He could see the dust collecting on it, although it hadn't been that long since he'd swept it off, which always brought some of the painted Styrofoam pieces down with it, which led to having to vacuum not only the floor, but the couch and chairs. Gavin had told him to let it be, it didn't matter, but it bugged him.

Now that he'd noticed it again, it bugged him again, on top of Isabel overreacting about his simple statement. But honestly, if she'd dated the guy for three straight years, what did she expect if it hadn't moved forward? Who would have stayed that long, living together and not living together? Could he? For three years? Not likely.

Of course if the guy was getting it elsewhere, that was a different story. He should have just left sooner and let her move on. Could be she tried to hold him too tight and he felt guilty about leaving completely, especially if they'd been friends so long first. He could understand that one, the way he let Davis stay for so long. He'd been a decent enough guy in school, despite his family issues, and they were pretty heavy issues, so it was no surprise he'd turned into an asshole. Sadly, too many were led that direction at home and it didn't matter what anyone else did to try to swerve them around.

He wanted to know more about Isabel's parents, her mom, especially. He'd gathered that her mom was Meladee Dillon's daughter, adopted by Meladee's husband. He got that Isabel was pissed at her for not getting away from her father the way Meladee had from her daughter's father…

Did she think that was how it worked? That you should run from your choices to make things easier? She respected her grandma who left her child's father, not her mother who stayed with her child's father. Seemed backward to him. Except kicking Isabel out wouldn't have been the worst her mother had done, so she'd said. He wanted to know what that was, what she thought was that bad, enough she couldn't forgive her own mother. It was hard for James to see any daughter of Meladee Dillon, based on the songs she'd written, grow up to be that awful of a parent. Could be she was only defending her husband. Over her daughter's interest? Or because of it? Hard to say.

He wouldn't be 'round…

Odd that Isabel was so obsessed with being left when she respected the female relative who'd left. Not only left, but took the kid away from the father and left. Had he objected? If he was trying to build a good home for them elsewhere, he seemed like he'd be a decent guy, right? Then why run? Why not at least let him help raise the kid? Could be that was her mom's thought, also, that maybe she should have grown up knowing her real father and she didn't want to do the same to her own daughter.

It didn't add up. Her *crazy mother*. She'd said Meladee's mother was crazy, and she spent food money on … on alcohol. Maybe a drunk rather than crazy, or a drunk because she had emotional issues she couldn't handle. Often, it was hard to tell which came first.

People had tried to blame his own alcoholism on his service, but it wasn't. It was the addiction that made him unable to deal with the job he'd signed up to do, not the other way around. It kept him cleaner than he would have been for some time, because he had to pass his tests, had to stay in decent shape. His unit, the other guys, had to be able to depend on him to have their backs. Not something he took lightly. It was the biggest reason he didn't reenlist. He was getting too undependable. That, more than anything, had pushed him to go home where someone would see he needed help.

Had Isabel ever had anyone rely on her before? An only child. No siblings to help look after. No young kids in the family. One friend who went her own way, sounded independent. Probably, she hadn't. How in the hell did she know she could do it for him if needed if she'd never had to do it for anyone else?

And she was angry. The defensiveness was covering anger. Maybe coaxing her to workout with him would help her deal with things, would give her a good outlet for the anger. It sure as hell did it for him. Running took his urges away. Could help her flush out old stuff that needed to be flushed. It was hard to escape from life while running, when it was just you and the pavement and the focus on your body working on strength and endurance, with your thoughts as company. He'd have to be careful about how he suggested it, though. The girl was incredibly touchy.

His mom asked if that was what he needed right now, while recovering, she meant but didn't say. No. Very likely it was exactly what he didn't need, but he was in too far by now to change course.

Twenty-four

Waking in his room, Isabel stretched lazily and looked at the clock. After eight. She should get up, she supposed, since it was Saturday and he'd be home instead of at work. The thought made her smile. They had the day together. The weekend, if she wanted.

After she'd gotten too defensive too fast the night before, she'd been afraid he would change his mind, but he'd kissed her goodnight, first on her lips and then on her head, and told her to sleep in as long as she wanted, that he'd take her to brunch and they could figure out what to do from there.

Pulling into her clothes, she stopped first at the bathroom and brushed her teeth so her breath would be fresh, and found him lying on the couch, his chest bare and stomach only half covered, his feet sticking out the other end of the blanket.

When he saw her, he sat up and shoved a hand through his hair. "Morning. I didn't expect you up so early."

She sat next to him, too close, maybe. He smelled of a trace of the aftershave he'd worn the night before plus a touch of body odor that wasn't terribly unpleasant, and only a touch. "I can sleep in every weekday morning until I find another job. Since you're home today, I'd rather spend the time with you."

Running a hand over her head, he gave her a soft kiss. "Let me shower real quick and I'll take you to breakfast. How about kayaking today? Supposed to be warm. Chance of rain, of course, but warm rain on a canoe isn't a big deal. Right?"

"As long as there's no lightning."

"Of course. They close if there's any risk of lightning. So, you'll be okay with getting rained on if we are?"

"Yeah. I won't melt, as Grandpa would say."

"I think, Isabel, you're the first girl I've asked to kayak in possible rain without getting *you're kidding me, right?* with a big roll of the eyes."

"I think, James, you've been dating the wrong girls."

He grinned. "Easy bet there." Getting up, he kissed her head. "Right back. Help yourself to the tea."

~~

After breakfast, canoeing instead of kayaking since she didn't trust herself enough for that (without rain, which kind of disappointed her), working on songs in the park, and then walking part of the bicycle trail to stretch their legs after sitting and working on songs, then cooking dinner for him, Isabel was exhausted and more than glad the show he'd checked into at the Mexican restaurant didn't work out so they could just sit and visit with Bruce and Abby, plus Gavin.

Gavin really wasn't much of a cretin when he wasn't influenced by Davis. She found his work at the jewelry shop interesting, and he was a reader. He talked books with Abby for some time. Isabel admitted she didn't read much, really, but now and then she could get into one if it pulled her attention well enough. Mainly she'd read musician autobiographies. Sting's was good, she said, even if she wasn't a huge fan. Eric Clapton's was interesting but made him sound a little pretentious, to which Gavin laughed and said something like who was surprised. She'd read *The Heroin Diaries*, but it took her forever to get through because it was sad and stunning and she could only handle it in parts.

Abby suggested a couple of novels she might like. Thanking her politely, Isabel figured she might not bother.

Bruce, who loved police thrillers, no surprise, asked James if he was headed to his parents' for Sunday dinner the next day. He was pushing, since it had apparently been some time since James had bothered. Instead of answering right away, James scratched his head and turned to her. "Interested?"

Her heart nearly stopped. "Me?"

"Yeah, you're staying tonight, right?"

"Um, I guess, but I can go on home in the morning so you can have family time."

"You're missing the point, Iz. I'd love for you to come meet the whole crew. And Dad did invite you in between his flirting."

Meet his family? He hadn't even met her grandpa yet.

"They won't bite. Not you, anyway." He grinned, his sweet green eyes sparkling. "Come with me. It'll make it easier to make myself go."

"Hell, J, you'll make it sound like you don't want to be there." Bruce rolled his eyes. "He means because, Heaven forbid, they'll ask how he's doing and he hates to be asked, never mind it's because they care about him. Freak. Get over it."

"No. I understand."

James tilted his head at her. "Do you?"

"I'll go if you want, but I don't have nice clothes here, just..."

"Whatever you have is fine. It's not fancy." He raised her hand to kiss her fingers. "Thank you."

It was impossible to say you're welcome since she was doing all she could not to back out. She did not want to go meet the family yet, even if she had met his parents. But she'd told him to lean on her, and if he needed her there, she couldn't very well turn him down.

~~

Walking her to his room, he stopped at the door. "Sleep well."

"I imagine I will since I'm absolutely exhausted. But you know if I'm sore tomorrow and I walk like I'm sore tomorrow, your family may get the wrong idea."

He laughed. "Careful with that kind of flirting, Iz. I'll think you have other things on your mind."

She ran fingers down the middle of his chest. "It's hard not to. And don't tell me you weren't purposely showing off today, taking your shirt off and…"

"It was hot."

"Uh huh."

"Fine. I was showing off." He ran his own fingertips along her bare shoulder. "To be honest, I've been showing off for you since we met. Can't help it. Men will be men, you know. When they see beautiful women, it's just instinct."

Sliding an arm around his shoulder, leaving the other hand on his chest, she kissed him. It turned hot fast and her hands ended up under his shirt, pressed against his back. Her breath was fast. Her kisses were deep, longing.

"Fuck, Isabel. I've gotta… um… back off now…"

Instead of releasing him, she held him tighter. Somehow, it turned into him lifting her into his arms, the door closing, and lowering onto his bed, his body over hers, her body pressing up against his. Moving into him. Holding him tight.

"Tell me you want this." He breathed it beside her ear. A stupid question, since he could damn well tell she wanted it. "Isabel, tell me you want this. Tonight."

Her fingers slid up his spine. Her breaths came faster. "I love you."

He kissed her neck, let his hand slide under her blouse, up to find … that she'd left her bra off after she showered. Allowing him to pull her shirt up and raising her arms to let him pull it over her head, she watched him remove his own and caressed fingertips gently over his stomach.

Lowering back against her, he kissed her deeply, and trailed his lips down to her beautiful full round breasts.

Her eyes were closed but her expression said yes and he unzipped her capris, slowly. No objection, only her guitar-callused fingertips clinging to his arms, locking him in. Moving to her side, still slowly as she allowed the release, he kissed her neck, her shoulder, and slid his fingers down, inside, to feel her softness, her warmth… her readiness. With soft groans, she touched him in return, over his jeans.

"Still yes?" At her soft nod, he moved away only long enough to reach over to his bed stand, pull the drawer open, and grab a condom, to be ready. To be sure she knew he would protect her…

Opening her eyes, she saw it, and pulled up to sitting, moving to the other side of the bed as though suddenly afraid of him. "I can't do this." Finding her T-shirt, she pulled it back on. "I'm sorry. I thought I could. I want to. But…"

Couldn't? After the yes? After the come on? "Okay, I'm confused as hell. You came onto me, Iz. I wasn't…"

"I know. I'm sorry." Pulling her zipper back up and yanking the shirt down over it, she stood, her arms crossed in front of her stomach. "Do you want me to go?"

"Fuck, stop asking me that." He shoved a hand through his hair.

"But I'll understand. I am sorry. James, I'm so sorry."

The girl looked too vulnerable to be mad at her, although he had to admit he wanted to be. With a sigh, he got up and went around the bed to stroke her hair. "What is going on with you?"

Her head shook.

"Okay. Come on." Taking her hands, unwrapping her arms, he coaxed her back to the bed, to sit. "You know what? I don't want you to leave. And I don't want to sleep on the couch." When her eyes raised, half curious, half concerned, he kissed her palm. "Change into whatever you brought for bed. I'll be back in a minute. I just want to lay beside you. Okay? Nothing more. Someday, Isabel…" He kissed her forehead. "Someday, you'll be willing to talk to me and I'll still be here."

Closing the door behind him, he took a deep breath, went to the bathroom to wash his hands and his face and change into the shorts he'd been wearing to sleep on the couch, then he headed to the kitchen to get two glasses of water. One. One would work. She could share it with him.

When he returned, knocking first to let her know he was coming in, she was in bed, covered up. Accepting a few swallows of water, she gave it back, waited for him to lie down, and cuddled in next to him.

Obviously, she was exhausted, probably mentally as well as physically, since she drifted off to sleep fast, holding his arm, her forehead against his shoulder.

She wanted to, wanted him, but the girl was deathly afraid of something. Maybe her first guy hadn't been gentle enough. Maybe he'd hurt her. Or he'd insisted. His gut churned. That would explain a lot. Her songs had some anger to them. But she seemed to regret losing him, so it didn't make sense. Did she miss him so much she didn't want anyone else? Was she hoping he'd come back?

Fuck, he hoped that wasn't the case. He needed her too much already. Wanted her too much.

Unable to resist, he brushed the hair alongside her face, saw her react but not wake up. "I'm going to help you be okay. We'll get through our shit together and we're both going to come out okay. Promise." He kissed her head. "I love you, my little songbird. Even if you don't believe it yet."

Twenty-five

Isabel wasn't sure what she expected, but still, she was surprised when he pulled onto a long paved driveway that broke a large neatly landscaped yard into two parts and ended in a circular drive with a parking area on each side. The two-and-a-half story house had ivory siding and stone-colored shutters, with matching stone around the bottom third. Unlike on some houses, the stone wrapped around to the sides rather than only decorating the front, and it looked like real stone, not a faux stone wrap.

The driveway aligned with the centered front door and the steps up to the wrap-around porch. The area in the middle of the circle boasted a perfectly maintained and mulched flower garden filled with gladiolus in shades of blue starting to fade out, yellow daylilies in full bloom, red short spiky things she didn't know the name of, and tiny white flowers around the front edge of it all. In the center was a tall flagpole with a large US flag flapping in the light breeze. Smaller poles were on each side, one with an MIA/POW flag, the other with an olive green flag with a circular logo in the middle. Both side flags had a large yellow ribbon attached to its pole.

James caught her studying it when he opened her door and offered a hand to help her out.

"This is beautiful." With a nod toward the house, she looked back at the flags. Is that an Army flag?"

"You know the Army symbol?"

"Sometimes I paid attention in class."

His eyebrows raised. "I don't remember learning shit about that in class. About anything military other than a general Veteran's Day thing."

"Okay, caught. I've maybe been looking stuff up. Your family is pretty supportive."

"You could say that. The POW flag was underneath the US flag, but when I joined, Dad wanted to put up the Army flag, too. Three on one pole were too many, so he added a couple of poles, and then the ribbon when I deployed."

"Why is it still there now that you're home?"

"For everyone who isn't, including my buddy. He's almost like family as often as he used to hang out here with me. Same with me and his family. Guess I should go see them again. It's been a while." His shoulders drooped for a moment with the drop of his eyes, but he shook it off. "Mom's oldest brother is MIA from Vietnam. She's always flown a flag for him and the rest who haven't been found."

Isabel wasn't sure what to say and luckily she didn't have time to respond before his mom came out to the porch, followed by a couple of men obviously older than James. One of them put his fists on his hips and yelled, "Nice of you to finally find the place again." He looked an awful lot like James, with dark blond hair and a square face. His build was more square, though, and he looked not quite as tall.

The other one came over, a darker haired man with blue eyes, framed a bit smaller than James with a rounder face. He eyed Isabel but spoke to James. "Felix told us you have a girlfriend, an *actual* girlfriend, even. You mean you really aren't gay? Because we were all starting to wonder about you and Bruce."

"Okay, thanks for that. And you wonder why I don't bring anyone here. Iz, this is Denny, second oldest. Isabel Dillon, yes, my actual girlfriend, so behave as well as you can manage." He waited through his brother's grinning hello. "That's Burt waiting on the porch because he's too lazy to walk this far. And as a warning, you're going to have to ignore at least half of what you hear. It never fails." Setting a hand on her back, he led her to the porch where a strong floral scent invaded her senses.

"That's jasmine you smell." His mom pointed at a vine covering a tall trellis sprinkled with small white star-shaped flowers. "Nice, isn't it? It's doing better this year than it has. It prefers southern climates, but I keep trying, anyway." Nora Gilbert gave her a smile. "It's nice to see you again, Isabel. Come on in."

James introduced her to his oldest brother, Burt, who seemed far more subdued than the other. His favorite. James had said Burt was his favorite brother. Meeting his brothers and being in his parents' home was terribly awkward, especially after the night before when they'd nearly taken things too far. He was being incredible, though. He hadn't said a word about it, had cooked eggs and hash browns and sausage links, and was every bit as loving and attentive as he'd been before.

Still, she felt ridiculously awkward. She wished she'd at least brought nicer clothes. His mom was in khaki pants and a pretty floral button-down blouse, looking very elegant but comfortable in her elegance. The boys were all in jeans, Burt in a polo, James and Denny in T-shirts, so her jeans and plain black blouse with a lightweight variegated blues scarf wrapped around was really fine, but compared to his mom, she felt underdressed and very awkward.

The house was spacious, casual but elegant and neat, just like its owner. The floors were hardwood, the walls cream-colored paint, without a scratch or stain anywhere Isabel could see. A wooden staircase curved around to the upper floor. An open floor plan. She could see much of the first floor from just past the entrance. And it was full of people, and loud.

Felix came over and said hello with a hug, which made her pull into herself, away from him. He raised an eyebrow at James but shrugged it off and started introducing her to the wives and the kids, lots of kids. One brother had four, two of which were in the back yard playing, the other had two little ones plus an older one, who hated being outside and barely pulled his head up from his phone to say hello. And then there was Felix's baby, a tiny little girl with dark hair, round cheeks, and big brown eyes.

Her gut twisted. She shouldn't have come. Isabel never should have given in to his request to join their Sunday dinner.

They were all talkative, every one of them, including the kids, other than the boy buried in his phone. They questioned James about how he and Isabel met which led to questions about her music which led to Felix saying they should have come out to Hicks for her show which led to what they were all doing that night and promises to get to another one...

And she wanted to leave.

"Tell us about your family." Nora Gilbert gave her another nice smile, which felt welcoming but still made her want to bolt. "You're from Pittsburgh originally?"

"Yes, and I don't have much, only my parents and grandparents and a half uncle I almost never see." She pulled her feet back when a toddler ran past.

"So you haven't been swamped by little ones?" Felix's wife pushed a strand of hair falling out of her loose bun back behind her ear. She was a pretty, petite thing with attitude written all over her. The one James said he'd had reservations about, if she remembered right.

Isabel admired the attitude. It wasn't rude, only … fiery. She figured any wife of Felix would have to be. "No, I haven't been around kids, really, other than seeing them while out and about."

"Well, here you go. Give it a try." She came over and held the baby toward her. "It'll be good practice."

She felt herself pull back. "No, I don't..."

"It's simple. She's holding her own head, so really, it's only about not dropping her."

Her heart skipped and her head shook. She was *not* taking that baby in her arms.

James was looking at her like she was some kind of alien. "You're afraid to hold a baby?"

"No. I just don't..." Her stomach hurt. She wanted to leave.

"I'll take her." James took the little thing in his arm and she smiled big at him while he talked to her. A beautiful child. Round cheeks and round eyes. A lot of dark hair already, with strands falling down over her forehead. Four months. He'd said Felix's baby was four months old. Five by now, maybe.

Someone said something about being unable to imagine not having children around, which led to more stories of children and how much work they were, how messy they were, but how they lit up the whole place. She had to not look at her James holding that baby girl. He was too comfortable with her, and he was good with her. The little one smiled at him constantly.

"She's missed Uncle J." Felix took his other side. "You're going to have to come around more often so she doesn't forget you."

"Funny." He tickled the baby, making her laugh. "You know where I live, you know."

"I'm not taking my daughter around those imbeciles you live with."

"Gavin's not an imbecile, and generally he's not a cretin, as Iz calls them."

Felix laughed. "Perfect word for your roommates, other than Bruce. Gavin depends on the day. He's a bit up and down." He addressed Isabel. "Bruce used to come around here with J a lot, when J still wanted to be around us. Nice of you to get him here again."

"Oh. I didn't..."

"Sure, you did. And don't worry, it won't take long to get used to the chaos." He ran fingers over his daughter's head.

"Dinner's ready." His mom interrupted and they all jumped up almost in unison. Someone went to call the other kids in and James asked again if she wanted to hold little Felicia, named after her parents Felix and Alicia, but she still couldn't look at him with that baby in his arm.

When his brother took the baby and walked away, James asked what was wrong.

Her head shook and while trying to answer, she saw the two little ones come in from the back yard, dirt streaking the face of the boy and the dress of the girl, to her parents' consternation and her uncle Felix joking they should have known better than to let them out before dinner. Then came more introductions. The girl with dark curly hair, Burt's youngest, smiled sweetly and introduced herself as Maggie and said she was almost nine years old...

And Isabel walked away. Out the front door, toward his truck. He hadn't locked the doors. She could wait in there for him. She wished she'd driven so she could leave. James followed, calling her name, but she couldn't look at him. She kept walking, past the truck, through the yard toward the road.

"Hey" He came up in front of her and grabbed her arms, gently. "What? You don't like kids?"

"I don't dislike them. I just... Can we go?"

"Now? Dinner's ready."

"I can't do this. This is ... too soon. Too much. Everything's just... It's too fast."

"Hey, it's just dinner, not a huge deal. Like they said, I used to bring Bruce all the time..."

"Not the same." She pulled her arms away and crossed them in front of her gut that was churning.

"Okay. So... Did someone say something I missed?"

Her head shook again and she grabbed a deep breath while gazing up toward the bright blue sky half filled with bright white clouds, birds flying around, a bee buzzing somewhere she could hear. She swallowed hard, trying to stay in control. She'd already embarrassed herself, and probably James, by running out the door.

Setting his hands alongside her face, he brought her eyes to his. "What about the kids is freaking you out?"

"I can wait out here. Go back to your family..."

"Not happening. Come on." Backing up, he grabbed his phone, messaged someone, and took her hand. "Let's walk a bit." He led her away from the house, to a partial clearing in the midst of trees where a little gazebo stood. Not so little. A large gazebo, screened. He opened the screen door that looked more like part of the side than like a door, and closed it behind them. The inner wall was lined with benches, like the one in that movie where the lovers escaped the rain. A fire pit stood in the middle, empty, and clean. A funnel dropped down and went up through the top, to keep the smoke out…

He lowered onto a bench and pulled her on top of his leg. "Okay, so, what's up? Don't say it's nothing."

How could she tell him? But how could she not? At this point, when they'd already had the sex conversation and almost went all the way with it, when she'd come onto him and backed off, had kissed him then backed off… All because of what he didn't know.

She figured he might as well know. If he was going to run, she'd rather find out than to have to keep doing the whole family thing with him. Swallowing hard, she grabbed a deep breath, let it out through pursed lips, slowly, and nodded. "Okay. So…" With another couple of breaths deep enough she nearly got dizzy on top of her nerves, Isabel forced it out. "She's the same age as my daughter. And she's…"

"What?" He stiffened. "Your…"

"My daughter. My beautiful dark-curly-haired little girl."

"You have a child?"

"Yes. And no."

"What the hell does that mean?"

Isabel got up and paced to the other side of the gazebo, faced away from him. No way could she look at him while she told him. Her big thing. The one he had to know if they were going farther. "Yes, I have a child, but no, I don't have her. She was adopted out just after she was born."

~~

James stared at her back. Her *daughter's* age? Felicia was four months old, nearly five months. He'd known Isabel … since May. At least he met her, first heard her sing, in May. It was September. She would have just had the baby…

He wouldn't stay 'round when she wanted and needed him…

The guy took off. So she gave up her child. His whole body cringed at the thought. Except she said she hadn't dated in two years. He'd left her two years ago. And she hadn't been with that one, only one before him. How could her child be…

Standing, he walked up behind her. "I'm a little lost."

"I've been lost for nine years."

Nine?

"She … reminds me too much of her. They both do. The dark curly hair, round face, those dark brown eyes. Too much. She was born with a lot of dark curly hair…"

"Four months ago?"

"What?"

"You said she was the same age."

Her head shook and she turned. Moist eyes met his. "As the nine-year-old, or almost nine. I was fifteen."

He felt his jaw drop and forced it closed.

"I still miss her. I haven't held a baby since then. Can't do it."

Nine years ago?

"He walked out on me as soon as I told him. Just disappeared. I don't know where he is, and it doesn't matter, but I still miss her. And I can't risk doing that to myself again."

Nine years ago. She had a child. She gave her child away. At fifteen.

Unable to even start to say anything, he turned and went back to sit, staring at the floor. Okay, getting tangled up with the wrong guy too young, he could understand. She had shitty parents, from what he knew, and she needed someone, but still, how could she give her child away? She was smart. She was capable. She had her grandparents. Wouldn't they have helped?

"You can take me home, if you want. Or to my car, anyway."

He looked up. Her daughter was nearly the age of Burt's youngest, Margaret India, nicknamed Maggie. Named for her grandmother and for her dark hair and dark eyes, like India ink, her mother said. Denton had joked about her initials. MIG. Suitable, with Maggie's fiery temperament and the speed at which she flew through the house chasing her older brothers. She adored Denton, said she was going to marry him when she was old enough. He teased, saying he'd wait for her, and Burt told him to be careful, she remembered everything and would hold him to it.

And her daughter... Isabel's *daughter* looked similar.

He shoved a hand through her hair to deal with the idea and to push thoughts of his buddy away again. She wanted to leave. But if he let her leave like this, he'd lose her. So far, he wasn't close to willing to take the chance. "You can't make it at least through dinner if I tell them not to push the baby at you?"

"I can." She crossed her arms in front of her stomach. "If you want. But if you'd rather not, I'll understand."

There was a question in her eyes, wondering if... expecting him to break it off. The hurt in her face, guarded by her clenched jaw and lifted chin about did him in. He went to her and took her hands, unwrapped her arms, and held her. "I'm sorry for what you've been through."

She cuddled into him. No way was he letting her leave, if for no other reason, to prove he wouldn't, that he wasn't the same as the asshole who'd walked out on her. "Okay, Iz. So that's the deep, dark secret you've been hiding? You wouldn't have had to hide it. You could have just told me."

"Maybe everybody doesn't run, but most do." Her voice was soft, shaky. Referring to the song. The one he'd meant as a message. "Even most of my friends did. They all deserted me. They all looked at me like I was ... beneath them, never mind a couple of them started sleeping with guys before I did. Still, they walked away. Except Libs, and now she has, too, because of some guy she married when she barely knew him and she'll end up..." A deep breath stopped her.

Of course her friends deserted her. They had to act above it, had to maintain their false image. No one had stayed. Not only the sperm donor, but *no one*. He considered throwing the 'you've dated the wrong girls' line back at her except with making the wrong friends, but that would be callous. "I'm not most people. I'm a hell of a lot stronger than I maybe seem so far. And I'm not running."

She held tighter and he remained still, just holding her, until the tension in her body lessened.

With a kiss to her head, he backed up. "Come on, let's go eat and we'll get out of here. If you're not sore from canoeing yesterday, maybe we can try kayaking today? It's a good day for it. And as well as you did with the canoe, you can easily handle your own kayak." He wasn't real sure he wanted to go kayaking, but he needed time to think, and he knew better than to make a rash decision.

"Are you as okay with this as you're acting? Because it is a big deal and I know it is. You can say so."

"Yeah. It's... a shock, to the say the least, but you know, let's... go have dinner and give me time to digest that a bit. If you're sure you can."

"I've been through a hell of a lot worse."

He nodded. And she'd run from it, was still running from it. He wasn't sure whether he was more bothered by the fact that she gave up her own child or that she was still running from her choices rather than owning up to them.

His family questioned him with looks but said nothing. They'd fed the kids and except for his mom who was watching over the now-sleeping baby in her bassinet, the moms had taken them all outside to use some energy. Burt mentioned meeting the family being overwhelming with as big as the crew was, trying to make Isabel feel better, and she apologized for walking out, but they brushed it off and settled into their usual conversation-filled dinner, about anything except kids and families.

Burt kept watching him. He knew something was up. Later, James would tell him, after he had time to think about it himself.

~~

By the time they pulled away from his family and got back to Green-ville, she was exhausted, physically from canoeing the day before topped by today's constantly tense muscles, and mentally from his reaction.

He was quiet, unusually quiet. She couldn't figure out whether he was annoyed about being embarrassed in front of his family, about leaving a lot earlier than he probably would have, or about knowing she'd had a child so young. She'd told him she'd snuck out a lot. She'd told him about her detentions and her rebellious period. How he could be surprised she'd get pregnant during all of that, she didn't know. They kind of went hand-in-hand.

Had he never risked a girl getting pregnant? She knew better. Maybe he had. Maybe... Maybe he'd walked away from a girl, too. Would he? During his drinking stage? Maybe it was guilt making him quiet.

Could she get past it if he admitted he'd done that to a girl?

Probably, she couldn't.

She needed to go home. But she was partly afraid if she left tonight, after the revelation, he wouldn't call again. And he seemed determined as all hell to get her to stay. When she said no to kayaking, he suggested a walk around the park. When she said no to that, he got fidgety, so she agreed to a movie but they couldn't find anything they both wanted to watch, so they decided on coffee and tea at Fresh Grounds. Except it was closed on Sundays. He suggested they could go get ice cream from Twin Temptations, but she didn't want ice cream. Her stomach was too knotted. And he was getting annoyed. So she said she should go home.

He raised his eyes to hers from where he'd been staring at the side-walk in the middle of town. "Fine." Opening his door, he helped her in and drove silently back to his building. She went to get her guitar and her small bag of clothes from his room and he walked her back down and out to her car. "Call me when you get home." He kissed the side of her face and stood back to let her get in.

She couldn't do more than nod.

Twenty-six

Watching her drive away, James pulled his phone out to call and ask her to come back, but changed his mind. He needed time to think. She hadn't held a baby in nine years, said she couldn't. Did that mean she'd be unwilling to have another one? Did it mean she'd never be able to hang out with his family without being uncomfortable? He loved helping with the kids. He loved the way eight-year-old Maggie had attached to him and followed him everywhere. The one nearly the same age as Isabel's daughter.

Her *daughter*. She had a child. Somewhere.

Fuck, he wanted a drink.

No. He needed to run. He'd been slacking on the running since she'd been around so often, since she hated running and wasn't fond of exercise much at all. And she'd given her own child away.

Fuck.

Starting up the stairs to his apartment, he changed his mind and sat on the steps. Bruce was up there. He'd tried to ask how dinner went and they barely answered him. He would know something was up. James didn't want to talk about it yet. He needed to run. But he was still in one of his nice T-shirts and jeans since he wouldn't dare go to his mom's for Sunday dinner not dressed at least that well.

He could walk, though. As soon as she called to say she made it home, he'd go walk. Or go up to change and run. Or head down to Steph's Pub and get a beer instead of a cola.

Hell with it.

He started walking that direction. Maybe he'd talk himself out of it by the time he got there. Maybe he wouldn't. Bruce would think he was at the coffee shop with Isabel. He could get one beer, maybe two, and leave it at that, walk it off before he went back to shower and wash out his mouth so he wouldn't get bitched at. He knew how to hide it. He'd done it often, for a hell of a long time.

On the way, he kept checking his watch. It was forty minutes to her place. She'd left about ten minutes ago. If he got to the bar before she called, he'd wait outside so she wouldn't hear where he was. Depending on how the phone call went, he'd get either beer or cola.

Thirty-five minutes. He was nearly in front of Steph's and she would be calling any minute.

Forty-five minutes. No call. He'd walked past the bar, down to the bridge over the river, and stood there waiting, getting honked at a couple of times for standing where he shouldn't, and no call.

So he called her. Three rings. Four. Five...

"Hey."

"Hey? Where in the hell are you? Was there a traffic jam?"

"No. Sorry."

"Are you home?"

Silence.

"Isabel? Are you at home?"

"No."

His heart constricted. "Where are you? What happened? Are you okay?" He imagined everything from her being stranded alongside the road to being in an ER somewhere...

"I'm fine. I'm sorry. I just ... couldn't go home yet."

Fine. She was fine. He caught up on the breath he'd been holding. "Where did you go?" Now he pictured some other guy...

"The park."

Park. "The one with the covered bridge along the trail?"

"No. Here. Riverside."

He was off the bridge and past the bar the other direction, headed home to get his truck... and he stopped, crouching on the sidewalk, his free hand pushing through his hair. Riverside. Just down the road. "Why didn't you tell me?"

"I didn't watch the time. I'm sorry. James..."

"Hold on. I'm coming that way."

"No, you don't..."

"Just stay put, okay? Please?"

Silence, then a quiet agreement. He stood again and half jogged, up Race Street over the bridge to Alan Avenue and into the park. She would be at the amphitheatre. He didn't have to ask.

Slowing his pace to try to catch his breath, he stopped when he saw her on the concrete platform, sitting cross-legged in the middle of it. Playing guitar. Kind of. Not great. Decently, but not her normal.

He pulled his shirt up to wipe the sweat from his forehead while he walked her way, wanting his breath to slow more before he got close enough to talk...

She was playing left-handed. He stopped walking when she looked up at him and she stopped playing. With a wave of anger surging, he moved up to the edge of the stage area. "What the hell are you doing?"

"I wanted to see how hard it would be. It's like starting back in the beginning."

"Yeah. You were doing pretty well."

"After working on it for a week or so. My fingers are starting to blister. I just wanted... Well, it was stupid to make the suggestion that you should do it this way without knowing how hard it would be, so I thought I should try it and, and then I felt like the cretin I called your buddies and so..."

She set the guitar beside her. "It was a stupid suggestion, James, and I shouldn't have made it. My mother always bitched at me for being too judgmental. It was usually when I told her she should just leave him, my father, since he didn't care enough to stop drinking, to stop making it hell for her, for me, and I thought she was only making excuses, but you know, she could be right. Maybe I am. There's too much I don't understand and I have no right, with my past, to judge, but I do. I just don't know if I'm ready for all of this."

James wasn't sure whether to go hug her, to walk away, or to yell. Instead, he jumped up onto the block, grabbed the guitar, her own guitar she'd restrunk upside down, sat facing her, and started playing one of his own songs. It was still awkward, but he played it decently enough to be able to sing with it.

By the end, tears ran down her cheeks.

"Told you I can't sing."

Her head shook. "You're crazy. You sing better than I do. Much better." She brushed at the moisture. "And you play beautifully. Even..."

"Even with the wrong hand."

"Yes. But... Your touch. Oh James, you are so much more a natural than I am. I've had to force every bit of it. Technically I do okay, but you, you're a natural. It's inside you."

He felt his jaw clench and gave it back to her. "Was."

"No." She took it but didn't seem to want it. "Are. You are. I wish..."

"You wish you could have heard me before?"

"Yeah. Sorry. Should I have said that?"

"I wish I would have met you before you gave your child away." Standing, he jumped down and treaded up the stone steps partly filled in with weeds.

A natural. Yeah, so he'd been told. What did it matter now? He didn't want it anymore. He'd stopped wanting it. He had to stop. And if she'd given up her child, she should just get the hell over it and stop letting it interfere, since she apparently hadn't wanted it to interfere.

She was out of breath by the time she caught up. Her heard her panting before her footsteps. For no good reason, that pissed him off, too, and he turned to her. "You're too out of shape for a singer. That's your biggest issue, you know. I mean other than the fact you're mourning things you should really let go. You made your choices. Fine. Deal with it and move the fuck on." He knew how bad it sounded as he said it, but truth was truth.

She stared a moment, then walked away, up the rest of the stone steps, through the small space at the top corner that led to a gravel parking area.

His heart tightened hard in his chest. What in the hell had just happened? Why in the fuck would he say that to her?

Crouching low enough to pull weeds coming up through the cracks in the stone, he heard a car door slam, heard the engine start, heard the crunch of tires on gravel; she was leaving.

Fuck. Knowing he'd gone way too far, he pulled out his phone and hit her number. Four rings. Five. Messages kicked in. She wouldn't answer, not that he blamed her. But damn, why did she have to be so damned touchy? He was the one fighting... and he wanted a drink. He wanted to go down to Sam's where he'd first seen her and...

Shit. He texted Bruce: SOS. At the park.

His phone rang and Bruce came over the line. "Are you serious? Where's Isabel?"

"On her way home. Probably just lost her."

"Where are you in the park?"

"Amphitheatre."

"Doing what?"

"Sitting here by myself trying hard not to go back for my fucking truck to go out to Sam's. Why the fuck else would I have sent that?"

"I'm headed your way. Already at the car. Keep your ass right there. I mean it, J. Don't move from that spot."

It would have been hard for James to ignore him and take off before he got there since Bruce kept talking until he came down the steps and sat next to him. "I'm proud of you, man."

"For needing another SOS after this long?"

"For using it, and for keeping your ass right here like I told you to. So what happened?"

"Fucking screwed up. Big time." He started up the steps. He had to move. Whether or not he should, he told Bruce the whole story, starting with Felix's baby and telling him about Isabel's daughter and playing left-handed guitar, how she did it far more easily than he ever could, which pissed him off since she still had a fully functioning left hand.

"You didn't break up with her because she has a kid she wasn't old enough to take care of?"

"No, but I did something just as stupid." He was at the top of the steps again and he started back down. "I was pissed, well, kind of ticked, not full out pissed, but..."

"What did you say to her?"

"I told her she was too out of shape for a singer."

"Fuck, J, you did not."

"It gets worse." Admitting what else he'd said, he crouched again, shoving a hand through his hair.

"Yeah." Bruce sat next to him. "That was a really huge-ass fuck up if I've ever heard one. So what did she say? Or do? Did she belt you in the jaw like she should have?"

"I wish she had. She stared at me a minute and walked away."

"Don't really blame her. Wouldn't blame her if she'd knocked your ass out, either."

James got up again and went back down, to the bottom, to where she'd been sitting. "Damn I need a drink. Just one."

"Like hell you do, and it wouldn't only be one. You know that. What you need to do is figure out how to get her back. You might have to give her some space first, but you've gotta stay clean while you do. There's not a chance in hell she'll come back if you don't."

"She's not coming back." He crouched and then lay back on the concrete, his knees pulled up, his chest heaving from exertion and anger, at himself. From wanting badly to knock his friend out so he'd be free to go to Sam's.

"She might."

"Bullshit. Would you?"

"No, but she's a better person than I am."

He closed his eyes. Right. And she deserved better. She deserved understanding, not anger.

"Is it worth the risk, J?"

"Which?"

Bruce punched him in the arm. Hard. "The girl, of course. Isabel. Is she worth staying dry so you can try again?"

"The question is: does she think I'm worth the risk? Why in the hell would she think so after that?"

"Because you are worth the risk."

He snickered.

"And because she's smart. She'll figure out you did as a defense mechanism."

"Don't start your psychobabble with me."

"Whatever, man. I know you did it on purpose, because you're afraid of how much she means to you and it'll be easier if she walks away. Looking for the easy out."

"Bullshit."

"Come on." Bruce tapped his shoulder. "I'm in the mood for Mexican. Let's hit up Compradres."

"They serve beer there."

"Yeah. So don't order it. If you do, I'll hit you even harder and then call your brothers. All of them."

"Do me a favor. Text Iz and make sure she got home okay."

"You do that, asshole. It's your job."

"She didn't answer when I called. Can't deal with that again."

"Fine, and I still don't blame her."

James lay still and kept his eyes closed. He wasn't moving, no matter how uncomfortable the stone was under his back, until he knew she was home safe. It took far too long before his phone buzzed and he sat up seeing her name:

Im home thanks for checking. Glad youre with Bruce

His chest swelled with tension release. Maybe she'd come back. Im so sorry Iz. Can I call?

Silence. For too long. Finally, it buzzed again: Not tonight. She'd even added the period at the end of the sentence, which she never did because she texted slow as it was. He couldn't leave it at that, but he had to think first.

~~

Isabel slammed her car door and then slammed her apartment door and slammed her keys down on the counter and then started throwing stuff into boxes. So what if it broke because she packed badly? It would likely sit in her grandparents' garage for months before she could find a place. It was just stuff. She had nothing valuable but her music and she would pack that last.

Her stomach growled since she'd barely been able to make herself eat at his parents' house with his brothers staring at her or avoiding her like she was some kind of freak. Maybe they should be looking at him that way instead. He was the one who pushed her to talk, convinced her it was safe to talk, and then turned around and proved why she shouldn't have. The first comment was too like her father. *Too out of shape for a singer.* No way could she get herself into that voluntarily after finally getting away from it. How often had she heard that girls tended to choose men like their fathers, whether or not they got along? She wouldn't do it. She wouldn't.

And the other comment. *Stop mourning and get over it.* Get over it? What the hell did he know about it? Gave up her baby? She didn't... He didn't even give her the chance to explain. He heard what he wanted to hear and nothing else. Talk about cold. He was too much like her mother, also. *Just get over it, Isabel. It's been long enough.*

How in the hell would either of them know?

He had no room to talk. At least she was functioning without getting bombed to try to forget. Fine, he went through things that were hard to deal with. So had she. Her worst vice was chocolate...

Which she needed. Badly.

Shuffling through her cabinets, she cursed when she realized she was out of anything chocolate. She had to go out and find it. Did she want it that much? Yes. Absolutely she wanted it that much.

She shoved her feet back into her shoes and, hand on the doorknob, she stopped. Her addiction was no better. Okay, it didn't mess up her head, didn't knock her out, didn't make her do stupid things. It calmed her, cleared her thoughts. Still, it was an addiction.

His ringtone made her jump, a text, and she looked at it where it sat on the counter across the room. She couldn't right now. She couldn't. She'd be too tempted to go to him, to tell herself it was fine, only a one-time mistake he wouldn't make again, when she knew better. She *knew* better. Yet she wanted him.

Ambling to her phone, she held it in her hand a moment before reading his text with a huge pit in her stomach:

I am sorry. Truly. It was a stupid thing to say. Let me know when you can talk.

She stared at it, but she couldn't answer. How often had her father apologized to her mother, making her stay just so she'd have to keep taking it day after day, year after year? No, Isabel would not do the same. Setting it back down, she went to rummage through her refrigerator to make her stomach stop grumbling, but there was nothing she wanted. She wanted to go back to Greenville, and...

"No, Isabel. You don't need to get into that mess you waited so long to escape. You don't need that."

Maybe she wouldn't go to Pittsburgh. Maybe, like her grandma, she would go somewhere else, somewhere new, to start over. Somewhere it would be easier to get her music out there, maybe find someone else to sing it for her, someone as good as James.

Why had he kept telling her he couldn't sing when his voice was so gorgeous? So, so much better than hers. He'd been lying to her ... about how many things? The singing. The guitar... He'd said he started to work at playing with the opposite hand but didn't get anywhere with it and yet he was far better than she'd been after all week of working at it. If it came that naturally, it wouldn't be a big thing to keep going. If it didn't, he'd worked at it a good bit more than he'd said.

What hadn't been a lie? What was he trying to accomplish?

The hell with it. She needed chocolate. And maybe food.

Turning her phone off so she wouldn't know if he texted again, she stuck it in her bag and went to find food. A Whopper. She wanted a messy Whopper with fries and ... a milkshake, with a chocolate chip cookie. No. A turtle Blizzard. The Dairy Queen was back down 19 across the creek, but she didn't care. She could stop at Burger King and eat her fries on the way to get ice cream and eat some of both on the way home, saving the hamburger until she could use both hands.

~~

James tried to concentrate on the movie, or on his roommates laughing at the movie, but he couldn't think of anything except the way she'd finally talked to him and he blew it. It was late. He'd have to get to bed soon so he could get up for work, but he wouldn't be able to sleep.

Getting up to pull his phone from the charger, he started to text, deleted it, then started again. B says you shouldve punched me in the jaw. He paced while waiting for a reply. After a few minutes, he realized it likely wouldn't come and he sat. Then stood again, trying to think what else he could say.

"Fuck, J, just go out and find some girl at Sam's, a less picky one this time." Davis laughed and chugged the rest of his beer.

Bruce jumped up. "Shut the fuck up, would you?" Standing in

James's path, he set a hand on his shoulder. "Give her time."

"Right." Davis snickered. "Time to meet some other loser in a bar. Probably has, you know. Why else would she play in bars?"

"You're an idiot." James rolled his eyes. "She's a singer. Where else is she going to play?"

"You mean what else is she playing at?" He laughed again through Gavin trying to get him to shut up. "The girl's easy. You can see it. She was even looking me up and down."

"You wish." Gavin shoved the jerk. "Knock it off already. J's right. You've gotta lay off this stuff."

"Fuck no, I don't. He can be a pansy ass if he wants. Not doing him any good. Still didn't get the girl." Davis made the mistake of wobbling up in front of him. "I've gotten it three times in the past week. Who's the loser, huh? Hell, one of 'em coulda been her for all I know..."

Bruce tried to push him away. "Knock it off or get out."

"She's a sweet innocent-looking little thing. You know that's too good to be wasted..."

His fist connected with the jaw before James even knew he was doing it. Davis slumped to the floor. He didn't care. He didn't give one fucking iota of a damn whether he'd killed him. Bruce put a hand on his chest as though he had to keep him from finishing the job if he hadn't and Gavin checked on the asshole, who was obviously still alive based on his sputtering and cursing.

"I'm going out." Ignoring it all, he went to the door.

Bruce stepped in front of him. "No, you're not."

"Move before I knock you to the floor, too."

"Not happening, J. You'll have to do it."

His hand clenched, and then released. As much as he wanted to, he couldn't deck Bruce. "Get him the fuck out of my apartment. And throw his stuff out with him."

Bruce nodded. "Yep. About time. Come on. Gavin can take care of him. Let's grab a popsicle." Code word for cool off. Where was Bruce with his codes when he was being stupid with Iz? By now, it didn't matter. She'd never come back.

Twenty-seven

He'd texted her three times a day for the past two and a half days. Still, she couldn't answer him. She was done packing. Everything but her music, a plate, a glass, a mug, and two pans, plus her bedding and a few clothes was in boxes, ready to go. She'd called her grandpa to say she was ready early, but the trailer he rented wasn't free until Saturday. He'd tried to ask what was wrong, he could hear something in her voice, but she side-stepped the question and said moving out of her own place felt like a step down. Which was true.

No matter how often he assured her it was a side-step, not a down-step, it felt like down. She felt ... just down. She should answer James. For what reason? She couldn't go back to that. She could not.

And yet, she'd barely been able to make herself eat, hadn't touched her guitar, hadn't even gone out for more chocolate. By now, she was pretty much living on peanut butter and Ritz crackers and dry cereal since she was out of milk and didn't want to buy more just to have to move it.

The door buzzer made her jump. Who would be at the door on Wednesday afternoon? She wasn't dressed for company. For the third day in a row, she was wearing his Madison Rising shirt and old sweats. She hadn't even brushed her hair.

Her heart thumped at the idea that he might be there, he might have left work early to come check on her since she refused to answer him. She even refused to answer Bruce last night when he tried to get an answer for his buddy. After she ignored Bruce, James texted again: Come on, Iz. Just tell me youre okay.

Okay? She wasn't okay. She was lost again, maybe more than ever before, almost. She ignored him.

The buzz at the door came again, pulling her out of her thoughts enough to check. Peeping through the hole, she saw flowers. Carnations. Red carnations mixed with red lilies. She opened it just a crack.

"Delivery for Isabel Dillon. Is that you?"

"Yes." Her heart thumped. "I don't want them."

"You sure?"

Was she sure? Maybe not.

"Will you at least sign for them so they know I got them here? Last thing I need is to get fired 'cause some chick don't appreciate flowers when a man sends them." The girl shook her head.

With a sigh, she unchained the door, keeping her foot on the inside of it while she signed that they'd been delivered.

"What do you want me to do with them?"

Isabel stared, unable to answer.

"Okay, then. I'll leave them right here. I'm sure someone will come along and be glad to have such beautiful flowers. Have a good day, then." The girl set them down and walked away.

What did she do with them? She did not want them in front of her door. She did not want one of her neighbors to knock to let her know they were there. And she definitely did not want someone to read whatever he wrote in the little card attached. With a sigh, Isabel picked them up.

She didn't want to read it, either, so she lay the wrapped bouquet on the table and went to ... do what? Maybe she'd go out. In case he did come. But she didn't want to go out. Flopping on the couch, she stared at the flowers for some time. She had nothing to put them in. Everything was packed. It didn't matter; she didn't want them.

"Hell." Scooching up on the couch, she grabbed the bouquet, pulled the card out, and tore the little envelope out of her way:

> *I may not be time—smoothed enough yet,*
> *but I would have stayed.*
> *Still would, and I'm still here.*
>
> *Love you, J.*

He was comparing himself to sea glass? Not time-smoothed. Still in progress. Who wasn't? Still… Sea glass. The beach. She wanted to be on the beach.

Dropping the card on the table, she went to dig through her box to find beach clothes, changed quickly, and pulled her messy hair back with a big wrap band. He would have stayed? Maybe, but he hadn't given her any kind of promise before trying to get her to sleep with him. Staying out of obligation wasn't something she wanted, either.

~~

She didn't answer. Her car wasn't in its usual parking spot at her building, and she didn't answer. Had she already moved? It was entirely possible. Except the flowers had been signed for, so they said. Could be they just marked it that way.

With a sigh, he dropped his head, wondering what to do next. Find her grandparents in Pittsburgh? Chances were they'd be unlisted. Meladee Dillon wouldn't necessarily want just anyone calling her. Sit there until she came home? But if she'd moved already...

A red petal caught his eye and he bent to pick it up. A carnation petal. So they at least made it this far.

James slumped to the floor, leaning against her door. When his phone buzzed, he jumped to grab it even though it wasn't her ring. Bruce. "Yeah?"

"Where the hell are you?"

"Isabel's. Since she wouldn't answer me."

"Tell me you went to work today."

"Yeah, I went to work. Just left there to come here. I've been here all of about five minutes."

A pause came over the line. "Find her?"

"No. No answer. Car's not here. Not sure what to do next."

"Come back home, J. You have to..."

"Give her time. Yeah, I got it, but I need to talk to her. I *have* to talk to her." He heard the heavy sigh, heard his buddy's question about whether he should drive up and sit with him, heard himself refuse. In a haze. Everything had been one big haze since she walked away from him, and he hadn't even touched alcohol. "I'm going to go grab something to eat and come back to see if she's here. Don't get all panicked. I'm good."

"Yeah, well, keep it that way. You've given her enough reason to be wary of you. Don't add to it. I like her, J. I'm hoping she'll give your pathetic ass another chance, too. Don't blow it."

Hanging up, he went back to his truck, sat there a while watching for her and deciding where to go, then headed to Cracker Barrel. Maybe he'd order two chicken fried chicken dinners and get one to go. If she still wasn't home, he could leave it in front of her door. Where the flower petal had been.

~~

Isabel got home way too late. It was past dark, and she hated to be out alone after dark. Holding her pepper spray tightly in her hand, she scanned the area, as well as she could see with only the glow of the street lights, while making her way from her car to her door, her keys out and ready, and she stopped just inside her building. There was a bag hanging from her doorknob. With another red carnation.

Her heart thumped. It smelled ... like food. And she was starving.

She'd run out the door so fast, she'd taken nothing but her license and keys, not even a debit card to grab something to eat. The blue Wal-Mart bag hanging on her doorknob had another bag inside, a white and brown bag, tied up tight, with a note taped to the outside:

I'm leaving this for you since you weren't here to go to dinner with me. Not leftovers. Didn't touch it. It's double tied, in two bags, tight enough you'll have to cut it, and if not, someone tampered with it. Text me, okay? LU, J.

Tears came to her eyes as she opened the door and took the bag inside, pressing the flower to her nose. The bouquet on her table was starting to wilt, so she took it into the kitchen, ran cold water into one side of the sink, cut the ends of the stems, and propped them to stay under water. The single one, she kept with her as she went to open the bags. They were still tied tight. Cutting it open, she pulled out the Styrofoam container. It was warm. He'd left it not long ago.

Her stomach growled at the and smell of the food, but first, she picked up her phone: Shouldve told me you were coming up here

She barely set it down before it buzzed: Hi to you too. Are you ok?

Okay? No, she wasn't okay. Im ... What? What did she tell him? What else could she tell him? ... lost. She wiped at a tear after hitting send.

Oh Isabel I am so sorry.
Where are you
Just pulled in at the apartment. You?
Home. Thank you for dinner. And the flowers
Can I call?
Not now

A pause. Too long. Okay. But ty for texting.
James...
Still here.
Youre still okay?
If you mean still sober yes.

If she meant still sober? Would he answer differently if she meant something else? At least there was that.

Iz? We can still keep in touch right? Or am I fired as your manager too?

She stared at that one for some time. Keep in touch. It sounded so ... so much like goodbye. She supposed it was fair since she'd made it seem like goodbye. But she didn't want it to be goodbye. She wanted him to come back and eat with her. Hard to fire you when I dont pay you

Funny. You know what I mean.

She stared at the food, trying to figure out how to answer. Only one way she could answer. Not saying goodbye just need time.

Good. Eat now before its colder. Night Iz.

The place was too quiet, so she pulled out her laptop and opened it to find the song he'd referenced early on, and the one that made her think about her own situation, about what he'd said. *Not Everybody Runs.* J.D. Eicher. She forgot to eat while she listened. With tears running down her face, she replayed it. Was he trying to tell her he was afraid, too? Had he bit back like that out of fear? Maybe she'd made him feel too cornered.

And maybe he wouldn't have run if she'd found him when she'd so desperately needed someone to be there for her. Maybe she would have had his child instead and she would still have her, with his help to raise her. Maybe he still wouldn't walk away, despite her meltdown.

Maybe she'd overreacted.

Twenty-eight

Her grandpa would be there in the morning with the U-Haul. Isabel let James know they had a last minute opening for the truck on Friday so she was leaving a day earlier than planned. He would be at work, but she didn't want to just go and not tell him when. He'd texted her daily to say good morning and before he went to bed to say good night, but otherwise, he'd left her alone.

Appreciative that he was giving her the space she requested, she also missed him already and she hadn't wanted her last week this close to him to go the way it had.

Pacing through the living room full of boxes, since she'd moved them all in there to make the morning easier and to make less hauling work for her grandpa, she suddenly wondered what she was doing.

Except she knew what she was doing. She was running. Her grandpa had asked if it was really what she wanted and although she hadn't admitted there was a man in the story, she assured him it was maybe not what she wanted, but what she needed. It was a cowardly thing to do. He'd said he knew he was a risk. James knew it was a risk, for him, also, and yet he'd jumped in full steam and she'd been the one to kiss him that started the whole thing. Well, he kissed her first and then apologized, so it didn't really count. It kind of counted. It did count. He kissed her first, but he backed away because ... because he was afraid.

He was every bit as afraid as she was, but he wasn't running.

Hell. What was she doing?

It was too late to change her plans now. She was packed. Her lease was up. Her grandpa had the truck rented. She'd told James...

She'd told him she loved him. And then she freaked out. Too easily.

Plopping onto the couch, Isabel opened his last message and hit reply. What should she say? It was late. He'd said he was going to bed more than an hour ago. Maybe she shouldn't. Setting it down again, she got up to wander, asked herself over and over what she was doing, plopped down on the couch, and let herself text him even if she shouldn't. Hey Gilbert still awake?

It came back faster than she expected. Gilbert?

Thought Id act like one of the guys

Please dont. Theyre all cretins.

Except Bruce

Including him. Whats up?

Just wanted to say... well... I guess I can be a cretin at times too. I have been lately. Still visiting me in the big city?

Never

Her heart nearly stopped. Never? He was done? Trying to decide how to answer, or even whether she should answer, she paced around the room until it buzzed again. She hesitated before looking, taking deep breaths to try to slow her now pounding heart.

Didn't mean to hit send yet. Youre never a cretin. Way too cute for that. And yes if you count Pitt as a big city.

Wow Gilbert. I nearly had to run to dq for an xl super chocolately blizzard

Huh?

Thought you were saying youd never visit me there

The reply was slow to come. Too slow. Maybe he had meant that and then changed his mind? Maybe... It rang. A call. Not a text. Hell. Biting her lip, she released it to answer. "Hey."

"Are you having second thoughts?"

She nearly cried at the sound of his voice. "About which thing?"

"Well, I meant ... moving. But ... about anything, I guess. Are you?"

"Oh. So many. Mainly about moving. I'm not sure I should have. Or at least not until I found my own place again."

"Well, since you're packed already, you could maybe ... move in here. Davis moved out, left the state, not sure where, but it's just as well. You can't save everyone. Anyway, I'll be power cleaning his room, so it would be safe. Until it's ready, you could have mine..."

"James." Isabel hardly knew what to say, but she couldn't agree.

"I'm only offering you a room. I won't push you."

"I can't. It's way too soon for that."

"Too soon? Not a no way in the world will that ever happen after I was such an ass?"

She shoved a hand through her hair. "Just too soon."

"Okay. I'll take that. It's nice to hear your voice, Iz. I've missed it. I've missed you."

"Me, too. Come down this weekend if you want, if you have time. You can meet my grandparents. Or..."

"Which day?"

"Either. I don't have plans yet."

"Saturday?"

"Sure. I'll text the address tomorrow."

Twenty-nine

Isabel hugged her grandpa tight enough and long enough he asked if she was alright. She nodded and then hugged her grandma, too. She hadn't expected her grandma to come and said as much.

"Someone has to supervise this thing. You know your grandfather is wonderful at a lot of things, but organizing?" She waved a hand as though she didn't need to say more and her grandpa introduced a tall, stocky guy he'd brought along. "This young man staring at you – watch it, son; this is my baby girl you're looking at that way – is Beckett, named after the playwright, no less. He's the grandson of one of my old platoon mates in the caverns of the Civic Arena and he had nothing better to do today, so he's going to use these muscles of his to help me move your furniture."

Isabel accepted the hand shake and said it was nice to meet him. He was about her age with dark sandy hair cut really short. And he looked nice enough. But he was really tall. A good bit taller than James, even. It was a little intimidating. "Thank you, but it wasn't really necessary. I can help move everything. There's nothing too heavy. I already pulled all of the drawers out of the dresser and I took the bed apart, so..."

"You save those hands for your guitar and let this boy do what he came to do. Now go show your grandmother what you want to go where and she'll start commanding the troops."

Her grandma shook her head at the rather pathetic labeling system Isabel used for the boxes. "Oh honey, I should have come up sooner to help you do this. How will you ever find anything?"

"I'll open them." She pointed at a few things separated from the rest. "These are the ones I need to keep with me, in my room. The rest can go wherever. I bought doughnuts and coffee, but um, I only planned for two." She barely looked at Beckett. "Sorry."

He grinned, a side of the mouth grin, and pulled a tall energy drink from his back pocket. "I'm covered, thanks."

Gramps rolled his eyes. "I don't get kids these days. What's wrong with good rich coffee?" He pulled it from the cardboard holder on the counter, added three sugar packets laying beside it, and grabbed a doughnut. "When I was that age, it was a privilege to get to have coffee."

"When you were their age, coffee had been barely thought of." Her grandma nudged his arm. "You old dinosaur. You don't need that doughnut, either, on top of all the sugar you're dumping into that good black coffee."

"My baby girl bought my favorite kind of doughnut, and I'm not insulting her by not eating one." He threw her a wink.

"Fine. For today, but Isabel, don't be a bad influence on this old man while you're with us. I want him around for a long time to come."

"So do I, Grandma. And I'll try."

"Okay, then. Let's get busy. Beckett, have a doughnut. It'll keep him from eating so many."

"Nah, I'm good, thanks."

"Now don't be shy around the girl..."

"Thank you, Mrs. Dillon, but I don't eat sweets. I'm in training." He looked at Isabel. "College football. Just a local college, nothing big, but I got a decent scholarship. You like football?"

"I don't really do sports." The conversation with James came back to mind.

"I can teach you the basics. Most girls don't like it only because they don't understand it. Once you do, it's different. I can get you into my games free."

She saw her grandpa's grin with a shake of the head. "Thank you, but..." But. She had a boyfriend. She should just say she did. Kind of. Maybe she still did.

"Well, you can let me know anytime. I help your grandfather out with stuff now and then, so we'll see each other. And call me Beck. All my friends do."

"Like Jeff Beck?"

"Huh? Who?"

Who? "Never mind." What kind of idiot didn't know the name Jeff Beck?

"Like in Beckett, but shorter." He looked at her like she was some kind of a moron, and like he was fine with that.

"Alright, Romeo. She knew what you meant. And you oughtta think about some music classes along with all those situps." Gramps pushed him away nnd asked where they should start.

Isabel nearly felt like she was in the way with her grandma supervising and Gramps and the football player lined up for orders. She wished she'd waited one more day. She wished she'd asked James to come help her, or just to come, to be there.

Unsure what to do, she gave into the huge pit deep in her stomach and sat with her tea and a doughnut against a far wall while they started moving her things out of her apartment. First the couch. And it was likely a good thing he'd brought help since it looked heavy even for the two of them. She asked if she should help but was told again to save her hands. Gramps was still strong for his age, and healthy, despite his wife's nagging, or maybe because of it. He kept up with Mr. Sports Scholarship just fine.

Staring into her tea, she clenched her jaw. She didn't want to move farther from him. She didn't want to lose the independence of having her own place. A stupid idea, moving back to Pittsburgh. Maybe Greenville would have a little one bedroom place she could afford. Or maybe she'd risk a roommate she didn't know. Or Abby. Or...

"Honey, what's wrong?" Her grandma lowered to the floor facing her, and she wanted to talk, but she had no idea where to start or what to say, so she shook her head. Her eyes watered.

"Oh, Isabel, honey. I know it's hard to start over, but you're going to be fine. You'll pick yourself right back up and..."

"It's not that." She rubbed her eyes to try to get them to stop.

"What is it, then?"

"I should be helping."

"You sit right here until you tell me what's wrong." Grasping Isabel's hand, she waited.

"There's um... I did something stupid. I think. But I'm not sure what part of it was stupid and I..."

"Are you okay? Physically?"

She knew exactly what her grandma was asking. "It's not physical this time." She saw the look of relief. Maybe Grams thought it couldn't be all that stupid as long as it wasn't the same stupid mistake. Maybe she was right. Maybe not. "I'm just afraid I might be getting into something I know better than to do and I'm not sure I want to stop it. I mean, maybe it's not the same and it'll be ... really worth it, but maybe I just hope it will be. I don't know."

"Baby girl, do these gentlemen belong to you?"

At her grandpa's question from across the room, she wiped her eyes and found Bruce just inside her door. And James. Her heart nearly stopped.

"They helped us get that old dresser into the truck. Said they were friends of yours. That right, or should I have young Beckett here kick them out?"

James looked over at Beckett as though daring him to try, then dismissed him and turned back to her. "Figured you could use a couple of strong backs to move your furniture. Is it okay that we're here?" His head tilted, studying her. "Are you okay, Iz?"

Isabel tried to say yes and then tried to ask why he wasn't at work, but she couldn't say anything, so she pushed herself up off the floor, went over to him, and grabbed him in a hug. He felt good. He smelled good. She'd missed him. Holding him reminded her how much she'd missed him.

"Since he's busy, I'm Bruce Means and this guy hanging onto your granddaughter is James Gilbert. Both from Greenville. He belongs to her. I'm just the nosy roommate who got dragged here to help out. Move to the side a bit, J, and we can work around you. Hi, Isabel."

Taking her out of the pathway while Gramps was questioning the *belong* comment and Grams was telling him to just give them a minute, James tilted his head to find her eyes. "I guess it's okay that we're here?"

"Shouldn't you both be at work?"

"We took the morning off."

"Just the morning?"

He grinned. "Being greedy?"

"Maybe. But I'll take what I can get. And yes, thank you. I'm glad you're here. Not for the help, but... just because." She slid her arms over his shoulders. "Really. I am glad. I've missed you. I've been stupid and I'm sorry. I..."

"Don't apologize. I was in the wrong. Am I getting another chance?"

Still unable to say what she wanted to say, she met his lips. Closing her arms around her back, he kissed her gently ... until a throat cleared behind her. Letting her hands trail back down his shoulders and over his chest before releasing him, Isabel introduced her grandparents.

James offered his hand to her grandpa first. "It's an honor to meet you, sir. I've heard a lot about you."

"Is that right? Funny I can't say the same."

Grams nudged him. "Be nice, Niall. It's lovely to meet you, James. You go by James, not Jim or..."

"J to my good friends, James to everyone else. I have an uncle Jim I don't choose to be confused with. It's an honor to meet you, ma'am. I'm a fan of your music."

"Meladee, please. And thank you. I have to say I'm surprised someone your age would know my name."

Isabel ran a hand over his back. "James has been helping me with my music, setting up shows, my own shows instead of open mics. And he's been marketing for me, on social media. He's very music knowledgeable. Obviously, we're seeing each other, too."

"Is that right?" Her grandpa looked him up and down. "Why haven't I heard about this young man? And not so young, I'd say. How old are you, son?"

"Thirty-one in a couple of weeks."

"Kind of old for her, aren't you?"

"Grandpa..."

"Well, sir, considering how mature she is for twenty-five, I think it works fine."

"Sir?" He looked at Isabel. "Did he call me *sir*?"

She wrapped her hand around James's arm. "He's just giving you a hard time. He does that."

Gramps laughed. "It's been a good long while since I've been able. Now, Baby Girl, why didn't we know about this? How long have you been seeing each other without telling us you had a new man in your life?"

Her grandma tried to hush him.

"No, I should have. I know. For ... a month or so, really. Before that it was only... I just... I've been kind of stupid about the whole thing. It *has* been a while..."

"Iz, you have to stop saying that." James stroked a hand along her face. "You're not stupid and it's not good to say it. You have to stop."

Her grandma echoed him and Bruce jumped in to harass James, telling her grandparents she was smart to not want to admit to anyone she was seeing the jerk, considering what a pain in the ass his buddy could be. Then he apologized for the language.

"This is a friend of yours?" Gramps looked between them.

"Yeah, he was. Up till now."

Bruce laughed and gave Mr. Football a directional signal with his head. "Fine. My new best buddy and I will do the moving thing. You just stand there and suck up to her grandparents. Don't worry. We got it."

~~

James wasn't sure what to make of her greeting. The way she held him said she was actually glad he was there. Still, she hadn't told her grandparents about him. It was hard not to let that irk him.

With the last of the furniture in the truck, they started on the boxes. His heart was heavy, and got heavier with each minute of helping her move out. Pittsburgh was too far away.

She insisted on carrying boxes, until he took her over to his truck to grab the thermos of warm tea he'd brought, Jasmine, the kind she'd almost always chosen when he offered her a selection, and ran fingers along her arm while she took a swallow.

She'd put a soft, long gray cardigan over her shirt ... his shirt. She was again wearing the one he gave her. There was a slight chill in the morning air, still fairly warm for September, and capping the thermos with thanks, she wrapped her arms in front of her stomach. Staying right there with him. Like she wanted to say something.

He figured he'd break the ice. "So who's this kid who keeps staring at you? Old friend?"

"No, I don't know him. He's the grandson of a friend of Gramps. And way too pushy. He already invited me to his football games."

"Football? He's still in high school?"

"College."

"Ah. Promising career ahead, maybe."

"Doesn't matter to me. He's creepy."

"You thought I was creepy at first, too."

"You were. I'm not big on too much in my face too fast."

"Okay. So any chance you'll change your mind about him? I mean, seeing as he likely lives down there, right? You'll see him?"

"I don't know." Catching his eyes, she brushed fingers through his hair. "I guess I'm not the only one with a jealous streak."

"Yeah. No, you're not. Iz..."

Meeting his lips, she wrapped her arms up around his shoulders and pressed in against his body. She sure as hell didn't feel like she wanted to move away from him. It was all he could do to keep from asking her not to, from begging her not to. It made going back to carrying boxes even more torture.

Finally, they finished and he pulled the truck door down, locked it, and checked to be sure it was locked.

When he turned, only her grandfather was still there. The old man eyed him. "Should I ask your intentions toward my baby girl?"

His intentions? He wasn't at all sure his intentions made one bit of difference. "It's fine, but at this point, we're a bit up in the air, so it's hard to answer."

"Honesty. I like that. Same thing she said. How about this, then? How do you feel about her moving farther away?"

"It sucks." He regrouped at the raised eyebrows. "Sorry, I mean I'm not happy about it, but it's what she needs to do."

"And you care about what she needs, for herself."

"Absolutely." James felt himself start to get emotional and pulled back, pulled it in.

"You don't think you're too old for her?"

"Except when she calls me ancient, no."

He laughed, a nice laugh, friendly. It matched his friendly eyes and tone. So very Irish, like his name. Niall Dillon looked very much like he could still handle himself well. "You think I'm too old for her?"

"She doesn't seem to think you are, and frankly, age is a small thing, more in the head than the body, although there are age things that come with these bodies... Either way, a few years here and there aren't a big thing. There are a few big things for me, though. Can we go that direction a ways?" Without getting an answer, Niall started toward the sidewalk and barely glanced over to be sure James was following. "Got a few things to ask you. Number one: you are single? And I mean legally and honestly single, not separated or occasionally seeing an ex-girlfriend single."

"Yes. Legally and honestly. I've never been married. I have no ex I see at all if I can help it. No kids. Just me." After he said it, he wondered if he should have mentioned kids.

"Why?"

"Excuse me?"

Niall shrugged. "A brawny good-looking guy like you. Why haven't you been caught already?"

"Haven't wanted to be caught. Not that I don't want to be, just haven't been before, not seriously. I spent four years away, mostly overseas. So there is that, too."

"Military?"

"Was. One sign up. Didn't stay in."

"Honorable discharge?"

"Yes."

"Okay. Good enough. Number two: You work?"

"Full time at the water treatment plant."

"That's a career path? Retirement and..."

"No, just what I'm doing now. Still looking for something I want as a career. I'm keeping busy and keeping bills paid in the meantime."

"You're nearly thirty-one and not sure yet what you want to do."

"About like that. I do have a thought, just haven't made a real move toward it yet. Strike one?"

Niall chuckled. "Nah, I'm well known as a jack of all trades. I find that much more interesting, as long as you're doing something worth doing and paying those bills."

"Always. I've been fully self-supporting since I was eighteen. I do computer work on the side and could go that way if I wanted."

"You moved out when you were eighteen?"

"Yeah, in with friends. I had money saved from all the farm work I did for neighbors. Learned it at home but that was just making myself useful, not for pay. I've worked since I was fourteen. For pay. Unlike a lot of my buddies, I saved most of it."

"I like your parents. Good for them."

"Yeah, so do I. Didn't always, until I grew up."

Niall slapped his shoulder. "Another good, honest answer. Okay, number three: Where do you stand with children?"

James stopped walking. They were a good ways down the sidewalk by now and that wasn't a question he felt the need to discuss with her grandfather. "About three and a half feet higher, or thereabout." It was a joke Felix had used more than once. Definitely came in handy.

"In other words, not my business."

"Too soon to worry about that."

"Is it?"

James knew what he was asking, but he also wasn't going there. "As I said, we're still a bit up in the air about how things will work, so that discussion isn't exactly on the agenda."

"Fair enough. Let me just say this, then. That little girl is much like my dear wife. So very tender hearted but tough enough to build her defenses as needed. You push that too far, build it too strong, and those defenses will keep her at a distance. No, wasn't me who did that to my wife, just some ne'er-do-well I'd still like to... Well, I don't want that happening again to my baby girl. She deserves better, and I'm still Irish scrapper enough to take care of things if needed."

Niall held his eyes. "And if you don't know what I mean, I'd say it's far too soon for the children conversation. If it's too soon for the conversation, it's too soon for the risk. Not that I have any say in the matter, but things happen you don't expect and I'd rather her get miffed at me for saying too much than for my baby girl to have to deal with some guy she thinks she can trust if she can't, and you know what I mean. Enough said." He patted James on the shoulder and headed back toward the apartment.

Before they got close enough to the others standing outside her building to be overheard, James figured he should say something. "I do know what you mean, Mr. Dillon. I know she's been left twice, and left with a child on the way once. Yeah, I know. I would never do the same. I love her, and I wouldn't have walked out on her. I would've been there."

"And your thoughts on her child?"

"I'm sorry she had to deal with it on her own, I mean without the father's support, and I hope she can find her someday. That's all I'm going to say right now."

"Also fair."

"I know about her father, too, and since we're getting things in the open, I might as well tell you I'm a recovering alcoholic, which is probably why she hasn't..."

"You're what?" Niall turned on him, staring him down hard enough that although the Irish scrapper was a good bit shorter than he was, James figured it might not matter.

"Recovering. Nearly ten months. That's not long, I know, but my buddy is diligent in making sure it stays that way, and I intend to keep it that way."

"That's why she didn't tell us about you." The man rubbed his chin with a frown.

"I would suppose so. But like I said, I want her to do what's best for her, what she needs to do. I told her straight out that if I ever relapse, she is to walk away, no question. It's a hell of a motivating factor for me, since I don't want to lose her."

"You're using her to recover?"

"No. I was in recovery before we met. If I hadn't been, I would have stayed away. Which, is the rest of the answer from before. I've tried to stay away from anyone I might hurt, until I pulled my act together enough to think I can hang onto it."

Niall was quiet for some time. When he gathered his thoughts, his voice was quieter. "In case she didn't tell you, I had to step in and take my baby girl into my home away from her father because she had been beaten down so far she accepted what she didn't deserve when we weren't paying enough attention, because we trusted her mother, our daughter, to take care of her better than that. Damn fool mistake. Her grandmother and I have had a hell of a road bringing her back up and repairing the damage, but once damaged that way, it's hard as hell to maintain if someone..."

"I know. She's wary, I know, and I understand it. I'm not pushing. I just want to..."

"Grandpa, stop torturing him, please." Isabel treaded toward them, with a scornful look.

"I'm doing no such thing, Baby Girl, just a man-to-man."

"Which you don't need to do." With an apologetic look, she took his side and gave him a soft hug. "Should I have interfered earlier?"

"No, it's fine." The way she looked at him said she didn't quite believe it. "The truck's packed and locked. So whenever you're ready..." Her sigh said she was very much unsure about what she was doing.

He nearly asked her again to stay with him instead. But he did want to give her time, and space. And her grandfather likely would have jumped all over his ass if he suggested it. Instead, he stroked the side of her head, brushing a strand of hair back from where the breeze pushed it nearly into her eye. "It's going to be fine. Okay?"

She held him and he clenched his eyes.

~~

"Ready to roll, Baby Girl?"

The empty apartment was locked. She'd dropped the key into her mailbox for Lisbon. Her friend volunteered to do the final check out stuff with the landlord, to include having the carpet cleaned. Isabel hoped she'd be there this morning, but again, no luck.

She looked at her grandpa beside the small U-haul filled with her stuff. Was she ready? "No."

"Forget something?"

She shook her head and slid her arm over James's back.

"Come on, Grandma. Let's leave the kids alone a minute. Hop up." He opened the passenger door on the truck.

"No, thank you, old man. I'm riding with Isabel. I had to put up with your driving all the way up here in that thing while you acted like you were at the Indy 5,000."

"500, dear one."

"Felt more like 5,000." Her grandma came to her. "Let me have your keys and I'll get it started for you. Take your time. It was nice to meet you, James. Visit whenever you like." She offered a hand and then said almost the same to Bruce, and went to Isabel's car as her husband shook his head and went to get in the truck. Apparently Mr. Football drove his own car. Bruce moved away to talk to him.

"Sure you still want this?" James ran fingers through the hair behind her ear and she shook her head against his chest. "It's as long or as temporary as you want, you know. Your grandparents don't have a lease you have to sign, right?"

She raised her face to his. "You'll visit me there?"

"Of course. And I'll work on getting shows in the city as well as the surrounding areas. This could be a good move for you."

Her body expanded in a deep breath as she nodded and tried to decide what to say.

James didn't bother with talking. He leaned down and kissed her, hard and long, with an arm around her back pulling her up against his body, the other hand entwining with her hair. She could feel his chest move in and out, hard and strong, when he released her lips. "I love you, Iz. Stay in touch. Let me know when you get there."

"I will." And he'd said he'd come the next day, but she still didn't want to let him go, unsure he actually would, that he wouldn't decide it was too far and not worth it.

"I'm not letting you go." His voice was low, soft, and deep beside her ear. "I know you want this, or at least I can see you could be interested in trying to make this a long-term thing, so you should know I'm not letting you go. I love you heart and soul, Isabel. I'd give my heart to you if you needed. Remember that when you're in the city with all of those guys hitting on you at shows. I'll get to them as much as I can, but if I can't, you remember that. And ... take your grandpa or someone else you trust. Don't go alone."

"I doubt Gramps would let me." She met his eyes, feeling the moisture in her own. "Call me if you need, Gilbert. You promised. Be okay. Be strong. And so will I. Yes?"

"Absolutely. But if you keep calling me Gilbert..."

"What are you going to do?"

"Probably nothing."

"But you'd rather I didn't."

"You know, as long as you keep calling me, I'd probably answer to most anything."

Isabel ran her fingers along his face and touched his lips. "I better go. Let me know when you get back to work. I'll have Grandma check my phone since I'm driving, so careful what you say." She stepped backward, sliding her hand along his arm to his fingers and finally releasing his fingertips. "I love you, too, James."

Following to her car, he opened her door and held it. "You don't have to act like it'll be months until I see you, you know. We agreed on tomorrow, right?"

"I guess I'm a little unsure you won't change your mind."

"Keep looking at me like that, Iz, and I'll follow you down there right now."

"Promises, promises." She grinned. "I'll see you tomorrow, unless you decide to follow me tonight." With a wink, she got in her car, rolled down her window, and made herself drive away.

~~

James had nearly followed her to Pittsburgh, but he went back to work and nearly jumped when she texted to say she was in and her boxes were unloaded and she was about to take a long shower to refresh and relax. He answered that he didn't need that much info in his head, but he'd call later.

By the time he got off work, he wasn't sure what to do with himself. He was still tempted to run south rather than north to his place, but he decided that would be too pushy. Instead, he went on home, grabbed the left-handed guitar he bought after she walked away from him, to replace the one he'd smashed a year ago when he was drinking and frustrated, and went back to working on it.

She enjoyed hearing him play. And sing. He'd never liked his voice. Ever. It was one thing that held him back before his injury. Playing well was great, but people expected words to songs, not just music, although he had quite a few original songs that were only music, technically innovative, or so he thought, meant for highly proficient guitarists, that he'd never gotten to play for anyone but Bruce before ... before he couldn't. He'd worked with singers, in bands, but nothing held together.

Maybe she could do it. Isabel was right that her playing was more technique than heart. She played well and her songs were full of emotion, but musically, she held back. She'd have to get past that and really let herself go like she did with her lyrics if she wanted to be more of a stand out on guitar, but if she'd let herself do that, she could do his songs. Maybe if he showed her that he listened to her, pushed himself to get decent again, she would let him help her let go with her music.

It was still frustrating as hell. As she said, it was like starting all over again. Not like. It was. He was starting again, except for already reading music and learning chords. That much he had under his belt. It was the technique of getting his fingers to bend just right so he didn't mute strings that weren't meant to be muted. It was making it feel natural and automatic. And it was playing upside-down, equivalent to learning to read books that were printed backward, he assumed.

Some left-handed guitarists did play upside down with right-handed guitars. He knew it could be done. Others, such as Hendrix, changed the strings around and turned the thing the other direction. James considered doing that with his beloved Seymour-Duncan, but he couldn't make himself do it. A lot of left-handers simply learned to play right-handed. He figured if they could do that, he could be a righty who learned to play left-handed.

No matter how frustrating it was, the idea of playing along with Isabel was too hard to resist.

~~

The last thing she'd wanted her first night back in her grandparents' home instead of her own place was for her parents to show up. Why they had to know she was there, Isabel didn't understand, but she was already emotional from having to move, farther from James, from being so indecisive about him, about how safe it was or wasn't to trust him as much as she wanted to trust him, and from having one room again instead of her own place. After twenty minutes of whys and hows and lectures about jumping jobs that would lead to no one ever hiring her, she couldn't deal with it any longer. So she walked out.

The farther she walked along the city sidewalks with cars flying past and radios throbbing deep bass music too loud and people honking at each other, the more she wanted to be back in Meadville walking the nature trail, or in Greenville walking the park and up and down the amphitheatre steps.

She'd asked if it was still used at all and he said he'd never heard of anything happening there. It had been built to entertain the troops stationed at Camp Reynolds nearby, but now it just sat there decaying. Any musical acts still playing in the park set up in the big pavilion instead since it had power for their equipment.

A shame. She would love to sit on the steps with him and listen to music, outside under the stars which she could actually see from there on a clear night or mostly clear night, unlike in the city where the ambient light interfered and all she could see was man-made lights everywhere she looked.

There were things she missed about the city, and she enjoyed the lights, especially the way they sparkled in the river, but...

It didn't feel like home anymore. Nowhere felt like home anymore.

But James would be there tomorrow, at least for tomorrow. And he'd said he would walk the river trail with her and stop for schnitzel. Which sounded good about now since she'd barely eaten during the day. They'd stopped for lunch at the Cheesecake Factory, since it was one of her grandma's favorite places, but she'd ordered a salad and didn't finish it. Her gut was in knots.

That got worse after she'd unpacked, first setting the boxes she would keep in her room in the entryway of the townhouse, and then helping to cart boxes into a storage space her grandpa rented for her while Mr. Football and a buddy he'd called for help moved the furniture. Isabel thought about just selling everything except her personal stuff so she wouldn't need the storage expense, but her grandpa convinced her it would be far less expensive to rent the space for a couple of months than to have to buy everything again. And he knew the owner, who gave him a break on the price. She wasn't sure her grandpa didn't know at least half of Pittsburgh.

He even had a job interview lined up for her already, through one of his contacts, at a music center. It wasn't a music job, only admin, but he said it was at least in line with what she wanted. How he knew what she wanted, other than selling songs, she couldn't imagine, since she didn't know herself. She would go, of course. Not that admin pay would be enough to move into her own place any time soon, but it would be something, she supposed, and it was walking distance. On "one of my routes," he said, so he could walk with her in the morning, at least.

It felt more conspiratorial than helpful, like he was in it with James to make her exercise more. *Too out of shape for a singer.* So often when it ran through her mind, her first thought was *screw you.* Even if he was right. Still, it was insulting. And a huge warning sign. And yet, she missed him already.

Stupid. It was stupid to miss him already. He would fuss about her calling herself that, but it was. Whatever.

Regardless of being tired, Isabel walked fast. Her pounding heart told her to slow down. She was ... too out of shape for such a fast, long walk, but she repeated *screw you* to herself, to her body's revolt, and kept going.

She was hungry, though. Walking past diners throwing out heavenly scents, at least heavenly when she was so hungry, she paused at the Smoothie Shack and considered going in for one to hold her until she got back for whatever her grandpa had been about to throw on his indoor grill when she'd walked out.

Wait. The Smoothie Shack was... With a full stop and breathing hard, she looked at where she was. Across from the big parking lot. Downtown? And it was dusk. Past dusk, more dark than dusk. She'd been walking since ... since before dinner, four o'clock?, and it was... She pulled her phone out to check the time.

Nothing. It was off. Why on earth was it off? She never turned it off. It was an older phone, four years. The company she used had badgered her to upgrade. Still, it should have a charge. She always plugged it in at night and it lasted all the next day and usually part of the next if she forgot. But it wouldn't turn on. Dead. She'd forgotten to plug it in the night before while she was so stressed about moving. She hoped she hadn't missed a text from James. She didn't even have money, or her ID. She'd grabbed her phone and walked out.

And she was a good distance from her grandparents.

With a cringe that went all the way through her core, Isabel told herself not to freak out, people went out by themselves all the time without a phone, or at least they used to. Her grandpa talked about it all the time, that no one learned to take care of themselves or to be defensive and aware because they all had their noses in their phones like that would do them much good in an emergency. Maybe for a slow growing heart attack it might, he said, but not much otherwise.

Okay, Grandpa. Let's see how your idea works. Since I don't have much choice.

Turning, she walked the other direction down Wylie Avenue. She'd stayed on the same road rather than zig-zagging as she often had in her younger days just to see if she could possibly lose herself. A stupid thing to do. Again, she heard James tell her to stop calling herself that. Okay, so a naive thing for a young person to do, but the young too often felt invincible, her grandpa often said. She'd never felt invincible; she just hadn't cared enough to worry much about it.

She kept her eyes on everything around her while she walked faster than normal, not that she didn't look around when she walked, anyway, when her phone wasn't dead and she was relying on it. Of course, she didn't always have her nose buried in it. She didn't even always have the thing on, until James. She'd used it more the past three months than she had in the past three years. It was hard to let her mind wander and come up with thoughts for songs when she was distracted by her phone, so she wasn't often. There were a couple of simple games on it for cases of extreme boredom, such as waiting for an oil change in a little closed-off room with some stupid television show blaring, but generally, she watched people instead.

No big deal. She could watch and walk without her phone. She knew where she was and where she was going. Isabel knew the area well, like James knew his area well, not only his town but those around him. She only knew her corner of Pittsburgh, but she did know that.

Her corner. As much as she hated to admit it, the more she walked, retracing old steps from her childhood, the more she felt like she was home after trying to escape home for something she didn't even know if she wanted.

Her legs started to hurt and one calf tried to cramp, so she slowed down. Her slip on boat shoes weren't meant for walking distances; they were meant to look cute with her capris. Still, she was proud to be able to walk so long, and some of it fast, without being more than somewhat tired. James and his workouts.

She badly wished he was there walking with her now.

~~

Getting off the phone, he was happy enough to have scored such a good gig for her, he had to text… No, he wanted to hear her voice, so he called to tell her. Her voicemail kicked in immediately and he waited for permission to leave a message. "Hey, Iz, call me back when you get a chance. I have something booked for you that should be good. Anyway, give me a call as soon as you're free. Hope all is well."

Since he didn't reach her, he went out to tell Bruce. Silence greeted him. No one was in the living room or kitchen. The TV was off. Where in the hell was everyone?

Too much quiet mixed with the fact that he hated her being so far away. Maybe her reception wasn't good in her grandparents' place. Often, he could get through with a text when he couldn't make a call. So he tried a quick text to ask her to call. And then he put on his running shoes and grabbed his keys.

Too much quiet, he couldn't handle tonight.

~~

She saw them on the other side of the street but kept her focus ahead. Still, one of them whistled. It was nearly full dark, with mainly the street lights letting her see where she was going, as well as the three figures in hoodies. They'd been standing, just laughing, but they started walking the direction she was going. On the other side of the street.

Just stay over there. She said it to herself and increased her pace somewhat. She did not want to look afraid. The sidewalks were empty otherwise. Figured. Why did people not go out walking anymore? Cars went past, like they always did...

"Hey girl, what's the rush?" The deep voice called from between passing cars.

How far now? A few blocks left. Too many. Her heart raced. Worse when they started to cross the street. Hell. Increasing her speed more in hopes they would be too lazy to bother to follow too fast, she felt a tightening in her chest. That slow-growing heart attack Gramps mentioned? She was too young and not really that out of shape.

Reaching for her pepper spray, a sick feeling in her gut reminded her she hadn't grabbed it. Only her phone. Her dead phone. She walked faster, now at almost a slow jog, which made her calf go ahead and cramp, which made her limp.

"Need a hand, girl? Maybe two or three or four hands?" A different voice, same group. Laughing. They were laughing. Probably, they were on something. Hell.

They were next to her now, one of them walking backward in front of her, laughing at her limp, imitating her. "On the way to work, or you work out here? How about a freebie or two or three?" He laughed and slowed down, right in front of her.

She moved around him and bumped into another one. Then she ran, pulling out her phone. They wouldn't follow if she ran. At least she hoped. And she hoped her leg wouldn't give out, that she wouldn't actually have a heart attack, that...

They were catching up, so she put the phone to her ear as though it wasn't dead, caught a glimpse of a street sign, and said loudly where she was, and that she was being followed. Slowing enough to keep from passing out from exhaustion and to be able to speak. But only that much.

"Cops are on the way." She yelled it through her heavy breathing.

They looked at each other, debating.

"I know you're on something. I'll tell them that."

One of them yanked the lead guy back by his arm. "Not worth it. Let's get outta here before they find our stash."

"Or we could grab the bitch and take her..."

"This one'll fight. No time for that, man."

With more hesitation, the lead guy warned her to keep her mouth shut and they turned and headed down an alley.

Isabel stopped only long enough to lean over and catch her breath, rubbing the cramp in her leg, and then forced herself to keep going, too fast, afraid they'd change their minds when cops didn't come.

~~

James got up to the top of the amphitheatre steps, again, and stopped, breathing heavy. In case he hadn't heard it, he pulled his phone out to check for a message or missed call. Nothing. "Where are you, Iz?" Debating whether to text again, he thought better of it and started the trek down the steps, using his flashlight app. Generally when he ran at night, he took a real flashlight, one with super bright LED bulbs. But he hadn't thought about it with his mind too wrapped up around her.

At the cement block, he stepped up and walked around the edge of it the way she had. And then he sat in the center and thought again about the way she'd been playing left-handed. With so much heart. Why would playing through struggle make her play with more heart? It only frustrated the hell out of him. He could hardly make himself... But it was for himself. He was trying to recapture his own ability. Isabel...

She'd done it to try to understand him, understand his frustration, his pain, to see how possible it was. It was for him, and he'd been a full-out asshole about it. "Fuck, Iz. Call me. Even if you shouldn't."

Getting up, he went over that night in his head. When he'd gotten too annoyed by her avoidance and ... tried to push her away. Was he? Was her neediness getting to him? Possible. Except that he also loved it. Would he continue to love it once he was fully recovered?

Maybe she wasn't sure. And maybe she wouldn't be so needy once she'd recovered. Although if it had been nine years by now and she'd chosen to give her child away, why wouldn't she be recovered? It was her choice. He knew how you could later regret a choice you wish you hadn't made, and obviously she regretted it, but still, she'd made it. Nine years ago. She'd been fifteen, nearly sixteen. Hardly the age to make such a huge choice. There was that.

And maybe it was more the guy she couldn't count on. Except she said she didn't care anymore. After two years, would she honestly stop caring within a couple of weeks or months?

Was he in Pittsburgh? Would she run into him again? Maybe that was her hesitation in going. "Call me, Iz. Just call me." Realizing he was the one sounding needy by now, James got up and jumped down off the block, away from the amphitheatre, walking down to the river where they'd canoed.

Planting himself on the damp ground, and it was hardly ever not damp given all the rain they got, and the near-constant clouds he hardly stopped to think about anymore other than when he got back from one of his east coast beach jaunts where sun was actually prevalent, he got on his phone and checked her sites. And her page. No activity there, but nothing unusual with that. She was rarely on it. Still, he sent a message, privately: Forget about me already down in the big city? He added a smiley face just to say he was teasing, although he wasn't terribly sure he was teasing. Okay, I know you're catching up with your grandparents, but how about a quick hello? Unless the kid with the arms has you too preoccupied. Teasing. LU.

Maybe he shouldn't have sent it, but at least she'd know he was thinking about her.

~~

She wanted James. She wanted to be in his apartment, in his arms. Right now, if he took her in his arms, she'd fall completely apart. Her legs throbbed. Her chest hurt. She had hardly stopped jogging since she got away from them. One more block. She had to slow down. Her feet hurt, too. Blisters, probably. She didn't even care. She just wanted to be home. Inside.

Finally reaching the door, she realized she didn't have the key to the house, either, and so rang the doorbell about five times while watching around her. All the movies with the hit and run vendettas or to keep someone quiet flashed through her head all the way back. She shouldn't have mentioned drugs. A stupid thing to do. They were on foot, though. Didn't mean they didn't have access to a car. "Come on, open the door." She knocked and it opened while she was knocking.

"Bella, what on earth…"

She pushed in, shoved the door closed, locked it, and clung to her grandma. Hardly breathing. No, breathing too fast. Shallow. Getting light-headed. Her legs cramping.

"What on earth happened? Isabel?" Her grandma stroked her head and then called out to her grandpa and she nearly fell when she tried to go in, the cramp in her calf now a full blown charley horse, incapacitating her, and she was lifted off her feet. Her grandpa.

"I'm… sweaty." And it hurt her chest to talk.

"Are you hurt?" He set her gently on the couch.

She shook her head. "Ran. Charley horse." She rubbed the spot but it made it worse so she stopped.

"You don't cry over pain. What happened?"

Cry? She hadn't noticed. With her grandpa insisting she talk, she got it out between breaths, in spurts, and sobbed on his shoulder until she was too tired.

"Come, Bella. Niall, bring her to the bath and I'll get her soaking in hot water and Epsom salts."

"I'm calling the cops." His voice was furious.

"No." The guy's voice telling her to keep her mouth shut echoed through her brain.

"Don't even try to stop me. I want those little assholes arrested."

"He's right, Bella. Don't argue." Her grandma stroked her face, her sweaty, hot face over her pounding head. She told Gramps to help get her to the bathroom first and then call.

~~

He had a sick feeling she wasn't coming back.

He'd been too rude. She'd avoided him for a week until he forced his presence on her. Yes, her greeting was nice, but it also felt desperate. Maybe getting away from it, from him, would make her see it wasn't a good idea, that he was too much risk, especially the way he'd come on to her after she'd said no. Stupid thing to do. It wasn't all him. She'd done her part to make him think she might. Still stupid.

Talk about a bad choice.

Couldn't *risk it*. She'd pulled away at the sight of the condom. Afraid to get pregnant again? Was it only that? He was offering protection, not that it always worked. Maybe it hadn't worked before.

But she was twenty-five, not fifteen, and he wouldn't walk away. He'd stay with her. He'd take care of his child. Not that he needed that in his life right now, until he was fully recovered and had been long enough he knew it would last. She was smart enough to know...

She wouldn't be back. Why would she? She had too much going for her, too many options.

Exhausted body and soul, he lay back on the grass, closed his eyes, and thought of the look on her face whenever he touched her. So beautiful. So afraid. But also trusting, or at least wanting to trust him.

And he'd blown it.

Maybe. Maybe they just had to go back to being professional, working together, and let other things wait until it was safer for both of them. She said she still wanted to work together. Hopefully, she meant it.

Thirty

Isabel woke up starving, with a headache. With a check of the time, she sat up fast and cringed, pressing a hand to the throbbing spot. Morning. And she hadn't plugged her phone in. She'd gone straight to bed after her bath. Her grandma had brought soup in for her, but she'd barely eaten it.

Where was her phone?

Getting up slowly, cringing at the pain in her head and her legs, her muscles stiff and heavy, she made her way out to the kitchen where she saw a light on.

"Bella." Her grandma came to her and helped her to a chair. "What hurts, honey?"

"Everything. Where's my phone?"

"It's here on the counter."

"Did James call?"

"I haven't heard any noise from it, but you said the battery died."

"Yes. I have to..." She tried to get up, but the pain got worse.

"Stay still. Your grandpa tried to plug it in, but his charger doesn't fit. If you tell me where yours is, I'll find it for you. In the meantime, I have hot tea ready." She went to pour a mug from her teapot and set it on the table. "What will you be able to eat?"

"Nothing."

"Oh, Isabel..."

"Toast? But I'll get it. You don't have to..."

"Nonsense. Sit still."

Giving in, she tried to think where her charger was, but the headache was making her brain fuzzy. She'd have to look, as soon as she could make herself move again. If she knew his number, the house phone would work, if he'd answer a number he didn't know. Sometimes he did. Sometimes not. Why hadn't she memorized it instead of relying on pulling up his name, or answering his last text? She could look him up online, but her laptop was among the boxes in her room, so she'd have to get up. She would, after some tea and toast. He could always look up her grandparents' number if he was too awful worried. They still had a landline and they were listed. It would be easy enough.

~~

Something pushed his shoulder and he threw a fist at the blurred face, felt the impact, tried to focus...

"It's just *me*, asshole." Bruce rubbed his jaw. "Fuck, that hurt. How in the hell drunk are you?"

James stared at his buddy in the bright light of ... morning? Was it morning? At the park. By the river. He scratched at his arms. Damned mosquitoes had taken advantage of him good. "It's morning. Saturday?"

"Yeah, and I think you broke my fucking jaw. What the hell?"

"Shit. Let me look."

"Are you kidding me?" Bruce shoved his hand away. "Are you part sober by now?"

"I'm fully sober. You startled me."

"Yeah, well, you might learn not to wake up swinging."

"Let me look."

"Wait." Bruce pulled James' eyes open wide one at a time. "You're seriously sober?"

"Didn't touch a drop."

His friend's chest rose and fell hard. "Good. You had us all worried like all hell, you know. I've been to every fucking bar in town looking for you. You've been out here all night?"

"Yeah." He rubbed his face and scratched at his arms. "Us? Us, who? Who did you call?"

"I have the whole posse out trying to find you. Guess I better call them off. How about you call your mom, though?"

His mom. "Fuck, why did you call her?"

"She called me. You were supposed to stop in last night."

"Last night?" He shoved a hand through his hair. "Forgot."

"Yeah, so call her."

While Bruce typed out whatever he thought necessary to whoever he was stupid enough to call before he knew it was necessary, James first checked his. His heart jumped. She'd answered. Finally.

Im so sorry. Phone was dead. Just plugged it in. Fighting headache. Call later okay?

It was dead all evening and all night before she noticed? The message was sent about an hour ago. They always said good night. Why wouldn't she have checked it?

"Army's called off. Sure you're okay?" Bruce nudged in. "What'd you do when you left the apartment? All of it. Before you call anyone, I want to know everything."

"I ran."

"Okay, Sherlock, but... Nothing more? No girls, right? No booze? Promise you're being straight with me."

"Neither. I wouldn't do that to her." Why had she not checked her phone last night?

"In that case, I'll forgive you for the broken jaw."

"It's not broken, or you wouldn't be talking so easily. How'd you find me here?"

"Isabel. Call her, J. She's pretty freaked out."

"Fuck, you didn't tell her you couldn't find me?"

"She called me a half hour ago when you didn't answer. I told her you were running and prayed I was right while I asked her, casually, where you most often ran these days. She's smart, though, probably caught on that I was worried. Call her and then call your mom, but do it while walking to the car. I'm heading back to get some sleep. About dead on my feet by now. Thanks for that, too."

He called his mom first since she would be the easiest and fastest to deal with. The relief in her voice made him guilty as hell and he promised to come for dinner the next day. He couldn't today. He was supposed to be headed to Pittsburgh to see Iz.

~~

Jumping when her phone rang, she pushed one hand against her head and grabbed the phone with the other. James. She sighed with relief as she answered. "Hey. I'm so sorry..."

"What's up, Iz?" He sounded testy.

"Um, my phone... I didn't know it was dead and I went for a walk." She wasn't about to tell him about the three guys. He'd worry and then he'd push her to come back and stay with him. She maybe wanted that, since she'd hardly thought of anything since it happened other than wanting to be in his arms, but it was too soon.

"All night? I waited up late for your call."

"I um, didn't feel good, so I took a hot bath and went to bed and I... I am sorry. Are you..."

"Didn't feel good? You seemed fine yesterday."

"I know. It... Nerves, I guess. This is harder than I thought."

"Come back up here if it's that hard to be there."

Hesitating, she fought back tears and tried to hide it from her grandma who'd been hovering all morning.

"Sorry." His voice softened. "I'm just... I missed saying good night, hearing your voice. Can't wait to see you. I'm going to shower and I can be on my way."

"Um, no, I..." She hurt. Her head, her calf, her feet, her body. He'd notice and she didn't want to talk about it.

"No? You don't want me to come?"

"I really need to rest today. Fighting a headache."

"I can rest with you. No need to go out."

She bit her lip and nearly agreed, but she had to go to the police station to file a report and ... and worrying him wouldn't help him, wouldn't help them be apart. "Maybe tomorrow instead?"

Silence. Briefly. "Can't. Promised Mom I'd be there for dinner. If I come, I want to at least spend the day."

At least. "Okay. Well..."

"I have a show lined up for you next weekend. Can you do it or should I cancel?"

"Where?"

"New Castle. The Confluence. Saturday five to seven. As a featured artist. Should be a decent audience. If you can do it."

"Of course. Thank you."

"You're welcome. Guess I'll see you then. Right?"

"James, don't be mad."

"I'm not mad. Gotta go. I reek and I need a shower." Bruce's voice came through the line although she couldn't hear what he said and James's voice softened. "I hope your head feels better. Call later, if you want."

"Thank you." She wiped tears from under her eyes. "I'll have my phone on. You can call anytime. Okay?"

"Yeah. Rest now. Talk to you later." He hung up.

Swallowing hard, she couldn't hold it back when her grandma hugged her and asked what was wrong. She told him he didn't buy her story and he'd think...

"Why didn't you tell him what happened?"

"He'd worry too much. He'd not want me to stay here."

"Do you want to stay here, Bella?" Taking her face in her hands, her grandma peered into her eyes. "Honestly. Is this what you want?"

"I don't know."

"I think you do."

She grabbed a deep breath and held it a few seconds. "I want to be with James, but ... I'm scared."

"Love is scary, honey. It's a good thing to be a little frightened of it.

That means you're thinking. But it's not a good thing to let it keep you from what you really want." Getting up, she ran a hand over Isabel's head with a grin. "Rest. I know you didn't sleep well. I'll be sure to wake you if he calls, and then we'll have a nice lunch before you have to go out."

~~

By Thursday, she was almost afraid to see him again. The police report had been taken, but she couldn't give them much detail since she'd been scared out of her mind and even had to guess at their heights, which she wasn't good at. They said it was a long shot to find them, but they'd call if they needed her to ID anyone. She hoped they wouldn't. She wanted to be done with it.

Her job interview had not gone well. They didn't like her looks and she could see they didn't. Just as well. She wasn't comfortable in the place, a small place, tight-knit, too cliquish. She'd been looking now and then, through job sites, but mostly she'd been writing. It felt good to be writing so much again, but it also made her wonder if she would have to stay in the city to be so inspired, or if it was the time away from him. Of course, it wasn't paying the bills or helping her find her own place where he could visit, and stay over.

And James was hardly talking to her. He only texted, hadn't asked to call, and his texts were only business. She was going to have to explain better. Her grandparents both thought she should if she respected him enough to think about making it long term.

Stuck on a phrasing that didn't sound right, she sighed, set her guitar aside, and picked up her phone. He'd be home by now, unless he'd stopped somewhere. She hoped he hadn't stopped somewhere, other than the grocery store. Of course, he could be running, too, but a quick text wouldn't bother him unless he wanted the excuse to take a short break. Otherwise, he could ignore it until he wanted to bother.

What should she say? She should have told him right away. Now it was harder. Starting with something simple to break the ice, something not professional, she gritted her jaw and sent the only thing she could think of. Hey Gilbert was that game bad or was it bad?

Readying herself to have to wait some time for a reply, she jumped when it came right away.

What game? Are we back to my last name?

Pirates. Last night. Did you watch?

Yeah and it was pretty bad. Did you?

Gramps had it on.

Ah.

And I was teasing. Sorry.

The reply was slow coming back. Don't be. Hi, Iz. How was your day?

A deep breath overtook her at the friendly tone. Long. Doubt the job will work out.

Sorry. Something better will come.

Ty. How was your day?

Long.

While she tried to figure out what to say next, how to lead into what she really had to say, he beat her to the punch. I miss you. Can I call?

Her eyes watered, and rather than answering in a text, she called him. They watered more at his voice, the friendly *Hey, Iz* that she loved by now. "I miss you, too."

"Good to know."

"Did you think I didn't? Or wouldn't?" Unable to sit, she got up and went to the long, narrow window in her room to watch traffic go by. She'd barely been out since that night, and only when her grandpa was with her.

"Wasn't sure. I thought maybe you were getting wrapped back up in your roots and thinking you were better off. Based on how quiet you've been and not wanting me there."

"No, I didn't... I did want you here. I just... I um, I wasn't sure I should tell you all of the reason it took so long to call you back. I don't want you to worry. It's fine. I'm being more careful."

"What's fine?"

She swallowed hard, trying not to let the fear creep back in, trying to make herself sound not terrified to be out on her own...

"Isabel? What is it? What happened?"

She told him, in maybe too much detail, more than she'd been able to give the detective because she'd been too nervous. All of it, that she'd been sore for three days and had done almost nothing but write to relieve tension, to try to get it out, that she didn't want him to worry.

"Should I come down there? Are you okay? I can leave now."

"You have work tomorrow."

"I'll skip it. Damn, Iz, you should have told me. That night, or at least the next morning."

"You were already worried about me being here."

"Yeah, well, turns out there was reason."

"No, I was just stupid. I won't be again."

"Stop calling yourself that. I'm coming down. Okay? Will you be at the house all night?"

"I will, but don't."

"Iz…"

"No. Really. This… It's not going to work if you think you have to run down here after me every time I get upset. It's fine, okay? Don't come." Silence came across the line. Much of her hoped he would ignore her plea and come anyway. "James? What are you doing now?"

"Pacing the apartment trying to decide whether to obey or just come to you, to make sure you're okay in person."

Her eyes clenched. "I love you, too. I'll see you in a couple of days, right? I am working. I'll have new songs for you. Maybe, um…" Did she dare suggest she could stay with him after the show until Monday when he left for work?

"Bring a few extra clothes. I have Davis's room cleared out, cleaned and bleached top to bottom. Honestly. I even bleached the ceiling, so it's… or you can have mine and I'll stay in there."

"Okay."

A pause. "Yeah?"

"I miss you."

"Me, too, baby. You're sure you're okay? You told me everything?"

"Yes. Both. Just scared and … and too out of shape." She shouldn't have said it. But he was right.

Silence came over the line again while she kicked herself for saying such a stupid thing, for rubbing it in.

"Waterfire's next weekend. How about staying for that, too? Can you do all week? I'll try to get you a gig on Friday to make it more worth it. Maybe a week night thing, also."

"Okay. But what's Waterfire?"

"Wow, Isabel. I'll explain later. Bring enough for a few days. I won't hold you to it, but you're welcome if you want to stay. As long as you want."

                              Thirty-one

James paced in front of the Confluence and watched every car that
pulled in. He expected her to be there already. More than half of his
family was there, as well as a few friends, even a couple of coworkers
from the plant. Where was she?

Giving in, he gave her a call. It went to voicemail. His stomach
churned. Something happened. She always made sure to have her phone
charged. Since her scare the day she moved back to Pittsburgh, she
always double-checked it before going anywhere, and she'd picked up a
car charger just in case. No way it was dead again.

"No sign yet?"

He jumped at his brother's voice. "Obviously not."

Denny set a hand on his back. "Relax, J. She probably hit traffic. It is
Saturday night coming out of Pitt."

"She'd answer her phone if it was just traffic."

"Unless it's dead or she forgot it or something. Chill out. A phone
isn't all that reliable, as you well know. Maybe you should give her a
necklace with a GPS tracker so you always know where she is, like the
dude in Star Trek."

"Funny." He paced more, headed toward the parking lot entrance.

"Getting hit by a car won't get her here faster. Come on, let me buy
you a... Hell, what do you drink these days?"

"Iced tea. Or iced coffee. Something with caffeine."

"Uh huh, herb tea might be more helpful." Denny stepped in front
of him to keep him from getting closer to the road. "She's fine, J. Come
on inside."

"Can't."

"Girls run late. It's what they do."

"Not Isabel. She doesn't. If she's less than ten minutes early, she
considers herself late." He shoved a hand through his hair and checked
his phone again. Nothing. "Come on, Iz. Where are you?"

Denny called over to Burt at the doorway. "Hey, help me get him to
calm down before he blows a gasket."

James rolled his eyes but didn't bother to answer.

Burt asked what was going on, but unlike Denny, he didn't seem to
think all was fine. Of course, James had told Burt what happened with

the three thugs. He hadn't told Denny because he didn't want any smartass comments about it. "Want me to go out and look for her? Is she coming up 18?"

"376 to the exit."

"That would make things harder."

"I can give Rob a call if you want and see if there's been an accident or anything."

Burt told Denny to shut the hell up, but James was tempted to let his brother call his buddy who worked for the state police. Instead, he paced and watched every car that pulled in. He nearly said he needed a drink, but it would only make his big brothers overreact and over protect again, and… He did want a drink. Hell. For the first time in… no, the second time since he'd been seeing her more than professionally, he badly wanted a whiskey. Scotch. Gin. Damned near anything. Her phone would be on. He knew it would be on. Something happened. She hadn't told him about the thugs for nearly a week because she didn't want him to be worried. What happened now that she didn't want to tell him?

He tried calling again. Still voicemail. He tried messaging. Nothing. "Fuck."

At five minutes after her scheduled start time, the manager came out and asked if she was still coming. James looked at Denny. "Call your buddy. Something's not right." While his brother was trying to get road info, James pulled up his traffic app. He'd tried already, but could be it would be updated now when it wasn't earlier.

Denny wandered away to talk, paused, hung up and came back. "Yeah, um…" He rubbed his chin. "There's a pile up on 376."

His knees gave out and he crouched to the sidewalk.

Bruce was right there. "Lots of people on the road, J. Don't assume she's involved. Stuck in it maybe, but…"

"If she was only stuck in it, she'd answer me. I gotta get there." He stood, heading to his truck.

His brothers stopped him. He'd never get to it, never get close enough, blah blah. Yeah, maybe, but…

At the ring of his phone, he about had a heart attack. Not a number he knew. Generally, he'd ignore it, but if it was… His hand shook as he answered with a wary hello.

"James. I'm glad you picked up."

"Iz. Thank God." He grabbed a deep breath. "Are you okay? Where are you calling from?"

"I'm fine. I'm on Gramps' phone. There's this big accident..."

"I know. I've called twenty times. Slight exaggeration. You're not hurt?"

"No. We were just barely behind it and it took forever to get off the road, but we're on 18 now. I know I'm late already. I'm sorry."

Breathing again, he shoved a hand through his hair. "Why didn't you answer me? It didn't get through?"

"I um, can't find my phone. I've looked all over the car, in my bag, everything. I know I had it. I did. I made sure I had it and it was fully charged, not taking chances, but..."

He laughed. A release. The girl was going to drive him crazy, but at least she was fine. "Okay, but you're okay?"

"Yes About twenty minutes out, Gramps says. I should have put your number in his phone because I don't know it; I'm bad at numbers, but I finally remembered it was on my website as management contact and I found it there. I'm so glad Gramps updated to a smart phone recently. I should have thought of doing that sooner, but I'll memorize it now. I'm so sorry I worried you."

"It's fine, baby. As long as you're okay. Take your time." He saw his brothers exchange glances. At the *baby*, he supposed, since he used to say he thought it was stupid to call a girlfriend that. He couldn't give an ounce of a fuck at the moment. They could harass him all they wanted.

"Will they still let me go on? I am sorry. I meant to leave sooner, in case of traffic, but..."

"It's fine. I'll let them know. Just get here safe."

"Thank you. See you soon."

"You better. Love you."

"I love you, too, James. Can't wait to see you."

He gasped a deep breath. The casual *love you* wasn't good enough. "Isabel?" She'd hung up. But she was safe. He lowered to a crouch again out of relief.

"Come on." Denny grabbed his arm. "I'll buy you a coffee."

"Bring it out here, if you don't mind. And let them know she'll be here in about twenty." He saw his brother's head shake, but he left and James lowered onto the sidewalk leaning back against the building, watching for her.

Burt lowered next to him. "So, this girl is..."

"The one I didn't know I needed." A phrase Burt gave him about his then-fiancé and now his wife and mother of four kids, who he still loved like crazy. It was in his eyes whenever he looked at her.

"Then why did you let her move farther away from you?"

"She wanted it. And it wasn't from me. It was..."

"From what?"

From what? She'd talked about looking for an apartment in Greenville and then backed out. Abby would have moved in with her. She could have done it if she hadn't quit her second job within a couple of months. From what? Or to what? He still didn't know where her baby's father was from or where he was now. Maybe he was in Meadville? Maybe she was again trying to escape her past?

Or she needed to keep distance from him until she was more sure. Maybe she'd moved away from him, nothing else. "Not sure. But it's not my place to tell her she can't, you know. I didn't let her. It was her call."

"And yet you didn't go with her. That's what I meant."

"My job's up in Greenville."

"A job you don't care about. A job for which you turned down a promotion."

James couldn't answer that one.

"What was her deal with the kids at dinner?"

"Yeah, I... can't say since I didn't ask if I could."

"But you know."

"Yeah. Maybe." And maybe there was a hell of a lot more to that story and he'd reacted so badly, she couldn't tell him.

"James." Burt shifted to face him better. "Be careful with this until you're more on your feet. I can see you're not. I can see you..."

"Wanted a drink? Yeah, I wanted a drink, but I didn't try to leave to get one."

"We wouldn't have let you, but as long as you're still craving it, you have to be careful with anything that might throw you."

"I know. And she knows I'm still recovering. She's watching for signs, and I know she is."

"Well, that's good, I guess, but you're my brother and I'm more worried about you. However that sounds. Is she going to stand by you if you bounce a bit?"

"Bounce? You mean fall off the wagon." He gulped a deep breath of air that was starting to cool with the lowering of the sun. "Not sure, to be honest. I don't intend to make her have to decide."

Burt let it go, for the moment, and the near silence of evening trying to fall into night mixed with the hush of rubber flying along pavement and a couple of crows in the distance squawking at each other took over, until a red Chevelle, '79, he thought, caught his attention. A gorgeous car, in perfect condition, it looked like. It pulled in close to him and Isabel got out of the back.

Jumping up to meet her, he grasped her in a tight hug and kissed her head, his tension dissolving with her touch, the way she clung to him so comforting. As soon as he could make himself release her enough, he set his hands alongside her head and just looked at her a moment.

"I scared you. I'm so sorry."

Unable to resist, he gave her a soft kiss and then held her eyes. "I love you so damned much. The thought of losing you in a fucking accident about killed me."

She held him again, resting her head on his shoulder.

"Alright, baby girl." Her grandpa interfered. "You're already late, and I found what you were looking for." He held up her phone. "Dropped it in the trunk beside your guitar."

James took the guitar. "Come in and unwind a bit while I get this tuned for you. Everything's set up, and you have a good crowd waiting."

~~

His family being there made her more nervous than anyone else being there, and it was a good audience, but his brothers joked with her before she went on and complimented her during her break, a short one since she started so late, and his mom asked if she'd come for Sunday dinner, since James made it obvious she was staying with him for a couple of days before going back to Pittsburgh.

She couldn't stay the week, as he'd asked. Two more job interviews prevented that, but as she told him, it would help toward her goal of getting back into her own place so he could come stay with her on weekends when she had shows down that direction. He had her booked the following Friday night up in Erie, so she agreed to stay with him next weekend. He'd mentioned that, also, like it was a claim or something. Or like he was telling his family this was a serious relationship and they'd have to get used to her.

She did well with the new crowd, and so did her tip jar. The manager invited her to come back and James said they'd arrange it. But as nice as it felt, she was glad when it was time to leave with him.

"You were incredible, Iz. And you look great." In the quiet and semi-dark of his truck, he stroked the side of her head and skimmed her shimmery gray tunic blouse that fell over what would be a pencil skirt if she was pencil shape but was more like an upside-down pear over her round thighs and butt. Luckily, it had a good stretch to it so it wasn't tight. The tunic covered her too-big parts well enough it looked okay, and she'd added color with a new scarf she'd found on the strip while out walking with Gramps, this one soft aqua and yellow that accented the green sea glass necklace. She'd planned to wrap it around her waist like a belt, but decided it emphasized her too-thick waist that way, so she draped it around her neck, letting one end fall over her right shoulder down her front and the other down her back, keeping the focus higher.

"Want to stop somewhere for dessert?"

"Thank you, but let's just go home. If that's okay."

"Home? As in my apartment?"

"Well, that's as close as I have to a home now."

"More than with your grandparents where you grew up?"

"Yes."

His head tilted in thought. "Meaning Greenville is growing on you?"

"No. Meaning you're my comfort zone more than anywhere else."

"Yeah?" He ran fingers through her hair. "More than the beach?"

If he was going to tease, she could play that game. "Well, at least as much as the beach."

"I'm flattered, and I'll take it." With a grin, he gave her a soft, quick kiss, and moved back to head toward home.

It wasn't far, really, from New Castle to Greenville, but it felt as though it was, and she was glad to finally see his building. He caught her eyes as though reading her thoughts, then got out and came around to help her out, grabbed her guitar, and took her hand. "I'll get the rest later."

Heat swirled between them, even in the cool dampness of the early fall evening. Not technically fall yet, but western PA fall, anyway. His intensity surrounded her all the way inside the building and up to his apartment. The desire. She could see it in him every bit as well as she could feel it within herself.

Bruce and Abby weren't home yet, although they left before she and James left. He texted his friend and got a quick reply. "They're doing a late movie. They'll be a couple of hours yet."

"So only one roommate tonight?" She kicked her boots off.

"He's out, too. Night fishing."

"Really? How will he see what he's doing?"

"Lanterns. I've done it. It can be fun. I'm grabbing water. Want a glass?"

"Sure. I'm going to change." Heading toward Davis's room, since he'd mentioned she could use it, although the thought was a bit creepy, she was stopped by his fingers taking hers. And his body pressed in, with a hand cupping the back of her head to pull her in for a deep kiss. A long, intense deep kiss that sent a shiver all the way to her toes.

"Mm." Moving his lips to her neck, he barely lightened his grip. "Damn I missed you this week."

"Me, too." Setting a hand on his chest, she could feel his rapid heartbeat.

"Use my room. I'll take his."

"You don't need to."

"I'd rather have you in mine. Don't ask why. Just a thing."

"Thank you." Isabel decided to run through the shower since her nerves made her sweat like crazy during her show. Making it fast, she started to pull on her sweats, but his roommates weren't there, wouldn't be there until after she'd be asleep. Instead, she wrapped the towel around her still damp body, took her things to his room, and borrowed one of his shirts, another music shirt, but a band she didn't know. Local, she expected. It reached just past her thighs, like a nightshirt. Instead of her thick sweatpants, she pulled short leggings on underneath, cringing at how bulky they made her look, especially while in bloated stage. She'd have to start doing something about her shape so she wouldn't cringe at the idea of James seeing her undressed when it was time for that. More than he had already. For now, his shirt covered it pretty well.

He was playing guitar when she went back out. Left-handed. It was stilted, like someone still learning, but he was playing. Her eyes watered and she went to him, stood in front of him, and watched.

He stopped and set it aside. "Long ways to go yet."

She tried to answer, but she couldn't find words, any words, that would be right. So she moved up between his legs, leaned down, and kissed him, not at all objecting when he gently pulled her down onto one leg and wrapped his arms around her waist, deepening the kiss. Or she was. Definitely, she was, and she decided she better ease back.

"I think I recognize that shirt." His voice was husky.

"Hope you don't mind."

He played with the sleeve while rubbing the backs of his fingers against her arm. "One of the local bands I supported before they broke up. Keep it if you want." He traced the small design of a whiskey jug and

MW over the left breast. "So what is it about girls wearing their boyfriend's clothes?"

"Has that happened to you a lot?"

He caught her eyes. "Is that a hidden question?"

"No. I mean, why do you ask?"

"Isn't it a thing? Seems to be, in movies."

"Oh. Well." Her hand on his chest, she leaned in to kiss his neck, and his jaw. "I can't say for others, but for me, I mean, I've actually never done it before and wouldn't have cared to, but ... it smells like you. And I can imagine it on you, so wearing it to bed is like having you there, kind of, especially when I have to be away from you. It's nice. Comforting. Does that sound weird?"

"Weird? No. It's a huge turn-on, to be honest. I was kind of hoping you'd say I was supposed to ask for it back."

"Hm. Not tonight. Maybe one of these nights, though." She nuzzled her face against his, savoring the mixture of warm, soft skin and prickly hair growing back in.

"You're killing me, Iz."

She couldn't help a slight grin. "Play more for me."

"Can I take that the way I want?"

Getting up, she handed the guitar back. "You switched the strings around. This isn't a left-handed guitar."

"You've been doing your homework."

"I borrowed one. To try. I gave it back after..."

"After I acted like an idiot. I am sorry."

"Play one of yours."

"How about I try to show you what I hear with your lyrics for *Not What I Saw*, since you asked."

"Yes. Of course." She listened with her eyes closed, thinking about the lyrics in her head while he played, struggling, but decent. When he started to get frustrated about having to struggle with the chords, she sang with it. He relaxed, played better to an extent, but got frustrated again.

Grabbing her own guitar, she played it with him, learning his music, and then adding some of her own, what she'd written for it. Blending and meshing the two. And he sang with her on the chorus, harmonizing.

Finally, they set the guitars aside and he reached for her hand to pull her back onto his leg, but she straddled him instead.

"It's a beautiful song, Iz."

"More so now. Much more. And you're right. It needs to be called *The Texture of Glass*. James..."

"Hm?" He kissed her neck.

"I love you like crazy, too."

Thirty-two

Pacing in front of his building while he watched cars moving anywhere close, James checked his phone again, for maybe the fiftieth time since she'd let him know she was leaving Pittsburgh. She wasn't late; he was only anxious after her recent close calls, one on the road.

She'd insisted on driving up herself since there was "no reason" to be driven by either her grandpa or by him when she had a car and a license and knew the way. Still, it was rainy and foggy and no matter how careful she was, too many were not. Since the advent of automatic lights, people had become too lazy about physically turning them on, as though they could trust the things to come on at the right times. Even with as much as he was into tech of any kind, he wouldn't think of relying on it that much. He even double-checked when his backup camera said everything was clear. Tech was often faulty. Often. He knew that well, since he was so often called to fix tech glitches.

He considered doing some advertising for his tech freelance work, leaving the plant, and building his own business up to have flexible hours and locations, but the plant included insurance and such that he'd lose, so until he was more stable, he didn't want to go that far. Although it would be nice to be able to spend the week in Pittsburgh with Isabel and bring her back with him on weekends to do area shows, including more around Erie. If he could get her more used to that area, maybe she'd consider a move up there so they'd be close to the lake. Of course, if she got a good job in Pitt, it might be hard to convince her to let it go and start again.

With a sigh, he decided to do his stretching since he'd gone for a long run before she was due in, running while she was driving. A good way to get the nerves out. He kept thinking about calling, but he didn't want her to pick up the phone while driving, so he waited. Even with taking Monday off to drive her back to her grandparents for her interviews during the week, and staying the day with her, coming home late enough that Tuesday had been rough and he'd crashed early that night, it was a long week and he was ready to have her home.

Home. He'd never thought much about calling his place home, since he still tended to think of his parents' place as that, but since she'd said it the week before, he had to admit it damned sure felt like home when she was there with him.

A girl whistled from a passing car. He'd taken his shirt off and left it on the building's front railing since it got drenched from the brief passing shower while he was running. Instead of rolling his eyes, he gave her a wave and got a big smile in return. Then he went on with his stretch. Arms high, he leaned backward and then slowly down to touch the sidewalk, pushed one foot behind him for a lunge to stretch the quads and glutes, then brought it back to stretch the other.

"You know it's raining, right?" Isabel, with her window rolled down, stopped in front of him.

Standing, he tried not to act as relieved as he was. "Hey baby, I was getting worried."

"It's foggy. Traffic was slow."

"Figured. Go park and let me show you how glad I am you got here okay."

With a grin, she cruised just over to the parking lot and he followed, opening her door as soon as the engine was off. He only leaned in to kiss her briefly, since he was wet from sweat and the misty rain, but she wrapped around him like it didn't matter. And she gave him a deep kiss.

"Damn. He's taken."

They both looked over at the voice, the girl from the car. It had circled back. There were two girls inside.

"Are you like, serious, or is this just..."

Isabel slid a hand up to his bare chest and eyed them. "Move along." When they did, with some comment he didn't quite catch, she looked up at him. "Someone you know?"

"Nope. They just went past and waved, so I waved back." Her hand was warm against his cool skin, and he loved the sensuality of it. "Jealous?"

"Jealous, no. Possessive, yes. I missed you."

Taking her hand, he kissed her fingers. "Let's go in."

Setting her bag in his room and letting her know there was warm water on the stove for tea, he ran through the shower. When he came out, she was working with the left-handed guitar he'd bought on Tuesday after work, when, tired as he was, he still wasn't in a hurry to go back to his place when she wouldn't be there. He left it on a stand in the corner of the apartment where he'd see it every time he sat down, as a reminder that, one, he should practice, and two, he could do it if he kept going.

She was playing one of her own songs. Badly. But again, he saw more heart in it than when she played right-handed. When he walked up in front of her, she shrugged. "Yes, that was a really bad job, but this guitar is beautiful. I love the string action and the natural wood look."

"Not an expensive one. Figured I should start low and see how it goes. It's a nice little dreadnought, though. The open pore mahogany gives it that rich sound." Reversing the scene from the other day, he took it gently from her hands and leaned down to kiss her. When her arms wrapped over his shoulders, he picked her up with his hands under her thighs and lowered onto the couch with her legs straddling his. "You know you have what it takes, right?"

"Um, should I guess what we're talking about?" Her eyes sparkled in a tease. "And you're ridiculously strong to be able to pick me up that way, without it even looking like any effort." She caressed his shoulders.

"I was talking music, and you're not all that heavy, Iz. Thanks for the compliment, though. Not only your songs, but ... you. Like I said, you can make it as a performer."

"You smell good." She nuzzled her face against his neck.

"Don't change the subject."

"I only want to sell songs, not perform."

"But..."

"You can sing them, if you want." She kissed his jaw. "And you just shaved."

"I don't sing well enough..."

"Your voice is far nicer than mine. Your pitch is perfect. Your tremor is gorgeous. Your phrasing. Your range. You're a singer, James. You're the singer I wish I could be, but I don't have your gift. Voice or guitar. You're..."

"I have dinner in the crock pot, should be ready soon. Thought we'd eat in before your show."

"It's only two o'clock, just after."

"We'll need to leave by four-thirty, latest, given the distance and weather. So I figured if we ate by three-thirty..."

"Who's changing the subject now?"

"Distracting myself." He kissed her nose. "And after your show, I'll take you for a late-night brunch of sorts. Sound good?"

She teased the hair at his nape. "You're management. Just let me know what to do."

A groan came from deep within his chest. "Careful."

"Well, I do only mean musically. And I will argue if I decide to."

"Hope you would, musically or not." Detaching until he was beside her instead of underneath her, since he'd missed her far too much to stay so close, he asked to hear about her job interviews. One of them sounded more promising, but the other she sounded more excited about, a possible music industry job, an assistant to an assistant, but in the industry. She said it was a huge long shot and she wouldn't get her hopes up, that the other paid better and she should hope for that instead.

"Iz, you hope high, not mediocre. Okay?"

"The one that sounds better is in downtown Pittsburgh. The other is up just north of Wexford, so it would be a drive every day until I move, but if I found a place up there, I'd be closer to you."

He raised her chin gently to meet her eyes. "You go after what you most want, not better logistics."

"Well, with the first one, I can still just stay with my grandparents. It's even walking distance, so it would be easier, but it would pay less. It'll take longer to save for an apartment."

"If that feels better to you, and you get a choice, take it. We can work around it."

"Sing with me." She touched his hair. "Please."

~~

Cuddling against him on the couch while James told Bruce and Abby how well she'd done at the Erie gig, that it was a shame the weather kept her audience so limited, but that she'd been asked back, Isabel wished she would have taken him up on the offer to get a hotel room up by the lake rather than driving back to Greenville so late. So she would have him alone. They could have gone to Presque Isle in the morning and then come back for Waterfire.

But she didn't want him to spend the money for the hotel and then breakfast and she couldn't afford it until she got a job, even with the decent tips she'd made from the small, but appreciative, audience. She also would have felt obligated to share one room to save money and then she would have felt like it was kind of expected that they would take things further, and she was not going to do it under expectations.

When she could hardly keep her eyes open and had to give in for the night, he walked her to his room, gave her a sweet longish kiss, and told her to sleep as long as she wanted in the morning, that he'd likely go for a run first thing.

Thirty-three

Checking his phone, he read the message from his little brother and put it back in his pocket. "My parents would love for you to come for dinner tomorrow." James took a big bite of the gyro and followed it with a swallow of Haitian coffee from the food truck. He'd stood in two lines at the Waterfire food court, a parking lot across the street from the Quaker Steak and Lube restaurant and out of the way of the street lined in vendors under white tents, in order to get both of his favorites.

Isabel licked tzaziki sauce off her fingers. "Your parents text you?"

"Felix. Passing along the message. And he actually said it would be nice if you could manage to drag me home again, but I wasn't supposed to say it that way because they don't want me to think they only want you there in order to get me there."

"I'm not the one who got you there."

"Well, you are, kind of. Probably wouldn't bother if I didn't want to show you off." He winked.

"Good try." From the curb they'd found as the only available space to sit while enjoying their elevated fair food, she watched the band set up on the temporary stage.

"Try? As in, too much too soon to go back again, or as in you don't believe me?"

"Hm." She sipped her coffee. "Both, maybe." Brushing hair from her face, she turned her eyes to the crowd.

For a damp, cloudy day, Sharon's Waterfire was still packing in crowds. He'd had to park at the far end of the Discount Shoes parking lot to find a space his truck would fit, hopefully without some idiot opening a door into it. They'd walked by all of the vendors already, sat a while to listen to an oldies group play songs they both knew well, and wandered down the river a ways. She'd bought him a large piece of green sea glass wrapped with silver wire into a tree shape pendant on a thick black cord because it was similar to hers. She said, away from the girl who'd made it, that she knew it wasn't close to the quality of the one he'd had made for her, but it was the best she could do for now.

He was glad to wear it, and glad she had hers on, highlighted over her nicely tanned skin by a V-neck dark green shirt that emphasized her breasts nicely and flared to cover the curves of her stomach and hips over tan-colored jeans, with a long sweater hanging barely from her shoulders for warmth. It covered even more of her backside, also. He liked her curves, but he knew she did not.

"You can go to dinner with your family tomorrow and I'll head back to Pitt, so I don't interfere. I have to go back Monday morning, latest, anyway..."

"Uh, no."

"My interview is Monday afternoon."

"Right. Monday. Not Sunday. Sunday's still mine. You don't want to go, I won't go. What do you think of the coffee?"

"It's wonderful. I love the brown sugar in it. But I don't need your family more annoyed with me than they probably are already."

Having taken a good bite of the gyro, he nearly swallowed far too fast and had to chew a few more times before he could answer. "What makes you think they are?"

"They have to be wondering what I have against kids."

"You have a right to your reasons. They can get over it."

"That doesn't make me feel better."

He shrugged before he could stop himself. "Well." Taking another bite, he wiped tzaziki sauce from his lips. "You make a choice, you deal with it, right? Whatever everyone else thinks?"

"But they don't understand, and I don't..."

"I don't either, really, but I know there's plenty I do and have done that you don't understand. That's life. We're all different."

"James." She'd started to unwrap her gyro more, but stopped and turned to him more directly. "You think it was my choice, don't you?"

"Of course it was." At her raised eyebrows, he regrouped. "Well, I don't mean getting pregnant. Obviously, I don't figure you were trying to do that, but... Okay. So, yeah, I'm glad you chose to have your child. So many take the easier way out."

"It wouldn't be easy to make that choice, or to deal with it. Or even easier. I can't imagine it would be."

"Maybe not. More convenient, then. Whatever. I'm glad you didn't do that. I just don't exactly understand how, even if you were so young, you could just give your child away. Some really should. I get that. Too many are parents who shouldn't be. But you, you're smart and hard working and kind. Resourceful. Courageous. Yeah, you are, so don't tell me you're not. You'd be a good mom, so..."

"You think so?"

"I know so. What? Did you think you wouldn't be? Is that what your mom did? She convinced you that you wouldn't be a good mom?"

"Well, she did think I wouldn't be, but ... it wasn't my choice." Her voice was soft, her eyes moist. "I didn't choose to give her up."

Letting that register, he kept his eyes on a few guys walking past closer than they would have needed, trailed by a scent he recognized well enough to be wary. But they went on by. "You mean you changed your mind? They don't just take them away."

"They do if you're fifteen and your mother forges your signature while you're too out of it to know she did."

"She what?"

"I didn't want to give her up, James. I wanted her. They knew I wanted her. No matter how often they told me I was too young, too irresponsible, that it would ruin not only my life, but hers, as well, I wanted her. Yes, I would have taken care of her. I would have quit school and found a job, any job I could find, and I would have taken care of her. I would have."

"Iz..."

"Mom kept saying the child could turn out too much like her father and I'd never be able to handle it and... She didn't want me or my child to embarrass her is what she meant. Heaven forbid Jocelyn Dillon-Sanderson, community icon, would have a grandchild before it fit into her schedule. She was actually worried my baby would be too much like me, too hard to handle, and she'd end up having to take care of another child who wasn't enough like her."

"She didn't say that."

"No, she said it was the father's genes she was worried about and that I would mess up my future, that I wasn't mature enough or responsible enough to take care of a child. But I'm not stupid. I know what she meant. I was too hard on her, is what she meant, and she didn't want to risk doing it again."

"How..?" James scratched the back of his head, trying to sort it out and to figure out what to say. "If she forged your name, wouldn't you know? Couldn't you tell them she did? How did they just take the child without you knowing? I can't imagine it would be that simple."

"I have to think they probably agreed it was for the best and let her do it without questioning it enough. Especially with my medical record."

"Meaning, drugs?"

"No. I never did that. I had a really hard pregnancy. My age, maybe.

I was sick a lot. I couldn't handle going to school so I homeschooled but I was so sick so often, I just couldn't do it. I failed Freshman year and I was in and out of the doctor's office all the time." Giving up on the gyro for the moment, she sipped at her coffee, her eyes anywhere but on him.

"Mom kept saying it was a sign I wasn't meant to do it yet and I shouldn't keep trying. Really, I think the stress at home is what made it so bad. And I was scared, of course. I needed..."

When she shrugged, James wrapped an arm around her and kissed the side of her head. "You needed support, not criticism. Where were your grandparents?"

"Away a lot. When they did come check on me, Mom sniped at them about their influence, about the way they'd carted me around with their musician friends in the wrong atmosphere that made me think it was okay to... Anyway, it led to a fight every time, and I just... I had to ask them not to come because I couldn't stand the fighting or to hear my grandparents being insulted because of my screw up."

"I can't imagine having parents like that."

"I'm glad you can't. Anyway, labor was bad, too. Nearly three days' worth. They finally had to do an emergency C-section because she just wouldn't come, even with drugs to make it faster, which also made it harder. They lost her heart rate and it scared them. I hurt too much to think about being scared. I didn't know it was possible to live through pain like that." With a deep breath, she took a couple more swallows of her coffee. "When she was finally out and I heard her cry, they tried not to let me see her, said they needed to go clean her up and so on, but I insisted. So they put her in my arm and she stopped crying and I started crying. Through all of that pain, I didn't, but when she was in my arm and comforted by my touch enough to cuddle into me like she knew she was mine and I was hers, I cried like I don't think I ever had before. She was so beautiful. Those huge brown eyes looked at me so trusting, and when they were done stitching me up, I told everyone to get out so I could just be with her and I nursed her on my own, not well, and it hurt but I didn't care. She was so beautiful. And she was mine. *Mine*, not his. I would have done my best for her. Maybe Mom's right. Maybe I would have messed up, but so did she. At least I would've put my child's needs first. I'm not sure how I could have done much worse than she did, to be honest."

When her voice faltered, James kissed her head again.

"They came back and said they were taking her to the nursery so I could sleep and to check her vitals and everything. And when I woke up enough to demand to see her, she was gone. Just like that. No warning. No goodbyes. They'd kept me knocked out for most of two days, for recovery, and by then, they'd given her away. I yelled. I told them to bring her back, but they said I'd signed the papers and she was already with another couple, a couple old enough to take care of her and it was for the best. I told them I signed nothing and I wanted her back, but they said I was only exhausted and confused... And she was gone."

"Damn, Iz." Goose bumps raised along his arms.

"I love my daughter. I love her more than anything. And I miss her. They kept saying I'd get over it. My grandparents came; they'd been out of state on business since she was early, and they were furious. But they couldn't do anything since it was all *legal* and final. They took me home with them when I was released and I stayed there from then on. I didn't speak to my parents for two years, at least. I still barely do."

"I'm sorry." It wasn't enough, of course, but what else could he say. He did hold her in close. "I'm so sorry, Iz."

"I look at your niece with her brown eyes and dark curly hair and I just..." Her head shook.

"Maybe we can find her."

"Her records are sealed until she's eighteen. For her protection. I tried. Grandpa tried. He tried for the longest time. Until she's eighteen, I can do nothing. And by then, she will have written me off, if she even knows. Maybe they didn't tell her she was adopted. Maybe she has no idea I'm out here thinking about her, or she knows and hates me because I gave her up. I'd just really like to see her and make sure she's safe and happy and with good people and I'd like to tell her, just once, how much I love her. Just once, whether or not she believes me."

There was nothing he could say, so he held her silently. His gut ached for her pain, for being too stupid to not ask more when she told him, for assuming... She was right; he assumed far too much. He was damned lucky she gave him another chance, and said as much.

"Can we skip the family thing this weekend? I won't always refuse. Okay? I just need time."

"Of course."

They sat and watched the band tune up on the little stage and he urged her to finish her gyro while they listened to the jazz trio that mixed in some contemporary stuff. He mentioned them doing so to keep their modern audience's interest. And then he took her to the bridge that had been closed to traffic. People thronged each side of it, looking out over the river or standing in groups talking and laughing.

Weaving up past the now-empty canopied platform beside the bank where they'd listened to music earlier, he took her over to the other side where they could see the huge American flag outside the Army surplus store building and then down farther until there was a clearing against the river's edge.

With her arms folded over the black metal railing, she watched the tall flickering flames inside large round braziers sticking up out of the river running in two lines. The flames reflected in the water, making each brazier look even larger than it was, and more significant. A row of ducks, a mother and her four babies, swam along in between, unconcerned about the fire or the crowd of people, their voices casting a subdued hum in the late afternoon light. A small drone buzzing around overhead filming the event caught her attention, and after watching it a while, she released the railing and snuggled in against him.

Dusk descended into dark while a small succession of boats rowed past. First came a local singer in a black dress, her face barely lit up by lights in the boat and the flames from the braziers. Next was a shirtless male fire dancer who captivated Isabel. Her eyes were on his every move all the way to where they stood and well past them. Next came a singer he knew, one James followed now and then when he heard about his shows. He stood, just him and his guitar and a mic, on the boat, and James couldn't help but wish he could do the same, with his love for water and boats.

Maybe he could get Isabel out there. He'd have to check into it. He could be one of the rowers and go with her. Next year. First, he needed to build her up more, get her to more shows in the area.

The local guy was apparently the last entertainer. Music faded out. People drifted away from the fences. The crowd around them cleared, still with murmurs of conversation, as though the fire had calmed their souls.. Still, she stared at the water, at the flames burning themselves out.

"Isabel." He kissed her head. "Tell me about her father. What drew you to him? You said you weren't in love with him, and yet..."

She looked up at him, then back at the water, the fire dancing in the soft flow of the river. "He was one of the small group I used to hang out with when I ditched school. A decent guy, really. He'd stood up for me a couple of times against less decent guys and kind of let everyone know they better not mess with me."

"Someone people didn't want to tangle with?"

"Right. Well, those who hung out in the streets didn't, anyway. He was quiet, but strong and good with his hands. Defensively, I mean. He never started anything, but you didn't want to push him. He um, wasn't treated well at home."

"Abused?"

"Yeah. I saw the marks now and then, although he tried to hide them. His mom's boyfriend. He talked about strangling him in his sleep but I told him he'd just end up in jail and he didn't deserve that. I said he should leave, just get out, since he was eighteen and could do it legally. I finally convinced him to at least consider leaving, starting somewhere else, for his safety, and he asked if I'd go with him since I wasn't happy at home, either. We weren't... We were only hanging out then. Of course, I wasn't old enough to leave, and I couldn't do it to my grandparents. Not to mention my parents would have found me, and dealing with that...

"After I said no, but maybe I'd catch up with him in a few years when I could do it legally and still stay in touch with my grandparents, I didn't see him for a few days. I figured he'd left."

Her fingers gripped the metal bar with a shake of her head. "About a week later, he showed up. He was covered in fading bruises. He never showed pain before, but he winced when I touched his side, and I cried. He said it was fine, he felt better for fighting back even if he got pummeled worse for it, and he wasn't going back there again. He'd only come to tell me he was leaving. I stayed out with him all night, even though I knew I'd be grounded forever, but after what he went through... I only meant to comfort him, but it led too far. He was surprised I cared so much and it just kind of happened." Her chest rose and fell.

"No, I wasn't in love with him, but he made me feel wanted, needed. He needed me. I could feel how much he needed me, and it was nice since my parents only acted like I was in their way and my grandparents were gone a lot for business. He started staying in an abandoned house at night and I kept sneaking out even though I was grounded, taking him food, using my saved allowance and such to buy it, along with grabbing stuff I'd usually snack on and giving it to him instead. He started looking for a job, said he could stay if he could find a place to live.

"Everything was good, until I told him I was pregnant. He freaked out and went for a walk to clear his head, and I never saw him again."

James slid a hand through her hair. "Do you miss him, too?"

"No. I hope he's okay. He's a good guy and he deserved better, but I wouldn't have gone with him even if I could have. So." She shrugged. "That's pretty much everything. You know my whole life story now."

"Did you ever go back to school?"

"I did it from home for the next year because I wouldn't go. I couldn't handle what they would say. Grandma called off her business trips and stayed with me and pushed me to keep up so I could get my diploma on time. She rewarded me by teaching me music after my studies were done. I did two years of work in one year at home and went back into school Junior year. She insisted I needed the experience and socialization. Since I type well and did well with English and computer classes, she helped me get an admin job after graduation." She turned from him, looking up at the dark sky that was too cloudy to see more than a couple of stars. "I'm not who you thought, right? You can say so."

His eyes clenched a moment and he wrapped his arms around from behind, kissing her neck. "You're beautiful. You're strong. You're caring and loving. And you're kind. I love you, Isabel. And just to be sure you know, I wouldn't have left you. Regardless of the consequences."

"Even now? After knowing..."

Turning her to face him, he claimed her mouth, pulling her body in against hers, making the kiss deep and long and tender and hard. "I love you. I'm not walking. Whatever happens, or doesn't happen. Okay? Got it yet? If not, I'll keep saying it until you believe me."

Her arms slid up around his shoulders and she dropped her face against his neck.

"Ready to go home?" He felt her nod and backed up to take her hand. They ambled along the mostly clear sidewalk to the still-crowded bridge they had to cross to get to the parking lot. Pausing, she tugged his hand, and he found the fire dancer who'd been on the boat setting up on the bridge to do a show. "Want to watch?" With her nod, he led her up to the front and she sat down, right there on the road. He sat mostly behind her, cuddling up against her body, being as close to an easy chair as he could be on the hard asphalt.

She was mesmerized while the guy twirled a flaming stick around his half naked body, including bare feet. His black pants looked like dancer's pants, leaving little to the imagination. But her focus seemed to be on the fire. Even when the guy looked over at her, more than once, she didn't acknowledge it. The fourth time he looked at her, James slipped an arm over her leg, his hand resting on her bare calf below her capris. The guy put his attention elsewhere.

Isabel looked up at him, curious. "What?"

"He is so flirting with you."

"No, he's not. He's entertaining the crowd."

"If you say so."

"You're cute when you're jealous." She gave him a quick kiss. "This is ... really sexy, though."

He groaned with an eye roll meant to make her laugh.

She didn't laugh. She reached around his head to bring him closer and kissed him. "Let's go home." It was a near whisper next to his lips.

With a light nod and his gut tightening at her look, he helped her up, saw her take a last look at the guy putting the flame down into his mouth, and led her away.

~~

They were silent on the way home. It *was* really sexy, not only the fire dancer, but the whole afternoon and evening into dark, the way he'd listened to her past, watched her, nearly cried for her. She could see it. The way he was so easy to be with, around. To talk to. To be silent with. The way he truly looked at her while telling her he loved her.

She had to hide a sigh when she saw Bruce's car there. Maybe she'd take the higher paying job just to be able to move out sooner, into her own place, so he could stay and ... stay. Whenever he wanted, on weekends. Even some weeknights maybe, if she lived up north of Wexford rather than in Pittsburgh. She couldn't afford Wexford, but maybe Cranberry...

"What are you thinking about?" He was holding his truck door open, waiting for her to get out.

"Um. Moving closer to you. So we could be alone on weekends."

He stared a moment, then lifted her up out of the truck into his arms. "They're both out tonight. Bruce went fishing with Gavin and another buddy, up in Conneaut somewhere. They're staying over. I was invited, but I had better plans."

After a fast, hard kiss, she tapped him to let her down. He rubbed an arm against her all the way inside and up to his apartment, kissed her head while letting her go in first, closed the door, and took her into his arms. Her body reacted fast. No denying she wanted it, wanted him. Whether she'd let herself was another story.

He was breathing fast when he released her, his forehead against hers. "Iced tea?"

"Okay, but I'm going to shower real quick to get the smoke smell out of my hair."

"You smell good, but go ahead."

"Right back." Making the shower quick and using her best body wash for both shampoo and her body since it was a soft, sensual scent and she didn't want her hair to smell different than her body, Isabel felt nerves move in while dressing in a low cut black tank top without a bra underneath and hi rise black bikini undies, then covered them with her M&M pajamas, since he'd found them so amusing. Not too showy or too suggestive. She felt suggestive, though, with the thoughts running through her head and down her body. Her toes nearly curled already.

She hoped she wouldn't chicken out.

He looked up from the couch where he was playing guitar, left-handed, one of her songs. The one he'd first heard her sing. She stood at the entrance of the room and he grinned at her pajamas, finished the phrase, and set the guitar to the side. Then he motioned to the table where a translucent plastic glass full of ice cream sat.

"Is that what I think it is?"

"My imitation of a Peanut Buster Parfait." He picked up the spoon and took a bite, slowly, watching her. "Vanilla ice cream." He took another bite. "Chocolate sauce." Another, watching her. "Caramel sauce." Putting more on the spoon, he held it out to her. "And peanuts. I do have M&Ms if you want me to add a few. Or a lot. Still love those pajamas, Iz."

Joining him, she sat close and let him put the ice cream in her mouth, holding his eyes while she closed her lips around it to pull it off, grinning at his teasing groan. They shared several bites, back and forth, and then she took it from his hand, set it on the table, and kissed him.

As a hint, or encouragement, she slid her hands up under his shirt. When he questioned her, silently, she kissed his neck.

"Have you decided I'm worth the risk?" His voice was husky, and soft, next to her ear.

"Yes." She planted a kiss on his jaw, and in front of his ear.

"Yes?" He pulled back to see her face.

"You're my forever, James. However that happens, you're... what I should have waited to find." Her heart raced as she wondered if she should have mentioned forever, if it would scare him off.

"You did." He smoothed fingers through his hair. "You're here. You're free." His fingers slid down to her neck, her shoulder. "And I badly want to make you mine, and not free."

"You already did that."

"No." Sliding his fingers down her arm, he picked up her hand. "We do this, Isabel, and I'm not letting you go. You better know that."

"If I wanted you to let go, I wouldn't be willing to do this."

"And yet you're wearing your cutesy pajamas. Don't get me wrong. They're adorable, but..."

Trying her best not to look nervous, she undid the buttons. Slowly. Watching him.

"Subterfuge?"

"What?"

"It's... never mind." He kissed her and smoothed the top off her shoulders, down her arms. "Now this..." He skimmed her with a grin. "This is sexy."

"Hm. Not as much as I'd like to be. But I also like ice cream."

Chuckling, he leaned back in and kissed her gently, lowering her against the couch, shifting to lay half way over top of her. "You're beautiful." He kissed her neck. "You're incredibly sexy." Trailed his lips down to the swell of her breast. "You're smart. Strong." His fingers sifted up under her tank to her stomach. "Funny. Talented." Up to her breast, cupping it gently. "Sweet. Gentle." His teeth nipped her over top of her tank. "And I want you to be mine."

Hearing herself groan, she arched up into him. "I am yours, James. I am. Take me to bed."

~~

She held him close and tight, her eyes clenched. At this point, she didn't even care if it wasn't permanent. Maybe she would later, if it wasn't, but for now, he belonged to her, he was hers, and she didn't want to be anywhere except exactly where she was. In his arms. Her naked skin against his, her body breathing hard to recover.

This...

What she'd done before, with her baby's sperm donor, was nothing. Nothing. This... She felt him shift, adding space between their bodies that made her shiver after the heat of him. Allowing it, barely, she reached up to touch his hair, the soft dark blond locks highlighted from the sun.

"I thought I loved you before." He kissed her nose. "But damn, Iz. Don't ever get sick of me, okay?"

Her head shook and she felt her eyes moisten. And he kissed her lips, a soft, sweet, tender, lingering kiss. She did not want to go back to the city Monday. She wanted to stay right here and see him off to work and be here when he got home and sleep beside him every night. But she couldn't tell him. She couldn't say anything. She barely allowed him to move away enough to lie beside her, on his back, his chest showing its attempted recovery. He was so beautiful. She couldn't help stroking his stomach, the curly dark blond hair weaving its way almost to his chest but not quite.

"Need to shower again."

She wasn't sure if he was saying he needed to or asking if she did. "I don't want to let go of you that long."

With a grin, he turned to his side and smoothed fingers through her hair. "If you want to join me, I'll wash your back."

"Okay."

"Yeah?"

Showering would be good. Getting on her feet and washing herself would be good. When he'd reached for a condom, she pulled him back, said she just wanted him, to feel him, at least once, that it should be safe at the moment. Still, peeing and washing would be good. Old wives' tales, probably, but she couldn't stand the thought of putting him in that situation. If it happened again, though, she wouldn't allow her parents in her room or around her child until she could see what they were doing. And she was twenty-five, not fifteen. She'd do whatever needed to support her baby.

And James said he wouldn't walk away.

"What are you so serious about all of a sudden?" He'd helped her to her feet and stroked her shoulder.

"Oh. Nothing. But I'm going to get cold standing here..."

He grabbed the towel he always kept in his room and draped it over her shoulders. Holding the front edge, he tugged it toward him and kissed her. "If it wasn't as safe as you think, I'll be here. Whatever. Okay? No one will do that to you again. I won't let it happen. Promise."

Wrapping around him, she lay her head on his chest. "I can do it myself now if I have to, but thank you. I love you. Whatever happens, I am..." At a loss for words, she bit her lip.

"Me, too. Come on."

~~

"Okay, gotta sleep. You exhausted me."

She chuckled. "Me, too."

He stroked hair from her face and kissed her forehead.

Isabel cuddled in next to him, pulled the blankets up over them both, and settled onto the pillow holding his arm, the strong warm bicep she adored. She loved his strength. His power. And the way he didn't try to use it with her. "I love you. Night."

He kissed her head. "I love you too, Iz. Sleep well."

She also loved his stamina. She would have to work on her own. Maybe that's what she'd do while in Pittsburgh, without him. But not after dusk by herself. She could walk in the park, the park where her grandparents had met. Where her mother hit her grandpa in the nose with a Frisbee, so the story went.

Or she'd join a gym, once she had money to do so, and avoid being by herself out in the open.

Thirty-four

Isabel stretched her bare legs underneath the soft sheets, feeling the effects of the long walk around Waterfire and the night's activity with James. Unlike Toby, Tobia by given name, which he hated and so went by Toby away from his family, James was in no hurry when they made love, as though he had all night and didn't care how much of it he spent with her before sleeping, or before worrying about his own needs. He talked with her in between, not about physical stuff she did not want to hear, but small talk, some teasing, some complimenting her features. He loved her curves. So he said. He did sound honest and he said he knew she didn't, but her fears about looking *too out of shape for a singer* dissolved under his touch, and his looks.

It was after nine and she told herself she should get up, but it was nice to lounge in his bed with thoughts of the night before circling her brain. The way it had been so easy to talk to him about her daughter, the way he'd listened, actually listened, not interrupting, only comforting.

The door opened quietly. "Morning." Coming in, he came to sit next to her. He was wearing only sweats, his hair still mussed. "Sleep okay?"

"Yes. Too long."

"Not even close." Leaning in, he kissed her head. "I haven't been up long, either. Only long enough to throw breakfast together. Hang on. Be right back." Disappearing, he came back and handed her a plate of pancakes topped by a good slab of butter and plenty of syrup with two dippy eggs and three sausage links on the side. The plate was on a wood folding tray and he held it while she sat up, moving the pillow against the headboard. A bag of orange jasmine tea was seeping its color into a mug of steaming water. There was also a small dish of fresh blueberries accented with a bit of whipped cream.

Before she could think how to say thank you, with as overwhelming as it all was, he left again and came back with his own plate and a mug. Setting his coffee on the nightstand, he sat next to her. "Look okay?"

"It's incredible. Be careful. I might skip the job hunt and never leave here."

"Promises, promises." With a wink, he dug in and barely swallowed before continuing. "Up to canoeing? We actually have sunshine. All day, they say. And 76 degrees. Or would you rather go up to the beach?"

"Aren't you tired?"

"Was last night. Not so much now."

"Okay, so I'm impressed. I'm also kind of wiped out. I have told you once or twice I'm ridiculously lazy, right?"

His grin was too adorable as he swept hair from her forehead. "I'd say you're not. I mean, based on last night alone, I'd have a hard time buying it."

"Hm. But today I'm tired."

"Then I'll paddle and you can sit and relax. Paint your toenails or whatever."

"Paint my toenails?"

"The polish is chipped."

"Yeah, they do that. Thanks for noticing."

He chuckled and leaned in to kiss her. A sweet, syrupy kiss. "I love that you're not too vain. It's nice. But if there's something else you'd rather do, say so. I'm open to new things."

Catching the glint in his eyes, she enjoyed her pancakes a while without answering, just to try to tell him he wasn't cute, although she couldn't stop thinking he was absolutely cute. And charming. And sexy. And spoiling her rotten.

"You know, we could stay in." She wouldn't mind a whole day of simply staying in with him, being lazy, maybe talking music or working on music...

"On a day like this when it's about to get too cold to do much outside?"

"Open the windows."

"Yeah, not good enough." He swallowed coffee, and shrugged. "Okay, so staying home isn't a great option for me. We could go to the park and you can write while I run."

"Seriously, James, you have way too much energy."

"Yeah, well, I'm feeling terribly energized today. We can always..." He ran a finger over her shoulder. "Do other things first. Still going to want to go out at some point, though."

"Canoeing sounds fine. If you don't expect much help."

"I'll do the work. You can sun bathe. Wear something skimpy."

"Not likely."

He laughed. "Someday, Iz. Stick with me long enough."

~~

Isabel stood at her car and tried to make herself leave. She had to go. She had an interview later in the day and was already pushing the time.

He stroked the side of her head, told her to drive safe, to keep in touch, to do well with her interviews and to take the one her gut told her she wanted without other reasons getting in the way. Without him getting in the way, was what he meant. That would be awfully hard to do, with as hard as it was to drive away, too far away from him.

"Go before I ask you to stay." He kissed her nose.

"I am."

"Not so much."

"I don't want to." She ran a hand down his chest.

"I have to get to work, anyway. And I have like ten minutes to get there, which I'm already unlikely to make, so…"

"Okay. I'm going." She sighed heavy, exaggerating it, and got in her car.

"Drive safe, baby."

"You said that."

"I mean it double. Love you. See you this weekend. Let me know when you're in. If I don't answer right away, I'm trying not to get fired."

"Don't get fired. I love you, too. Have a good day." Letting him close her door, she put the window down and accepted a sweet, short kiss. Too short. It was going to be a long week.

Thirty-five

The buzz in his pocket made him slow his stride. At her name on the screen, James felt the tension drop away. A call, not a text. "Hey baby. How'd your interview go?"

"Are you okay?"

"Yep. Out running."

"Already? Didn't you just get home?"

"Got home, changed clothes, and went out. I have a big IT job to work on tonight, so I wanted to get this out of the way early."

"Nice. Same client you were working on?"

"New one. Bigger. May take a few weeks. They left a message this morning and I called during lunch. That's why I only had a minute to talk to you. Sorry I cut you off."

"No, it's fine. I'm glad. It'll help keep you busy when I can't."

"Don't remind me. Why do you think I had to go running?"

"Sorry."

"Isabel." He stopped walking. "No need to be sorry. I love missing you. I love more when you're here, but I mean I love that I enjoy your company so much I miss you when you're not here. It's a really strange feeling, not one I'm used to, but don't apologize."

"Thank you." Her voice was soft. "Me, too."

"So? Your interview?"

"Well." She sounded tired.

"Didn't go well?"

"No, it did. But it's ... well, it's more involved than anything I've done and they're willing to let me give it a try, even offered more training, but it would have to be done after work hours, weekends, mainly, and I..."

He started walking again. "Weekends."

"Yeah, I told them I can't do weekends. It's good pay. They'd even do extra for transportation because I'd have to travel between two offices. I could do the trainings at night after work. It's online. But it would take a lot of my music time away, and..."

"Is the job something you want to do?"

"No. But they pay $20 an hour and that's really hard to pass up. With that, I could move out sooner."

"You have another interview Wednesday, right?"

"Yes."

"The one you're more interested in."

"Yes, but it's $14 an hour. So..."

"Did you answer them already?"

"No. I told them I had another interview I didn't want to cancel."

"Good for you. Even if you take it, they need to know you have other options."

"So you think I should take it?"

"I didn't say that. I only mean you should go to the other one and see how it feels and take the one that seems right for you. Not just for the money, the one that you want."

"But..."

"And if my IT work keeps growing, it'll be easier for me to move down that way, so we could..."

"Split the rent?"

His heart nearly stopped. He was glad she said it so it wouldn't sound like he was pushing. "Something like that."

"Would you? Move this way?"

"Might. Depending."

"It's a lot farther from the beach."

"But a lot closer to you. I'm finding that matters a hell of a lot more to me. Also a strange feeling."

She was silent a moment. "I love you."

Thoughts of quitting first thing in the morning and moving to Pittsburgh circled his brain. As Bruce had accused him of, he was entirely obsessed with this girl. He hoped it was a good thing. "I love you, too, Lizzy from Erie."

She chuckled. "Okay, Gilbert. I'll let you finish your run, because I can hear I'm interrupting, so you can get back to work."

"What are you doing tonight?"

"Working on the new songs."

"Management praise. Can I call before bed?"

"Of course."

Hanging up, James stood where he was for a moment, then turned back toward the apartment. Walking. Thinking of her, of how damned badly he missed her already, although she'd just left that morning. Of moving south, away from his buddy who'd been his main source of stability the past year. Was he ready for that? Their relationship was still fairly new. She was still getting used to the idea that he was an alcoholic, with having such a hard past because of it, or partly because of the alcohol. If he didn't let it interfere, she should be good with it.

But it was still new. He'd been her first in ... ten years. Was that right? She'd been fifteen and was twenty-five now and said the first guy, her baby's father, was her only one before him. Ten years. Hard to imagine. He should maybe not start making big plans yet. He'd barely kept himself from asking if she was willing to have more children when the time was right. But it had been her idea not to use protection the first time.

Why? If she was so afraid of the results? She'd said she could manage it herself if it happened. How? She was having enough trouble staying in one job and they weren't family supporting jobs. She'd stay with her grandparents, probably. Except he wouldn't have it. Whatever happened between them, if they had a child together, he would be a parent all the way, not just a weekend, child-support part-time dad.

She chose to be with him. She'd have to deal with him being fully involved.

~~

Isabel grabbed her phone from her pocket at the buzz and slowed her ascent up the hill. She was glad it was a text rather than a call since she was far too out of breath for the short distance she'd walked, although she was pushing herself to walk faster than she would normally. Taking his tip to deal with missing him, she'd eaten a light lunch and then told her grandma she was going for a walk. Being sure she had her phone and it was charged, along with her pepper spray and debit card, just in case, she headed the opposite direction she had last time. While she had to be away from him, she could at least work at getting in better shape for a singer. Or just because she would feel better about herself, and be better able to keep up with him. If he needed to go for a run to avoid what he shouldn't do, she wanted to be able to go with him. Maybe he'd fast walk instead. She could work up to that.

His message was brief, abrupt: Sorry I was grouchy earlier. Hope your day is going well. He was on afternoon break. During his lunch half hour, he'd called, sounding grouchy, said he was hot and sick of chemical smells and ready for the weekend. Break wasn't long enough to call and still be able to grab a snack and drink. It was long enough to flirt a bit, though. So she did: Wish I cud wash ur back n help you unwind tonit

His reply came fast: So not fair Iz. Can't wait for the weekend.

Not sorry. Me too

What are you doing now?

She chuckled. He asked every time he called or texted. Sometimes she gave him a straight answer. Often she didn't. Not this time. Rnnin to Sharon to look for fire guy

Pick me up on the way. Will chaperone.

U wish

You're in a mood. Wish I could take advantage.

Me too

Love you. Have to go.

LU2

Glad he let her smart aleck answer work, she put it back in her pocket and increased her pace even more, up Squirrel Hill. She didn't want to tell him yet she'd started an exercise regimen. Before she told him, she wanted it to be an actual regimen, not just a walk here and there when she felt like it, and she wanted to see the effects of it, or see if he'd see the effects of it.

Her phone buzzed again. Expecting it was Gramps checking on her since James said he had to go, she shook her head seeing his name.

Didnt say what youre actually doing

Arent u working

Yep sh dont tell

To cover her tracks, she sat down and pulled out her notebook before she answered. Wrkng on a song in the park

A slight pause made her wonder if he'd had to put it away. Until it buzzed again. By yourself?

Yes ?

Another pause. Be careful. Phone charged well?

Yes n peppr spray at hand. Will be in long b4 dusk.

Good. LU

He was worried. Not that she could blame him. Still, she had to not let herself be afraid to go out alone. It was daylight. Lots of people were around. It was fine.

Thirty-six

With a deep breath, Isabel looked at the glass front office building and opened the passenger door.

"Call when you're done, Baby Girl. I doubt this rain is going to let up any time soon." Gramps looked up at the sky, even though he'd already checked the forecast more than once.

"I could have driven myself, you know."

"Had to venture out anyway. Your grandmother has to have her pomegranates while they're in season. No need for you to mess around finding a parking spot and walking around in the rain while you're all prettied up. You can drive when they give you a spot in the deck."

"If they do."

"When they do. Think positive and keep your head up."

"Now you sound like James."

"Good for him. Listen to us both." He patted her hand and gave her an encouraging grin. "Break a leg, baby girl."

"Thank you. Love you." Opening her umbrella before stepping out onto the sidewalk that would take her to her second job interview of the week, the one she actually wanted, her heart pounded. Nerves. Think positive. Right. Except she barely graduated since she only did what she had to in school and no more, and she'd left four jobs since then... no, five. She'd left five jobs already. Why would they take a chance on her? She'd put her grandpa down as a reference since he insisted, although they were supposed to be non-relatives. They knew him, he insisted, and it would be fine. She was going to put James down, but he suggested Abby might be better, with her job as a school counselor and his not-so-hot record. She needed three, and debated whether to use Libs or Bruce. Bruce's work as a public defender was impressive, but she hadn't known him long. She'd finally gone with Lisbon and hoped it was the right call.

Just inside, she closed her umbrella, slipped it into its sleeve so it wouldn't drip, and wiped her shoes on the mat. She'd worn the skirt outfit she'd bought for her promo photos and had to wear her black sandals with it since she didn't have anything more dressy. Her hair was pulled back with two small barrettes to try to make it look neat. And her heart pounded like crazy.

To calm herself, she texted him. Fingers crossed? Waiting a bit, she sighed when she didn't get a reply. It was time for his lunch break, but she hadn't heard from him. Checking the time, she decided to try again. Figuratively of course. Would be hard to text that way.

Still nothing. And she had to go. Making sure it was on silent, she took another deep breath, touched her hair to see if it was sticking up anywhere, and made her way to the front desk. The receptionist's greeting was pleasant and the girl directed her to the elevator that would take her up to the office she needed.

"Be sure your phone is off before you step out of the elevator. They'll tell you to leave immediately if it buzzes at all. Good luck."

So far, so good, she figured, except she really wanted to hear from him. Holding it while waiting for the door to open, she sighed and turned it off once inside. No service, anyway. Maybe he didn't want to wish her luck for the job that would keep her farther away? He had told her this morning to think positive and keep her chin up and shoulders back so she looked like she thought she deserved the job, so it sounded like he hoped she'd get it. Maybe he was having second thoughts. Maybe he was wishing he hadn't somewhat offered to move to Pittsburgh.

Think about it later, Isabel. Just do this right now. Chin up, shoulders straight. You deserve this job. Why, I'm not sure, but you do. Act like you do.

~~

"So much for *call anytime*." James slammed the phone down, not giving a fuck whether or not he broke the thing, since she wouldn't answer, anyway. He didn't want to read texts. He needed to hear her voice. "Fuck, Denton, why didn't you keep your fucking head down like I told you to?" He paced over to the photo of himself with his battle buddy, studied the face of the always over-eager adventure loving friend who was like a brother, and shoved a hand through his hair.

"What can I do, J?"

Brushing Bruce aside, he set the photo back on the bookcase and grabbed his keys. "Going out."

"No, you're not. Not like this." His roommate jumped between him and the door. "Have you called Isabel?"

"*Four fucking times*. Once from work, just after I called you, twice on the way, and again now. She's not fucking *answering*. So much for..." He swerved around the body in his way. "Whatever. I'm going out."

"I'm going with you."

"The hell you are."

Bruce grabbed his arm and wrestled the keys from his hand, shoving them down his pants, the one sure way he knew James would not go after them.

"You're a fucking asshole."

"No, I'm your friend. And you're not doing this."

"Keep them. I'll walk."

"I'm still going with you."

"Just back the fuck *off*."

"J..."

"You don't *get* it. You weren't *there*. This guy, hell, *he* should have come home. *I* shouldn't have. This..." Clenching his jaw, he shoved Bruce nearly off his feet and bolted out the door, slamming it behind him. Taking advantage of the time it would take his roommate to dig his fucking keys out of his crotch, he ran down the stairs and around the back of the building to throw the asshole off when he came after him.

He had to talk to Isabel... Hell, he'd left his phone. Whatever. She hadn't answered. So much for *call anytime*. Fucking great lifeline she made. Had she been serious about the fire guy in Sharon? She didn't answer right away the other day when he asked what she was doing. Probably didn't want to say. Maybe she was already realizing he wasn't a good bet. Who in the hell could blame her?

He had to run. He wanted a drink. Or two. Three. Four. Why the fuck not? Why Denton? *Why?* Why any of them? What in the fuck was the point, anyway, when they'd just handed back everything they'd fought for, died for, what so many came home maimed for. Another fucking Vietnam is what it had become. Shouldn't have been. Didn't start that way. They'd had the capability...

Stop thinking about it. Just stop. You can't change it. He'd told himself the same a million times. Only thing that would stop it now was for guys to stop signing up, though that likely wouldn't work, either. They'd just go back to the draft.

Stop.

Doing his best to shove the voices from his head, to think of Isabel instead... Not Isabel. She wasn't answering. For the past how long now? An hour? More like two. Instead, he thought about his buddy. His buddy who should have come home. He fucking *should have* come *home*. And he'd had to hear about it at work. Guys talking about it. What a shame. Anyone here know him? With sad faces. Right. What did they know? They had no idea who he was. He'd heard the talk, about *a local guy*, and the name, looked it up... and walked out. Calling Bruce. His friend had left work to meet up with him, was there when he got home. And Isabel wouldn't even answer her damned phone.

He supposed he should have checked the texts he'd missed while his phone had been off for work hours. But he didn't want to read texts. He wanted to hear her voice.

Out of habit, he ran to the park, using back roads to evade Bruce. Just to go nowhere, just to go. He ran all the way there, to the amphitheatre, up and down the wide, high steps, until his lungs burned, until his heart thumped hard and fast. Then he slowed to a walk, back up the steps where he and Isabel talked, played, laughed, made out. Damn, he needed her now. Just her voice, or a text to ask what was wrong. Something.

Crouching at the top, leaned back against the tall wall that needed repair before it crumbled to the ground, he looked down at the cement block where she'd sat cross-legged playing guitar left-handed, showing more emotion playing through struggling to do it right than in the position she was comfortable with.

He'd been thinking about that, but hadn't reconciled it.

Lowering to sit on the top step, he felt his body try to recover from the exertion, the anger, the fear... Fear. Of... Of falling back to his vice, his escape. Except he hadn't even thought about it until Bruce looked at him as though he was thinking about it. He'd just wanted to talk to Iz.

He needed to tell her. About his buddy. And that he only needed to hear her voice to help him through it.

Getting up again, he walked down the steps and past the raised square, across the road and the field of grass, to the little branch of the river, and lay down in the grass still damp from the earlier passing shower to look up at whatever sky he could see beyond the trees and through the quick-moving clouds.

He had to go back and get his phone and tell her, if she'd answer. She would answer. Something just had her distracted.

Or... The last time she hadn't answered, she'd been followed by thugs and... And she'd been out by herself the day before. At the park. Alone. Had she gone out there again?

Fuck. Jumping up, he started back home to get his phone. Soon, he was running, despite the cramp in his leg from running, not stretching, and running again. Like she'd had. A charley horse from running from those assholes, the ones who were never caught. His heart thumped part from exertion but more from fear. She would answer if she could. She'd promised not to go out without her phone again, to always be sure it was charged first. He'd even bought her an instant charger to keep in her bag just in case.

Something was wrong.

~~

Thanking her new boss, Isabel tried hard not to bolt. She'd taken it. After two hours, the first half of which was mostly waiting through another interview that ran late because the girl showed up late, and then filling out paperwork including a personal survey, and a very long talk with an assistant first and then the boss in charge of hiring, she was offered the job. And she'd said yes. Just like that. Even if it would keep her farther from James. He'd said she should, and it felt right. It was the first time in her life she'd been excited about a job.

But her phone had been off more than two hours now and she wanted to call him, first in case he'd tried to answer and also to tell him she got it and it sounded perfect and she was excited.

Forcing herself not to turn it on until she was back off the elevator and in the lobby, she answered the receptionist who asked how it went, got a sweet congratulations and a 'look forward to seeing you,' and noticed the rain had stopped.

Calling her grandpa first to say she was going to walk home and would tell him about it when she got there, her phone buzzed to say she'd missed messages and calls. He'd called. More than once.

Instead of taking the time to listen to voicemail, she called him. No answer. His messaging service kicked in, so she said she'd been in the interview and was free now, and then she played the first message.

"Hey, Iz, where are you? Call me, okay?"

He didn't sound right. He knew she had an interview. It was from nearly two hours ago. He should have been working then.

The next was longer. "Okay, I remember your interview, but you've got to be done by now. Just give me a minute. Need to hear your voice."

Her gut clenched. Her pace slowed. And she tried calling again. No answer. Where was he? Work. He'd still be at work for about an hour. Why was he calling from work?

At the third message, she stopped walking.

"Come on, baby. Where are you? Gotta talk to you."

Her heart nearly stopped at the desperation in his voice. She had to reach him. If nothing else, she'd drive up there. But she had to get back first, to her grandparents' place, and to her car.

~~

Good thing the apartment was unlocked, since Bruce still had his fucking keys. Grabbing his phone off the counter, he cursed when the screen didn't respond. He tried holding the start button. Nothing. Tried plugging it in. Nothing. "*Bruce.*" He'd use his buddy's phone to call her. Where in the hell was he?

Empty. The whole fucking apartment was empty. He was out? Now? His keys... If Bruce had gone out, he was maybe looking for him and he wouldn't have left his keys if he was afraid James would give in and go for a drink. "Come on, man. Where are you?" His spare. He had a spare key in his night stand.

Rushing to get it, he knocked his leg into the corner bed post, cursed, and scrimmaged through his drawer. Where was it? It was always there. Bruce... Fuck. No phone and no truck. Fucking fine. There was always another option. Denton had taught him that years ago.

Flying back down the stairs, he kept up his pace as well as possible with one leg yelling about the cramp remnants and the other about a probable big-ass bruise from the bed post, toward his nearest friendly neighborhood bar. To use the phone. To call her. He just had to make sure she was okay, and the rest, he'd deal with later.

~~

Isabel debated calling her grandpa to pick her up to take less time, but she was on a one way street and he'd have to circle around and by the time he found her, it probably wouldn't take less time, so she kept walking fast, unsure what she'd do when she got back if she hadn't heard from anyone. Bruce hadn't answered, either.

She jumped when her phone rang. A number she didn't know. Another spammer. They'd become ridiculous, even calling through business numbers trying to get an answer. Ignoring it, she told herself he was fine, Bruce was right there and watching him. James said he was good, stable.

He'd also warned her it hadn't been long yet.

Despite the coolness of the late October afternoon and the nice breeze, Isabel was sweating from the fast walk and from the worry. It felt like a ridiculously long walk, since she was moving so fast and still not getting there fast enough. Two thirds, or thereabout. Unable to wait until she got home, she tried Bruce again.

Finally, an answer. "Hey, Isabel. I was about to call you."

"What's wrong? Where is he?"

"He's here. Getting him back home. Can he call you in a bit? He'll be using my phone."

There was noise in the background, but it was hard to decipher through the pulse in her head. Back home? "Put him on."

"Um, in a few, okay? I won't forget…"

"No. You said he's there."

"He is, but…"

"I don't care. Put him on. Please."

"Fine, but don't take anything he says seriously right now. Okay?"

Her gut twisted. She knew what that meant. *Getting him home.* He'd been drinking. Her eyes watered, but she held it back. "I know how it works. Just put him on." While she waited, the noises became more distinct: voices talking, laughing, music… a bar. It sounded like a bar.

"Where've you been?" His voice was loud, but clear.

"Hey. What's up?"

"Don't fucking give me *what's up?* Where have you been? Tried to reach you half the day."

She heard Bruce trying to calm him, telling him it wasn't close to half a day. "My interview. I had to turn my phone off. I didn't expect it to take so long."

"Half a damn day? No interview takes that long. Go find that fire guy, did you?"

She stopped walking. Again Bruce told him to calm down, to knock it off. "It took two hours. I've been trying to call you since the minute I walked out their door. Are you okay?"

"Where are you?"

"I'm on the way back to my grandparents' place."

"By yourself?"

"Yes." She nearly said why? but she knew better. The more he talked, the more she could tell he'd been drinking.

"Driving?"

"Walking. I've been walking more. You know, management suggestion to be in better shape." Probably, she shouldn't have said that, even if she was teasing.

"Walking by yourself? You didn't learn anything from that last time?"

"James, I'm fine and I'm sorry if I worried you. But it's still broad daylight and I have my phone, and my pepper spray, and I'm in a better area. It's okay."

"It's fucking *not* okay. I lost *one* fucking person I love already this week. Can't *handle* anymore."

Lost? "Who? What happened?"

"Forget it. Text me when you're in. Actually, text Bruce since I broke my fucking phone. No, you know what? Just stay on the fucking line until you're inside so I know you are. I don't care who's trying to call. They can wait."

"I'm coming up there. Okay? I can be there in a couple of hours. Tell Bruce I'll text him when I'm leaving."

"*Don't* hang up."

"I won't. I'm here. We'll talk more when I come, but I'll stay on the line as long as you need."

Silence came from the other end. A car honked in the distance. Bruce must have gotten him outside.

"James?"

"Still here. ...I'm walking. ...Don't want to be in your fucking car, okay?" Bruce was talking to him in the background, offering to walk with him... "I know the fucking way." Bruce argued again.

"Hey. Hello?" She wanted his attention back.

"Sorry baby. Want to tell this asshole I know my own way home?"

"He knows you do." She heard Bruce say something about public disturbance and another arrest. "Hey, talk to me."

"Thinks he fucking owns my ass just because..." He mumbled something away from the phone.

"James. Let him take you home, please. Do it for me. Okay? You know he's trying to help."

"What? Don't want to stay on the phone?"

"Of course I do."

"You're walking alone. Why the fuck shouldn't I? You about there yet?"

"Almost. I'm nearly home. Let Bruce drive you and then we can talk more when we're both in. Okay?"

"*Don't* fucking hang up."

"No. I'm not." She heard Bruce tell him to be nice.

"She's *my* fucking girlfriend. Stay the fuck *out* of it."

"If you want her to stay your girlfriend, be nice to her. And come on, get in before someone calls the cops on you. We don't need that again."

Again. She had to swallow hard. She wanted to tell Bruce to stop talking for a minute. "James? Hey, listen to me, okay? Please get in with Bruce. I'm coming up to see you. I'll walk with you. As far as you want.

Just get in for now and..."

He snickered. "Far as I want? 'Cause you can keep up with that?"

Shoving a hand through her hair, she gritted her jaw and told herself it was fine.

"Hey, Isabel." Bruce. "Grabbed my phone back. Sorry about that. As I've said..."

"Is he okay?"

"Not at the moment, as you heard. He will be. He is getting in the car, so there's that. Let me get him home and I'll call you later."

"I'm coming up."

"Well, that might be good, helpful, if you can handle it, but he's..."

"I'm back at the house. I'll text when I'm on the way. Does he need me to talk again? You can tell him I'm in. Well, at the door."

"Good enough. See you soon. Drive safe."

When the silence said he'd hung up, she grabbed a deep breath, crouched against the front door, and closed her eyes, calming herself before she went in to face her grandparents. They would ask about her interview. She had to be able to tell them about it without breaking down.

But she couldn't care about the job right now. He was drinking again. "James, no." Wiping a quick tear, she pushed herself up, took a couple more deep breaths, gritted her jaw, put on her brave face, once she'd practiced far too often, sat with her grandparents long enough to tell them she got it and she was nervous and sweaty from walking so fast, and was going up to see James to tell him about it. First, she showered. To get unsweaty and to unwind.

~~

As requested, Isabel texted Bruce to let him know she was at their apartment instead of going straight up. Then she called her grandpa to let him know she made it. He knew something was up, but she couldn't bring herself to tell him James was drinking. It was only once, anyway. He could stop again. It would be fine.

Pacing in front of the building, she'd convinced herself it was true by the time Bruce came down to meet her. With his greeting, he ran a hand through his dark locks, looking defeated and tired.

"How is he?"

"I probably should have told you not to come."

"You could have told me a hundred times not to come, but I still would have. I need to see him."

Bruce caught her arm when she tried to go around him. "Okay, a couple of things you've gotta know first. Sit a minute." He motioned to the front steps. "Please." Sitting next to her, he heaved a deep sigh and pushed the hand back through his hair. "Okay, so..."

"How bad?"

"He's coming up out of it at the moment. Burt's here. His oldest brother, if you don't remember. He's good at getting J sobered up. But I won't even try to tell you it's a one-time thing and won't happen again. Okay? You have to know that. He's..." His head shook and he dropped his elbows to his knees. "Has he mentioned his buddy, Denton, to you at all?"

"The one who dared him to join the Army and stayed in."

"Right. They grew up together. They've been close as you can be to someone not family since about second grade."

"That's what he said."

"He was killed overseas a few days ago."

Isabel's heart dropped and her eyes watered. "No."

"J found out today, at work. The guy's a mess. He may be a mess for some time. We'll watch him, but..."

"I'll stay and help."

"Not a good idea. Really, I should have told you not to come."

"Bruce..."

"The thing is, J drinking isn't so scary. He's kind of fun and easy-going when he drinks."

"They say it brings out who you really are."

"Yeah, may be true, but, J sobering up is a whole different story. He's rude, obnoxious, crude. We know it's coming and it's not a big thing to us, but Isabel, Burt agrees with me. You shouldn't be here right now. Go stay with his parents tonight. His mom invited you. And maybe go the memorial tomorrow to help him through it.

"Tomorrow? That was fast."

"Yeah well, they didn't want to put it off and give the wrong element time to get here and make a scene, so yeah, it's fast. They tried to call J yesterday but didn't have his new number, I guess. Anyway, if you can deal with being there tomorrow, go back home afterward and let us..."

"No. Yes, I'll go with him tomorrow, but I'm staying with him. I'm not walking out."

"Isabel."

"No. Bruce, this isn't... I told him I'd be here. I promised he could count on me. I can't…"

"You won't, though. And I'm not being cruel. I'm being honest. He'll try to make you leave. He'll say things to you he shouldn't…"

"Won't be the first time someone's done it to me. I'll deal with it."

His chest heaved and he paced in front of the building. Obviously, he was trying to decide how to convince her to go.

Taking his side, she met his gaze. "He's my forever. Through anything. I'm not walking away just because he slipped up."

Silent for some time, Bruce tilted his head in a surrender. "Fine. I warned you. Just don't take anything he says to heart. Don't let it hurt you. And the big thing: don't fuel him."

"That, I know."

He looked like he didn't quite believe her, but she remembered that lesson vividly. Stay calm and quiet and disappear as well as possible. She wouldn't disappear with James, but the rest, she knew how to do.

No matter how prepared she thought she was, when she walked into the apartment and saw him slumped on the couch, bent forward with his arms propped on his legs and his head hanging nearly between his legs, Isabel had to grit her teeth and swallow hard a few times to keep from crying her eyes out. His brother gave her a nod and she tried to return it, but she could only see her James. If Bruce looked partially defeated, James looked full-out defeated. It hurt her inside and out.

Knowing words would be pointless, she went to him, set a hand gently on his shoulder, got no acknowledgement, and sat next to him, lowering the hand to his back. Finally, he looked at her. His eyes were bloodshot. Purple bags circled them. He looked full-out heartbroken, the way she'd felt when she realized her baby girl was gone, taken from her.

"You shouldn't have come." The words were mumbled, rough. And didn't sound at all sincere.

Unable to answer, she wrapped him in her arms as much as he would allow, feeling the resistance, until he stopped resisting and fell into her, shaking. She cried with him, since she couldn't stop, and stroked his hair. They sat like that for the longest time until Bruce said there was food and James needed to eat.

He didn't want it, tried to brush them off, but she insisted, pushing it at him slowly. Until he looked too exhausted to even put it in his mouth and she said he should lie down. It was late. Dark. Gavin had come in and tried to talk to James but didn't get an answer, so he retired to his room. Bruce and Burt tried to talk to him. He mainly stared into space, but he did acknowledge Isabel when she tried. Mostly, she didn't try. She just wanted to be there.

By now, though, she thought it would be good for him to lie down. "I'll walk back with you."

"How'd your interview go?"

Isabel had to catch the lump in her throat to be able to answer. "Um, good."

"Yeah?"

"I got the job."

He raised his eyes to hers. "Already?"

"I start Monday."

He nodded. "Good. Congratulations." Then he jumped up and went back to his room, slamming the door.

She looked at Bruce. "Should I not have told him?"

"Doesn't matter. This is just the beginning. Burt is staying tonight, in Davis's old room. If you want mine, I'll take the couch. Or I'll take you out to his parents' place."

"No, I'm staying." Lowering her voice, she glanced over at where his brother was coming from his room, checking on him. "Will he care if I stay with James?"

"Nah, but Iz, I don't think..."

"I'm staying here with him."

Burt obviously heard her, based on his raised eyebrows. While studying her, he scratched his chin. "Tell you what. I'll take the couch so the other room is free, so at any point, you can move over there if you need. That okay?"

"You don't have to."

"You haven't seen him this way. Don't get me wrong. I'm glad you're here. Might help. But look after yourself first. He's never hurt anyone, physically, while drinking or withdrawing, but..."

"I'll be fine."

"Okay, then, the room will be free just in case. Yell for us if you need, and don't lock the door." Burt gave her a soft, long hug. "I think you might make this a hell of a lot easier for him. Thanks for coming."

Giving in to a cup of hot tea when Bruce offered, Isabel sat with them at the table while they gave her some insight on James and Denton – Ryan Denton, but they called each other Gilbert and Denton and joked about putting a band together under the name The GD Garage Dudes, or GDGD to imitate CBGB in New York. Ryan played drums, not well,

Burt laughed, but he played. He'd often said backing James, it wouldn't matter how bad he was because no one would hear anyone else, anyway.

James was that good on guitar. Had been.

Which made Isabel have to wipe her eyes again.

"Sorry. Maybe not the time to tell you all of this." Bruce set a hand on her lower arm.

"Since it was one time, this won't be hard for him to come out of again, right?"

They looked at each other and Burt answered softly. "He said you understood alcoholism. Your father? Is that right?"

"Yes, but he never quit, never even tried, so I only know it from..." She stopped. It was unnecessary to say more.

"Ah, well, this is a horse of a whole different color, then. J quit for a short time before, but only a week or two, so this has been his longest dry spell since high school, probably. We used to joke about it, about his high tolerance, until it started worrying us because it wasn't just a weekend thing, which we didn't know for way too long, and mentioning the possibility that he was an addict made him fly off the handle and avoid us. Hardly saw him for the longest time, and then before we knew it, he'd joined up with Denton. We hoped they'd help shape him up and get him on track. Didn't turn out that way. So, to be honest, we don't know for sure what's going to happen next with this. And, whatever you need to do, we'll understand." With a swallow of coffee, Burt stood. "I'm going to check on him."

"I will." Isabel stood. "Please. Let me." A light shrug of the head told her Burt wasn't sure she should, but he wouldn't argue. It made her feel maybe he understood her relationship with his brother wasn't a minor thing, wasn't temporary. So she hoped.

Knocking softly, she didn't hear anything, so she opened the door quietly. He was lying on his bed, atop the comforter, fully dressed, eyes closed. She went over and watched his chest rise and fall. Deeply. Asleep. Her beautiful, sad Adonis. Not Adonis. Ares? No, not right, either. Prometheus, maybe.

Sitting next to him, she stroked the blond hair beside his temple and he stirred. She held still trying not to wake him, but he opened his eyes, stared at her a moment, and pulled her in, kissing her hard as he grasped the back of her head. His hand slid up under her shirt and pulled her bra out of the way.

"James." She managed to escape his lips only enough to whisper his name.

"I need to feel alive, Iz. Help a guy out."

"You're very much alive."

He pulled her closer, and yanked the other half of her bra away.

"Let me close the door. We're not here alone." Somewhat wary of his insistence, she was also glad he still wanted her there and took advantage of a slight release of his hand from her head to go close the door. Against his brother's advice, she also locked it. She did not want them walking in.

Undressing her fast, he shoved his own clothes off, lowered on top of her...

"Wait."

"No." With his eyes locked on hers, he pushed into her, gently, and gathered her up into his arms tight and close.

He wasn't protected. It wasn't a safe time. Not that any time was especially safe, but some more than others, and... and maybe he'd said he wouldn't leave, but he was sober then and his brother couldn't guarantee he'd come out of it again, back to recovery, or that he'd stay in recovery, and she couldn't do it to a child, even if she chose to do it to herself. They had to wait on that.

"James. I want you. I do. But..."

"You've got me." Sitting up, still gripping her, keeping her tight against his body, he pulled her onto his legs, wrapping them around his waist.

"We're not protected. Just... before..."

He kissed her, stopping her protest, a very light protest since the last thing she actually wanted was for him to stop, to move away... the next to last thing. The last thing she wanted was to have a child with an unrecovered alcoholic. She barely thought she could consider having one with a recovered alcoholic, since it was never guaranteed.

But she loved his urgency. She loved the way he made her feel, the attention he gave her, to every aspect of their love-making. She loved him. She wanted him. Needed him.

And he needed her. More now than ever. But he'd wanted her before he needed her, so it was okay. She hoped.

When he was finally spent and released her to flop onto the bed, she stroked his hair and asked him to move just enough to get under the blankets.

A groan escaped. "Gotta find food. Starving now." He patted her bare hip. "Come on."

The second next to last thing she wanted was to go out and find food knowing his roommate and brother were out there and would know darn well what they'd been doing since he only pulled his jeans back on, without even clasping the belt.

"Iz?" He was sitting now, running a finger along her skin, between her breasts.

"I think I'll stay here."

"I'm not so much in the mood for the breakfast in bed thing, or dinner in bed."

"I'm not asking you to. But Bruce and Burt are out there."

"So? Not like Bruce doesn't know we're screwing, and I don't give a fuck if my brother knows."

Really? Isabel gave him a look.

"Sorry. I get crude when I'm hungry. Whatever you want to call it. Ashamed of being with me?"

"No, but..."

With a roll of the eyes, he got up. "Fine. I'm getting food. Come out if you decide you're hungry."

Watching him leave the room, she gritted her jaw. Bruce warned her. She should have listened. What now? Hide out in his room so they would know she was embarrassed and stay there all night, starving? No. She would not. Getting her back up, she grabbed... Her things were still in a bag out in the living room. Fine. She grabbed one of his T-shirts and a pair of his sweats, and went to the bathroom to run through the shower. Except she took her time, enjoying the hot water and the memory of his hands on her skin. And she told her body not to accept his sperm, to just say no if they tried to make their way through. Not that having a child with James would be all bad. When the time was right. Not now. For now, she would keep telling herself not to accept it, that she would not get pregnant that way. Not again.

Before she got so relaxed she couldn't control her emotions, she got out, scrubbed herself dry, put his clothes on, and went out to find them in the kitchen.

Bruce tried to hide a grin. Burt raised his eyebrows. James turned, skimmed her, and said he would have brought her bag in.

"You didn't, so I made do. What smells good?"

"Pizza. Almost done." Bruce handed her an unopened can of soda.

"Thanks, but I'll get water."

"There's other kinds if you want something else." He nodded toward the three cartons of soda, all different.

"I'm mainly drinking water now."

James snickered. "Yeah, with tea and a ton of sugar. Soda's just as healthy as that, you know."

Bruce argued there was at least no corn syrup and fake flavoring in tea, trying to head his friend off, Isabel assumed. She didn't bother to answer. Making herself at home, she grabbed a glass and a couple of cubes of ice and ran water from the faucet. And she stood beside Bruce against the counter. No need to push her presence too close if he didn't want her to be.

James was too adorable with his hair was sticking up in places. And he was too withdrawn. She hated seeing him so inside himself, looking as though ... as though his best friend in the world had died.

"So you have a new job." Bruce broke the silence. "What is it?"

"Assistant to an assistant. Nothing impressive, but it's..."

"Music." James took a couple of swallows of coffee, leaning back in his chair. "She landed herself a job in the music industry."

"Well. Barely. I'm an assistant."

"You said that already." He scratched his head. "No need to downplay it. She's editing sheet music for a publishing company. Nice start to a real music job. Good connections."

"Well, a different music job, no more real."

"More real, and you know it. She'll be one of the bigwigs down in the big city of west PA before you know it and she'll forget all about little Greenville."

"Knock it off, J." Bruce threw him a look. "What you mean is: Congratulations, Isabel, you deserve it. Right?"

"Yeah." James gulped the rest of his coffee.

"Refill?" Burt took his mug.

"Whiskey?"

"Not funny." While refilling the coffee mug, his brother asked more about her job, said that if they had more openings, she should try to get James in, except that he'd given up on music, which led Bruce to saying he'd gone back to it, to an extent, partially as Isabel's manager, but also himself, with a left-handed guitar...

"Shut the fuck up." James jumped up from the table. "If I'd wanted him to know, I would have told him." Leaving the coffee, he stormed out of the kitchen.

"Told you he'd be a bear." Bruce shook his head. "Really, you don't have to stay."

"He's hurting. Deeply. I did stupid things when I was hurting that deeply, too. And I'm staying." Setting her glass on the counter, she followed to find him staring out the window. The rain had cleared, and a red glow from the setting sun illuminated his face and chest. Risking a rebuff, she went to him, from behind, and slid her arms around his stomach. When he didn't flinch or push her away, she lay her head between his shoulder blades.

"Sky's blood red. Appropriate." His voice was hoarse, soft.

"I'm sorry you lost him."

"I want a fucking drink."

"I know." She kissed his warm skin.

"Want to go out with me?"

She had to think about how to answer that. She'd never be able to stop him by herself, physically, if he decided not to listen to her, but if he wanted to go out, she didn't want to refuse. "To the park?"

"Fuck no. Can't even take a drink there, much less get one."

She saw his roommate and brother come in, but decided not to acknowledge them. "We can walk."

He snickered, which she took as a no.

"You want to talk to me about him?"

"No." He pushed away and treaded half way across the room before turning back. "You shouldn't be here. Go home."

"I don't have a home other than here."

"You know fucking well I mean your grandparents' house. That's home, right? It's where you ran to when I scared you off. Go back."

"You didn't scare me off."

"Come on, Isabel. At least be fucking honest with yourself if not with everyone else."

"I *am* honest. You did *not* scare me off, James. I scared myself. Because I fell in love with you when I didn't want to. But I'm glad I'm did. You're worth the risk."

"Like hell I am. Go home. I made you promise to leave me if I did this again. *Go home.*"

His brother looked like he wanted to interfere, but so far, he and Bruce were staying out of it. Luckily. And maybe arguing with him would count as setting him off, but if it did, it did. She wasn't backing down.

"No." With a hard swallow, she pulled her chin up and moved closer until he met her eyes. "You asked me to walk away if you did to me what my father did to me. You haven't. And I didn't agree that I would. So…" She moved all the way up to him and set her hands aside his face. "You chased me, Gilbert, and you know you did. You wouldn't give up, wouldn't back away, because you knew I didn't want you to give up on me like everyone else has. Fine. It worked. Now you're stuck with me. I love you, and I'm staying."

His shoulders slumped. "I don't have the strength to fight this again. You don't understand how hard it was the first time. Now…"

"I understand hard. I understand losing someone you think you can't ever move on from. I do. I understand being what you don't think you can be in order to move forward. Not just move on, but move forward, which I didn't let myself do until you pushed me to do it. My turn. It's okay to fall apart. I'm right here. So is your family. We'll hold you up until you regain your strength. I'm not letting go, and I'm not running." She stroked her thumb across his temple. "Not everyone runs, James. You showed me that."

Dropping his head down beside hers, he held her in, his body heaving. After a few minutes, she heard Bruce say pizza was ready and she gently led James back that way. When he detoured to grab a shirt, she went with him and gave him a deep kiss before taking his hand and leading him to the kitchen.

Despite him saying he didn't want to talk about Denton, that's where conversation went while they ate. Burt's phone rang a few times. His family, he said, checking in. James wouldn't talk to any of them. He wouldn't talk about his friend, either. He let the others do that, including Gavin, who had come back out to grab a midnight snack since he smelled it. Gavin knew Ryan Denton to some extent, but not well.

When James got up and walked out of the kitchen, she figured he was just using the bathroom, but after a few minutes, she got nervous so she went to check on him. He was in his room, lying on his bed, arms folded under his head, staring at the ceiling. She went to sit next to him.

"Can't listen to anymore tonight. Turning in. If you want my room, I'll take the other one."

"Can I stay here with you?"

"Sure you want to?"

"Yes." She stroked his hair.

"Come in whenever you're ready."

With a light kiss, she went out to tell them he was calling it a night and that she was going to sit with him. Coercing him under the blankets after coaxing him out of most of his clothes to be more comfortable, she slipped out of his sweatpants, leaving the T-shirt on, and cuddled in next to him.

He stayed still for some time, until she thought he might be asleep, but then he rolled to his side and pulled her in gently, with a kiss to her head. "I'm sorry. For earlier. I shouldn't have..."

Stopping him with a kiss, she stroked his face, noting the sadness in his eyes in the glow of the moon through his window that never had the curtain drawn. "I'm strong enough to deal with this. With you. I am. You don't have to test me."

"You think that's what I was doing?"

"Partly." She smoothed the back of her fingers along his shoulder.

"You scared the hell out of me when you didn't answer. I kept thinking of those thugs that bothered you and that they weren't caught and... Stupid way to express my fear, but on top of Denton..."

"I'm sorry I scared you."

"I'm sorry I was an ass. And I can't guarantee I won't be again."

"I know." She kissed him again. "Just try not to be and I'll try not to be offended when you slip up. Okay?"

"Iz?"

She let her fingers wander along his chest. "Hm?"

"Don't walk out on me." It was a near whisper against her ear as he rolled her onto her back and slipped a hand under the borrowed tee to her stomach.

"I won't."

"Mm. Thank you." He teased her softly. "Let me have you again tonight."

"Yes, but only if..."

"I'll use protection. I'm sorry for that, too. Tell me it's still the wrong time."

How could she tell him the truth? She couldn't. Not tonight, after everything, with everything he was dealing with. "It should be fine."

Thirty-seven

Friday morning. The memorial service was tonight. Damn, he want-ed a drink. The possibility of getting out to find one was low as hell, though, with the guard dogs in his apartment. And Isabel.

With a start, he realized she was at his side, curled up against him, holding his arm. She shouldn't have come. And yet, he couldn't imagine getting through the next two days without her. She'd said, before she fell asleep, that she would call and cancel her show Saturday night, but he wanted her to do it, wanted something to look forward to after...

Maybe he'd move with her. Her job was a good step, could easily help jump her career better than he could with the little shows he was setting up for her. She needed to do the shows. She did. Everyone needed to pay their dues and start at the bottom to truly understand the business, the music. All of the book learning, so to speak, in the world didn't teach you what paying your dues at the bottom rungs could. Pittsburgh shows would be a better test of what she could do, what she could handle. He could schedule her around there instead.

It wouldn't be bad to get a new start, himself. He could move to the city. The three rivers weren't the beach, but it was something. He'd walk the river edge with her as she'd asked and they'd escape up to Lake Erie now and then. Together, they could afford a place, maybe only a small place, but their own. If he saved pennies, they could travel to an ocean on her time off from work. It wasn't like beach hopping most of the summer, but a week with her would be better than a full month on her own, or with just someone he grabbed to go with him.

First things first. He had to get through the memorial service and the funeral while trying to fight the urge to walk away and find the nearest bar.

Funeral. For his non-blood brother, his battle buddy. They'd been close before, but going to battle together, standing side-by-side through shit no one should have to go through, strengthened that. Every step they'd taken, every challenge they pushed each other through, had created a stronger bond. It started back as kids playing whatever sport they could talk their parents into letting them play, and went through high school when their biggest mutual dare had been asking out girls who were way above their playing field, older girls full of themselves.

Strangely, it hadn't stayed a challenge long. They fast became the two guys most girls wanted to have ask them out, for the prestige of being thought of as above anyone's playing field, which by now he was old enough to realize was a myth. No such thing.

He'd been an arrogant ass back then. Maybe he still was.

But Isabel, the way she looked at him... The girl saw something in him, something that made her break out of her self-imposed personal protection prison to give him a chance. She was the real thing. If she was strong enough. Could be he'd have to not make her be. There was that. No way should she have to be.

The thought circled his mind and the image of his buddy mixed with her image. Ryan would have liked her, would have teased her mercilessly, partly as a test, but he would have liked her. James hadn't even written him lately. His buddy hadn't even known about his little songbird.

Tears fell. His buddy. His brother-in-arms. The one who should have come home. Gone.

Shit. Getting up carefully, trying not to wake her, he paused when she stirred. Her eyes flickered, but he didn't want her awake yet, so he spoke gently into her ear to tell her to go back to sleep.

"Are you okay?" Her beautiful voice was a very bright candle in the darkest forest.

"I'm going to shower. Sleep, Iz. It's going to be a long couple of days." With a kiss to her forehead, he went to take a very hot shower.

~~

She could see he was getting edgy.

He'd eaten brunch, consisting of several things Gavin had gone to grab from a local bakery, while jumping up and down several times for different reasons, which made her wonder if he'd burned more calories than he'd consumed. Now, he paced the apartment, watching the time. She'd tried to ask him about his IT job, the new one that would last a few weeks, but he brushed it off. She asked if he wanted to go over music, if he wanted to okay songs for her show the next night, since he insisted she do the show, but he said whatever she did would be fine, which rankled her somewhat, as though it didn't matter.

With a deep breath, she went to where he stood at the window, watching the mist try to decide whether or not to turn into rain. "We could go for a run." She rubbed his back.

"It's wet. Probably going to downpour."

"I know you run in the rain when it's warm enough."

"It's not." He turned his head slightly. "And you don't run."

"No, but I could give it a shot. You might have to do circles around me, but..."

"You don't have to do that."

"I don't mind."

"I mind. Just stop, okay? I'm not looking for something to do." He walked away from her.

Burt had gone home first thing in the morning to see the kids off to school and to feed the animals so his wife wouldn't have to do it, and Bruce had just gone into work, but he promised not to be long and gave her his direct line in case James got out of hand. Gavin had been there when Bruce left, but he got called about a client who would only work with him, and after getting Isabel's okay, said he'd only be about an hour. For the moment, she was on her own to try to figure out what to do.

Not willing to work on music in his apartment when he wouldn't even talk about it, she grabbed her phone just to keep her hands busy and looked up the first thing she could think of to look up. Apartments in Pittsburgh. When he stopped behind her to see what she was looking at, she started to ask what he thought about a little one bedroom place on the outskirts of the strip district, but he walked away, grabbed his keys, and headed out the door.

She caught up fast. "Where are you headed?"

"Don't start acting like my fucking wife just because we've screwed a couple of times."

She started to yell and knew that would make things worse and then she started to not give a shit if she made things worse and then she thought about calling Bruce, but she didn't want to do that, either. No matter how pissed she was, she didn't want him out alone, so she grabbed her shoes and jacket and her phone, and followed him, locking the door behind her. She had to jog to catch up before he got in his truck. "Hey." She grabbed his arm. "Don't talk to me that way. I only wondered if I could go with you because I'm a bit house bound since I don't know what to do with myself at your place."

"Practice songs. Or write songs. Isn't that what you do?"

"Not in the mood."

"What are you in the mood for?"

"Honestly?"

"No. Lie to me Isabel, because that will help everything right now."

"Don't be an ass to me, James. Okay? I didn't do this. And I'm seriously in the mood for a huge ice cream sundae with a hell of a lot of chocolate sauce and caramel and whipped cream. So, if you're going by somewhere that has that, maybe drop me off and do what you need to do and swing back by to pick me up."

"You have a car."

"Yeah, but I don't have a key to your place and I just locked myself out. Guess where my car keys are, Einstein."

He stared a moment, then took a deep breath and shook his head. "Come on." Walking her around to the other side of the truck, he opened the door and helped her in, then took his place behind the wheel. "I'm headed to get a new phone, since I broke mine. Help me pick one out and then I'll take you somewhere for ice cream. I could use that, too." He started the truck, put it in gear, and sat, staring into space.

She risked taking his hand.

"Going to forgive me if I get fries with ranch?"

"I'll wait till you wash it down with something else before I kiss you. I think it'll be fine."

He met her gaze. "Why in the hell do you still want to?"

"Want to what?"

"Kiss me. Or anything. Why are you still here?"

"You really are asking for the Einstein comment today, you know." She squeezed his fingers. "Because I'm in love with you. Stop trying to change that, or test me, or whatever. I'm here because I want to be here, and because I want you to be here. And you know what I mean."

His chest rose and fell and he raised her hand to kiss her fingers. "I don't deserve you."

"Well then, try harder. I'm patient."

"Damn I love you."

"Good. But I need ice cream."

~~

James tried not to be sick when they turned onto the road that led to the funeral home. The town had flooded the street with American flags and a legion of bikers stood across the road, standing guard. Veterans, he supposed. Their bikes were filed down the crossing street behind them. The funeral home parking lot was filled to capacity, and every available spot along the road was taken.

Bruce had driven, with Abby and Isabel in the back. He'd said it would be easier to park his car than to find space for James's truck. An excuse, but he didn't want to drive, so he accepted it. His family was behind them. The whole crew. Denton had been nearly one of them, had stayed over many weekends. Other weekends, James stayed at his place. Until they could drive and get themselves wherever and then they'd taken turns.

"Best bet is likely around the corner at the shopping complex."

He didn't answer. It didn't matter. The girls brought umbrellas. He didn't care if he got soaked through. Currently, it was only the damned mist again. Maybe he'd move somewhere without constant mist/ rain/ sleet/ snow/ clouds. Out of western Pennsylvania. Somewhere there was a beach within walking distance.

Just away.

Except Isabel was about to get entrenched in Pittsburgh. Maybe he'd ask her to reject the job, to pick up and move with him. Away. They could both start fresh.

Going through the motions when Bruce parked and they all filed out of the cars and walked toward the funeral home, James wished for a downpour. Full out. Hard core. Most wouldn't like it, he knew, but he didn't give a damn. Denton would laugh. Everyone dressed up nice to come say goodbye getting drenched by a hard rain would make him bust a gut laughing.

He stopped, looked up at the sky, and swallowed hard. Felt Isabel take his hand, saying nothing, just being there.

"It's alright, J. We've got your back." Felix set a hand between his shoulder blades.

"I was supposed to have his back. I should have stayed there with him."

"If you had, we would have lost you over there, too. You wouldn't have stopped him from saving those kids. You would've been beside him."

"Should have been."

Isabel squeezed his hand and dropped her head.

"No, honey." His mom moved in front of him and set her hands on his face. "Don't stand here and tell me I should have lost you. I lost my brother to a war. I don't need to lose my son to one, too."

He swallowed hard again, and nodded. He'd put her through enough already. It wouldn't be fair...

"Gonna rain soon. Let's go, J." Burt this time. "The women won't appreciate you making them soak their shoes." A running family joke, ever since Burt's wife fussed at him a few years back about holding her up talking to someone until it suddenly poured and soaked her brand new heels, along with her feet.

Giving in, he tensed more the closer they got. By now, there was a line leading into the home, a waiting line, outside the door and down the sidewalk. Staff, with help from some of the bikers, was setting up canopies to try to keep people dry while they waited, but he just wanted to leave. Go find a bar. Maybe start at Mortals Keys along Pymatuning and then over to Jacob's for cheaper beer and fried mushrooms, where he and Denton spent a lot of weekends, more than he'd ever admit to his mother.

Another canopy tent was going up and James stepped in to help. Until he was recognized. Denton's uncle, organizing the tent raisings. No surprise. "What are you doing out here?" He gave James a hug. "You should be in with the family. They've been wondering about you."

"No, I'll wait. Have the whole group here."

He looked over and greeted everyone. "Come in, come in. We have space for family. Don't argue. He'd want you in there with us, James. All of you." Taking his arm, the man pulled him toward the entrance.

With no real choice, he let himself be part dragged, part pushed, until he was inside face-to-face with the Dentons. Damn, he wanted a beer or two or three or...

~~

Isabel felt like a total outsider, especially since Bruce introduced her when James didn't. He was inside himself, quiet, sullen, speaking softly to his friend's family when they spoke to him directly, but not otherwise. She wasn't sure he even remembered she was there. Which was fine. Except she'd wanted to help him and she only felt in the way.

The hug he got from his friend's younger sister made Isabel wonder if there had been anything between them. The way the girl hung on him made her think she'd definitely be okay with something going on if there hadn't been. She was probably Isabel's age. A cute girl with curly blonde hair, highlighted by a few red streaks, and a little round face with an upturned cutesy nose. She wasn't wearing black, or even navy. The girl sported a royal blue dress, a clingy knit thing that showed off her cute, but too straight build, topped by a long vest in red and white plaid, a small plaid, not a big, gaudy plaid. She was obviously paying tribute to her big brother, and Isabel would have had an issue with the way she clung to James if her eyes weren't red and swollen, and if she didn't keep sniffing and wiping her nose when sniffing failed.

Mainly, Isabel stuck to Abby. Bruce's girlfriend hadn't known Sergeant Ryan Denton, either, so she was support crew as much as Isabel was. They both stayed nearby, but not directly in line where everyone filing in stopped to give sympathies to the family.

When James approached the casket, he looked shaky. His brothers were there, and Bruce, and Ryan's sister, but she wanted to be there for him, too, so, with the line clearing, holding back, she made her way over to take his arm. Not that he noticed.

Sergeant Denton looked just like the guy in the photo, but without the smile. He was wearing a blue uniform jacket, sporting medals on one side of his chest. The lower half of his body was covered up; half the casket was closed and a black sheet was tucked up underneath the jacket. Bruce told her the guy had stepped on a mine while clearing some local kids out of the marked minefield. Saved them, but he hadn't had a chance.

James picked up one of the circular disks hanging from a ribbon, ran a thumb over it, and replaced it. Then he set his hand over the still chest. "Should have come home with me, bud. Just once, you should have listened to me." His voice was low, shaky, then he swallowed hard, set a hand aside his friend's head, and backed away. Quickly, ignoring one of his brothers calling his name, he slipped away, out the back door.

Isabel stayed right with him. It was raining hard now, but she didn't care. She didn't care how drenched she was getting. She didn't care about her shoes, or that her hair she'd spent time on to try to look nice enough to be worthy of being by his side was soaked and dripping and would frizz into a horrible mess. She stayed with him while he walked. Fast.

Bruce caught up. "Where are you headed, J?"

His head shook, but he didn't slow down.

"Isabel, go on back. I'll stay with him."

"No."

"You'll get cold."

"I don't care."

James stopped and turned his face up toward the rain, eyes closed. She moved in front of him and held him. His heart was pounding. She heard it through his suit jacket. When she shivered, his chest heaved and he ran a hand over her head. "Come on. You'll freeze."

"I'm fine."

"It'll be hard to sing tomorrow if you're sick."

"Doesn't matter."

Roughly, he set his hands alongside her face and raised it to his. "It does matter. It absolutely *does* fucking matter. Don't you *get* it? You can still do what you love. You didn't lame yourself being stupid. You didn't get yourself killed being a hero. You still *can*, Isabel, so yes, it fucking *matters*."

"J, lighten up." Bruce pulled him away.

Taking her hand, James headed back to the funeral home, half pulling her, went in through the back door, and asked someone to get her a towel. A woman who seemed to know him led Isabel to the restroom saying it was warm in there and would help her dry.

It didn't matter how warm it was. She couldn't stop the tears. And she couldn't go back out there, since the tears weren't for the guest of honor. They weren't for herself. They were for James, and she couldn't stop them. Before she knew it, Abby was there and the woman was gone.

Abby put an arm around her. "Bruce said to tell you he'll be okay. It'll take a while, but they'll bring him back around again."

The comfort only made her cry harder.

"So, his recent ex girlfriend is here and he doesn't want to talk to her. How about coming with me to get rid of her?"

~~

He'd been too harsh. James knew he'd been too harsh. But he was jittery, shaky, and fighting himself not to give in and disappear to go find a beer. One. Just one. He'd have one to calm the jitters and leave and then he could be reasonable again. No one had to know.

It didn't matter? Maybe she hadn't meant it that way, as Bruce told him. Still, the girl had everything ahead of her and she didn't get it. She'd already quit once. So easy. Just walk away from something you loved that you could still do only because some people heckled. So what? People were jerks. He should know. He was a jerk, too. She'd have to get over it, or just keep hiding, keep stalling her life because of a little insulted pride. There were a hell of a lot of worse things than insulted pride...

"Hello again."

Looking up from where he'd planted himself on a chair out of the way but still close enough to watch over Denton's family, he felt his eyes roll. He'd been trying to avoid her, hoping she'd have the decency to leave him alone. "Jackie, why are you here?"

"Paying my respects. Why else would I be here?"

"Did you know him?"

"No. I knew of him. His uncle is a friend of my father's."

"His uncle is a friend of everyone's father. And?"

She smiled and sat next to him. "He is quite the socializer, isn't he? Have to admire that. So, you haven't called lately. Been busy?"

"Yeah. And I'm not up for chit chat," He stood, hoping she'd take the hint.

She took his arm, pressing in. "So call me this week. Maybe I can help relax you."

Relax him? She was talking about sex at his buddy's memorial? He couldn't even...

~~

Isabel saw his face. Annoyed. Or at least she chose to think he was. With Abby pushing her, she went to him, to his other side, and politely said hello to the girl. The one she'd seen at the park on the Fourth of July, if she wasn't mistaken. Ignoring the raised eyebrows that said her hair was a mess and maybe her eyes, too, she put her attention on James. "Can I get you anything?"

His head shook, but the girl jumped in. "Oh, you're working here? Is there bottled water? Spring water, preferably."

"She doesn't work here and it's not a fucking restaurant." Taking Isabel's hand, he went to let his family know he was leaving, that he didn't want to go out to their place for the evening, and he'd see them the next day. Felix gave Isabel a hug and quietly asked her to hang in there. Next, with his hand still gripping hers, he stopped to tell Ryan's parents to let him know if they needed anything, politely refused the request to come by the house where a buffet was set up with the excuse that she was wet and needed to find dry clothes, and pulled her out amid someone trying to give him condolences.

The car was silent other than wheels on the pavement and the whoosh of cars going by in the other lane until Bruce ran through Wendy's and ordered food for everyone, refusing to let her or James help pay for it. She didn't want it, but she ate because everyone else was.

The apartment was just as quiet and after changing into sweats, she sat and played a game on her phone while he showered. The way he was acting, she wasn't sure he'd want to share his room, but after hardly watching the movie Bruce put on to fill the quiet, he said he was heading to bed and said she could come in whenever she was ready, no rush. Of course she went with him. He didn't talk to her; he just lay looking at the ceiling until his eyes closed.

Refusing to let herself dwell on his words, his actions, reminding herself that Bruce warned her and she said she could handle it, Isabel thought about lyrics instead. Something unrelated. As always, though, current events sifted through.

> *You ask me not to leave/ I promise I'll stay*
> *You say I should go/ I tell you no way*
> *I'm here, I'm around, I can stand the pain/ that you give when you're down*
> *as long as I know you won't run/ once you've healed...*

Thirty-eight

Why are you still here?

His question ran through her head while he fully ignored her in favor of getting lost within his family. Despite James telling them he wanted to be left alone until the funeral, they'd descended on his apartment, the adults and two oldest kids, the rest left with sitters, except for Felix's baby who was still nursing.

Isabel thought she was doing well, playing hostess, being friendly to everyone although they could see he was ignoring her, as though she was a leech he couldn't get rid of. She'd even held little Felicia and managed to enjoy holding her, cuddling the sweet little girl who smiled at her, loving the new baby smell she still had. James had looked over, noticing her holding his niece, doing fine with it, and still, he kept his distance.

Why was she still there? The thought crept in more often the closer it came to having to leave for the funeral, and suddenly, she had to escape, only for a few minutes. Telling Bruce she'd be back shortly, she grabbed her jacket and her phone and left the apartment. A cool breeze took her breath away for a moment, but she let the door close and wandered around to the back of his building, to the little play area that was luckily abandoned since it was chilly verging on cold.

Lowering onto a wooden swing that looked as though it had been freshly painted in the spring, in bright teal instead of old-fashioned red, which kind of made her sad, she rocked herself with her toes while holding the cold metal chain. What was she doing? He didn't need her. He was enmeshed in his big family and his good friends and she didn't fit in his life. That Jackie girl fit better. She was open and talkative and ... and pretty. Thin. Svelte. Composed and sure of herself. Definitely more his type. Maybe even athletic.

You don't run. He'd said it with derision, a criticism. *You're too out of shape for a singer.* He'd apologized, but that didn't erase the words. He meant too out of shape for him. He meant, as he'd said when they first met, that she wasn't his type. In which case, why? Why had he kissed her? Why did his eyes sparkle so often when he looked at her? Why in the hell had he slept with her?

Don't act like my wife because we've screwed a couple of times.

Jerk. He was such a jerk. She should go. She didn't need him to set up her shows. She could do it. Or if she didn't, so what? Her job, as he said, would likely help more than any and every show he could book for her. It was about her songs, not her singing.

But it wasn't her music that was keeping her with him anymore. Maybe it was never about that. Maybe she was only using it as an excuse to be with him, around him. Soaking up his humor and smiles and outgoing friendliness that attracted her the way ships in a storm were grateful to and attracted by a big lit-up lighthouse.

Even lighthouse bulbs burnt out at times. Their foundations cracked. The ocean tried to come in and sweep them away. Then they depended on someone who cared to help repair them. It would be unfair to feed off his outgoing friendliness and walk away when his light burned out.

Is that why her mom stayed with her dad? Had he been different, friendly and outgoing? Could be. She had seen sparks of that at times. Rare times, but at times.

Wiping sudden tears from under her eyes, she looked up at the cloudy gray sky that threatened more rain and was pulled by someone approaching.

James. Ambling toward her, his fingers, the pointer fingers, stuck in his front pockets. Looking like a five-year-old who was made to go apologize, he lowered onto the swing beside her. His fingers gripped the metal chains, the "useless" fingers hanging there mocking her, or him. Did he feel that way about it? He'd seemed unsure it was lucky they were still there.

She watched him while he looked at the patchy grass in front of his feet. Such a mix of arrogance and uncertainty reflected from his expression, from his whole body, his arms taut but his shoulders slumped. Like he was trying hard just to hang on.

"I shouldn't have asked you not to leave." His voice was soft, reluctant. "Thursday night. I won't hold you to your answer."

"I'm not leaving."

He looked over at her. "I made you cry. I never wanted to do that." His head shook. "Go back home, Isabel. This isn't fair to you."

"It's not fair to you, either."

"It was my doing..."

"No, it's not."

"Really? Is that what your dad says? That it's not his fault, that he can't help it, it's a chemical or a disease or whatever? Did he make your mom believe that crap?"

"It is a disease."

"Yeah, so is a cold, but people don't purposely try to make it last longer, do they? They do what they can to get over it."

"So are you. Trying to get past it."

His chest heaved and he got up to walk away.

Isabel caught up and walked with him. Away from the building.

"It was a choice. I made the conscious choice to go get a drink, despite knowing what it would do. I don't deserve for you to stick around. And I told you not to. I told you, if I ever treated you that way, you need to leave. So do that."

"No. James..."

"I don't *want* you here. I don't want you to go to the funeral. I don't want you to be part of this. You... You have to go." He took her hand. "You can stay here until your show. Practice. Unwind. Whatever. We'll do your show and come back here so you don't have to drive to Pitt that late at night, and..."

"And what?" The lump in her throat nearly strangled her.

"You were going home tomorrow, anyway. Take your things. Maybe someday I can get it together and if you haven't found anyone else..." Raising her hand, he kissed her palm. "I need you to not be here for a while so I can... find my balance."

Staring, she couldn't even react. She was numb. Stunned. In full disbelief that it could end that fast. After he'd chased her. He had chased her. She tried to avoid it, but he kept pushing. Until he got what he wanted, got her in bed. Maybe it wasn't what he hoped it would be. Maybe she was too held back, too reserved. Something.

Feeling herself nod, she let him take her back into the apartment, stayed silent while he told his family she was skipping the funeral in order to get ready for her show. Their looks said they knew better, but they said nothing.

He got dressed in a nice black suit with a soft blue shirt and matching blue and black thin tie, like some kind of hot rock star dressed for a damned award acceptance, looking ridiculously sexy, then he gave her a kiss, aside her face, not on her lips, left an apartment key on the table in case she needed to go out, and left. With his family and his friends. To go to a funeral for part of his life she wasn't a part of, that he didn't want her to be a part of.

No way was she staying in his apartment. After leaving a note on the table beside the key to say she'd meet him at the show, she grabbed her things, including her guitar and little amp, and headed out to Grove City to be close to her venue, to sit and write somewhere she wouldn't be too alone. Until time for her show.

After her show, she'd go home. To Pittsburgh. The hell with what time it was. If he didn't want her involved in his life, she would not go back to his place.

As though she needed the message, she turned the radio on to Lewis Capaldi's *Someone You Loved*. Maybe he'd only been meant to help numb her pain for a while until she could move on. Maybe it wasn't meant to be permanent. It nearly killed her to admit it, but she would not repeat the past two years of refusing to accept the end when it came.

After nearly two hours of sitting in the back corner of Eat'n Park writing a song that came to her while thinking of him at his friend's funeral, and trying not to be angry at the guy she didn't even know for getting himself killed and throwing her James into a whirlpool, she wanted to add the music. It was written, on paper, in her head. She could hear it. But she wanted to do it with her guitar, so she headed to the park she'd seen the other day when they drove by it, grabbed her guitar and her notebook, and found an empty shelter near the pond to sit and work.

> *I didn't know you, but I see how you matter,*
> *those you've left behind are shaken and shattered*
> *Your dreams have disappeared, burnt to ashes and dust*
> *the shifting sand you walked on now tinged with rust-*
> *colored tears of they who remain, ashamed and afraid*
>
> *We could have been friends, you and I and him*
> *You're a part of his life he doesn't want to let go, but could have shared*
> *Instead, you're taking him away, he won't stay with me when*
> *I didn't know you, don't understand what was or should have been*
> *and I can't compete with your ghost*

As a title, she wrote across the top: Ode to an Unknown Could've Been Friend.

Rereading it, she stopped at *shaken and shattered*. It was familiar. Had she used that phrase already? She didn't think she had. Closing her eyes, she focused on the phrase, where she'd heard it, on the music that went with it... Oh. A Ryan Reynauld song from years ago when he was still solo. *You've been shattered and shaken, afraid... afraid to make a move...* To the girl who became his wife. Wasn't she his wife now? Isabel wasn't sure if he'd ever bothered to marry her. She also wasn't sure she believed he and Infiniti's lead singer weren't involved. Infiniti. She hadn't done one of their songs lately. Maybe she'd slip one in tonight.

Either way, she couldn't use the phrase, could she? Would he sue her over one phrase? Maybe he wouldn't, but his label might. If anyone ever heard it, which was a long shot. This one, she might not let anyone hear.

Better safe than sorry, though. Better to change it.

I didn't know you, but I see how you matter,
  those you've left behind are sorrowful and ...

No. Just no.

those you've left behind...

She'd have to think about it later. It was time to head to the venue. She hoped he would have called her by now.

Where was he? Five minutes till show time and all she had was a guitar and amp. No mic, no speakers. Open mics always had that stuff set up. She didn't own a mic or speaker. The venue manager asked if she was ready to go, and she nearly said no way in the world could she go on without mic or speaker, or more importantly, her manager at her side.

But she was there, and she had an audience waiting, a decent one. Gathering her nerve, she said she'd be ready in four minutes. And then her gut ached. So she stepped outside for fresh air and tried to call him. It went straight to voicemail, so she left a message: *Hey, how'd it go? Call me later, okay? I'm heading to the stage, so my phone will be off, but I'll check it on break. Love you. Be okay for me.*

A heavy sigh overtook her body and she channeled the frustration and worry into adrenaline for her show. On her own. Without him. But he needed to know she could. He needed to know she didn't need him in order to move on, to keep moving, but she wanted him, anyway. It would take the pressure off, and hopefully let him know she only wanted him for himself, not for any help he could give her.

~~

Be okay for me.

James listened to her message several times in a row. Be okay. Too fucking late for that. He'd slipped away from the funeral, when everyone was standing around in the cemetery paying last respects, whatever the hell that meant, and walked down to the closest bar to grab a six-pack. Would've been easier to get it from the convenience store like people in other states could. Stupid law. If they wanted it, they were going to get it, even if it was less convenient to get it. Like he did. Just made him even more annoyed to have to go farther for it.

He'd at least waited to get away from everyone before he opened the first can.

She would be about halfway through her show about now, he figured. If she'd gone on as planned. Oh, fuck. He had her equipment. She only had her guitar and amp. Did she have her amp or was it with his stuff? Her guitar was an acoustic/electric mix so she could play it without the amp. Still... Where was her venue? He couldn't remember. She'd apparently gone on, though, since she said her phone would be off.

Already he'd let her down. First he made her cry... No, first he was a rude ass, like Bruce told him, then he made her cry, and now she was at a show not equipped well because he decided to grab beer and then couldn't go. He hoped she still went on. Mostly, he hoped she still went on. Partly, he wished she'd cancel and come back to him, even if she shouldn't. No, he didn't. Not like this. If she caught him sitting at the park alone, drinking, she'd be gone.

Good and gone.

Long gone.

There was a song...

Who gave a fuck? The point was she couldn't come back like this. He had to get back to his place, try to sober up before she got done and came... No. She couldn't come. Not tonight.

He didn't dare call and leave a message. She'd hear it. He was on beer number ... five? already? Hell. He wrote a text instead, studying it five times to be sure it made sense since he was buzzy already. He laughed about being buzzy after only five beers. Been a while, huh, James? Losing your touch. When he stopped laughing enough to read it again, he shrugged and hit send:. Not home so dont come tonight. you can stay with my parents. Hope it was good without my stuff to use

After sending, he considered whether it made sense and sounded like him. Whatever. She could put her big girl panties on and deal with the fact he couldn't always be what she wanted. Maybe she'd find some professional type guy at work. Just as well. Might as well tell her to do so: Going to be busy a while. With the family. No point you sticking around. Find a good guy who dsn need nythng from u

Shit. Stupid thing to say. He realized it after he sent it, but just as well. Cracking the last beer, he chugged half of it and stumbled down to the river's edge, getting his feet wet, his shoes, and lay in the wet grass.

~~

The engine was running. But she couldn't shift it out of park. Which direction? The parking lot was nearly empty, with only a few cars from employees still waiting around. Her doors were locked. She needed to get going if she was heading back to Pitt. It was already late. She'd been scheduled till nine but kept getting asked for another song, requests, and she did a few until management said they were about to close, telling the audience more than her, thanking her and asking that she call and schedule with them again. She nearly referred them to James, but she wasn't sure that would be a good idea.

His messages at first hurt her heart, made her consider driving back home and staying there and shoving the whole thing: James, her shows, all of it. But then she reread them. They weren't him. He didn't abbreviate texts. He used capitalization and punctuation, the way she didn't. And full sentences. She tried to tell herself he was tired and overwrought and nothing more, but she knew better.

South to Pitt or right to Greenville? She would not go crash his parents' house. That was not on the even possible list. She'd already told her grandparents she'd be staying at his place instead of driving back so late. If she went home, she'd have to explain. But how could she go to his place when he asked her not to?

Which direction? Run from it or face it?

Maybe somewhere in between to give herself time to think.

Putting it in reverse, she backed slowly, then headed to the hotel she'd seen across from the outlets. Somewhere in between. To give herself time to think. To give him the space he apparently wanted for the night. In the morning, she'd decide her direction.

Once she was checked in, she texted her grandpa to let him know she was in for the night and the show went well and said good night. She considered whether to text James, also, but decided against it. He'd asked her not to come, told her to go home. If he wanted to know if she was okay or where she was, he could ask her.

Restless, Isabel wished she had a swimsuit since the Comfort Inn had a nice indoor pool. It was too late by now, but she could have gotten up early to swim, then shower and dress before checkout time. Not that she would have. Maybe she'd linger in her room all morning, enjoy the quiet, and go wander the outlets across the street before heading home.

Or to see James. Whichever.

Thirty-nine

When he sat up, pain flashed through his skull and exploded like a hand grenade went off inside his head, or next to his head. Pressing his palms against it, he barely realized he was in his own room and had no idea how he got there. Last he knew, he had a couple of beers in the park. That wouldn't have made him unaware of where he was or what he was doing.

He was still in his clothes, had been lying over top his comforter. Mud covered it where his lower legs had been. His jeans were muddy, dried but muddy, up to his knees. "What the fuck?" Forcing himself up, he grasped whatever he could reach to steady himself and worked his way to the bathroom. He had to shower. A nice, long...

Where was Isabel? She was supposed to come back to his place after her show.

Starting out to the living room, he turned back when his gut lurched and barely made it to the toilet. From a fucking six-pack? Couldn't have been. He never got sick from so little. It was the funeral. Nerves. Anger.

Whatever it was, he flushed it away, cleaned out his mouth, and went to find Iz. But it was Burt who looked over at him from the newspaper he was reading. "Sleep well?" His brother had that look in his face.

"Don't be a smartass. Where's Isabel?

"She went home, I suppose, like you told her to. Left a note to say she went ahead to her show and would meet you there. Not that you bothered to come back and find it."

"She was supposed to come here after the show."

"After those messages you sent her, jerk-off?" Bruce came up behind him. "Think that girl will ever come back? She shouldn't."

"I didn't..." Messages? "I haven't sent her any texts since..."

"A whole case of beer, J. A whole fucking *case*. What the hell?"

"What?" He held a hand against his pounding head.

"That's what we found beside your passed out ass by the river close to the bridge. Lucky you didn't drown your dumb ass, or is that what you were trying to do?"

"Uh, I got a six pack. Okay, I shouldn't have but..."

"We found your trail and where you got it. You bought a case. Tell me you didn't have a girl there with you."

"No." A case? No way he got a case.

"Sure?"

"No one was there."

"Which means you drank the whole thing yourself. And then you were stupid enough to text your girlfriend that way."

The pain in his head exploded down through his gut. "Holy hell. Where's my phone?"

~~

Isabel thought about going to Primanti's, by herself, but decided the memory would be too hard and went to the food court at the outlets instead. Walking along the sidewalk toward the food, she saw a chocolate shop and splurged on some incredible caramel pecan clusters and a lot of chocolate almonds, grabbing a water to go with it. She passed a small playground where a couple of kids were running back and forth on the wooden bridge to slide down and run back to the ladder while a woman in a too-tight T-shirt and leggings that were not made for her size, at least not without a long shirt over top, ignored them in favor of whatever was so interesting on her phone. Even when they looked over and called "Mom, look!" an uninterested "uh-huh" answered, without eye contact. Sad. She hoped it wasn't an everyday occurrence, but she expected it was. At least the kids were outside playing. There was that.

The food court was full and loud, being Saturday, and she wandered up and down to see what was there before deciding on the bourbon chicken after accepting a sample from a pretty Asian girl offering it.

Wandering through the tables, she found one by the windows that was free. It wasn't clean, but it was by the window, so she left her food on the tray and was careful not to touch anything on the table while gazing out at the cloudy sky with a tease of blue here and there, studying people walking past, some in small groups, many alone, and a few couples. A middle-aged couple walked hand-in-hand, with the man carrying a bag that had to belong to the woman. It was marked as intimate apparel. Isabel wondered if he'd gone into the store with her or waited outside.

Would James go into an underwear store with her? If they stayed together long enough, would he be comfortable with it? He very well might. In fact, she was pretty sure he would. Nothing much embarrassed him, it seemed.

She thought about texting Bruce to see how James was doing, but she wasn't giving in, or looking desperate. If James wanted to know more, he would have to contact her.

~~

His hands shook.

He wasn't sure whether it was from feeling like crap, being dehydrated as hell, or nerves about what she might say, whether she would even answer. He had to try, though. After reading what he'd written to her the night before, he'd sat, head in hands, on the couch for some time telling himself how stupid it was, then telling himself not to call himself names, or put himself down, and then arguing back that he very well should be calling himself names. He'd told her to walk away if he ever did what he'd just done. But he didn't want her to walk away. Selfish. He was too entirely selfish. Not full-out selfish, he supposed, since he was at least trying to make himself let her go and move on, to apologize vastly and sincerely and ask her to please find someone who would be good for her and help her move up and on and ... and maybe give her the baby he knew she wanted. Even if she didn't know it herself, he knew she did after watching her with Felix's little one. It would never replace the child that was taken from her, but it would be healing. At least he thought it would be.

But what in the hell did he know? He didn't even know what to say to her.

"Staring at it won't help anything. You've got to actually send a text. Or better, call her. She deserves your voice."

"Yeah. Maybe. But I'm..."

"She likely already knows what you've done to yourself. Not like you're going to be able to hide it. And you shouldn't, not if you respect her at all."

With a sigh, he nodded at his brother and looked at his phone again. Text or call? Say what? "What do I say to her?"

"What do you always say to your girls after you've done this to them?"

"Different."

"Why?"

"Because it is."

Burt gave up the questioning, but Bruce squatted in front of him, forcing attention. "Huh uh. Why is it different?"

"Back the fuck off, would you?"

"Nope. Why is it different? I'm staying right here in your face until you answer me. Why's it different? Why don't you play it off like it's a big joke the way you did with your other girls? Not so hard, right? Just do that."

"Can't do that to her." He pushed a hand against his head. Maybe he could think what to say if his head would stop throbbing.

"Why can't you?"

Fine. He wanted an answer. He could have one. "Because I'm in fucking *love* with her. Okay?"

"Yeah. I know that. Just hoped you did. So tell her the absolute truth, that your best buddy was right, you are a full-out jackass when you're coming down out of a binge, and apologize your ass off. Then hope she might give you another chance, even if she shouldn't."

"But she shouldn't. So I should tell her that."

"Yeah. Tell her that, and then ask if maybe she will, anyway." With a hard slap on the back of his shoulder, Bruce told him to call, not text, and walked away to give him privacy.

~~

She'd finished lunch, but she still wasn't sure where to go, so Isabel did some unneeded shopping, enjoying some of the chocolates she'd picked up while meandering up and down the sidewalks, on both sides. Along with the candy she didn't need, she bought too many lotions at Bath & Body Works, and a sweater that would look nice on stage. She couldn't afford any of it. When her credit card bill came in, she'd kick herself. But she was in the mood to be indulgent.

Actually, she was ridiculously stressed out, due to being ridiculously indecisive, and ridiculously wanting to just drive to Greenville and tell him he was absolutely not giving up on her, on them, because he lost a buddy. More, that he was not giving up on himself.

That was her worst fear, that he'd given up on himself.

So, go up there or go home? She couldn't spend another night at the hotel only because she wasn't sure of her direction.

Walking by another store advertising chocolate, homemade exotic-sounding fudge, she forced herself to go past, then hesitated, turned back to put her hand on the door handle, hesitated again, and figured why not? The moment she stepped inside, her phone rang. She almost didn't bother to check, but she at least had to silence it so she wouldn't be one of those obnoxious people who let their phones ring or talk loudly on them inside a business.

James. Not a text. A call. Her heart pounded. Should she answer? Stupid question. Just like going in to get more chocolate when she shouldn't, of course she did. Giving the clerk who'd greeted her an apologetic smile, she stepped back outside as she cautiously said hello.

"Hey, Iz."

Her knees nearly collapsed at his simple, friendly greeting. Like nothing was wrong. Like he hadn't been such a jerk. "Hi." Should she ask how he was or would that be insulting, or condescending, or questioning?

"You said that already." Humor reflected in his voice.

She considered teasing back, being a smartass and saying something like, no, I said hello, not hi, and one was just to say I answered, but she wasn't in the teasing mood, even if he was, and she wasn't sure she was okay with him being in teasing mode. "I guess I'm not sure what else to say." Okay, that was kind of a figurative punch in the gut, but really...

"That's fair. I'm glad you answered. I wasn't sure you would."

Biting her lip, she moved farther down the sidewalk, away from the group of teenagers laughing and shoving each other as though trying to see who would push who into the little marshland area between sidewalks.

"I wouldn't have blamed you if you hadn't. I um... I'm not sure how to say this because it's not enough, but I'm truly sorry. It wasn't... um... I didn't even know I... Shit. Can we meet up? Are you back home by now? I'm guessing you are."

"I'm at the outlets. Grove City." Why had she told him that?

"Yeah? So can I meet you there? I can buy you lunch."

"It's nearly three. I've had lunch."

"Right. Dinner, then."

"You don't need to." She found herself walking faster to try to keep up with her racing heart.

"Meaning you don't want to see me."

"No." When he didn't reply, she realized how that sounded. "I mean, no, that's not what I meant. Yes, we can meet, but you don't need to buy dinner. Do you want me to come up there? If you don't, say so." She clenched the bags in her hand tighter. *Please don't say no...*

"I don't mind, but I don't want to put you out if you're headed the other direction soon. Where'd you stay last night? My parents?"

She started to breathe again. He didn't mind. It was something, at least. "A hotel right here. Instead of driving to the city."

"They would have been glad to have you."

"Couldn't."

Silence came over the line a moment. "Okay, I guess I get that. Were you about to head back to the city?"

She was getting light-headed with the fast breaths, then no breath, and walking faster than normal. He was right; she was too out of shape for a singer. Mostly, it was the ridiculously mixed emotions. "Um, I don't know. That's why I stayed here. I wasn't sure what to do."

"Damn, Isabel, I'm so sorry. Come back, okay? I know you have to work Monday, your new job, but we've gotta talk and I, um, shouldn't..."

"Shouldn't what?"

A pause. "Okay. You have to know. I shouldn't drive today. I'm hung over as hell. I'm sorry. I just..."

Her eyes clenched as she stopped walking. She wanted to yell at him, but mostly she wanted to yell at fate or whatever for doing this to him.

Then a thought struck her. "Bruce said you were fun and friendly while drinking but a jerk while coming out of it."

"Yeah, he's right as always."

"You were coming out of it last night when you texted me? How? You were fine when I left. I mean you were..."

"Sober. You can say it. Yeah. No, I was fully out of it when I sent those. I don't even remember doing it, to be honest. It's not an excuse."

"You're not drinking now?"

"No. I'm coming out of it." A pause. "Huh. Guess I am doing things ass-backward this time. Don't know why. I feel like crap, headache and all, but otherwise, I'm..."

"Safe enough to be around? You sound like you are."

Another pause. "Yeah. I think so. I mean, I understand if you'd rather just talk over the phone."

"I want to come see you."

He sighed, loud. "Come on up. I'm at home. Still have shopping to finish, or..."

"No, I was just wandering. I'll come now."

~~

James paced outside his building knowing full well Bruce was sitting on the front steps making sure he didn't go anywhere before she got there. A good thing, probably. His brain kept nagging him to slip away, insisting it would be easier to give in to his craving than to have to deal with his mistake. For most girls, he'd listen to that voice. He always had before. Couldn't do it this time.

He wanted to run. Well, his brain wanted to run. His body told him if he tried, it would go right ahead and explode like that hand grenade. He was already shaky from upchucking however many times it had been.

The sight of her car coming down the road, slowing to turn into the parking lot, made his heart pound. What was he doing? He wasn't up to this. He had to tell her whether she should hang on, ask her if she could hang on and wait it out, or to suggest she move on. He had no idea yet which he would do. Playing by ear was his typical M.O., but he should have played this differently.

She was in the capris she'd worn when he first met her, and a top he didn't recognize. New, maybe. For her new job? Didn't matter. She was there. She looked wary and gave Bruce a grin at his greeting, but she came to him, her gorgeous eyes studying him. "Hi. Yes, I know I said that a bit ago, but in person is different."

He hugged her. No way he could stop it. He wrapped his arms tightly around her, kissed the side of her head, and clenched his eyes. "Hi."

"Are you okay?"

He nearly collapsed in her arms. "Not close. I'm such an asshole. I can't imagine why you're here."

"No, you're not. You hurt. Don't talk about yourself that way."

Despite the fact he was about to burst after all of the hell of the last few days, he chuckled at her turning his words around on him, and then his body shook and he couldn't stop the tears. "Shit." Pulling away, he turned from her, trying to hide it.

"It's okay." Following, moving back around, she touched his face, sliding her fingers through his hair to pull his head back down to her shoulder. "Come inside."

Damn, he wanted to take that in a way she didn't mean it. Bruce was there, coercing him, and he managed to pull it together enough to get up to his apartment without embarrassing the holy hell out of himself, and then he wrapped back into her. "Why are you here? Isabel…"

"Because I love you, even if you are a jerk, and you *are* a jerk."

"I won't argue."

"It might be easier if you did."

"Because it would be easier to walk out?"

"Yeah."

His gut clenched. "You can. You should. You know I told you to, if I ever did this again"

"Yeah, but you know what? You don't get to decide that. You took this too far. And I mean, we've taken this too far. *I* get to decide whether or not I can deal with it. You don't. It's not up to you."

Studying her, he sifted fingers through her hair. "That's fair, too. Let me take you to dinner. You might have to drive..."

"I don't want to go out. I can cook."

"Nope." Bruce's voice made her jump since she'd forgotten he was there. "Ordering in. You know the deal, J. Not letting you out of my sight for a couple of days."

Forty

Tired of walking, although to be honest, she was more tired of her up and down emotions, Isabel moved to the edge of the water, as close as she could get without getting wet, and sat cross-legged to stare out at Lake Erie.

He'd slept at her side after insisting she not drive back to Pittsburgh since it was so late after they'd talked. And he hadn't said much of anything, other than sharing some memories of his buddy, and that talking to Denton's little sister had put him over the edge. She was a sweet girl, he said, always doing volunteer work. Denton had been very protective of her, and as close as he and James were, he'd warned James not to even think about it.

He wouldn't have. She was like his little sister. Seeing so much pain in her face had about killed him. Instead, he went to grab a six pack, although Bruce insisted he'd bought a case, not a six-pack. He wasn't even sure.

When he asked if she'd go up the lake with him, Isabel hesitated. The night before, he'd been as sweet as could be, but by morning, he was grouchy and nearly unresponsive. After sniping at her for asking if she could make him eggs after he told Bruce he didn't want anything, he came back and hugged her. And asked if she'd go up to Presque Isle.

She didn't agree until Bruce said he and Abby would go, also.

He took her back to where they'd met and she wasn't sure if it was a hint or whatever, but he was barely talking to her. He'd gone for a swim, with Bruce at his side while Abby talked with Isabel about stuff that didn't matter. Small talk. Abby was good at it. Isabel was not. As soon as Bruce reclaimed his girlfriend, Isabel went to sit by herself.

She wondered if the little pink troll had been found by its owner. Hopefully it was at least found by some little one who was glad to have it. One who wouldn't lose it.

Her eyes watered. Swallowing hard, she got up and started gathering sand into a castle. A bad one, since she again didn't have a shovel or mold or anything, but it felt better to be building a castle the lake would eventually overtake than to sit and do nothing. At least there was pleasure in the doing.

At least her little girl was out there, hopefully with someone who truly loved and wanted her. Isabel would always have that.

Not enough, but...

Not enough. She wanted her daughter. She wanted James. She wanted parents who were real parents. Her new job was something to look forward to, a good direction, but not enough. She wanted... and needed...

"Can I help?"

James appeared in front of her suddenly, blurry through the moisture in her eyes. "Iz?"

"Um." She wiped them with her sleeve and kept building. "Sure." She supposed he meant the sand castle.

"You okay?"

"I'm... I don't know." Gathering more damp sand, she carefully added it to the top of the wall she'd started and shaped it.

He did the same, building beside her, adding to the outside to strengthen it. "It'll hold better if the walls are thicker and graduated from the bottom. Like this."

She gave him enough room to add a mild incline around the outer base of her castle. Barely enough room. She liked having him so close. He'd put his shirt back on, but his hair was still damp from swimming, as were his trunks. She would be freezing in a half wet swimsuit since it was only 60-something, on the high end of 60 but that was cold for her. She'd worn a long sleeved tunic over leggings and had a sweater along, in case she needed it. So far, it was just sunny enough she was fine.

The castle was fairly tall when a child playing Frisbee nearby hit the top and knocked part of it in, then acted like he'd just taken down the Taj Mahal. James assured him it didn't matter. A young boy, maybe five or six, who was impressed with their castle. James talked with him about castles and dragons and knights while they built it back up.

"You can play with it." Isabel stood and brushed sand from her hands.

"Cool!" He called to another boy, excited, and she walked away as they descended on the castle.

James kept her side, silent for some time, until he bent to pick something up. "This one's nice." His open palm held a deep blue piece of polished glass. He tried to give it to her.

"Keep that one. They're hard to find in that color."

Taking her hand, he kissed her palm and set the sea glass over the spot he'd kissed. "Then it should definitely be yours." He closed her fingers around it and kept her fist in his own hands.

Her eyes watered again. Her emotions were too on edge. She tried to wipe them subtly, like she had sand or something in them.

"I'm sorry. I didn't want to do this to you."

"You've already said that."

"I know. I'm just not sure what else to say. I know you should throw up your hands and get on with things, find someone easier to deal with..."

She walked away. She was not close to the right emotional state to listen to it.

He followed. "What do you want to do, Iz? I hope you'll at least let me keep setting up shows for you."

"Will you come?"

"Do you want me to come?"

"Yes."

He stopped her to slide fingers up along her face and around the side of her head. "Then I'll come. By next weekend, I should be okay enough. I'm sorry I missed it last night."

"No, it's fine. You shouldn't have even thought about going. I should have cancelled to stay with you, to be there when you got home."

"I shouldn't have asked you not to go to the funeral."

"Why did you?"

"Because... I didn't want you associated with that memory. You're the best thing I've had in my life for a hell of a long time and I didn't want the memory of you at that funeral to mess it up. You're my light. I can't stand the thought of dimming that. At all."

At a deep intake of air, she gritted her jaw and looked up at the seagulls circling a small family sitting on towels snacking on something they'd brought.

"Why did you think?"

The thought of the food made her hungry. She'd barely eaten breakfast since he was being so snippy, and she still wasn't terribly hungry when they stopped at the Chick-fil-A just before driving onto the Isle, so she only ordered nuggets and a side salad and it hadn't lasted long.

"Iz? Tell me what you thought."

What she thought. About why he'd pushed her aside. With a soft shrug, she told him the part of it she could stand to admit. "I figured I'm not part of your past and you don't want me to interfere in it. And, you don't particularly need me since your family's there, which is good, I'm glad they are, but it leaves me..." Unable to say more, she gave him another shrug.

"Oh, Isabel." His head shook and dipped lower toward hers. "No. Damn, I'm sorry."

"Stop, okay? I don't want you to keep apologizing."

"But..."

She kissed him. A short kiss, but real, her eyes staying closed to linger in the moment, in his scent, his warmth, his personal space, for a moment. "I love you, James. We're going to get through this. Okay? Just..."

"Don't give into it again. I know. I'll do my best."

"I was going to ask you to remember to call me when you need to talk. Whatever time."

"You'll be working."

"Oh. Yes, but I'll see if I can leave my phone on, at least for a week or so, and I can check it at lunch."

"Bruce does that. You don't need to."

She walked away. His family. Bruce. Even Gavin. He had plenty of people there for him.

His hand closed around her arm, encouraging her to stop. "I didn't mean I'd rather call Bruce. Okay? I'd far rather talk to you anytime, but he can do it without risking his job. He's well established. His schedule is somewhat flexible. It's not a risk to him. It would be for you, with a brand new job, and I do not want you to risk your job. That's it, all I meant. Okay? You go back and knock them out. Show them who you are and what you can do and get where you want to be. I'll leave a message when I need to talk and you can call back on lunch or break or whatever, but don't risk your job for me, Iz. That's exactly counter to what I wanted to do."

"This isn't all about me, you know."

"You're the one with the direction. I have nothing right now but a paycheck from a job I don't care about, so..."

"So redirect."

"What do you think I've been working on?"

"With your IT jobs?"

"No, Iz. That's just a paycheck." He brushed his fingers against her temple and behind her ear. "You. Music. I can't do it myself, but I've been working on heading back into it differently."

"You want to go into artist management."

"Well, A&R, really, but you have to start somewhere to get your foot in the door. I have to prove I know music, and I can market it. And I have to get noticed by the right people who see I know what will work and what won't. So, it is about you, and I mean aside from us, it's about your career."

She walked away again, down to the water. About her career. Was that why he was trying to be nice to her when it seemed hard to be nice? *At least let me keep setting up shows for you.* About her career. Maybe it should have been left at that, as she'd told herself a hundred times before they got involved.

Stopping at the edge of the water to where it barely came in up over her feet, she shivered and crossed her arms in front of her stomach. Soon, he was behind her, warming her with his own heat, his arms wrapped around hers.

"Not only that. It's never been only that." He kissed her head. "You do know as much, right?"

Did she? To be honest, she wasn't sure. And she was far more concerned about their personal relationship than their work relationship. Even if he felt the opposite. "It's not about that to me. It's not. It's about us. I don't want to push my music career that far without you. If you're not there doing shows with me, I'll go back to sending my songs in and skip doing shows. Not because I'm afraid; because I don't want to do it if you aren't there. Remember that." Turning in his arms, she slid her hands up his chest and around his neck. "*Remember* that. It's about *us.* We do it together or I don't do it at all." Meeting his lips, she hoped to rekindle his fire, the one that was set to a huge burning flame the night they watched it dancing along the river.

~~

It was hard as hell to let her go back to the city. He needed her to stay for the week. Needed her encouragement, her hugs. Damn did he need her hugs. More than anything.

And she offered, but missing her first week of work at a new job would likely lose her the job. He didn't want that. He did, and he didn't. He couldn't do it to her, so he acted like it was fine, he was good, and he'd be at work, so there was no point in her staying.

Walking her to her car and giving her a nice kiss, he asked her to drive safe and let him know when she got in, and he managed to do it all without letting the shakiness he felt show on the outside.

Good thing Bruce walked out with them. Otherwise, as soon as her car was out of sight, he would have been headed to find another six pack.

Or whatever he got last time.

"Come on, man. I know what you're thinking, and you did a good thing letting her go."

"I hope like fuck she'll be back." Squatting on the sidewalk, he shoved a hand through his hair.

"She'll be back."

"Sure of that?"

"Yep. And you better come on up with me now and stay clean to make it worth her coming back. You should take the next couple of days off, too. I'll do the same."

"No." He stood and headed back into the building.

"Are you sure? It's going to be a trigger for a while, being that that's where you heard it."

"Can't be helped. Gotta save funds to move to Pitt soon."

"Yeah? That's your plan?"

"As soon as I think she's sure enough of me. I hate being so fucking far from her."

Forty-one

Only Wednesday.

Isabel enjoyed her job and the days went by fast. The people she worked with were great, supportive, helpful, and friendly. She was writing well, inspired by the work she was seeing on a daily basis, both the good work and the not so good work. Both were equally inspiring.

But she missed James.

He texted during his lunch hour, which was earlier than hers, so she didn't get his reply to her reply until his late break, and she didn't get that until she was off at five. But he was friendly and said he was doing fine. On the phone every night when they talked, he sounded jittery and like he was covering.

She considered texting Bruce to see if he was actually doing okay, but it felt disloyal, so she just sent a thought up into the universe or wherever it went for him to be okay, to be strong.

Saying goodbye to her coworkers, Isabel forced herself to wait until she was out of the building and on the sidewalk before checking her texts. Strange. He hadn't replied. Maybe her service was being slow to catch up. Before trying again, she walked down to the parking deck, phone in one hand and pepper spray in the other, made her way to the space along the front where it was open rather than somewhere in the middle of the thing or along the back, got in her car and locked it behind her, and frowned about still getting nothing. Had she said something wrong? They mainly talked about their work and music. Nothing, really.

When she pulled into her driveway, her grandparents' driveway, she gave him a call rather than texting or waiting. It went to voicemail. Since she didn't want him to think she was worried about what he was doing, she left a teasing message: "Hey, Gilbert. Off work yet or do they have you doing overtime because they can't stand to let you go? Couldn't blame them. I'm home, so you can call if you want."

She was barely in the door when she got the text, not a call.

Not feeling great. At home. Will be in touch when Im up to it. Hope your day was good.

With a frown, she sent a quick reply: Sorry youre sick. Hope its not too bad. Sleep and get well. At least she hoped he was only sick, even if it was horrible to wish someone sick.

~~

By Friday morning when she still hadn't heard from him, Isabel gave in, rather than let his "when I'm up to it" text keep her from badgering him, no matter how often she worried. It kept distracting her at work. In the parking deck, she started to call but figured he'd be at work if he was better and so texted with a simple: How are you doing by now?

Not expecting an answer until sometime later, she jumped as she closed her door. A text: Have u booked tomorrow at a brewery on main in butler.. new venue but should be good.. will meet you at six. tell me if you cant

Really? She stared at the message like it would reveal more the longer she stared, felt her ire rise, and reminded herself he was sick and men were babies when they were sick. Even her grandpa got grouchy when he was sick. While ambling along the parking deck toward work, she answered, briefly. See you then. I need the name of the place. Any particular playlist?

Will send later

That was it? At least he'd answered. It was something. Business only, but something. Isabel was starting to have an almost definite feeling that they should have kept their relationship business-friendly and no more.

A brewery. Should he have booked a brewery already? She hoped Bruce or one of his brothers would be with him. Isabel would ask Gramps to go.

In case he didn't show up.

Her heart pounded when she pulled up in front of the venue. It was a big place, nice, elegant, judging from the outside. She didn't see his truck. The last she'd heard from him was the night before when he sent her the venue details and said it was posted on her page. She'd checked before she left to be sure it was still there and the venue was still advertising it. Lots of likes were under the post featuring her picture, the one he took of her with her guitar on the amphitheatre steps. Nearly 60. It only made her incredibly nervous.

And he wasn't there.

Her grandparents had wanted to come, but her grandma had an event she couldn't skip and Isabel insisted her grandpa go with her instead, as he should. She was meeting James. It was fine.

But he wasn't there. Which meant not only no moral support, but no mic or speakers. Again, she only had her guitar and her little amp. But he would be there. He'd said he would and he hadn't bothered to say he wouldn't, so she had to believe he would be.

Gritting her jaw, she forced herself out of her car and grabbed her things to at least tell them she was there and to check the place out a bit. Some guy held the door for her with a smile, which made her nervous, but she thanked him and made her way to the greeter's desk, told the girl who she was, getting a big smile from her, also, and followed to a manager.

His large hand took hers firmly. "Nice to meet you, Isabel. I was expecting to see James with you."

"He should be here soon. You know him?"

"For years. He used to play for us now and then back when I ran a little club in New Castle. Glad to see he's back into music. Such a shame about his accident. Come let me show you around while we're waiting on him. I'll take those." He reached for her guitar and amp, but she only agreed to let him take the amp.

The stares from diners and from employees made her want to run right back out to her car, but she set up her amp and tuned her guitar and watched her phone for any message from him. Finally, she sent him a text to ask if he'd forgotten.

The friendly manager came back and teased about giving him a hard time for being late, figuring out he had the rest of her equipment. He'd brought her a glass of water and asked if she wanted anything else, which she did not, and still there was no sight of her manager.

So she stepped outside to call him. Voicemail answered. He wouldn't return texts while driving, but he always answered his phone, since it was hooked into his truck. She had to try not to sound panicked while she left a message: "Hey, are you still sick? I could have come up to grab stuff. Are you okay? Let me know. If you don't show tonight, I'm coming up there to find you. Consider that fair warning."

Maybe she shouldn't have mentioned the equipment. It was him she was most concerned about. And by now, she thought maybe she should cancel the show and just go find him. *Bruce.* She called Bruce since she couldn't get James. Voicemail. Cursing, she left him a message asking if he would let her know where James was, said she was supposed to go on in five minutes, but could cancel, to please call.

Waiting and watching for his truck as long as she dared, she went back in, shrugged at the manager, and found herself agreeing to again work without mic or speaker.

Whether or not she should, she checked her messages after every couple of songs in the guise of checking her playlist. Still, the audience was good and the tables filled in fast. Dinner time. But they were paying attention rather than talking and ignoring her. A good thing. Applause was good. Some guy at a back table said he couldn't hear her well enough and she thought about telling him to look up her manager on her social media sites and complain to him, but instead, she apologized and said she was missing some equipment due to management illness and would try to be louder. Someone else commented about not being prepared and she tried to brush it off, but between the comments and worrying about James, she fumbled her words, and then the chords, pushed through to finish the song, and excused herself for a break. Early.

Barely outside, she dialed him again and shivered. The temperature was dropping. A storm was trying to move in. She hoped it would pass above or below… Again, his voicemail. "James, please, just send me a couple of words to say you're okay. Please. Should I come? Or do you want space? I'll do…" She waited while an older couple went by. "Either one. Just say so. Please just be okay."

Hanging up, she stared out at the stars in the dusk. She could only see the brightest few, since heavy clouds were blocking most of them and making it dark faster than normal. She had to be okay without him. If there was one thing she learned from her mother she wanted to keep, it was that she had to be able to hold herself together, whatever he did.

With a deep breath, she went back to finish her show.

She still heard nothing from James or Bruce by the time she'd talked with a few who wanted to talk and then packed up and got to her car, walked out by the manager.

Not willing to add another hotel night to her fast-growing credit card balance, Isabel went home. Back to Pittsburgh. He was right; Pittsburgh was home.

It was nearly eleven before she pulled into the driveway and she held her pepper spray in her right hand, her guitar case over her shoulder and her amp in her left hand. Her grandparents weren't home yet, so she set her things down just inside the door, holding the spray while she walked through turning every light on downstairs and then upstairs. Satisfied she was alone, she went back for her things, stored them in her room, thought about eating since she hadn't been able before her show, and decided against it. Her stomach was still in knots. Where was he?

She'd never be able to sleep, so she pulled her guitar out and played with a melody...

At a sudden noise, she jumped up to sitting. Daylight streamed through the window, through the sheer white curtains falling gently over the oak blinds. Years ago, she'd done her room at her grandma's in an ocean feel and it had been left that way. Still hers. A reminder it would always be her home, her grandma said.

The noise... her phone. James. It was the ring tone she used only for him. A text, not a call. Reaching to grab it, she noted the time. 7:15. On a Sunday morning. "Please be okay." Opening the message, she had to read it three times.

Heard you made a big splash. Nice.

Nothing more. Did he mean at her show or at her job? Who would have told him either? Since she was far too tired and she'd lost her patience by now, she returned with Hello to you too. Guess youre still alive. Good to know.

Told you I was down.

You said not feeling great. Could mean many things. Didnt get my texts at all?

A long pause elapsed before he bothered to answer, during which time she realized she'd fallen asleep fully dressed and her guitar on the floor looked like it might have fallen, so she picked it up to inspect. Luckily it looked and sounded fine.

And it buzzed again. I did. Want to come up today?

Isabel nearly threw her phone against the wall. No, she did not want to go up and see him if he couldn't even take five seconds to say he was still sick, or down, or drunk or whatever and wouldn't make it her show. Ignoring the question while she went to the bathroom, washed her face, brushed her hair, and changed into clean clothes, she calmed enough to simply say No.

It was fair. Why should she? It felt like he only offered for her sake, not because he wanted her there. No, not like that. Not because she'd been stupid, again, and slept with him and he felt obligated...

Want me to come down?

That was harder to answer. It took more effort to come see her than to let her drive up. But he asked if she *wanted* him to come, not whether it was okay if he did because he wanted to see her. That was a whole different thing.

She paced while trying to decide how to answer. She had to move things back to professional and leave it at that until he decided what he wanted. You should rest after being down so long. Maybe next weekend. Working on new songs. Show went fine. Manager said to tell you hello. Perfect. Not angry. Not pushy or clingy. Just professional. His move.

Except he didn't answer.

She had brunch with her grandparents, since her grandpa loved making a big brunch on Sundays, let them know her show went well, saying nothing about James although she could see them wondering, listened to funny stories from their gala, then worked on her songs. Still, nothing. Fine, he was mad. Not that he had the right to be.

Forty-two

By Tuesday morning, when she still hadn't heard from him, Isabel took a chance and asked if she should be ready for a show over the weekend. Still, he didn't answer, and nothing was posted on her page, or on his. She couldn't stand the thought of another full work day without knowing anything, so just before she left, she tried Bruce again with a simple Good morning.

This time, he answered immediately. Hi Isabel. How are things?

At least you answered this time. Thanks for that.

What?

You didn't answer me a few days ago.

You didn't text me. Have you texted J at all?

Really? Yes I did. Both.

A pause, then he called. "Hi, um, I don't have any missed texts or calls from you. Okay time to talk?"

"It is, and I tried to reach you Saturday when he didn't come to my show when he said he would."

"You had a show Saturday?"

"Um, yeah. He set it up. What's going on?"

"He said he'd been in touch with you, but you were too busy to come up or anything."

Flopping onto her bed, she wasn't even sure how to respond.

"He has been in touch?"

"Kind of. Not since Sunday morning."

"Um, I guess he isn't with you, then."

"No." Her heart lurched. "Where is he?"

"Well, that's kind of..."

"Bruce?" Unable to sit, she got up to pace. "Where is he?"

"I'm ... not real sure."

"You mean tonight? Is it okay to let him be on his own by now?" When she got silence, her heart raced enough she could hardly breathe. "Since when? Was he at work today?"

"Okay, so don't panic, but he didn't show up at work, today or yesterday. I haven't seen him since Sunday morning when he said he was headed to his parents' for dinner. They never saw him. We're trying to find him."

Lowering, but missing the bed and landing on the floor when her knees gave out, she shoved a hand through her hair, her eyes clenched.

"We'll find him. Not the first time."

"Is that supposed to make me feel better?"

"I'll call you as soon as we find him."

"I'm coming up."

A pause. "You might as well wait until..."

"No. I'm coming up. I'll be there in about an hour and a half. Will you be at the apartment?"

"Yeah, I can be. Drive safe. Getting into an accident won't help us find him any easier."

After calling in to work for a personal day, she gritted her jaw and explained to her grandparents. She tried to argue when Gramps said he was going with her, but it was pointless to argue, especially when her grandma said she was going, as well.

They kept trying to talk to her on the way to Greenville, but she couldn't answer them. She texted with Bruce to find out where they'd looked already, asked about the park, the kayak place, Presque Isle. They'd hit all of them, plus every bar in Greenville, Mercer, Grove City, even Jamestown and Conneaut Lake. She suggested the coffee shop and he said he'd send someone, but he doubted James would be there. He had a whole army out looking, from the way it sounded, including some of Denton's family who heard that he went off the deep end after the funeral and wanted to help before they lost "another one."

She wasn't sure whether to be comforted by the fact or more worried. She finally got it out of Bruce that James hadn't taken anything but his truck and wallet, not even his phone. He wasn't using any of his cards. He'd pulled a bunch of cash out of his account.

Isabel started to think he might have chosen a new place along the coast to go beach-hopping, since he'd mentioned it had been a while. Where else would he be? Bruce suggested she should have stayed at her grandparents because maybe he'd gone to find her. When she mentioned that to them, her grandma called her next door neighbor and asked her to keep an eye out for him.

On the way up, she asked to stop at the Confluence and at an Irish bar in New Castle he said he liked. In Grove City, she stopped at Primanti's and considered the coffee shop but Bruce said he'd have someone nearby check there and she didn't want to take that much of a detour. His parents had been all through Mercer, so she didn't stop there, either.

Where else? In Greenville, they took a swing around the park just in case, and she got out to walk down along the river. She knew they'd been checking the park, but she wanted time to think, needed to unwind enough to think. Being near the water always...

He wouldn't go anywhere very populated if he wanted to be alone.

Making her way back to the car, in a near jog that tired her out since she was already exhausted from not sleeping well and from her heart being in a constant race from anxiety, she gave her grandpa directions to the apartment building.

Bruce and two of James's brothers were outside when they pulled up and Isabel nearly jumped out of the car before it stopped all the way, but her grandpa hit the brakes while her grandma called her name and she went straight to Bruce. "Tell me you've heard something."

"You look like hell."

"Thank you. I don't care..."

"Sleeping at all?"

"Did you check... There's a place on Presque Isle he used to hike to before it flooded, or... was cut off. He said he used to..."

"Already checked it, and we have the island staff watching for him." He set an arm around her. "Isabel, you've got to calm down. Come inside. Have you eaten at all today?"

"No. It doesn't matter. Where else did he used to go? You checked Sam's, right?"

"Several times already." Felix cut in. "Any other ideas? We've looked everywhere we know to look."

Setting a hand over her stomach as it churned, she shook her head. Bruce greeted her grandparents, introduced Felix and Burt, and insisted they go inside. Isabel went straight to the bathroom. He was right. She looked like hell, even in her skirt and blouse, her work clothes. She hadn't taken time to change or grab clothes.

Washing her face and brushing her hair with his comb, she went to his room and pulled out the knit pants she used as house clothes at his place. She had a couple of T-shirts there, also, but instead, she grabbed one of his. She wished she had her deodorant. Since she didn't, she used his. Better than smelling like sweat.

Her grandpa raised his eyebrows at her change of clothes and Bruce told her that one looked better on her than on J, too. Trying to sound not as worried as he looked. Didn't work. He offered a sandwich...

She shook her head and paced, jumping when her phone buzzed.

"Lisbon. My friend." Since every eye was on her, hoping it was him as much as she hoped it was, she answered curtly. "Yeah?"

"Hi, Izzy! How's it going down in the big city? Want a couple of visitors?"

"Libs, I can't talk now."

"You're mad at me. I'm sorry I've been so unavailable, but I have news and I want to tell you..."

"I'm not mad. James is missing. I have to keep the line open. I'll call later." Lisbon. Meadville. A thought crossed her mind and she hung up and went to grab Bruce's hand. "Come on."

Burt, the oldest brother, tilted his head at her. "You have an idea where he might be."

"Yes. Long shot, but maybe. It's one of our places, in Meadville, and maybe I shouldn't assume he'd go to one of our places. "

"Let's go. I'll drive."

Her grandparents tried to come, but she asked them to please stay in case he came back, wrote Bruce's number down for them in case her service got iffy, and headed out the door, hearing Felix assure them they'd look after her. Bruce grabbed the jacket James usually wore plus a denim bag and one of James's sweatshirts, handing the latter to Isabel since she also hadn't grabbed her coat.

She sat up front with Burt, and Felix and Bruce jumped in back. Giving directions, they flew up I-79 and turned off into 322 toward Bean's Trailhead. "There are different places to park along the trail, but this is where..." Her heart pounded and she pointed. His truck.

Again jumping out before the car stopped all the way, she went to it. The door was locked. No sign of him. Bruce pulled keys out and lifted the canopy covering the bed. He nodded inside. Beer cans. A lot of them.

"Come on." Isabel grabbed the closest hand, not caring whose it was, and pulled it, leading them down the trail toward the covered bridge. A good place to be alone. A good place to hide. In the mostly dark. Anyone actually riding on the trail would likely veer around him and move along without questions.

Between her heart pounding and her near-jog – she couldn't risk actually running since the trail was three miles or so in this part of it, the part they'd walked, and he could be anywhere – she had to fight off dizziness, hearing them talk, someone on the phone saying where they were and they'd let them know, hearing Felix ask if she was okay or if she needed to stop a minute, but she focused her attention along both sides of the path, realizing Bruce and Burt had their heads together enough to split up and each watch a different side of the path, and that Felix was slowing her down with her hand gripped tightly in his.

When the covered bridge came into view, she yanked it away and ran up and inside. Nothing. Doubling over enough to try to catch her breath, she felt someone pull her in.

"Unwind, Isabel. No sign is a good sign so far. Okay?" Bruce gently raised her face to his. "We've done this more than once. You have to unwind before you make yourself sick."

More than once. She hugged him and fought back tears and started walking again, slower, still trying to let her body catch up from the exertion.

At the two mile marker, she collapsed into the grass alongside the trail. A wild goose chase. He could be anywhere. He could have parked his truck and hitched a ride, with a girl, maybe, and threw them off track purposely. Why would he be there? Why would he be anywhere they'd gone together after she wasn't there for him when he tried to call her like she promised she would be? After she'd gone back to Pittsburgh for work when he was struggling with the loss of his friend who was like a brother? Why would he? And why wouldn't he be unwilling to talk to her?

"If you want to take her back to the car, we'll go the rest of the way up the trail." Burt. Talking to Bruce.

"No." She got up. "I'm not giving up."

"Neither are we, but..."

"No." Continuing down the paved trail, she also knew he could have gone off the trail. His brothers were on each side watching for any sign of that. Bruce was beside her.

They were coming up to the small clearing beside the creek where she'd sat to write and he'd startled when she touched him, and her pace increased. The bench... someone was on the bench, lying down... a foot stuck out.

"James." She hurried around to him. He was on his back, his left leg and arm dangling over the side, the right leg sticking off the end, an arm over his stomach. His eyes were closed.

Bruce kept her from getting too close. "Let me. He may swing." Setting fingers against his friend's neck, checking for a pulse, Bruce gave the two brothers a nod and Felix put an arm around her, holding her back.

"J." Bruce tapped his face. "Come on, man. I know you're alive. Your heart's beating. Wake up." He tapped harder and blocked an arm that flew up at him. "Not this time, bud. Good try, though."

"Go away." The words were hard to understand.

"Nope. Get your pathetic ass up. We've been looking all over hell for you. Time to go home. Get up." Bruce pulled at him, and with Burt's help, got him to sitting.

"Good to see you, little brother." Burt tousled his hair. "Even like this. Guess we start all over, huh?"

"How'd the fuck'd you find me?" His words were slurred.

"Isabel found you. Good thing. You're shivering. Got your system depressed to all hell and it's about to get cold."

"Iz? Where?"

She moved closer, but Felix stopped her from getting far.

"You swing at her, J, and I'm knocking you right back out. Got it? You awake and with it enough to let her get close?" Bruce pulled his eyelids up one at a time. "Fuck, you reek. Get this off." Yanking the T-shirt up over his head with Burt's help, he wrapped James's jacket around him and felt his pulse again. "Gotta get some water in him."

Burt pulled a large bottle of water out of the bag and handed it to James, helping him when his hand shook. "Come on, little brother. Let's get you home." He pulled one of James's arms over his shoulder and lifted him with Bruce on the other side. At jerking motions, they pulled him next to the shrubs and doubled him over enough not to get the vomit all over his clothes.

Felix moved in front of her, blocking the view. "Is there a shorter way out of here?"

Pointing the way they'd been walking, she said it was only about a mile to another parking area and Felix mentioned getting the car and bringing it around, but James was back on the bench after rinsing and spitting to clear his mouth and she went to his side. "Hey."

Bloodshot eyes met hers. "Why are you here? Told you to stay away if I did this again. You promised..."

"No." She ran a hand through his hair. It badly needed washed. "I said okay, as in I hear you. I did not promise I would."

Shaky hands reached up to cup her face. "Not fair to you. Find someone you don't have to do this with..."

She saw Bruce ready to grab James if needed, watching to keep her safe, but she kept her attention on her love. Whatever else he was, he was her love, her world. "I love you, James Gilbert, and I'm not leaving. We'll get through it together."

He wrapped around her. For the first time since she met him, he smelled bad, a mix of heavy body odor and old alcohol and dirt. Still, she cradled him in her arms, felt his body heave from cold and exhaustion, she expected, heard his brothers talking and Felix say he'd go get the car and find his way to the closer parking area.

He did reek, even with the shirt off, but she didn't care. She held her arms around his cold skin under the jacket, trying, hoping to warm him.

"Here, J." With a hand on Isabel's back, Bruce offered a wet washcloth for his face, and then a clean tee. "Up to walking if we take it slow?"

"Head's splitting." He pressed a hand against it.

"Yeah, no surprise. I've got a couple of protein bars and more water. If you can get some of it down, I'll add aspirin."

Burt handed James an open snack bar, and a hand to help him stand. "Okay?"

"My truck is... um..."

"We found it." Bruce pulled a couple of plastic bags from the canvas bag and told Burt if he wanted to start out, he'd grab the trash James left and wrap his "nasty" shirt and catch up.

He didn't talk on the way back to his place other than refusing when Burt asked if they should go straight to the ER to have him looked over. He did sip on the water and eat the protein bars Bruce pushed him to eat. By the time they arrived, he was far less shaky, and his apartment was packed. His parents and the middle brother were there, along with two people she recognized from the memorial service, one his buddy's little sister, the other not family, she thought.

James disappeared into the bathroom for a shower and Felix let them know Isabel was the one who figured out where he was and between the thank yous she didn't want, she felt herself being pulled away. Her grandpa took her as far from the crowd as possible, and she fell into her grandma's arms.

"I think we should get you home now."

She raised her head enough to see Gramps. He was concerned, but also angry. It showed all over his face.

"Now, Niall. You just calm down." With a warning look he never ignored, her grandma stroked her head. "He looks all right overall." At Isabel's nod, she grinned. "Good. Now listen. Your grandfather is going to try to insist you come on home with us, and before I know whether to agree with him, I need to ask you one question."

"I'm not going." She held her grandma's gaze, her chin up.

"I suppose there's no need to ask you to leave, then. Niall, just hold on a minute." She stopped him when he tried to argue. "My Bella, I'm going to ask you this, anyway, because I feel I must. You don't need to answer, but you think about it. Will he be as loyal to you as you are to him? By that, I mean whatever happens, will he do as much for you as you are for him?"

Her eyes watered and she swallowed hard. "Yes. He already has. And he took the risk first."

"Did he?"

"I've kept a lot of distance, more than was fair, and still, he just keeps waiting for me, to let my guard down. Thank you. For everything. For tonight, I have to stay. I'm not sure yet from there."

"You realize calling off work twice within a week of starting may result in you being fired."

"Maybe. But I'll have to take the chance."

"You're sure he's worth it?"

"Yes. He's been there for me through more than you know, and I have to do the same."

"Have to or want to?"

"Both. It wouldn't be right not to give as much effort to this as he has. And I want to. I want this."

"Well, that's too rational to argue. Remember whatever happens, your room is open anytime you need it. No questions, only ears. Remember that, Isabel. There's no choice that can't be remedied. Don't try to keep yourself from choosing in order to try to avoid mistakes. Not choosing is usually the worst mistake. Take the reins. It's time."

She swallowed hard, hugged them both, and promised to call in the morning.

Before they got out the door, James came back out, showered, in clean clothes, and thanked everyone for their concern but asked them to leave. Everyone. Ryan's sister gave him a hug and told him to hang in there because she couldn't lose him, too, and left with the other guy.

Isabel tried to stop her grandpa from going to him, but it wasn't possible. Looking James in the eyes, Gramps warned him to be good to his little girl or there would be hell to pay.

James looked past him, to her. "Go home with them."

"No."

"Isabel, go home. Go. You have a job. A career. I told you to leave. You shouldn't be here."

Felix pushed up against his brother, trying to calm him. "You know if she hadn't come to help, you'd still be lying out there freezing your ass off. You might be more grateful."

"Fine. I'm grateful. Thank you." He came over to her, with Bruce at his side watching him, her grandparents at hers. "But go home. I don't want you here. Like I told you. Go."

"I want to help."

"If you want to help, then fucking *leave*, like I asked."

Bruce shoved him. "Knock it off or I swear I'll knock you out."

"Fine. You tell her to go. Tell her why she should. I'm starving." He turned and went to the kitchen.

Isabel felt the stares while she tried to decide whether to listen, heard Bruce apologize, reminding her this was just J when he was coming down, and shook her head. "No, it's fine. Really. He can contact me if he wants. I'll leave him be unless he does. Just let me grab my things." Going to his room, she quickly changed into her own blouse, lay the T-shirt she'd been wearing on his bed, and grabbed anything of hers she found.

Unclasping the necklace she always wore, her sea glass pendant, she turned to set it on his dresser, the taller one, and caught sight of a notebook with his handwriting. Lyrics. Aware it was a privacy invasion, she reached for it. *I'm Not Sayin'* was scrawled across the top.

I'm not saying you don't have the right to walk away
and I'm not saying things will be better if you stay
I just want you to know
I may fall apart if you go but you should anyway
because I'm not sayin' I'll ever be okay
enough... for you

So go on and do your thing, shine your light, bright
like a beacon in someone's dark life
it matters

you matter. Let it show, go on and go

you've gotta do you

and I've got a lotta working on me to do

so go, be bold, do your own show

and shine

That was it. It was unfinished. *Go. Do your own show.* Fine.

Unable to resist, Isabel took a photo of it with her phone, made sure the words were clear enough to read, and set the notebook back in place. Then she reclasped the sea glass pendant around her neck and tucked it under her shirt. She couldn't quite leave it.

Finding him sitting at the table, a shaky hand trying to put chips into his mouth, she hugged him from behind, whispered into his ear that she loved him and to be okay, and left with a fast goodbye to his parents and brothers.

Take the reins. Fine. She took them. She had work in the morning, a job she liked in the city where she was comfortable, as much as she was comfortable anywhere, and she was going to forge the path she wanted.

Maybe someday, it could include him again.

If it didn't, she'd live with that, too.

Forty-three

Isabel gave Lisbon a long hug and then introduced Charlie to her grandparents. She hadn't heard from James since he'd kicked her out a week before, but Libs had been calling every day checking in. Charlie picked up tickets to see The Clarks at Stage AE on North Shore and invited Isabel. Libs told her to bring whoever she liked, meaning a date, she supposed. A not-so-subtle hint to start seeing someone else.

Her grandpa suggested the young man who helped them move her, as a thank you, but that wasn't going to happen. She'd rather be a third wheel than to take someone just to take someone. And she wasn't giving up on James. She was only waiting him out.

Leaving them to talk, she went to change into something less nice than work clothes and nicer than the old sweats she wore around the house. Choosing jeans with a purposeful hole in the knee and a loose gray sweater over a black tank top, she frowned when the jeans didn't want to go over her hips. Too tight? Already? When had she last worn them? Spring, probably. She'd been wearing beach clothes, work clothes, or sweats since then. Hardly ever jeans.

With a check in the mirror once she managed to get them up and zipped, Isabel shook her head and took them off. The only other decent pair she had were also too tight. She wouldn't go. She'd just tell Libs she wasn't up to it and stay home and have a couple of scoops of ice cream with caramel and chocolate and...

Plopping onto her bed in her sweater and undies, she studied the bulge of her thighs. "This is *not* okay. *None* of this is okay." She missed James. She missed the beach. She missed doing shows. And she missed the small part of her that used to care about her appearance, her health.

You're too out of shape for a singer. His voice echoed through her head. It had hurt more than she should have let it. Because he was right and because she hated that she didn't care if she was.

Take the reins. Her grandma's voice replaced James and herself. "Take the reins, Isabel. It's time."

Fine. Going to the small closet, she found a stretchy black maxi skirt to wear instead of jeans and went out to make herself enjoy the thought of going to see one of the biggest bands to come out of her area.

She did wish James was there to go with her.

Keeping the smile plastered on her face through Libs and Charlie dropping her off before they headed to their hotel with an indoor swimming pool and a view of the city over by Tenth Street Bridge, Isabel told her grandma the concert was nice, that The Clarks were not only technically good but entertaining, and she liked their songs, then answered Gramps about details of the show and the stage set up and said he should have come with her. She'd invited him, and Charlie invited him, but he didn't want to interfere with the young people, so he said.

Through it all, the pit in her gut that had grown the whole time she'd been there because she knew James would enjoy it, knew he was a fan of The Clarks because she'd seen it on one of his T-shirts, and knew there was a chance he was at the show and hadn't bothered to tell her, maybe with another date for all she knew, burst into billions of pieces that shot through her system and came out as tears. Escaping to her room with the excuse of being tired, hoping she'd gotten away before they noticed, she closed the door and plopped onto her bed, leaned back against the headboard.

Go home. I don't want you here.

His words got stronger the longer she didn't hear from him. It was getting too hard to believe he meant it for her good. Two weeks. He should have been cleaned out enough to just say hello or something. Anything. If it was for her good, he would do that. He'd apologize for being such a jerk.

It wasn't for her. The drinking was an excuse, just like it was for her father. She couldn't let him keep taking her for a ride. She would not turn into her mother and keep looking the other way.

"Bella?"

Grabbing more tissue, she wiped her face and her nose and refused to look at her grandma when she came in.

"Did something happen tonight?"

"No. I'm fine. Really."

"Hm. Yes, it looks like you're fine, really." Coming over, she sat on the bed facing her. "Have you heard from your James at all? I haven't wanted to ask."

Her head shook and the tears strengthened.

"I'm sorry, honey." Taking Isabel's hand, she gently rubbed the inside of her wrist, as she had often when she was young to help calm her. "I'm sorry you hurt so. Have you tried to call?"

"No. He said to leave him alone." She sniffed hard and then reached for more tissue, her body jumping with sobs she tried to hold back.

"I heard him, but I rather think he didn't honestly mean it. People say stupid things while being defensive, when their pride is hurt. I know. I did it to your grandfather often enough. I'm glad he was strong enough to stand by me through it. Otherwise, I would have lost one of the best things to ever happen to me."

Her chest heaved. One of the best things. Like James. Or she'd thought he was. She wasn't sure anymore.

"You feel the same about your young man."

"I don't know."

"Oh, Bella. You may not know right this minute, but you know. Things have a way of working themselves out with enough time and determination. Maybe he's not your one. Maybe he is. Either way, you'll get past this. Just keep moving."

Her head shook. She didn't want to keep moving. She wanted to lie down and hide in bed until it didn't hurt anymore.

"Okay, so it's the weekend. Take the weekend to roam the house in your pajamas carrying your tissue, and on Monday, pick yourself up and move forward. Take one more step toward whatever your goals are. It will make you feel in control, whether or not you are, and the way you feel about yourself matters more than anything. Take the weekend to think about it. We'll leave you be for that long. Come Monday, grab the reins again." She stroked Isabel's hair and kissed her head. "Go on and take a hot bath and get to bed and cry yourself to sleep if that's what you need. A few tears never hurt anything. You'll be fine."

With the silence that came with the soft click of the door, her tears stopped. Deep, cleansing breaths took over. Monday. Yes, Monday, she would take the reins. Somehow. But first she was going to accept the permission to indulge in a good, long sulk. With ice cream.

~~

James shivered as he stared out at the high waves. End of October. Two weeks since he'd seen Iz. Three days since his last binge. Burt figured getting him out on the beach might help clear his head, but it was fucking cold. And she wasn't there. At least he expected she wouldn't be on the Isle on a cold damp windy day. If not for Burt pushing him there, he wouldn't be, either.

Burt's three boys had come along while his wife and daughter had a girls' day out. The boys bickered and laughed and teased each other all the way there until James finally exploded and told them to quiet the fuck down and Burt told him not to talk to his kids that way. Maybe he shouldn't have, but his head still wanted to explode from three days ago and he wasn't up to the squabbling.

They'd been avoiding him since then, more than two hours later. The cold didn't bother them at all. They weren't in the water, but they played along the edge, kicking a ball back and forth at the moment. Like he and his brothers had done as kids.

Isabel had never had that, never had siblings to hang with, to fight with, to torment, to trust with secrets and tears. Her only girlfriend didn't seem too awfully close, either. He couldn't imagine.

He hoped she was doing well in Pittsburgh. And he hoped she wasn't, that she'd give up the city and move closer. She wouldn't, though. She'd find some stable, probably boring, guy who would give her an easier road, maybe an industry guy who'd push her songs to someone who would care because of her married name combined with her grandma's name, since that was generally the way to get up to the top. He couldn't give her that. Or much of anything she needed.

Loving her wasn't anywhere near fucking enough. It wasn't.

Shoving up from the sand, he wandered down to the water. Too far. The waves rushed in farther than he expected and soaked his shoes. He shivered again, but stayed where he was. Took a step out farther. Focused on the cold, on how the cold waned after a few minutes, got numb instead. Numb would be good, if he could manage it. Just don't feel. Don't want.

Don't give into it.

He heard her voice. Easy for her to say. She gave into her chocolate craving whenever she wanted. She gave into her laziness, as she called it. She gave into her fear.

She'd given in to him when he told her to leave. She'd said she wouldn't, but she had. Maybe not everyone walked out during hard times, but most people did, even those you needed most.

Taking a few steps farther, he felt the water splash his knees, his thighs. Since he was half soaked anyway, he figured he might as well let the cold numb him more. He nearly changed his mind when it hit his crotch. But what the hell? What fucking difference did it make if he couldn't hold onto the one thing he'd actually wanted since he lost his hand and his music? Why not just ... walk out...

"What the hell are you *doing*?"

The numbness dissolved at his brother's face suddenly in front of his. Holding his arm. No. Grabbing his arm. Clenched.

"J?"

Now the oldest boy was there, too, staring.

"Enjoying the water."

"It's too damned cold to be in the water."

"You brought me to it."

Burt's mouth opened, staring, and closed, his jaw gritted as though James was about to get punched in the gut. But even though he knew the look, from years ago, he did nothing to defend himself. And his brother's face softened. "Come on, little brother. Time to go." Urging him back to shore, with his kid on the other side not holding on like Burt was, but close enough he easily could and tall enough he could make it hard to fight against them both if he was so inclined, Burt released his arm once they were on dry land. Instructing his kids to grab their stuff, he didn't move from James' side until back in the parking area.

"We're going to have to strip before getting in my truck. I'm not having my leather seats soaked."

Out of the water, it was far colder, particularly in the mostly deserted parking area where the three of them pulled their jeans off. Nothing numb about that. Especially in the crotch.

"Leave your skivvies on, if you don't mind, and sit on your coats. Would have brought towels if I thought you were crazy enough to get in the water."

"You plan to kick me out nearly naked in front of my building?"

"No. I'm taking you out to stay with Mom and Dad a while. Mom can turn her head for a few until you're..."

"The fuck you are."

"Don't talk that way in front of my kids. And don't bother to argue. Not asking your opinion this time."

Behind the wheel, Burt turned the heater on full while mumbling something about extra clothes and insanity, with an apology to his kid who got soaked for no reason.

Forty-four

After spending the weekend lazing in front of the television, watching a couple of newish movies Gramps picked up – he never bought them brand new; he always waited until the big hype passed, he said – and checking her social media pages, mainly to see whether he'd answered any messages lately and answering herself when she found he hadn't, Isabel was ready to get up and out to work Monday morning.

In between being lazy and pouting, she'd checked around on how to take a step toward a new goal.

After work, she went straight to the gym she'd found that was close enough to walk from work and then home, for a reasonable membership fee. Her heart pounded when she went in. Talk about way out of her comfort zone. Doing her own shows was nothing compared to walking into a gym by herself when she had no idea what she was doing or where to start.

The man at the front desk was luckily friendly and very helpful. Once she was signed up, he called one of their trainers over to show her around and help her get started. Of course it had to be a nice-looking guy instead of someone homely or a girl or something. A very nice-looking guy with a chest that was hard not to focus on under this very well fitting gym T-shirt. After stammering her name in greeting while taking the offered hand and completely missing his name due to nerves, she blanched when he asked what level she was at. Expecting it would be obvious once she got started, Isabel was honest about how out of shape she was.

"Hey, that's why we're here, right?" The guy smiled. "It doesn't matter where you are now, only that you're starting. Our focus is overall health, so if you're interested, we have nutrition information available and we're always willing to answer questions about how to best support yourself dietary-wise, with supplements and such, for where you are and where you want to be. Do you have specific goals in mind?"

"Um." Specific? Not really. "I guess I'd like to not get tired so easily, and I'd like to fit in my jeans again." Her nerves kicked in higher at the personal information she hadn't wanted to share. "Is that what you mean? I'm really new to this. I went canoeing and kayaking a few times over the summer, and I walk now and then, but otherwise..."

"Perfect place to start. So, stamina and fat burn. They do tend to go hand-in-hand. Is it the water you like or the action of rowing that made you go canoeing?"

"Um, I ... just agreed to go with my boyfriend. He had to push me into it. Really, I'm very lazy, but I'd rather not be, I guess."

"Are you doing this for him or for yourself?"

"For me."

"Good. Doing it to impress someone else never works well. It's how you feel that matters. So. How about we start simple, on the treadmill, and just walk a bit? There's a changing room back there." He glanced at the bag she carried and then behind her. "I'll wait here to get you started. Sound good?"

Changed into loose sweats and a long T-shirt, she felt every bit as awkward as when James had stood in front of her at Sam's, or more so maybe, when he led her to a fancy treadmill, showed her the basics of how to use it, and led her through some light warm-ups first. For a minute or two, she felt like she was back in high school and rebelled at the thought of being made to stretch, but Isabel reminded herself it was for her own good. And this time, it was her choice.

By the time the half hour she'd allowed herself was up, she'd walked a mile plus a couple of tenths, on a slight incline. The trainer who got her started came over and checked her settings. It had taken twenty-seven minutes. "Not bad. That gives us a good base to start from. We'll work up from here. Before you know it, you'll be doing twenty minute miles up and down hills." He winked with a grin, accenting the blue eyes with ridiculously long lashes. "How do you feel?"

"Tired."

"That's a good thing. But you're okay, right? Just tired, no pain?"

"Yes. Just tired. Thank you."

"That's why we're here. You'll want to stretch your legs again, like this." He raised one leg at a time, the knee bent, all the way up to his stomach. Without holding on.

She had to grasp the handle of the treadmill, which was also embarrassing.

"Don't worry. That balance will come in time, also, as we strengthen your core. How often do you plan to come?"

"Every day after work."

"Nice." He looked surprised, as though he didn't expect her to be back at all. Asking about her work while they continued to stretch, he at least acted impressed by her job as an assistant music editor. She couldn't admit to this guy that she was a songwriter. He knew too much already. Seeing her grandpa at the entrance gave her an excuse to end the conversation. "My ride's here." Her walking partner, actually. He'd said he would come meet her.

"It was nice to meet you, Isabel." He offered a hand with another smile. "See you tomorrow." He had a pretty smile to go with his nice gym trainer build. Shorter than James, he was also broader than James, with medium brown hair kind of shagged into a neat but not rigid cut barely touching his shoulders, and a nice tan that looked like he spent a lot of time outdoors.

Gramps gave her a smile and asked how it went.

"Good. I might actually have enjoyed it a tiny bit."

He laughed. "Sounds like every job I didn't want to do but accepted anyway." Holding the door with a goodbye to the desk clerk, he set a hand on her back. "I'm proud of you, Baby Girl."

"For getting back in shape? I don't know how long I'll be able to make myself do it."

"For taking the step. For caring about yourself enough to take the step. I love you exactly as you are, but I want you to be happy with you as you are, so if you think you need this, good for you for doing it. Your grandmother has something healthy and hearty ready for dinner to encourage your quest." He leaned in like he was telling her a secret. "And I may have stashed away a couple of double chocolate chip cookies for dessert. Always remember balance is important, too."

~~

"Let's go, son."

With a groan, James turned over to his other side, away from the door, away from his father trying to get him up.

"Don't make me get cold water." The tone said he meant it. The man wasn't playing. "I've given you a week to get yourself together on your own. You don't seem to be doing it, so as of now, you work for me again. Until you find someone else who'll give you another chance. Get up. Hay needs to be bailed and it won't do it itself."

"You have people to do that." He pulled the covers up farther over his shoulder.

"And for now, you're one of them. Get up, James. I'm not asking. You've got five minutes to be in the kitchen grabbing your coffee."

Fucking Burt had to bring him to his parents and tell them he was not only not working but that he'd walked out into the lake. So the fuck what? It was water. He knew how to swim. And he did not want to go back to farm work. It's how he lost his fucking hand. What made his father think he'd want to do it again?

Let him bring the cold water. Wouldn't be worse than the lake was. Or the fucking virus he'd picked up two days later. So he'd lost his fucking job. So the fuck what? He still had his IT work.

Maybe. How long had it been? When was the deadline? Maybe he didn't. What in the fuck difference did it make?

"James, honey. Come on out and have breakfast while your father will still let me give it to you." His mom this time. With a mug of steaming coffee in her hand that she set on his dresser. Not his. The guest room he was crashing in until they decided to release him to his own recognizance.

He couldn't refuse his mom, so he sat up. Shoved hair from his face. Scratched the growing beard he hadn't bothered with. "I don't want to do farm work again. Didn't like it in the first place."

"Well, then, I suggest you start getting yourself on track and find what you do want."

"Found it. Lost it. Blew it like everything else."

"Water treatment?"

"Fuck no. Sorry. No." He couldn't do it, couldn't say her name out loud.

"Isabel."

Clenching his eyes, he shoved the hand back over his head and leaned down over his legs.

"Have you called her at all?"

"Can't. Not like this."

"Well, then, get yourself back into a place where you can."

"No strength left. I can't do it again."

Moving up next to him, she cuddled him in against her warm skin, her soft shoulder. "Yes, you can. Your family will be your strength. You're going to come through this like you have everything else. With our help. Now, get up, go shave off that mess on your face, get dressed, come have a hearty breakfast, and get out to work."

He almost said again that he couldn't handle going back out to the bailer, that the thought terrified him, but he'd pushed Isabel to do it, to keep doing shows even though it terrified her after her ordeal. And he'd said he would be there for her. He wasn't. He'd skipped her show and she did it anyway. It had pissed him off. But by now…

If she could do it, so could he.

~~

Two weeks in, and Isabel already felt the results. Instead of pushing for a twenty minute mile, which Kenny said she should be able to do fairly easily, she was now at an 18.5 minute mile on the treadmill. On weekends, she walked the sidewalks and found herself jogging at times. She wasn't sure how far she went, but she was pushing. And it showed at the gym. Kenny was impressed. He'd asked her out for coffee one night as she was leaving, but she turned him down.

She hadn't heard anything from James. The thought of it, the anger, and Journey on her workout playlist, spurred her on. She jogged. There on the treadmill in front of people. It felt good. She hated to admit that it felt good, but it did. Her heart pounded along with her feet, and she saw Kenny look over from the heavy lady he was currently working with and give her a smile and a nod. Isabel bypassed him and gave the lady huge kudos for being there, for trying to help herself.

Slowing again, she saw that she was at the two mile mark and did the math in her head to figure her speed for the second mile. She did the math three times. 17.6. A *seventeen point six* minute mile? A record. Her own record. The thought fueled her and she kept going to finish mile number three while she was on a roll. At the end of it, Kenny came to check on her, and she couldn't help but brag a bit.

He smiled again. "Nice progress, Isabel. Very nice. You're working up fast."

"I'm jogging on weekends. Well, walking mainly, but I add some jogging, too."

"Where?"

"Around the city."

"By yourself?"

"Yes. Gramps says his running days are over and I'm going too far for him. Grandma said his running days were over as soon as he got out of his last gym class and didn't have to do it anymore. Anyway…"

"How about letting me jog with you on weekends so you're not out there alone?"

"Oh. No, I'm okay. And I can't afford a personal trainer. This is hard enough on my budget." She slowed more, since it was getting hard to talk through her increased breathing.

"I'm offering as a friend, or at least as someone who'd like to see you off duty. I run on weekends, anyway, so it's no skin off my teeth to do it together. I'll come to wherever you are."

A friend? After asking her for coffee earlier? "I'm sure I'm far too slow for you."

"No problem. I'll use it as a warm up and track your miles." He raised his wrist to show off his fitness watch. "You should get your own, but until then, I'm glad to do it. And maybe we can stop for iced coffee in between as more impetus to go farther?"

She hoped he meant farther as in walking. "I don't drink coffee." Flashbacks of telling James the same thing made her feel guilty for even considering Kenny's offer. And Kenny could see she was considering it.

"Good for you. Neither do I. I know a good healthy smoothie place, though. Just as friends. I get that you have a boyfriend."

Did she? Maybe. Maybe not. And it would be nice not to walk alone.

"Tell you what." Kenny walked her toward the weights where they'd been working on her upper body strength after her walk/jogs. "I have some friends throwing their annual fall pre-hibernation bash this weekend. Bring your boyfriend so we can meet and I can make the same offer just to show you I'm on the up-and-up."

Bring her boyfriend? If he was there, she'd be walking/jogging with him. But she never talked about him. When Kenny had asked why it was never him meeting her at the gym, she'd just said he was working. Isabel hoped he was still working. Either way, it wasn't very likely she'd ever introduce him to James. "I'm not sure you'd want his reaction, and I really can't accept, but thank you."

~~

You make us search for you again, and I'm taking you back to rehab. Behave, and you can stay here instead.

His father's words kept drifting back at him every time he considered walking the five miles into town to find a beer. It'd be easy enough to do. A couple of hours or less and he'd find somewhere to buy a six-pack. Somewhere that hadn't been alerted by his family. Or that had been and would take a bit extra to keep their mouths shut.

But he wouldn't. And it wasn't the words, the threat. It was the look in their eyes. Couldn't do it to them again. Almost could, though. Every time he picked up his phone to text Isabel and then couldn't do it. Best he could do was to keep checking her media accounts for more of her replies to people posting there. The more he ignored it, the more she took over. Good to see. But there were no new shows booked. People asked. She said she'd keep them informed.

He should at least do that. Just book one and text to let her know if he should cancel. Get her back out there before she lost what she'd gained. Fans were fickle. They'd move along. At least for a mostly unknown singer, they would.

But if he booked her and she didn't cancel, he'd have to go. Or not go. No way to know which would be worse. He'd done enough damage.

Four weeks now since he'd seen her, or talked to her. Four weeks said she was done, wasn't coming back. Maybe he'd hit up a fall festival somewhere and… Like hell he would. They'd all have booze there. And girls. Not something he could risk being around yet.

~~

Three weeks she'd been going to the gym. Five weeks since she'd heard anything from him. So often, she thought about texting Bruce to check in, just to be sure he was okay, but James had asked her to leave him alone and she wanted to respect his wishes. She missed him. The way she missed him fueled her workouts, along with the anger she felt about being used and tossed aside. Again.

On angry days, she tuned her iPod to Nickelback and Anna Nalick and Pink and Matchbox Twenty and Melissa Etheridge… She'd set up different playlists for different moods. On determined days, she mainly streamed the soundtrack for *The Greatest Showman* and altered her workout to match the tempo of each song. *This Is Me* felt like her anthem. It had taken her some time to get through the whole soundtrack without stopping and she was proud of the fact that she could now do that, including slow jogging through the two fastest songs, and then repeating them at the end to finish the hour.

On bad missing him days, she put it on her softer songs, including J.D. Eicher since James had hooked her on his music, and she often repeated Lewis Capaldi's *Someone You Loved* for the emotional purge, but mostly she was angry. It worked to her benefit, physically. She was even up to jogging more than walking on the treadmill, often did 5K speed walks with some jogging in between, and had just managed a sixteen minute mile, followed by a twenty minute mile, after a twenty minute upper body workout with the trainer who was still hitting on her, but carefully.

It was raining by the time she finished. She'd already called Gramps and told him not to come walk with her since he was fighting a bit of a cold and she didn't want him to get worse. She walked quickly, between the chill of the November air and the quick-growing dark and her need to get home to find a warm shower and then dinner. Probably home-made chicken noodle soup since Gramps was sick. One of Isabel's favorite meals.

She was finding she liked to walk in the rain after a good workout. She was even enjoying her workouts. She felt good. She felt her vocals strengthening along with her muscles and her better cardio health. She was seeing her legs and stomach getting firm, her face thin out. Definitely, she was getting addicted to this new-found interest.

Her cycle starting had slowed her progress for a couple of days, but it also brought a hell of a lot of relief since it was late and she getting worried that she'd done it to herself again, mixed with some thoughts that she might not mind too much even if he didn't come back into her life any other way. Mostly, she was relieved. Never mind that she'd cried. It felt like another loss of something that she wanted.

By now, she was feeling full steam ahead and ready to start scheduling her own shows. Fans were asking. Gramps offered to help her get a microphone and a small speaker, but her job was going well and if she could do it in installments, she could do it. At this point, there was no hurry to move out, so she wasn't worried about saving for that and could splurge on herself for a change.

Nearing the house, she noticed some guy in a dark rain coat, his head covered, get out of a parked car and walk up to the porch. Stopping, she waited, saw her grandma answer, and both heads turn toward her.

Bruce. Her heart nearly stopped. Something happened. Something drastic for him to come in person rather than call. He came toward her and she held her ground, unable to move, to walk toward...

"Hey, Isabel. Aren't you cold?" He glanced at her soaked hair.

"What happened?" She could barely get it out.

"Can I come in? Your grandma said it's up to you."

"No."

His eyebrows raised. "I guess you're mad at me, too? I suppose I don't blame you, but he did ask me not to bother you. Maybe I shouldn't have listened."

"Asked you?" The rain was coming down hard now. It dripped off her bangs and into her eyes. She shivered and wiped it out.

"Yeah. You okay?"

"Is he?"

"Well, more or less. Can I just have a couple of minutes?"

More or less. She expected that meant he was still alive. Relief flooded her system and she nodded, led him to the door, and stripped out of her soaked shoes and coat while he did the same.

"Wow, so, you look good." He scanned her workout clothes, long leggings with a long clingy tank that covered her butt with a long-sleeved quick-dry fitted shirt over top.

"I just came from the gym."

"The gym? Really?"

"How about not looking so shocked, okay? Yes, I've been going to the gym. Had to find a way to work out my anger, and yes, if he's still alive and all, I'm still mad at him. Come in."

His grandparents greeted him like he was family, asking if he'd stay for dinner if it was okay with her. It was fine, but she was showering first.

More or less. James was *more or less* okay. Great. That made both of them, she supposed. She didn't particularly want to hurry through the shower, but she knew they'd wait to eat and she didn't know how long Bruce would want to stay since it was a work night, so she washed under nearly full heat and got right back out, pulled into ... no, not sweats. If he was there to go back and report to James, Isabel wanted him to tell the jerk how well she was doing without him. Petty. Whatever. He deserved petty from her by now.

Trying her jeans for the first time since realizing they were too tight, she nearly held her breath hoping they'd fit. They were loose. *Loose.* Her jeans had a gap. Not much of a gap, but a gap.

With a quick catch of her breath, she chose a fitted tee and tucked it in, checking the mirror. Not bad. She nearly cried at the thought that she didn't hate the way she looked. Even her hair had grown out enough in the back to look cute and professional. She combed it with her fingers, threw just a touch of gel in it to keep it tamed and a little scrunched up, and went out for dinner with her chain raised enough to show Bruce she hadn't been kicked down too far by his buddy. In case that's what he wanted to know.

His head tilted in a question. "You have plans tonight?"

"Working on songs. Why?"

"You, um... You look great. Maybe I can take you out for coffee, or tea, rather, after dinner, since you're dressed anyway?"

Gramps joked that she didn't need *the drunk's* buddy hitting on her any more than she'd needed what he'd put her through. Grams told him to behave and told Isabel to grab bowls to set on the table.

"Yeah, don't worry about that." Bruce flushed lightly. "Abby and I are looking at setting a date. For a wedding."

"You're engaged?"

"She's been really great through all of this, with James and all, and I can't imagine not being with her, so I figured I might as well make it official." He thanked her grandpa for the cola. "I do hope you'll come." He barely looked at Isabel. "Whatever happens with James. I still consider you a friend and so does Abby."

She considered saying a friend wouldn't leave her in the dark for over a month, but Libs had done it to her, also, and Isabel still would have been there for her wedding if she'd had one. "When?"

He shrugged while taking a sip of the soup. "Wow, this is good." He barely waited for her grandma's appreciative thanks. "Not sure. Depends on ... um, how soon we can get J back around again. It's not going so well right now. Last couple of weeks were good. This week..."

"Meaning he's still drinking." Gramps threw an icy stare.

"Mostly not, but someone brought it in on Halloween, his parents' place; they had a party since they're too far out for trick-or-treaters and didn't want James to go out. Was supposed to be only family, mainly for the kids, but I guess he called a few people. I want him as my best man, but I've gotta be sure he'll be dependable, you know."

"So you came here to tell Isabel she's right to stay away?"

"Niall." Her grandma reached for Grampus's hand to quiet him and looked at Bruce. "He is trying to fight it still?"

"He is, and mostly doing okay. He just has moments he can't get past. I came, well, as a last ditch effort, really. Even if it isn't fair to ask." He looked directly at her. "Can I take you for dessert or something after dinner? I mean, if you still do dessert at all."

"I do, just not so often. Yes. If you think I can help, I want to know how."

Forty-five

It was raining again, and cold, but Isabel didn't care. She didn't want to go back to the gym, not for a few days until she had time to gather herself, but she needed to walk. Fast.

Bruce, on Monday night, had given her a CD of original songs written and played by James, as well as a DVD of clips from a bunch of his gigs. She'd stayed up far too late listening to and watching all of it: over three hours' worth. She woke Tuesday groggy and achy. She figured it was from only about four hours of sleep plus the heavier workout plus the walk home in the rain, but part way through the work day, she'd had to leave. On top of everything, she'd caught her grandpa's cold, except more of it.

She couldn't stand to go back to work until Thursday and she'd still been far too tired to work out, but she went, anyway, after taking two days off, and then her flirting trainer asked if she was okay while she struggled to walk through *Photograph*, the Ed Sheeran song that was far too appropriate and far too heart-wrenching to be able to deal with after watching James rock the stage, so confident, so beautiful, and being too tired and too slow in recovering, and then through *Small Bump* since her iPod often played two from the same artist in a row, which she hadn't needed just then, and she'd broken down in tears when Kenny said she looked like she was trying to work out a heartache, that he understood, and asked her again to go out with him when he was off, maybe to a little sports bar he knew, for drinks...

And she packed up and left. Again, in the rain. She was sick of the damned rain. She needed the beach. She needed sun and warmth. And she needed ... she needed to run.

So Friday, instead of going to the gym after work, she went home, changed into her workout clothes, adding sweats over leggings for warmth, hooked her iPod into her ears, and took off. Toward the Point. Her goal was to go all the way to Point State Park and back. She did have her phone, so if it was too much, she could call Gramps to pick her up. But she wanted to go all the way. To prove to herself she could.

Her grandma said not to push so fast after a bad illness, or to at least eat first, but Isabel assured her she felt fine and would feel better with the fresh air after being in the office all day with the heater too high. If she waited to eat, it would be dark before she got back and she did not want that. Stupid short fall nights. One of the worst things about the cold seasons. She missed the long days.

While she walked, his music that had been floating in her head since she listened to it threatened to overtake the music playing through her headphones, so she turned it louder and quickened her pace, until she was running. Not even jogging, but running. And it felt good. It felt incredibly good.

Nickelback and Journey pushed her on, down Smallman Street as far as she could go. Triumph took over about the time she had to route around to Fort Duquesne Boulevard, avoiding the more major roads. *Music Power* accompanied her a good part of the rest of the way, since she replayed it twice and sang with it the third time. Some people turned to look, but she didn't care. She ran and she sang and she was at the water fountain by the time Taylor John Williams sang *Wicked Game* into her ears and she slowed to a walk, catching her breath, thinking of how she'd talked to James about his music.

She should have stuck to her guns and not fallen in love with him. She'd known better. No matter how hard she tried, no matter how loud she turned her music, Isabel couldn't block him out. So she gave in.

Sitting on the fountain, facing the convergence of the Monongahela, the Allegheny, and the Ohio rivers, she switched playlists to James' songs. And she listened again. Such incredible songs. Such a beautiful voice. And that guitar. Damn, he was good on that guitar.

Bruce said he'd stopped playing, and he'd barely saved the new left-handed guitar from destruction when James was on a roll one night. It was hidden with Felix until safe to give back.

James was spending a lot of his time at Riverside Park sitting on the amphitheatre steps. And he was fighting it. Off and on was what people saw. Bruce knew it was constant. He'd lost his job because he'd missed too much work, leaving early to get beer and take it to the park to sit and get plastered. They were back on constant watch, Bruce and Gavin and James's family and a couple of Denton's family members, including the little sister. Trading off so the rest of them didn't lose their jobs.

Closing her eyes, Isabel focused on his voice, his lyrics, his guitar. It would be hard as hell to lose skill like that.

And yet, she hadn't made herself book any shows. *You can still do it.* His voice taunted her. His anger that she still could and was willing to give it up. And he was right.

He was right.

She gave up too easily. With too many things.

Standing, she stretched her tired muscles so they wouldn't cramp, and headed back home.

Not home. To her grandparents' townhouse. That wasn't home. She had yet to make her own home. It was time to grab the reins. Grabbing her phone, she sent a quick text to Bruce as she walked.

It was growing dark by the time she made it back, since her return route was slower than the first half. Because much of her anger had drained by the time she left the water fountain. Because too much of her energy was drained from being sick and emotional. Because Bruce had given her a thumbs up, with a bonus attached.

After a hot shower and a too generous helping of Grams' meatloaf and fried potatoes, Isabel said good night and closed her bedroom door to work. Like usual. Except this time, she had a specific purpose.

You captivated me that night at Sam's and I can't stop thinking about the way I felt while listening to you, to your words, how much they affected me. If I feel that way, so will others, and ... music ... it's a life saver. It is. I want your stuff out there to help others, and I want to help make that happen. Lots of people need to hear what you have to say. Honestly.

His words from back barely after they met had been flooding her the past week since Bruce had come. A life saver. He'd called her music, music in general, but also her music, a life saver. She hadn't really let it in at the time, hadn't understood. But now...

Tuning her guitar to E major, she ran through her newest song to be sure she had it down, and then set up her laptop to record. She half considered doing a live thing, but she wasn't that sure of her emotional control yet, so she wanted to see it before it went out.

> *Say it louder or don't say it at all*
> *I hear you, I feel you, I know you are there*
> *but I need your words. I need your world.*
> *I need you to know I am yours however far down you fall,*
> *the hole in your ground doesn't lead far.*
> *Climb back up, love, I'm here and I need you to hear me,*
> *need you to feel me, to love me, to say*
>
> *I captivated you and conquered you*
> *showed you your own spirit come true*

your dreams and your quest are the same now,
they're one
with my own, love, we're true
no need now to stay blue and dazed, confused,
curtained
I'm yours and you're mine and that's stage left
come on home

Instead of leaving a break between songs, Isabel segued right into the one he'd asked her to play from Sam's, the one that captivated him.

She choked up slightly in the middle, but she kept going, then played it all back and decided to leave it exactly as it was. It took forever to come up with a message to add. Finally, she decided to keep it simple:

Here's a sample of what's to come at my next appearance, tomorrow night at Sam's Shack in Greenville, Pennsylvania at their open mic night. I'm honored to have been asked to close the show. Come by if you can. This goes out to someone who needs the healing power of music about now. Climb back up, love. I'm still with you.

Considering it for some time, she took the "love" back out to keep it more general. It wasn't a secret that she'd been dating her manager, but it wasn't public knowledge, either. No sense getting too personal.

Hitting "post," Isabel felt her heart race and shut her laptop down. She didn't want to see any comments right now, couldn't handle it. She only hoped it would work.

~~

Sam's. She was going back to Sam's.

James slumped down onto the couch and listened to her new song again. It had only been a few days since his last binge. Not close to soon enough to go to Sam's. He couldn't. He had to get better first, if not fully recovered, then at least on the way.

Climb back up. Apparently someone told her he'd fallen again. No surprise. No one could keep their fucking mouth shut. Bruce, probably, since he was such a fucking fan of hers. Whenever Bruce asked if he'd talked with Isabel yet, James told him to let it go. Asshole never listened.

She was playing Sam's. And this song... This was number one material. Not that he was any kind of judge of that. Not that he was any kind of judge of anything.

Still, she was back at Sam's for open mic night instead of doing her own shows? Why? The equipment. She used his stuff and he hadn't been there. So she'd quit again? Figured. Maybe she was right. She didn't have it in her to be a singer. Songwriter, maybe. Her stuff was good. But if she wasn't willing to pay the dues to keep getting them heard, what did it matter? As far as he knew, there was no reality show for songwriters. You had to sing, perform. You had to stand out as you.

He was wrong to push her when she didn't have what it took inside to keep going on her own. Open mic, for her, was going backward.

"Good stuff, huh?"

He jumped at his buddy's voice and closed his phone out.

"Not listening to the other one?"

"I've heard the other one."

"Yeah. So? Thought you liked it. Wait; if you know what it is, you've watched the whole thing already. How many times now?"

"Fuck off, would you?" He got up and headed... nowhere.

"Whatever, man. But I'll be there to support her, whether you go or not. If you don't, you're a huge asshole, by the way. I'm headed out a while. How about staying home? Safe to leave you here yet?"

"Just get the hell out." Shoving the television on, he dropped back onto the couch. Stay home. Right. He wasn't sure why they thought it was a good idea to leave him alone already, suddenly, but just as well. Having them stay on his tail non-stop drove him nuts. The only one he'd want to stay on his tail was ... Isabel. And she was in Pittsburgh doing her own thing. He should contact her. Apologize. Should've done it long ago. By now...

Climb back up. I'm still with you.

She hadn't given up. Unless it was someone else she meant, maybe some guy she'd met and was talking to. Couldn't be. Not with posting the song that had reeled him in at Sam's with that message.

Still with you. Why? Why was she hanging in?

Not that she was actually still with him. She'd run down to her city, to her family, away from him. When he needed her the most. Like hell, she was still with him. Still willing, though, it sounded, at least for some kind of relationship. Maybe only work. Possible. But unlikely. She wasn't the type to sleep with a guy to raise herself up. Not by a long shot. Especially not with someone so fucking low on the totem pole who likely couldn't help her half as well as she could help herself. So it was for him. For them. Why?

Fuck. He had to go see her. By now, a phone apology wouldn't cut it by a long shot. But was he ready to handle it?

Forty-six

Gravel crunched under the tires and Isabel's heart pounded at the sight of Sam's. The weather-beaten formerly-white wide board siding was tinged pink by the setting sun filtering between the pines and maples lining the road leading up to and partly hiding the iconic bar. Two birch trees acted like columns at the private entrance road, their branches meeting high above the line of cars that passed beneath. It reminded her of the walkway arch at Thiel College down the road, where one of the Raucous guitarists had gone to school, which was why he was in Greenville when he wasn't from the area. The story surrounding that varied upon who told it, like everything did over time.

The weight of the significance of the place belted her in the gut. Her grandma was looking at it fondly. Isabel knew how much she still wished she could have talked to him again, her guitarist, or had met any of his bandmates, back in the day. Or even now. Isabel had to wonder if anyone could ever look back and feel that way about her, because of her music, because of the impact it made on their lives. If it ever would. She had to keep going, whatever the obstacles, because it mattered. At least it mattered to her. Her songs mattered to her. During the time she'd walked away from it, thinking it didn't, thinking there was already so much good music out there that adding her own wouldn't make even a drop in the bucket and so why was she bothering, something welled up deep within and came back at her like a flair. *See* me, it said. This is urgent. This... *This* is important. Do it anyway, because you *need* to.

Because you still can.

Her eyes were watering by the time Gramps parked and she brushed it aside to get out. To take the next step. To keep going because she had to, and she still could.

The parking lot was already filling in, and it was early. A good sign, maybe. Of course there were others playing first, so the cars could be their fans and/or family. His brother had offered to get a bunch of people to her shows way back when, so it was possible someone had done the same for another act or two...

Or they'd done it for her. But why would they, after she'd walked away from him? Because they felt bad for what he'd said, what he'd done? Maybe. Or it could be people from her page, her sites.

By the time she got to the door, her hands were shaking. And it wasn't due to the possible crowd. Her foremost thought was whether he would be there. Maybe it would be easier if he wasn't. But then she'd know it was over, if he wouldn't even go across town for her. It wasn't the fear of seeing him so much as the fear of not seeing him.

Gramps reached over to hold the door and Grams told her to take a deep breath, she would be fine. Would she? Along with the whole James situation, the memory of her last appearance at the club shook her. Between the two, her head swirled badly enough it nearly made her dizzy.

Several people looked her way while she headed toward the performance area. She was carrying a guitar, so it was no surprise. Until a couple of young girls came over with a black Sharpie and asked if she would sign their T-shirts. Light gray shirts with her picture ironed on the front and her name printed across the bottom. The photo from her social media. Between them saying they had them made and hoped she didn't mind and trying to grasp the idea of someone wearing her face, she somewhat managed to sign her name on the front of their shoulders, the least awkward spot she could find, and managed to thank them for coming, but her head still spun. The whole thing was foggy, blurred. She could hardly focus on where she was.

The open mic host greeted her, using her right name this time, thanked her for coming back, pointed out her reserved table, and said she could warm up before they officially got started if she wanted to. She did not want to do so. She'd warmed up by singing in the car to the radio on the way there, from the time they were going through Mercer, sometimes with Gramps singing along to help keep her loose and somewhat relaxed. But she had to sit.

The host introduced her to the other singers as they came in and Isabel was fully amazed by the recognition and respect they offered. They had all either been to a show or followed her page and videos. A couple of them knew James and asked how he was. Since she had no idea how well they knew him, she just said she hoped he'd be there so they could ask him in person.

Her voice shook the slightest bit while she said it and she sipped the hot peppermint tea with lemon that she'd brought in a thermal cup for her voice while she studied the bar, the scuffed and water-stained wood tables, the indented wood plank floors, warped from years of use, the old bar that also served as a counter top for wings and wraps and such that helped to absorb some of the ridiculous amount of alcohol that flowed all night long. Maybe he wouldn't be able to be there. What if he was cleaned out by now and coming to hear her would trigger him, with everyone drinking around him? Should she have done this? Too late to back out. Maybe he wouldn't come. She wouldn't blame him, wouldn't write him off, if he didn't, if he had to protect himself by staying away. For whatever reason.

While listening to the other acts, she kept an eye on the door. Every time it opened, her gut clenched. Libs. This time it was Lisbon, and Charlie. Isabel smiled and waved them over. After quick hugs and ordering drinks, Libs leaned in to ask if she'd seen him yet. Isabel shook her head but couldn't answer. She had to keep focus on her own part of the show to come, as much as possible.

Her breath caught when she saw the trainer from the gym come in. Why was he there? Alone, even. Not alone. With another couple of guys. She turned her eyes away pretending she didn't see him, but it didn't work. He came up behind her, set a hand on her back, and said hello.

She did her best to sound casual. "Um, hi. Is this one of your usual hangouts?"

He laughed. "Not by a long shot. I saw on your page you'd be here, so we thought we'd come up to the boonies to add to the audience." He introduced his buddies who had apparently heard about her already, and, in turn, she introduced her grandparents and friends, and Libs invited them to sit. With not enough chairs available, his buddies said they were going to wander, but he pulled one up beside her, too close. Leaned forward, forearms on his legs, he watched the trio perform *Say Something I'm Giving Up On You*, a song that was nearly making Isabel cry already because it was too close to home, and asked where her boyfriend was, if he had better places to be.

"He's, um, not feeling well. I'm not sure he'll be able to come."

"That's too bad. I'd hate to miss it if I were him."

"How do you know? You haven't heard me sing."

"Sure I have. Videos. Online. They are public, you know. So, might he be the one you mentioned who needs a lift with music?"

Trying to figure out how to answer, her gut twisted when she saw his brothers come in. All three. And Bruce and Abby. Gavin. And James. He was there. She clenched her jaw and looked away before he saw her staring and emotional. He was there.

And this guy was sitting far too close, talking in her ear. Flirting. Not knowing what else to do, she moved her chair a bit away from him, closer to her grandpa.

Gramps looked from the door to her with a knowing gaze. "Still okay, Baby Girl?"

Leaning in close to keep it private, assisted by the music overwhelming the place, she caught her breath. "No. Can I just go?"

"You absolutely cannot. You stand your ground, do your thing, and don't allow him to have that much control over your emotions."

"But ... he does." She wiped a tear before it could fall.

"Well, I guess you can't help that." He set a hand softly over her shoulders. "Don't let him control your actions, then. That has to be under your own control."

Her control. She'd thought she'd regained it. Maybe not so much.

"Hey, Isabel." Bruce stood behind her, somewhat between her and ... and the trainer. She couldn't think of his name at the moment.

Because she didn't know what else to say, she asked Bruce if he remembered Lisbon, apologized when he said they hadn't met, and let Libs introduce her husband. He said hello to her grandparents. And he looked at the trainer.

She stumbled over what to say. "Bruce Means..." Still, she could not come up with his name. "Um..."

"Kenny Richards." He introduced himself.

When Bruce nodded, too obviously wondering what the relationship was, Isabel had to say something. James was there. He would ask. "He's a trainer at the gym I go to. I never expected him to come all the way out for this. Or all of you, either. I mean..."

"His brothers? Yeah, well, they're still very appreciative, shall we say. Anyway, are you on soon? Not sure how long we can..." With a look at Kenny, he stopped.

How long they could keep James there, he meant. He shouldn't be in a bar. She wasn't sure how long he'd been sober, if more than just tonight, since he seemed to be tonight. "I'm next."

"Good. Break a leg." He set a hand on her shoulder. "I look forward to hearing it again. Been a while. Live, that is. Loved the new video." With a smile, he returned to wherever they were sitting, if they were sitting. The place was packed by now. She doubted they found a table but she couldn't make herself look.

"Forget my name?"

"Oh. Sorry, I get inside my head before shows, so I'm..."

"Yeah, I'm guessing one of those guys that just came in is the boyfriend, or at least related. So." He stood. "I'm going to get out of your way. I look forward to hearing you live, too, Isabel. Good luck."

She cringed when he walked away. You didn't tell performers good luck before shows. It was ridiculously bad luck, although she didn't know why. And she was at Sam's again. The last thing she needed, with James there in the place they met, was bad luck.

A silly superstition. Nothing more. Her grandparents were there. Libs was there. It was fine. It was.

And yet, when the trio ended their set to the nice applause they deserved and the host announced she would be up next, she badly wanted to run outside and throw up, and then leave. Gramps took her hand and went with her to set her equipment up, or in the guise of helping her set up. It was for moral support. And she loved him to death for it.

She watched her grandma now and then while she tuned and warmed up her fingers, getting an encouraging nod and smile, took a few hundred deep breaths to try to calm her racing heart, and nodded to the host that she was ready.

She wasn't ready. She wasn't close to ready.

"And now a special treat for yunz tonight." The host gave her a quick smile during smattered applause, likely from some drunk guys in the back. And maybe the girls wearing her face. The whistle was Bruce; that, she knew, but she still didn't look over there. "We have the fast-rising local celebrity from Pittsburgh here to close out our show. How 'bout some hands for Isabel Dillon."

Applause thundered through her ears, through her soul. Good thing the strap was holding her guitar or she might have dropped it. Never did she expect this. Fast-rising? Celebrity? Not even close. Still, she thanked him and the audience. She wasn't sure they heard her, even with the microphone. Had they found out who her grandma was? Why else would they be so excited when she hadn't performed yet? Or even if she had?

With a few chords to work into the music and try to quiet the noise, mainly the noise in her head, she took another deep breath. "Thank you. I'm going to start with one of my long-time favorite songs. It's an old one, back from about the time Sam's was made somewhat famous, at least locally." Triumph was a bit later to hit than Raucous, but in the scheme of things, it was about the same time. She refused to look at James while singing her soft version of *Music Power*, or anywhere except at her own support system and tables beside it where she knew no one.

She managed to get through several songs, mainly her own, but also one of The Clarks' that she heard at their show and had been learning since then, giving them acknowledgement as one of the area's biggest acts. The audience was highly appreciative of that, and some sang along with it. Amazingly, quite a few people sang along with her songs, as well. Her videos James had recorded and uploaded and promoted. Had to be. The thought was truly overwhelming.

Then she made the mistake of looking toward the back of the room and caught his eyes. Her gut lurched. He was studying her the way he had the first time, as well as she could tell through the distance and dim lighting. With a deep breath, she said she was debuting a new cover song from another local artist, this one barely across the border in Ohio. Her nerves shot through the roof while doing J.D. Eicher's *What We're Not*, fully a message to James. She didn't dare look at him while she sang. It was hard enough knowing he was there. Again, the applause stunned her. Taking a chance after the song ended, she looked over at him. He gave her a salute with his glass. Cola, she hoped. But nothing more.

Jumping back to a more comfortable cover song, she did Infiniti's *Now I Can't* to let herself stabilize, then gave Kenny Rogers a nod by doing *Something Inside So Strong*, although it was a far more folksy version, and also a message to James. Then she asked the audience if they wanted a cover next or one of hers. Honored when they overwhelmingly asked for one of hers, Isabel did an early original, one of the first he'd recorded and uploaded because it was one of his favorites, and thanked them sincerely for the applause.

"I have time for a couple more." She grinned when a few people threw out different titles of her songs. "Thank you. But I think some of you are here after seeing the two videos I posted last night. Yes, I actually figured out how to post stuff on my own recently, after so much help getting started. I'll admit to being very non-tech, but I'm taking baby steps." A few chuckles filtered through.

She got through *Stage Left* fine by not looking at him, by focusing on the music, the audience, her growing tip jar. As she thanked them for the applause, Isabel debated whether she could do the one that had drawn him in during her first show at Sam's. She knew she *had* to do it. Maybe just for herself, to prove she could.

Halfway through *No Words*, she congratulated herself for keeping her voice strong and steady, her guitar work controlled and precise ... and then he walked up closer, slowly, but in a direct path to the stage area, and stood right in front of her like he had that night. His gaze was thoughtful. Studying her like she'd been some kind of experiment.

A couple of people yelled "down in front," but he didn't acknowledge them and she guessed someone told them who he was since they stopped yelling. The bar was hushed, far more than it had been yet. He watched, studying her, with nearly no emotion, even less than the first time he'd haunted her while singing. If she mattered to him, if she *really* mattered, he wouldn't be able to just stand there studying her. But he did. He just stood there watching.

Isabel didn't need to throw up anymore. She needed to run out the door and break down in tears. But she wouldn't do either. This was her reclamation show. At Sam's where she'd been chased out. In front of her ex who told her to leave, that he didn't want her there when he most needed help. With her grandma there, at the bar where her nearly life-long crush had gotten started on his huge career path and made her choose to move away from home and settle out there, where she'd met her own real life-long love. Full circle. This mattered too much. Isabel was taking the reins, and she could do this. No matter how hard he stared or how close he stood. A test? Seeing if she would actually pack up and run again?

Not this time. This time, she finished the song and thanked the audience, remembering to remind them of her name. When they yelled for an encore, he turned and walked away. But the bar manager gave her a nod, permission to keep going if she wanted.

Fine. He got the point. But she would get the break point, or whatever the hell he'd called it. She would prove she wasn't giving up. "One more, then. How about a brand new song never played in public before?" She waited through applause. "This one goes out to ... to the one who taught me not to throw away what you can still have only because things aren't going right."

Maybe it was a bit of a low blow, but he did have it coming. And he stopped walking.

She played the opening to *Even If I Haven't* twice before she could make herself sing. Her voice was shaky, unsteady, but she kept going.

That night you looked at me/ I ran
That should have told you to go, run/ don't look back
But you found me/ Do you ever wish you hadn't?
He turned to look at her.
Even if I haven't given you reason/ please say you're still glad you did/ that you

gave us the chance to be right/ to be amazing, or at least okay/ with our pasts and our new lives/ that we have bits of each other/ to take away, to last

Turning again, he went to the door. Went out. Left the bar.

With a slight hesitation, she continued, managed to finish the song. And then, thanking the audience, Isabel headed stage left. She supposed that was that.

Swallowing hard about a hundred times while she packed up and thanked those who came over to say how much they enjoyed the show and answered those who asked if she was okay, she nearly hugged Libs when her friend interfered, asking them to give her space. Gramps took her guitar and Grams gave her a long, tight hug and told her she'd been wonderful, a real success. She didn't feel like a success. She felt like she'd failed. With James. Which felt far more important than any show. Wiping a couple of tears, she made her way outside. She needed to be outside.

Isabel would give herself a couple of weeks to pout, to mourn what she thought she'd had while praying his family and friends would see him through and help him get straight, and then she'd get up and start again.

The cold darkness was refreshing, although it stung her eyes. Or maybe it was the dust kicked up from the gravel parking area from cars leaving, flashing their headlights out to where small lights sparkled just above the grass, within the trees bordering the parking lot. Lightning bugs. She loved lightning bugs, even used to play with them.

Maybe she'd learn that song, too, the one about fireflies and what she used to be before.

"You okay?"

At Lisbon's hug, she wiped the moisture from her eyes. "Yeah. Thanks for coming."

"Oh, Isabel, you were wonderful. And he's a huge jerk for walking out on you. Really. He doesn't deserve you. Forget him."

She tried to hush her friend's naturally loud voice as Felix and Burt came up behind her. They'd obviously heard Libs. "Sorry. This is my long-time friend, Lisbon. She's kind of protective."

Felix threw an understanding grin. "Nice to meet you, Lisbon, and you're right." He looked back at Isabel. "We're really sorry he's such a jerk."

Burt nudged his little brother to shut him up. "You were great tonight. Isabel. The new songs are nice. I'm glad Bruce let us know you'd be here. If we can help you in any way, professionally, let us know. The offer's still good."

"Thank you, but it's really not necessary."

"Why? Plan to quit again?"

She startled at James' voice behind her. Beside, really. Nearly touching her by now.

"Come on, J, play nice for a change. You can handle it for five minutes." Bruce apologized for his friend, and complimented her, told her he loved the new song even if it was wasted on such an undeserving ass...

But she could hardly hear him. Or anything. James hadn't left. He was there, looking at her like ... like he was impressed and captivated and sorry and ... and lost. He looked as lost as she had felt the first time she'd played Sam's and had been chased out. He was thinner, pale, had bags under his eyes, and he needed a haircut and a shave. Still, he was there, right in front of her, looking like maybe he still wanted her but was afraid to say so. Or it was her wishful thinking.

His dark green eyes shone bright under the lights from the door, like a cat, or a cougar. A jaguar, with its sleek strength and stealthy moves, standing there just watching her. Waiting.

Isabel didn't back down even half an iota while he scanned her body, her straight skirt and fitted hi-low thin sweater that showed she had lost weight, was pretty well toned. She'd tied a long blue and green striped scarf around her waist, letting the corner hang down one hip, as an accent, a way to add color to her black outfit. And her sea glass pendant lay over her chest, pulling out the colors of the scarf. She'd bought the scarf because it matched her pendant...

"You look really good, Iz." Reaching behind her head, he fingered a strand of hair. "This is different."

The streaks of color. Dark blue and light green. She'd splurged and gone to a salon to have peekaboo highlights added to the bottom of her hair, underneath the top layer, an imitation of the lake and the way the color flowed with movement.

He lowered his hand and tucked it into his jacket pocket. "So I guess you've decided to go all out for the singer thing rather than just the songwriter gig."

"What?"

"You did a lot of covers. Good for audiences, less so for getting your work heard."

"It's hard to get my work heard if I don't attract audiences first. Someone told me as much recently."

His chest rose and fell. Gramps said it was time to go, with a hand on her back. Grams hushed him and pulled him away. Likely not very far away. His brothers and Bruce did the same, gave them space. Libs told her to call later and gave her another hug with her goodbye, plus a glance at James that could have been taken as a glare.

"So, um." He dropped his head enough to look ... more lost. And contrite. Not a look she was used to seeing from him. "Bruce said the guy sitting with you earlier is your trainer."

"Not my trainer. He just works at the gym." She heard the annoyance in her voice. It was unintentional, but also deserved.

"Not a boyfriend? Not that I'd blame you. He's..."

She eyed the lump under his shirt and the chain around the back of his neck. He was still wearing the sea glass pendant she'd bought him. "He's not my type. And I'm waiting for you."

His eyes raised. "Why?"

"Because I love you, even if you are a jerk."

His chest rose and fell again and his head shook slightly. "I lost my job. So I'm unemployed as well as a jerk. And I think jerk is putting it mildly. So, if the trainer asked you out..."

"He did. I declined."

"You should maybe take him up on it. I mean, he did come up here for your show, right? More than I've done lately."

"Tell me you still want me, that you still want us."

He was quiet too long, his eyes lowered. His jaw tightened and released. Silence was filled with crunching gravel, murmured voices, and the pang of bugs hitting nearby lights as they tried again and again to get to the source and failed. Isabel felt their pain.

Finally, he shoved a hand through his hair and met her gaze. "You fucking walked out on me. So really, it doesn't matter what I want."

Her heart nearly stopped when he turned away. But she wasn't giving in that easily. "I didn't walk out. You told me to go. Twice. At least."

He turned back. "Because you *wanted* to go. I made it easy for you. Fine. You walked. As I said you should. Glad you listened. It means you have some kind of common sense. So why are you back here? Why the whole show of it?"

She saw Bruce moving closer, watching. There was no way they didn't hear James with as loud as he was. But she ignored him, and the stares. "I did *not* want to go. I did not. *You* were afraid of this, afraid I wouldn't stay, and so you pushed me out."

"You took a job in the city."

"Yes, for us. To start building something. To help make a good start for us."

"Bullshit. It was an escape."

Her head shook. She swallowed hard. "No." At his raised eyebrows, she backtracked slightly. "Okay. Maybe it was to an extent. But it wasn't only me. You were supposed to call me. I told you to call me if you ever needed me. And you didn't. So I guess you didn't need me, or didn't want me enough. Fine. But *don't* put it on me. *I* didn't walk out. *You* did. You turned back to alcohol instead of to me. *You* walked out on us. I waited for your call. I waited over a month, James. I would have come the instant you called if you had, but you didn't. You're the one who ran."

"Good try, but you knew where I was. And by the way, you know that glass you've been collecting? They're fucking *beer* bottles. So I guess you can say my habit is supporting yours."

Swallowing hard, she forced herself to answer. "They aren't all."

He laughed, a sarcastic laugh. "A damn high percent of it is, especially all the green, like this one. One of my favorite brands." Pulling his necklace from under his shirt, he laughed again. "It's fucking hilarious, if you think about it."

Unable to speak, she stood, fighting her emotions she would not allow him to see.

"Go find yourself a real life, Isabel. You've got no future with me." Turning again, he walked away. Felix caught up with him, tried to stop him, then coaxed him into the car when he wouldn't turn back. Bruce apologized and Abby hugged her tight and Isabel said good night and went to her grandparents.

~~

Looking out through the dark, Isabel watched what she could see of his hometown slip past. *You've got no future with me.* You... *You fucking walked away from me.* As though he hadn't wanted her to...

He hadn't wanted her to go. It was her future he was focusing on. Not himself. *You've got no future with me.* Protecting her. As always. He was always...

When she saw the exit sign leading to 79, her heart jumped and her head shook. "Turn around."

"Are you all right, Bella?" Her grandma turned from the front seat to see her.

"I have to go back. Please. Go back."

"Are you out of your mind, Baby Girl?"

"Niall. Be gentle." She set a hand on his arm and nodded toward a little gas station, hinting to her husband he should pull over.

"That boy is nothing but trouble."

"So were you, old man, but I stuck by you, anyway. Pull in there and let's talk a minute." When he slowed, but was still considering, Grams got more firm. "Niall Dillon, this girl is old enough to make her choices. We wanted her to be independent. She is. Pull over, as she asked."

With a frown, he did as ordered, but didn't turn off the engine. Instead, he propped an arm over the seat and eyed her. The lights from the gas station made him look far more stern than she knew he was. "Alright, so tell us why you want to go back. Need to tell him off more since you let him off easy? That, I'm all for doing. Anything else..."

"He needs me."

"He has family."

"It's not the same. You know it's not. Gramps, I love him, and it's not like Toby who was an escape or like Mickey who was ... comfortable. I didn't really love him. I was comfortable with him. And that wasn't enough. I'm not comfortable with James. I mean, I am and I'm not and I like it better that way, even if it doesn't make sense. But I finally understand why Mom stayed. She had to stay because he needed her and she loved him and so she made the less comfortable choice..."

"She made the wrong choice."

"Niall."

"Meladee, you know our girl made the wrong choice. She made all kinds of wrong choices and I kept my mouth shut because it was her life, she was grown, so she said, but I won't do that again. We made the wrong choice, too. We kept silent too much. Not this time. Baby Girl, you deserve better than what your mother did to herself. She deserved better, too. I can't have you living that way, too."

"There's a difference, Grandpa. There is."

"And what is that?"

"James loves me. He really, honestly loves me, and he's trying..."

"After the way he talked to you?"

"He's hurting. I should have stayed. He trusted that I would stay even when he told me to go and I didn't. He's hurt. And I have to fix it. He can't do it right now. It's my turn. He didn't give up on me and I won't give up on him."

"You're not drowning yourself in alcohol as an excuse."

"No. I was drowning myself in fear. In my grief. It's no better. For ten years, I've been hiding behind what I lost and he pulled me out of it to where I want to really *live* again, not just get through the days. I have to do it for him. I *have* to, Grandpa. I can't lose him."

"And what will it do to you?"

She had to think about that one a minute, but only for a minute. "It'll give me what I most need."

"That boy is what you most need? What about your music? Your career?"

"No. Not the boy. Or not only the boy. Strength to face what comes. If I run now, I'll just keep running. I don't need James. I *want* James. I *need* to be able to find the courage to go after what I want. And now I understand why Mom made the harder choice instead of the more comfortable choice. It didn't work for her, I don't think, but, James isn't Dad. He's trying. He is. And he needs my hand to help hold him up while he's trying."

"Bella." Grams reached for her hand and patted it. "You've grown up to be exactly what I knew you could be. But you have one thing backward. Your mother did not make the harder choice. She made the comfortable choice. Your father was her comfort zone, and that's why she stayed. She never loved him enough and I tried to tell her as much, but she pulled away from me. You, my dearest one, have your head on straight and I know you're going to pull your James up with you rather than letting him pull you down the way your mother did. Niall, turn the car around."

"Now, Meladee. It's after my bedtime already. We turn around and..."

"You just turn this thing around. We'll drop the girl off and go check out that pretty hotel we just went by so we'll be close if she needs us and you can get your beauty sleep, because heaven knows you need it."

Gramps gave her a friendly scowl. "This." He looked back at Isabel. "This is what you want to put up with?"

"Yes. This is what I want." Isabel gave him a grin. "James reminds me of you. When he's sober, he does. Honestly."

Gramps groaned and turned back to the wheel. "Then I'm taking you right home instead."

"You'll do no such thing. You take this girl where she wants to go. And then we'll go break in that hotel room right."

Isabel covered her ears, as she always did when they started flirting with each other. When Gramps pulled back onto the road, back toward Greenville, her tears started. Tears that said she knew it wasn't going to be easy, but she didn't care because she loved him and she wanted him, and she had the courage to make it work.

~~

"Come on inside, J. It's getting cold out here."

He shook his head, trying to convince Felix to go in and leave him be. Lying on his back in his parents' yard, he went over the conversation in his head, and her songs, her expressions. He was supposed to call. He was the one who walked away. As much as he wanted to argue, he couldn't do it. She was right. After all the times he'd criticized her for giving into her fear, he'd done the same.

He was too afraid of her walking away. So he'd pushed her away, and walked away himself. As if that was any better.

Fuck, he wanted a drink.

No. He wanted Isabel. And he'd scared her off.

Who could blame her? Even his family took her side. Bruce took her side. Said he was a huge asshole and he'd just lost the best thing to ever happen to him. But she didn't deserve to have to put up with it. Again. She'd been through enough. Maybe he could...

He sat up. Maybe he could find her daughter. Sealed records didn't mean shit if you went through the right channels, or the wrong channels, or found the right person to get through the red tape. Sealed didn't equal gone. They were there. Someone knew. Maybe he could find out for her.

"Coming in?" Felix shivered.

"Yeah." Getting up, he ambled toward the house with his brother. Hot coffee sounded good.

Coffee sounded good. He wanted coffee. And he wanted his laptop so he could start searching, or finding out how to search. Maybe she'd hang on long enough he could get himself up out of it, get sober and stay that way, and find her child. Her daughter. James wanted to find her daughter. He wanted to meet Isabel's daughter.

He wanted ... everything to do with her. Her music. Her daughter. *Her.* And ... he wanted to have kids with her. The thought struck him hard and he stopped walking.

"J?"

"I've got to talk to her."

"Yeah." Felix set a hand on his shoulder. "You do. Because I think she'll be willing to try again if you stop being such an ass. But not tonight. It's late."

"I don't want her to go all the way back to the city thinking..." He couldn't even say it.

"Thinking it's over?"

With a shudder, he squatted, wrapping his arms over his head. No amount of pleading from Felix coerced him into the house. If she went back to the city, it would be over. Not for the moment. Forever. And yet it had to be her choice. He couldn't ask her to stay. It wasn't fair to her. He shouldn't have turned to alcohol. She's right. He hit a wall and ran from it. Why in the fuck should she come back?

Sniffing back his thoughts, his fear that she would never trust him again, never want anything to do with him, and worse, that he would never want anything more to do with himself, he forced deep breaths, trying to find a good reason to ... to just keep trying.

"Come inside, son." His dad's voice at his side startled him. "Tomorrow's a new day. We'll start again."

Same thing he always said. But some things were just over when they were over. Like his guitar playing. The use of his fingers. Denton. Now Iz. At least his family was still hanging in so far. "I'm sorry I've screwed this up again."

"Well, that's step two. Just keep stepping along the path and we'll get through it."

"How often?" His strength was gone. He couldn't do it again.

"As often as it takes until it holds." His dad was sitting next to him now, a hand on his back, over top of the jacket he'd set over his shoulders. "You're my son, James. And you're a Gilbert. We don't give up. We just keep plugging away. You're going to make it, because your mother and brothers and I won't let you do otherwise. Come inside now. Your mom has a fresh pot of coffee ready."

~~

Isabel knocked on his door with her heart racing. She'd told her grandparents they could wait in the car and she'd text them to tell them to go ahead back to the hotel, but they insisted on walking up with her. Well, Gramps insisted. Grams came because Gramps did, to watch his temper for him, she said.

It felt like forever until the door opened. Bruce. Not James.

"Can I come in? I know he told me to leave, but I don't care. I don't want to leave. I don't want to give up. And I need to tell him."

"You sure?" Bruce had changed into old sweats and his hair was mussed.

"Yes. Is he asleep?"

"He's not here."

Her heart sank. Her eyes watered. She swallowed hard. "Where is he? Tell me the truth. Tell me you know where he is."

"Relax, Isabel. He's fine. He's with his parents. They're keeping an eye on him until he's good again."

With a deep breath, she heard Abby ask who it was and she came to the door. "Well let her in, for pete's sake."

"No, I... Um." What now? She didn't want to ask her grandparents to take her to Mercer.

"Come on back to the hotel with us tonight, Bella." Her grandma put an arm around her. "We'll help you find him in the morning."

"I need to talk to him tonight. I should have brought my car."

Abby grabbed her hand. "We'll take you out there."

Bruce raised his eyebrows at his girlfriend. Fiancée. They were engaged. "It's nearly eleven."

"It's not a work night. You'll be okay. Get your shoes and your keys."

"You don't have to." Isabel tried to argue, even if she didn't want to argue. She wanted to go see him, without her grandparents hovering.

"Yeah, I kinda do." Bruce shrugged with a look at Abby. "Okay. So we'll take you over. Let me give him a head's up."

"No. Don't tell him."

"Text Felix." Abby slipped into her shoes and grabbed her coat. "Felix is staying there with him tonight. Tell him not to say anything. You have things in the car you need?" She was asking Isabel.

"Um." Her guitar. She hadn't brought clothes. No, she did. He'd grabbed her overnight bag. In case of... In case. Because she'd been making a habit of it.

Transferring her things to Bruce's car, she gave her grandparents hugs and Bruce told them not to worry, he'd watch over her and take her back to the apartment if needed.

~~

When his little brother again checked his phone, James stood from where they'd been playing Bones at the kitchen table. Judging from the expression, Felix's wife wasn't real happy that he was away at night again. Raised a city girl, she didn't like being out in the country on her own, never had, although she loved being out in the country and it was her idea to be out there on a five acre lot with nothing on it but a big old house that she loved working on. It was largely Felix's country boy qualities that made her fall for him. His little brother could keep up with his own marksman skills decently, even though he was only hunting trained rather than hunting and Army trained. She also liked that Felix wasn't "so big" as she often said. Meaning the smallest of the four Gilbert boys. A surprise baby who came almost exactly ten years after the oldest. Nora Gilbert often teased her youngest, who came when she was 32 years old, about interrupting when she was finally starting to do something other than change diapers and clean messes. She also absolutely adored him. Hell, everyone adored the kid. Pretty impossible not to.

Still not small, Felix was a good 5'11, and shoulder strong but svelte, more than the rest of them. Made him look better in his clothes when he wore something other than the tees and flannel shirts over loose jeans barely held up by his belt.

"Are we done with the game just 'cause you're losing?" And that smile could charm even the Cheshire cat.

"Can't sit in here right now." He refilled his coffee, although he knew it would keep him up all night. Thirty-two. His mom was a year older than James was now when she had her youngest.

His phone buzzed again. Felix lost that smile when he checked it. Definitely his wife didn't want him gone. Days alone were fine with her. Nights were different. And it was worse now that she had a little one.

"Go home to your wife. I know she hates having you away at night."

"She's fine. Gives her a reason to badger me." Felix glanced up in between answering the message. "And you know the deal. We take turns doing this until you're good to be on your own."

"I'm good. Going to do some work on the computer and then head to bed. Go home."

"Is that right? Just like that, you're good? After fighting with the girl you should have apologized to instead? Not buying it."

Unable to argue, he shuffled out to the front porch and lowered onto the top step. The breeze sent a shiver up his back and he held the mug between his hands for the warmth. Felix sat next to him. Of course his brother had been smart enough to put a jacket on. "Your laptop's out here, is it?"

"When did you turn into such a smartass? Hanging out with Denny these days?"

He laughed. "Nah, he's far too busy with his big business down in shiny town. Good for him, you know, but not my thing."

"Yeah, so how's the bed and breakfast thing working? Don't think you've said lately."

"You haven't asked lately." Checking his phone again, he propped his elbows on his legs. "Just got done building a big garden, fenced in to keep the deer and rabbits out. She says our guests will love the fresh produce. I'm not gonna love weeding the thing when she's too busy." He shrugged. "To be honest, I'm kind of tired of the monotony and extra work of it, but the wife is loving it, so I guess we keep going. It's doing well, more than paying for itself, so there's that, anyway."

"Thought that might happen."

"Which? Doing well or me getting bored with it?"

"Both. It fits your social skills and Alicia is like the ultimate hostess, but I figured it wouldn't stay exciting enough for you."

"Yeah." Felix pulled up a weed pushing its way through the neat garden along the front of the house. "Not like being out on the road together, huh? You and me and Ryan, only one of us with talent. We coulda been your roadies, though. Would've been fun."

"Your wife wouldn't have married you if you'd done that."

He laughed. "There is that. Guess it was a better trade."

"You guess? Things are good, right?"

"With Alicia? Yeah. She's still incredible. I just need ... something other than eight hours at the store and then clean up and maintenance around the house day after day after day. Maybe just new dad blues or whatever. Restlessness, really. Maybe when you're up to beach hopping again, I'll plead with the wife to let me go with you."

"Not sure when that's going to happen, and not likely she'd let you go without her."

"Probably right. At least not for a month like you used to do. Wouldn't do that, anyway, not with my baby girl growing as fast as she is. Can't believe she's ten months already."

He shivered and thought about grabbing a jacket. Baby girl. Isabel's grandpa called her Baby Girl like it was her name. Checking his watch, he figured she'd be back in Pittsburgh by now.

"Want to go in?"

"No." He should text her. Or call. What would he say?

"Grab a coat?"

"I'm good."

"If you say so. Anyway, no, it's all good, as Pete would say."

"Pete who?"

"The cat. You know, Pete the Cat." Felix rolled his eyes. "I'm a big expert in kids' books already. Licia reads to the baby every night. I know. I've gotta find a hobby."

"Or add to your B&B, something to make it more interesting."

"Like?"

"Like, I don't know. You're great at socializing. Host something there. Group paintings are big. You paint anymore?"

"Hell, not for years, other than the front porch and walls..."

"Shame. You were getting good. Take it up again. Hold painting parties. Or card game parties. You're a whiz at cards, too. Could be fun. No gambling, but just cards or painting or something you want to do, to bring others in to do it with you."

"Don't have a lot of space for that, and guests might not want a bunch of strangers in the house when they're there to relax."

"Don't do it in the house. It wouldn't be hard to build a good-sized gazebo far enough from the house not to bother anyone. You've got space. Or make it a screened in sun porch. Wouldn't be too expensive, and if you get it going, it would pay for itself fast. I'd help you do it. Got nothing else to do these days."

"Yeah? That could be cool. And you know, maybe..." His head shook and he got up to wander. The boy never sat still long.

"Maybe what?"

"Nothing." Felix turned to face him, hands in his jacket pockets. Then he checked his phone and returned to sit again. "So."

"No way. What?" James bumped his arm. "Don't be all jumpy with me like you used to be. What were you going to say?"

"I was young then. Ever going to let that go?"

"Probably not. What were you going to say?"

"Well. If we do that, we'll need a grand opening to get it started. With music. No party is right without live music. So, maybe the singer we know might not charge me a whole lot. You think?"

Isabel. Singing at his brother's grand opening party? "The one I just royally screwed it up with? She probably wouldn't charge much, if anything, and she might still do it if you ask her. I might have to promise not to be there, though."

"Nah, wouldn't take that deal. My big brother being there matters more."

"Those things usually involve alcohol along with music, so it would make more sense to have her come."

"Doesn't have to. We'll break the mold and make it a dry party. And the group things could be painting and coffee. Right? I mean, not everyone wants to do the alcohol thing. Might get a different audience. Alicia would go for that easier, anyway."

"Not everyone does coffee, either. Might add tea to that."

"For Isabel."

"Well, if you can get her, but there have to be a few others who don't drink coffee. Not that I understand it."

"Yeah, me either." He yawned.

"Go on in to bed if you won't go home. I'm not going anywhere."

"Guess it would be hard for you to do, considering you have no wheels."

"Great. Hijack a guy, take his wheels away, and rub it in."

"We wouldn't have if you hadn't been half lit." His voice lowered. "Does she know you were drinking before you went to her show?"

"No idea. Not like I told her."

"Still don't know how you managed to get it. Don't suppose you want to tell me."

"No."

"In case you want to do it again?"

"I'm trying, alright? Wasn't sure I wanted to see her."

"Glad you didn't tell her you had to drink to be able to see her. How about keeping that between us?" Felix stood and set a hand on his shoulder. "Don't even think about walking anywhere or calling anyone. Going in because it's cold, but I'm keeping an eye out until you're snoring." Running a hand up the back of his head, because he knew it annoyed him, Felix went inside.

James stared up at the sky, shivered at a cold wind gust, and longed for summer's return. He needed beach weather. Swimming. Walking or running in a tank or tee. Hot sun on his face. Lightning bugs flickering in the distance. Iz loved watching them. Damn, he missed her. Did she know? Good question. Not that it mattered.

It was a great little summer romance, he supposed. There was that. Once he stabilized, he'd have to go on another beach jaunt.

Except he didn't want to go alone. He wanted to go with ... Lizzie from Erie. His fiery, nervous, but headstrong little songbird. It could have been good.

Turning on his phone to find the saved messages, he started reading them again. Everything she'd sent. Not everything. The what time kind of things, he'd deleted for space. But everything real. He read them, seeing her face, looking closer at what she'd actually said.

This girl actually loved him. Not a fleeting thing. Not an only if thing. She'd waited, sent him a message on her page, had come to him most of the way, asking him to come the rest of the distance. She still wanted him.

And he was an incredible ass. Too defensive. Because he'd been half lit. He needed to tell someone where his hiding spot was, where he hid money to be replaced with gin that he poured into his water or ginger ale. It had been hard to get away from Bruce long enough to find it, but he'd managed to get there. Stupid thing to do. Being lit made him an asshole to her. Why he did things backward with Iz, he still didn't know. He'd never been an asshole while lit, only while coming up from it. Why had that changed?

Turning the screen off, he closed his eyes. He would find her daughter. Screw the beach jaunt. He would spend all of his time trying to find her daughter for her. Not all. Most. In between, he would work on building his IT business and see what he could do to help Felix build his new project, get it ready for a spring opening. James had done enough wiring as one of his temporary jobs to be able to wire a gazebo for basic lights and a heat source. It could be payback for all Felix had done, had given up, to help him get back on track. Burt and Denny could go in on it with him, make it a nice one, maybe with glass windows for cooler weather events. He could scrounge for used windows. People were always selling them. Alicia would love the thought of that, reusing...

Headlights going past caught his eye. Someone out late partying, probably. He hoped they had a DD. That's one thing he'd never done, well, not since he was young and stupid and lucky enough not to kill anyone doing it. He would never have pulled back up from that.

The car didn't go past. It pulled into the drive. After midnight. Standing, he watched it come toward him. Slowly. Who in the hell would come to his parents' house at this time of night?

Keeping his eyes on it, he backed into the house to grab one of his father's shotguns. Except he had to ask Felix where the key to the gun cabinet was since his father was keeping them locked up these days.

"Why?" His little brother looked suddenly wary.

"Someone's pulling in. I can at least still protect the family, let them know they're screwing with…"

"No need. It's Bruce."

"What? How do you know?"

Felix raised his phone. "Go on back out."

By now, he could see the front of the car. His roommate's car. "Why the fuck is he here at this time of night? Am I getting kicked out since I wouldn't tell you where my hiding place is?"

"Come on, J. You know better. As Dad said, we're in this with you as long as it takes. Go ask him why he's here."

Wary of his buddy's intentions, he stepped back out onto the porch but held his ground. Could be Bruce was kicking him out of the apartment since he'd started drinking again. Except he couldn't. It was in *his* name. It was *his* place. He and Denton talked about it while still overseas, that they'd get a place together. When James found the place, it was unusually big but low rent because it was a shit hole. He'd spent the time and money fixing it up, then invited Bruce…

A girl was in the car, too. He barely saw her with the glow of the porch light. His heart nearly stopped until the car stopped and he saw that it was Abby. Was his buddy eloping? He wouldn't, couldn't do that. Not now.

His roommate stepped out. "Hey. So what kind of a mood are you in by now?"

"Why the fuck are you asking? And why are you here? You know your family will have your fucking head if you elope with the girl instead of having an actual wedding."

"Okay. Well that tells me it was not the time to come. Going to chill out a bit?"

"Why are you here?"

The back door opened. His heart raced. Isabel. Still in the outfit from Sam's. Even with her long coat over top, he could see that she'd lost weight, gained muscle. She looked incredible, life-saving incredible. And he couldn't move, couldn't make himself take one step toward her. The gin was mainly out of his system by now, but…

She came toward him. Slowly. Watching what he'd do, he guessed. And she stopped at the bottom of the steps, with Bruce and Abby both just behind her. She paid no attention to them. "I'm sorry. You're right. I *was* afraid." She moved up two steps and glanced behind him.

"Hey, Isabel." Felix sounded apologetic, as though he had anything to apologize for. "Come on in, guys. J made a whole pot of coffee. Might as well help him drink it."

Waiting for Bruce and Abby to go past her, Isabel didn't answer Bruce when he said the car was unlocked and she could text him if she wanted to leave. He gave James a warning glance on his way in.

Iz crossed her arms in front of her stomach.

Her defensive posture annoyed the fuck out of him. "Thought you were headed back to Pittsburgh tonight."

"We were. I changed my mind before we hit the interstate exit. I had a time convincing Gramps to turn around."

"He's a smart man. You should probably listen to him."

"You want me to listen to him?"

Gritting his jaw, he tried to tell her yes. It would be better for her. But he couldn't quite. He'd told her to leave. More than once, he told her to leave, even if it was the last thing he wanted. And still, she was there. Again. Apologizing to him. As though she had any reason to apologize.

"What if I want to stay?"

His gut lurched, and he rubbed the stubble on his jaw as an attempt not to jump at her offer. "It's not fair to you. You should have kept going."

~~

"Not fair?" Isabel wasn't sure whether to laugh or to cry. "What's not fair is not letting me be there for you, with you, when I want to be. That's not fair, James. It's not."

"Why in the hell do you *want* to be? I'm..."

"Struggling again."

"Major understatement." He shoved the hand up through his hair, making some of it stick up. "I can't fight it off this time. I try. But this..." His head shook. "Last time I didn't want to fight it off. This time, I try. I've been trying. But I just, I can't seem to..."

"You can. I know you can. I want to help."

"Why? You've made it very clear how you feel about *stupid drunks*."

"I never called you that."

"Not in so many words."

"No. Never. If that's what you heard, that's in your head, not mine. Yes, I said I don't like it when people get stupid with it, and you know I have reason. But you're not stupid."

"I am a drunk."

"Not the same thing. You're not like Davis. He's a stupid drunk.

You're..."

"I'm still part lit from earlier tonight. That's what I am. Yes, I was drinking before your show. Only way I could make myself be there. So I'm also a coward. At least when it comes to personal relationships. I've never been able to stick to one. I dated mainly the wrong girls for a reason. This... this shit is too hard. And I shouldn't have told you I was drinking tonight, also shouldn't have done it. I knew I shouldn't. Yet I did."

Too hard? "You think this isn't hard for me? Relationships are hard for everyone, James. They are."

"Like fuck they are. My brothers just fell into it like it's all natural and was written in the fucking stars or some corny shit like that. Same with Bruce. No big deal. Just decide it's right, say so, and move along. Great, but..."

"But they don't have the same complication you have. You can't compare yourself..."

"Because they choose not to get bombed to deal with shit. Why in the fuck can't I?"

"I don't know. Why did I choose to hide for nine years instead of moving on? It's hardly a new thing for girls to get left with a child on the way, or to have shitty parents, or to lose a child. It happens all the time and they choose to move on. I chose to hide, to close myself in. You chose alcohol. But I've decided not to choose that anymore. And you can choose to stop, too. You did before. You can again."

"For how long this time?" His shoulders slumped, his defensiveness dropping. "Don't you get it? It's what I do. Why in the hell do you want to put up with this?"

"I love you."

"I know, Iz." His voice shook. "But that's not what I asked. You know that's not enough." Lowering to the porch floor, he leaned back against the door.

Moisture welled in her eyes and she tried to hide it, tried to let the cold breeze dry it up. "It's my choice. I choose to accept the hard, because you're worth it to me. Isn't that enough?"

"I don't want to make you cry."

"There are far worse things." Wandering over to him, she lowered, facing him.

He wiped the tear that escaped. "Your tears, hurting you, is not something I can handle."

"Then don't push me away."

"Damn, Iz. You don't get it." Jumping up, he jogged down the steps, and treaded out a few steps into the grass. The light from the kitchen window shone on his hair, the top of his shoulders. And he shivered. He wasn't even wearing a coat. Only a long-sleeve shirt, the one he had on at the bar. And he'd had to drink to be able to go see her.

She didn't get it, of course. How could she? She couldn't truly understand his alcoholism any more than he could truly understand her fear. "I don't care." It was a near whisper through the dark, through crickets hidden in the trees bordering the yard, through the pretty chimes hanging from the Gilberts' front porch that sounded like music. The key of A, she thought.

Getting up, she walked up behind him and wrapped her arms around his stomach. It was too gaunt, like his face. It made her eyes water more. "I don't care if I don't get it, James. I really don't. Because what I do get is that we're good together. I also get that you're scared. Trust me, fear is something I understand. Except mine was for myself and yours is for everyone around you. You're hurting yourself trying to protect everyone who loves you, despite what you want, but it's not working like you think. It's only hurting me and probably everyone else you love when you try to push us away, to keep us at a distance. But you know, that's why I'm still here. Because it matters to you. Because you don't want to hurt me. Because you so deeply care about others, you're so protective of everyone else, that you're willing to hurt yourself more to try to protect us. But you're going about it wrong. Just like I was, thinking only of my songs getting out there and not enough about the audience needs. You were right. I missed the bigger part of the equation. So are you."

She lay her head against his back and closed her eyes. "We *want* to be here for you, even if you don't understand it. You can't do it this time because you're thinking too much of others and not enough of yourself. You have to stop that. We're your audience. We're part of you, of your show, of your recovery, and it's *our* choice. You have to stop denying us, stop doing all of your own songs, and start letting us provide some covers. Start leaning on us."

When he moved, she released him, allowing it, ready to follow if he walked away. Instead, he turned toward her. "I don't know how to do that. I'm..."

"Like me. You're like me, James. We're independent-natured, too much for our own good. We have to do it all ourselves. I do get it. But I let you jump in and help me when I was about to give up. It's your turn. It's only fair."

His jaw clenched. Fighting the idea.

"The funny thing about all of this is that I finally understand my mom. At least to a better extent. I worried her because I would never let her in, never talked to her or let her help me. I had to deal with stuff on my own. Always. She had enough to deal with and I couldn't add to that. Now you're doing it to me and I can see how it feels. It's frustrating and ego-killing and it makes me feel helpless. I don't want to be helpless."

"Damn, Iz. You're not. You're far from it."

"You think I'm too weak to deal with it. How am I supposed to feel?"

"You're supposed to understand that I *don't* fucking *want* to put you through it. I'm... Hell, I don't even know *what* I am anymore."

"Lost." She stroked the side of his head, his gorgeous hair. "You're lost. I know. I see it. But James, I can deal with it and I can help you. I *can*. And I *want* to." Pulling the chain out from under his shirt, she was relieved that it was the sea glass pendant. "You still want me or you wouldn't still be wearing this."

"Of course I want you. That's not the issue."

Her chest heaved in a relieved sigh. Of course he wanted her. *Of course.* As though she should have known. Maybe she should have.

Wiping more tears from her cheeks, he slid a strong, chilled hand alongside her head. "The issue is ... yes, you should listen to your grandfather. He knows this is not going to be an easy road. He knows it's not fair to you." He shivered again.

Isabel wrapped her arms up around his sides, trying to share what little warmth she still had. "Okay, but you know what he tells me more than anything else? He tells me he wants me to be happy. So, fine, I'll listen to him. Because my being happy does depend largely on you. Yes, I could learn to be happy without you. At this point, I know I could, because you taught me that. But I want to be happy *with* you, not without you." Sifting her fingers back through his hair and around behind his head, she pulled his face toward hers. "I love you, and I'm not giving up on us. I'm not. You can tell me every day to leave, but it won't matter, because until I believe you actually mean it, I'm not listening to you. You can be rude. You can keep testing me, keep trying to push me away, but I'm not leaving. You can keep slipping off the wagon and I'll keep helping you back up. I won't stop trying to keep you on it, though, so..."

He met her lips, and she pulled him in, pressing up against his body while his arms slid around her and held her tight. It was a long, deep, exquisitely passionate kiss that brought more tears to her eyes.

When he released her mouth, he kissed the side of her face. "Damn I'm glad you came back." The stubble on his chin poked her face as he lined kisses down to her neck. "Thought about calling you about a thousand times but I didn't know what to say and I didn't know if I should even try or to let you be. I've been fighting the fuck out of myself just trying to decide what I should do and it's been driving me out of my fucking mind. Sorry. I don't control my language well when I'm..."

"I don't care." She set her hands alongside his head. "James, I don't care about your language. I don't care if this is hard on me. I don't want you to question whether you should or shouldn't with me. If you want me, I want you to tell me you want me. If you need me, tell me that. It's okay to need me until you don't. It's okay. It is. When you don't need me anymore, I hope you'll still want me. Because I'm still going to be here. Because I love you like crazy and I'm not losing you."

Hugging her close, his body heaved heavily, his arms held tight, strong, gentle, his need showing through every part. She felt fully one with him, fully connected, like she had while they'd made love after Waterfire. It had been far more than sex, and it ... it wasn't making love that gave her the feeling, because she felt it again. A belonging that was impossible to explain. She felt his need of her, like she had with Tobia, but it was a different need. It was ... a need coming from connection, love. He hadn't been lying when he said he loved her. He did. She honestly felt it. Her breath caught and she stroked his hair, clenching her eyes. "You're mine, Gilbert. You are. Might as well stop trying to deny it, or run from it. We belong together, and you know it as well as I do."

He nodded against her shoulder. "Okay, then, Lizzie from Erie, since I'm apparently stuck with you, I guess I'll have to quit."

"Drinking or pushing me away?"

He caught her eyes. "Both."

"Yeah?"

"Yeah." He kissed her nose. "I'm not promising it's going to work. I did that before, told my family I was done, and look at me. But I'll try again."

"You're going to make it this time. You know why? Because I'm staying right by your side until you're good to be out on your own."

"That's going to be hard to do from Pitt."

Her head shook. "I'm not going back. I'm staying. You offered me the extra room and I'm taking you up on it."

"Iz." He shivered. "You love your job. I can't do that to you."

"I don't love my job. I like my job, but it's just a job. I love *you*. You matter far, far more."

His head shook and he shivered again, harder.

"We need to go in."

"Too crowded in there. I just want you right now."

Taking his hand, she led him to Bruce's car, pulling him into the back with her. It wasn't warm, but at least it blocked the wind. Cuddling up against him, she ran a hand along his arm, trying to warm him. He smelled of grass and soap, mixed with a leftover whiff of whatever he'd been drinking. The thought made her eyes water, but she pushed it back, kissed his shoulder, his neck, ignoring the stubble on his chin.

"Your grandparents would hate me for pulling you out of a career that could be really good for you."

"They won't hate you. I'll hear about it, but I don't care."

"Okay, maybe I'd hate myself for doing it to you, on top of everything else I've done."

"Well, let me tell you something you should know." She met his eyes and set a hand on his cold cheek. "A couple of weeks ago I was starting to think I was pregnant." Her eyes watered at the memory. "Actually, I was pretty sure I was."

"Iz…"

"I'm not. But you know what? As much as I kept praying I wasn't, telling myself it was a bad time and I didn't want to do it that way, when I found out I wasn't, I cried. Because I felt like…" She sniffed and swallowed. "Like I'd lost something I very much wanted. Again. I wanted it, James. Regardless of circumstances. It's not the right time, I know, and I'd never try to hold you that way, but…"

"You want kids with me?"

"Yes." It was nearly a whisper, and she ran fingers down his chest. "I want everything with you. You are my one. Once we're stable enough, once you can say *recovered* instead of *recovering*, yes, I want a baby with you, one we get to raise. But first, I need to know it'll be okay for a child. I won't put my child through what I went through."

Pulling her body against his, he kissed her hard. Like the night after they found him on the trail. Leaning her backward, adjusting them both until he was over top of her, an arm under her head acting as a pillow, his body heat warmed her enough his cold hand shocked the bare skin under her blouse.

She kissed his neck, felt his heat rising, and her own. "Tell me you can quit. All the way. For good."

"You're staying with me?"

"Yes."

"If I slip again?"

"I'll still be here."

His body heaved in a deep sigh. "Yes. I can do it. Not gonna say it'll be easy. On either of us…"

"Nothing's easy. You're worth it. *We're* worth it."

"I hope I am."

"I know you are, and we're going to be incredible together, just like your brothers and their wives. We are."

His chest heaved again. "Okay, baby. I'll do my best to believe you."

"You better, because I really want to have babies with you."

He kissed her neck, and in front of her ear. And he fingered her hair. "This…" His fingers slid through one strand and then another. "This is really sexy."

"Not just *different?*"

He grimaced. "Also a stupid thing to say. Sorry for that, too. It's definitely sexy. It suits you." Nudging her jacket and blouse out of the way, he kissed her shoulder, sliding his still-chilled hand up under her blouse. "Can we practice for the having kids thing until it's time to try?"

"Not here."

"It's dark. They're all inside."

Her eyes clenched at his touch, at the pressure she felt against his hip showing her he was ready. In Bruce's car? It would be different in her own car. Still…

"Fuck." He backed away. "We can't."

Grasping his shirt, she pulled him closer. "Was that supposed to be a tease?"

"I have no protection with me. Haven't needed it."

"It's okay. I took care of it. We're safe, until we don't want to be, at least mostly safe, and I'm willing to risk the one percent or whatever it is. Come here, Gilbert. This is day one of the next 364 until you can say *recovered* instead of *recovering*. Got it? Because you're not getting any younger, you know. We don't have a long time to wait."

He groaned. "Again with the age thing. How about I remind you how much that doesn't matter?"

"You do that."

~~

The cold was starting to seep back in, or his body was cooling enough to notice it. He shivered.

"We need to get you home and in a hot shower." She slid fingers through his bangs.

"Damn I love you."

"I know."

"And I want to be a really good dad. I want our children to respect me, to trust me. I want to always be there for them. And for you."

"You will be. And I think we should take a beach trip. Just the two of us. Somewhere warm. As soon as you think you're up to it. I can maybe do some shows along the way to help pay for it..."

He kissed her. "The first of many. Yeah?"

"I hope so."

"Let's go home, Lizzie from Erie."

She nearly pulled him into the house, insisting he shouldn't get too cold again.

"You fogged up my windows." Bruce shrugged when Abby pushed at him, the diamond on her finger flickering under the light.

"But we didn't write on them, so they should be clear by now." Iz squeezed his fingers to let him know it was fine, even through the snickers. "I'm moving in, by the way. He offered me the extra room..."

"Extra room, hell. You're staying with me."

She looked up at him. "Okay." And back at Bruce. "He should get home and in the shower now. He's too cold."

"Yeah, anyone with brains would've worn a jacket out there." Bruce stood. "Ready when you are. It's way past my bedtime."

"Not to sound bad, but.." Felix interrupted. "You sure about this, J? I mean, you're still in stay-with-family mode right now."

"I have him." Bruce yawned. "At least till Monday morning. Can't skip work Monday, so if you can come at least part of the day..."

"No need." Isabel wrapped her hand around his arm. "I have him. We'll be fine. And we'll be back for dinner tomorrow."

James met her eyes. "You sure? You don't have to do the family thing just because you decided to give me another chance."

"I know I don't have to. I want to. Let's go home and get some beauty sleep first so I don't look like a wreck."

"Next to me, baby, you look like Miss America. And really, you do look good. Your trainer did a good job." He skimmed a glance down her body.

"No. My manager did a good job. My trainer couldn't have helped if I hadn't been motivated to do it. For myself. And it's time to get you moving again, too, since I can see you haven't been."

"Might have to give me a few days."

"Nope. We're going for a short run in the morning."

"Run? You don't run." His eyes sparkled.

"I do now. Going to keep up?"

Scooping her into his arms, he kissed her forehead. "I'll do my best. Take that however you want." With a gentle *I'm glad you came back* kiss on her beautiful soft lips, he whispered into her ear. "I love you. Thank you."

Forty-seven

Isabel woke with the sun, as she was used to doing by now because of her work schedule. James was naked beside her and mostly uncovered, as usual since he got hot so easily. She wanted to run fingers over his skin, over the muscles, over the soft skin of his lower abdomen where the V shape of his pelvic bones enticed her every time he wore his shorts low around the house. It was the sexiest part of a man, in her opinion, that V. She'd often let her fingers roam along it. But she didn't want to wake him.

With a soft kiss to his shoulder, she got up gently and started to pull into her clothes from the night before. She'd taken all of her clothes that day he told her to go, and her bag was in her granparents' car. Would he have reclaimed the drawer she'd been using? Quietly, she pulled it open. A pair of her beach capris were there. They must have been in the laundry. And the pair of his smaller sweats she'd borrowed once or twice. There was also an old tee that wasn't hers. Triumph. An old concert shirt. He wouldn't have been old enough to see them. Had he found it for her? It smelled freshly laundered, so she put it on along with his sweats. They were even looser on her now, but they'd stay up okay with the string drawn tight.

Deciding to turn the favor around and make him breakfast in bed, she was glad Bruce and Abby were still asleep also. It was early, too early to make noise cooking. So she grabbed her phone and started looking for jobs nearby. Isabel couldn't say she was terribly okay with losing the one she had, but it would be worth it in the long run. In the morning, she'd call and explain. Maybe they'd be lenient if she told them ... what? That her boyfriend was an alcoholic and she couldn't leave him? She couldn't say that. It was his personal business and not fair to share it. She could say a sick family member needed her, but that wasn't quite truthful, either. Maybe she'd just have to tell them it was personal issues. It wouldn't save her job, but it wouldn't be a lie or invasive.

It didn't matter. He was worth it. Whatever it took, she was going to help him stay on track.

~~

"Wake up, lazy. Time to get moving."

James forced his eyes open to Isabel, sitting on his bed, her fingers stroking his hair. "Morning, baby." He took her hand and kissed her long, slim, soft fingers. "Damn, it's nice waking up with you. Why are you dressed already?"

"We're going running and we have to be back and cleaned up to meet my grandparents at eleven. Get up. Let's go."

"What time is it?"

"Just after eight." She pulled his blanket back. "Come on. I made breakfast."

He yawned and scratched at his chin. He needed a shave, and a couple hours' more sleep. "Why so early?"

"I told you. We're going running before dealing with the family stuff."

"Thought you were joking."

"Not joking."

With a quick movement, he pulled her down on top of him, rolled her to the other side of the bed, and raised her shirt to smooth a hand over her abs. "Is that why you look so hot? You've been running?"

"Well, I started with walking and worked up to speed walking and occasional jogs. I'm still not doing long distance or anything, and I have to walk in between, but I can tell you haven't done any of it for some time, so maybe we'll be closer to equal stamina."

"I look that bad, do I?"

"You look like you haven't taken care of yourself. I want to change that."

"All about my looks, is it?"

She pulled back. "That's not funny."

"It was meant to be." Bringing her gently closer, he kissed the side of her head. "I know it's not about that. And hey, I'm so sorry about what I said, about, well, your physical stamina."

"That I was too out of shape for a singer? Well, you were right. I was. And I was holding myself back. I was thinking too small, letting my fear rule me. I quit too easily. You were right about all of it. I was mad at first. No, I was hurt at first, then I was mad, and then I said screw being hurt or mad and I faced the truth. The truth is, yes, you can be a jerk, but you were also right and I needed to hear it even if you didn't say it the way you could have. Probably it wouldn't have mattered, though. How you said it. I still would have been hurt and mad. Because I knew you were right. So, I did something about it. Now it's your turn. You look like hell, which means you're not healthy, and I can't have that because I need... I want you. I want you for a very long time to come. So..."

He claimed her mouth, gently, deeply, brushing his fingertips along her soft, toned abs, sliding them up to find her even softer skin...

"No time for this." She whispered against his lips. "We're going running."

"Okay." He found the front hook of her bra, a slinky but supportive black bra that pushed her breasts up nicely.

"James."

"I'll run with you. At whatever pace you set. First..." He kissed her neck and undid the hook.

"Breakfast is already getting cold."

"I'll warm it."

"We're supposed to meet my grandparents at eleven. I have to tell them I'm staying with you."

He groaned. "That's not going to be fun. We can do a short run. Not up to more than that now, anyway."

"Then you should save your energy."

"Isabel?"

"Hm?" Her eyes were closed and she'd stopped trying to stop him.

"I love you. Thank you. For not running. Away, I mean."

Her eyes met his. "Promise you'll let me stay."

"As long as you can stand me."

"No matter what?"

"No matter what. And I'll try not to be such an ass. If I do..."

"I'll go for a walk if I need. And then I'll come back."

"It's about to get cold."

"I don't mind walking in the cold. I even ran in the cold rain up to the Point the other day while I was getting over being sick. I think it helped to flush it out."

"You what?"

"Two and a half miles, running all the way. Honestly. And I listened to your music there. Bruce brought it to me, along with some videos of you playing in a band. Wow, you're good. I mean, really good. It was incredible."

"I *was* good. Past tense. Why'd he do that?"

"He wanted me to understand. He said you were classically trained, with years of not just guitar, but also piano and..."

"Fucking jerk. Can't keep his mouth shut. So you came back because he asked you to come back?" He started to get up.

"No." She sat up and grabbed him from behind. "No. I came back because I want you, I love you, and ... and I finished your song."

Trying to tamp down the anger, he gritted his teeth and forced a long, deep breath. "What song?"

"The one that was on your dresser the day you told me to leave."

He shook his head. He hadn't written in forever, at least not full songs. "I don't know what you're talking about. I was probably drunk or getting there, so..."

"*I'm not saying you don't have the right to walk away...*" Singing. She was singing to him. Acapella.

"*and I'm not saying things will be better if you stay/ I just want you to know/ I may fall apart if you go, but you should anyway...*"

That one. That one, he remembered, even with as much as he tried to forget. When she stopped singing, he turned, and continued the song. "*because I'm not sayin' I'll ever be okay/ enough... for you.*" His voice was hoarse, out of practice, and emotional. "Did I screw up your music?"

Her eyes watered with the soft shake of her head. "*So go on and do your thing, shine your light, bright/ like a beacon in someone's dark life...*"

He took over, guessing at where she was going musically. "*you've gotta do you/ and I've got a lotta working on me to do/ so go, be bold, do your own show/ and shine.*" He ran fingers across her thigh. "That's all I had. Not even sure I have the words right and can't check since I tossed it."

"Why?"

"It was killing me. Telling you to go. I still think you should have. You should. But..." He swallowed hard and leaned in against her, dropping his head to her shoulder. "I don't want you to go. I've tried very hard not to need you, for your sake, maybe for mine. Defensive. Just figured..."

"You took a bigger risk than I understood." She stroked his hair. "*I'm not saying it doesn't scare me to say I'll stay/ and I'm not saying I can be strong for you every day/ But I want you to know/ Though I'll fall apart on some days, I'll stay with you anyway/ because I'm not sayin' I'll ever be okay/ if I never have you.*"

"I'm not sure I'm exactly on pitch." She stroked his shoulder.

"It's beautiful. You finished it?"

"Hm, mm hm."

He planted a kiss behind her ear. "Keep going."

"*So come on and let's do our thing, together we'll shine bright/ like a beacon for those who need light/ we matter/ love matters. Let it show, let them all know/ we've gotta get through/ and I know we can do what we need to do/ so be bold and stay,*" *help me to say/ it's fine, we can shine...*

"*Because together we're stronger/ and we'll always rise again/ If you say you'll hang in there,/ I'll keep letting you win/ Each beat of my heart will add/ a knot in the rope,/ so climb in and hang on and say ... I can stay...*"

She hummed a few measures he assumed was a refrain.

"*I'm not sayin' this'll be easy/ I just want us to try/ no goodbyes*" She shrugged. "It can be tweaked. Or thrown out. I was just..."

"Iz." Slipping his fingers behind her head, entwining them with her hair, he kissed her nose. "It's far better than I could've done."

"It's not. Your stuff is incredible, James. Can I, maybe..."

"You want to sing anything I wrote, you're welcome to it."

She kissed his shoulder. "Thank you."

"So, can breakfast wait a bit?"

Wrapping her arms around his neck, she pushed him down to the bed.

~~

"Okay, I give."

Isabel stopped and turned to James when he sat in the middle of the amphitheatre steps, his chest rising and falling fast and hard. Going to his side, she wiped sweat from her forehead with her jacket sleeve, a workout jacket she borrowed from him and had to roll up a ways to find her hands, and felt her own heavy breaths start to calm.

Forearms propped on his legs, he looked up at her. "How'd you do it so fast?"

"Do what?" She stretched her legs by pulling them up to her chest one at a time.

"Get in shape like this. It usually takes a good bit of time to work up, with plenty of falling back and starting again."

"I used to take gymnastics. My coach said I build muscle fast." She shrugged at his surprise. "I wasn't always lazy. I walked everywhere when I was in Pittsburgh. It was easier. I only got lazy when I moved up to Meadville with Libs. And..."

"Because you were nursing a heartache."

"That, too. I just kind of gave up."

"So, this time, I mean, after what I put you through, why did it..."

"Do the opposite? Simple." She sat next to him. "I hadn't given up on you, on us. And I guess I realized if I wanted to be worthy enough for the kind of guy I wanted, I had to feel worthy. And I don't mean... It's not about looks. It's about not being lazy, not giving up. For myself."

"I get it."

"Yeah?"

"Yeah." He claimed her hand and kissed her palm. "But you know you're worthy of far better than me."

"You only say that because you don't like where you are right now. But I'm going to get you past that like you did for me." She brushed fingertips through his sweaty but chilled-from-the-cold hair.

"Sure you won't like this humiliated side better?"

"Humbled. Not humiliated."

"No, I meant what I said. Never wanted you to see me that way. That's why I got so rude. I am sorry. It was..."

"Defensive."

"Inexcusable. And I don't want you to excuse it."

"Okay. So then, maybe try to accept that I'm stronger than you think I am and I can handle you when you're disgusting and when you're struggling and when you're weak and whatever else. The only thing I can't handle is to be pushed away, because you didn't have that right. I am a bit needy. Fine. I need to be with you, to be there for you, to feel like I'm part of everything with you, not just what you want me to see. Got it?"

"Even if you shouldn't have to?"

"My choice, Gilbert. Not yours."

Wrapping her in his arms, he let his hands wander as he kissed her, feeling her curves. "Hm, so." Pressing his lips together to absorb the moisture from the kiss, he smoothed his hands along each side of her waist. "This isn't only from running, is it? I mean, you've..."

"I lost ten pounds."

"Only ten? Are you sure?"

"Well, I gained muscle, too."

"It's a big change for one month. Tell me you didn't starve yourself to do this."

"No. Mainly I gave up sugar. Almost. I slide a bit on that now and then, but only in small amounts. No more full sundaes or medium Blizzards. If I get one, it's small and I split it with Gramps. If I have to eat out, I do grilled chicken with no mayo and take the bread off. No fries, and only unsweet tea or water instead of soda. Grandma's been good about having stuff other than pasta or sugary sauces for me. It's been tough, but it makes such a huge difference."

"So you kind of get what I'm dealing with. Avoiding that stuff you really want."

"I'm sure it's not the same."

"I don't know, Iz. As strong as your sugar addiction is, or was…" With a grin, he kissed her fingers.

"Is. I still want it. I just say no. Usually. So it's not really the same. I can have a bit now and then and it's good. I don't have to go cold turkey and always say no, so it can't be as hard."

"I love you."

She hesitated at the depth of his expression, his tone. There was nothing casual about it. It was deep and full force. "I think you've said that a couple times already today."

"Yeah, well, I kind of got backlogged on it. Gotta catch up. On this, too." With a soft kiss, he caressed the side of her face, around her ear.

She got up. "Come on. We still have to run home and get cleaned up. My grandparents will be waiting."

"How about we walk and save energy for the cleaning up thing?"

When he stood in front of her, she set her hands on his chest. "What? Did you miss me?"

"Oh, Iz. I can't even tell you how much."

"You could have just said so."

"Should have. And you know, Denton would like you. He'd give me a bunch of crap about you being too good for me, but he'd like you. Actually, he probably would've fought me for you."

"Wouldn't have worked." She stroked fingers down his chest.

"How do you know?"

"No one else would work for me. You know, we could name our first one after him."

"First what?" At her look, he grabbed a deep breath. "Oh. Yeah? I mean, if it's a boy, we could. If you're sure."

"If it's a girl, we could do Ryanna, unless you want to wait for a boy and just do Ryan."

"You're beautiful." He kissed her forehead.

"Will you talk to me about him?"

"Yeah. When I'm…"

"More recovered. I'll take it. Right now, we need to get home and cleaned up. Ready to run?"

"How about we walk?"

"If we walk, we won't have time to clean up together and still meet with my grandparents before making dinner with your family."

"About that…" James pulled his phone out and texted while they made their way down the stone steps. By the time they reached the bottom, he had a reply. "How about calling your grandparents and inviting them out to my parents' place for dinner?"

She stopped walking. "Why?"

"Thought it would be good for them to get better acquainted. And it's one family thing instead of two, which gives us more time before we have to go anywhere."

"Um, you know Gramps won't be thrilled that I'm giving up my job to stay here with you."

"You can deal with me, I can deal with him." Raising her hand, he kissed her palm. "Isabel, you stay with me now and I'm going to plan on you staying. Not just for now."

"Always. And you better. I wouldn't have given myself to you if I didn't intend to stay."

"Yeah? So…" Caressing her hand, he held her eyes. "Marry me. And I don't mean anytime soon. We can wait and see how this goes. Maybe a pre-engagement? Just so you understand…"

Her eyes watered. "James. If I say yes, it won't be a pre-yes or a maybe-yes depending on whatever. It will just be yes, and I'll expect you not to back out. So you better mean it all the way if you're asking."

He lowered to one knee. "Marry me, Isabel. As soon as I'm steady enough. I will be. Promise."

"Through better and worse?"

"Absolutely. And you can wait to answer if you'd rather. I get it."

"Come here." She tugged his hand until he stood in front of her. "You know I may get lazy again at times, right? I probably won't always look like this."

He chuckled. "Yeah, that's usually how it goes. Up and down. I don't care. I love you lazy, too. And I can row when you're not up to it."

"Same here, and I'll never get too lazy to be able to take over at times. Promise."

His head tilted closer. "Teamwork will get us through anything, right?"

"Right. We make a good team."

"We do. Marry me."

"Okay."

"Okay?"

"Yes. I would love to marry you. Better?"

"Much." With a light kiss, he enveloped her in his arms. "Can we just walk home now and then spend a good bit of time cleaning up?"

"Did you propose just to get me to agree to walk instead?"

He laughed and took her hand to head toward home.

"Do I get to tell my grandparents today that we're engaged?"

"Tell anyone you damned well please." He kissed her fingers. "And I'll do something about a ring soon."

"Don't feel like you have to. Your promise is enough. But now I feel like running. Try to keep up." She chuckled at his groan.

~~

"It's seriously time for another girls' day out." Alicia winked at Felix and focused on Isabel. "That's when we leave all of the little ones with the boys and go out and doing something fun or relaxing or both on our own. We take most of the day, so we'll have to find a time that works for you, too. You have to come with us."

Isabel glanced over at him, and then scanned the other wives for their reactions.

"Definitely. It's been too long. We should do the Bent Fork. I bet you'd love it. Or have you been there already?" Denny's Krista sent their oldest farther away when she kept chattering about being old enough to be included by now, to which the women said definitely not, nearly as a chorus.

"I haven't. What is it?"

"A fun little diner. You really have to try it. What day will work best for you? We usually do a Monday since I have Sundays and Mondays off, but I can maybe change it."

"I'm pretty free right now, so whatever you want to do works for me. I mean, if you're sure I won't intrude."

"Of course you're not intruding. This is the first time J's had a steady long enough to include in our plans, and we've been looking forward to it. We do gossip about our men when we're by ourselves, you know. Part of the fun."

"I thought you were working in Pittsburgh now." His mom interrupted Denny telling his wife it was too soon to include Isabel in family gossip.

"Yes. I am. Was. But I'm..."

Her hesitation said she was unsure how much to say, so James jumped in. "Change of plans. She's moving in with me. Starting, well, last night."

Her grandpa got up and walked away. Her grandma followed him.

"Are you sure, Isabel?" His mom looked at him, somewhat accusing, it seemed, or it was his own conscience making him think so. "From what James said, it sounds like the perfect thing for you."

"It's ... yes, but..."

"She's doing it for me." He leaned forward, bracing his arms on his legs. Asking the two kids still close enough to hear to go check on the younger ones, he grabbed a deep breath. "I promised her I'm done drinking. She's staying to help me get past the initial cravings. I've told her she can call any of you if needed, but I don't plan to make it needed. I'm done for good this time. And I know you've heard it before. Don't blame you for not believing it. But I can't have my fiancée changing her mind on me, so that's pretty strong motivation."

"I won't." Iz grabbed his hand, pulling his arm over to her own leg. "I'm here, and I'm staying."

Silence. And then congratulatory chaos, starting with Felix.

James accepted his family's congratulations with more hesitation than he wish he had. It was her choice. He understood that. But it was *his* responsibility, since he asked her to stay. It wasn't planned. He'd had no intention of proposing so soon. But when she started talking about baby names, and naming their *first* after Ryan, what else could he do?

Her smile lit up his mom's living room when they pulled her onto her feet for hugs. When they asked to see the ring, he had to jump in to say it was a spontaneous thing earlier in the day so he hadn't gotten that far yet. Iz again said he didn't need to, she had the sea glass necklace and that worked well enough. He would, of course, get her a ring, and said as much. No need for his brothers to jump on him for being cheap or whatever.

She was meshing right in with his family. She'd even held Felicia just after they arrived and the baby gave her big hugs. It had turned rainy by the time they got there, so all of the kids were inside, and still, she didn't flinch from the noise or the kids or his brothers. She'd teased Felix, who seemed to be her favorite of his brothers, in return for his teasing. She'd helped with dinner and got along with his mom easily. She even put up with his dad's flirting, or testing, as James told her it was, without so much as a blush.

"You're sure you should have done this already?"

Trust Burt to question it. His voice was low enough, no one would have heard, other than Bruce still at his side. He hadn't wanted James to drive out to Mercer, so he invited himself and Abby. He'd asked the same before they left the apartment, in front of Isabel.

James decided to answer it the same. "Not at all." His brother's eyebrows raised. "For her sake, I'm not. For myself, hell yes. That girl's the best thing to happen to me. Nothing has ever felt this right." When he'd said it front of her earlier, she'd held him and said she thought the same.

Burt rubbed his chin and mouth. "Well. You better keep your promise to her, J. You've done a lot of stupid shit, but messing this up now that she came back to let you try again would be…"

"I know. I got it." He cut off further assurances when she came toward him.

"I'm going to go talk to my grandparents. I'll be right back." She brushed fingers through his hair. "Everything okay?"

"Yeah." He could see his parents in the sun room talking with her grandparents. "Want me to come with you?"

"Not yet. Give me a minute. Then you can if you want."

Sipping at his water, he watched her, saw his mom give her a grin and walk away to let them talk. The kids were all getting the news of his engagement by now and most had come to be loud and excited in his face, asking if they could be in the wedding and other questions he couldn't answer at all at this point.

"Okay, all of you back up out of your uncle's face. If they want your help, they'll ask you for it." His mom shooed them away and took Isabel's chair.

"If you're going to warn me to keep my promise to her, it's been handled already."

She gave him a soft grin. "I'm sure it has, but I'm also sure you will."

"Are you?"

"She's good for you. And I can see your love for her. Try to never make her regret it. And, part of that, I think, might be for you to reconsider letting her quit her job."

"I told her she shouldn't, that we'd work it out, but she wants to be with me, to help…"

"Why don't you move there with her? Wouldn't that be the better option, since she's the one with a job?"

"Is that a slam?"

"Oh, honey, you know it's not. It's only a fact. You need something better for you, anyway. I've thought so since you took that job."

"Nothing wrong with the job."

"No. But it's not your path. It was a hiding spot. Now, though…"

"Now, I'm trying to climb back onto my feet. Moving away while I'm still so deep in the grip of it…"

"A change of pace could be good for you. Start fresh. Find something more in your line, which will be easier with more opportunity."

"I'm not sure I'm ready for that." He took a gulp of ice water.

"She's going to be worth it for you, if you treat her right. Part of that is respecting her work, her career. Her path." She set a hand on his shoulder as she got up. "I'm going to pull dessert out. Think about it. We'll still be right there if you need us. An hour is nothing, really. And Denny's even closer, barely down the road. However, I doubt you'll need us now like you have before. You chose well. Now do right by her."

~~

"The worst thing, Baby Girl…" Gramps took her hand in both of his. "Is that you know what you're doing to yourself. You've lived it. I couldn't convince your mother not to do it and it's killing me to think about you doing the same."

"It's not the same."

"Of course you think it'll be different. We all think it'll be different, that it won't happen to us."

"It's not the same. James isn't Dad. He has so much good inside. He cares about people so deeply."

"And yet he's willing to let you quit a job you love."

"No. He told me not to. He said I should stay in Pittsburgh and follow my career and my passion and not let anything interfere. Including him. He said he'd visit and we'd make it work, but I don't want to do it that way. I want to be with him, to help him. I love him, Gramps. I didn't even know I could possibly feel so much for anyone. When he's stable, he's willing to move with me and we can start again together. Until then, I have to stay with him. I *have* to."

His chest rose and fell and he looked at Grams, getting that *you know when you're beat so just give in* look that Isabel had seen so often. "Well, then. What do we do to help the lad out so he can stay on the straight and narrow?"

With relief swelling through her body, she hugged him tight. "Don't give up on him."

"Am I interrupting?"

Looking over to find James, not too close, looking like he was truly afraid to approach, she offered her hand. "No. Never. But we may head back soon so I can pack some things and bring my car up here. Do you want to come?"

He hesitated, with a look back at his mom in the next room.

"If you'd rather stay here, that's fine. I'll come back by this way and pick you up. It'll be ... about three hours or so, though..."

"Well, how about instead of that, you come back to the apartment and let me pack a few things?"

"Um... Why?"

"I don't want you to give up your job. I have enough money saved I can find a little hotel for a few days while I look for a cheap apartment."

"James." Her heart thumped. "You need your family right now. Close, I mean."

"Nah. I only need you. And I want you to keep your job. So." He faced her grandpa. "If you have recommendations about the best cheap place to stay or where to start apartment hunting, I'll gladly take it. If you'd rather not help with that, I'll understand, since I do plan to ask her to move in with me." His mom came up behind him, and he acknowledged her, but continued to address her grandparents. "I know you're concerned. I understand. But I do love her and all she is, and I'm going to try my damnedest to be even half as good for her as she is for me."

"You're already far more than that." Isabel hugged him. "You don't have to do this. Really."

"I know I don't have to. I want to. For us. And before you argue, you should know that Mom thinks I should, so you'd have to argue with both of us."

Nora Gilbert gave her a warm smile. "You can call us anytime you need, Isabel. We're not throwing him at you and dusting our hands. And I hope you'll be able to make our girls' day out. They'll do it on a Sunday so it works with your schedule. One of his brothers can entertain him for the day."

Still unsure she should accept, she met his eyes. "Are you sure?"

"Yep. You still owe me that schnitzel and a walk along the river. Careful, though, we might have to make it a habit."

"Thank you."

"No. Don't thank me yet. Let's see how this goes. Okay?"

"Of course. I'll still be willing to come back here if it doesn't work for you. Remember that."

"Well, son." Gramps stepped forward. "If you're intent on taking our baby girl out of our home, you need to give her better than a cheap little apartment."

"Yes, sir. I didn't mean to imply that I wouldn't find something decent. I will."

"And you'll need a good job for that."

"Of course. I'll find something I can do. I adapt well, I learn fast, and I like to stay busy. I'll get two jobs if needed, along with my IT work that's coming along well."

"No, you can't." Isabel grasped his arm. "You're still my manager, too, so you need to be off weekends to go to shows with me and manage my schedule, and..."

"Don't worry, Iz. That'll come first."

"But you don't need to be overwhelmed."

"If you'll both let me finish." Gramps set his hand against his hip. "I might happen to know of a computer engineering job in that big monstrosity that took the place of the Civic Arena. I'll never forgive that, I can guarantee. Anyway, I have a contact who'd be willing to give you a looksie, if I ask him. Can't guarantee you anything, but I can get your foot in the door to be looked at. I do that, though, you better be reliable. I have a reputation in the industry I don't want blown."

"Absolutely. But, why, when I know you'd rather never see my face again, not that I blame you."

"My baby girl has her mind set, so best I can do now is help her out. I want her to stay in her job until she can make the connections she needs to make for what she wants most. Since you seem to want the same and you're willing to make the sacrifice to let her do it, seems to me helping you do okay with the sacrifice might be the best way to help her. Don't get me wrong, son. You hurt her and I'll be right there doing my best to pull her away from you. Got it?"

"Loud and clear."

"Glad we understand each other. And Baby Girl, you remember you can always come home. No matter what. And I'm 'sposed to ask..." With a scratch to the back of his head, and a glance at Grams, he sighed heavy and gave Isabel a soft shrug. "Yinz can stay with us till you can find a place of your own. We can keep a good eye on your boy while you're working, that way." He shrugged when Grams nudged him. "Truth is truth. It's the only reason I'm agreeing to the living-in thing under my roof without the license."

"Behave for a change, old man. She's an adult, whether or not you want to accept that. And we didn't have the license when you moved in, either, so don't act so haughty." Grams gave James a smile. "What he means is we'll be glad for the chance to get to know you better before you officially join the family. Please, stay with us as long as you need until you're ready to get settled together. We'll give you space and quiet to work when you want it and be glad for the company when you're not working."

~~

James opted for the guest room although Iz's grandma said there was no need to be so old-fashioned. Her grandpa was wary of him, and he didn't feel right sharing her room there. Calling it a night early, with as long as the day had been, he pulled the left-hand guitar out of its case.

It was slow-going, since his right hand was still clumsy with the chords, but he kept it simple, using those chords that worked easiest so far, and wrote the music for her lyrics, the one she'd asked him for, so she would know what he heard before she shared her own music. He'd been working it out on his mom's piano, melody only, since he could do that with his right hand.

He jumped at a tap on his door. Was he keeping them up? It was an acoustic, quiet.

The door opened slowly and Isabel stepped halfway through. "Heard you playing." She was in her M&M pajamas, topped by a fuzzy robe. "Can I come in?"

"Of course."

Sitting on the bed facing him, she pulled a leg up. "What are you working on?"

"The music for *What I Saw*, since you asked what I heard while reading your lyrics. Sounds crappy so far, not quite what I heard, but as close as I can get. Stupid fingers."

"Can I hear it?"

"Sure." It didn't take long to get frustrated with the chords, so he ignored the guitar and sang it instead.

> *Browns and tans and shards/   all most ever see*
> *the sea-smoothed edges/   of what I'm meant to be*
> *But underneath the polish/   I'm the texture of glass*
> *sharp enough to cut/   rough enough to shine*

His head shook. "It's better in my head."

"It's beautiful. And actually, I think that'll work better, or a blend..." Her eyes closed and he could tell she was concentrating on the music, the song, blending it...

"Play it again."

"I'm having trouble with the chords."

"I know. I don't care. Play it again."

Of course, he agreed. She took what he was doing and expanded on it, using his pauses while he tried to get it right to fill in a different melody which somehow, as she said, blended right in with what he had.

"Hold on." Getting up, she left the room and came right back with her own guitar. "Okay, so, do some of your harmony with it."

Through a good bit of back and forth and start and stops, they re-worked the song together, fitting their styles around to change it into something unique, and perfect.

Finally going all the way through once, while he added harmony with his voice as well as guitar, she set her guitar down and smiled. A gorgeous smile. "We make a good team."

"We do. It's a beautiful song, Iz."

"Much more so now that the edges are smoother and the texture is stronger. And it's called The Texture of Glass. I like your title better." Taking his guitar from his hands, she moved in, gripped his shirt over his chest, and took him in for a deep kiss. The passion grew fast and she leaned him back onto the bed, lying on top of his strong, warm body, her arms wrapped around his neck. "Be with me, James. I want to celebrate being your fiancée."

Forty-eight

Doing a New Year's Eve show at Sam's was maybe not a good idea. James was surrounded by revelers drinking and laughing in between listening to her. He'd been booking her at quieter venues, mainly coffee shops and some bar & grills, a couple of indoor craft fairs, avoiding straight-out bars while still pulling back onto the wagon. His family was there with him, though. He'd be okay.

It had been nearly two months since he quit drinking and moved to Pittsburgh, and he'd had moments of anger and defensiveness. Some days he would hardly talk and pulled away. Isabel brushed it off and gave him space until he calmed down and made it up to her. When she got too edgy, with thoughts of the similarity of her parents creeping in and bringing major doubts about their future, she went for short walks with Gramps or to the gym to run, since it was too cold to run far outside. Or she worked on her music at their place, asking her grandma for her thoughts.

His brothers had come to visit now and then, just because, they said. But it was always during his moody times, so she knew they were checking in with him, and better, that he was being honest with them. Most Sundays, they went up to Mercer for his family dinner, and some Saturdays, they stayed at the apartment with Bruce and Abby, if he wasn't working and she had a show nearby.

With his computer tech business growing, James worked a lot of hours, sometimes from home helping people remotely or working on laptops screwed up by viruses, other times going to their houses to fix issues, along with his evening and occasional weekend job at the arena that he had to book her shows around since she wouldn't go to city venues without him. On days they both worked, he dropped her off in the morning and picked her up again, then took her for a quick dinner or had it ready when he took her home to their little apartment on the outside edge of the strip district, close to her grandma's first apartment. He'd opted to leave his truck at his parents' for the time-being, since they had only on-street parking and her Aveo worked better for that. Once they hit Mercer, though, any running they did in the area was in his truck.

Along with her job, her songwriting, and shows, Isabel was teaching a couple of young girls how to play guitar. It was hard at first, since the youngest was near her daughter's age and Isabel couldn't help wondering if her own little one would be interested in the guitar, or music in general. But she enjoyed teaching. And it turned out she was good with them. James often said as much, with a shine in his eyes whenever the kid conversation arose or when she played with his nieces and nephews. So far, they were still using protection. They both wanted time to steady themselves and their relationship before adding another child to the mix. And he always said "another child" when he mentioned it; he never failed to acknowledge her little girl as part of the family, even if she had no idea where her baby was yet. She loved him for that, for so many things, really, but mainly for how hard he was trying to stay sober.

Her shows were off and on, being that they both worked so many hours already, but her audiences were good, and growing. The tip jar was doing well and her name was getting well recognized by venues in the area. Tips were especially nice during the songs James came up and sang with her. She still had to beg him to do it, but it was getting easier. Now and then, he played, also, since he was getting the hang of the left-handed guitar pretty well. Not enough for his own liking, so he rarely played, but more and more, he gave in to add harmonies or to do duets, including the one he'd started to write and she finished. They also sang it that way, as a duet. It always went over well.

Sam's was harder on him, and she could see it was, especially on New Year's Eve. But he smiled at her whenever she caught his eyes, and he gave her a wink once or twice.

For her next-to-last song, she chose the one she'd been writing on the beach the day they'd met. He said it was his favorite, even more than the one that caught him the first time at Sam's, which she'd started with.

> *"He said the right words, he spoke the right tune*
> *until she was so gone she knew what she would do*
> *when he asked... and then..."*

Swallowing hard, Isabel focused on her James. *Her* James. Who made the liar not matter anymore. Not quite true. *She* made him not matter anymore by letting go and moving on. Her sea glass vase wasn't full, but it didn't matter because her heart was. The vase sat on their dining room table, and he often added small bouquets of fresh wildflowers to it. When they wilted, he tossed them and washed the whole thing out to keep them "pretty and shiny" for her.

> *"He was gone with the breeze like the nightingale's lie*
> *and she was so struck down, she couldn't even cry, 'cause she knew*

She wanted his need of her, wanted his truths
to be lies full of blossoms and honeys and sighs,
she wanted what came of him, all that he left her,
and then it was gone like the breath of a cold night
in white wisps of blue."

James had figured out what she meant. She meant her child. It had started out about the ex and transformed into a song about her daughter. It was a healing song, a moving on and forward song.

"She wanted and needed him and no one could tell her
and no one could sell her the truth,
that he wouldn't stay long, he wouldn't be 'round
when her need said he'd stay and his lips said he may,
and she knew she was wrong, yet she felt she belonged..."

Pausing, she looked over at James and saw a touch of moisture in his eyes. A mix of hurting for her and pride in her, so he said before when he'd done the same. Her James. Whatever happened. They'd pulled each other up and would continue to hang on during the struggles to come.

Isabel knew they would. She knew. No indecisiveness.

She belonged with him. She'd just had to wait to find him and then hang in with him. And together, they were starting again, on a new joined path neither would have found alone.

The applause was nice. Respectfully subdued.

"Thank you. I have one more for the night. This one goes out to my manager, my best friend. My love." She gave him a smile during applause and some whistles. From his brothers. She saw Felix nudging him, but James kept his attention on her.

Life doesn't go as you plan, does it ever?
We trail along chasing our dreams
while they flee into the weeds
and the dark of the gravel-dust night
like the crickets and toads you hear but can't reach

And yet, at moments, a light flashes through
the dirty faux stained glass curved panes
mocking benignly as you sing
offering scratched and stained hope
that all of your hard-earned lessons will teach
a few truths...

> *Didn't know what I was looking for*
> *when I walked through the old door*
> *through I thought I was sure*
> *   of what I wanted and didn't and couldn't and would*
> *But life is a game, it's a risk and a gamble*
> *   it laughs and it mocks, but then it rolls back*
> *and holds a mirror in your face in the least likely place*
> *   showing not what you wanted or dreamed of, or planned*
> *   but what you didn't know you needed*
> *And me, I found it at Sam's*

It was 11:30 when she finished her set, and the bar manager put the countdown show on their big televisions that highlighted each side of the bar. James came over as she packed her guitar and gave her a brief kiss. Then he wrapped up cables and his brothers helped him take the gear to the truck while a few fans talked with her, asking for autographs on shirts and such.

Just before midnight, they made their way back to his family, and Gramps and Grams, and Libs and Charlie. Isabel set a hand on his chest while cuddling against him. "I hope it was okay to make that so public in your hometown."

"That I'm your manager?" His eyes sparkled.

"I think that's already well known. I mean us."

"I'd say that's fairly well known by now, also, you know, since you're hanging on me every chance you get."

"Really?" She answered his teasing by backing away a couple of steps. "I can change that."

"Don't you dare." Gripping her fingers, he pulled her back in. "If I cared about anyone knowing, I wouldn't have proposed, so you were kind of asking me to be a smartass."

"I guess that's fair." Except to be honest, he'd said nothing more about getting married since that day, so it was also fair to wonder if he'd meant it.

Raising her face to his, he met her lips gently. "You were incredible tonight, Iz."

"You always say that."

"Because you always are." He looked over at a group of guys nearby toasting each other early, beer glasses in hand, raising them like they were showing them off.

Burt leaned in. "He's right. You were incredible as always. Great job, Isabel, although I think he could have booked you somewhere nicer for tonight." He eyed James. "Ready to get out of here since she's done?"

"Nah, I'm good. And this is where we met."

"Yeah, I get that, but…"

"I'm good, bro."

"Sure?"

"Yeah." He wrapped Isabel in for a soft, but firm, hug. "I've got my girl and my family. I'm more than good."

She kissed him, meaning for it to be a quick, casual kiss since they were surrounded by family and strangers, but she didn't argue when he made it deeper. When he released her lips, she moved them close to his ear. "I'll give you something else to think about when we get home. You know, to remind you why it's worth staying sober."

"Oh, Iz. Even without that, you're very much worth it." Pressing back into her lips, he released her to tell her happy new year when the cheers and toasts swirled the air. As Auld Lang Syne began, his forehead rested against hers. "I love you, Isabel. And I was as wrong as I could possibly be the day I found you at the beach."

"About which thing?"

"The biggest thing. You are very much my type."

"Hm, no, I'm not, really."

Pulling back, his head tilted.

"I'm not, or at least I wasn't. And that's okay, because I want you even if we don't fit like … like the perfect couple, if there is such a thing. I don't care. Because I think we can grow together enough to become that, if you can stand me that long. And I think that matters more than where we started."

"You are such a poet." His expression teased.

"Meaning that was really corny?"

"To be honest, I'm not sure if it was really corny or highly philosophical. But it's good, either way. And I kind of think that does make you my type."

"If you say so."

Grasping her hand, he lowered to one knee. "I know I technically did this already, but I want to ask again, now that you've had some time to think about it."

Voices hushed around them, creating a quiet mist in the middle of the storm.

James reached into his jeans pocket and held up a ring. "You are definitely my type. No one else would ever work for me like you do. And I want forever, Iz. I'll keep doing my best for you. For us. Through good and bad and anything else. I promise I won't run again. Tell me you still want to be my wife."

His wife. His *wife*. What an incredible sound that was. He hadn't changed his mind. He was only giving her time. She couldn't even...

"Don't blame you, Isabel. Make him wonder if you've come to your senses by now." Felix laughed, but his wife hushed him.

"He has it coming and he knows it." Bruce this time. "But, he is coming along, and we'll still be around if you need us. In case you're nervous about the idea of getting stuck to him, and we wouldn't blame you."

James rolled his eyes. "Guess I should have done this away from the peanut gallery. But I won't hold you to it. From before, when I was..."

"I would be honored to be your wife. I wouldn't have said yes the first time if I didn't mean it. *Yes*. And me, too. Forever." Her hands shook while he slipped the ring onto her finger. Or maybe it was his hand shaking. Or both.

"Forever." He squeezed her fingers lightly and smiled into her eyes.

Through the pandemonium of everyone they loved jumping in to congratulate them, and strangers, as well, with Felix and Bruce offering her their condolences through their smiles, Isabel hung on to him, refusing to let go. Only when it calmed did she even look at the ring more than enough to see that it was an engagement ring. Green sea glass accented the swirled silver sides, showing off the diamond in the middle. "It's the same color as my necklace."

"It's the same glass. I had Gavin save the chips. There's resin over top to protect it from breaking."

"I had a hell of a time figuring out how to make it not shiny so it still looked like it came from the sea." Gavin jumped in from behind, startling her. "Bought some to play with first. Think it worked out okay."

"It's gorgeous. Thank you."

"Nah, my pleasure. Probably the thing I'm most proud to have been able to make. Congratulations, Isabel, and good luck." With a grin, he gave James a hug and congratulations and moved away with a girl stuck to his side.

Admiring the ring, she moved back in against her fiancé. "You know the glass is probably from a beer bottle, right?"

He laughed and kissed her head. "Probably is. A reminder that beauty can come from brokenness."

"With enough smoothing time." She threw her arms around his neck. "Let's go home, James."

"Do you feel okay?" James handed Isabel the perspiring translucent green water bottle she always carried and ran the backs of his fingers alongside her face. "It's hot for this. Especially now. I didn't expect it would be when I booked it for you."

"Thank you. I'm fine. And this is nice." She glanced around the courthouse square from under the canopy set up on the circular bandstand edged with a black metal railing. It was usually used by Mercer's Community Band for Friday night concerts, but currently, it was also hosting hour-long lunchtime concerts during the week. The crowd wasn't big, but it was nice. Courthouse employees mingled on the building's steps behind her or congregated around one of the wood benches planted along the sidewalks facing the bandstand. Others, more casually dressed, brought folding chairs and sat eating sandwiches in brown bags they'd picked up from one of the restaurants around the square, and there were several young kids running around in the grass chasing butterflies or moths. A couple of the little ones danced now and then and Isabel had trouble not just watching them.

"Let me know if you need a break. They'll understand." He set a hand against her round stomach. They'd become less careful about protection after their engagement was formally announced and they were both entrenched in their jobs and doing well living together, so by the time they got married on the beach in June, the place they met, one year from the day they met, she was already four months along. By now, she was right at six months and James was being ridiculously protective.

"I'm fine. Sing with me while you're up here."

When he agreed, she strummed a bit of the beginning of *I'm Not Sayin'* and spoke to the small audience. "You're getting a bonus today. My incredible manager, who also happens to be my even more incredible husband, actually gave in to sing with me." She waited through a smattering of applause. "This is one we wrote together."

Isabel couldn't help watching his face much of the time. He was more than incredible. He was her superstar. Eight months since the last time he'd had a drink, and he didn't even have to bother telling her or his family that he was "good." They could see it. His energy was back. His humor and smartass tendencies, which she actually loved, were back.

And he again looked like a super sexy rock star, with his hair grown out just a bit and his summer tan highlighting the sun-streaked blond.

Just the opposite, she was gaining too much during the pregnancy, since he kept treating her with Jones' shakes in all different flavors every Sunday after dinner with his family, along with cooking for her or bringing home her favorites while telling her to kick back and put her feet up. They did still work out together, but by now she was walking instead of running. Her energy level was lagging horribly, even with Gramps continually bringing over fresh-from-someone's-garden veggies, which she couldn't get enough of. James even made sure to bring her a stool so she could sit while she sang. On good days, she didn't bother with it. Today, she'd started without it but was sitting by now.

As usual, when the duet ended, the reaction was good. James directed the applause to her, gave her a kiss on the head, and backed away to let her continue on her own.

A woman walking around supervising the dancing kids asked if she would do her cover of Infiniti's *When I Tell You*. She hadn't planned to do that one, but when one of the little girls jumped up and down clapping, her eyes full of expectation, Isabel couldn't refuse. She watched James through much of it. As usual, he was wandering, listening to the sound from different locations and occasionally talking to someone. Now and then he returned to their own group: his mom, Burt and his two youngest kids, Felix and his family, and Gramps and Grams. They said they wanted her to have a good turnout for the show since it would be a small audience. They were about a third of it.

At the end of the song, Isabel smiled at the girl who clapped loud and was again jumping up and down, then moved into another one of her own. When it ended, she grabbed some water and looked over at James for a time check. He held up two fingers from where he stood in the distance with a small group who had set up just in front of the community events sign. He was talking to a man with dark, slightly graying hair, who looked sixtyish, and not local. Someone music related? Her husband had brought people in to listen to her now and then, A&R people mostly. She didn't know why he would bring them to a short outdoor show with a small audience, but not much surprised her about him anymore.

Before she continued, she remembered to do her promo. "Thank you for coming out today. If you'd like to follow me, I'm at Isabel Dillon Gilbert dot com, and there are links to my social networks there. James has cards, in case he hasn't forced one on you yet. We are working on a full CD, but in the meantime, there are free samples here on the step, so grab one if you want it, or grab two if you want to share with someone who couldn't be here." She grinned when the little dancing girl dropped a five dollar bill in her tip jar and grabbed a CD with a big smile. "Thank you." She got a sweet "I love your music" and returned with "I love your dancing" before the little one rushed off again.

"I have time for two more songs, so I want to do one..."

"Do *Someday When I Find You.*" James had come up close to the stage. He wanted her to do the one she'd written to her daughter? She hadn't done it publicly and she almost refused. It was hard not to get emotional whenever she sang it, and here, between her unsteady hormones and the heat and knowing James had been working with some guy he'd hired months ago to see if he could find a lead, she wasn't sure she could. Still, she'd never been able to turn him down when he requested a song. He almost never did. And his expression was pleading with her.

"Okay, I guess you get to hear another one I haven't done in public yet. I'll try not to screw it up too much, since I wasn't prepared to do it." She glanced at her husband, who only grinned and shrugged. Before she started, she grabbed a couple of good swallows of water and mopped her forehead and neck with the cool wet towel that wasn't cool anymore.

"Still okay?" He leaned on the railing along the steps.

She wanted air conditioning and a cool shower, but she gave him a nod and started the song.

> *Someday when I find you/ because someday I will*
> *I'll tell you all my heart hides,/ has held inside for years*
> *We were children, he and I/ but one of us stood up while the other flew*
>
> *I wanted you. Only this you need to know*
> *above all else, above all I could say,*
> *if I can say only three words before you fly*
> *I would tell you how I wanted you/ and I still do...*

Getting through it decently enough, she grabbed her water bottle, more as distraction than need, let the cool water soothe her nerves, and started the chords for her last song. A couple of older people cheered before she even announced it.

"This is a song that has been very inspirational to me throughout the years. Some of you might remember it, although my version is pretty scaled back." At the end of *Magic Power*, one of those who had started cheering whistled approval. The man James had been talking to nodded with a smile. Had to be a music person.

"Thank you for coming out. You can check with my manager about more show dates in the area." Setting her guitar on its stand, she stepped down off the bandstand, accepting her husband's arm although she didn't particularly need it, and talked with those who came for CDs to be signed. Isabel was glad to hear so many say they would look her up and follow her, but by now, she really just wanted to sit and get cool.

Instead of unplugging her amp and speakers right away, as he usually would, James took her guitar from the stand and hung it over his back, then pulled her in for a soft hug. "You were amazing as always."

"Did the song sound okay? You should have warned me to go over it before the show."

"It was beautiful, Iz. Thank you for doing it."

"Why did you ask for it?"

"Come with me a minute before I answer that." He took her hand, suggesting she follow.

"Can we pack this up first? I need somewhere cool. And a chair." She cradled her stomach with her free hand.

"Are you okay?"

"Yes, I'm just hot and tired and I want lunch. Inside. In air conditioning."

With a grin, he kissed her forehead. "I'll take care of all of that in a minute. Burt and Felix will get everything to the truck so we don't have to worry with it. Just come with me, Iz. I have a surprise for you." Giving her his arm as though she needed the help to walk, he forced himself to go slower than he wanted. She always knew when he was making himself slow down. It showed in his stride. After months of keeping up with him pretty well, she was back to slowing him down. Which he said didn't mind at all.

In a funny twist, he now ran with Kenny, her trainer, when he needed to go farther and faster than she could. They even doubled a couple of times with Kenny's girlfriend, also a trainer. The couple often came to Isabel's shows.

James stopped to thank the music store owners who hosted the event and left the rest of the CDs with them to give away at their store. He stopped again when Felicia ran to Isabel wanting to be picked up, and picking her up himself instead.

"I'll let you sit beside her at lunch, Miss Rambunctious. For now, stay with Mom and I'll come back to get you." Giving the child back to Alicia, despite the protest, he teased that he'd been replaced as the girl's favorite. She attached herself to Isabel every chance she got.

"Right back." Isabel gave the one-year-old the sign for "right back," even though the girl knew what "right back" meant, and let James lead her to the man he'd been talking with. The guy looked familiar. She couldn't place why, but he stepped up in front of the couple and two girls who'd been sitting behind them and were still straggling behind. Dragged there, probably. Wanting to get out of the heat as much as she did, she was quite sure.

"Iz." James set a hand on her back. "This is Dan O'Neil. Isabel Dillon Gilbert." He used her business name. With most, he only used her first name, sometimes first and last. She'd kept her grandparents name and added his after they got married. Generally, he only used his. Theirs.

"It is nice to meet you, Isabel. Your voice is beautiful. James said most of the songs are your own?" He had an accent. A softened accent, but still an accent.

"Thank you. Yes." She noted Gramps and Gram coming up behind them. Odd. They usually stayed out of the way when she talked to fans after her shows. He had to be someone from the business. She wished she'd practiced that song more... That song... Her gut clenched.

"I know of someone who may like to hear them, since James said you're looking to sell your songs. If you would be at all interested."

"Oh. Thank you. Maybe." Some of them, yes. Not all of them. She looked up at James, waiting for more information.

He kissed her head. "We can get back to that when you're off your feet. For now, there's someone here who wants to meet you."

Mr. O'Neil stepped aside and motioned for one of the girls to come forward. A young girl, about ten or so, with dark wavy hair and...

Isabel's heart nearly stopped. Her eyes watered. "Neala."

"Kerrie." The girl looked up at the couple at her side. "It's not her. That's not my name."

A woman set an arm around her back. "You didn't officially have a name when we adopted you. But you had this." She pulled a folder from her shoulder bag.

Through her now-racing heart beat making her head swim, Isabel could hardly make out the writing on the pink-edged paper. The *Baby*

Girl Sanderson sign from the hospital crib. Isabel had crossed out "Baby Girl" and written *Neala Dillon* above it. The name she'd given her daughter. Dillon was going to be Neala's middle name...

"You're my birth mother."

She could only nod while she studied her baby's face. The same face. The same dark curly hair, now past her shoulders and wavy instead of curly, but barely lighter. And her father's round, dark brown eyes. "You're beautiful. Look at you." And healthy. Happy. She looked incredibly well.

"You wrote that song to me? You've been looking for me?"

"Yes. Since the day they took you away. Yes."

"You wanted me."

"Oh, baby. Yes. Very much. I've missed you every day of your life."

Neala walked up close, studied Isabel's face a moment, and threw her petite but strong arms around her. "I'm glad you found me. I love my parents. They're wonderful. But I've always wanted to know."

Wonderful. They were wonderful. She was happy and healthy and well cared-for. And beautiful. Unable to control the tears, she found James and gave him a smile.

Notes and Acknowledgements

Many western Pennsylvania locales and businesses were mentioned in this story. I have no affiliation with them and they are used fictitiously. Some of them have changed or closed over the five years the book has been in progress, but I chose to leave them in as the way I first remember them. Mention of the businesses are honorary/story fodder only; it is not, in any way, an endorsement. Supporting local in general, however, is something I believe in.

The Greenville amphitheatre is real. It was built as part of Camp Reynolds during WW2 and was sitting abandoned when I began this story. The way it is described is the way I first saw it. During the writing of this book, it got a wonderful revamp and is now used for community concerts.

Sam's Shack, the bar where James first hears Isabel sing, is entirely fictional. It was first mentioned in the *Rehearsal* series under LK Hunsaker and was drawn into this story to connect them.

Many singers and bands are mentioned in the story, as well. Most of them are real, used fictitiously, and I also have no affiliation with them, other than following/supporting the mentioned locals. I do love to follow and support local music.

Infiniti, Dani, Ryan Reynauld, and Raucous are entirely fictional. Raucous is the band *Rehearsal* centers around. Infiniti and Dani will be brought to life in its sequel, which is in progress. Ryan is the main character in *Off The Moon*, published in 2009 under LK Hunsaker.

The novella *A Melody in the Dark*, first published as part of the *Music of the Heart* anthology by Fire Star Press (2017), is the story of songwriter Melodee Lerner and Jack-of-all-trades turned roadie Niall Dillon.

Thank you to all those running area information pages and sites that helped with the research I didn't do in person. Links for those pages, along with area information, will be listed on Isabel's website: IsabelDillonGilbert.com

A note about the alcoholism and PTSD issues addressed within the story:

Much of what I wrote, I have seen at different points in my life from different people. The rest, I researched. I am not an expert. I have no medical qualifications. I do have a psychology background, but I am not a licensed therapist. Nothing in the story is intended as medical or mental health advice.

My thoughts, while writing this story, and otherwise, are with those affected by addiction and/or trauma.

As always, thank you to my loyal readers for continuing to follow me and to new readers for finding this book and giving it a chance. I am truly grateful.

About the Author

Ella M. Kaye uses her art and psychology background to create contemporary love stories with mental health issues set around the creative arts. Each of her novels and novellas fall under one of three series: Dancers & Lighthouses, Artists & Cottages, and Songwriters & Cities. Kaye has been writing romantically inclined literary fiction that branches into straight mainstream in both novel and short story form under the name LK Hunsaker for more than two decades. After many moves as a military spouse, she is settled in western Pennsylvania where she enjoys the abundant foliage and recreational lakes along with the hilly vistas.

Find her at EllaMKaye.com and LKHunsaker.com.

Other Books By Ella M. Kaye

Pier Lights (2013)
Dancers & Lighthouses

Caroline was a relevé away from becoming prima ballerina when, partly due to her own actions, she was damaged enough to never be allowed en Pointe again. Returning to her hometown area, she finds a grittier dancing job and determines to land on top this time.

Dio hides away on his farm near Charleston, South Carolina, and ventures out only when he can be in disguise. He uses his swordsman skills to work out aggression and connect with others while he maintains distance. When the two collide on the beach in the glow of the lights from the pier, their personal scars push them away, and pull them in, just as the ebb and flow of the Atlantic.

~~

Shadowed Lights (2014)
Dancers & Lighthouses

When her sister loses her house to Hurricane Sandy, Delaney Griffin welcomes the family into her home. Months later, with five noisy kids and an overbearing brother-in-law threatening her sanity, Delaney spends much of her free time at the wildlife refuge, which also works as her refuge. Still, the lack of privacy, along with space to dance, her only passionate release, causes her debilitating social anxiety to escalate.

Eli Forrester has come from small town Indiana to Barnegat, New Jersey with his company to help restore the coast. A high rise worker who loves new people and new places, he fears nothing, except water. When he accidentally kicks one of the sea critters Delaney is trying to help rescue, he is drawn to the quiet New Jersey girl. Unwilling to take her cues to leave her alone, Eli is alternately put off and turned on by her odd behavior.

Under shadow of devastation, fear, and forced separation, Delaney and Eli search for their own rescue light.

~~

Pieces of Light (2014)
Dancers & Lighthouses

A Cape Cod grade school teacher. An Irish ballroom teacher visiting for the summer. A little girl who needs a lot of guidance and understanding.

On the shores of Provincetown, Massachusetts, three independent spirits are brought together by unpredictable tides of rapid change. Emma has survived an unsupportive marriage while supporting her family. Fillan is trying to balance his passion for dance with the realities of obligation. Eleven-year-old Patty has been tossed around by her mother's inability to deal with her own life, much less her daughter's autism. When fate brings them together, they must determine whether joining their lifeboats will provide an even keel or throw them further off-balance.

~~

Shadows of Greens & Memories (2015)
Artists & Cottages

Francis Barrett returns to her hometown of Storm Lake, Iowa to take care of the family holdings, such as they are, after her father passes. While turning his garden shed into a small but livable cottage, she runs into an old flame she admired from afar but never dared speak with during their high school days. Using her secret passion of oil painting to unwind from long days of clearing out the mess, Francis finds her father also had a secret passion and left behind a tale of a man she didn't truly know.

George Frederick McKenry never left the Midwest town where he was born other than brief travels with his four children, who he now has custody of since his ex moved into a condo with her new boyfriend. Running into the one girl from school who rebuffed him when he asked her out, G.F. can't help checking on her and making sure she's getting along alright. False assumptions and past resentments fade as Fran and G.F. let down their guards in order to create new memories.

~~

Shadows of Blues & Echoes (2016)
Artists & Cottages

Gillian Hart has big ambitions while working as a reporter for a small circulation paper in Denver, Colorado. When her editor and friend assigns a story about some rich businessman who chucks it all to live in the woods alone outside Durango, she does her best to fight it. With no choice but to give in, Gillian determines to use it as a stepping stone.

Hank Dennison wants nothing but solitude while he recovers from a life-changing devastation he has managed to hide from the public. The last thing he wants is another nosy journalist badgering him, especially one who knows nothing about survival in the wilderness and taxes his waning strength. Noticing the darkness of depression that weighs her down, despite her attempt to hide it, Hank determines to keep her off the path that led him to his own illness.

~~

Shadows of Rust & Reels (2017)
Artists & Cottages

By day, Holli Jacoby is a jewelry artist in her hometown of Williamstown, West Virginia. Abandoned by her family, Holli mainly stays to herself, preferring her potter's wheel to the risk of letting others see, and take advantage of, the uncontrollable effects of her bipolar disorder.

Isaac Bradshaw is a welder who spends much of his off time assisting his parents due to his father's declining health. While playing pool, he notices a fiery brunette eye him as though she knows him. He soon learns "fiery" is an understatement, and his buddy warns him against the girl, but something keeps him drawn to her.

Despite their earlier crossed paths and a shared love of adventure, Holli's roller coaster life might be more than Isaac is willing to handle. When the bottom falls out beneath her, their relationship hits a critical test.

~~ ~~ ~~

Watch for more of each series from Ella M. Kaye.
All novels are stand-alone and can be read separately or in any order.
The series are related by art form and setting, with some limited character mingling.

In Memory

Rest in Peace, Kenny Rogers (March 20, 2020).
I don't have the words to say how much your music has meant to me throughout most of my life.

I would be remiss not to mention Alan Longmuir (July 2018), Ian Mitchell (Sep 2020), and Les McKeown (Apr 2021), all members of the Bay City Rollers and partial inspiration for the *Rehearsal* series. The music will never die.

To David McClain (March 2021), fellow author and friend, one of my biggest writing encouragers. Almosta Ranch will live on through your words and our memories.

Also, to Annette McRoberts, who lost her battle against M.S. in 2021, one of my beta readers who often apologized for asking so often if I had anything new yet. No apology needed. Thank you, Annette, for your constant encouragement and your assistance in fine-tuning the stories you loved to read.

~~ ~~ ~~

Sipping iced tea from the large plastic glass his mom kept in her cabinet for him, even through fussing that it didn't match the rest of her dishes and it took so much space, James watched Isabel talk with her daughter from across the room.

She was a sweet, beautiful child, with a smile as incredible as her mom's. Kerrie was all Isabel when she smiled. She was small, short for her age, he thought. From her biological father, he supposed. Her skin tone showed his Italian heritage. One of Kerrie's first questions, after learning why she'd been adopted out, had been about her father. Isabel told her it was his family he left, not her, really, that he was only afraid of being a father, but he was a good person with a kind heart and she hoped he was doing well. It was far more generous than James would have been, but it pacified Kerrie. The girl had asked if he was kind of her dad, too, since he was the father of her sibling-to-come. Honored beyond the ability to show it, he gave her a big hug and invited her to stay with them anytime her parents said it was okay. Throwing the power back to them, since he could see they were somewhat wary of Iz's intentions.

Once Isabel assured them she didn't want to interfere, but she'd like to see Kerrie at times if it was okay, also leaving the power in their hands, they relaxed. In an odd twist, they'd known his parents for a lot of years and had been to the house for something to do with work. A good thing, since it made them comfortable to come over and let Kerrie hang out with her mom for a while.

Kerrie also asked about her name, the one Isabel meant to give her. Neala, the Irish feminine version of Niall, was named after her great grandpa, which seemed appropriate since James saw a lot of similarities between the two and they were getting along like they'd always known each other. The name Neala, Isabel said, means female warrior, which pleased the girl. James could see her as a warrior, with her quick wit and obvious independent streak, and the way she was in several sports. He'd bit his tongue about that one, but he would, for sure, harass his wife about passing along a sports gene she didn't have. Kerrie asked if she could add it to her name, make herself Kerrie Neala Woodson, since she hated her middle name and the great aunt she'd got it from but had never liked had passed, anyway. Her parents offered to consider it.

His family tried to give them some space, but the kids buzzed around and asked her to play and Burt had to tell Ronnie to stop flirting, the girl was family. The twelve-year-old turned all kinds of red, but Kerrie just laughed and said she'd always wanted siblings and cousins and didn't have either. Maggie, only three months younger than Kerrie, was already acting like her best buddy. With their hair color and facial structures, they looked like they could easily be cousins. Burt offered to host a play date any time.

Alternately joining the conversation with Iz and Kerrie's parents and giving them space, he also watched Iz's grandma talk with Dan O'Neil as though they were old friends. Dan and his daughter, who looked awfully young to be his daughter, being that he had to be closing in on 70 and she was maybe 18, if that, came from the UK where they lived, to take the case, but he sounded very familiar with the States, as though he'd spent a good bit of time running around the country. For his work, possibly. He'd become one of the foremost experts in finding and reuniting people, and he refused all payment. He did it for personal reasons, he said.

When dinner plans began and his brothers headed home, Dan and his daughter came to say they were leaving. James took him over to Iz to let her know.

She stood and gave him a hug. "Thank you. How do I repay you? James said you don't accept payment, but..."

"I do not, and there is no need. I am always happy when I can help."

"But you came so far."

"It gave me a gud reason to come back this way. I stayed up in Greenville for a few weeks way back when. It was nice to see it again and to see it has not changed to a great extent. We will be visiting family in another part of the state when we leave here, and so it was only a bit of a detour." He set an arm on his daughter's shoulders. "And we should go or they will wonder what has become of us."

"We've met, right?" Isabel was studying his face.

"No, I would say we have not. You would not have been born yet when I was in this area last."

"But you look familiar."

He grinned. "I have tha' kind of a face, so I hear. Congratulations, and let me know how things work for you. Your grandmother has my contact information."

Niall stepped in. "We'll walk you out. We have to be headed back to the city before it's dark and hard to see. The old eyes don't work the way they used to." He and Meladee gave Isabel a hug, and then her daughter.

Kerrie gladly returned the embraces with a sweet, "Bye, Grandma and Grandpa."

With a kiss to his wife's head, James helped her sit again and told her he'd be back in a minute. After more thanks to the O'Neils, he and Niall hung back when Dan asked Meladee if she'd go to his car with him. Opening the trunk, he handed her an old guitar case. She tried not to accept it, obvious through her head and hand motions, but with a few words that had to be an explanation, he got her to give in and take it. She gave him a long hug, said something to his daughter, and stepped back to let them leave.

When the car pulled out, they joined her where she stood watching it go, and Niall raised his eyebrows at his wife. "Should I be jealous about you getting gifts from a more handsome man than me?"

"Don't be silly, old man. You're still, and will always be, my prince, when you're charming and when you're not." Her eyes sparkling with emotion, she grinned at James and patted the guitar case. "This is a story I'll share another day. You and Isabel come on over for dinner when you get a chance. Let us know what works for you."

"We will. Thank you."

"No, James. Thank you. You've brought such a light to our girl as we'd never seen. And you helped to find our granddaughter. We're forever grateful."

Niall took his hand. "She's right. You did good, son."

When they drove away, he returned to the house and stood at the door of the sun room where his wife sat cradling their child with one hand and holding the fingers of her oldest with the other. Little Felicia was at Kerrie's side again and Felix was inviting the girl and her parents to one of their paint and stirs, since Kerrie was into art.

Isabel glanced up and saw him and excused herself to come over. "Everything okay?"

Okay didn't begin to describe it. "Everything is absolutely beautiful, just like you." He kissed her forehead. "Is it going as you hoped?"

"Better." Her eyes lit up. "She's hoping we have a lot of kids because she always wanted siblings."

"Well." Wrapping his wife in his arms, he gave her a soft kiss. "I guess we better get back to working on that as soon as you're up to it after this one comes. I'm not getting any younger, you know."

She laughed. "I don't know. I'm not sure you aren't. Me, I'm a different story, so I guess it's good you have a few years on me. Don't want you to go looking for a younger woman with you being all rock star hot and everything."

"Damn, I love you. And that, my little songbird, will never happen. Have to save my energy to give our daughter more siblings, right?"

Her arms slid up around his neck and her baby bulge, their child protected so well by his beautiful wife, pressed against his stomach. "You better. Because I love you like crazy, and I'm finding it pretty cool to be a mom."

"Cool? Did you just say cool? Wow, Iz, we've gotta get you updated to the right decade."

"I don't know. Maybe I can just teach my kids that our growing up decades were pretty cool. All things considered."

"Now, that might be the right idea. Come on. Let's go ask her if she wants to grab ice cream."

"You know, I think you're enjoying the dad thing pretty well, too."

"Absolutely. She's a great kid. You did good."

"Not me. Her parents."

"Nah, Iz. Her inner being still comes from you and it shows all over her. What they are when they're born matters. What you did before she was born matters. You did good, and I am incredibly proud to be your manager."

She laughed again. "Okay, Mr. Manager. Let's go celebrate our success with ice cream."

"And when we get home, you can explain why Mr. O'Neil might have given your grandma a priceless guitar, if I'm right about what was in that case he gave her before he left."

"He gave her a guitar case?"

"Yep. An old one."

"I think I know why he looked so familiar." Her jaw dropped a moment. "It wouldn't be..."

"Maybe?"

Silent a moment, she shrugged. "Maybe."

www.ingramcontent.com/pod-product-compliance
Lightning Source LLC
Chambersburg PA
CBHW010838190726
48286CB00012BA/2899